BORGO

Ferrel D Moore

ISBN-13: 978-1-958557-06-8

To my lovely wife, Beth.

Copyright © 2022 Ferrel D Moore

All rights reserved. No portion of this book may be reproduced, stored in a retrieval system, or transmitted in any form or by any means electronic, mechanical, photocopy, recording, scanning, or other   except for brief quotations in critical reviews or articles, without the prior written permission of the publisher.

This novel is a work of fiction. The characters in this story are fictitious. Any resemblance to persons living or dead is coincidental.

Published by White Cat Publications

PART ONE

1

"Mr. President."

"Please, sit down, Miss Corvasce."

The president waved his hand, and only when she was seated on the rich blue and gold divan did he sit in the leather chair across from her. The royal blue curtains were closed, and the room was lit by only one Aladdin Vertique lamp with a base formed of rich yellow glass shaped like a goblet. She kept her eyes on the man across from her. It vividly impressed every element of the room into her consciousness. Marla's back was sore from being locked into place and forced to sit on a metal bench for hours and hours. They stared at each other, each of them taking the other's measure. He seemed at ease, but she knew it was an act.

"May I call you Marla?"

"Of course."

"Thank you. I will only speak with you for a short while, Marla. Please don't interrupt me with questions. I am not being autocratic. It is only the way it must be because of the situation. So, please listen to what I have to say. More than you know depends on it. Then go with the men who will escort you to your mission location. Everything will become clear when you meet the man to whom you will be reporting. His name is Traverse Nations. He has mission authority, unless you find he has become unstable or determine that he is under the influence of our enemy."

Marla said nothing, but a warning bell went off inside her mind.

"Do not ask me today about the situation or its ramifications. Do not inquire as to your resources or limitations. You will learn all of that from Mr. Nations or on your own as you are able. Now I will speak to you as your President. Next, I will speak to you as a fellow citizen and as a human being. When I am through, I will allow you one question before you leave and one question only. I wish it were not so, but it is. If I can answer your question, I will. If I cannot, so be it."

Filament cameras would be invisible to the eye. The invasive technology had to be accepted. There was little to be done about it. The whereabouts of the security personnel were likewise a mystery to her. They were the ultimate professionals with the most advanced weaponry and tactics in the world. So, she did not bother to locate either them or the monitoring equipment. It would be seen as a micro-aggression, and such behavior would have consequences. They were protecting the leader of the free world, which was difficult enough, but President Mahomed Usman was also the first Muslim President of the United States. The number of men and women his election had enraged, caused a staggering increase in their already heightened awareness.

For the president himself to ask for a private meeting with her was something she could never have imagined. It was unthinkable, unless something of great consequence was at stake. The President did not meet with field operatives. She realized she was being sent to the Middle East, and that whatever was involved was so incredibly delicate and dangerous, that he and his advisers thought this meeting was called for. That thought both thrilled and excited her.

"I have but little time to spend with you, Marla. In fact, I have," he smiled, "no time at all to spend with you, but here I am. I can tell you with complete surety that only a few people on this earth know where I am at this moment. Our secrecy must be absolute. The brevity of this meeting helps ensure that. After tonight, I will never see you again. You will accomplish your mission and then disappear."

Marla inclined her head to acknowledge the serious nature of the situation, whatever it was. Do the job. Get gone.

"Good," he said, steepling his hands before his chest as though praying. "I imagine you have an idea that I am about to send you to the Middle East."

Again, she nodded.

"That would be wrong. That would be much too easy. Where I am sending you is right here, inside our own country. Its location is kept secret. So you will once again be traveling in the blacked-out van. You have, I am assured, the stamina to do this."

This time, Marla did not move at all. She'd made the mistake of signaling her thoughts once. She wouldn't make that mistake again. It was difficult to repress the question of where and why, but she kept her mouth shut. He would tell her in his own time.

"Do you know, Marla, that when I became President, a part of me thought my most challenging task would be to stay alive long enough to make a difference? Before that, at every campaign stop we made, I and my security detail, the press and multitudes of others feared suicide bombers and assassins would plague us. The thought of innocents dying simply because I stopped in their towns to campaign kept me awake at night. My campaign handlers would have had a nervous breakdown if it ever leaked that I took sleeping pills to sleep at night and daily doses of Xanax to keep my anxieties under control in those days. The reason I am telling you this is that shortly after assuming office, I learned for the first time in my life the meaning of actual fear, and it had nothing to do with suicide bombers."

On the ride over, she had tried desperately to work out where she was being taken to, but had finally given up. She could feel the road's twists and turns, and make guesses about the terrain, but with a black bag over her head, cotton stuffed in her ears and her wrists and ankles chained to a solidly mounted steel pillar bolted to the van's floor and ceiling, there was no way to make a good guess.

"I am a Muslim American, Marla. I love this country with a passion that sometimes eludes my fellow citizens and my brethren around the world. They struggle to believe that I am both a faithful Muslim and a loyal American. If I use the name Allah to refer to our divine creator, many of my fellow Americans are certain I wish to enforce Sharia law across our country. If I use the name God to refer to our divine creator, many of my brethren around the world believe that I am a traitor to Allah. It is an impossible line to walk at worst, and nearly impossible.

"I came to this office with a campaign promise to restore true openness to our political process and to unite citizens of all faiths and, in that, I include those with no faith. This last offends the religious. The religious offend the atheists. Ah, well, there you have it."

President Usman sat comfortably reclined in the wing backed leather chair. He seemed completely at ease, but Marla had too much time in the field not to notice the haunted look in his eyes. They were restless, flitting about the room as though looking for hidden attackers. That, of course, was impossible. With the level of security at his command, she doubted if even a determined ant could have invaded the room. But besides his nervous eyes, his fingers also tapped on his legs. She doubted he realized it. For a man as skilled in statesmanship as President Usman, it would take a lot of pressure to crack his composure.

"Only when I came to the office, I was informed of something so monstrous there was no responsible way to pull it into the sunlight to be examined and dealt with, if that could ever be accomplished at all. It is a secret our government has kept for just under a century. No one truly knows of his origin. But I can tell you, both as your President and as a citizen, that it is a danger to every man, woman and child in the entire world. I am at great pains to impart to you that this is not in the slightest an exaggeration. There is a great evil in our country, Marla, and I do not mean terrorists or criminal gangs or foreign agents of espionage. I do not mean an impending natural disaster or a plague or even a nuclear attack. It is something much, much worse. You must stop it. We are all in great peril. Your mission, your only goal, is to destroy it."

She did not understand what he was talking about or where he was going with this, but that did not worry her so much as the fact that he'd slipped once and referred to the evil as a "he" instead of an "it."

"I speak to you now as a husband and father. I have two sons and a daughter. They and my wife are everything in this life I value. As a family man, I love this country and the best of what it stands for. As a citizen of the human family, too, I am concerned. You may think I'm making a speech. And I am. I feel compelled to. I am making a speech to you that, I hope, will be impassioned enough to give you strength when you will most need it. As a prudent man, I have many fears about the future of humanity. I work hard to contribute to the peace, security and equality of all people as a family man. As a man devoted to God, I pray every day that we all turn our hearts to heaven for love and mercy. These are not words from a campaign speech, Marla. They are words from my heart. But from this day forward, I will pray for your victory and your safe return, especially for your safe return. Remember what I say, and it may give you strength in the days ahead. Now you may ask me your one question. I remind you, do not ask what I cannot answer."

For the first time, she noticed what he was wearing. A navy blue sweater with a crew neck. His shirt collar stuck up above it. The French vanilla khaki pants, with the crisp pressed line running down the front of each leg. The casual shoes. His thin beard and mustache, his firm chin and unlined face. Even at fifty-eight, he looked able-bodied and fit, thoughtful and intelligent, and, most important, the compassion on his face appeared to be genuine. Too good to be true, but he was the President of the United States. Marla knew about politicians, but some were better than others.

"Why me?"

He looked away from her as he answered.

"Because it asked for you," he whispered in a hoarse voice. "Your grandfather stole something that it wants returned."

When he turned back, he added, "Your files say that you are an expert at what you do, Marla, and that your performance in the field is exemplary. You are completely mission focused. I pray you are much, much better than that, because I do not wish to live to see the total enslavement of humanity."

With that, he left her alone in the room.

Seven seconds later, they came to take her away.

2

President Usman sat behind the same table in the Treaty Room that President Obama and President George W. Bush had used as their private study. It was President Usman's favorite room in the entire White House, as it had been for many of his predecessors. The grandfather clock to his left ticked softly, measuring out the time left until a monster returned to the world. A monster that could not be stopped.

On such nights as these, his Isha would be performed very late indeed, because the worm of fear and rage slithered through the sick lake of hopelessness that roiled his stomach. The phone sat still on the desk. The phone that only rang if it called.

Some nights, he sat at this table and could feel the eyes of the world staring at him. He could hear the whisperings of his brother Muslims, some strident, some pleading and all demanding Sharia law. He remembered the No Sharia signs bobbing up and down at his campaign rallies. The never-ending baiting him with hostile reporters eager to show that he was Muslim first and American second. Worse were the sycophants, who wanted to show their opening-mindedness by getting him elected because he was a Muslim. But these were pleasant night meditations compared to those when he remembered the thing lurking in Borgo, Michigan. The rattling breath of evil that haunted his sleep. The thing threatening that it would soon return.

The monster that every president since President Harry Truman had feared. One by one, each of them had determined to put an end to the creature who now held sway in a world separate, but tangential, to their own. One way in, no way out. Borgo, Michigan.

And like those presidents before him, President Usman had sent sacrifices to appease the monster because he knew the consequences of disobedience. He tried not to think of the Corvasce woman. She would never be seen again. What would happen to her was unthinkable. He had no choice, though. Some must die that others may live.

When he had taken the oath of office, he had steeled himself against the trials and tribulations of his Presidency, and yet determined to make a difference for the better. He was born and raised in Hamtramck, Michigan. He loved Michigan. And now, knowing what he knew, he hated the entire state of Michigan.

The people were wildly diverse, and it was not a melting pot of culture. No, it was a robust and thriving, contentious and a brilliantly interactive climate for both high tech and hard living. But, to his everlasting shame and regret, Michigan was where the portal to the town of Borgo stood, between the inexplicable giant wooden poles thrusting up into the sky north of Lansing. The landmark known as "Polehenge."

It was there that masked agents put a hooded and bound Marla Corvasce into the remotely operated van to send her through the portal. Traverse Nations had already explained to the president that if Marla died in Borgo, he would see to her remains. If there were bone fragments left, he would bury them. There was a young systems analyst he could have to say an appropriate prayer for her. Her family, although long dead, was Catholic. She would need Catholic rites or at least as close to that as Traverse could arrange, said the president. Traverse hadn't responded to that request, but President Usman hadn't pressed him. Traverse Nations was all that stood between Hiram Abiff and the world as everyone knew it.

The phone, that awful phone, stared back at him.

President Usman dreaded the sound of its ring. Only one person ever called that phone, and that was Hiram Abiff. Once, early in his term, President Usman had refused to answer it when it rang. The next morning, when his daughter had turned a faucet handle in the bathroom, blood had come pouring out. He heard screams but was pushed and dragged away by well-meaning Secret Service personnel. The President had to be protected at all costs, even while his daughter screamed for him. Later, when his daughter had been sedated, they showed him the blood writing on the mirror above the sink that read, "Always answer my calls."

The phone, that awful phone, the big one with the rotary dial and no phone cord connected to it. The only connection he was allowed to the town of Borgo.

It rang.

Feeling nauseous, he closed his eyes and, as he picked the receiver with them still squeezed shut, he heard the growling through the earpiece. A dog. Maybe a wolf. Maybe a monster gone mad. The president sat up straight up in his chair when heard thunder and then came the sound of something sniffing at the phone at the other end of the line.

A hunter's sniff—not slow and sensitive—but harsh and demanding, looking for prey. Hungry for prey.

Then the line went dead.

Rage seized him and he clenched his teeth so hard his jaw hurt. Then, President Usman put his hands against his face and wept. But not for Marla Corvasce, himself or his family. He wept for the world.

3

"What do you have for me, Jimmy?"

Jimmy cringed.

Wherever Traverse went, Marla Corvasce was sure to follow. And although Jimmy liked Marla a lot—any man would—he didn't like the idea of her standing behind him. It made him feel uncomfortable. No reason, really. They were both on the same side, after all. It was just the little piece of rope with the knot in the middle she always carried around. He'd read what things like that were used for. Made him want to scrunch his head down tight on his shoulders so his throat was safe.

"Jimmy?"

"Sorry, Mr. Nations. I've got nothing. I thought the new program would make sense of the scrambled visual data feed, but it's pretty well useless. It's like the old man just disappeared. I had him right until he was a block away from the Masonic lodge, but as soon as he passed the stop sign, he was just… gone, like usual."

"Shit," said Traverse. "All this money on equipment, all these people and still nothing."

"Want me to go after him?"

Marla's voice sounded like Marla looked. Lithe. Supple. Provocative.

Traverse flipped an empty Styrofoam coffee cup into a trash can.

Took out his phone, looked at the caller ID and then shoved it back into his pocket. He shook his head.

"No."

"I can take care of myself," she said.

The irritation in her voice caused Jimmy to hunker down over his keyboard.

"What? I'm not talking about you. Too much to lose—as in if we piss him off, it's all over. You're just not in his league."

Ignoring the cold look in Marla's eyes, Traverse stepped back to study the wide array of screens. He studied the feeds from the security cameras across town. Everything from military installed equipment to the ATMs and the optical fibers embedded in the TV's, bedroom walls and even data from the RFIDs in the townspeople's clothing. Too much data. Not enough data.

Borgo, Michigan, USA was a locked down town.

Traverse felt the need to do something violent.

Most of the main screens were blank or useless. There was more government equipment tied up in his operation than they'd spent in Iraq. Iraq only lasted ten years. Operation Borgo had been going on for seventy.

The new equipment failures started happening sporadically over the last six months. Something causing it, something they couldn't identify. It wasn't the old man, he didn't think. When he made something go dead, it died spectacularly. None of this fade-out and come back crap. But it bothered Traverse. Maybe it was because in his experience, strange questions you couldn't answer in Borgo, Michigan, always had really, really bad explanations.

"I wish the NSA could see this place," he told Jimmy.

"They still can't see anything, including us. They can't even find this place with their satellites."

"Yeah, I know. Shit. Forget I said it."

A tech called out from the other side of the room.

"All eyes are blind," she said.

"What?" asked Traverse.

"Every visual feed in town is dead. We are completely blind, sir."

"Sure you don't want me to go check on him?" asked Marla.

Traverse Nations thought about it. They were flying blind here.

He couldn't afford to make a wrong move. Too much at stake for too many years. But no, the old man had asked for Marla. Best not to fuck with the old man's new toy.

"Stay put, Marla."

His jaw ached from the constant tension.

"Director Nations?"

Traverse turned to see Major Lansdale coming at him, flanked by two soldiers.

"I'm busy."

Landsdale was tall and had wiry white hair cropped in a short buzz. Strong features with a stone jaw, and bright blue eyes. Walked like a robot on steroids. Or a military zombie.

"The Secretary of Defense would like you to answer your phone."

"I'll call him back."

Landsdale and his two bodyguards stopped at exactly the same moment, only three feet away from Traverse.

"Sir, the Secretary of Defense orders you to answer your phone."

The background noise went down in the big room and the tension ratcheted up.

"Major, I don't work for him — you do. Are we clear on that? I work for the president. And as concerns Operation Borgo, the Secretary of Defense reports to me, as does everyone else in this country, including you."

"I'm afraid—"

"No, you're not," said Traverse. "If you want to be afraid, you have to cross me first."

"We have orders to take you into custody if you don't comply. Sir."

"Major, the only two people I report to are the President of these United States and God," roared Traverse, "and I don't think you want to bother either of them."

Marla was on her feet, moving in. Traverse shook his head, and she went over to lean against the water cooler.

"Mr. Nations?"

It was Jimmy.

"What is it?"

"Now all the cameras across town are working, but the old man's gone."

Traverse had no idea what that meant.

"Can you get hold of the teams?"

"No, sir."

Shit.

"Are we through here, Major? If so, take your men and get back to work. I'm busy. I'll call President Usman and have him replace the Secretary."

Major Landsdale flushed. Too bad. Chain of command was chain of command.

A slight nod of the head and Traverse knew it was over. He'd have to kill him again later, though. He just knew it.

"Sorry to have bothered you, Mr. Nations."

In his head, Traverse translated that as I'm going to murder you, motherfucker. But Traverse didn't waste time thinking about it. Later, the Major would get his. He knew worse things than death were headed their way, anyway. Felt it the way old people felt the weather in their bones. Things were coming to a close in Borgo. He didn't know how he knew it; he just did.

The lights went out, and the room was plunged into darkness. The emergency lights flashed. Traverse looked where he had last seen Marla. Her eyes were fixed on the wall of computer screens. She'd seen something there before everything went black. A glimpse of something that startled her. For the first time since she worked for him, Traverse saw fear grip her lovely face.

Traverse had seen a glimpse, too, before the power went out. The old man, his face on all the screens at once, staring at them. Nearly bald, wearing an old flannel shirt and wire-rim glasses. The lenses glowed an eerie electric blue, concealing his eyes.

Time was running out; the Freemasons would come soon enough. That's when it would really start getting bad. That's what Eva told him, and Eva knew things.

Time to bring Marla up to speed. The president sent her, so she had to be good. But that wasn't why he'd sent her. Good didn't cut it in Borgo. The old man asked for her and that was enough. The old man was where everything started and ended in this town. At least she looked nice, too. Most of the other women in Borgo were already dead.

****

"This way," said Traverse.

Marla Corvasce hustled after his broad back and tangled mass of silver hair as he strode down the hallway. She caught up to him at the elevator just as the door was opening.

"Minus Eight," he said to an unseen sensor.

They were at full power again, the techs still huddled around their screens. The scientists trying to figure out what the hell was going on, and the military personnel balanced on the knife edge of feeling the threat but unable to locate the enemy.

She slipped in just before the doors closed and the elevator began its descent eight stories below ground. Traverse noted her presence and then drifted off to another place in his mind. Most men his age were likely struck by her looks. Unfulfilled desires. Lost loves. Lost youth. Not him. He was on a mission.

Traverse Nations was sixty-six years old. He walked like a manic Marine and talked like a newscaster with a gun. The kind of guy who'd stand out in a crowd easy enough for a long-distance sniper to put him down and be confident he got the right guy. But Traverse didn't care. He had one mission only, and that's why he squashed the Secretary of Defense without a second thought.

"You have been here two days now, right?" he said.

"Almost."

"You've done good, so far. I told you no questions. I told you to watch and learn, and you look like you've been doing both."

"And?" she said.

"What do you think so far?"

"I don't know."

"Scared?"

The elevator came to a stop.

"No," she said.

The stainless-steel doors opened with a soft hiss.

"Too bad," he said. "I thought you were smarter than that."

It was her first time on Minus Eight and the sight of so much free firing electricity was so completely unexpected that Traverse got a ten-foot head start on her. The air pulsed with scarlet light from banks of twenty-foot-tall glass tubes where ribbons of electricity twisted and coiled like living DNA. Traverse was headed toward a giant blue crystal lifted that was ten feet in the air on a pedestal made of what looked stainless steel. She stared at it all incredulously. A few moments passed before she noticed the room's temperature. It was like walking into a freezer. She wondered if the president knew about this place, or if Traverse kept it from him.

"You coming?" Traverse called over his shoulder.

Marla shook off her sense of astonishment and hustled to catch up.

"Time you got to know what's going on here," he said when she'd drawn even.

They were ten feet from the base of the stainless-steel platform. The temperature grew warmer the closer they got, as though the overhead crystal were a radiant heater. She gaged the room to be two hundred and fifty feet long by two hundred feet wide. Floor to ceiling, around thirty to forty feet. It was hard to tell with the distracting lights and arrays of flashing tubes.

Traverse turned and faced her.

"This floor houses our weapon of last resort. The one that brings the big pain."

She stared at him, one part of her brain trying to understand just how dangerous he was, another shocked by the equipment in Minus Eight, and another part of her mind still struggled with the dread she'd felt when she'd seen the face on the screens upstairs. When the president had suddenly assigned her to this facility, she did not know her next assignment would be like this. Now she wished she was in the Middle East.

"It—this entire floor—is a dislocational weapon," said Traverse. "Go ahead. Ask."

"All right," she said. "What is a dislocational weapon?"

Traverse took a step closer and searched her eyes.

"First, tell me what you saw on the screens upstairs."

He spoke softly, but his voice carried more impact than if he'd barked at her.

"A face. On all the screens. Old man, glasses glowing like neon."

"And who do you think that was, Marla?"

"I don't know."

"Come on," said Traverse. "Tell daddy what scared you. Was it the moment you figured out that it was the old man who asked the president to send you here?"

His mouth was set in a dark, knowing smile.

She wanted to wrap her rope around his neck and yank it so hard his face would turn rose-hip red, and his eyes would bulge like those of a drunken fish.

But he was right.

She was scared.

"Do you know anything about the Freemasons, Marla?" asked Traverse.

"What?" she asked.

Where the hell was he going with this?

"Your file says all the men in your family were Freemasons."

"So?"

"That old man you saw on the screens thinks one of them went rogue and took something he wants. He thinks your grandfather was the one who took it. It's a thin little book. A journal. It's called The Confessions of Mr. Hyde or something. Do you know where it is?"

"What the hell are you talking about, Traverse?"

Traverse put his hands on his hips, and his eyes seemed to stare past her. He looked like Superman in his senior years, minus his cape, posing for the world as he looked out over the Metropolis cityscape with old, wise eyes.

"Somebody's always got to pay," he said in his deep, resonant voice.

4

"We think it has stuff in it about him, stuff he doesn't want us or anyone else to know," Traverse said. "He wants it badly. Can't talk about it anywhere else in Borgo or he'll hear what we're saying and maybe get pissed. We can talk here because of all this high energy interference tied in with the Minus Eight dislocational weaponry. The science assholes think there are a lot of places in this complex he can't hear us.

"You and I, we're going to need to talk sometimes where no one else, including public enemy number one, can hear what we're saying. He doesn't like it if, though, so we can't stay here too long. You got that? Think hard and think fast. Were there any Masonic papers handed down to you by the men in your family? Or do you know if your grandfather's estate included any Masonic papers or journals? Come on, Marla, think."

He'd taken a step back to put a more comfortable distance between them. Writhing black ribbons from the pulsing light slid across his body like shadow snakes. She kept her breathing even and tried to block out the sense of threat and the strange equipment packed into the level called Minus Eight.

"My grandfather was a dirt-poor farmer," she said irritably. "Whatever land or possessions he had were seized by Mussolini's fascists."

Traverse smiled, and she actually thought he was going to laugh, but he went serious at the last second.

"Hold it," he said and pulled his phone from his inside pocket.

His smile broadened as he looked at the screen.

"What is it?" asked Marla.

When he glanced up at her, he grinned like a big, silver-haired wolf.

"Change of plans. Minus Eight is ready. Time to watch a trial run."

****

The caravan of three cars stopped in the middle of the gravel road beside a row of wrinkly fingered trees. Snow was piled about in random drifts. Marla rode in the second car with Traverse. The car ahead and the car behind each contained four grim-faced soldiers. All three cars switched off their headlights at the same instant and then the night was on them.

A faint silver glow lit a small patch of sky where the moon slowly suffocated behind clouds the color of oily rags. After her eyes adjusted, she saw islands of water scattered among dead cattails and frozen rushes ringed by snow.

"We're going to test Minus Eight here?"

"Lot of rocks around here. Bottles and old sinks and whatever other trash the good citizens of this city can get away with dumping here. Easy to break an ankle in the dark," said Traverse.

Cold air rushed in when Traverse opened the driver's side door and stepped out into the night. Something dark flapped by the car and disappeared out over the water before one soldier fear-shot it.

Gravel crunched beneath her feet as she stepped out onto the road. The night air was cold and clean. She pulled on her night vision goggles and activated them. The night lit up in ghostly hues.

"Lead the way, sergeant," said Traverse.

Two soldiers flanked them on either side as they moved forward, the sergeant in the lead and one more bringing up the rear. Frozen branches and weeds snapped and cracked as they made their way through the snow-covered brush. They maneuvered their way through the tree line and saw an open field of snow. In the middle of the field, thirty feet away, was a small stand of trees.

"You're going to need these," said Traverse as he handed her a set of night-vision binoculars.

"Why?"

"So, you can see the action."

"Where?"

He extended a finger toward the stand of trees.

Something didn't feel right to Marla. She scanned the area, looking for anything out of place. Nothing. But she had a feeling, and she didn't like it.

"Showtime," said Traverse, and he raised his own night-vision binoculars.

Marla did the same.

The shock of what she saw was like a punch in the gut.

Six men were staked to poles by what appeared to be wire cable. Black hoods covered their heads and were cinched around their necks. Their hands were tied behind their backs. They stood completely still, like goats staked out for a lion. Afraid to move. Afraid they'd be noticed. Afraid they'd be pounced on. She was glad she couldn't see their faces.

"Convicts," said Traverse before she could ask. "Every one of them sentenced to lethal injection."

She lowered her binoculars and stared at him.

"You're going to test Minus Eight on them?"

He didn't so much as look at her. His silver hair sprouted from beneath a pullover cap. He stood formidably straight and tall. A captain looking out over Her Majesty's ocean of snow.

"Had to try it on somebody. They're all going to die, anyway."

Marla had killed up close and had killed from a distance. But never like this.

"There's got to be another way."

"Don't pussy out on me now, Marla. We have to know for sure what Minus Eight can do."

He lowered his binoculars, pulled out his phone, and pushed a button. The screen lit up.

"Don't do this, Traverse."

"Shut up Marla."

He removed one glove and touched the screen, then lifted his binoculars again and looked toward the area where the men stood.

Marla looked around at the others. They didn't appear to notice or care. It was out of her hands.

She raised her binoculars.

Sparks of ionized air surrounded the men, who panicked and pulled at their cables. She saw their heads thrash back and forth and thought she heard muffled screams. And then they were gone.

Blackness, instant blackness where they'd stood.

It lasted only a fraction of a section, then the night returned to normal.

Six lives snuffed out like someone had turned off a switch.

"Old man, you are soon to be one dead-assed freak," screamed Traverse.

His voice was filled with a raging wildness.

"You just killed six men," she said.

"They had it coming anyway," he said after a prolonged, almost painful inhalation of night air. "For once, they did something good. It works, Marla, it works. The son of a bitch works. We are going to win this war now."

They'd both lowered their binoculars. Traverse was looking around at his men like a bionic alpha male. Marla still had the bad feeling. She turned back toward where the men had disappeared and raised her binoculars again.

"Sergeant, this night will go down in history," said Traverse.

"There's someone still out there," said Marla.

"Bullshit. They're all gone. I saw it. You saw it."

"Look again."

From the corner of her eye, she saw him raise his binoculars. She knew he was seeing what she was seeing. An old man standing where the convicts had been tethered. He wore a flannel shirt and jeans. No coat. No hat. Marla saw a glint off the man's glasses as he raised his finger and pointed at them.

"Can't be," choked Traverse. "Can't be."

The old man's lenses were the color of cold blue neon. They grew brighter. Brighter. Without warning, they flashed so brightly that Marla and Traverse both dropped their binoculars and shielded their eyes. Marla was instantly blinded. She heard men screaming all around her as she dropped to the ground. Pressing her gloves over her ears, she rolled back and forth, trying to drown out their dying.

5

Traverse was ten minutes on the phone with the president while six body bags were being "cataloged" by the scientists. Marla had seen some blood in her time, but she'd never seen six bodies split open like overripe fruit. Clothing soaked with gore. Faces split apart. Hands burst open. Bloody lips blown up and cracked cheeks. Only so much you could look at. Only so much you could "catalog" before you quit functioning.

Everyone on the main floor knew something horrible had happened. She could see it in the soldiers' eyes and by the way the technical people and the scientists tried not to look at the soldiers. Men and women were dying because the scientists couldn't give them weapons to fight their enemy. The tension between the two groups was like a low microwave hum. No one was saying anything, but things were getting hotter.

"Minus Eight is one heck of a lot of melted titanium," said Jimmy.

"Does Traverse know?" asked Marla.

"Traverse knows everything."

"I don't think he saw this coming," said Marla.

"No," said Jimmy. "Somebody's going to have to pay."

"What did you say?"

Jimmy looked away.

"I have to get back to work now. Re-route around level eight."

It wasn't what he said; it was what he didn't say. She moved closer to him, violated his space.

"Jimmy, what exactly do you do here? Exactly?"

They were only inches apart. She turned up the wattage. Breathed a little slower and parted her lips.

He backed away.

"Nice one," he said. "Almost had me."

As he was about to turn his back on her, an impulse question popped into her consciousness.

"What is the old man?"

For a moment, she thought he was thinking of an answer. Right until Traverse Nations stepped into her field of vision.

"Let's go down to look at Minus Eight and have a talk," he said to her. To Jimmy, he said, "Get back to work. Check every weapons system we've got. Scientists tell me everything's running. If they're wrong, I'm going to have one of them shot in the head while they're in the cafeteria eating lunch with their pals. I mean it. No room for error here. Somebody's got to pay."

The look on Jimmy's face told Marla all she needed to know.

It wouldn't be the first time.

****

As the elevator slid down toward Minus Eight, Marla looked at the small screen displaying their depth and what level they were approaching. Traverse was looking at her, sizing her up, staring at her like he wanted to see if she could take it. Older men could be like that. Younger men, too. Both were dangerous.

"Somebody has to pay," Traverse said as they came to Minus Eight again. "I think that prick Landsdale has gone over. I never trusted him. We're at war here, you see that, Marla? An enemy that looks like a little old man. But it's an actual war. You see that, don't you?"

"What is he?" she asked.

Traverse inched a little closer and she could feel her back muscles tighten.

"He's an American citizen is what he is, and we're trying to contain or kill his ass with everything this country has got to throw at him. Seventy years later and nothing to show for it but a bunch of dead bodies and billions of dollars of black expenditures. Problem is, I don't think he's from around here, if you know what I mean."

"And?" she said.

"Either way, you have to keep the troops in line. Somebody's got to pay. I never liked Major Landsdale. He doesn't belong in Borgo, or maybe he likes it too much."

Soft chimes as the elevator completely stopped.

"Discipline's the only way. It's not my idea. Dr. Grayson's got it all mapped out for me. People go crazy in an operation like this. Got to keep them under control. People look up to you long enough, eventually, you got to look down at them. Only way. Are you hearing me on this, Marla?"

Not for the first time in the last two days, she wondered exactly what President Usman had gotten her into.

The stainless-steel elevator doors slid open to reveal the extent of the disaster. Because the HAZMAT teams had installed specialized filtration units, the air was breathable. A team of electrical engineers and electricians had the lights back on, but one look at the damage and she didn't understand why they wasted the time. Floors, walls and ceiling were fine. Desks and chairs were coated with dull metallic dust, but otherwise looked ready to sit on. But the Minus Eight equipment had melted into blobs of iridescent silver.

"What the hell happened here?" she asked.

Traverse ignored her and wandered off. The old man in the field happened here. They both knew it. She just wanted to hear him say it. Remembering the president's last words to her, she prayed she was up to this task. She had a job to do, and she was wondering if, for the first time in her life, she wasn't up to her assigned mission.

Traverse was walking between the masses of multi-colored, shiny mounds, swearing to himself. Once, he stopped and screamed. His arms spread out at his sides, fingers splayed wide as he went primal for the cameras. Somewhere no one would ever find, there'd be filament lenses. Special Aides to the president would watch in dark rooms. Psych profiles would be updated. Analysts would be called in.

The President would be briefed. The president would nod, show some anger, show some anguish and show some steel. Traverse would get a call, Traverse would talk, the President would talk and nothing would change. She saw all that in an instant. They didn't know what to do.

Where did one old man get the power to resist the entire government of the United States? No one seemed to know. At least she was getting answers to the questions the president knew, but refused to tell her before she was taken away. She remembered him saying, "It asked for you."

To hell with that.

She remembered his face filling the computer screens. Remembered seeing him standing where the hooded convicts had stood, pointing his finger at her team. Remembered the flash of painful light. Waking up to the dead men lying in pools of their own blood on the cold ground.

Impossible that this could all be below the media's radar. How did Traverse keep it out of the news? How did the president?

But she'd seen a lot of impossible things in the last few days.

Traverse screamed so loudly she thought his lungs would burst. His long, silver hair was wild. In his jeans, cowboy boots and corduroy jacket, he looked like a ranch hand going crazy at the moon. He picked up a table and ran down the aisle shouting. Papers flew madly behind him. Marla's eyebrows went up in surprise as he spun around in circles and then threw the table at a wall-mounted fire extinguisher.

"You missed," she said.

When he turned to face her, his white hair stuck out as though electrified, and from his spastic hand gestures, she thought he was going to come running at her, but he started laughing.

They were the only two people on the whole level now, as far as she could tell, because the sound of his laughter crashed back and forth like images bouncing off fun house mirrors. He gasped for breath, bent forward and slapped his knees. Finally, he sat down on the floor cross-legged, like a cowboy guru settling into the lotus position.

"Get up," said Marla. "I'm too wired to sit and I'm tired of being kept in the dark. What's really happening here?"

She extended a hand to Traverse, who grabbed hold and allowed her to help him to his feet. But he hung on to her hand and didn't let go, peering at her as though seeing her for the first time. The realization that they were alone rose in her thoughts like a flashing red sign.

"We're at war here, Marla," he croaked, "with a man or something that looks like a man but that we absolutely cannot kill."

"Let go of my hand," she said.

"What? Sorry, I got carried away."

He loosened his grip, then shot forward with incredible speed and hit her with both palms. The impact was so powerful and unexpected that she blacked out in flight but snapped back to consciousness in time to hit a round mound of metal. It knocked the air out of her lungs and left her gulping desperately for air as she slid down to the floor. He was on her instantly, slapping her and ripping at her clothes. His breath stunk like rancid meat.

His weight held her in place as she struggled to stay conscious. When she brought her head up for a breath, he head-butted her so hard her skull cracked back against the floor, and she was momentarily blind for the second time in a day.

"Somebody's got to pay. Your turn, your turn."

Growling and spitting the words like an enraged animal. One hand in her hair, pulling hard now.

A blurred demon mask hung above her, and she screamed. Had to kill this thing. Had to kill it. It was it or her. She got a hand free, slammed it upward, and connected with its chin. Heard the howl. Heard the animal pain and rage. It pulled back, gave her enough space between them for her to brace her foot and flip it off her.

"Enough."

Marla was on her knees, pulling out her thin black rope as the room spun dizzily around her. Then she processed the voice and saw the creature she'd thrown off her. Not Traverse. She froze.

Yellow, rheumy eyes, mottled green skin and a hideous mouth open wide and showing rows of razor-sharp teeth. Long arms and sharp talons. Ears that swept up into points and tufts of rough hair sprouting from its skin. Two blunt, gnarled horns jutted up from the top of its head.

It stared at her with seething hatred blazing in its huge yellow eyes.

"Don't move," said a commanding voice.

Six feet away, a tall woman dressed in black silk held her palm out.

"Hiram's creatures are mine to command," she said. "But they are hungry, always hungry. Never tempt them."

The beast snarled.

"Enough, I say."

Its eyes glanced over at the woman, then down to the floor. With a few quick, bent-legged leaps, it was at its mistress's side.

For the first time Marla saw Traverse Nations was standing like a statue, his hand outstretched as though still holding on to her. His face was a stretched mask; his mouth wide open and stuck in that position. He was a mannequin stranded on the thirteenth floor of life.

"Your grandfather chose sides badly," said the woman. "If the Fascists had found him first, he would have at least died as a human being."

"What did you say?"

She stayed in her crouch, unwilling to risk an attack by the creature, confused by what the woman was saying. How she got there, what the beast was, and why Traverse did not move were questions she would only think of later. Right then, all that mattered was the woman who held the creature back.

Tall, unbelievably beautiful. Long, dark hair that hung about her shoulders and a hideous creature that obeyed her.

"Do not stand in my way, sister. I will have the journal back. Prepare to return it to me or die a death worse than that of your grandfather's."

Then she was gone. The creature was gone. Traverse Nations lowered his arm and spoke.

"What the hell happened to you?" he said.

She got up slowly, ignoring the pain in her head, her back, and her chest.

"That bitch," she said. "That fucking bitch."

6

Traverse Nations leaned back in his black, plush leather chair, held the glass of bourbon in front of his eyes and admired the ice cubes floating in the amber covered liquid. After a moment's thought, he brought it to his lips, closed his eyes and knocked it back. He savored it as it slid down his throat. It had taken a while to quiet Marla Corvasce down. A phone call from the president interrupted their argument, and he told her he'd fill her in on all the details of what was going on in Borgo in the morning. That wasn't completely true, but it worked. She wasn't happy. In fact, she'd been flat out furious. He'd thought he was going to have to shoot her in the kneecap or call the guards to baton her into unconsciousness. But she'd eventually quieted down. She was still red-hot angry at being put off after being knocked to the concrete floor by a hairy monster with horns, but she womaned up and put it in neutral. Hard to argue with a man who had the president on the phone. And it gave him time to think of how to explain to Marla who the woman was who had appeared in Minus Eight. Eva Morgan was not a simple woman to explain.

The president had been easier. He took in Traverse's report, wanted to know his next moves, and then let him get back to it. President Usman was an okay duck for a Muslim. He sent the weapons, the food and the personnel like the other presidents. At first, he'd try to get hold of Project Borgo, to understand just what the hell was really going on. But they were all like that, thought Traverse. They had so much control over so many things that they thought they should be able to fix everything. A couple weeks on the job disabused them of that, especially for Project Borgo. Some had wanted to load in more firepower, others wanted to close down shop, pretend the whole thing never happened. They eventually figured out that wasn't an option. Eventually, the old man with the glowing eyes would return to the real world, and they just couldn't let that happen without a fight.

Except Usman. He was a fatalist. He knew the end of the world when it looked him in the face. So, he didn't put up a fight at all. Usman was dickless, like all the rest of them. George W. Bush wanted to attack Borgo with everything the country had, but after Iraq, he lost his faith in war. He'd turned it all over to Traverse. That's how two generations of Nations men had headed up Operation Borgo. It was their curse after what happened to that prick Truman.

Traverse missed his father and his grandfather. Both had disappeared into the Borgo portal to take over the fight against the old man. But better dead than alive in Borgo.

Now, here he was alone in his office with the lights off and the whiskey flowing. He was remembering how it had all had started with Eva Morgan. When she'd shown up again, he was less shocked that she looked to be only thirty years old than by the fact she existed at all. She was real. His childhood nightmare was real.

With a second round poured, he tapped his fingers on his glass and chrome desk and remembered their first meeting.

****

Trenton, Michigan USA July 15, 1955

"Old people can't have babies," the girl said.

"Why not?" asked the boy.

"Because," the girl said.

"Because why?" persisted the boy.

"They're cursed, that's why," the girl said.

"I'm seven," he said.

"You'll die, too," said the girl.

The boy looked around for his mother. He looked to his right and saw that she was still waiting in line to buy his fudge bar at the little shack with the concrete casting of an ice cream cone as big as his older brother.

The little girl came from nowhere and sat down next to him on the red and white picnic blanket in the shade of a tree that blocked the sunlight like a giant beach umbrella. He had watched wide-eyed as she lifted one side of the picnic basket lid and rummaged through the knives and forks and pickle jars and sealed plastic containers of sliced tomatoes and yellow-white cheese. The girl had pulled out press-locked plastic bags of ham, cream cheese, and chives. A loaf of bread was against one side of the woven basket, as though resting.

"That's ours," said the boy.

The girl set a plastic bowl full of fruit the size of a bisected beach ball next to his right foot. She looked at him and smiled, pried open the lid of another container, plucked out a deviled egg, and pushed the entire thing into her mouth.

"My mom's there," said the boy, pointing at the ice cream shack.

The girl chewed, swallowed, then gulped and said, "She'll drop your ice cream."

"I'm older than you," said the boy.

"You'll die first," said the girl.

She had hair as white as spun sugar, eyes blue as wildflowers, fair skin sprinkled with freckles, and a smile bright as a toothpaste commercial.

"Will not," said the boy.

The air was as moist and hot as an open oven door. Patches of burned grass scarred the park as though blasted by ray guns. The pony rides were closed until the temperature dropped below ninety. On the other side of the parched baseball field, the red lights of a parked ambulance with open back doors flashed and spun. A man and a woman in white uniforms were sliding someone onto a stretcher. Six women with hunched backs, thin white hair, and big black sunglasses huddled close by as though one of them was next.

"Your brother wants to bury you in the backyard," said the girl.

"Mom," yelled the boy.

"What's the matter, baby?" his mother called back.

He looked at the girl. She was batting her eyes and waving at his mother. After a sideways glance at him, she even blew his mother a kiss.

"Are you coming back soon?" he called to his mother.

"In a minute," she said. "You just wait there for me."

He looked at the girl.

"She can't see me," she said.

"She can too," said the boy.

Overhead, in the tree, the boy heard a bird's angry chatter. He glanced up and saw an orange-chested robin on a branch flapping its wings. The branch shook, but the robin's claws stayed fixed to it as though glued. The boy looked back at the girl.

"Nobody can see me except you," she said.

"You want to play catch?" asked the boy.

"First, we have to make lunch," said the girl.

"Huh?" asked the boy.

"In the kitchen," said the girl, and pointed to a white plastic stove and a red plastic table and chairs that had not been there a moment ago. "First, we play kitchen, and then we can play catch."

"No," said the boy.

"Yes," said the girl.

"How come?" asked the boy.

"We always do what I want first, then what you want. Always."

"What's your name?" he asked.

"Eva," she said, and curtsied.

"You're weird," said the boy.

He looked toward the river and imagined a cool breeze coming off its waters.

"If you go near the river," Eva said, "I'll drown you."

"Mom," called the boy.

"Mommy's coming," his mother called back. "I just have to pay this nice man and I'll be right back. Just keep your little pants on."

Overhead, a dirty-gray seagull flew in circles and screamed for food.

"Go away," the boy told Eva.

"You know what happened when your grandma died?" asked Eva.

The boy slapped his hands over his ears and closed his eyes.

"She died by herself, and she just laid there on the kitchen floor for three days," said Eva.

"La, la, la," chanted the boy.

"You remember her dog?" asked Eva.

The boy nodded while he continued to chant. His long blonde hair bounced up and down as though fluffed by puffs of wind.

"He didn't have any food in his bowl, so he ate your grandmother."

The boy screamed.

"What, baby? What?" called his mother. She dropped the fudge bar and broke into a run.

"She's bad," wailed the boy.

His mother laid her purse on the ground next to him, grabbed his shoulders, and dropped to one knee so that she could look right into his eyes.

"You scared me to death, little man," she said. "Are you okay?"

"She's bad," said the boy again, and he pointed at Eva.

He saw his mother look where he was pointing, squinting as though looking into the sun, then she looked back at him and said, "Who, Adam, who's bad?"

The boy pointed at Eva again.

"There's nobody there," said his mother.

"Told you," said Eva.

"I don't see anybody, son. Is something wrong with you? Does it hurt somewhere?"

"She's there, right there," cried the boy. His mother squeezed his shoulders, then released her grip and smiled. "Oh," she said. "You mean your imaginary friend? Okay, now I see her, honey."

"Your mother is a liar," said Eva.

"I had an imaginary friend when I was your age," softened his mother.

"She thinks you're a retard," said Eva.

"Am not," said the boy.

"Not what, honey?" asked his mother.

"Not a retard," said the boy.

"Of course you're not, honey," said his mother. "Are those boys in school calling you names?"

"Her," said the boy, pointing again at Eva. "She says I'm a retard."

His mother told him, "Well, she's wrong. Maybe she just thinks you're cute, honey, and wants your attention. Little girls are like that, even imaginary little girls. What else did she say?"

The boy looked at his mother and knew that he couldn't tell her about his grandmother and her dog.

"Nothing," said the boy.

"You're a liar, too," said Eva, "just like your mother."

"Nothing?" pressed his mother.

"She said bad things," the boy blurted out.

"Maybe it's your tummy talking to you," his mother said. She rubbed his stomach with her free hand, describing circles the size of a softball.

"God's mad at you," said Eva.

"Is not," said the boy, and he stomped his right foot in protest.

His mother pulled back and examined his face as though inspecting him for a rash.

"Let's try some fruit," his mother suggested. "Will mommy's little man try a banana for her?"

"Don't eat the apple," warned Eva. "There's a worm inside."

"No," said the boy, and he shrank back and leaned into his mother.

"You don't have to get upset, baby," said his mother.

"She thinks you're a retarded baby," said Eva.

"Because you don't have to eat a banana," said his mother. "There are oranges and apples and grapes, too."

The boy closed his eyes.

"Do you want an orange?" his mother asked.

"I'll still be here when you open your eyes," said Eva.

"No," said the boy, and he closed his eyes tighter.

"Okay," said his mother, "that's no to bananas and no to oranges. You want an apple?"

"Do you want me to go away?" whispered Eva.

"Yes," said the boy, and popped his eyes open.

She was still there.

"Well, there you go," said his mother. "An apple it is."

"I hate you," said the boy.

"Now, that's no way to talk to me," said his mother.

"Not you," said the boy. "Her. I hate her."

"Is she being bad again?" asked his mother, her eyes following Adam's extended finger.

"God told me why he's angry with you," said Eva. "Want to know?"

"Maybe," said the boy.

"Can't tell you," said Eva, and she stuck out her tongue.

The boy's mother had polished the apple to a waxy bright shine.

"Here you are, little man," said his mother. She extended it to him, as though it was an award.

The boy took the apple and turned it over, looking for a wormhole.

"Take a bite," said Eva. "Your mother wants you to."

"Oh look, honey," said his mother, "it's a little baby robin, right there."

The boy looked where his mother pointed and saw a baby bird hopping in the park grass. "Can I have him, mom?" he asked.

"I don't know," said his mother. "It could have rabies or something. It's a wild animal, son. "

Eva waved her hand in front of the boy's face to get his attention, and then smiled when he looked at her. "If you take a bite of the apple, I'll know you're my friend," said Eva.

"So?" asked the boy.

"If you're my friend," said Eva, "I won't kill the birdie."

"Better not," said the boy.

"Well," said his mother, "you never know. Bats have rabies."

The boy was about to say something, but his mother's pager went off. She extended her arm and pointed at the tiny, scrolling text with one finger. "It's him, it's him, honey. He came to see me."

"Mom —," began the boy.

"Shhhh," said his mother.

He saw a middle-aged man with thinning brown hair walking toward them.

"Mom —," said the boy.

"Shhhh," said his mother, then added, "I'll be right back. I'll just be with Tad for a little while."

From fifteen feet away, he heard her say, "Hello, Tad," in her breathy boyfriend voice.

Eva mimed his mother blowing kisses, inserted her right index finger into her mouth, pulled back her cheek, and then pretended to gag.

"Stop it," said the boy.

His mother waved him into silence, then she and Tad walked over to another tree, still talking as she walked away. She turned back to look at him and held a finger up to her lips.

"God said if you won't be my friend I can kill the birdie," said Eva.

"You're mean," said the boy.

"Will you be my friend?" asked Eva.

The boy looked at the bird, then back at Eva.

"I won't let you," said the boy.

"Die birdie," said Eva.

And the baby bird fell over dead.

The boy's mouth opened in horror.

"If you tell your mother," said Eva. "I'll kill her, too."

The boy looked at the bird, then at his mother.

"If you tell, I'll kill her. Now will you be my friend?" asked Eva.

The boy ran to the bird, kneeled down and looked at it, still clutching the apple. He poked the feathered corpse with a finger and then rolled it on its side. The grass underneath it was blackened into a perfect outline of the bird's body. The boy rolled the bird onto its back again.

"Wake up, birdie," he said

It lay there.

"Take a bite of the apple and I'll know you're my friend," said Eva.

The boy looked back at her, but couldn't think of anything to say.

"That's why God is mad at you," said Eva, "because you won't be my friend."

"But you're mean," protested the boy.

"If you take a bite of the apple, I'll know you're my friend. That's what God wants," said Eva.

The boy began to cry. He looked toward his mother and saw that she and Tad were standing very close. They were looking absently at two girls sitting near the river, and she was laughing.

"Will you be my friend?" persisted Eva.

"You won't hurt her?" sniffed the boy, pointing at his mother.

"Not if you're my friend," said Eva.

The boy bit into the apple.

Eva clapped.

"Don't hurt my mom," said the boy after swallowing his first bite.

He heard his mother laugh again.

"Now that we're friends," said Eva, "we can hold hands."

She extended her hand for the boy to take.

He walked back to where she stood. She had a big smile on her face.

"Don't hurt my mom," repeated the boy.

"Grab my hand," said Eva. "Don't make me mad."

The boy looked down at the apple.

"There's no worm," he said.

She stuck her hand out further, and, after another desperate look at his mother, he took it.

"The worm's in your stomach now," said Eva as she tightened her grip on his hand.

The boy gagged and bent forward, spitting out tiny pieces of apple.

"We'll always be friends," said Eva.

"I hate you," said the boy.

"You know where mommies die?" asked Eva.

"You said you wouldn't hurt her," said the boy.

"In the basement," said Eva. "Bad things happen to mommies in the basement. If you're ever not my friend, I'll wait for her in the basement when it's dark. When she comes down the stairs, I'll make her die, just like the birdie."

"No," said the boy.

He yanked back on his hand as hard as he could, but Eva would not let go. He grabbed her fingers with his other hand and tried to pry them off, but she only giggled. He kicked her in the shins and she laughed.

The boy dropped to his knees and cried again.

"Let me go," he whimpered.

"No," said Eva. "We'll always be friends. I'll come back again one day and be your best friend forever."

He did what scared his mother. He puffed his cheeks out and stopped breathing.

Eva smiled and squeezed his right hand so hard that his eyes glazed over from the pain and lack of air.

And then she was gone. Eva was gone.

The boy was the only one who even knew she had been there.

Everything was good after that.

Everything was fine after that. The mom and her boy lived well. Nothing was wrong. The boy forgot everything. That was good, too.

****

But, sixty years later—one year ago tonight—when Adam Traverse Nations was halfway through the construction of the Minus Eight weapon, she had returned and claimed him. He poured himself a third glass of bourbon and closed his eyes again.

7

John Amrozi tucked his shirt into his pants, zipped up, and buckled his belt.

She's an animal, he thought.

Traverse Nations gave him a lot of perks in his job, but introducing him to Eva Morgan topped them all. He was not doing too badly for a guy charged with treason. He'd been about to make John Snowden look like a piker when they busted him. But that was then, and this was now. Traverse had sent people looking for him, saved his ass from prison and for the last five years Amrozi had worked full time in the sweet town of Borgo on what he appropriately now called the Borgo virus, although it was really much more than that. Much more than a virus.

He'd modeled it after the SETI program, infiltrated as many computers as he could to accomplish the big man's goal, and used them as hardworking little robots in the John Amrozi army. By the time he was through, he'd turned the Internet into his own private workforce. It was a weird, very weird thing the old man was after, but with Eva Morgan thrown in the mix, how could he say no? It was a crazy plan, but if it made his perfect minx happy, he was the man to get it done.

Seeing his reflection in the full-length mirror across her bedroom, he puffed up his chest and turned his chin to the side. I get better looking every year, he thought. I look great, I'm brilliant, about to be sinfully rich and I've made the slickest computer program in the world.

Too bad no one would ever know. His looks, brains and money would be obvious, but the Borgo virus, revolutionary though it was, couldn't even be detected, much less talked about. With the money and the rest going for him, he could live without the notoriety. He could live very well indeed. It was better than being court martialed. As long as Eva came along for the ride.

"Are you going to stand there admiring yourself, or will you come have a drink with a lonely woman?"

Eva Morgan's voice was soft as Turkish Angora fur. She radiated mind-numbing sexuality.

"I think I can arrange that," said Amrozi.

She was so hot the air conditioner kicked on when she licked her lips.

He was lifting his cream-colored shirt when she slid in close and plucked it out of his hand. With an elegant flick of her wrist, she tossed onto the bed. It landed in a heap on the royal blue silk sheets.

"Oh no," she said. "No need for that."

She reached around him and slid her hands onto his stomach.

"I adore your abs," she said.

Their reflection in the mirror was almost more than he could take. He felt like a voyeur, spying on his own life. He smelled her musky rich perfume, saw her perfect chest pressed against his back, and watched as her right hand slid up to caress his chest muscles. He shivered with pleasure. Her lips brushed against the back of his neck.

"You are an incredible woman," he said, and half closed his eyes.

She stretched up on her toes and whispered close to his ear.

"It's working," she said.

"Oh yes. I can go another around."

"Not you, dearest. I meant the Borgo virus. Traverse says it's working."

If Traverse Nation's scientists were happy, that meant the project was a success. And that meant he got the big payoff. The ultimate check. Fifty million dollars.

"He's thrilled," she purred.

Her hands floated up to his shoulders, and she kneaded his muscles. She was so good. His mind drifted. The Borgo virus. Altering the screen patterns on a monitor ever so slightly. Traverse Nation's scientists had given him the mathematical algorithms to embed. He never knew exactly what the changes did. Something about changing brain wave patterns for whoever was looking at the monitor. Why? He wasn't sure exactly why. Perhaps it elevated their frontal lobe energy.

She was nibbling on his ear. It was hard to think.

Traverse Nations was bat shit crazy. Television and the Internet did the same thing anyway, every day and every night. Spoon fed visual shit to the masses. No wonder nobody could think clearly anymore. He at least had an excuse. He had Eva Morgan.

"Two o'clock tonight at Traverse's house. I'll meet you there. He has a surprise for you. He's thrilled with what you've done."

"He's up that late?"

"Don't worry, I'll take you to him."

Amrozi sighed. He felt so good, so very good. Damn, life could be exquisite with a woman like Eva around all the time.

He never knew where the knife came from. He saw a brief flash of silver in the mirror and the red line of blood across his throat.

His last memory was of two golden cat eyes glowing in the mirror in the spreading blackness of his death. His eyes had glassed over by the time Eva Morgan bent down, cut them out, and then slid them into a black silk bag lined with clear plastic. Goblins were always hungry, and hers were more than most. Without looking back, she went to the kitchen, set the bag on the black marble counter, and washed her hands in the highly polished stainless steel sink. As the warm water ran over her hands, she thought of how angry Traverse would be when he found out what she'd done.

Good, she thought. Eventually, he had to learn who was the pawn in whose chess game.

She used a paper towel to dry her hands, then threw it into the wastebasket. There was no need to worry about fingerprints. By the time she and Hiram were through, there wouldn't be enough left of Borgo, Michigan, to find with an electron microscope. Too bad Traverse didn't know that.

Carrying the black bag in one hand, she stepped over Amrozi's eyeless head again just because she enjoyed doing it. Her black cape, the one she had worn to the Mihaloff farm, was hanging on a wall hook. She threw it over one shoulder, wrapped its cord around the catch near her throat, shook her shoulders to let it settle smoothly and let herself out. As her stiletto heels clicked out the number of steps to the sidewalk, she remembered her failure at the Mihaloff farm and decided that Brother Mihaloff's daughter would have to pay for that.

Boiling oil was always good, but a little old-fashioned for her taste.

****

As she stepped outside, she saw the pack of three goblins surrounding the porch in a semi-circle. Pairs of yellow-green eyes stared at her. Then, in unison, they dropped and touched their foreheads to the ground. The night fog clung to their haunches, and their rich musk mingled with it. She looked up to the imaginary stars that twinkled above Borgo like nightlights in a canopied mausoleum. She smiled, then she told them to rise. It was the only trick she had ever taught them. With four quick jabs of her right forefinger, then a jab of her thumb toward the open front door, she sent the beasts into the house to eat John Amrozi's corpse. The three of them raced past her, their claws raking the cement. Moments later, she heard the ripping and tearing and the crunching of bones. They would eat until nothing of his body remained.

As she waited, she looked up and down the streets at the darkened buildings lit only by the soft lights of gas streetlamps. Hiram preferred them to electric streetlamps. Memories, she thought, of his days in Old England and the horrors he had wrought there.

Eva had seen many terrible things in her long span of years as she inhabited first one body and then another, but standing on the deserted streets of this created town of the living dead was one of the strangest of the carnival of horrors that was her existence. Only ten blocks away was the massive underground complex manned by Traverse and his doomed soldiers and scientists. But that was not her destination. Instead, she would go to her master and report on her success. Her master. The thought enraged her.

Hiram Abiff was no fallen angel—he was a hideous created creature vacant of a soul. His body had been constructed by the Nephilim darkness with a poisonous magic beyond her present understanding. He was a soulless creature, infested by a legion of demonic spirits. They would torture and torment him until he subdued them one by one and absorbed their festering powers to make them his own.

Cursed for his desecration of the architecture of the Divine, he was now a captive of the Nephilim darkness that had suborned him. A loathsome thing whose body gathered and re-formed when violated. A male presence whose existence was like a lash cutting away at her pride. But like all males of whatever station, he could eventually be brought down by seduction and stolen power. If she could just find the journal.

The Confessions of Mr. Hyde contained the answers to Hiram's purpose and his weakness, but there was only one copy in existence, and the Freemasons had it, but it was lost within their vast network of hiding places. The Nephilim darkness, no matter how much she had begged and pleaded, would tell her little of the details of Hiram's background.

So far, she could not find the journal. With the death of Bartok, the book would in theory pass to Worshipful Master Frank Mihaloff, she thought. Worshipful Master. A male's title. She would gladly have her goblins tear pieces from him until he told her where it was. But Hiram had warned her about harming the man, however insignificant, until he was through with him. For now, the old man had the power to force her obedience.

She was sure that it was in the man's house, but her pistol-toting daughter had been an unpleasant surprise. Hiram had not been pleased with her failure. His eyes had glowed faint blue, and she'd thought he was going to punish her again, but then they had returned to normal as he told her that if she did not find the journal soon, he would devour her instead of simply destroying her. The idea of being trapped within the creature known as Hiram Abiff was worse than oblivion.

She would be careful from now on, very careful, but she could not let go of her need to feed the Worshipful Master Mihaloff's daughter to her monsters and feel the ecstasy of watching them rend her flesh. And she had to find The Confessions of Mr. Hyde and learn the secrets that would allow her to seize the power it contained. She was certain that the daughter knew something of value.

She looked at the cameras positioned up and down the streets, cameras that would only see what Hiram allowed them to see. They could not see her or her goblins. All they could see with all of their high-tech wizardry were empty streets. When night fell in Borgo, very few walked its vacant streets. Sometimes, Traverse would send military men out to learn what they could about Hiram; sometimes Hiram would let them return alive. More frequently, he did not.

Behind her, she heard the goblins scrabbling down the steps and smelled their satiated blood lust as they lined up behind her.

"Follow," she said to them, as she walked with an imperiously languid stride down the street to the Borgo Masonic Temple where Hiram Abiff waited, shrouded in darkness and mystery.

Along the way, she passed an ice cream shop, a small bookstore, and a clothing store. Hiram had created them. When he lured the first soldiers into the town, the only thing moving in Borgo had been Hiram himself. Over time, the bodies of those Hiram had killed and reanimated left Traverse's complex and occupied the homes and the stores. Creatures with clouded memories of who they had once been now arranged inventory Hiram provided, sold to the other reanimated dead for whom he created money to buy products in his attempts to make the town an insane parody of small town life. His purpose in this was still a mystery to Eva, as with so much about this creature of darkness.

The grand plan she thought she understood. The Borgo virus would allow him to seize the energy of computer users all over the world. When she had possession of the Blazing Star, she would use it to trap that energy for him, to deceive people into thinking he was the Antichrist. He could then reconstruct the Temple in Jerusalem, and the Nephilim darkness could captive a body, so that once again it could walk the earth in physical form. These things she grasped and would use them to seize control of both Hiram and the Nephilim darkness. But this ridiculous town—luring in soldiers and scientists seemed to her to be a waste of time.

No matter, she was smarter than Hiram Abiff, the creature with a brain infested by the raging dead and unclean spirits. She was cleverer, she thought, than the Nephilim darkness itself.

Eva Morgan would never again call any man Master.

When she and her beasts reached the Borgo Masonic Temple, she looked up the steps and saw the doors swing open.

She hesitated before walking up them. Her goblins whimpered and flattened themselves against the sidewalk pavement. The sickening smell of their urine pervaded the misty night.

Her goblins knew who was Master of Borgo.

For now, she thought.

Once inside, standing on the tiled Masonic emblem, she looked about and felt the emptiness. As she stepped up the next flight of stairs to the right of the building, she glanced up and saw the doors of the temple room swing open as the doors behind her swung closed. Eva kept her mind free, even as her muscles tensed and her stomach soured. There were no lights on anywhere in the entire Masonic Temple. Like the predators they both were, she and Hiram could see in the dark. Eva stopped at the doorway and saw him seated in the East.

His eyes glowed that soft neon blue she feared.

"Go, tell Traverse Nations that I would see the Corvasce woman," he said with a faint menace to his voice. "And that I will have what is mine. The time is close to us. I must have that journal. The Confessions of Mr. Hyde reveals too much about me that could prevent my return. The world can never know about me before then."

"I will," she said.

She had heard these words over and again from this monstrosity. What was in that journal that could be so damning?

"And Eva," said Hiram. "Soon the Nephilim's brother will have the Blazing Star of Freemasonry. That is the most important of all. You will leave after speaking with Miss Corvasce and meet with Mr. Chirac. You will follow his instructions exactly and return to me."

If Eva got her hands on The Confessions of Mr. Hyde first, perhaps she would then have the delicious pleasure of murdering Hiram Abiff. Of course, then she would need to kill a creature long since dead. Perhaps she would first practice on Mr. Chirac.

8

Marla Corvasce felt like she was losing her mind.

She was trapped in a military complex housed beneath a viaduct in a small town with a few hundred scientists, soldiers and computer people. They all armed to the teeth with the most sophisticated weaponry she'd ever seen, and all aimed at what? A little old man with impossible powers? She'd learned that the town's citizens were several thousand soldiers who were part of the military machine locking down the town. The entire city was off the map, like Los Alamos, when it was known only as PO Box 1663. And she was trapped under the powerful thumb of Traverse Nations, who, in her opinion, was a psychotic episode with sixty seconds left on the timer. And if she got out alive, she would not vote for President Usman even if he ran for another term.

The president had sent her to… to do what, exactly? Destroy the old man? With what? All these soldiers and they hadn't been able to do anything. He might just as well have sent her to crawl into a metal shredder while blindfolded.

She washed up, geared up, and left her bunk. As President Usman's special operative, at least she got her own room. Which was odd, she knew, because so far all she'd done was follow Traverse around like his own personal bodyguard. Her access chip, he'd told her, would let her into almost any place in the complex, except certain areas that he would neither identify nor discuss.

The hallways were always bustling with scientists in their lab coats walking in different directions, talking in low tones to their tablet computers. They never seemed to look at each other, but always at the electronic tablets. And it was never clear to Marla why so many of the staff wore lab coats. To the best of her knowledge, she had seen only one chemistry lab and most of the weapons research that went on in the facility had everything to do with physics and almost nothing to do with chemistry.

She was about to enter the elevator when an MP held up a hand and said, "Sorry, miss, but this elevator is reserved."

Before she could ask for whom it was reserved for, she saw two men rolling a cot containing a body bag toward the elevator. She raised an eyebrow at the MP who'd held the elevator up for the men rolling the gurney.

"Major Landsdale. Had a major heart attack or something."

"But I just saw him—" she began.

The MP looked away.

Marla heard Traverse Nations in her head repeating the phrase, "Somebody's got to pay."

After the gurney was maneuvered into place in the elevator, the MP stepped in with the other two guards and the doors closed. Marla stood there remembering Major Landsdale challenging Traverse to take the call from the Secretary of Defense. He was tall, square shouldered and military proud. He probably ran more miles in a day than most people walked in a week. A heart attack was not likely. She was about to turn and find another elevator, when she noticed by the light bar over the elevator doors that the elevator was going down, not up toward the surface. She would have thought the elevator would go up to take the body to be buried. Why on earth would it go further underground?

Jimmy walked by and said a quick hello. When she looked over at him, he saw the look on her face and walked faster to put distance between them. He knew something, and she was going to find out what that was. No need to follow just now. She could find him any time she wanted. The trick would be finding him separated from Traverse. Finding him alone. She could squeeze some answers out of him then. Jimmy looked pain averse. He ran the entire electronic surveillance operation and maybe much more. That made him prime meat, and Marla was hungry for answers.

She took the elevator up one level and stepped out into the antiseptic hallway. White walls, pale blue floors. The LED lighting made everything look bright as day. At the end of the fifty-foot hallway was Traverse's office. She looked to the left and right as she walked, but there was nothing but closed, unmarked doors. Each door had a number. Each number grew smaller as she came closer to the door marked number one. There were so many doors that she wondered how Traverse could control what was happening throughout the complex and the town outside.

Somebody's got to pay.

What was it that happened in the still lower levels? Why were they taking the body down there? Jimmy would know the answer. She felt it in her gut. The nice ones were always guilty.

She took the elevator to Traverses's floor, got off and walked past seeming endless bland doors until she came to the one marked with a one. Knocking, she waited for a full minute, until she heard a voice say, "Come in," and went inside. Traverse Nations, his silver blond hair swept back like an old-time movie star, was holding a bottle of Maker's Mark in one hand and a glass filled with ice cubes in the other.

"Want a drink?" was the first thing he'd said.

It was a terrible start. Marla's intuition, honed by years of working with dangerous people, immediately flashed another red mental warning light.

She shook her head, determined to ignore the small talk and gestures.

Traverse shrugged and drained half his glass, which he then set on a cork coaster on his desk.

"Okay, then. You'll want one before we're through. But, right now, down to business. You've got questions, I've got answers. So, I'll tell you the story of what we're up against, why you're here and what the plan is. You want to break in with a question, go for it, but it will go quicker if you just let me tell the story. Sound good? Then here goes.

"First, what we're up against. On August sixth, 1945, we dropped a nuke on Hiroshima. Bad day for Japan. Switch over to Potsdam, Germany, where Truman learns it was a success, depending on your point of view. Some people say we saved a million lives by that move and the subsequent dropping of another bomb on Nagasaki. Some people say it was cruel and unnecessary. We'll leave all that to the political scientists and the philosophers. What is more important to what we're up against is the fact that Truman and six guards were in a room in Potsdam after he'd learned the nuke drop actually worked. Are you with me so far?"

"Yes," said Marla. "I'm with you so far."

The lights dimmed to half strength. Traverse took another drink and then topped up his glass. The amber liquor darkened as though it had thickened in the darkness.

"Fucking power in this place. Anyway, so that's when it all started. That's the first known appearance of the old man. He just appeared in the room. The door was closed, you understand. The windows were closed. Truman was sitting at a desk surrounded by a room full of armed guards. No fade in, no flash of light, no thunderclap. He was just there and looking at the man whose orders had just vaporized about a hundred thousand people, depending upon who was trying to cover up what with their estimates.

"The American government wanted to minimize the casualties. Some other people wanted to maximize and give bigger numbers. But the fact is," and here Traverse stabbed a finger at her face, "that President Harry Truman was at that moment the most dangerous man alive. He killed with his word. You see that, don't you? And he knew when he was sitting at that desk the incredible destructive power he'd let loose. Can you form this picture in your mind, Marla? Truman went from being a man pumped up by the sheer fact of his own personal power to being a bureaucrat terrified by an old man with the power to simply appear in front of him.

"The president—and I can tell you this from having read his private diary—cringed and pissed himself. Like a kid pulling up the covers over his head because he knew, just knew, that any moment the closet door would pop open and something would be waiting there for him. Truman could accept giving the word to his military flunkies to fry roughly one hundred thousand people, but he couldn't accept the fact that he was powerless to prevent this old man from invading his space. Fucking-A incredible."

People did not just appear in a room. Despite herself, she created a minimalist image of what Traverse was describing and she felt her stomach rebel.

"What happened?" she asked finally.

"The guards went bat-shit crazy. Some of them blocked the line of sight to Truman. Others started shooting. The old man got pumped full of bullets, one of which blew half his head apart. Blood and brains all over. Two guards hustled the president toward the door to get him to safety. Not the smartest move, but understandable. They got to where the door was a second ago, and it wasn't there anymore. They were looking—as far as Truman's notes say—at a blank wall. No windows. They were in a box with no way out. Truman was having a conniption fit. He was the most powerful man in the world back then. Hell, he'd just authorized dropping a nuclear weapon on an entire city. And suddenly, he couldn't even get out of a room."

Traverse suddenly pushed his chair back on its rollers and stood up. His right hand brushed against his glass and almost knocked it over. He began pacing, straightening pictures on the wall, tightening up books. His face seemed stretched and sallow in the reduced lighting. From across the room, he stared up at the ceiling and started talking again, not even looking at her. The energy of his movements, and the building intensity of his voice, set off warning signals in her mind again.

Train coming, she thought. Don't walk on the tracks when the red lights are flashing.

"See this happening in your mind, Marla. Smell the gun smoke filling the room like caustic gas. Hear the explosions and the ringing in your own ears as the shots are fired. The screams—not from the old man—but from the president, the all-powerful president, as he watched the blood bursts blossom from the old man's body as each round impacted him. See his little accountant's face twist in terror as one bullet blows part of the old man's skull apart. Watch it happen as two guards rush the blood-spattered president toward the door. And then, the horror paralyzes their facial expressions as all of them, everyone still living in the room, realize that there is no escape from the carnage of their new prison. Imagine what that does to their minds. The president, and this is in his own handwriting, Marla, gibbered. I don't even like to think of that word. The president, our president, gibbers and then, felt the warmth when his bladder let go. Like I said, he pissed his pants."

Traverse stopped for a moment and seemed to drift off. Like he'd taken an unscheduled visit to a mental prison of his own making.

The realization that she would have to escape Operation Borgo and its deranged leader was now a certainty. There had to be a way out of this armed lunatic asylum.

"But it was about to get worse," Traverse continued, snapping back to the moment. "They looked at the old man. He was covered in blood. His brains and blood were everywhere. The president vomited. And then, the old man's head started putting itself back together."

He stopped telling the story again and absently scratched his forehead. He kept scratching. Marla saw blood trickle down to his eyebrows, and she almost took out her nine-millimeter and shot him. It was that creepy. His pulled-tight sallow face and haunted eyes were visible in the darkened room. The story of the old man's head. The way Traverse had paced the room with his nervous, coiled energy and his rapid fire telling of the story were like an angry cobra discharging a machine gun.

He noticed her staring at him, shook his head and got a Kleenex to wipe the blood away.

"You live in this place long enough, you get some pretty weird nervous ticks."

With a flick of his wrist, the balled up bloody tissue flew in an arc, which then disappeared into a stainless-steel wastebasket.

"We only have two sources for this report. The first is the president's diary, and the second is the report filed by the only guard to survive the event. So, the view I'm giving you is a combination of what they said. When I told you the old man's head started putting itself together, I'm not sure what happened. Not in every detail. But you think about it."

He turned to look at her. To stare at her, looking for a sign of support, any sign she believed him. Blood still seeped from the thin gash he'd cut into his own forehead.

"Trapped in the room with this corpse that impossibly—I can't think of another word—starts reassembling. And then it stands up. Alive again. A fatal head wound takes the old man out, but he comes back right in front of them. In a room full of armed men, Marla, that old man was the most terrifying thing in the room."

"And?" she prompted.

"They killed him again. They killed him until they ran out of bullets. He reassembled. He rose again. His clothes looked like shit, but he kept coming back. Now comes the scary part."

Traverse returned to his desk and sat down again. With a motion smooth as the liquor itself, he drained the glass. For the first time, Marla registered the framed black-and-white photo behind his desk. It was a grainy black and white blown up so that its details were obscure, like a French impressionist painting drained of color, drained of life. The world's first use of the power of the atom to annihilate life. The human mind caught on camera redefining the true meaning of horror in a once anonymous city named Hiroshima.

"By that time," Traverse continued, "there was so much gun smoke in the closed room it must have smelled like a dynamite blast in a small cave. Hard to breathe. Everyone was deaf from the noise. Every guard was lucky they hadn't caught a bullet from one of the other guards. Really lucky one of their rounds hadn't killed President Truman.

"Now what comes next is why I'm going to have another drink."

And he poured another drink. His hand, thought Marla, was shaking.

"By this time, the guards were out of their minds. This wasn't combat. This had nothing to do with war. This was not for the human mind to see. One of them had enough brain cells to take out his knife and stab the old man in the stomach. Like that should do it?

"The old man opened his mouth, and you'd think it'd be to scream, but these black oily red phantasms—that's what Truman called it in his diary—came crawling out from between the old man's lips and their skin is like nothing the president had ever seen or imagined. Let me read you the next part from his diary."

It didn't look like a safe, but when it came sliding down from the ceiling like a stainless bright tube, she knew she was looking at an upgrade in the world of portable vaults. Traverse held his hand on one side of it, then breathed into a small opening on the gleaming side. A door slid back and around on the body of the device, and inside she could just barely see a leather-bound book, with little tabs sticking out from the sides in retrograde defiance of modern technology. Traverse reached in for the book and she saw the laser grid flit over his hand as he took the volume out and carefully laid it on the desktop next to his whiskey glass. One of the two, she thought, kept him sane while the other slowly drove him mad.

Carefully, as though he were handling a priceless antique, Traverse opened to a bookmarked page.

"So, here's what it says: 'These things, these black segmented spirits fastened on to the soldier's necks despite the men's heroic efforts to beat them off with their spent weapons and their bare hands. They fought these supernatural creatures with all the valor that men can call upon. I can still behold it happening all over again in my mind whenever I close my eyes. Such debauchery and horror as I saw that day was a searing fire burned into my consciousness as though branded there. These things, these demons, had many arms that clicked and clacked like telegraph keys as these nightmarish denizens of evil tore into those fine men whose sole mission was to protect me.'"

Expelling a quick breath, he slammed the book shut, this time as though it were an outdated textbook.

"What a bunch of bullshit, eh? Sounds like something out of a romance novel. All that's missing are some bare-breasted women and square-jawed pirates. I checked into how big the room was. Twenty feet by twenty feet, give or take a few inches. The way I see it, Truman was hunkered down in the corner, bawling like a baby. The guards were near insane because they'd seen an old man come back from the dead after they'd emptied every bullet they had into him. And there had to be screaming. Lots of screaming as they went nuts. There's blood on the floor, demons crawling out of the old man's mouth that rip them apart and then eat them. That's the way it ended for the guards. Five out of the six shredded and digested right in front of Truman. Everybody pissing their pants as they died."

"I think I'll take that drink now," said Marla.

Taking another glass from the tray behind him on the credenza beneath the photo of the nuclear blast, he asked, "Ice?"

"Straight."

"On the house," said Traverse.

After a long drink, Marla asked, "What happened to the other guard?"

"He lived," said Traverse.

"How?"

"The question you should've asked isn't how, it's why the demons didn't devour him like a ripe grape like they did the other guards. He was standing scared shitless in front of Truman, ready to defend the president with his life, but he didn't attack the old man. Maybe he was saving his bullets for a last attempted defense. But it's a fact that he took no overt action against the old man. From what we'd call the after action report and from an inspection of his weapon afterward, he didn't even fire a single round. Now you might think that's why the old man let him live. But I don't think so. I'll tell you why I think he did it later.

"Anyway, according to the guard's report and Truman's report, once the demons were done with the carnage, the old man opened his mouth and sucked them back in. Then he looked at the two left standing—or cowering in the case of Truman—and just disappeared. The doors were there again, just like they were before. The windows came back, too. But the bones and blood and little chunks of flesh were splattered all over the room. It was real. It happened. He could have killed Truman and the other man if he wanted to. And that, Marla, is when the United States of America decided to go to war with the old man you saw on the screens. In self-defense, of course."

The dim light flickered and then went out. The room's plunge into suffocating darkness was immediate and total.

"That's disturbing," said Traverse said again.

9

Beneath the skin of his left hand, Hiram Abiff felt something squirming to rip through to freedom. Tiny claws punctured his wrinkled skin. Hiram lifted the hand closer to his face, then smiled as his hand burst into bright violet-green flames. As his hand blackened and his skin sloughed away to expose the bone, he saw the screaming little creature writhing between what was left of his fingers. His smile widened as he picked it up by its tiny wings, using his other hand and, with the little creature still burning, he brought it to his mouth and chewed.

He was invisible to the soldiers, spies, and scientists of Borgo. The laws of reality, as they knew them back in their world, simply did not apply in Borgo. The town was the Nephilim's test tube, where he allowed the men sent by the government into his world-prison to attack Hiram with their weapons and their science. The people were mortal, and he was not. They could die and he could not. He was, in fact, already dead.

Hiram sat on the bottom front step of the Borgo Masonic Temple and watched his hand re-form in the gathering gloom. Directly above his age-spotted bald head shone the lighted Masonic symbol of the square and compass. Hiram twisted to look up at it. To him, it was a symbol of freedom from this hideous created world that had been his prison for the seventy or so years since the Nephilim darkness had cast him into it.

His imprisonment in Borgo was both a penalty and a test. A penalty for having told his story to a man he thought was dying, not knowing the fool would write it down and pass it to the Freemasons to hide it from him. It was also a penalty for him revealing himself to President Truman. And a test for him to battle the weaponry of the mortals as he simultaneously developed mastery of the demonic spirits that twisted through him in the space left by the loss of his soul.

The artificial dark clustered about him like a personal protective guard. In the town of Borgo, there was, of course, no sun and no moon. This entire town was a magically created environment, a creation of the Nephilim. The soil, the air, the water, and the town itself all bore the imprint of the demon's occult machinations. The streetlamps, the streets, the sewer system, the electrical grid, the birds, and the insects, too, were all the results of its magical incantations. The fallen angel had no such power in the world of men, but here, in a dimension of its own creation, it reigned supreme with Hiram and the witch as his appointed stewards. He could create false daylight for his own amusement. He could cause snow to fall one day and rain the next.

The time of his exile to Borgo was nearing its end. He would soon reenter the mortal world for the first time in decades, although, truth to tell, mere decades were nothing to a creature such as himself. Since his resurrection by the fallen angel, he had lived for over three thousand years as a wretched thing reborn of dark magic and the fallen angel's fury. Twice, they had attempted to rebuild the Jerusalem temple in a way that suited the Nephilim. Twice he had failed his dark angelic master, but this time, when he re-entered the world as Grandmaster Hiram Abiff, leader of millions of Freemasons, he and his dark angel would overcome both God and humanity to reduce the world of the living to a pool of blood.

The sound of approaching footsteps confirmed that the witch Eva Morgan had arrived. He knew of her return long before she came close. The demon spirits trapped within him always screamed and shrieked as she came near. Her closeness drove them into a chaotic frenzy. She was the fallen angel's own, and they both feared her and were driven to a ravenous frenzy by her presence. Hiram was tormented by the need to use her and devour her, but the fallen angel would not allow her destruction. She was his to use, but her role in the coming conflagration was set. He was not allowed to destroy her. But in the core of his soulless being, the desire to shred and consume her was difficult to repress.

"I spoke to Traverse as you instructed, but I believe," she said deferentially, "that Brother Mihaloff has the book in his house. I felt it in his thoughts."

"The granddaughter of Enzo Corvasce does not have it?" he asked.

"One or the other has it. The granddaughter will soon be summoned and we may deal with her then. But in the meantime, dear Brother Mihaloff is hiding something from me somehow, so I will start with his house, then return to press hard on the Corvasce woman you asked for. One of them will have it for us. My marker is on Brother Mihaloff."

He did not look up at her. From where he sat on the hard step, he saw one of her high-heeled patent leather boots come to rest inches from his leg. Her long coat was open, and he could see the creamy white color of her calf muscle.

Hiram felt the sudden raging of trapped spirits bursting into fire inside what was left of his being.

"Get me that journal," he screamed up at her in a sudden explosion of vitriol. "And bring me the head of his daughter."

"And if Brother Mihaloff gets in the way?" Eva asked in a voice like velvet ice.

"Devour him," he said. "No, wait. Devour, his daughter. I need Brother Frank Mihaloff to be alive for my return to their world. Why must I repeat myself to you? Someone must introduce me. He and his fellow Freemasons will be rewarded for their loyalty by being the first subjects in my kingdom. They are blind men and suited only to be slaves."

His jaw extended as he said this, and in the recesses of his mouth, the squirming things blinked against the light.

As she transformed into a snake, the length of a man's body with golden green goblin eyes, the demons inside him clawed at his innards, enraged at the insult of her having the freedom to roam between both worlds while they did not. She slid up the steps of the Borgo Masonic temple to leave through the portal beneath the Empty Chair.

Hiram rose from the steps and looked around at his prison. He saw the shops manned by dead men and women, the houses full of inarticulate creatures, and, thirteen blocks from where he stood, the viaduct. Beneath its brick and concrete arches was the military installation erected by Traverse Nations and his predecessors. In an inverted structure descending thirty stories below ground were their armaments, housing for their soldiers and scientists, their laboratories, advanced monitoring devices and space-age weaponry. And above all, their computers. Fah, they thought they were a match for him with all their electronics. They could only see him when he wished for them to see him. Their cameras and listening devices were primitive compared to his magic. And one by one, he was killing them and, in the deepest levels beneath their complex, he and the Nephilim labored to reanimate their dead. The only way for Hiram to be free to die was if the Nephilim finally acquired a body. And Traverse and his soldiers and scientists could not stop him. They could only hear Hiram approach when he chose for them to hear him. And when they did hear him, they knew that death had arrived.

He looked around again, seeing the distant horizon that demarcated the border between the world of Borgo and the mortal world. It was hidden within the tree line. But that dimensional line was all that kept Borgo intact. There was only one way in and no way out, save for the connection between worlds beneath the Empty Chair inside the Masonic Temple. But only he and Eva knew about that. Mortals that entered Borgo through the Polehenge gate could never leave. The Borgo Pass, the magical construction that connected the worlds, was a membranous tunnel through Hell itself. Few save the spellbound had the courage to pass through it.

Hiram remembered again how, in a haze of wild anger, he had been beaten by Enzo Corvasce near the end of the war. Enzo Corvasce—a mortal without the mental faculties to read or write. To this day, the thought of that failed confrontation drove him to rage. Because of that insult, come what may, on his return to the dimension of the living, Hiram Abiff would rain down his revenge on whatever pitiful remnant was left of the Corvasce family.

A squadron of soldiers came walking down the street toward him as these thoughts burned through his consciousness. It was one of Traverse Nations' night patrols coming his way, unaware that he was there. It was beyond even his mind why the Director of Project Borgo sent his soldiers out at night. They and their brothers-in-arms would walk their grid, canvassing the town as though it was a crime scene instead of a combined prison and laboratory. It angered him that the Nephilim darkness would not allow him to reveal his true self to them. He would allow him to burn them, to vivisect them, and even to eat them, but he would not tolerate the revelation of who he was to them.

His memory was a rat pen. Three thousand years of un-life could do that to a being's brain. Three thousand years of invading spirits possessing him, ripping apart his thoughts as though they were tissue paper and pouring burning psychic oil through his eyes and into his essence. Through the eyes, he thought. Evil always came in through the eyes.

He looked again at the soldiers.

The Nephilim darkness had confined him here after he almost destroyed three thousand years of secrecy. He attacked the President of the United States near the end of World War II, but that had been the fault of the demonic presences tearing at his mind. In those days, before he gained control of those raging phantasms, he could not stop himself. He was, he could now admit to himself, insane back then.

Now, he could suppress the dark spirits that forced him to think violent thoughts. Not always, he had to acknowledge, but on most days.

But though he had been resurrected from death by the Nephilim darkness without a soul, he still felt hunger.

Yes, he decided, he would eat these soldiers. Even someone such as him must eat.

10

Marla had her pistol up and the barrel flashlight on.

"You're blinding me," said Traverse. "Point it somewhere else."

She wondered if he ever got so drunk he slurred his words.

"How long for the emergency power to kick in?" she asked.

"Should be on already. If he wants it on."

"I'm through with this," said Marla. "I'm getting out of here."

She got to her feet, turned, and walked to the door. Or thought she did. Where she had entered the room, there was no longer a door. Nothing but a smooth expanse of wall. She turned her head from side to side, following the beam of the flashlight, looking for the door that was no longer there.

"This is bullshit," said Marla.

"You want another drink?" asked Traverse.

For the first time in her life, Marla felt the skin on the back of her neck pimple with fear. It made her angry. What was wrong with him? He acted like nothing bizarre was happening. He was in his own drunken world. And that made her even more angry. The Director of Operation Borgo was lost somewhere between shit and useless.

"I want to put a bullet in your brain," she said.

"Me, too," he said. "And that is when I'm sober, Marla. That is when I'm sober."

"What happens next? Lights go out, the door disappears, and we're trapped. You know what's going on here, don't you? What's next, Traverse? What's next?"

From outside, at least what she thought was outside of the room they were in, she heard a deep, ugly growling. There was a loud boom and then the floor shook. The wall stretched and bowed inward. She jumped to one side and went to the same side of the desk as Traverse Nations.

"I was sitting in one lab downstairs, maybe a year ago," he said, "when it happened just like this. I'm talking to this scientist working on a contact poison we thought maybe we could use to kill the old man when the lights go out. We started looking for ways out, too. Just like this. Then the scientist starts screaming and screaming and won't shut up and I'm losing my mind. I wasn't drinking as much back then, but I sure did after that."

From wherever outside of the room was, Marla thought she heard breathing.

Traverse kept talking.

"So, I turn to look at him and wham, just like that, he splits into two halves like someone sliced him down the middle with a samurai sword."

"Shut up," said Marla. "Just shut up."

Something was prowling the hallway, looking for them. She could hear it sniff the air, tracking their scent. With sudden clarity, she lifted her pistol and fired a round straight at the wall. Whatever was on the other side of the wall screamed in pain and rage. She stepped closer and fired to the right. Another scream and then something slammed into the wall, bowing it inward as the entire room seemed to shake.

When it got quiet again, Traverse drained what was left of his glass. He set it back on the desk and made too much noise doing it.

"Blood everywhere," he said as he poured another shot.

She scanned the ceiling, looking for an air ventilation duct. When she found one inset over the table, she moved to the table and hauled herself up to a standing position on it. No way she could fit through the air duct, but the ceiling tiles were another matter. She saw a tall metal floor lamp in the far corner of the room and hopped back down to get it. Yanking the plug out of the wall was easy if she found the cord. For a moment, she panicked when she couldn't find it and was afraid it was hard wired beneath the floor. It was a solid piece of pewter colored metal and would make a good battering ram.

The growling and banging continued as she dragged the lamp back to the table and climbed up. She shone her pistol flashlight on Traverse, who was still nursing his drink.

Not my problem, she thought as he raised the glass for another round. His mouth opened as it neared his lips, and Marla froze in place, crouched down on the tabletop, the lamp stand held tight in one hand and her pistol in the other. Traverse Nations' mouth split open so wide it hid his face. Dark, swirling clouds came pouring out between his teeth and stretched-wide lips. Marla slammed the lamp stand straight up into the ceiling, butt end first. The impact jolted so hard she felt it all the way down her spine. The ceiling tiles should have shot up with the blow, but they were like iron squares welded in place. She looked wildly around the room for any other way out.

The darkness pouring out from Traverse's open mouth coalesced into a shape, a shape lit with a writhing scarlet pinpoint of light at its center. Marla leaped from the table, landed and swung the lamp stand at it and let go. It flew through the dark, swirling mist without slowing down and clattered off the wall behind it. In desperation, she swung her pistol up, waiting for the smoke-like apparition to solidify into something she could hurt. Traverse sat frozen in his chair and she wondered again if she should shoot him. Maybe whatever was pouring out of his mouth could not be hurt, but if she killed Traverse, she might stop it from turning into something worse. The thought that she would get the death penalty for shooting her boss never crossed her mind. She needed to survive first.

But a form emerged from the mist, a caped figure that stood motionless in the glare of her flashlight's beam. Marla settled into a two-arm shooter's stance and placed the illuminated sights of her pistol center mass on the figure. The face that stepped from the shadowed vortex was a young woman with wide-set dark eyes and a full head of dark hair that hung to her shoulders. She looked straight into Marla's eyes as Marla fired twice into her chest. The noise was deafening, but the alternative seemed to Marla to be much worse. Partial hearing loss was better than total death.

The two bullets hung incomprehensibly in the air between them, vibrating like plucked strings.

Twin columns of darkness formed on either side of the woman and two horned creatures covered with wiry, twisted hair appeared. Marla stepped back until she bumped into the conference table. In the flashlight's beam, she saw the two creatures cover their eyes and then growl. She risked a glance at Traverse, still frozen with his mouth stretched open wider than humanly possible.

"Human males are the most susceptible of all," said the woman.

The twin bullets still hung humming in the air between them, like angry bees pressed against an invisible wall. Marla tried to slow her breathing, but her whole body was jacked up with adrenaline. She wanted to run headlong into the wall behind her in the hopes she could crash through it. Even with her own bullets obviously stuck between the two of them and by some kind of magic going nowhere, she felt the urge to keep pulling the trigger until the slide locked back.

The caped woman stepped closer, raised a hand, touched one bullet and sent it rocketing past her right shoulder, then did the same with the other and sent it shooting past her left shoulder. Marla kept her pistol up, the flashlight shining right in the woman's eyes. No fear there, not even with the pistol pointed right between her eyes. No hand up to shield her eyes from the bright beam. Not human, she thought.

"Sister—" began the caped woman.

Marla fired the remaining nine rounds straight into her face. The sound was so loud it rang her eardrums like they were giant timpani. If she lived, she'd be deaf for a year. But before that thought flew across her conscious mind, she'd dropped to a crouch and had her knife out. She moved forward and slashed across the inside of the woman's thigh to open her femoral artery. Except that wasn't what happened. The woman was no longer there, so instead she'd blown apart the skull of one of her creatures, then sliced its leg open so slick and quick that she was hit with its burning hot blood spray before she could move out of range.

Her scalp felt like it'd been ripped off her head and she was suddenly pulled backward and slammed onto the hard surface of the conference table. The air was knocked out of her lungs by the impact. Fireworks exploded in front of her eyes. She saw a circle of light dance wildly over the walls as her pistol with its rail mounted flashlight was ripped away from her hand and sent bouncing across the room.

Through her confused vision, she saw the furious face of the caped woman. Twisting to one side, she tried to flip off the far edge of the table, but felt an iron grip clamp onto her neck and slam her hard onto her back again. One more attempt to twist away, but she couldn't move. Her body wasn't receiving muscle commands from her brain anymore. She was paralyzed from the neck down. The caped woman's beautiful face appeared above her, twisted with rage in the thin light cast by the flashlight.

"You killed one of mine," she hissed. "Your heart is now mine."

The woman's free hand arced up and morphed into thick talons. With an impossible rush of terror, Marla realized that the woman meant to stab those claws right through her ribcage and rip out her still beating heart. Marla couldn't move. Her last sight on earth would be that of her heart fountaining blood down onto her own face.

As though an ultrasonic whistle had been blown, the caped woman's claws stopped before thrusting downward toward her chest. She cocked her head to listen to something Marla couldn't even hear, then slowly looked back down at Marla.

"You have been given a reprieve," she said in a strangled voice. "He will see you in two days hence, at midnight."

The hand compressed her throat so tightly that Marla could hardly breathe. She felt hot and sweaty. It was terrifying and frustrating at the same time. She could feel her body, but she couldn't move it.

"What do you want?" she rasped.

"Bring the papers," answered the woman. "Bring the journal or die."

"I don't know what you're talking about. What are you—"

"Your family secrets, Marla. When your uncle died, the papers passed to you and now my master wants them. The Masons must not see them. My master must have them back. He will have them, or he will twist the organs out of your body."

"Who… who are you?" croaked Marla as she fought to suck in a breath.

The caped woman opened her mouth and for just a brief fraction of a second, Marla saw the tips of sharp teeth and a searing glimpse of red light. As the woman leaned closer, she tried to press back into the table, to get as far away from those teeth and that light as she could, but her body would not respond. She could feel the woman's need to bite into her face. When her open mouth was only a hand's length away, the woman's hair fell down over her face and onto Marla's.

"I am," she hissed, "the Scarlet Whore of Babylon and I bring destruction with me like an enraged beast."

The caped woman moved back, still facing Marla, hidden in the shadows as she blocked the vague light from the pistol's flashlight where it lay over to one side. The remaining creature clutched its dead companion like a broken rag doll. It growled and bared finger-length teeth.

"You are the second woman to murder one of my children in as many days. I will roast you over an eternal spit."

She turned and looked first back at Traverse, who sat with his mouth open wide like an airplane hangar, then back at Marla. With the woman's iron grip removed from her throat, Marla felt control return to her body. When the Scarlet Whore of Babylon turned and began to slowly dissolve into a dark, writhing smoke and the horned creature turned to do the same, Marla arched her back and released the wire cable from her belt. She rolled off the table and was up and moving toward the beast. Her fingers found the handles as she unwound the rough-edged wire, and by the time she'd looped it around its hairy neck, she had a solid grip and pulled them in opposite directions. Instead of an enraged roar from the creature, she heard a rush of air and blood explode from the cut. The angry scarlet light flared in the smoke as it poured back down Traverse's throat, but disappeared as the beast's severed head struck the floor.

Traverse Nations' mouth slowly closed. Marla felt nauseous. The thought of that woman, that thing, occupying his body was beyond disturbing. He remained still, like a wax recreation of a human being. Was that what he was? Could it be possible that Traverse Nations wasn't a human being at all? She could hear the blood roaring in her ears at the thought.

No time to think. She retrieved her pistol, then swiveled to point its flashlight at his face. A tiny wisp of smoke trailed from the corner of his mouth. Was he even alive? Or did the Scarlett Whore of Babylon use his body as a portal? Should she kill him? There would be no explaining it either to the soldiers in Borgo or the president. No, whatever Traverse was—human or not, alive or not—her real problem wasn't him. Her real problem was that she had to get out of the complex, out of the town and back to sanity. Borgo was dangerous to her life and her sanity; she wasn't sure what she could accomplish by staying except her own death.

With a glance at the floor, she saw the creature's head dissolve into fine powder. The lights came back on without warning, causing her to step back and protect her eyes. The door to the office was now behind her. When she looked back, she saw Traverse's eyes flutter.

Realizing suddenly what it would look like if he returned to consciousness and saw her pointing her pistol at his face, she quickly holstered it. She knew instinctively that she was in the most dangerous situation of her life, and she thought that if she let Traverse know what had just happened, she would be a dead woman. She had to cover it up. It had to look like nothing had happened. Nothing at all. That was her only hope. Judgment call.

Looking around the room, she located her shell casings and started picking them up and pocketing them as she heard a low moan issue from Traverse's lips. She finished tidying up as fast as she could, then returned to the chair in front of his desk and sat down. She saw the fine powder on her clothes and brushed it off. Creature blood turned to particulate grit like the thing's head. She took a deep breath to slow her breathing.

Traverse shook himself, like he was emerging from a fugue state.

"Did I nod off?" he asked. His voice was slightly slurred.

Who was speaking? she wondered.

Was it the woman who entered the room like a wraith through his body? Or was he totally unaware of how he was being used and was he now speaking for himself? Was she somehow inside of him, listening to everything that was said to him? Or was she gone?

"Power was off for a bit," she said, "and we both dozed. Just now it came back on."

"How long was it off?"

"Not long," she said.

Traverse grabbed a bottle of water from a nearby shelf, unscrewed the cap, and sat back down while he swallowed the contents in a few quick gulps.

"I needed that. I felt dehydrated."

Or, like you've had demon smoke going in and out of your mouth, she thought.

"So, let me pick it up where I left off. Now you know how we found out about the old man. In the last few days, you've got an idea of what we're up against. This man, this thing or whatever it is—and let me say it straight out, we don't even know if he or it is from this planet—anyway, we've tried a lot of ways to kill him. Our body count keeps piling up while he's still around. You do not know how hard it is to say that, Marla. Even with Minus Eight, we couldn't kill him and paid a price for trying. That's how it's been since the day we found him. We thought we had him surrounded. Well, we're wondering if we're looking at it wrong. But you want to know why you're really here, and who the woman that appeared near the ruins of Minus Eight."

"Tell me who the woman is," said Marla.

A smile split his craggy face.

"She's our secret weapon. With Minus Eight melted to slag, she's the only chance we've got short of a nuclear weapon and I'm not even sure that would work. Eva is a witch, Marla, a real-life witch. But she's a witch on our side."

Out of Traverse's line of sight, Marla's hands were still trembling. During her years of training and work as a field agent, she had experienced high-stress situations and kept her cool, but they had been nothing like what she'd just gone through. She was terrified, but she couldn't let it show. She was in real danger every moment she was still in Borgo, and she knew it. Never had she felt the level of high alert she did at that moment. She had just seen Traverse Nations used as a demon portal and he had no clue. Did the president know his Director of Borgo Operations was infected with a demon witch? The last time the witch had appeared, Traverse had gone through a similar transformation and had not known what happened either. Now she knew he was dangerous to be around. The fear roiled her stomach, and she wondered for the hundredth time just what the hell she had been sent into.

But now she had a name for the witch—Eva. It was at least shorter than the Scarlet Whore of Babylon. But incomprehensibly, Traverse thought she was on their side in the fight against the old man. Marla was fairly certain Traverse was out of his mind and that the witch was on the old man's side. And, she wondered, where the hell had the witch came from? Witches and demons were not possible in the real world. But in Borgo, Michigan, well, anything was possible.

How powerful is she? Marla wondered. She seemed to toss magic around like something out of a sword and sorcery novel. Without warning, she seemed to be able to appear anywhere she wanted. She stopped bullets in midair, and she was protected by hairy monstrosities which, at least, seemed vulnerable to bullets. Again, at least in Borgo, Michigan.

Taking her silence for doubt, Traverse spoke up again.

"I know it sounds crazy, Marla, but it's true."

That, thought Marla, is an understatement.

"When we found her," continued Traverse, "we knew we had a chance if Minus Eight failed. When she came up with a way we could boost her power, we put the full resources of Operation Borgo behind it."

He said it with an expectant yet hesitant grin, as though he deserved praise, but wasn't sure he'd get it.

"What, exactly," said Marla, "do you mean she's a witch and why do you want to boost her power?"

"Good question. We put a lot of scientists on the issue, and I'll try to condense it down to layman's language. But before I do that, let me assure you that not only is she on our side, I can arrange a meeting with her to prove it. You'll like her. You two got off to a bad start last time. She thought you were a threat. I'll explain to her that you're working for me. I told her once, but I think she was... jealous. She'll talk to you then. But, if you get me, she's protective of my safety. Trust me, you two will end up being good friends and teammates."

Marla remembered the witch saying that she would roast her over an eternal spit, but nodded as though she agreed.

Traverse looked thoughtful for a moment and then said, "I'm tired of sitting here, Marla. There's some people I have to introduce you to. You've got a right to hear what they tell you."

As he headed toward the door, Marla found herself reluctant to follow him. A big part of her didn't want to know anything else about the place. Outside of the underground Borgo military and science complex was a town populated by military and technical staff, giving an appearance of normalcy to the environment. But, outside of that, according to Traverse and his staff was nothing. Simply nothing. They were all trapped in a city that floated in the realm of fairy dust and string theory, attached to the normal world by... what? No, Marla really wasn't sure that she really wanted to learn anything else about Borgo, Michigan.

11

"In here," said Traverse.

He opened a door leading to an enormous conference room with a table as long as a school bus.

"Jimmy and the others are on the way," he said.

Soft lighting from behind brushed stainless-steel molding two feet below the twelve-foot ceiling made the room feel hushed and dreamlike.

"What others?" Marla asked as she followed him into the room.

The effects of her adrenaline rush were wearing off. Her vision blurred, then returned. A soft buzzing filled her ears as though bees were passing through her head. She stopped and steadied herself against the door.

"Jimmy, a couple of our top people, two guards and a mystery guest."

"A mystery guest?"

For a panic-filled moment, she thought it might be the witch, but his next words dispensed with that idea.

"He's a guy you already know. Don't worry. But I'm giving you warning, Marla. What will happen here in a little while is nothing like what it looks like. You got that? So, don't get wired and react. Don't spook the guards. Personnel in this complex have reason to be a little jumpy. No matter what happens, just stay calm and everything will return to normal. It's hard on the head at first, but you get used to it around here. And say nothing until I tell you it's okay to speak. You'll understand that, too, by tomorrow. Sit down, here comes everybody. Anywhere, it's okay. Just sit anywhere."

They had only been in the room a minute or two, but already Marla felt her anxieties rise. She re-visited her original idea that the President was sending her to a war zone in the Middle East. Now she wished he had. Suicide bombers had nothing on Borgo.

As she sat down in the seat closest to the door, she saw Traverse wink at her. Two men and one woman filed in one after the other and took seats on the far side of the enormous mahogany table. Jimmy sat directly across from her, then a white-haired man in his early fifties with a round, kindly face but a grim set to his smallish mouth. The other was a spindle thin, anorexic woman with a pinched face, acne scars and ears large as her palms. Even her grandmother-white hair did nothing to soften her hostile stare.

"I'll introduce everybody in a minute," Traverse explained.

A muscular guard with a shaved head came in next and stood to one side of the door, which was opened all the way inward. The man who stepped into the room next caused Marla to take in a quick breath. It was Major Landsdale, who, the last she'd seen, was being wheeled into an elevator on a gurney so he could be taken, she'd supposed, to a makeshift morgue.

"Miss Corvasce," he said, nodding his head.

Another soldier, who looked like a life-sized rough and ready Ken doll, entered behind him and stood on the other side of the door.

"Thanks for coming, Major," said Traverse. To the guards, he said, "Shoot him."

While Major Landsdale stood staring at Traverse with a shocked expression on his otherwise nonplussed face, the two guards drew their pistols and shot him in the back. As large as the conference room was, the noise was like a sonic boom. Marla flinched, her ears ringing like she was trapped inside a cathedral bell tower.

These people were crazy. She knew that now. Totally. But her instincts told her that the safest thing to do was to stay completely still, and that's what she did. She looked at the guards and saw that their faces were unreadable. They holstered their weapons as Major Lansdale cried out and dropped to one knee on the carpeted floor. His right hand caught the blood spattered back of the chair next to Marla, then he coughed once and shuddered as he fell the rest of the way to the floor.

No one made a move to help him.

"Don't worry," said Traverse. "He was already dead, anyway. Get the body out of here, corporal. Try not to leave too much of a blood trail in the hallway."

Marla's hand was on the grip of her revolver, but she didn't draw. Her back ached with the tension of holding her posture rigid. She kept her face neutral. However bad things had been in Traverse's office, she thought they were about to get much worse.

"Jimmy, how many times have I killed that son of a bitch?"

The young man held up three fingers, then lowered them back to the tabletop. He looked at Marla, then back at Traverse.

"Three times I've killed him?"

"No. Three times before tonight," said Jimmy.

Traverse considered it for a moment, then continued.

"I'm going to have to kill him again before the week is done. You watch."

Both guards left, carrying the body of the major and closing the door behind them. Marla looked up from the bloody chair and over at Traverse. No wonder the president suspected Traverse was crazy or under the influence. Her boss looked back at her with his unblinking hazel eyes. He was a man who knew too much, and the magnitude of what he knew was killing him inside. She didn't want it to kill her, too. He'd just shot a man in cold blood and actually said it was no problem because he was already dead. Traverse Nations was a step beyond sociopathic.

"That's right," said Traverse. "I've killed him four times now. You see the problem, don't you, Marla? First person who died in this place, the old man passed a note to Borgo's Director of Operations. My grandfather. Said to lower the body down the shaft with a long, long rope. These instructions were in an envelope that just appeared on his desk. Like a magic trick, only real. There was a map inside; it led them to a place on one of the lower floors. A door was set into the wall where there wasn't a door a few hours before. Nobody knew how it got there back then and we still don't know now. But you open the door and there's a deep hole that goes straight down.

"They didn't think about it too much that day. Nobody wanted to piss off the old guy. So, they just did what it said in the letter. They lowered the dead man down the hole. It took a lot of ropes tied together; don't ask me how many. It didn't say in the report.

"The guy—his name doesn't make any difference, does it Jimmy—was dead when they dropped him in. All the records are clear on that. They keep letting out rope and letting out rope and finally it hit bottom. We think. Nobody really knows what's down there. Nobody wants to go down and find out. Then the rope started shaking and jerking like something got hold of it. Scared the piss out of them, even after being in a place like this, and that's saying a lot.

"When it suddenly snapped stiff, it was so unexpected it almost pulled the two men down the hole, but they let loose and then, suddenly, the rope went slack. They waited a few minutes, and then they started pulling the rope back up. When they reached the end, they saw that the knotted loop was undone, and blood smeared the rope for the last ten feet. That caused a lot of talk around the office, let me tell you."

"Show her the gate," said the round-faced man.

Traverse did something with a matte black device he took from one pocket. The far wall to the left lit up to show a stand of trees.

"Happy?" he asked. "That is the only way into this town. You drive through Polehenge, and you end up here. Trucks drive through and here they are. It's a one-way access, though. Nothing ever leaves Borgo. Nothing. One way only. Now, back to the story."

Traverse turned toward her again, a look of mad glee on his face.

"A week later, the same guy they lowered down the hole was back at work in his lab. Said hello to his co-workers, got his lab coat and safety glasses out of his locker and picked up where he left off on his last experiment.

"People die, and they go down the hole just like the old man said they should. Eventually, some of them come back up. We don't know what happens to the ones that don't. We've scoured every inch of this place and can't find anywhere the recycled ones are sneaking back in. None of them remember dying. They aren't zombies, Marla. They don't walk around with their arms waving in front of them trying to find brains to eat. They look normal. However badly they were torn up before we put them down the hole, they came back with no injuries. If they lost an eye before they died, they have two normal ones when they come back. Don't ask how I know that.

"But this town was empty before we got here. Only person here was the old man and the guy who found him. He thought he was going to get a medal for the employee of the month for finding the bastard. How could he know anyone that enters Borgo never leaves?"

"They're dead and they come back to life?" asked Marla.

It was everything she could do to keep a neutral face.

She caught the wary look in Jimmy's eyes out of the corner of her eye.

"Remember how big the population of Borgo is? Remember what I told you?"

"Yes."

"Most of the people here died one way or the other and came back. The government keeps sending up more people. He kills them, then they come back. The first time they come back, it takes a while to notice, but there's something different about them. They give off some kind of weird vibe, don't they, Doc?"

The white-haired, pinched-face woman tilted her head to one side as though she could hear a sound the others could not, but then answered.

"My name is Dr. Lydia Grayson, Marla. You may call me Doc. It's what everyone else around here does—both the living and the dead."

That last statement scared Marla as much as the story of the hole. She tried to size her up, but there really wasn't anything about her to grab hold of. She reminded Marla of one of those character actors, at home in any part they were given as long as it required a pinched face.

"What kind of doctor are you?" asked Marla.

"Psychology," she said. "I had the misfortune of being tenured faculty at the University of Michigan. I say misfortune, because Borgo is situated geographically north of Lansing. Because of that, I was chosen by the security powers that be to send here as the town's resident therapist."

"To keep us all sane, isn't that right, Doc?"

Traverse smiled a crooked smile. An inside joke. Something dark lit the corner of his eyes. It was hard for her to keep down the feeling that at any moment, he would tilt his head back with his mouth wide open and something dark, viscous and malevolent would come rolling out. She drew in a breath and held it to calm down. As she released it slowly, she wondered what made her question whether or not Traverse was actually alive.

"Are you saying," she asked Traverse, "that thousands of the people here are dead but still working for you?"

It was again the doctor who answered. She could feel the woman's eyes on her. Looking at her the way doctors looked at their patients. At that moment, she didn't know who was more menacing—Traverse or Dr. Grayson.

"I'm a psychologist, Marla," said the pinched-faced woman. "I'd be the first to know if we were all crazy. Believe me, I wish we were all crazy. But we're not. We're suffering from a disorder I have created called disruption dissociative disorder. It is similar to PTSD, but it's brought on by prolonged exposure to disorienting, disrupting conditions that are not necessarily violent, but that seem to violate reality. You've only been here a short while, but your profile suggests you adapt well to... extreme conditions. Even so, may I ask you how I feel about everything that you've seen?"

"Shut up," said Marla to Dr. Grayson.

"Nice," said Traverse. "I'd say she will do better than most."

"Who's he?"

"The white-haired guy with the face round as a range target? He's the nuclear guy. We brought him in to nuke the whole town, including the old man. It didn't work, though, did it Terry?"

"I still have a few tricks up my sleeve," said the man. "Working on a fuel oxidant bomb that might just do the job."

"Uh-huh. Like Minus Eight? The billion-dollar slag heap, that's what we call it now. Anyway, Marla, Professor Terry Grieves and the Doc and Jimmy and I are the only four people I'm really sure are living, as in really living except for you. Not dead and brought back to life, right Jimmy? There may be a few hundred more. Maybe minus the hundred and fifty in the cage, too."

Jimmy looked at Traverse, held his gaze, saying nothing, and then looked away.

"In the cage?" asked Marla.

"Later," said Jimmy. "Don't ask now."

"That's four of us and you make five, Marla," said Traverse as though he hadn't heard the exchange. "Maybe more. It's hard to be sure. This place is so big. But welcome to the club. Five known living, breathing human beings in the land of the walking dead and one old guy that all we know for sure about him is that whatever he is, the only thing he isn't is human."

"Traverse," asked Marla, "I need to let the president know what's going on."

"You don't do that," said Traverse. "And besides, it's technically none of his business. I know you were hooded on the way here, and although you might think you're in Michigan, like the Doc says, we're not exactly in the United States, in case you haven't figured that out by now."

"I have to let him know. He's the President of the United States. I have a job to do."

12

"Marla, I don't care if he's the Pope's grandson," shouted Traverse.

"He's the President of the United States," she shot back.

"I'll say it again—case you didn't hear me the last time," said Traverse. "We aren't exactly in the United States."

Marla was on her feet, the chair pushed back with her clenched fists pushing on the table.

"But he told me, the president told me, we were in the United States."

Her voice trembled with barely suppressed rage. She'd had enough of these crazy assholes.

"Yeah, well, he's totally out of his mind. I don't care that he's the President. I don't care that he's the first Muslim president. Why the hell would I care about any of that? Like I said, I don't care if he's the Pope's grandson. He is out of his mind if he thinks he knows where this place really is or that he's in control. None of them, not one single president since this started, has ever really understood what's happening here or even where we are. Hell, we don't understand what's going on here and we're the ones trapped here. None of our firepower, none of our scientific know-how, and none of our think tanks have been any use here at all. You think we're crazy, I know you do. Don't say you don't. Well, we were crazy. You want to know how crazy we were? Do you? I'll show you, so you can see what we were like before we got a grip."

His face was contorted with anger, and his cheeks were flushed red. With a touch of his finger on the screen before him, the lights came on in the darkened section of the conference room. Marla froze when she saw what was there.

"Yeah," Traverse said, "Take a good look."

On the far wall, she saw leather straps bolted in place and knew immediately what it was. Two straps where the ankles would be, one that looked like an over-sized bell where the waist would be, two for each wrist, one higher for the neck, and where the head would be, was a metal framed structure with restraining clamps to hold the head. Blood spatters outlined where the body would be. Marla felt her stomach shrivel in disgust.

Traverse sprang from his chair and strode to one side of it like a lecturer preparing to discuss a lecture slide. His face was alive with manic twitching as he waved one hand at his exhibit. Marla glanced at the psychologist, Dr. Grayson. She was staring straight at Marla, daring her to call them all insane.

"We were dying here, Marla," said Traverse. "Everything we tried against the old man went nowhere. We tried blowing him up, which was less than satisfying, let me tell you. C4 didn't work. Rocket-launched grenades didn't work. We sectioned off the plumbing to his house when he was out and poured poison into his drinking water. Nothing. We disconnected the gas lines leading into his house and pumped poison gas in there. Same."

Traverse looked as though someone had walked over his grave as he rushed the pace, like the more words he put between what he'd just said and what he was saying now, the safer he would be.

"So, we were up against the wall. Going out of our fucking minds. So, we stole some moves from the CIA. We brought in the writers. That's when we started going bad. They fucked us up, Marla. It was the writers' fault.

"You remember that movie Seven Days of the Condor or something like that? Robert Redford was the main guy. The CIA had these analysts reading books to look for ideas they could use. I think that was it. Anyway, we had the president send in a bunch of writers. We had to figure out what was going on here, before we all died or went insane. We asked for science fiction writers, horror writers and fantasy writers. That's how we brought it down on ourselves. We thought they'd have all these creative insights and ideas, maybe bring a new way of looking at things. This room was built just for them to sit in and brainstorm."

"What happened?" asked Marla.

"Lydia, why don't you tell her?" said Traverse. "I'm thinking I'll go nuts if I talk about it."

My God, thought Marla. Does the President of the United States know that the Director of the Borgo Project is both demon-possessed and insane?

It was hard to read Dr. Grayson's expression. Her eyes were sunken, her stringy hair lay flat against her head. She had the look of a sullen child holding back a confession.

"It became," she said, "the basis for my theory of disturbance dissociative disorder."

"Just tell her," said Professor Grieves.

Dr. Grayson swiveled her head to glare at him, then turned back to look at Marla.

"As I was about to say, what happened to the writers provided me with a testable hypothesis."

"Are we going to be here all night?" asked the physicist. "Just tell her. Nobody cares about your bullshit psychological theory."

Dr. Grayson shoved back her chair, straightened to her full height and slammed her bony fist into the side of the physicist's head. The blow knocked him sideways in his chair, which then fell against Jimmy, who pulled back in horror. The physicist's chair rocked in place as Dr. Grayson was on him like a professional wrestler, snaking her forearm around his neck and pulling him upward and backward.

"Enough," shouted Traverse.

Dr. Grayson stared straight at him as she choked the physicist unconscious, then rolled him off the chair and onto the floor. Her breathing was difficult, and her cheeks were flushed.

"The fuck is the matter with you?" said Traverse.

Marla remained motionless during the entire episode, watching warily. Her attention was now on Jimmy, who looked at her and shook his head. Not now, he seemed to say. Not in front of them. You can't trust them.

"He was at me again. Egging me on," said Dr. Grayson.

She glared at Traverse defiantly, then kicked Professor Grieves in the side of the head.

Reaching beneath his sweater, Traverse pulled out a pistol and aimed it directly between Dr. Grayson's eyes. There was no fear in the woman's face, Marla noted. There was instead a look of acceptance. Almost a look of pleading. She seemed to say please. Please shoot me. Please.

Traverse looked down and saw Jimmy staring at him. He lowered his weapon and tucked it back beneath his sweater.

"Sorry, Jimmy. I just… you know… I went backwards a little. Sorry. Lydia, sit back down and don't kick him again. Don't step on his fingers either. I won't shoot you. But I can still have you put in the cage, you understand. I will do that if you don't settle down."

Marla observed a small reaction in Dr. Lydia Grayson's face this time. Apparently, she would rather be shot than put in the cage.

"Jimmy, can you help me get him back in the chair? Lydia, don't touch him. Marla, stay where you are. Just give us a minute."

The two of them dragged Professor Grieves back up and into his chair, while Lydia watched with disdain. Marla, as she had done so often during this madhouse event, kept her cool and said nothing. Waiting. Watching. Learning.

Jimmy took a handful of napkins, dipped them in a water carafe, and wiped down the unconscious man's face. He sputtered, coughed and looked around wildly as though he didn't know where he was. Then he saw Dr. Grayson and lunged for her. Traverse and Jimmy both were ready for the move and held him back until he quieted.

"You're going to get yours, Lydia," he rasped. "You're going to get yours."

"Yeah, yeah. Enough," said Traverse. "This is screwed up enough as it is. Can you handle that, Terry? If you can't, I'm going to get the guards in here and have you dragged out and have them slap some restraints on you. We'll talk this out later. Somebody's going to have to pay. But right now, I want to fill Marla in. We need her, remember? We need her. She's our chance. Her and Eva. The rest of this can wait. I'll let you smack her around later. Oh, sorry Jimmy. I didn't mean that. I was just trying to calm everybody down. Wasn't thinking."

The physicist looked back and forth between Traverse, Dr.

Grayson, and Jimmy.

"Don't say anything, Lydia," warned Traverse. "Just keep your mouth shut."

After a moment's hesitation, as though he wasn't completely sure the two of them would abide by the truce, he headed back to the end of the table and resumed.

"Where was I before this bullshit? Wait, I've got it. It was that fucking twilight zone episode, that one with the little kid. That's what started it. We got these writers together thinking they'd come up with some creative ideas as to what the hell was going on here. Had the presidents—Bush and Obama—ship them in on a flatbed. We tried it twice. Neither President liked doing it. Some kind of conscience bullshit. Anyway, we got them together in this room. This room. Sometimes I'd sit in, sometimes Dr. Lydia here, and we'd lay everything out and wait for them to come up with some answers. But writers aren't all that creative sometimes. In fact, they like to repeat the same shit over and over. They're like psychotic tape recorders on a reboot rant.

"The science fiction people started the problem. This one guy, he says that this whole thing reminds him of that episode on the Twilight Zone with Billy Mumy. The one where that kid has the power to do things with his mind, including reading people's thoughts. The people in the town are scared shitless of him and they keep telling him everything is good so he won't send them into the cornfield, which was bad, or turn them into human jack-in-the-boxes. Okay, so there were some similarities to what we've got going on here, but it wasn't really the same. The old man is not a kid, and he can't read our thoughts. So, we tell him that and ask him to keep thinking.

"Then, all the crackhead writers started doing the same thing, no matter if they wrote science fiction, fantasy, horror or... what's that other one, Jimmy?"

"Magical realism," said Jimmy.

Traverse snapped his fingers.

"Yeah, that's it. Magical realism like that Dresden file stuff. Anyway, they all keep going back to this story or that story. Magic or aliens or Area 51 experiments they've read about. They can't get off it. Then this same writer brings up Billy Mumy, and the Twilight Zone again. We tell him to get back on track. It kept going like this, Marla.

They'd try to figure out how our situation here was the same as this story or that story or similar to this novel or that novel. They started getting on our nerves big time. You can see why, right? They couldn't come up with anything new. People should die for that—I mean figuratively, Jimmy.

"So, some of them got on this trope bullshit. You ever hear the word trope before? I hadn't. Now I know I'd rather die rolling around in a Laundromat dryer than hear that word again. Anyway, there's nothing new, they say—got to be a trope that matches what's going on here. One lady says, well, if it's like a novel and this old guy is the super villain, there must be a superhero to defeat him because all stories have to have villains and heroes of approximately the same strength. We called her an idiot. Me and Lydia both. We called her an idiot and told her to try harder. Lydia slapped her a couple of times.

"But then, the asshole pops in again with Billy Mumy and the Twilight Zone episode. Do you understand where this is going? We couldn't take it. Some of the other science people—most of them are dead now and have come back, but back then they were alive—start getting so they couldn't stand it either. Every time that little prick brought up Billy Mumy, we wanted to kill him.

"So, one day, we did."

Traverse twisted his head against his shoulder like he had a sudden nerve spasm.

"Fuck, that hurt. Anyway, one night, after one more of those never-ending writer meetings, some of the technical guys come back and bolt these straps on the wall. I didn't know about it, Lydia didn't know about it, and Terry didn't know about it. Major Landsdale was the guy that got everyone worked up when he had the idea and the next day, they had the lights at this end of the room dimmed so it was hard to see what they'd done. Hey Jimmy, could you pray for me? I'm getting a little tense. Could you do it for me? I don't want to lose it."

Jimmy nodded and bowed his head. Marla wondered who he was praying for, Traverse or himself.

"Thanks, Jimmy. And, Marla, this was before Jimmy came here, all right? Just to get that straight. We went crazy and it would have been worse if it wasn't for him. Jimmy saved us. Saved our sanity. Jimmy's like our guardian saint."

I don't think so, thought Marla.

Traverse picked up where he left off.

"The meeting got going. Landsdale and his tech guys got ready. An hour and a half into the meeting and that little fuck of a writer brings up Billy Mumy again. That's when they got up and grabbed him. They dragged him over there and strapped him up. Screaming and kicking like he was having a psychotic break. That metal thing on top kept his head still without covering his forehead. The other writers tried to stop what was going on, but Major Landsdale had that figured out in advance. Couple of his troops busted in and beat them senseless. Then Major Landsdale picks up this big hammer and a metal spike and says, 'Say it again. Say Billy Mumy.' The writer is crying and begging at this point. He pissed his pants."

Marla's exposure to the town of Borgo had gotten progressively darker and now she felt like it was suffocating her. She knew what was coming next. She could see the dried, dark bloodstains around the hole where the man's head would have been. She wanted to scream or shoot someone.

"The writer wouldn't say it because I think he knew what was coming. But, after they'd broken him, he finally said 'Billy Mumy.' That's when Major Landsdale says, 'I knew you'd say that,' and he pounds the spike right through the guy's forehead."

Marla fought back the bile rising in her throat.

"Grim, huh?" said Traverse. "You still praying for me, Jimmy? Good. I need it, Jimmy. It kept going that way, Marla. Even after the beating and the spiking, these moronic dumbassed writers couldn't stop."

Traverse's face distorted with rage, and Marla cringed.

"Billy Mumy. Billy Mumy. Twilight Zone. Twilight Zone. What the fuck was wrong with them? They kept saying it, we kept staking them. It got out of control, okay, but they deserved it because if there was ever any fucking group of people on the planet ever deserved a stake through their heads, it was them. Sometimes we'd leave one of them up there for a couple of days. But then we'd remember what the old man wanted, and we'd take them down, drag their bodies to that door a few floors down, and lower them into the pit by that long rope. We did it a lot.

"Then one of them brings up pocket dimensions. Then another. Fucking writers can't come up with anything new. They think about something somebody else did and start harping on it. You can guess the rest. Anytime one of them says, 'pocket dimension,' they get strapped to the wall and get a spike through the forehead. It kept on going. We kept getting… worse."

"May I continue for you, Traverse? I am better now," said Dr. Grayson.

Traverse nodded.

"Yeah, sure. Sure. You take over. Terry, don't you say a fucking thing, or I'll stomp your head in."

13

"No," said Marla. "I don't want to hear any more about this. I wasn't sent here to listen to your mental condition. My mission is to destroy this old man, or whatever it is he actually is. That's why the president sent me here. And that's what I will do. So, tell me about the secret weapon. Tell me about the witch."

"But the research that went into developing my disturbance dissociated disorder will immeasurably help you understand what we—" Dr. Grayson started to say.

"Research?" interrupted Professor Grieves. "You were one of the subjects, you stupid bitch. How can one of the subjects be objective? Can you tell me that?"

His words were slurred and the right side of his mouth, the one toward Dr. Grayson, was purple and starting to swell.

"I—"

"And," he continued, "you had sex with at least three men we later found out had been dead and reanimated. How's that for objective, you dumbass? Real scientists don't orgasm with the dead."

This time it was Marla who brought up her gun. She aimed it right in the center of Professor Grieves's face. She wasn't planning on shooting anyone, but she desperately needed to get them back on track.

"Shut up," she said. "Both of you just shut up or you'll be the next two bodies lowered down the hole. And Lydia, I can see what you're thinking, so unless you want to be the first with a bullet in her forehead, I'd calm down."

Traverse and Jimmy watched almost disinterestedly. Scenes like this must have played out many times in the past. Professor Grieves, staring nervously at the pistol pointed at his head, finally said, "Okay."

Marla automatically swiveled the pistol to point at Dr. Grayson. Lydia looked straight back at her, ignoring the pistol. "Go ahead, pull the trigger. Shoot me if you're brave enough."

Jimmy shook his head slightly.

Don't do it, he was saying.

Was she already dead? Marla wondered. Is there something about her Jimmy knows that I need to know?

"Talk or die," said Marla. "Not about your research. Tell me about the plan and the witch, or none of you are any use to me."

She was tired of them all, tired of Borgo. She wanted to do something instead of getting kicked around by a witch and her pet monsters and listen to these mental incompetents piss and moan. She wanted to find a way to hurt the old man. More than that, to kill him. Marla didn't need to know what he was or why he was. She just needed to destroy him, whatever he was. Or she needed to find a way out of Borgo.

"We created a program," said Lydia. "One of the most gifted computer programmers alive built it for us."

Marla returned the gun to her holster.

"What kind of program?" asked Marla. "Who created it?"

"A young man selected by the government after an extensive and rigorous search."

"Name?" asked Marla.

Dr. Grayson looked toward Traverse.

"He won't save you," said Marla. "If you don't tell me, I will kill you."

Ignoring Marla, Traverse gave a nod.

"His name was John Amrozi. He created the program."

"Is he here?"

"He was," put in Traverse. "We found what was left of his body yesterday. Someone cut his throat and bled him out, we think."

"What do you mean, you think?"

"Well, the head and neck were left and a little underneath that, but the rest was, well, just scraps."

"Maybe those parts didn't taste as good to whatever ate him," giggled Dr. Grieves.

"Shut up," said Traverse.

"Who? Did you catch who did it?" asked Marla.

"We're living in a town of re-animated dead and one old man who can kill us all, Marla. So, no, we don't have a clue who did it. And we don't care."

"If the old man has a confederate in here—" began Marla.

"Where's your head?" said Traverse. "He probably found out and terminated the sleazy prick. Get over it. And that old man doesn't need an inside man or woman. He probably controls the reanimated dead. Hell, for all we know, he reads their thoughts or controls their thoughts if they really have any thoughts. Is that even possible, Terry? Scientifically, I mean."

"Who gives a fuck?" said Professor Grieves. "He does what he does. Perfectly good uranium comes in here so we can go nuclear and kill him and all the rest of us, but somehow, he makes it so it's not radioactive. That's not possible. Every time we talk about the science or psychology of this, we have to fall back on the same answers. We don't know shit. Is that scientific enough for you?"

Mission, thought Marla. Keep your mind on the mission. Nothing matters but accomplishing the mission. Destroy the old man or find out how he could be destroyed and get the hell out if she couldn't do it by herself. But listening to these maniacs made it hard to focus on the mission. They were beginning to sound as dangerous as the old man himself.

"You see why we don't know who killed him?" asked Traverse. "We don't have anything to go on that makes any sense."

"What was the program supposed to do?" asked Marla.

Dr. Grayson answered. She looked a little more in control of herself now, but Marla could see a thin film of sweat on her upper lip. Why was it, she wondered, that everyone beside herself and Jimmy seemed to always be on the edge of a homicidal rage or a cold-blooded killing spree? Were there demons inside them all like the ones she had seen burst out of Traverse?

Mission. She had to keep her mind on the mission. And her mission was to destroy the old man.

"It was supposed to subliminally interrupt and control the thoughts of everyone in the real world who was sitting at their computer," said Dr. Grayson.

"Why?" asked Marla.

"I'll tell you," said Traverse. "It's because of Eva. The one you call the witch. She's been helping us, but she can't take on the old man himself. She's not powerful enough."

"I'm not following you."

"Brainwaves," said Professor Grieves. "This is more my area than these two. She told Traverse that if we could create a mental harmonic—millions of minds thinking the same thought at the same time—that she could create a magical ritual to harvest that energy. Like when you jump start one car from a power grid."

Marla had no idea what he meant. She looked over at the wall, splattered with dried blood, and pockmarked with spike holes.

"You're serious," she said when she'd turned back to look at Professor Grieves.

"Marla, how the fuck would any of us know if it works? Do I look like I know anything about magic? It's like when one soldier got so tired of hearing about magic that he and the janitors started spiking any one of the writers who would say something about the Dresden Files. This is not Chicago and Harry Dresden is fucking imaginary. Somebody had to spike them or—"

Marla had raised her pistol and aimed it at him again.

"Sorry," he said, raising both hands palm out. "Sorry. Won't happen again. It's just that… okay, everybody thinking the same thought at the same time may create an energy harmonic, whatever that means. Maybe. Like Tesla's research into energy harmonics? I don't know. Fuck, I can't even get uranium to work in here. But let's say it created a massive amount of energy that Eva's magical ritual could harvest. If she powered up with that, maybe she could blast the old man. Maybe, just maybe, she could kill him using that energy."

Although Professor Grieves was looking at her for approval,

Marla was thinking of what he'd said differently. What if, she wondered, she was harvesting it for the old man? What if she and the old man were working together? That made a hell of a lot more sense than her performing an act of kindness for the remaining residents of Borgo. But why? What was their end game?

"This program," said Marla, "how could it do that?"

"Borgo," said Dr. Grayson. "We call it the Borgo Virus. With the approval and help of what used to be called DARPA, John Amrozi infected every computer in the world connected to the Internet, including the Internet of Things. Amrozi was supposed to be from DARPA. None of us know who he really was, though. There was so much secrecy about his being brought here."

"Did he know no one can ever leave Borgo?"

"No, Marla, he didn't," said Traverse. "You think we're crazy? If he did, he would never have come here. And we told DARPA he had to do it from here, according to Eva, in order for it to work."

"Was that true?"

"No. We lied. We were desperate. We couldn't take the chance the president would say no to the plan part way through it and shut the whole thing down. If he did that, we'd be trapped in here, don't you see? That can't happen. One way or the other, Marla, we're getting out of here."

Jimmy was still praying. The only person Marla had ever seen praying like that was her grandmother. That old woman could pray for hours and hours. Marla vividly remembered at that moment waking up early one morning to find her grandmother praying at the dining room table, looking as if she hadn't moved from the night before where she'd been praying that she and her grandfather could die at the same moment. Her grandfather was in the hospital and her father and mother made the old woman come back home with them to get some rest before returning to the hospital. She'd stubbornly sat praying at the table until Marla's parents had finally given up and gone to bed.

"Did he complete the software program?" she asked. "Did it launch?"

She felt her stomach tighten as she asked the question. If it launched, it was too late.

"Yes," said Professor Grieves. "It launched."

A sudden thought struck her.

"What day, what time does it take effect, Professor?"

Professor Grieves rubbed the back of his hand over the tender right side of his head, then touched the corner of his mouth with his fingertips.

"Shit," he said. "This is going to swell up badly. And bruise, too." He glared at Dr. Grayson.

"When exactly does it take effect?" snapped Marla. "I want an answer now."

"Well," he said, "we don't really know."

"Soon," said Traverse. "It's going to happen soon. She didn't want us to know exactly when, in case the old man could read our thoughts. He wasn't always able to do things like that, but we think that he's getting stronger."

"I believe he is dynamically involving," said Dr. Grayson. "As opposed to evolving in an environment where a species would change in response to environmental or competitive matrices. His very being is turning inward and metamorphosing into a higher order."

Jimmy still prayed, his hands folded in front of him. His elbows rested on the table and his head leaned forward as though, by the act itself, he was submitting to the will of the divine.

"Psychologists are full of shit," said Professor Grieves. "The old man is getting stronger. Nobody knows why, nobody knows how, and nobody understands enough to even guess. Maybe he's always been this strong, but has been toying with us. Or he sees that we've acclimated a little to the tension, so he ratchets up the stakes."

"Or maybe he's like a cat playing with a mouse," said Marla. "Ready to break our necks when he's ready to eat."

The room was silent for a few seconds. Then Traverse said, "I like the way you put that, I really do. Maybe that's why he asked for you. Maybe he's ready to eat."

"It's not that," said Jimmy. "It's something else. Right now, he's in the Masonic Temple in the center of town. Why does he go there every Wednesday night? Is he a Mason? That wouldn't make any sense. None of us in this room believes he's even human. So why does he go there? What does he do in there? When we sent over men one night to break into the temple, they photographed and videoed everything. It was like any other Masonic Temple. We left fiber optic cameras and micro mikes there, too. Nothing ever happened. Except every Wednesday night, when that old man stepped into the Masonic Temple, and all of our audio and video equipment would quit working."

Traverse, Dr. Grayson and Professor Grieves went silent when Jimmy talked. Marla wasn't sure when he quit praying and started talking, but she was glad he did.

"How long has this been going on?" asked Marla.

Jimmy and the others turned toward Traverse, not only because he was the Director of Operation Borgo, but because he had been there longer than anybody.

"Since the beginning," he said. "After the old man disappeared in Germany, an early version of the Identikit used in police work was used to create a portrait of the old man. We made statues that were the same height. Took pictures of the paintings and sketches and the statues. The President's watchers were in full panic mode. Mock-ups were made of the room where it all happened.

"They grilled the soldier that stood between the old man and President Truman worse than a hot dog at a high school band concert. When you think about it, it was obvious. It was after the assassination of President McKinley back at the beginning of the twentieth century that started the secret service protecting the president. The situation with the old man started—at least as far as we know—in war time.

"Think what it was like, Marla. An old man demon monster traps the President of the United States in an alternate reality and kills all his guards except for one. Who do you think both the Secret Service and the military are going to come down on? Easy to figure out, isn't it? That one soldier was the only possible scapegoat. No one really believed that what the President said went on in that room actually happened, but he was the President. Maybe they thought Truman went crazy and butchered all those men and that the one soldier was covering up for him. Maybe they thought the two of them were in it together. Nobody writes those kind of thoughts down. But the President had other ideas.

"It would have been over for that soldier if the President hadn't stepped in and protected him. The President was actually there. The

President actually saw what happened, and he also saw that lone soldier put himself between him and the old man. He realized only one man beside himself really saw the old man, and that if that man was both relentless and brave, then he was the only one with the chance to hunt that old man down. Toward that end, that soldier was appointed the First Director of Project Borgo, my grandfather."

Marla thought this over before answering. She didn't want to keep going backward, but she sensed that if she let Traverse continue, there was something important she might learn.

"And how did they find him?"

Traverse ran a hand through his luxurious mane of silver gray hair, lost in thought for a minute.

"It differed from that," he finally said. "I think he led us to him. Understand the hysteria after the day he popped in on Truman. No one really believed the President at first… but the bodies and the room were hard to explain away. The longer they analyzed the evidence, the more real it became. So, the artists' sketches made their way to the field. Treason was what they finally settled on for a cover story. J. Edgar Hoover was finally brought into the loop a few months into it. He was so strong even back then that there was no way to keep him out. Hoover was a little creepy, but he had the manpower to snag the old man if he showed up in the U.S., and he eventually did. An FBI agent ID'd him in Michigan, called in and followed the old man up US 127 until it turned into US 27 and kept on heading north until they eventually came even with Polehenge."

"What happened next?"

"The agent waited there for reinforcements to arrive. Thirty-six top notch agents showed up to cordon off the area, and then the military. They brought serious hardware, Marla. Serious hardware. When they were all set up, a convoy of soldiers went down the road. About fifty yards down, the entire convoy disappeared and reappeared here, in the town of what we now call Borgo, Michigan. It was a complete town, empty of life except for the old man. You can guess what happened.

"I won't go into the details, but after they disappeared, the soldier who stood between the old man and President went in leading a team of specialists. They never came out. No one who enters Borgo ever leaves. And now you're one of us because the old man asked for you.

Like I said before, he's never asked for anyone specifically before. According to Eva, he thinks you know where something is that he wants. So, you're going to get to see him face to face."

"He thinks I know about something he wants? What in the hell is he looking for?"

"Some Masonic journal. Like a little book. Eva wouldn't say exactly. I don't know if she knows what's in it. But he's angry, and he wants it back. It's not good when he's angry. Something one of your relatives had, but that has gone missing, she said. Most of the men in your family were Masons, right?"

"A lot, why?"

"The Masons are the key to this whole thing. That's what Eva says. For a while, the CIA tried to torture it out of some of the higher ranking Masons around the country, but that ended badly. Very badly. He didn't like that. We got the message to leave them alone, and that was it. Eva is the only person who can go back and forth between this town and the normal world. She was looking around for the papers, too, but she can't find them yet either."

Marla had her doubts whether Eva could be classified as a person.

"I know what you're thinking," said Traverse. "If she can get out of here, why doesn't she get us out, too? But she can't. She doesn't have the power to do that. Just enough to get herself through. If the Borgo program works, she says maybe after she crushes the old man, she can use what's left of the power to get us out, too."

"Maybe?"

Marla trusted nothing, the witch said. It was better, she thought, to believe the opposite of what she said.

Traverse, Dr. Grayson, Professor Grieves and Jimmy stayed silent.

"Maybe?" she asked again.

"We don't know," said Professor Grieves. "None of us understand magic."

"How does she do it? How can she leave this place and re-enter the normal world?"

Traverse shrugged.

"Magic."

"Look," said Marla, "my mission is to destroy this old man and so far, all you've told me is what doesn't work. How about telling me something that does work or did work? Isn't there anything that's ever hurt him? Nothing you've done that's ever caused him pain?"

"We tried holy water once," said Professor Grieves. "We pumped it into the water system in his house. Once, when he was walking down the street, we turned on sprinklers that sprayed him with it."

"And?"

"No effect."

"There is one thing which has never been tried," said Dr. Grayson cautiously.

Marla sat up straighter.

"And what is that?"

"No one from this complex has ever spoken to him. Really spoken to him. You will be the first, except, of course, for Eva Morgan. We were hoping you could plead with him on all of our behalf. Try to reason with him. Ask him if he will allow us to leave this place. Tell him we'll do anything he wants if he lets us go. We mean him no harm."

"Eva says the Masons are coming soon to take him away, back to the normal world," said Professor Grieves.

"There are people coming to take this thing, this monster back to the normal world? Are they crazy? Don't they understand what he could do once he is loose? And how would they get him out? How would they even get in to take him out?"

"Eva says they're zealots, true believers," said Traverse. "They're Masons, you know? They wear aprons at their meetings. What kind of men wear aprons?"

"What meetings? Why would they take this monster out of here?"

"How the hell would I know? They're out of their fucking minds if they think anything good can come out of letting him loose. Is this bullshit or what? You wonder why I think every president is an asshole? Because they can't get us out and they don't care about us. But the Freemasons can? That's just plain bullshit. Who's running the USA—the Freemasons or the president? And you know what's worse? I think those same Masons are going to leave us all behind. With the reanimated dead. Eva thinks that when the old man is gone, they'll turn on us. The reanimated dead, that is. Scares me so bad I can hardly sleep. You think I want Major Landsdale coming for me?"

"That's why you must plead with the old man," said Dr. Grayson. "If you know where his papers or books are, tell him. Find them for him. Give them to him. If you don't, tell him that. But beg him to set us free. Maybe you could do that for us? Could you do that, Marla?"

Marla wanted so badly to put a bullet into Dr. Lydia Grayson's brain.

"There's one thing," said Professor Grieves, "that hasn't hurt him, but that disturbs him."

"What might that be?" asked Marla.

"Jimmy," said the Professor. "He seems almost afraid of Jimmy."

Traverse, Dr. Grayson and Professor Grieves all turned to look at the young man at the same time.

Focus on the mission, she thought. Find something to hurt the old man.

Jimmy looked at her. There was something in his soft brown eyes that begged her not to pursue this in front of the others. But right now, Jimmy was the only option she had. He had the shoulders and forearms of a computer jockey. And the thick glasses. Dressed in black slacks held up by a black belt, and he wore black shoes and a white shirt. The only thing missing was a copy of the Book of Mormon and the Pearl of Great Price. If the old man was afraid of a clean-cut young man like Jimmy, maybe he did have an exploitable weakness.

"He's not afraid of me," said Jimmy.

"No? Then what is he afraid?"

"I don't know."

"Forget about that," said Traverse. "Concentrate on what you have to do when you meet the old man. You've got to persuade him somehow to get us out of here. Lie to him. Beg for mercy. Get us out of here."

"What if I don't go?"

The room became so quiet she could hear herself breathe.

When no one answered, she asked Traverse, "Well, would you do it?"

Traverse looked pensive, and Jimmy just stared at her.

"Well? Traverse?"

"Only if I took Eva with me."

Marla wasn't about to take Eva with her. She didn't really

understand who the witch was, but whatever she was, she definitely wasn't on their side.

"Then there is only one way I'll go," said Marla. "I'll do it if I take Jimmy with me. He'll be my ace."

"Not a fucking chance," shouted Traverse. "You're not taking him with you. He's the only sanity we've got in this place. No way. Not happening. I'd rather feed you to Major Landsdale and his dead-again soldiers."

"You can't have him," said Professor Grieves.

"He's with us," hissed Dr. Grayson. "He's one of us. You can't take him to see that—"

"Devil," finished Professor Grieves.

"What did you say?" asked Marla.

There had been something in the physicist's voice. A sound of genuine, agonizing fear that, for the first time, had the feeling of truth.

"He's the devil," whispered Professor Grieves. "Right now, he's in that empty Masonic lodge. Just him and those empty chairs and the officer's stations, with no one to recite the pagan Masonic rituals. What is he doing there? What is he doing there?"

"But you said," pressed Marla, "that he's the—"

"The devil. Yes, I said it. He's the devil. That old man is Satan himself. Were you expecting the Devil to have a pitchfork or something? Red skin and a pointy beard?"

Professor Grieves' voice had risen in pitch until it was almost a shriek.

"Shut up," said Traverse.

"Why do you think he's the Devil?" asked Marla. "Why?"

"Leave him alone, Marla," said Traverse, and he was on his feet again.

His big hands were planted face down on the conference room table. It was easy to forget how big Traverse was until he glared down at you.

"You know who the first Director of Project Borgo was?" he growled.

In the tense atmosphere of the room, in the complete silence of the others when he asked that question, the sound of his voice seemed magnified, as though it was the sound of a vicious dog warning another predator away from his territory.

"No," she said, and she worked hard to keep the sound of her voice calm.

Inside, she was not calm at all. She felt an overwhelming desire to throw up. She'd been trained to handle a lot of difficult scenarios in her career, but nothing like this. Nothing remotely like this. She was surrounded in this underground complex, if Traverse, Dr. Grayson and Professor Grieves could be believed, by thousands of men and women who had been killed and then come back to life after being lowered by a rope a long way down a mysterious shaft. And then there was the witch, her demon-beasts and their ability to burst out of someone's mouth and into existence. All this before taking into account the old man. The personage Professor Grieves had called the Devil.

"It was my grandfather. And the Director after that was my father. That son of a bitch has murdered every Nations that he's ever laid eyes on. But one day, when he was looking back at me through the computer monitors, Jimmy walked between us, and I saw that old devil recoil. It was just an instant, but I knew right then that Jimmy was our crucifix against him. The only one that made him back off. I don't know how the old man can watch us back through our own cameras, but he does. And when he saw Jimmy, well, you should have seen his face. So, let me ask you this, Marla—if you were in a pit surrounded by vampires and you had one crucifix, one fucking crucifix—would you give it to somebody else who was leaving the pit? You aren't taking Jimmy. End of story."

"Let's Jimmy decide," said Marla.

"I'm in charge here," said Traverse. "I'm the one with the ultimate authority to say what's what. Nobody, not even the president, tells me what to do in Borgo, Michigan."

"I'll go with you, Marla," said Jimmy.

From the look of horror that seized the other three faces, Marla knew she'd made the right call.

"How are you with a knife?" she asked Jimmy.

"I'm not."

"Traverse, we need schematics for the Masonic Temple," said Marla. "We're not going in there blind."

If looks could kill, Marla knew she would already be dead.

14

Marla and Jimmy went to his rooms to talk, but fatigue was dragging her down and when she walked in behind him, she looked covetously at the bed beyond the open bedroom door. They had a lot to talk about, but first she needed sleep.

"Nice place," she told him.

Jimmy turned and grinned at her. It was the type of dark humor two inmates on death row would exchange. What did it matter what comforts you had in life when you were going to die soon?

"I decorated it myself."

"I can tell. Postmodern computer chic. Very Avant Garde. Pretty bad when you've got more computers than chairs. But I need some sleep, as in really need some sleep. You mind if I use your bed for an hour or two while you guard against Traverse and the rest of the maniacs?"

She couldn't help herself. She raised her hands overhead her head and stretched.

"You stay here in the living room," she said. "I'll be in there on the bed, but I'll have my pistol with me. I'll warn you now, if I get spooked in my sleep, I wake up firing. Got that?"

"Yes, ma'am," said Jimmy.

She hoped he got the point. He didn't look like the type who'd try to molest a woman in her sleep, but better to get the law laid down up front.

She was on the bed for less than three minutes before she was asleep.

Five minutes later, she was dreaming. In her dream, the witch Eva Morgan spellbound her and transported her to a farm with a broken-down barn and a rickety farm house.

"My gift to you," said Eva Morgan. "Watch and learn."

It was snowing hard, and from the dark smile on Eva's face, Marla felt that something terrible was about to happen.

"Where am I?" asked Marla.

"In the dark beginnings of your troubles," said the witch.

****

Italy, the winter of 1944

The heavy wooden door swung back with a screech of rusty hinges and cracked against the barn wall like a rifle shot. Inside, huddled behind stacks of frozen hay, Enzo Corvasce trembled and peered from between the bales, looking out into the framed darkness. He crossed himself, pulled down his thick, ice-crusted woolen scarf below his unshaven chin, then closed his eyes and prayed to the Blessed Virgin. With blood still leaking inside his mouth from the stump of his severed tongue, he prayed. On that night of darkness and killing cold, it was his only comfort.

No wind, no sound.

Enzo cracked his eyelids and looked around him. The horses, skittish for the last hour, were now silent. The wind, which had been rattling the barn's wooden plank walls with icy blasts, was as still as the dead eye of a winter hurricane.

Ice cold tears gathered in the corner of Enzo's eyes as he stared through the open doorway into the soft white blackness haloed by the awful aura of his pain. Moonlight lit the snow with a diffuse pale blue glow, and he saw falling white flakes spiraling down, shimmering as they sparkled the night like incandescent fairy dust. His mind wavered as the agony behind his clenched teeth tried to force a scream past the potato vodka soaked rags he had stuffed in his mouth. He longed to run out into the night and fall face first into the snow and cool the burning fever that tormented him.

But within the snowfall, darkness moved.

Enzo kneeled behind the stacked hay as though before a protective shrine, afraid of what he might see, but more afraid of what might come upon him unseen. Red starpoints danced before his eyes and he knew he could not last much longer without sleep. But he could not rest.

Hiram Abiff was coming.

I will walk your nightmares…

The voice was inside his head; the fear was in his heart.

****

The *fascio di combattimento* had taken away his wife and daughter. He sometimes prayed they were alive and sometimes prayed they were dead. The dead could not be tortured. But the thought of them was all that was between him and insanity. The Corvasces were hard men and women who did what needed to be done. Someday, he told himself, someone in his family would rise up and revenge themselves on the evil that was coming. One of them would wipe this evil off the very face of the earth. He knew that as surely as he knew the pain that ate away at him. One day a Corvasce would make his death worthwhile.

I will chew on your dreams…

Not real. The voices in his head were not real. They couldn't be. It was the potato vodka that swirled through his brain and dissolved his thoughts.

He shivered. Kneeling on the hard dirt with the smell of old straw, horse manure, and old wood in his nose, he hugged himself and rocked back and forth. From between bales, he looked straight into the night's dark maw through an opening in the boards. He clenched his fists and his massively corded forearms spasmed and ached from the constant pain.

The voices in his head began at sundown, after he'd cut out most of his own tongue to keep from ever telling the Black Shirts his secret. He drank half a bottle of vodka, took his sharpest knife and, after a silent prayer for mercy, grabbed his tongue with one hand and sliced it through with the other. Pain flared like a torch in his mouth, and he dropped and rolled on the rough floor, grunting and wailing like a wounded dog. A noise like angry sirens shrieked in his ears and he rolled about on the hard wooden planks in agony. When he could finally stand, he'd pressed a bloody mess of rags soaked in more vodka into his mouth and nearly choked to death on his own blood. If he died, so mote it be.

He could never reveal what he knew to anyone. He had left the journal wrapped in a wax paper at the drop, and that was enough for a simple Mason like him to do, live or die. Someone else, he did not know who, would carry them to the next drop and another courier would take it to the next and so on, until they eventually would arrive at the right man. Someone who would know what to do. But he had done what was required of him. He would keep his silence, for he was a Freemason, and he would rather die than break his Masonic oath. No one would ever know to whom he had sent the papers or by what route they would travel to get there. And Enzo could no longer speak.

Footsteps scrabbled across the roof, as though a giant crab were working its way across the shingles. Enzo jerked his head upward, his fingers clenching together so tightly his nails drew blood, but he did not feel it trickle or see it drip toward the broken spines of hay covering the floor.

I will disembowel your soul…

He closed his eyes to shut out the whispered threat in his fevered mind. His body raced with heat despite the deep cold, and he trembled.

Silence rushed in.

Why the roof? he wondered as he hugged himself with all the strength left in his tortured muscles.

Did Il Duce's Black Shirts or something worse expect to find him crouched in the loft, cowering beneath the hay? He was too weak to climb that high. He could only lay in the dirt, where he knew they would eventually find him, with his eyes closed and a fever burning through his brain.

A gust of restless spirits sprung up outside, rushed through the open door, and hunted for him. His eyes popped open, and although they were accustomed to the darkness, he saw nothing.

Phantoms, he thought. I am captive to phantoms. Forced to my knees in my own barn in the dead of night, hiding from the wind.

****

A boy's scream snapped his head up. It was his son.

No, he thought. It can't be real. It's a trick.

Enzo felt a pressure build in his chest and he doubled over again in despair.

Fast behind the scream came a piercing shriek as the howling of the storm raced into combat with the darkness.

Please let it be one of his tricks.

Both the Black Shirts and Hiram Abiff had their tricks.

If only I had a gun, he thought.

But what would he do with it?

Enzo Corvasce against Mussolini's fascio di combattimento? Against Hiram Abiff, who was once human, but now, by all accounts, was not?

He was surely cursed. Acidic liquid washed and gurgled in his stomach. The surrounding barn blurred. Vomit rushed from his mouth and sprayed the bales of hay. The awful stench was the congealed horror dripping from his mouth, drops of it falling to the hardened floor. He took a rag from his pocket and whimpered as he wiped his lips and chin.

"Enzo..." his wife's voice wailed through the bitter night.

He balled his fists and beat them against his head.

"Enzo...."

Dear Lord, let it be a trick. Let it be the imaginings of his horrified mind.

To his right was the wooden slot ladder leading to the loft. He stared at it as though it was a stairway leading up — not down — to hell itself. Up there he saw a deeper darkness, a moving blackness like a spill of ink. It pooled down and onto the hay strewn barn floor, then surged upward into the shape of a man formed from black pitch. As it stepped forward toward Enzo, he heard the suction and release snap sound of the demon's footsteps as though it were walking through tar. Enzo made soft mewling sounds and felt pain in the ruined stump of his tongue. He convulsed as though shaken by strong yet invisible hands and wept again. The advancing specter stopped and cocked its dark head as though to listen.

Then the oily surface of the figure sloughed away, and from beneath it, like a snake slithering away from its molted, discarded skin, came the figure of a small, older man dressed in rough clothes, work boots and a corduroy billed hat. It was the very commonness of the man standing before him that terrified Enzo. His tan canvas coat with the fleece lining jutting up above the collar. His old man's face with the narrow chin with a day's stubble visible even in the thin moonglow. The viscous black pitch that fell away from him like diseased skin.

"The journal," came the voice raspy as a rake dragged over rough ground. "Where is the journal?"

Enzo felt compelled to answer by the man's softly glowing blue eyes, but all that came out was an agonized mewling.

The steel rims of the old man's glasses began to glow an angry, brighter blue now, like the tip of a torch. His hands clenched into fists. His eyes compressed into slits. Even in the pallid light, Enzo could see the thing's lips pull back, exposing small, ivory colored teeth. In a panic, Enzo recited the Lord's Prayer in his mind.

The old man-thing exploded in a burst of ragged rage and lunged toward Enzo.

"You," it hissed, "you think you are so clever."

Its right hand was up and twisting like an agitated snake looking for prey.

"I must have that journal. I will have that journal. I will not be stopped. I will have my soul back if I must ravage and destroy every living being on this planet to get it. No one must know my secret before the time of my unveiling comes. No one, do you understand, you filthy little worm? Who have you given it to? You don't know, do you? I can see it in your fear-addled mind. And yet you can't speak.

You dare to cut out your own tongue so you can't tell me? Yes? Then of what use are you?"

Enzo cowered, pressing his back against a roof support. He understood. Within that thin journal were the secrets of what this demonic creature was.

"I will find it if I have to chew the bones of every member of your family, do you hear me? I will curse you and yours for generations to come."

The man-thing shrieked and threw its hands in the air. Enzo's heart pressed against his rib cage with such force he thought it would rip apart. The pain and blood in his mouth and the terror racking his body twisted and pulled at his mind so that he could no longer think coherent thoughts. The old man-thing stopped, and Enzo saw its jaws stretch impossibly wide and within the darkness of its mouth he saw pinpoints of red light and movement. Wider still, it opened with a horrible wailing. Clawed fingers gripped the edge of the thing's lips and began pulling themselves through and out. The sight of shiny fangs and red eyes made Enzo close his eyes, trying to blot out the sight of the winged creatures crawling out of the old man's mouth.

He banged his head against the wooden support, praying he could strike it with enough force to crack his skull and kill himself. But before he could swing his head backward again, his head was stopped in midair as though by a giant hand. He opened his eyes as clawed hands punctured his face and began peeling back his skin.

A swarm of red-eyed demons lifted him into the air, their tenebrous wings flapping like those of rabid bats. He could not process what he saw. The blood loss and pain and the sight of these things were more than he could comprehend. When one creature bit off his genitals, Enzo could no longer even scream. He hung in midair, stretched between the horrors that pulled and bit at him.

Enzo Corvasce was already dead when Hiram Abiff stepped over to him, unhinged his jaws again and swallowed what was left of the man and the shrieking demons. He spared only Enzo's head, which, after glaring angrily at it, he threw it to the floor and then kicked it. He watched the disfigured, bloodied thing roll and bounce until it collided with a rusted and worn four tined pitchfork, and finally lay still, staring toward the underside of the barn's roof.

"Hiram…"

Being thwarted by an illiterate Freemason was more than he could bear. Hiram leaned back his head, opened his mouth and breathed a pillar of fire up to the rafters. As he closed his jaws and the flames disappeared, the angry beings trapped within him again shrieked excitedly.

"Hiram..."

The voice was deep, disturbing, and insistent. Without turning his head, Hiram knew that the oily discards of blackness pooled on the barn floor were re-forming, coagulating into the atramentous shape of the dark being who had stolen his soul over three millennia ago, then returned him to life with that most precious part of his existence missing. At this thought, a bright bubble of orange rage expanded within him and surged upward. He felt the fire singe his throat again as he turned to confront the demonic darkness, but as the fire touched his lips, the dark metal points of the pitchforks shot up and into the soft flesh beneath his chin and he was lifted upward into the air and backward. The floor slammed into his head as he was paralyzed by the tremendous force of the tine points thrusting up through his head and backward until they pinned him to the ground. He lay there flopping like a fish speared in cold, dark waters.

"Hiram, can you hear me?" it hissed with a voice that popped and crackled like the sound of burning flesh.

With a quick twist of the tines through his brain, Hiram felt the debilitating inward loathing of total helplessness. The spirits inside him thrashed and screamed at the recognition of their tormentor.

"Ah, but you cannot speak, so you may yet listen with a finer ear."

Blood leaked from both of Hiram's ears and from each nostril as the pressure of the tines forced it out onto the ground like trickles of diseased water. The dark demon, with no features at all, but like a man wrapped in slick black oil, leaned heavily on the pitchfork. Hiram's jaws could no longer open and close to scream.

"It is a hideous tribulation to be unable to die, is it not? Suspended between two worlds, but more dead than living. You feel pain, but no pleasure. You are always raging, but never delighted, and are always and forever guilty, but never innocent."

A quick, forceful sideways lurch and an agonized rush of burbling dribbled from Hiram's mouth.

"Do not be afraid, Hiram. No matter how often I puncture and impale your brain, it will always re-form. I have saved you from death, have I not? You cannot die until I release your harrowed soul, lest you find neither paradise nor oblivion. And the Temple Guardians will now hunt you. Your time of freedom on this earth grows short."

With a glance to its right, the darkness saw a rusted sickle close to Enzo's mutilated head and, leaving the pitchfork in place, it retrieved the rusty blade and floated back to the incapacitated Hiram Abiff. The Nephilim darkness hovered above Hiram like a Stygian judgment.

"I have prepared a place for you where you will be tested and test others. Twice before you have failed me, but you will not fail me again, for I now give you a companion formed from the impenetrable Abyss of my pride. When the time is right, you shall enter the world of mortals together. Then you will bring me forth to stand with my brother ,who has already returned to this world."

One hand of the Darkness held the sickle. The other he extended as it began to coil, and twist, and grow. As it grew, it became encased in a sheath of iridescence. A split tongue emerged from its mouth. The snake-thing was now the length of Hiram's body. A membrane slid back from its miasmic yellow eyes as its now fully formed body plopped to the ground and glissaded like a viper up and over Hiram's still tremoring body, and flowed into his still open bloody mouth. Hiram began to whip back and forth as the cold-scaled serpent flowed like vomit past the spear and down his collapsing throat.

"From my essence, you will birth her into your sanctuary. Use her as you will. She is now flesh of our flesh, essence of our essence, the Scarlet Whore of this realm and those beyond. She will quiet the demons who infest you when you are most in need of surcease. I gift you this tenderness before I leave you for a time."

As the demonic darkness slashed and cut with the rusty sickle over and over again, Hiram could feel the painful slashes as they cut through his face, his chest, and his organs until his mortified flesh was reduced to the consistency of butchered meat.

15

Marla twisted hard to her left, grabbed a handful of hair and yanked downward.

"Easy," said Jimmy in a strangled, pain-filled voice. "It's me."

His face was inches from her own. She could feel his breath on her face and the sag of the mattress as his body landed next to hers. The light was dim, and she was disoriented. Jimmy's dark eyes stared into hers.

"Nightmare," she gasped. "She showed me a nightmare. A real nightmare."

Her breath was coming in quick gulps, like she'd just finished running for her life.

"Okay," he said. "You're safe now. Can you let go of my hair? You're pulling it out by the roots."

She released her grip.

"Sorry," she said.

"I will sit up now," he said.

Her free hand shot out, and she grabbed his shirt collar.

"It was her. In my dream. That witch. She was really in my dream, Jimmy. Really. It wasn't my imagination. I felt her touch my arm. I could smell her. I could see the color of her eyes. I was really there and so was she."

"I know. Let me sit up."

"You don't understand," screamed Marla, and she yanked him forward to within an inch of her face. They were lying next to each other like lovers.

"I know. You were screaming in your sleep. That's why I woke you."

"We were at a farm. It was snowing, it was dark. We were in an old farmhouse. I don't know how, but she took me there."

Jimmy tried to pull her hand away, but her grip was desperate with strength.

"This man, this farmer, was in the kitchen, sawing at his own tongue with a kitchen knife."

Marla caught sight of her face in the mirror of Jimmy's glasses, and in the faint light from the computer monitors, with her hair unruly and her bloodshot eyes, she looked like an angry zombie angling to bite his face.

"I know."

"No," she said, "you don't. You weren't there."

"But it was just a dream," he said. "Would you like something to calm your nerves? How about a Xanax?"

She heard the edge of fear in his voice, as though he thought she'd ramp psychotic on him at any moment.

"I don't need pills, Jimmy. You need to know what I saw. I was there. I was really there. I don't know how she did it. It was more than a dream. I know what a dream is like, Jimmy. I know what a nightmare is like. But this was real. I saw the blood. I know what blood looks like. It was real. I saw his bloody tongue on the table. She told me why he did it. She whispered it."

"Hiram Abiff was coming for him."

"Who?"

"Hiram Abiff. The old man. He'd made a mistake. He'd confided the secrets of who he was to a Freemason, who he thought was dying and wouldn't be around to spread the truth."

"What?"

"But," Jimmy tried to shrug his shoulders, though Marla had him in an iron grip, "the Freemason lived and wrote it down in a journal and passed it on to another Mason under Masonic secrecy. From there, they passed it to your grandfather, who voluntarily made himself the last in the chain so the old man would never know where it went from there."

"How do you know this?" she snapped.

"We've been after the old man for centuries, Marla."

Jimmy gave up trying to pry her grip from his collar, and instead just lay back on the pillow next to her. Marla rose and straddled him. She kept her grip tight on his shirt collar. Beneath her weight, Jimmy stiffened. Lowering her face down to within six inches of his, she spoke with an intensity just shy of an asylum inmate.

"He drank vodka from a bottle and then stuffed rags in his mouth. There was blood everywhere. I thought he was going to die. His face was gray. It was my grandfather's blood. She told me. There was a lamp turned down low on the counter. The shadows were awful—alive. I could see them move, Jimmy. Why would that witch show me that? Why, Jimmy, why?"

She grabbed onto her own hair like she would pull it out.

"Get off me, Marla. Please."

"There's more," she whispered in a voice like the rush of wind down the empty hallways of a haunted building.

Her weight against his hips was uncomfortable. It had been a long time for Jimmy, a very long time. The ends of her long, dark hair brushed against his cheek. With a look of wild fury, she grabbed his collar again and shook him.

"You know what's going on, don't you? Tell me. Tell me or I'll—"

"I can tell you what I know," said Jimmy. "But first get off me and let me stand. You're scaring me."

And she was. The wild look in her eyes frightened him.

Slowly, she let go of his collar and angled off the bed. She flexed and curled her fingers, like she was warming them up to choke someone. Jimmy got up just as slowly as she had, so he wouldn't spook her. He brushed himself off.

"Do you want some water?" he asked.

"I want a drink."

"I don't have any alcohol here. All I've got is bottled water and coffee. Can we sit down?"

"No alcohol? In a place like this?"

"I didn't say I didn't drink," said Jimmy. "I just can't afford to in this town. I need to stay alert. So, do you want water or coffee?"

Without waiting for her to answer, he went back into the other room and collapsed into a computer chair. She left the bedroom and followed him into the room.

"I saw that thing—the old man—bite off the farmer's head, Jimmy. He came down from the rafters of the barn and opened his mouth three feet wide and just bit off his head. Then he—"

"Don't tell me anymore, Marla. I already know. Others of us have had the same dream."

"Who the living hell are you, Jimmy? Who is this we you're talking about? Tell me. I have to know. Can whoever you are with stop them?"

"Marla, the entire United States government hasn't been able to stop that old man. Their weapons do nothing to him. He just reassembles."

"Who are you, Jimmy?" she asked again, her face flush with anger.

There was a ragged, desperate edge embedded in her question.

"I'm a priest," he said with a shrug.

"You're a little young for that, aren't you?"

"I'm older than I look, Marla, and I'm serious. It's why I was chosen to infiltrate this place. That, and the fact I'm good with systems analysis."

"Can you communicate with the outside world?"

Jimmy ran a hand across his lightly freckled forehead.

"No. The only communications that get through are the ones the old man wants to. The Church must think I'm already dead."

"Why are you here?" she asked.

Jimmy looked down at his hands for a long time before answering.

"Because," he said, "we, the Church, we thought he was the Antichrist. Or might be. Don't look at me like that, like I'm crazy. It's what we believed."

But sitting in the darkened room, lit only by panels of computer screens, she thought it wasn't so insane.

"You really believe that?" she asked, anyway.

"I used to. Now…. I don't. Everything we know about the Antichrist is from the Bible, and there is nothing like Hiram Abiff anywhere in the Bible. I've read Revelations more times than most people back in the real world, so I should know. And no, not anymore. Hiram Abiff is neither the Biblical Beast nor the Antichrist. But here's my disturbing idea: he might be trying to deceive us into thinking he is. I know that sounds crazy, Marla, but try this one on for size—what's the one question you haven't asked? Knowing what you know now, what is the most important question you should ask?"

"I have no idea," she said, "and if you don't tell me, I swear I'll strangle you."

"The question you should be asking is why now?"

"Why now what?"

"Why," asked Jimmy, "is Hiram getting ready to return to the real world? He's been hiding here since after the Second World War. And he rules here, Marla. He runs this place. Life and death and all of that. If the witch is really telling the truth and he's about to return to the regular world, then why now? Think about it. He's safe here. He's totally safe here. Nothing we've thrown at him has hurt him in any way. What Traverse was telling you was true. None of us understand it.

"None of the scientists can explain why it's impossible to detonate a nuclear weapon in this town. We don't understand why poison gas doesn't affect him or how he can be shot fifty times, but still reassemble. And think about this: he vanished after he appeared in front of President Truman and killed all his protective guards except one—Traverse's grandfather. They completely lost track of him until the day he showed himself and lured us here, to Borgo. Like I said, we haven't been able to hurt him even a little, no matter what we throw at him in all the time we've been sending soldiers and scientists here. In fact, we couldn't touch him in the real world either. So, ask yourself if he's leaving here and returning to the real world, why is he getting ready to do it now? What's changed, Marla? Why now?"

"I don't know."

"If he was going to take on the world, don't you think he would have done it before now? Every year that passes, our weaponry gets more and more advanced. Maybe it will even be dangerous to him, but that only explains why he might eventually return, not why he's doing it in a few days."

"I don't get it," she said.

"Well, wouldn't it have been better for Hiram to go after the world when we were less sophisticated? Back when we didn't have the weapons systems we have now, if you see what I mean?"

"I do."

"Here's what I think has changed—what we think has changed."

"Tell me."

"For the first time in history, the United States has a Muslim president, don't you see? Doesn't it seem like she's trying to throw confusion into religious and political institutions at the same time? All to further the idea that Hiram Abiff is the Antichrist."

"No. What has that got to do with anything? Who cares about that crap?"

Jimmy looked away, and then back. He looked somehow older.

"I think Hiram will use that. I don't know how, but I know it will be bad. Maybe try to sow confusion and fear and cause everyone to look to him as the answer man—a divinely appointed savior. Or maybe... maybe something else has changed. Maybe something we don't know and never knew. Maybe Hiram's changed. Maybe he's accomplished something here—"

"We should just kill them," said Marla. "I've just had enough of this incomprehensible crap."

"Kill them with what?"

"Holy water? Crosses? I don't know—you're the priest."

"They're not vampires, Marla. But I think you're right on one point. Hiram is definitely un-dead or never been dead. I don't know which. That's why nothing they tried here ever worked. You can't kill what's already dead. He just... re-assembles. I don't know about the witch. Can't even figure her out. But we don't even know what he's made of or how that's possible. She seems different from him, but what the difference is... that's beyond me."

Marla ran her hands through her hair, stood up and began to pace.

"Tell me this," she said. "How did he die the first time?"

"What?"

"He's un-dead, you said. Or never dead. But I think he must have been alive once. What killed him? And what brought him back?"

A pained look came over Jimmy's face.

"What?" she asked.

"In all the centuries we've been following Hiram, I don't think anyone, including me, ever thought to ask that question. And now that you've brought it up, if someone brought him back to life in the first place..."

Jimmy's voice drifted off as he thought.

"Did it ever occur to you," she said, "that person or whatever might still be around? If someone brought him back?"

Jimmy was staring at the monitors.

"There is, here in Borgo, a more terrifying darkness than Hiram Abiff. Something much worse than him," he said.

"Bullshit," said Marla.

"Can't you feel it?" asked Jimmy. "An overarching evil?"

Marla clearly didn't.

"Did you ever read the Book of Revelations?" Jimmy asked.

"No, and I don't plan on it, either. Religion and I don't get along."

"There are no sidelines," said Jimmy, and this time it was he who flashed with anger. "This is war. The oldest war in the world. Are you Catholic?"

"How did that woman enter my dreams? Who is she and where does she get her power?"

She was ignoring his point. But she was right, in a way.

Religion, he thought, was no longer important. Religion, codified religion, like Hiram, was dead a long time ago. Faith used to be the world's biggest fight club; now different faiths were so busy trying to get along that finding the truth, the true power of the right faith, was too lost to be found. Jimmy looked around the room, looking away from her to make thinking easier. She was an attractive woman, and, after having lived in a town full of the reanimated dead for the last five years, it was harder for him to think clearly around her than it should be.

"I don't know, Marla. I just don't know. But if Traverse is right, the man in the dream who cut out his tongue was your great-grandfather. He was one tough man. A Freemason who would rather cut out his tongue than tell Hiram who he gave the journal to. That took guts."

"I'll kill her."

"I would do it myself if I knew how. I've tried to exorcise him, but it didn't take."

"I'll find a way," she said.

The anger in her voice was annoying. She'd been here just over a week, and she was, in her own way, demanding answers. Her nightmare was terrifying, and, to give her credit, she'd seen some horrific things since she came to Borgo, but she hadn't seen what he had. Not by a long shot. She wanted all the answers, everything they'd found out over more than hundreds of years, and she wanted it now. Jimmy didn't know if there was anyone left alive he would trust with that information. But in about eighteen hours, it would be just the two of them, face to face with the monster.

Marla looked like she was going to pull out her wire cable and strangle him.

"We can't just sit here," said Marla. "We have to do something or by midnight tomorrow we'll both be dead."

"Like what?" Jimmy said and flung out his hands in frustration. "We're sitting here in my rooms a couple of levels below ground with a viaduct running over top of us. At its peak, this place had four thousand soldiers. Four thousand, Marla. What is it you think we should do that they didn't do? And don't forget that most of the people here are already dead. We've been here so long about a third of the men and women here have drifted away from this complex and work in the town. The Postmaster at the Borgo Post Office used to be our Ordinance Officer. The Mayor used to be our Director of Materials Testing. The woman who runs the ice cream stand was an MP. This town went from a war zone between the U.S. Military and one little old man, to a normal town populated by the reanimated dead. So, do you really think there's anything we can do tomorrow to stop him from taking over the world?"

"Isn't there any kind of weapon here that might work against him? Maybe a research project that got pushed to the side and never used that we could try? There has to be something, Jimmy."

If he were a different man, if he'd made different choices in his life, the sight of her leaning forward toward him would have sped up his heart rate.

"Look, it's four o'clock in the morning. Maybe you should try to get some sleep."

"I don't know if I'll ever sleep again, Jimmy," she said. "If we can't stop them, we need to get out of here before they do. Haven't you been able to find any way out? How about that shaft where you lower the bodies to be re-animated? There has to be some way this place is connected to the outside world."

"It's connected, all right, but not to the outside world," said Jimmy. "I think we're in a one-way passage to hell. So, if we're looking for a way out of here at the last minute, I will vote no on that one. I never want to know what goes on below here."

He saw the reflected look of revulsion on his face reflected on the computer monitor and shuddered.

"We have enough munitions to destroy this entire town, don't we?" asked Marla.

"I don't think so," said Jimmy, who felt frustrated anger flushing his face. "You still don't understand the way this place works and what's already gone on here. If the old man doesn't like it, it doesn't happen here. That's the condensed laws of physics, Borgo style. Second, don't you think we already thought of trying to find some way out of here? Since the day the first soldiers filed into here and figured out how much power the old man has, that's what's been on everyone's mind right after killing him. When we figured out we couldn't kill him, it became our number one priority."

"So, you're saying that after all these years, there's nothing we can do? Nothing?"

"We can pray. That's the main thing."

"You take care of that," she said. "I'd like something a little higher tech."

"You don't get it yet. We've tried high tech. It doesn't work."

That made Marla angry.

"Jimmy, I will not walk into that Masonic Temple with you like a sheep to be slaughtered."

"Quiet," he said, and his whole body stiffened.

"What?"

"Look."

"Look at what is going on in Traverse's room. Look who's with him."

He pointed behind her.

"Look at that screen."

16

"Tell me about the woman, Traverse."

Eva's voice was a soft and sultry purr as she ran her fingers through his hair.

"She's becoming a problem," he said as he leaned back in his chair.

"More," she said as she licked his ear.

His office door was locked at all times, and he was always glad of it when Eva came. Eva did not use doors. Traverse could never find out how she did it, but when she came to him, he lost all interest in the topic. She leaned in and kissed him just below his left earlobe. He closed his eyes and shivered with pleasure.

"The president sent her."

"I already know that. Are there more... interesting things you can tell me about her?"

"Why?"

She nuzzled the spot on his neck that drove him crazy, then brought her hands to his shoulders and massaged the tension away.

"Such tension," she said. "Your muscles are so... hard. Let me stimulate them with my fingers."

"Marla's just another government killer," he said. "Just like all the others, they sent, only better looking."

She lowered one hand and stroked between his legs.

"You think she's better looking than me?" she asked.

"Nobody's better looking than you."

Traverse pulled her down and kissed her. She gave in for a minute, then pushed him away, saying, "I don't like her."

"You going to kill her?" he asked.

"Do you want to keep her?"

He thought it over.

"I think I'll kill her," he said.

Eva's eyebrows rose in surprise.

He reached for the knot that held her black robe together, hands eager for her breasts, but his fingers wouldn't cooperate to untie the knot.

"Traverse," she said in a low voice.

"What?"

"It's almost over."

Without knowing why, Traverse tried to keep from crying. Everything was ending. He'd known it before she said it. It was Marla. She was the one bringing everything down. All these years and the old man never asked for anyone. No one. And then, he asks for her. He should have known it was a bad sign, but they'd been so close with Minus Eight. It should have worked. It should have obliterated the old man. Fucking Professor Grieves. In fact, everything they'd tried should have worked, but especially the dislocation weapon the professor had dubbed Minus Eight.

"He's finally going to kill us?" he asked.

"Not all of you, darling."

His anger rushed through him like a flash flood, and he jumped up with his fists clenched so hard they hurt.

"Damn him," he said. "Damn him."

"But it's not your fault," she whispered. "You see that, don't you, dearest? All the death, all this—" she waved her hand vaguely around his office. "This underground complex, all the soldiers, all the weaponry, all the science, all the failure, it's not your fault."

With a brutal, quick motion, Traverse grabbed a bottle of whiskey from the shelf behind him and threw it against the far wall, where it smashed into jagged pieces. His face twisted in rage; he took a step toward Eva.

"I know it's not my fault," he growled. "This is the most fucked up situation there ever was. Ever. I want out of this place, Eva. You said you could get me out."

She slid up onto his desk and crossed her legs as he came to within an arm's length.

"What about the others?" she asked.

"Get me out of here. Everybody else is on their own. This isn't reality. It's some twisted Big Rock Candy Mountain."

"Sugar Candy Mountain," corrected Eva.

"I don't care. You know what I mean. We're all going to get turned to glue."

She tapped a fingernail against his chest.

"Everyone but you," she said.

He grabbed her wrist and yanked her in closer.

"And Jimmy. You've got to get Jimmy out."

She grinned.

His temper flared again.

"What happened to John Amrozi?" he said.

His face was distorted with rage, and for a second, he saw his hands going for her throat. With a husky laugh, she leaned in to kiss him. By a trick of the light and his intense emotion, he saw metallicine scales on the side of her throat, but when she pressed her lips to his, he forgot all about it. When her tongue found his, however, Traverse stiffened, shuddered and then passed out when he realized its tip was double-pointed.

****

"Wake up, Traverse. It's time to be a prophet."

The voice was soft and far away. Traverse felt sluggish and disoriented, as though someone had drugged him. He opened his eyes, looked to one side and saw gauzy light and indistinct shapes.

"How did I get here?" he asked in a thick voice.

He felt her hand on his head, warm—almost hot—and soothing. As she ran her fingers over his face, with each caress he felt more and

119

more like he was floating above the bed.

"I brought you," said Eva. "You were feeling lightheaded and then you passed out. The stress is weighing on you. So much responsibility. The weight of the world on your shoulders. So hard to stand. Lie here and rest. Rest. Rest."

Traverse's eyes widened at a sudden memory. He turned to look at her again, turned to look at her neck. As his eyes refocused, he could see the pale smoothness of it. There were no scales. It was the stress, just the stress making him see things. Another memory, harsher than the first. He looked at her face, saw her licking her lower lip with the tip of her tongue. It was normal, completely normal. Just the stress. He relaxed.

"Rest, my love, just rest."

"But—"

She touched his temples in a gentle, circling motion.

He was floating again.

"I have something for you," she said. "It will help you stay relaxed and safe while I tell you everything I've learned. Everything about you and me and why we will always be together. Let me help you up. That's it; lean on your elbow. Yes. Now drink this. It's very good for you. It will help you stay calm."

So tired. As Traverse lifted himself up onto his elbow, he smelled the cup of aromatic liquid she extended toward him. The odor was so pungent it was like his head was wrapped in a steaming wet towel.

"What is it?"

"Drink."

Traverse hesitated, a flash of memory of the scales on the side or her neck, causing him to recoil in fear.

"Do you remember the little bird from back when I first met you?"

Traverse drank the pungent liquid down in one quick gulp. He would never forget the blackened ground that outlined the bird's body. And the smell. The whiff of burned feathers and flesh. Short and quick. Gone in a second. The bird was alive. Then Eva had told it to be dead.

"Soon you'll feel so much better."

I am the Director, he thought. I'm not helpless. I'm the Director of Project Borgo. No, the only person in charge of everything in this town is an old man with glowing eyes. But no one messes with me. I keep the President of the United States on hold.

"Do you know why I am?"

"What?"

The room was dim, as though overlaid with gauze.

"I am because of you."

Traverse clenched his fists. He tried to feel strong. I'm a big guy, he thought. But it was just a memory. People always thought I played football.

"That's it," she soothed. "Try to hold on to who you are. Clench your fists together as the sands of your memories pour out between your fingers, while I, your beloved, replace them with the truth."

No, he thought. I'm drowning in a sensory deprivation tank. Her voice is my safety rope while I dangle in warm liquid nothingness.

"The journal, Traverse, President Truman's journal, was nothing but lies written by a man empty of morality. When Hiram appeared to him in that German hotel, he came to talk. Only to talk. To beg President Truman, this man who had obliterated by atomic fire two entire. So what really happened in that German hotel? President Truman ordered his men to kill Hiram. You see that, don't you?"

"Who?" asked Traverse.

He was sweating profusely. Even his sideburns were wet with perspiration.

"His name is Hiram. Hiram Abiff. Truman lied to your grandfather. All presidents lie. One after another, they lied to your grandfather, then your father, and then you. Each one of you was in turn directors of Operation Borgo. Each of you was lied to. And what is the mission of Operation Borgo? Kill Hiram Abiff, the man who begged the president to never again use a nuclear weapon. An entire country against one old man."

"Yes," said Traverse. "One man."

"One very special old man," said Eva.

"The spirits," said Traverse. "In the journal. The spirits... the demons..."

"There were none," she whispered into his ear. "Lies by a man who irradiated one hundred thousand people. So hot. So hot that the outlines of children were burned into the concrete. A man who said it was to end the war. The war was already ending, my love. President Truman wanted to test his new weapon, to establish his dominance of the entire world. Would you believe the written words of a man like that?"

"What?"

"You were lied to. Hiram Abiff was an innocent, appearing to plead humanity's case before a mass murderer."

"Bad," said Traverse.

"Yes, bad. But one man didn't bend the knee to the order to kill Hiram. Hiram never forgot that."

"He didn't die," said Traverse. "They shot him to death and he... he... didn't die."

The will required to create a coherent sentence was dissipating. Thinking was hard work. Very hard work.

"I'll tell you Hiram's story now. Drink my words like milk from my breasts. Cherish these new memories. Make them yours. Make them your truth. Remember that Hiram was born over three thousand years ago, chosen by King Solomon—the wisest of Israel's kings—to oversee the construction of his temple to the Divine. A very special man. A man given a task to complete."

"Special," said Traverse. "Yes, special."

"Near the end of its construction, however, Hiram was killed for refusing to change the Temple design that went contrary to the instructions of the Divine. Do you understand? Nod if you do, yes, like that."

He couldn't tell whether he'd nodded. His memories and his participation in the present moment seemed disturbingly surreal.

"But then, a miracle happened, Traverse. A miracle. King Solomon, who admired and loved Hiram's work above all others, sank into deep despair. How could the mighty Temple of Jerusalem be completed without the guidance and architectural genius of Hiram? Stay awake, stay awake, love."

Hiram Abiff, he thought. What was Hiram Abiff?

"The Temple of the Divine was at stake. What could he do? How far would he go to not be defeated? I'll tell you how far he would go—he resurrected Hiram Abiff. Since that remarkable day, when the Great Architect of the Universe brought Hiram the Temple Builder back to life, he has lived for only one purpose—to build the last and final Temple, the one that will stand forever. Two have been built and destroyed. He was there for both of them. Now, he will build that third Temple. He will return to the world to complete his divinely ordained mission.

"You have agonized for most of your adult life where Borgo, Michigan, really is and why it exists at all. Why did Hiram come here?"

Hiram Abiff, thought Traverse. So that's what the initials on his mailbox stood for. H. A. Hiram Abiff.

"Borgo is in a space the size of a grain of sand," she said. "His angel created this tiny world for him to be safe from those who would destroy him. He created Borgo — every aspect, every detail of this town. For centuries Hiram had kept his secret, but he was always on the run, always hiding, always persecuted. Imagine—kept alive only by the grace of the Great Architect of the Universe, tasked to accomplish one last rebuilding of the Jerusalem Temple. A miracle. A miracle of miracles. A divine mission. But he is not immortal, Traverse. He lives only until that goal is accomplished. Then he becomes a mortal man again, to live a few short years and die as he should have three thousand years ago. His angel built this place, this Borgo, to stay alive until that day when divine grace calls him again to lead the peoples of the world. A place where he could be safe until the Great Architect of the Universe called him to his final task. When that is done, perhaps peace can finally exist for us all."

"His angel?" asked Traverse.

"Hiram has grown in accumulated power over the centuries. An incomprehensible ascension. And his mind has grown as well as his understanding. Three thousand years and more of life will do that to a man's mind. He has the knowledge and wisdom to finally bring peace and unity to mankind."

As she spoke, Eva's mind was elsewhere. She could recite what she was telling Traverse without so much as thinking about it. The hypnogogic drug he'd drank combined with the effects of her magic left his mind impressionable to whatever she told him. If she made a mistake, she could simply go back and correct it. His mind would not know the difference. Best of all, when he woke from the combined influence, he would remember nothing at all about what had occurred. So, while she spoke, her mind was fixed on the two women who had humiliated her by killing her beasts. Tomorrow night, Marla, the one sent by President Usman, would die like all the others who had come to Borgo. Tonight, with or without Hiram's approval, she would kill the other, the daughter of Frank Mihaloff, Worshipful Master of the Temple Guardians. The night was still young.

She kept talking. With one palm, she rubbed his chest.

"Hiram only sought solitude in Borgo, but when your government sent soldiers and weapons in after him, he was once again forced to defend himself. Worst of all, they sent your grandfather here to lead the assault. Do you know why the only person spared the day the president's guards attacked Hiram was your grandfather? It was because your grandfather did not even fire one shot at Hiram. Not one."

Marla would be fed to the horned beasts tomorrow night. The bitch had killed two of her children, but tomorrow night at midnight she would come with no weapons at all. Now that Eva would collect the Blazing Star of Freemasonry from the Frenchman, everything else was irrelevant. Only four days until the unveiling of Hiram Abiff to the world in the Unfinished Theater at the Detroit Masonic Temple. Only one day's worth of work to accomplish here in Borgo. Then she would return to the outside world to create the spell to harvest the mental energies of millions of people and channel it into the Blazing Star. When that was finished, Hiram would unleash it on the assembled Masons. All accounts would be settled, save one. Emile Chirac needed a comeuppance. A permanent comeuppance. He had dared to have his thug Ricci lay hands on her. Both Mr. Chirac and Ricci would die horribly. A special death.

"Remember what I am telling you, Traverse. Remember. Remember that the struggle changed. With so many soldiers pouring into this town of Borgo and so much weaponry aimed at him, it began a struggle for Hiram to survive. A test if he was still worthy. Because of the accumulated military strengths of countries around the world, Hiram feared he could not face their united resistance. The temple must be built in Jerusalem. The Jews, the Muslims and the Christians would stand against him. Russia and Europe would join with the unbelievers to fight Hiram. So, this town became his testing ground. Military might against the Architect of the Divine. If he could not stand up against America, he could never face down the combined might of the nations that would gather to destroy him. Here, in this microscopic town where his angel has twisted time and space to his own ends, he has been learning from his life and death struggle with your government. He has been testing you, seeing if you are a worthy foe, fulfilling his silent promise to your grandfather that one of his line would stand with him, shoulder to shoulder in the fight to restore for all eternity the Temple of Jerusalem.

"And you succeeded, Traverse. Faced with terrors that would have broken a lesser man, you have survived with your sanity intact."

Traverse tried to say something in response to this, but his lips felt like soft rubber and only foamy drool came out of the corner of his mouth.

"Yes, your sanity is intact," she repeated.

Perhaps she had mixed in too much of the hypnogogic drug. More likely, she had projected too much magic into his simple mind. But he would remember what she told him. Drooling or not.

"Jimmy," he said in a burst of foam filled words. It was as though he'd swallowed bubble soap. "You, we…"

More pink bubbly drool. He shook his head back and forth.

"Ah… oh… Jimmy, too good to stay. Save Jimmy. Get him out, too."

Even in her disgust, she was impressed. In the enhanced hypnogogic state, he should not be able to voice an independent, coherent thought.

"I will."

"She…"

He wrenched his head to one side as though he was going to throw up, and Eva instinctively pulled back.

"Bitch taking him. Bitch… blurry… Ahhh… taking him with her tomorrow… alublaaa… tomorrow night."

Unexpected, she thought. Traverse could be so full of surprises for a simple man. He'd taken too much of the hypnogogic to give him more, but she had to calm him down. Who would have thought Marla Corvasce would take Jimmy in tow? Nice move. Dangerous move.

"Relax," she said, patting him on the forearm. "Jimmy will be safe.

I'll protect him. I'll take him out of here myself. He'll be so happy to be free, and you and I will be the ones who saved him. Won't that be wonderful?"

"Nice," said Traverse, and this time his words were foam free.

"Hiram is divinely chosen," she continued, "and you will be his voice to the world. Together, we will reveal what Hiram knows about the Old Testament, the New Testament, and the Koran. He was there. He saw it all. He was commissioned by King Solomon himself. And the power Hiram has accumulated and nurtured for all these centuries, he will share with us. When we speak, his power will be with us. It's time to clean up the world, Traverse."

"Mm-huh," mumbled Traverse.

"All you have to do is make three phone calls. I will teach you what to say and you will remember it as your own. First, you call this number."

She recited it slowly.

"You will tell the Pope's secretary this—that you have in your possession the Scrolls of Barsabas the Body Thief and the artifacts as well. Tell him you will produce them for the public soon. You will hang up before he can reply. Do you understand? Can you repeat what I just told you?"

He nodded twice.

She knew that under the influence of this particular drug and her magic, he would have a complete memory of everything she instructed him to remember, but nothing else. It brought a slight smile to her face.

"Next, you will call the president and tell him you have learned the secret of Borgo and that the old man is the Mahdi and will return to the world in two weeks. You will immediately hang up before he replies. Do you understand? Can you repeat what I just told you?"

Again, he nodded twice.

"Next, you will call this number for the Temple Institute in Israel, and when they ask who is calling, you will say that the Messiah is returning soon. Hang up before they answer."

She gave him the numbers.

"Do you understand? Can you repeat what I just told you?"

Two more nods.

She drew in a long breath, centered herself, and then said, "Now for your final instructions. Major Landsdale returns in the morning, and you must put him to work."

His body was so still as she continued talking that it appeared as though he was dead.

****

In another room, three levels lower and at the other end of the labyrinth complex, Marla sat with Jimmy before a bank of computers in his living quarters, watching what played out between Traverse and Eva. They stared at the screens as though mesmerized.

"Scrolls of Barsabas the Body Thief? What the fuck is that?" asked Marla.

"They're—"

"I don't care what they are," she shouted. "I will kill that bitch."

"How?" agreed Jimmy.

"There has to be a way. I want to shoot both of them. If they get back to the real world, I can't even think what they'll do."

"Rule the world," said Jimmy. "I think that's what the Borgo virus is all about. Everyone thinking the same thought at the same time while she harvests the energy of that synchronicity. But she's not strong enough to do anything with it; she will harvest it for him."

"For the old man? Hiram?"

"Yes."

"How do you know that, Jimmy?"

"I've been here a while longer than you, Marla."

In the pale glow of the screen's light, Jimmy still looked too young to be here. It was as though he'd quit aging when he hit nineteen.

"Why not for herself?"

"I'm not sure I can't answer many more of your questions, Marla. Facts have always been thin here. I've got my own ideas, though."

"Lay them out for me."

"Okay," said Jimmy. "I think Eva is of a different order than Hiram. That's what I think. I think the Borgo virus and the harnessed power of everyone's thoughts would destroy her if she tried to ride that type of energy."

"What is she?" asked Marla.

"I don't know."

"Have you seen her turn into smoke and disappear into his mouth?"

Jimmy gave her a hard stare.

"I have. I didn't know anyone else had. You have to understand; we've been tracking him—whatever Hiram is—for a long time. She's a relatively recent phenomenon. One thing I'm sure of, though. He summoned her."

"We? Who are you, Jimmy? Who are you a priest with?"

"Doesn't matter right now."

"The Vatican?"

Jimmy actually tilted his back and laughed while he stared at the ceiling.

"No. Don't ask. Believe me, we don't have time now. No agency or organization in the world can help us, anyway. It's just me and you and God."

"How about Professor Grieves and Dr. Grayson?"

"I think they're under the influence of the witch, too."

"How do you know?"

"I've got eyes," said Jimmy, pointing at the computer screens.

"How long have you been doing this? I mean, watching Traverse and the others?" asked Marla.

It was an oddly creepy occupation, which made Jimmy an oddly creepy man.

"Took me a couple of weeks to set it up after I got here," said Jimmy. "I've been watching Traverse and the rest since then. Couple years. Didn't take long to figure out that watching the old man was a waste of time."

"She says she's going to get you out of here," said Marla.

Jimmy half snorted and half gagged.

"Get me out of here? In a body bag, maybe."

"What's with the name?" asked Marla. "What kind of name is Hiram?"

"He's the secret behind Freemasonry. He's the god-man of the

Craft."

"I hate conspiracies," said Marla.

"Yes, but tomorrow night we'll be standing toe to toe with one."

"I just want to be standing toe to toe with his dead body."

"That would be too easy," said Jimmy.

Marla was quiet for a moment, trying to figure out just what the hell that meant.

"I've got to talk to the president," she said. "I need to communicate with the outside world, Jimmy. Can you get me through?"

Jimmy shook his head.

"Hiram won't let anything get through. I've tried. We're on our own."

"Then how is Traverse going to call out?"

"He's not," said Jimmy. "There's no communication. The witch will make him think he's talking to them. That's what I think. It's all lies that she told him to say. They're just trying to cause confusion. It's impossible to tell the truth from a lie."

"I have to speak with the President. There has to be a way."

"Marla, we're living in a world the size of a grain of sand located in a field off US 127 in midwestern Michigan. No one can see us, no one can figure out how things and people go in or out of here and you want me to tell you there is a way to talk to the President? I just found out that I live in a world less than an eighth of an inch tall. I need a few minutes to get myself together. Now I understand why social media never stumbled onto this place. It's too small to see. But maybe the size thing is a lie, too. I really don't know what to think."

"Yeah, well, if this dick Hiram leaves here and gets out into our world again, there's going to be a lot of dead people, so we have to do something. I saw what he can do."

"Me, too," said Jimmy. "And there's more you don't know."

"Can we stop him?"

"I don't know. And I'd really like to get out of here before Major Landsdale opens the cages down below."

"Where does Traverse have all the people locked in cages?"

"They're not people, Marla."

She went quiet while that sank in. Too much information and all of it is bad. For the first time in her life, despite all her training and experience, Marla felt helpless.

"I'd better go get some sleep," she said. "Tomorrow's going to be a long day. Then maybe we can come up with a plan."

"Would you spend the night with me?" asked Jimmy.

"You want to explain that?" she asked with an arched eyebrow.

"No, no, that's not what I meant."

An uncomfortable look, almost embarrassment, flickered across his face.

"Then what did you mean?"

"It's a matter of personal safety. Neither of us should be alone tonight. They might try to separate us, lock me up so that you have to go it alone. Or... worse."

"Jimmy, I can stay here, but considering what we just saw, I don't know if I can protect you."

"I wasn't worried about me," said Jimmy.

Then he pointed past her at the computer monitors again. She swiveled and looked in the general direction of where he was pointing.

She turned to look, but saw nothing unusual on any of the screens.

"What are you pointing at?"

"That one," said Jimmy quietly. "The one that shows the city."

She went from one screen, showing an empty hallway. The next showing Traverse with his head leaning forward onto his desk, sound asleep. Another showing a cafeteria half full of soldiers on break. Another. Another. Another. Then a screen showing nothing but billowing gray mist.

"You see it?" prompted Jimmy. "The fog."

"So?"

Jimmy slid his chair forward and tapped on the gray screen.

"What?" she asked.

"Since the first day I got here," he said. "The weather has been the same day after day, night after night."

"And?"

"Marla, there's never been fog in Borgo. Never."

"Is that bad?"

"Change is always bad in this town."

"Get up," said Marla as she finally noticed movement at the bottom of the door.

"What?" asked Jimmy, who still stared at the screen, looking for an explanation of why the town of Borgo was buried under fog.

"It's in the room," Marla said.

Maybe it wasn't fog. It may have been gas. Maybe it was something worse. Maybe something inside the thick, billowing whiteness was worse still. She backed up against Jimmy and looked wildly around the room. The fog was so thick, so dense that they could not see into it or past it. A solid mass of white vapor blocked the doorway and the walls.

"Take a deep breath and we'll try to run through it," she said.

"To where?" asked Jimmy.

There was no escape. On the screens, all of Borgo lay under the enveloping cloud. Every hallway within the Operation Borgo complex, every stairwell and every room was filling with the suffocating miasma. Marla had never before experienced anything like the creeping horror of white that pressed forward on them like a wall of death. She didn't understand what it was and didn't know what it could do. No way to run around it, under it or over it. It was a physical presence in the room, rising like a specter come to claim them and take them away.

<h1 style="text-align:center">17</h1>

Marla knew the feeling. Floating back into your body while the hypnogogic drugs wiped away your memories of the immediate past. A little unsteady. Speech just a touch slurred depending on which of the drugs were used. She'd been in a lot of hospitals. But as her vision returned to normal, she realized even in the faint light she wasn't in a hospital. She was in someone else's room, lying on the floor and with a lump on the back of her head that hurt like hell. Just a few feet from where she lay, Jimmy was sprawled on the floor, a chair tipped over next to him. Jimmy had a display of computer holograms and screens in the room. The menacing fog, or whatever it was, had completely disappeared. The question was, how long they had been unconscious?

It was lucky that when she'd fallen, she hadn't hit her temple or head. She peered into one monitor and studied her reflection. No cuts, no bruising, she could see. Her neck ached as though she'd twisted it, but other than that, she felt good to go. Except, she realized, where she was called to go was to the Borgo Masonic Temple. Summoned by the old man—the author of all horror.

She debated leaving without him and looking for a way out. She'd given up on her mission to destroy the old man. President Usman did not know what kind of danger lived in the town of Borgo. Or maybe he did, and that's why the President of the United States always gave him what he wanted. If they did, the old man stayed in this world, wherever and whatever it was.

President Usman didn't really think she could destroy the old man. He didn't really think she could stop him. In fact, he knew she would die. She was a sacrificial appeasement to the demon god who called himself Hiram Abiff. And it would do no good, because he would not be staying in Borgo for much longer, according to the witch.

From what Traverse had said, the old man wanted a journal about him he didn't want known by the outside world. He thought she had or knew or could find the journal and demanded that they deliver her to him. But after she told them knew nothing about it…

Jimmy differed from the rest of them in some way that she couldn't quite get. Why would a priest voluntarily enter the town of no return? What was the point? There was something more to Jimmy than what she was seeing. Looking around his room, she saw nothing that stuck out as a clue or a hiding place. That was the thing about trying to uncover secrets—you never knew where to begin, and that was especially painful when you had very little time to find whatever it was you needed to know.

No, it was easier to charm or choke it out of Jimmy. Just asking would not cut it. She needed answers fast. President Usman had sent her because the old man had asked for her by name. She wondered how Hiram Abiff had that information. He seemed consigned to this world, so how did he know what was going on in the outside world? Did he have spies in her world or confederates? Did he have one or two such people, or hundreds, maybe even thousands? Or was the witch—as Traverse said—able to travel between worlds? Marla really had only one person to interrogate. First, she'd have to wake him up.

She went to one knee, pulled him up a foot off the floor, and shook him. A mumbled something spilled out of his mouth, so she dropped him back to the floor, got up and rummaged about the room until she saw a bottle of water on top of an old Bible. She picked it up and, after a moment's thought, she lifted the book's cover up and looked at the first page. It was an old, leather bound bible. Inside, on that first page, embossed in gold ink, was the Masonic square and compass, and inside that was the single letter "G." Without warning, Jimmy snored.

Secrets within secrets, she thought. It was the Masonic way. Peel back one layer of concealment and you would always find layer after layer of concealment after that.

Was Jimmy a Mason as well as a priest? You couldn't tell by looking at him. But she thought she remembered the Catholics excommunicating Masons or something like that. She thumbed through the Bible's pages, looking for marks, handwritten commentary, sections that were underlined and anything else that might help her, including folded up notes. In the Borgo Complex, who else but her would bother looking for spies? Hiram didn't need spies—he, and he alone, held the ultimate power in this world. Especially when it came to Jimmy. From the way the others treated him, he was above suspicion. Traverse treated him like Saint Jimmy.

After closing the cover, she walked over to where he lay, unscrewed the water bottle's cap, took a quick swig and then poured the rest of it down and onto Jimmy's upturned face. He shook his head back and forth as he swatted at the stream and coughed and gagged like he was being waterboarded.

He had his eyes scrunched tight and Marla thought whoever Jimmy really was, he was no secret agent. He was like a choirboy trapped in a Nicaraguan midnight massacre who'd dived under the bed and closed his eyes tight, clapped his hands over his ears and pretended he wasn't there while he rocked back and forth. She kicked him in the ribs.

"No," he shouted as his eyes popped open, and he sat straight up like his back was spring loaded.

"Easy, Jimmy. You don't want to wake the monsters."

She'd kneeled down on her haunches and was face to face with him. His eyes were wide like he was on drugs, but she saw the fear in them. When his hand shot out and grabbed her wrist, he was so quick she felt his fingers wrap around her before she saw the after-motion blur.

"Did you see them?" he asked.

All the color had drained from his face.

"What?"

Marla didn't pry his fingers from her wrist. It hurt, but she didn't want to interrupt him. Jimmy had visited the world of nightmares, and she was eager to know what he'd seen.

This time it was Jimmy who leaned in close to her. So close that his breath tickled her nose.

"Them. The things from the cages in the subbasement. Traverse let them loose. They were… they were… eating… no, feeding. We have to get out of here, Marla. It's going to happen soon. She told me in my dream."

His shocked face telegraphed his stress.

She knew who he meant. The witch. In his dreams.

Marla pried his fingers from her arm.

"Jimmy," she said without looking up at him. "In your dream, did you see a way out?"

"What? No—I saw them—"

"Tell me something I can use," she screamed. She slapped him hard across the face. "This whole place is like the Little Town of Horrors. I already know you saw them. You and I have to focus in on one thing and one thing only—are you listening to me? We need to find a way out. That witch comes and goes between our world and this piss-ant town, and I want to know how she does it. Did you see anything in your dream that will help with that?"

Jimmy's face was red where she hit him, but the light from the computer screens was too weak to see if he was blushing. He was at first bewildered by her sudden explosion and then angry. Now he was looking at her. Really looking at her.

"No. Nothing. I saw nothing, and I know nothing that will get us out of here."

He wiped the back of his hand over the area she'd slapped, then he pulled it away to see if there was blood. When he took it away from his face, he held it up and scrutinized it as if it were evidence at a trial. The pity in his eyes as he looked at her again infuriated her.

"You disgust me—all of you," she shouted. "You've already given up."

"We are already beaten," said Jimmy, and the sadness in his boyish face was hard to look at. "It didn't take long for me to realize once I got here that I was never leaving. No one who comes here will ever leave, except Hiram Abiff and his witch."

"But there's more, isn't there?" she asked. "You're holding back something from me, aren't you?"

Reluctantly, Jimmy nodded.

"Well, what in God's name is it?"

Jimmy slowly got to his feet, and Marla did the same. He put his hands on her shoulders and for a moment Marla thought he was working up the courage to kiss her, but then he said, "Marla, like I said, there is something much worse living here than Hiram Abiff."

It was the way he said it that made her heart stop.

When they both found a chair and sat down, she asked, "What?"

"You've seen the time?" he asked.

She nodded. The time was in the corner of every computer screen in the room. One hour and a half until they had to meet Hiram Abiff. Half an hour before they had to report to Traverse Nations. The power of the witch, she thought. Marla had given up trying to understand the power of Hiram and his witch. That was no longer a priority. The priority was to get the hell out of Borgo.

"Then you understand that there is not much time left. We can't defeat either of them, Marla. But, here is what I think—not what I know, Marla. What I think. If there is any way out of this hell, it is through the Masonic Temple."

Marla leaned forward, grabbed his shoulders, pulled him forward and kissed him hard on the lips.

"Now you're talking," she said.

An embarrassed Jimmy pulled away and wiped his mouth. "You know, you shouldn't kiss a priest without an indulgence."

"Tell me what's worse than the old man or I'll kiss you again."

"Yes, well, there is something else here."

"Jimmy, I'm going to smack you again if you don't quit stalling."

For a moment, Jimmy seemed to consider the situation, but then he talked.

"I had a dream or a vision when I first came here," he said.

She glared at him.

He held up his hands.

"All right. I just feel that this is real. I don't know it, okay? Are you good with that?"

"Talk, or I'm going to get mad."

Jimmy looked around the room, then turned and stared back at her. The intensity in his eyes was startling.

"Do you know about the Nephilim? Do you know what they are?"

"No. Tell me."

Marla got the feeling that Jimmy was finally going to tell her something useful.

"This is from the Bible, so just run with it for a minute. There were these sons of God in Genesis—it's a book of the Bible."

"I know about the Book of Genesis, you dickhead."

"Okay. Sorry, but you said that you don't read the Bible."

"We're running out of time, Jimmy."

"So, here's a quote from the Book of Genesis: 'Now it came about, when men multiplied on the face of the land, and daughters were born to them, that the sons of God saw that the daughters of men were beautiful; and they took wives for themselves, whomever they chose. Then the LORD said, 'My Spirit shall not strive with man forever, because he also is flesh; nevertheless, his days shall be one hundred and twenty years.' The Nephilim were on the earth in those days, and also afterward, when the sons of God came in to the daughters of men, and they bore children to them. Those were the mighty men who were of old, men of renown. Then the LORD saw that the wickedness of man was great on the earth, and that every intent of the thoughts of his heart was only evil continually.'"

"Just what the hell does that mean?" asked Marla.

"There are a few interpretations—" began Jimmy.

"Just tell me one that helps me understand what's going on here, and how it relates to getting out of this place and back to our world."

"It's not that simple, but—I know, I know, I'll just get to it. The Nephilim were the offspring of fallen angels. Don't give me that look, Marla. Just hear me out. The Nephilim were giants in this world, children of the fallen Sons of God, but they and the lines of people descended from them were cursed because of their origin since the whole mess had angered God."

"Okay…"

"The curse was that when one of the Nephilim died, they went to neither heaven nor hell. They were cursed to roam the earth as demonic spirits. This place, this town of Borgo and whatever space/time continuum it exists in, was created by one of the Nephilim. The worst of the Nephilim, the most feared of these demonic spirits, was known as the Nephilim Darkness. No one ever recorded his real name, but I think that it's here, Marla. That Nephilim—the king of the Nephilim—is here."

"Well, that's bullshit, Jimmy, but thanks for the story."

"I'm not asking you to believe it, Marla. I'm asking you to remember it."

Marla was so sick of Borgo. She was sick of the old man. Sick of the witch. Sick to death of the underground complex built beneath a fucking viaduct. Sick, even, of Jimmy. She wanted to shoot somebody— anybody. Except Jimmy. She was sick of him, but he was okay. Weirder than she'd thought, but still okay.

"Tell me why. Why, in God's name, would I want to remember what you just said?"

"Because if you get out of here, there will be someone waiting for you on the other side. He'll need to know the story."

"What the hell are you saying, Jimmy? If I get out? Are you saying for sure there's a way out of here and that you think it's somewhere in the Masonic Temple? Give me something solid to go on here."

For a moment, he stared at the row of computer monitors. The red hair and the freckles did it, Marla thought. For however long he lived to be, he would always look like Superman's best friend Jimmy Olsen.

"You know how I ended up here, Marla?"

"No, and I don't care. Don't be such an asshole. Tell me why you think the way out is through the Borgo Masonic Temple and how you know it's there."

For the first time in the short time since she met him, Jimmy grinned.

"Marla, I don't know for sure. It's just my best guess. It feels right. I've been watching every square inch of this little world for the last five years, and that's the one place in this entire demon-created place that the old man stays close to."

That at least made sense. It was Jimmy's job to monitor the entire town of Borgo with his computers. He had infrared detectors all over the place, sound sensors, vibration sensors, ELF units, and God knew what else around the place. If anybody would have a clue to where the escape hatch was, if there really was, he would. But the old man himself would be in the Temple when they showed up, so how would they get past him to find it? Marla's hopes withered at the thought of it.

"How do you know there will be someone waiting for me? What

aren't you telling me?"

"Why I'm here. If you're going to grasp that, keep quiet. Don't judge, don't reason it out. Here's what it is. A little over five years ago, I was sleeping, but I shot straight up in bed in the middle of the night. I don't really know if I was awake or asleep. I heard a voice speaking to me. It told me clearly who to go see and what to tell them to be sent here, to this forsaken place.

"I thought I had been given these instructions by divine providence. Borgo was a place I had never heard of. I didn't know what the Nephilim Darkness was and, I swear to you, I had never heard of Hiram Abiff. But, I was directed to come here, and I did what I was told.

"You have to understand, Marla, that I had never heard a divine command before. I'd read of such things in my studies at seminary. It's just that it was more... possible than real to me. Most sane people would have thought they were dreaming, but it never crossed my mind. It was real, and I knew it. So, the church—which, even with a Muslim president—is well connected in more ways than you can imagine. I really don't know how they did it. There wasn't any need for me to know.

"But, six months to the day after the command, I was brought through the same one-way portal that you were brought through, and I've been here ever since. And in my vision, I was told about the Nephilim. But it was just a vision. Or maybe prophetic. Learning that much was apparently above my pay grade.

"So here I've been ever since then. Waiting for someone to come who I was supposed to tell everything that I learned here, and that person was supposed to tell that to someone on the other side. I was given to know that I would never leave here. I waited, and I waited, but that person never came. I thought it was just a dream. As much as I could, I put it out of my head. Until you came along, Marla. At first, I doubted it could be you. You're not what I expected. But now I believe you are that person."

"You're not crazy, are you Jimmy? And you're not one of the walking dead people, are you?"

After a grim smile, Jimmy said, "No, I'm not crazy and I'm not one of the walking dead."

"If we find a way out of here, we can both get out. Vision or not,

I'm not leaving you here."

"There are higher powers at work here, Marla. We're not really in charge."

"Uh-huh. Look, we have to get ready to go meet Traverse."

"There's nothing to get ready, Marla. What's going to happen will happen. There's nothing to prepare that will make a difference. It will be in the hands of God."

"Yeah, well," she said. "If I'm going to die, I'd like a shower and a change of clothes first."

****

Jimmy walked Marla to her room, down two floors where she showered, changed clothes and added a belt that when she pressed a button on the buckle would release two thin, coiled cables with roughened edges that could cut loose a head from its neck in less than a second. The problem was, Hiram Abiff wasn't human. In her cargo pants pockets, she hid a pair of thin steel rods that could pierce straight through a person's temple. She added a pocket watch that, when two of its buttons were depressed, turned it into a powerful explosive. Her hair was in a tight bun on top of her head and, after a moment's thought, she inserted an enameled steel needle into it.

"You look like a ninja all dressed in black," said Jimmy.

"Shut up."

"It won't do any good. It will be in God's hands."

"Like I said," she said as she pushed Jimmy out of the way and opened the door, "shut up."

Down the hall and into the elevator, passing men with clipboards and HoloLens glasses. The same hum of activity she'd encountered when she'd arrived in Borgo in the back of a truck. Everyone studying, analyzing the world of Borgo and its demonic resident. Plowing the same ground over and again. Seventy-five years of sampling the environment, coming up with ways to kill the old man, running the tests and failing to destroy Hiram. Still, they continued doing the same thing over and over again, falling backward after each attempt like

Sisyphus pushing the stone up and hill while being cursed by the gods with having it roll back to the bottom each time he got it to the top.

They took the elevator to the surface level, walked out into the command center, where soldiers and scientists in white lab coats manned the monitoring and the sensing devices scattered throughout Borgo. Marla glanced over at them as they walked down the bullet-proof glass hallway that led to the reinforced steel doors that led to the town of Borgo. They are damned, she thought. Damned to re-live their hopeless militaristic and scientific efforts to destroy Hiram Abiff.

At the giant, automated doors, Traverse Nations, Dr. Lydia Grayson and Professor Terry Grieves stood waiting. Their faces showed a mixture of terror and submission. No one, she thought, really cares about me going to see Hiram, but they are filled with dread at the thought of Jimmy going. Jimmy was their talisman against the old man, their hope of eventual freedom. None of them, she thought, believes he's about to die.

Traverse was dressed in a black suit and a soft gray colored shirt. His shoes reflected the overhead fluorescent lights. With his white hair swept back, he was a cross between a funeral director and a television evangelist. Professor Terry Grieves stood with his hands folded in front of him, a haunted look in his sunken eyes. A professor, she thought, about to deliver a lecture to the dead. The narrow-faced Dr. Lydia Grayson was clearly stricken, as though she had just received an undisputed medical diagnosis of her impending demise.

Considering what the witch had told Traverse in his waking dream state, that diagnosis was about to come true. If Traverse released whatever creatures were caged down below, all the personnel were about to become food on a menu for monsters.

The Director of Operation Borgo looked down at his electronic smart watch and said to both of them, "Are you ready?"

Jimmy said yes; Marla said nothing.

"I don't like you going," said Traverse to Jimmy.

"I know," said Jimmy, "but it's important."

"Eva said you're going to be all right."

Jimmy shuddered at the thought.

"There was a lot of fog last night," said Traverse, "but it's dissipated. Just enough of it left it so it looks like a scene from Casablanca out there."

Marla had never seen the movie, but got the point.

"So, Jimmy..." said Traverse, at a loss for words. Eventually, he gave up, stepped forward and hugged the younger man.

The sight of this disturbed Marla. She remembered all too well the night when the witch entered Traverse's office through his outstretched mouth. Was she in there at this very moment? She shuddered at the thought.

Then Professor Grieves stepped forward.

"You be careful, kid," he said, then stepped back.

Marla could see the tears welling up in his eyes. Why, she wondered, did everyone in Borgo think of Jimmy as a kid? And why were they so attached to him? Maybe it was because he was the only truly sane person in the complex.

"You know what you have to do," Traverse told her.

To his credit, demon infested or not, he didn't look away when she locked her eyes on him.

"Yeah," she said. "Take one for the team."

"Hey, that's not—" began Professor Grieves, but Traverse held up a hand.

"Leave it, Professor," he said. "Lady's got a tough job."

For the briefest of moments, Traverse looked away. If the witch were inside him, decided Marla, that wouldn't have happened.

Dr. Lydia Grayson looked as though for some time during the night she'd been mummified in paraffin at Madame Tussaud's Wax Museum. The fluorescent lights made her acne pits shine, and she wore black-rimmed squarish glasses, which made her thin nose look even smaller. Her mouth was a tight line, holding back the anger she felt at Jimmy leaving.

"Don't come back changed," she said to Jimmy. To Marla, she said, "I hope you don't come back at all."

And I, thought Marla, hope that when Traverse releases the creatures in the cage deep in the complex's basement, that they find you first.

"That's enough," snapped Traverse, then he nodded to a soldier to open the doors to the night.

18

The night air was cool and brisk as they walked out from beneath the viaduct and onto the street.

"Well," said Marla as she touched the top of her hair to make sure the steel needle was in place, "that was a warm goodbye."

"Careful," said Jimmy, "they can still hear you with the parabolic microphones."

He pointed a finger upward toward the underside of the viaduct. She didn't look up, but kept walking.

"I don't give a damn," she said.

There were mounds of fluffy snow piled along the way, as though Hiram had made only a half-hearted attempt at weather control. There were blankets of snow on the small houses that lined the street, and Marla wondered if any of the dead slept inside. Maybe, she thought, they never sleep, but lie down and close their eyes as though mimicking the behavior of the living.

Eight blocks to go.

The trees were now barren of leaves, and the dark fingers of their branches did not move.

No wind, she thought.

"Tell me about the creatures in the cage and what happens down in the hole," she said.

Jimmy shot her a glance.

A gray-smeared image of a moon hung in the sky, and it was the color of old bones. The clouds kept away from it, as though it was unclean. She listened for the sound of footsteps following them, but heard nothing. A few blocks ahead, though, the reanimated dead lined the streets they would walk to get to the Borgo Masonic Temple.

"I think that's where the Nephilim and Hiram experiment with bodies. In the hole beneath the complex, I mean."

"To accomplish what?"

"To see if the demonic spirits of the Nephilim can inhabit their bodies. The demons that were once the Nephilim always lust to be free of the void and to inhabit a body again. Once, they were the children of the fallen sons of God. They exulted in this in the same way that the fallen sons of God lusted for earthly women. These Nephilim now have no bodies, as I told you before, and they are driven to discovering a way to defy God himself by once again becoming flesh and blood."

"I'm guessing it didn't work out," said Marla as they grew closer to the re-animated dead.

"I don't think so," said Jimmy, "but I think that is their unholy endgame. Now we should be quiet. Don't talk in front of them."

He nodded to the reanimated dead.

As they passed them, the dead fell in behind them. In another four blocks, Marla and Jimmy would enter the small downtown of Borgo, where, in the middle of Main Street, the Borgo Masonic Temple and the master of Borgo waited for them. The sound of shuffling footsteps behind them was disturbing. He knew what was following them. Those who had been lowered down the mysterious shaft as corpses and yet returned.

Up ahead, more of them lined the streets, and when they passed them, they joined the pack of silent followers. Marla shivered as they walked, not from the cool night air, but from fear. She looked over to Jimmy, who walked beside her, a look of grim faith on his face. His chin was up as though he were walking into an invisible wind. The streetlamps that lined Main Street glowed softly, and the absolute insanity of what they were doing struck her. Inside the Borgo Masonic Temple, waited the most terrifying man she could imagine.

"Jimmy," she said.

"Don't talk."

"Why are they following us?"

"They're not," he said tersely. "They're herding us."

And it was true. The reanimated dead formed an inhuman funnel ending in the Borgo Masonic Temple.

They passed the darkened flower shop and the thought of it was as terrifying in its own way as the night she saw the witch pouring out of Traverse's impossibly stretched mouth. Flowers in this town of the dead and the terrible? She would have laughed were it not so horrifying. Although she thought nothing could be more bizarre, another block later she passed the Borgo Funeral Parlor.

"Jimmy?"

He grabbed her elbow and kept her walking. Since the day she'd arrived in this false world, she'd been focused on the dark power of the old man, but now she saw a malevolent dark humor that mocked the soldiers and scientists of Borgo with a pure hatred of their lives. The Borgo Masonic Temple loomed ahead of them, a chilling blue-yellow light radiating from a single window.

"Marla?"

"What?"

"Pray with me as we walk."

The frightening realization that she not only did not know how to pray, but who to pray to paralyzed her. God was an abstraction. A church recitation with no meaning to her at all. She and Jimmy were alone in this forsaken world.

"I don't know how."

"I'll lead you."

"Not in front of them," and she shook her head toward the rows of reanimated dead they were passing.

One or two of them, she thought she recognized. A soldier who'd led her in to meet Traverse her first night in Borgo, although she realized that there really was no such thing in Borgo, the town of eternal night. A doctor—what was his name—peeled away from the curb to join the now massive crowd behind them. But she really couldn't be sure if she recognized any of them—their vacant stares and blank faces blurred their identities.

"The Lord is my shepherd; I shall not want," Jimmy began.

Behind them, she heard guttural growls from the creatures. Marla touched the metal rods in her cargo pants pockets.

"He maketh me to lie down in green pastures: he leadeth me beside the still waters…"

Her footsteps sounded suddenly too loud. Each of her boots had a mechanism that, simply by clicking the heels together, would cause a sharp blade to shoot out the tips of her shoes. Two feet, two boots and two blades against the mob of the undead closing in around them.

"He restoreth my soul; he leadeth me in the paths of righteousness for his name's sake…"

Low, angry mutterings from the undead.

"Yea, though I walk through the valley of the shadow of death, I will fear no evil: for thou art with me; thy rod and thy staff, they comfort me."

One block left to go.

The black, billowing clouds overhead began to move. Marla felt it before she looked up and saw it.

"Jimmy…"

"Thou preparest a table before me in the presence of mine enemies," he continued in a stronger voice, "… thou anointest my head with oil; my cup runneth over."

A red lightning bolt cracked across the sky, followed by the first thunderclap she had ever heard in Borgo. An angry, raucous howl broke out from behind them.

"Surely goodness and mercy shall follow me all the days of my life: and I will dwell in the house of the Lord forever. Amen," finished Jimmy.

They stood at the base of the steps leading up to the brooding presence of the Borgo Masonic Temple. Marla looked up to see that the doors were closed. On a sudden, inexplicable impulse, she turned to look at the sea of undead standing behind them, stopped now, too, staring straight ahead, seeing nothing.

"Jimmy—" she began but stopped when the doors to the Borgo Temple swung toward them without a hand—human or inhuman—propelling them outward.

"No time, Marla," said Jimmy as he began walking up the steps.

19

The lobby was dimly lit by the glow from the open door halfway up to the main lodge room. The air was damp and heavy, with a musky smell that reminded Marla of a tiger cage. Her muscles were sore with tension. At the top of the stairs in the lodge room, she would face Hiram Abiff. No matter what the horrors she had faced in this town of magic and death, somewhere inside she knew that this would be the worst of it. She did not believe that either she or Jimmy would leave the place alive. She would not go down without a fight, but up against a being like Hiram Abiff, the outcome was not in doubt, no matter what Jimmy had told her about a possible way out.

There would, she knew, be no time to escape even if Jimmy knew exactly where the exit was. She remembered how she had seen Hiram Abiff kill the soldiers. Remembered the stories Traverse had told about him. Nothing could kill Hiram Abiff. In this world, he was the master. When Jimmy grabbed her elbow, she nearly screamed. She turned to look at him and saw the temple doors closing. In the lambent light outside, she saw the crowds of incurious dead staring at them. After the doors had clicked closed, she wondered if they were still staring.

It feels like a tomb, she thought. She stared at Jimmy before taking another step. A look of almost eager anticipation animated his face and yet, there was a sadness. He was dressed in what she thought of as priest's garb. His white collar yellowed in the candlelight's light that spilled from the lodge room. They stood in a square, ceramic tiled space, where the stairs to the left led downward to a cafeteria and/or event space, while the stairs to the right led up to the actual lodge room. Where Hiram waited.

Jimmy took a small vial from his inside pocket, unscrewed the cap and wetted the tip of his forefinger. He swiped the sign of the cross on her forehead while saying something about in the name of the Father, the Son, and the Holy Spirit. She did not catch the rest of it, because as he spoke the words, she felt an angry energy spring up in the room. It had been a long time since Marla Corvasce had heard what she called church words. It would have been appropriate for her to add a few words of gratitude for the priest's blessing, but instead, she felt for the spring-loaded sheathed blade strapped to her forearm. Jimmy nodded, then began walking up the stairs to the lodge room.

I can't let him die, she thought, and followed him up the stairs. She felt as though they were about to step into dark waters.

At the top of the stairs, she saw a row of old photos of men dressed in Masonic regalia, and in the middle of them, a large wall clock with the Masonic square and compass emblazoned on its face. Against the wall to the right was a wooden bench seat beneath a window facing the city street they had just left. Marla leaned toward it and saw the mass of undead still staring at the double doors through which they had entered the building. They were dark, immobile figures, like an army of statues.

She could not make out their faces, and that was good. Humanizing the enemy was a bad mistake. She turned to see Jimmy standing before the two open double doors that led into the lodge proper. As she walked toward him, the air seemed to grow still thicker. It was a trick of the mind, she knew from her training. The brain tries to slow the body from walking into danger and the legs and arms feel heavier. She knew her body was right, but there was no choice. There was nowhere to run. And in the town of Borgo, there was really no place to hide from Hiram Abiff.

"Enter," said a sultry voice.

"Uh-oh," said Jimmy.

It was the voice of Eva Morgan.

Then, as though he'd been training for this moment since he

arrived in Borgo, Jimmy straightened his shoulders and walked through into the candlelit room, with Marla just a step behind him.

At the far end of the room sat the old man in the Worshipful Master's chair, higher than all the other officer's chairs. Hiram Abiff as the Worshipful Master in the East. A demon in a man's body, and from it radiated evil so real that Marla could feel it. An evil so much larger than the little old man that it seemed to fill the room. Some part of her brain screamed to turn and run before the thing that looked like an old man annihilated her. Something gigantic and malevolent looked across the room at them with palpable rage, not at them, but at the fact of their existence.

An empty wood and leather chair flanked him to his right and to his left. There were positioned two rectangular wooden pillars with flat tops three feet in height off to either side of the Master's chair so that those approaching him had a clear view of the Worshipful Master's imposing presence. On the wall behind each of the three chairs on the Master's dais were great looping wooden moldings that formed an archway over it all. The entire platform was elevated three steps above the floor. She noticed these details the way a death row inmate noticed the wiring on the electric chair as they entered the execution chamber.

To their left as they entered, Eva Morgan sat lounging languorously in the Senior Deacon's chair, her legs crossed, revealing the creamy white of her thighs. Her long black hair was pulled back over her left shoulder. To either side of her were two fluted wooden pillars with globes mounted at the top of them. At that moment, Marla wanted to strangle her so that her fingers ached as she squeezed them into fists. The monster in the worshipful master's chair was beyond her reach and she knew that, but the witch, Marla, could kill the witch —she would find a way.

Eva found Marla's reaction mildly amusing. Her dark eyes locked on Marla and ran approvingly over her body.

"Welcome sister," she said.

To Jimmy, she added, "We get so very few priests as visitors to this Masonic lodge. Enter and be welcome."

She smiled as she said this, revealing long, sharp, bright white teeth.

Marla wanted to take out one of her blades and cut her throat, but she would have to wait until the time was right. If there was ever a right time—she knew that with a single blast of magical energy, the old man could kill both her and Jimmy. She had seen that at the Minus Eight site. Marla's legs felt weak as she remembered who this old man was, how many weapons the military had sent in and how useless it had all been to kill or even stop him.

"Thank you for coming," said Hiram Abiff.

His voice was a hollow echo in a funeral parlor. A man used to conversing about and with the dead. Marla and Jimmy exchanged a glance. They hadn't considered which of them would do the talking.

Finally, Jimmy said, "Of course. We welcomed the chance to meet the Mayor of Borgo."

There was a dark humor in Jimmy's voice that was almost brave.

Hiram Abiff smiled. Marla felt disoriented by it. His teeth were impossibly long and sharp. It was a bending and twisting and shattering of reality that allowed monsters to smile.

"The Mayor of Borgo? Yes, the Mayor of Borgo."

Hearing Hiram Abiff speak like a normal man was almost too much for Marla. This thing, this creature of such immense power, spoke like a kindly old man. His wire-rimmed glasses were horrifyingly mundane. What did a being like Hiram Abiff need glasses for?

Marla was certain that it was not to see more clearly. It was like a mask, to fool whoever was looking at him into thinking he was an ordinary old man, like his old man's face and drooping physique. The flannel shirt and his jeans were just more elements of his disguise, something that allowed him to pass. She wondered what he would like if he dropped all the fakery. A demon, she thought. He could transform into a hideous demon from hell. Like the demon who had killed her grandfather in her nightmare.

"You asked us here to inquire about a journal," said Jimmy.

The old man nodded.

"I did. Eva has informed me, to my great disappointment, that she," he indicated Marla with a nod of his chin, "does not have it or know where it is. But I want to hear it from her own lips. Traverse and his ilk would lie to me about this. But you, I think, will not. Tell me, Marla, is it true? Do you truly not know where it is? Speak carefully; I will know if you are lying to me."

In the dim light, his cheeks were hollowed shadows, and his eyes were flat, discolored coins.

"Why," said Marla. "You're going to kill us anyway, aren't you?"

She found her heart beating hard in her chest. Again, she realized how inadequate her concealed weapons were against him. This was a creature who had killed thousands of scientists and soldiers in this awful town. Yet if she could get close enough to cut off his head…

But Hiram shook his head from side to side.

"No, young woman, I will not kill you. Have you not seen in your brief stay here that I only deal retribution to those who attack me? Never have I initiated violence. Never. I only respond."

The statement took Marla by surprise. The fact was that she had seen no evidence that Hiram had initiated force against anyone who had not first attacked him. Except… in her dream. And this thing lied because he was built from lies.

"What about the soldiers you killed?"

As soon as she'd said it, she wished she'd hadn't. Why antagonize someone who literally had the power of life and death over the two of them? But to her relief and surprise, he answered the question.

"They murdered those men they had staked out in cold blood," said Hiram indifferently. "I was appalled at their actions and retaliated on behalf of those defenseless creatures. Who else could bring them to justice? You, who stood by and watched them die? The priest at your side who sits and prays, but does nothing to help those in need? No, I did what I did for justice."

There was nothing Marla could think of to say. She, in fact, was appalled at what Traverse had done. And yet, she knew that behind her, sat the witch who took over Traverse's body and brought those hideous beasts with her. The witch was pure evil, and Hiram was worse. Talking with them as though they normal was like living in a Franz Kafka novel. He'd promised not to kill her, but she knew she couldn't trust anything at all that Hiram said. Hiram was master of all the evil that infested Borgo. Hiram was, in fact, the source of all evil in Borgo.

"Now tell me," said the old man, "and tell me truly—do you not have the journal I have been searching for all these long years? Or do you know where to find it? Do you know anything at all about its whereabouts?"

She remembered the dream. Her grandfather's farm. The nightmare of this old man and the dark thing lurking behind him. For a moment, fear gripped her so completely that she could not speak.

But then, her mouth seemed to have a mind of its own as she responded, "Why do you want it? What's in it?"

She could not see Jimmy's face because she was focused on Hiram Abiff, but she was certain he wished she'd shut up.

"It contains," said the old man, "all that I personally witnessed of the man named Jesus. I divulged it in a moment of weakness to a man who swore to me that what I told him he would keep confidential on his Masonic oath. Later, I learned he had betrayed that confidence by writing it down. If the world learns of its contents, it will be disastrous and create chaos. Many will die in the outrage and conflict that follows. It would shake Christianity to its foundations, and I do not wish to cause that. I was there, you see, at his supposed Crucifixion, and I will carry the secrets of that day and those that followed to my eventual grave. I will protect the secrets even of Mohammed and Moses—and yes, I knew both of them—and, unfortunately, who they really were. I will return to the world soon from my self-imposed sabbatical, and I will enter that world peacefully, bringing only good news to the Masons who have protected me all these long centuries. I will come, as they say, in peace instead of dissension."

"You lie," said Jimmy.

The force in his voice made Marla turn and stare at him. Was he crazy? Making Hiram Abiff angry was insane.

"Sit down, Eva," said Hiram in a stern voice.

Marla turned to see Eva, only three feet away from Jimmy, her left hand extended toward him and floating in the air. The witch gave Hiram a withering stare, but then obediently floated back to the Senior Deacon's chair as though nothing at all had happened. Compared to the other things Marla had seen in Borgo, this was less disturbing than it perhaps it should have been.

"I was not speaking to you, priest. You have your mythology to uphold. Again, I ask you, Marla," said Hiram. "Do you know where the journal called The Confessions of Mr. Hyde might be found?"

The intensity of his stare made her take a step back. Then she caught hold of herself. She had no idea where the journal was.

"No, I don't," she said. "All my grandfather left behind were some old pictures of him and his family. Nothing else. I'd never even heard of this journal before you had me brought here."

He stared at her for a long time as Marla held her breath. She was so out of her element. None of her training as an operative could help her in this place. She could only stand straight and try very hard not to look afraid, although her insides felt as though they were melting.

Finally, Hiram nodded.

"Very well, then."

Slowly, he stood up from the Master's chair like an arthritic old man and began walking down the steps toward her and Jimmy. Hiram Abiff was a few inches shorter than her when he stepped down to the lodge floor. The wispy tufts of gray-white hair that ringed his head gave him a disheveled look. There was nothing about him to suggest that he was anything but an old man, no different from any other senior citizen. But Marla knew better. Hiram Abiff was the walking embodiment of evil. She'd seen it in her nightmare.

And then came the horrifying anticlimax. The polite dismal, with an undertone of death.

"Now that you have told me that which I wished to know, I will leave you in peace. Eva will depart with me and arrange an escort to return the two of you to your own world. You don't want to be here, too, when I bring down retribution on the heads of those who have tormented me all these many years before I leave. She," he nodded at Eva, "will return in a half an hour with those who will lead you to the hidden exit from this world. Do not leave before then. That would displease me. You truly," he growled, "do not wish to displease me."

Before either Marla or Jimmy could respond, the old man and his witch walked out the through the double lodge doors, which then swung shut so hard behind them that the building itself shuddered. There was a loud click as locks snapped shut like coffin latches at an angry funeral. For a second, Marla saw herself looking up at the closing lid of a velvet lined casket lid.

"Hurry," said Jimmy. "Search this room for an exit. I'll go downstairs and you do the same. I know the layout better than you, and we don't have time to waste."

His voice was tight with urgency, and his eyes were stern. She felt locked into position, like a confused statue.

"Get moving," he yelled over his shoulder as he ran toward the doorway to the side of the Worshipful Master's dais.

Jimmy's command broke the spell. Marla didn't need to be told again. She looked frantically around the room for anything that might conceal a doorway, but saw nothing. If there was a doorway hidden somewhere, where would it go? Outside the building? What good would that do them?

A sudden thought hit her. Maybe they weren't looking for a normal doorway, but a portal between Borgo and her own world. Maybe they could just find and pull a hidden lever and they could walk through the suddenly revealed opening and instantly appear back in the real world. She spun around, looking for any kind of clue to a hidden opening, but nothing looked promising. What would an inter-dimensional doorway look like, anyway? She looked at her watch. Twenty-one minutes remaining.

Jimmy, I hope you're doing better than I am, she thought.

The wall lighting? Could it be something as simple as that? She ran up to the first of them in line—there were four mounted on each of the side walls. Since all the lights were turned off because Hiram apparently preferred candlelight, she grabbed its base and twisted. Nothing, no magically created opening to her own world. No turning gears, no sound of whirring electric motors or mysterious guardians appearing to defend the portal.

Suddenly, she felt the weight of hopelessness settle on her shoulders. What if Hiram Abiff was lying to them? She tried every single light fixture with no results. Her eyes fell upon the Worshipful Master's chair. She pushed and pulled on every fixture. Nothing. Then she looked at the floor carpet, jumped from the dais, fell to her knees and ran her hands over the carpet, looking for trap doors. Sweat drenched the back of her neck and her scalp and ran down toward her forehead and eyes. But she did not wipe it away until she'd covered one third of the entire lodge floor. By the time she made it to the halfway mark, she heard Jimmy coming back up the stairs.

"Nothing," he called out. "I can't find a blessed thing and we're about out of time."

"How much left?" she said, without looking back at him.

"Seven minutes," he said, then got to his knees and started feeling the carpet, too, desperate to find a hidden door.

"We'd better get up and get ready to make a stand for it," she said.

Jimmy looked at his watch, shook his head, and got to his feet.

"Remember what I said," he told her.

They both turned at the sound of the lock on the lodge doors disengaging.

"Remember," he repeated.

But Marla could no longer remember what he was talking about. As the doors swung open, the witch Eva Morgan stepped in. The temperature dropped in the room.

"Your escorts are here," she said with a smile, and stepped aside.

A swarm of creatures scrabbled into the room past her. Their skin was the green-black color of mold in the room's candle light. A few moved on all fours; the rest walked upright on two legs with backward pointing joints. Their hands were tipped with sharp claws that made snapping sounds as they opened and closed them in anticipation. The smell of rotting meat permeated the air and nearly gagged her. Black pustules spotted their skin with thick hairs sticking out from them. Their jaws were long and as their dark tongues flicked in and out between them and Marla saw rows of sharp teeth that looked like they could rip through Kevlar. Their sharply domed heads were hairless, and their eyes, their yellow-green eyes, bulged from their sockets. As she drew out her two knives, the creatures hissed and barked like infected dogs.

"I warned you, sister," the witch said to Marla, then turned and walked out the door as she called back to her creatures without turning around, "Even their bones are yours. You should have known never to believe the child of the lying one."

Marla heard the lock click into place behind.

"Get behind me, Jimmy," she said.

When he didn't move, she stepped in front of him. There was no time to waste. As the lead monster took a step forward, Marla pointed a knife at the candlesticks.

"Fire," she said to Jimmy.

The first creature leaped at her, its clawed hand savagely swiping to rip out her throat. Marla slipped beneath the claws, spun low and sliced open its abdomen. The beast screeched in pain and dropped to the floor behind her. She didn't retreat but moved forward and shoved the point of her other blade in the nearest creature's eye, then cut open its throat with the other. She felt its warm blood spurt over her hand. As another came at her, she went low again, then thrust straight upward, driving it through the soft place of its lower jaw and into its upper palette so hard that it stuck there. Its gurgled anguish blended with the screams of the other two as they died. She didn't yank it out. Stopping was death.

With her empty hand, she withdrew one of the two steel rods from the pocket in her cargo pants and smacked it hard against the next beasts clawed hands, spun and hit it so hard across its eyes that both burst with a spray of green fluid. She didn't keep count, she just kept moving. But a beast she didn't see coming slashed her left shoulder, causing her to scream out in pain and drop the knife. She hit it across the nose with the steel rod and it leaped back, howling in pain. The remaining creatures backed away and she tensed, waiting for a mass attack, but instead, she realized they were backing away in fear. The answer to why they were backing off came as Jimmy stepped beside her, holding the two candlestick holders in front of him.

"Fire," he said. "You're right—they're afraid of fire."

Pain flared in Marla's shoulder where the beast had wounded her.

"The floor," she gasped through clenched teeth. "The carpeting. Set it on fire."

Jimmy's eyes widened, then he stooped down and lay one set of burning candlesticks on the floor. A moment later, a small flame rose from the carpet. The creatures howled in frustration and began chomping their teeth together with a sound like bear traps snapping shut over and again.

"Back up," she said.

"To where?" asked Jimmy.

"Toward that big chair," said Marla, her eyes never leaving the pack of snarling monsters.

She gestured toward the chair opposite the Junior Warden's chair, which was known in Masonic circles as the Empty Chair.

"Before you do," she added, "try to make a half circle of fire around us."

Three creatures had broken away from the others and were running around toward the Worshipful Master's chair to block the door beside it, cutting them off from any exit.

Blood was running down Marla's arm and she felt lightheaded.

Going to kill them all, she was thinking. Every damned one of them.

Jimmy kneeled down again and tried to catch a small bit of the carpeting on fire. Marla kept glancing between what he was doing and the horde of creatures surrounding them.

"More fire," she shouted.

"I'm trying," he snapped back. "This stuff doesn't burn as easy as the other part did."

The carpet wasn't kindling. It would catch for a second, seem like it was ready to catch fire, only to smolder and die out seconds later. Three of the five candles left had gone out.

"You have any matches?" he asked.

Marla turned back to look at him.

"What?" she asked.

Jimmy's eyes widened, and his mouth opened in horror. Before Marla could turn to see what he was looking at, Jimmy sprang to his feet and jumped past her. As she followed his leap, she saw him barrel into one creature and the two of them went rolling. She looked up to check what was going on with the rest of the beasts, who were still back behind the fire line save the three near the Worshipful Master's chair, who were now in motion toward her.

Jimmy and the beast rolled to a stop with Jimmy on top with his hands wrapped around a goblin's neck. He was shouting and shrieking and banging the thing's head on the floor over and over. Marla was only two steps away when the creature's clawed hand shot up between and through Jimmy's arms and plunged its talons into his throat, ripped out his windpipe and threw it over its shoulder. It squirmed out from beneath Jimmy and opened its mouth to bite the priest in the face when Marla stabbed her last knife into the base of its head and sunk the blade all the way to the hilt. The red blood gushing out from Jimmy's savaged throat merged with the green goblin blood in a nightmarish mix. As she jerked back around, she unsnapped the belt cable with its stainless-steel wire out from the sheath she wore wrapped around her waist.

Smoke hung in the room like acrid fog, and she gagged on it. Tears filled her eyes, but she whipped her belt cable out at one creature who ran straight for her. As the rough metal coated wire wrapped around its neck, she slid forward and pulled hard. Stepping up and over the creature, she tugged it the other way, sawing off its head completely. As she moved back toward the big chair, she saw its head bounce on the floor, roll and come to a stop, staring at the blood and gore-stained carpet. The savage roar from the remaining creatures was deafening. They were closing in on her, tightening the half circle so there was no escape.

No way I'm going to die, she thought. No way.

So tight was her focus on the advancing creatures, that she stepped on Jimmy's body without realizing it and almost fell, but caught her balance. Her shoulder felt hot and her face was flecked with blood as she snapped the wire cable out and back with her other arm, hoping to keep them at bay. One of them snapped its tongue out at her, then pulled it back, mimicking the motion of her weapon.

You first, thought Marla. If I go down, I'm taking you with me.

They were moving like a pack now, only fifteen feet away. No longer afraid of her. The smell of her blood fired that lust for her flesh. She'd seen this before with wolves in Eastern Europe, but even wolves would show more mercy than these creatures. She had to keep swiveling her head from side to side to keep up with their advance because she could hardly hear anything over their howls. One broke rank and shot straight at her; Marla whipped out her wire and it would have caught it in the neck if its forehead hadn't exploded as it was knocked backward. The pack went wild and charged. She fell back, felt herself pushed aside and almost went down.

A muzzle flash from an automatic weapon and three, then two more were blown backward. More muzzle flashes to her other side, and her ears went numb. Two more of the creatures fell back with holes in their chest. Marla turned and saw a man to her left and a woman to her right. The man turned and pointed behind them with his free hand. Marla pushed it away as she slashed the cable across a charging creature's eyes. Its clawed hands went up to its face as another shot blew a hole through its neck.

More urgent directions by the man, pushing her to get behind them.

"Look out, Rebecca," he screamed.

After another burst of shots from behind her, Marla turned again and saw an opening where the chair had been. The woman named

Rebecca was still firing with an automatic weapon, literally ripping apart the rest of the creatures. Marla saw the man's mouth form the word run as he took off for the opening, stopped and motioned for her to follow. Behind them, the room was filled with the sound and fury of destruction. The woman backed up against her, turned and smiled an insane smile. Marla thought she said let's go, but could not hear because she was nearly deaf. Then the woman stopped, turned back to face the room, and took something out of her pocket. Marla saw that the lodge doors were open and the witch floating through them. The woman next to her took whatever was in her hand, pulled a ring loose from it and threw it toward the witch with one hand as she raised her weapon with the other and started firing again.

The witch held out a hand, and the bullets ricocheted away from her. Hanging in the smoke and fog, hovering over the bodies of her creatures, she smiled at Marla and Marla felt her stomach shrivel. But at just that moment, the phosphorus grenade came to a stop beneath the witch's feet and the woman who had thrown it spun, turned Marla's body around and shoved her forward to follow the man into the opening. The explosion of fire behind them sent a percussive wave of heat after them as they ran for their lives. They disappeared into the darkness as one of the burned and wounded creatures bounded into the opening after them.

As they ran through a nightmarish, membranous tunnel of red lightning and screams, Marla wondered for a brief moment about who the woman named Rebecca was. She forgot that when she heard a bestial howl from somewhere close behind them and the terror caused adrenaline to jack her body into high gear as she ran with unthinkable urgency.

PART TWO

20

In the narcotic fog, she had no eyes.

Rebecca's hand and forearm burned where claws would soon scrape her bones, and her nostrils filled with the demon's odor. Even when blind, the voice of the witch was always with her and the knowledge of who she was sickened her. As nausea washed over her, Rebecca Mihaloff's vision returned as though being slowly revealed by the raising of a theater curtain. The streets of Detroit burned with scarlet flames. Buildings were crushed flat, exploded into concrete sinkholes of broken pipes and melted electrical wirings. Amid the miles of destruction, only one building remained—the Detroit Masonic Temple, which stood like a Temple of Darkness towering above the streets of Hell. Through the broken concrete of its streets ran packs of reptilian demon-men that hunted the remnants of the living. The night sky raged with spidery, crackling bursts of lightning.

In the narcotic fog, she had no mouth.

As she gazed up at the revealed Masonic Temple, she saw the acid-washed bone face of the world's tallest mausoleum. It was the charnel house for every deception of every false god that ever railed against the Divine. Through its empty halls walked only the unliving, ruined relics of the occult philosophies where succubus and incubus disguised as angels of light prowled for prey. In her bodiless state, she heard their scrabbling claws carom across the shiny, perfectly waxed marble floors of Masonic lies. The panic grew inside her like a living thing, clawing at her insides, chewing on her organs in a rabid bid to eat its way free of the confines of her body. She had no mouth, but she most definitely could and did scream.

Her terrified spirit suddenly flew up and toward the roof of the Masonic Temple where she could see, standing at the edge of its parapet, the old man whose eyes showed the cold blue flame of magical power. Rebecca willed herself to stop, to fall back to the broken sidewalks. She would rather die than get closer. But still closer she flew, pushed by an unseen maleficent force, until she hung above the city, barely ten feet away from the thing of horror.

In the narcotic fog, she had no ears.

The old man's mouth opened wide and his face shook with rage as he bellowed. She felt the spray of his saliva projectile vomited onto her face. As she wiped it away, the wind buffeted her, and rain broke loose from the tormented clouds to splash against her face like waves. He lifted his head and once again screamed cacophonous words. With the falling away of his cowl, she saw that the Masonic Square and Compass were scarified onto the flesh of his forehead, and that by his side now stood the Scarlet Whore of Babylon.

21

Rebecca Mihaloff jerked straight up in bed and screamed. She clutched her quilt to her chest and hitched in quick breaths of the night air. Cold air spilled through the partially opened window as a nervous moon took refuge behind a dark, protective curtain of clouds.

Not a nightmare, she thought. It was a warning.

And she knew what night it was—Walpurgis night.

Her eyes were open so wide they hurt. She jerked her head from side to side, looking for the source of her anxiety. Was there something hiding behind the long billowy window curtains? Impossible. The closet door was open at the far side of her shadowed bedroom. Hadn't she closed that? She realized to her horror, that it had a handle on the inside and the outside surface of the door. What if something had opened it from the inside?

"Lord Jesus, protect me," she whispered.

Her father was still out. A quick look at the bedroom clock showed it was only ten o'clock and when he went to the Detroit Masonic Temple, he was never, ever home before midnight. He'd been there in that horrible place the night her mother died. The memory caused a flush of anger to color her thoughts. She didn't need him. He was never there when she needed him, anyway. Never there for his cancer-stricken wife when she needed him. Too busy with his brother Masons.

She could take care of herself.

The bedroom window overlooking the woods was fogged, so she could only see the moonlight as a blurry outline surrounded by dark swirls and tiny smears of light. A window version of Van Gogh's Starry Night. Her mother's old chest of drawers towered against the far wall and always looked in danger of falling over to one side and blocking the door. A foot-high statue of St. Michael stabbing a dragon with a long sword stood atop it. It was a statue her father had bought for her mother, long before the cancer took her. Her mother had kept it on her dresser as long as Rebecca could remember. This had been her mother's room. Full of beautiful memories and nightmares, too.

She looked around the room again. Slowly, this time.

Nothing.

The night suddenly shrieked outside her bedroom window and this time she reached for the .25 Raven she kept in her nightstand. She snapped the safety off and chambered a round, even as she realized it was the car alarm going off.

Car's locked in the garage, she thought. Something must have broken in and triggered the alarm.

Rebecca had her jeans on and was throwing on a denim shirt when realized she'd thought something had broken into the garage and not someone. Forty miles out of town never seemed so stupid. She could call 911, but what would she say? I had a bad dream, and my car alarm went off?

The Raven felt too small. From the drawer in her desk alongside her bed, she took out her Smith and Wesson .38 Model 642 LaserMax revolver and two speed loaders. Felt the weight in her hand. That was more like it. After she'd put on her dark navy pea coat, she pushed the. 25 in her left coat pocket and shoved the speed loaders for the .38 in her right. With a few keystrokes and mouse clicks, she brought up the screen on her computer and scanned the video from her web cam security cameras. Ran it back fifteen minutes and then wished she hadn't.

Loping out of the tree line was something the size of a Great Dane. It was covered with silver-green fur that rolled and bunched with the movement of its massive musculature. It moved like a big monkey — shoulders higher than its hips as it pawed the ground. Long jaws and sharp black teeth. There was enough moonlight to get a view of it without switching to thermal. It swung its head from side to side, stopping to sniff the air, eyes flashing an ugly yellow. Her breath caught in her throat when she saw the horns.

Witchcraft.

What had her father done? What was he involved in now?

It hit the attached garage first, ripping the wooden doors off in a shower of splinters. Her adrenaline kicked in so quickly her arms and legs shook and her mind went blank. She felt like she did the time she'd blundered into the path of a rabid dog. Knew she would die. Afraid to run, afraid to scream.

"Oh no," she said. "Can't be real. Can't. Just can't."

She squeezed the .38 so hard her fingers hurt. Then she got hold of herself and switched to the house cams. Did a room search, hallway search and finally the stairs. Nothing. Whatever it was, it was contained in the garage.

Her heart beat so fast she felt light-headed. Closing her eyes, Rebecca Mihaloff leaned her head forward and prayed. After a few moments, a gentle peace settled over her. Her pulse seemed to slow, and she took in a long breath. When she opened her eyes, she checked the screens again and saw that whatever it was hadn't entered the house.

Panic room, she thought.

She had to get to the panic room.

From downstairs, she heard an explosion of wood and knew it was too late. The panic room was on the first floor.

She said another prayer as she stood up straight, slid on her jeans and her loafers, checked her gun and headed for the door. If whatever was down there could bust through the door from the garage, she wasn't any safer in her room. A quick check of the inside cams showed it snarling in the kitchen. She turned the volume up on the speakers and heard it now, huffing like an angry gorilla. It picked up the kitchen table and threw it toward the dining room. Missed, hit the wall and she heard it splinter with a loud crack like it had been hit with a sledgehammer.

Was she really going to do this?

She could barricade the door to her bedroom. Thought about that for a second and then stuffed the idea into her mental waste basket.

She would head for the panic room. Gently she opened her bedroom door, took the .25 out of her pocket and with both guns held out in front of her, started softly padding down the hallway.

The stairway was five steps ahead. The beast, whatever it was, was busy destroying the kitchen. Down the stairway, one jog to the right, down the second stairway would put her just outside the living room. A quick sprint to the panic room door, enter the six-digit code and she'd be behind a three-inch-thick steel plate door. Down ten more steps and she'd be in the concrete bunker. If the thing saw her, she'd open fire and blow its face off.

No telltale creaks as she descended to the floor, but the beast was making so much noise trashing the place it wouldn't have heard her, anyway. Four steps to the edge of the landing, then a quick look at the gold framed painting of her mother and father before starting down the last stairway. The air was suffused with a musky scent, like the smell from a big carnivore's cage mixed with the odor of rotted meat. She felt the denim shirt like a warm wet cloth on her back. A drop of sweat slid down her nose and she wiped it away with her forearm.

Each step down the last flight of stairs, she was ready to pull the triggers and empty both guns into whatever it was if it came at her. She'd taught concealed carry classes and wasn't afraid of a one-on-one if it came to it with another person. But whatever was downstairs wasn't remotely human.

One step more and she'd be at the bottom of the stairs.

She heard it near the den, hammering on something with its fists or paws or whatever the hell it had. Glass shattered like a chair had been thrown against the trophy cabinet and she was around the corner and running down the hall for all she was worth. A sudden roar from behind her as she made it to the first panic room door and started punching numbers on the keypad, but even when the lock disengaged, she knew she was out of time. The pounding footsteps were too close. She yanked the door open and got halfway behind it as she started firing. She felt a terrible pain as the .25 was slashed away from her hand and bounced down the hallway.

But she got in three shots to its center of mass as she took in the yellow eyes, long sharp fangs and the awful horns. It howled in pain and fell against one wall, sprang back up and struggled to balance on the edge of the stairs leading to the vault. With blood pouring down her left arm, she pulled out from behind the door, shot the beast in the thigh with her .38, and as it moved back with another enraged howl, she fired again at its thick hairy throat, and then got inside and slammed the steel door behind her.

Her left arm and hand going rapidly numb, she pocketed the .38 and forced the bolt home with her right. She gasped with pain and leaned against the stair railing, breathing heavily and brushing her hair away from her eyes. After a quick look down at the bloody floor, she turned away. She had to get the vault before she passed out.

The .25 was somewhere back in the hallway outside the panic room door, and it could stay there. Her ears were ringing, and she hoped she hadn't blown out an eardrum. Her arm was throbbing. Please God, not an artery. No time to think about that. Medical supplies in the vault. She had to keep going.

She got moving down the stairs, leaning against the wall for support. The soft glow of the filament lighting running along the ceiling was better than being blind. The second bunker door was only a few feet away when she heard the thing crashing like a hairy tank against the door at the top of the stairs.

Too much steel for it to get through, she thought.

She hurried down to the cement landing, entered the second set of codes, and held her breath until the door slid open. For the first time in her life, Rebecca Mihaloff was very, very glad her father was a rabid survivalist.

****

Blood dribbled down her arm and onto the laundry room floor as she staggered forward. The bunker was a twenty-four hundred square foot rectangle. Complete with laundry room, plant room, decked out kitchen, living room, four sleeping rooms, meat locker, food storage, bathrooms, independent water supply, filtered air, independent escape tunnel and, thank God, a complete medical room.

The lights turned on automatically as she stepped into it, and she took a step back and swung her gun up when she saw herself in the mirror. Bloody tangled hair, blood-soaked shirt. More blood smeared across her face where she'd wiped a blood trickle away from her eyes. Her left sleeve was ripped open, and she could see the ugly gash that cut across her forearm. The skin on the back of her hand was ripped and torn back. She could feel shock taking over.

Bandages and adhesive tape. Peroxide. With her one good hand, she raided the cabinet and carried the supplies over to the sink, and placed them on a stainless steel tray. The throbbing pain helped her focus, as long as she didn't think too much about what she would do. But it was hard not to notice that everything she'd touched was smeared with blood.

No time for anything fancy. She picked up a pair of stainless-steel scissors and cut away as much of her shirt as she could one-handed and let the bloody material drop to the black and white tiled floor. The urge to stumble over to a nearby cot, flop down on it and just close her eyes seemed like a great idea, except she didn't want to bleed to death. Instead, she used her left armpit to hold the big bottle of hydrogen peroxide and unscrewed it with her right hand. The top dropped to the floor and onto the bloody shirt scraps.

She upended the bottle over her arm and hand and let it pour while she held her jaws clamped shut in an ugly grimace. With surreal fascination, she watched the pink blood water foam and drain down the sink. Maybe she should have just used water, but she wasn't that clearheaded, and she didn't want her wounds to get infected. That thing's claws had ripped her good.

A horned monster clawed me, doctor.

No, that just wouldn't fly. And calling 911 would be no good with that thing out there.

With the wound as clean and disinfected as she knew how, she dropped the peroxide bottle, put one end of a roll of surgical gauze in her teeth and started winding it around her left arm with her right. Blood was still seeping, and it bloomed red against the whiteness of the gauze, but she kept winding. She bit back the pain and struggled to stay conscious.

When she was finished, she went back to the cabinet and got Amoxicillin and Narco. Sitting down in front of the computer security system, she opened the bottles and swallowed two pills from each. As she did so, she remembered TV shows complaining that people took antibiotics for minor wounds, and other advertisements warning that pain pills were addictive. This caused her to remember why she quit watching TV.

She washed the pills down with a bottle of spring water from the tiny fridge under the desk. Nothing had ever tasted so sweet as that water. She went over to the computer and fell back against a chair.

The system booted quickly and brought up more of the same cams she'd used upstairs. A click of the mouse and she was looking at the hallway outside the panic room.

Things had changed.

In the computer-enhanced light, she could see a woman crouched next to the monster on the floor. No doubt about it—if there ever was—it was a beast from the world of nightmares. Face like an ape, wolf and a raptor. Its head was lying in the woman's lap, staring right up at the camera. Almost like it knew Rebecca was staring down at them. Its rheumy yellow eyes compressed at the corners, its mouth opened and she saw hair fly back from the woman's face but didn't hear a sound. She realized the speakers were off, and then, after thinking about it first, she turned them on.

"You," came the furious voice from the speakers. "Who are you?"

Even the pain flaring along her arm like a vein of fire didn't take away her shock at hearing the words.

With a trembling finger, Rebecca muted the microphone. Never, her father had taught her, give information to an enemy. This woman on the security screen gently cradling the head of the mottled-skin creature that had clawed her arm and hand so badly was definitely an enemy.

She wore a dark robe with a hood pulled back and to one side. Long, thick, luxurious hair that hung over her shoulders like a glossy black mantle. Wide eyes, high cheekbones and eyes that would make a cat jealous. Something dark smudged the woman's forehead. Seething with anger and the need to take it out on someone. An enraged priestess holding her demon while its lifeblood dripped on Rebecca's father's new carpet.

It was a witching moon. She should have known the terrors would begin this night.

The pain pills were hitting her faster than she would have thought. Her focus blurred in and out. But the woman and the monster were still there. Pain throbbed inside the windings of her bandaged arm and her hand felt numb. She felt herself weaving back and forth. Time to make a call before she fell out of the chair.

Before she could punch in the numbers, the woman's voice came through the speakers again.

"I will have what is his."

Her voice had a sultry, commanding quality to it. She stood up as she spoke, dropping the monster's head to one side as she rose, and it turned to sand. It hit the floor and stayed down. Up and toward the camera, the darkly exotic woman came. She stared directly at it with every step she took.

As she got closer, Rebecca could see that what she had thought was a dark smudge on the woman's forehead was the number 666. Before taking another breath, Rebecca punched in the number of her father's cell phone and listened to it ring before it finally went to voicemail. The fear helped her focus enough to leave a nearly coherent message, and then weakness overcame her totally and she fell out of the chair, unconscious.

22

Rebecca lay on the floor in a bloody heap. Her breathing was stertorous and came in shuddering gasps. The floor was cool, black-and-white marble smeared with red blood. Her mouth was half-open and a mixture of saliva and blood leaked onto the floor. For a while, she floated in dark unconsciousness, but then dreamed prophetic visions from long ago of the monster who was coming…

****

Beneath the Temple Mount- Jerusalem 1118

"Send them away."

The heat was scarcely bearable, even underground. It felt as though by digging so far down that they were getting closer and closer to hell. The underground air, normally still as a dead man's chest, now sighed through the tunnels and gasped in the cavern where they stood talking in low tones.

"But they can still dig."

"At once, I tell you."

"Has something happened?" Geoffrey tried to look past his commander, but the man stepped even with him to continue blocking his view.

"At once," repeated Hugh de Payens. The intensity of his stare shocked Knight Geoffrey.

"Yes, Commander."

"Disperse them quietly. Do this quickly. Our lives may depend on this. Then gather your brother knights and return to me, leaving Rossal and Gondamer to guard the entrance."

Geoffrey saw, for the first time since he had known Hugh de Payens, a look of haunted terror that stiffened the man's posture and kept his eyes nervously roaming along the walls of the anteroom.

"I will, Commander. What do you prefer I tell them?"

"Tell them," began the commander, "that... that... that today is a day of sacred remembrance to us and that we will spend the rest of the day in prayer and reading our sacred texts. Or whatever you think best. Each of you must return armed for battle. Step with urgency."

"Battle?" asked a confused Geoffrey.

"Something walks beneath our feet," said Hugh de Payens, "and we must decide whether to kill it or save it."

A now nervous Geoffrey looked down at the dust and rock beneath his sandals. What did this mean? How could something walk beneath his feet? How could his commander see beneath the stone? Yet, the commander often saw things that others did not. Twice he had been visited by angelic messengers. Thrice he had rebuked demonic presences that held priests enthralled. No, he did not doubt Hugh de Payens' sanity. The two things his commander was closest to were God and death. On any given day, it was a matter of consideration which stood nearest to him. Tonight, nearly thirty feet below the Al-Aqsa Mosque, Geoffrey passionately hoped it was the Almighty who stood closest to him.

"Hurry," said Hughes de Payens as he drew his sword. "I will hold back what I can hold back until you return. Let no one see your fear. It is bad enough that the devil smells it."

****

The pitch torches spat and sputtered along the rough rock walls as the chastised Geoffrey hurried purposefully back down the tunnel. His sword gripped in his left hand and a torch in the other, he led them to the remaining knights save Rossal and Gondamer, who remained behind to guard the entrance to the excavated tunnel as instructed. Andre and Archambaud had insisted on the torches. They had more experience in these matters than Geoffrey, and knew that demons recoiled from fire. Archambaud kept a vial of water thrice blessed by the Holy Father tied to his belt. Godfrey de Saint-Omer and Payne de Monteverdi brought up the rear. They were men more seasoned in combat with other men than with spiritual warfare. "A sword slices through flesh and spirit alike and cleaves it clean," was Godfrey's belief, and Payne de Monteverdi was of one accord with that idea.

Seven knights and the commander made eight. Geoffrey prayed they were enough to prevail against whatever had terrified their commander.

They rounded the corner that led them to the downward leading stairs they had discovered after six months of backbreaking excavation. Geoffrey stopped before them and held up his sword. He could hear only in his right ear, and he turned his head to discern the sounds more clearly.

"What is it?" whispered Archambaud from behind.

Geoffrey thought he heard voices.

"Voices ahead."

"But you said there was no one left down here but Hugh de Payens," said Archambaud.

"He missed someone," said Andre in a voice soft enough not to carry.

"No," said Geoffrey. "I missed no one."

"But you said you heard voices, as in more than one voice," protested Archambaud.

"Aye," said Geoffrey.

In a tunnel with no side legs, it was impossible for him to have missed anyone trying to conceal themselves. Who then was the other man speaking with their commander?

"What are they saying?" whispered Archambaud.

"I can't tell. I can hear the commander, but I can scarcely hear the other. It is like a whisper."

"Let's go find out," said Andre.

Geoffrey looked back to see the other knights nodding in agreement.

Still, something in the voices coming from below made him feel uneasy. Perhaps it was his certainty that when he left, the only man in the cavern below had been Hugh de Payens. Was there yet another tunnel that led to the surface?

There was no really good plan to make use of as they stepped onto the stairs and began their downward trek, swords in one hand and torches in the other. There was not enough breadth to go down two abreast. It was a soldier's nightmare. And their torches would be seen as they approached. There was no help for that either, as to approach in total darkness was madness. So careful were they as they stepped, that the occasional crackling of the torch flames made more noise than their feet during the descent.

As they neared the last step, Geoffrey's heart and lungs pumped like an overheated bellows. The air in the tunnel seemed to thicken, and without thinking, he prayed the Knight's Prayer over and again. At the bottom of the steps was the archway covered with strange markings that led to the cavern where he had left Hugh de Payens. As the five knights stepped through that arch and into the open area, they saw to their amazement their commander on his knees, talking excitedly to the floor.

****

"How long?" asked Geoffrey for the third time.

He leaned forward as close to the hole in the floor as he could, but yet off to the side just enough that a blade shoved through from beneath the floor would not put out his eyes or do worse damage.

"Let me out," echoed the voice from the chamber below.

"How long?" repeated Geoffrey.

The other knights were gathered around him at each point of the compass. Hugh de Payens rose and stood off to the side, stroking his beard and shaking his head as he had since they had arrived. The mystery of it all confounded him. Down many broken stone floors below was a man who, according to him, had been secured by chains since before the destruction of the second temple.

"Mercy, have mercy; I'm dying of thirst."

"I doubt it," whispered Archambaud to Hugh de Payens. "The son of a jackal has been chained and buried beneath the earth for over two thousand years and he is going to die of thirst now? Fah. Demon-possessed, I tell you. I've heard that the wretches who are demon-possessed can live for thousands of years. Difficult to kill, commander, but not impossible. We can make a length of rope half a pied du roi in length, lower ourselves down and cut him in half. An old man told me once they'd finally had to quarter one such as this and bury him the length of a man deep. They dug him up a year later and his head was still talking like a crow."

Hugh de Payens looked at Archambaud, betraying no reaction. The man was afraid of nothing, true to the One Faith, more loyal than a hound, and yet, he was the most gullible man the commander had ever met.

"I heard that," said the man far below. "I know not why, but I thirst."

"And if he is not alone?" asked Hugh de Payens calmly. "What then? Also, have you considered that he may be unchained?"

"Have you considered," said Archambaud, "that he may not be human?"

Geoffrey looked over at the big man in alarm as he scooted away from the enlarged crack. They had found it easy to chip away at the opening. Over a matter of hours, they had enlarged it so it would comfortably allow two men with supported ropes to descend at a time. But they did not. All were very nervous at just who might wait for them at the bottom. At first, they could see nothing at all in the darkness. After much discussion, they had decided that Geoffrey should drop a lighted pitch torch over the edge. It fell too quickly for him to see much at all except for broken stone and abrupt blackness as it flared like a corposant rushing to eternal darkness. When it finally struck, it burst like a hive of fireflies and then was swallowed whole by the gloom.

"Human or not," said Andre nervously, "I am re-thinking this. Perhaps we should fill this opening with rock again and seal it over with pitch. It is unholy enough for this creature who speaks like a man to be alive for so long."

A thought struck Geoffrey.

"How is it we can understand it? How is it able to comprehend our speech? If it was indeed buried beneath the destruction of the second temple, should it not be speaking an old tongue?"

Hugh de Payens considered the question, realizing that the being below alone held the answer to the riddle.

"Ask it," he said.

Geoffrey leaned toward the opening and asked the question. His voice echoed down the hole, and he marveled again at the way his voice and that of the thing below carried so easily.

"How is it you speak our language?"

Moments passed, as though it were considering.

"I was," it finally replied, "present at the day of Pentecost, when the tongues of fire descended on many of us and gave some the gift of tongues."

"Impossible," said Archambaud, and he crossed himself quickly.

Godfrey de Saint-Omer and Payne de Monteverdi were on the far side of the ragged, elongated opening.

"Send us down," said Godfrey, "to reason with it."

He patted his sword affectionately as he spoke. He was a big man, almost the size of Rossal and Gondamer, the two bearded hulks who guarded the entrance.

Payne de Monteverdi, who could have been Godfrey's twin save for missing most of his left ear—which was honorably lost in battle and why he grew his hair thick and long to cover it—grunted his approval.

"Keep the shrewd men up top," said Payne, "and send the bluntest to the bottom."

Hugh de Payens ruffled his thick beard as he mulled over Payne's suggestion. There was merit in it, but it was the tactics involved which he did not appreciate. From the torch's descent, they had estimated that the voice who claimed to be a prisoner was in a dungeon cell three levels below. It was difficult to estimate the actual distance, but Archambaud had been right when he suggested they connect a long length of rope to lower them to where this man or thing was trapped. Yet only one man could realistically be lowered at a time.

"Ask it its name first," said Archambaud. "No demon will reveal its name."

Hugh de Payens nodded his approval to Geoffrey.

Geoffrey was not sure if a demon would refuse to give its name, but he asked anyway.

"You below," he called into the pit. "What is your name?"

A minute, then two passed with no answer.

"Aha," said Archambaud.

"Hiram Abiff," came the belated, drawn-out response. "My name is Hiram Abiff. I have not been asked for so many centuries, I had almost forgotten my reply. I was the Great Architect of the first Jerusalem temple and the Great Architect for the second temple as well."

"It proves nothing," said Archambaud. "How do we know it is his true name? Hiram Abiff? I have not heard a name such as that ever before."

Hugh de Payens stood and ambled away from the pit. With a wave of his hand, he motioned the others to follow. One by one, Geoffrey, Archambaud, Andre, Payne de Monteverdi, and Godfrey followed him to huddle two steps away from a hissing torch held in place by an iron bracket they had pounded into the wall.

"I must decide," began their commander, "whether to confront this troubling matter or simply bury it. Before doing so, I would hear your advisements. What have you to say?"

It was no dispersion upon their discernment or their will to act that they were confounded so long before responding. Never had knights of the cross been confronted with such a dilemma. They were men of differing character, but had in common the hard life of knights and their unshakable faith in their Lord and Savior. What they faced now was not the sharp steel of a determined enemy, but a question of faith. Was it possible that God himself had ordained the wretch buried beneath the rubble at their feet to live for a thousand years?

"God gave it to Methuselah to live for nearly a thousand years," said Archambaud. "It is possible that he also appointed another to do the same or longer. And Adam lived nearly as long. Yet, if whatever it is chained up down there is lying, we must forever bury it away from men."

"If it lies, we should cut off its head and send it straight back to hell," said Andre.

There followed murmurs of agreement and furtive glances back toward the pit. Never had men faced such a decision.

"I have a question to pose," said Godfrey.

The tone in his voice caused the others to quiet and wait expectantly. Godfrey's usual response to most of life's conundrums was whether to pull his sword or return it to its sheath.

"If the thing below is chained, who chained it and why?"

"Perhaps it was a prisoner," said Andre. "A prisoner awaiting judgment. A murderer or a captured enemy. If it is, as it says from the days of the second temple, it may have been a Jew fighting against the Romans."

"That makes no sense," said Geoffrey. "Why would the Romans chain a Jew beneath the second temple instead of executing him? They could have crucified him, as they did our Lord."

His voice trailed off and a look of wonderment crossed his grime-covered features. He rubbed the side of his calloused forefinger on the bridge of his nose.

"Speak," said Hugh de Payens. "What is it?"

When Geoffrey turned to face his fellow knights, his expression was that of a man who has seen a great wonder. In the lambent torch light, his face seemed to glow with excitement even as though they were surrounded by shadows and dust.

"Could he have been alive during the time of our Lord? Could he have seen Christ as a man? Is that possible? Can we have unwittingly come upon a living witness to the crucifixion?"

"Stop," said Archambaud. "Think. If it is a demon, it will say whatever you want to hear. It is their way."

The thought of that sobered them all. A living witness kept alive by the power of God or a demon who would say that same thing only to deceive them?

"Have we no criterion to measure this question?" asked a distraught Hugh de Payens.

"My sword," said a grim-faced Godfrey.

"And mine," said Andre.

"He has neither eaten nor drunk, he says, in over a thousand years," mused Geoffrey. "How is it he lives?"

"That was not my question," said Hugh de Payens. "Against what criterion can we measure this thing?"

"But that is what I am thinking. He has neither eaten nor drunk, but he asked us for water. Have we not water to test him?"

"How will that test him?" asked Archambaud. "What will that prove? Cannot a demon drink water?"

"I think so, but can he drink that water?"

Geoffrey pointed at the flask that always hung at Archambaud's belt. The flask that held water thrice blessed by the Holy Father.

"Never," said Archambaud.

He said it so forcefully that for a moment, it appeared he would draw his sword.

"How could you suggest such a thing? This water was given to me by the hand of the Holy Father himself. It is three times blessed."

"Yes," said Geoffrey patiently. "I know. And that is the point—can a demon drink holy water? He has asked us for water. What say we give it to him without revealing its sacred nature? If he drinks it and lives, then he lives by God's allowance, and we must assist and even rescue him. If he dies, then one less demon will desecrate this world."

Archambaud's affronted look gradually waned and was replaced with a look of resolve. He squared his shoulders as though standing for inspection. This was a course of action he could endorse with his whole spirit. He released the leather thong that held it tight to his belt and handed it to Geoffrey.

"It is yours," he said simply.

"No," said their commander. "It must be you who unmasks the truth of this thing. The thrice blessed water is yours, given to your charge by the hand of the Holy Father himself. You must be the one, and you must go alone."

"Will you pray for me before my descent?" asked Archambaud.

"We will pray for your safe return," said Hugh de Payens.

****

The last face Knight Archambaud saw as the others slowly let out the knotted rope was that of his commander, Hugh de Payens, leader of the Knights of the Temple. He wondered as he was lowered into the darkness if Hugh's would be the last human face he ever saw.

It had taken three days and the blessing of the King of Jerusalem to secure sufficient rope and other materials for Knight Archambaud to be lowered into the pit. He did not know what stories the commander had invented to get the rope, the cage and the wheel made, but it had taken half a day just to transport the mechanical assemblage and half a day more to mount it to the floor of the cavern. A curved sheet of brass had been placed over the lip of the pit to prevent the rope from being frayed by its jagged edge. With each spike pounded in the floor to secure it, Archambaud had to force himself not to shudder at what a straight drop into darkness and instant death would be like. He decided it might be a better way to die than being eaten by a demon. As the wood and rope cage jerked with each turn of the ratchet and wheel, it was like his heart skipping a beat.

"How are you?" he heard Geoffrey ask.

"He's only down ten yards," said Andre. "I can still see his torch."

"Remember to keep the torch away from the rope," said Geoffrey.

"Yes, mother," he called back.

The ancient space beneath the mosque carried sound like a music chamber, he thought.

"Can you see anything?" asked Hugh de Payens.

Remarkable. It appeared his commander was calling to him from three yards away. It must be something in the sacred geometry of the second sacred temple. He remembered the scripture that said, "And all the people shouted with a great shout, when they praised the LORD, because the foundation of the house of the LORD was laid. But many of the priests and Levites and heads of fathers' houses, old men who had seen the first house, wept with a loud voice when they saw the foundation of this house being laid, though many shouted aloud for joy; so that the people could not distinguish the sound of the joyful shout from the sound of the people's weeping, for the people shouted with a great shout, and the sound was heard afar."

Never had he thought of the second temple constructed to magnify sound, but now he understood how they could so easily communicate with the person or thing that waited below. The Architect of the first and second temples. It sounded blasphemous, for was not the Lord God himself truly the Great Architect of these things? As sweat soaked the cloth wrapped around his chest, he attempted to re-balance himself in the cage they had constructed and found that to be a bad idea, as the sudden swaying and creaking of the ropes made him nauseated.

"I see nothing beyond the torchlight, my commander, except broken stone blocks and what look like fallen columns. It is difficult to see."

"Do you hear anything?" called Hugh de Payens.

"No. Nothing."

Nothing, he thought, except the icy fingers of death clawing toward me in this tenebrous tomb where a thing calling itself a man claims to have lived over a thousand years in darkness.

Lower.

He was lowered still further. But in the darkness, he wondered if he'd moved at all.

"How far down?" he called up.

"Fifteen yards," said Geoffrey.

How many yards left to go? If a demon waited below, how many yards would it be to his own death? He closed his eyes and prayed for strength. As he did so, his fingers tightened reflexively around the hilt of his sword.

When he opened them, he was still in darkness, save for the fiery light of the torch. Then, a flash of coppery gold. Archambaud blinked, then blinked again.

"Twenty yards," he heard Geoffrey call down to him.

"I've seen something," he called back up.

"Tell me," commanded Hugh de Payens.

"Tell him," came the obscene voice from below.

It seemed to him as if it was taunting.

"Something. Something bright to my right side. I can't say how far away, but it flashed golden in the torch's light."

The cage slowly stopped jerking and swaying as though Andre had engaged the ratchet lock. For long seconds, he seemed to hang suspended between heaven and hell.

"Did you say gold?" asked Hugh de Payens.

From down below, in the black pool of tar that was the pit, Archambaud heard soft laughter.

23

"A statue? You say a statue did this?"

Too much on his to-do list to be involved in this, but Ian Hunter desperately needed the rest of his uncle Bartok's papers. The Detroit Masons had them, and he wanted them. More than anything in the world, he wanted those papers. If he had to spend a few minutes talking to a crazy man to get them, it was worth it. Besides, he and Moser had received a Masonic summons to go to Detroit and help with a "paranormal" problem. So, they were killing two birds with one stone.

They'd had no luck hunting for the piece of alien crystal Bartok had said was in Atlanta. When they'd descended on the darkened house miles from the city, they'd found only the ripped-to-pieces remains of a tentacled creature in the basement and a blackened hole blown in the concrete floor. A twisted safe lay on the cement, its door broken away from the hinges and thrown in a metal laundry tub like discarded scrap.

"Let me unstrap his neck brace," said the doctor. "It will make it easier for him to talk."

The other five men watched intently as the neck brace came away and exposed the patchwork of yellow-purple bruises that circled Mike Leasing's thick neck like a death scarf. Leasing closed his eyes while they stared at him. Brothers Mihaloff, Kaufman and Cook had already seen the damage, but it was the first time Hunter and Moser had gotten a look.

Hunter swung his phone up and took a picture.

"No pictures," snapped Brother Mihaloff.

"I've got my reasons and we'll talk about it later," said Hunter, with a trace of irritation in his voice. He said it with enough edge that Brother Mihaloff scowled, thought better of it, then leaned back again in his chair. When it came to the paranormal, Hunter didn't take instructions, he gave them. It was the way his uncle Bartok had taught him.

"Can you talk?" Hunter asked Leasing.

He knew taking the man's neck brace away would not improve his ability to talk—but it made it easier to see the damage. Just something to say to get things moving.

"It hurts," Leasing half-croaked, "but I can manage."

His tone was flat; like he didn't want to use his vocal cords too much. Hunter winced just looking at what looked like the man's tattoo art hematoma. Moser didn't seem upset by the twisted mass of bruising and blood blotches on Leasing's neck. Hunter knew he'd seen worse. But Moser was definitely paying attention.

Hunter looked over at Brother Mihaloff. The older man with the long, white beard nodded for him to go ahead. Mihaloff looked like a cross between Nostradamus and Santa Claus. The only thing that ruined that image was his expensive black business suit. He re-focused on Leasing.

"You know why I'm here?" asked Hunter. "That is, do you know who I am?"

Leasing nodded and then shook his head no to the second question.

Hunter tried to imagine stone fingers crushing the man's throat and could almost see it, but not quite. It was a little too weird and not too possible. And the whole thing had been dropped on him out of the blue. He'd gotten a phone call in the middle of the night at the tail end of a dreadful nightmare. Worshipful Master of his Masonic Lodge told him there was Masonic business to take care of in Detroit. He'd been asked for specifically.

"Why do the Detroit Freemasons need a paranormal

investigator?" he'd asked.

"This is Masonic business. You're under obligation to keep it to yourself."

"When do they want me there?" he'd asked again.

"Now. Get there now. They sounded nervous. But remember, keep it to yourself."

"Can I take Moser?"

"Why?"

"We work as a team," he'd said.

"He's a brother so he will be allowed," said the Worshipful Master. "Get him and catch the next flight. I'll call ahead and tell them."

"Better to drive," he'd said. "I've got our equipment packed in the trunk."

"Godspeed, Brother," said the Worshipful Master.

"Worshipful, wait. Who's paying for this?"

But the phone connection was dead.

A ten-hour drive to Detroit. Then straight in to get the heads up from the Brothers Mihaloff, Kaufman and Cook at the Detroit Masonic Temple. The largest Masonic Temple in the entire world. Hunter had researched it on his tablet on the way in, looking for anything that could tell him about the paranormal history of the place, but there was barely anything to find.

"Listen to his story. Tell us if you've ever heard of anything like it," said Brother Mihaloff when they got there. A big, imposing man with an authoritative voice. He was the one who did most of the talking when they'd arrived. "Then, do what you do. Investigate. We need you on this. Big things going on here. Enormous. Can't have anything that would stop the event. You must sort this out."

"Why can't you tell me what happened?"

"You need to hear it for yourself," said Brother Cook.

"Why is it so important?"

This time it was Brother Kaufman who answered.

"Because you're a fellow Mason. That should be enough."

"That's it?" he asked.

"That's it," said Brother Cook.

Moser gave him the eye.

"Okay, we'll do it," said Hunter

But he'd had a bad feeling about agreeing to it. He wondered if they'd used the Grand Hailing sign over Skype to the Worshipful Master of his own lodge and it almost made him laugh until they walked by a row of windows in the lodge, and he realized with a start that it was coming up on dark again. Outside, the Detroit night was crowding against the Temple's stained-glass windows like a killer looking for victims.

Keep moving, he thought. Get this over with.

"My name is Ian Hunter and I'm a paranormal investigator," he said to Brother Leasing. "I investigate the paranormal and write books about the supernatural. I have a lot of experience in the technical aspects of things that go bump in the night. I'm also an engineer, but I'm a fellow Mason. And I'm under Masonic oath. What you tell me stays with those of us in this room, unless you decide otherwise, brother."

With a slight jerk of his head, Leasing indicated Moser.

"Same with me," said Moser.

Enid Moser was less into talking than he was listening.

"Tell me what happened," said Hunter.

The doctor took a chair beside Leasing, then slid back to put a little distance between them.

Crazy might be contagious, thought Hunter.

"I know it will sound like I've lost my mind, but I'm not nuts," said Leasing. There was a careful, constricted quality to his voice. His bloodshot eyes were hard to look at. "Just give me a second."

"Could the pressure on his neck have broken blood vessels in his eyes?" Hunter asked the doctor while Leasing pulled himself together.

"Maybe," said the doctor.

The doctor's name was easy enough to remember. Smith. Dr. Smith. Ian Hunter wondered if that was that was his real name. It was hard to imagine a Mason meeting another Mason using an alias, but so far, the whole thing was very, very weird.

"Okay," Hunter said to Leasing, "Just tell me what happened. Don't worry if it sounds crazy. Moser and I have heard and seen lots of crazy. Hauntings, spirit voices, ghosts, demons, curses. I draw the line at vampires, werewolves and Bigfoot, but other than that, I try to keep an open mind."

He smiled slightly, trying to keep it light. Leasing wasn't having any of it. He looked like he was about to have a breakdown. Whether it was from the anxiety of recounting something horrific or the effort of keeping up a lie in front of so many people, Hunter couldn't tell. Or maybe he was just a crazy working up to another psychotic break. He wished they hadn't left their guns in the car. Since the events at Townsend Mountain, Hunter rarely went anywhere without a firearm.

"Before we get started, Mike, are you on any medications?" asked Hunter.

Dr. Smith placed his hand on Mike Leasing's forearm and answered for him by shaking his head.

"Just Xanax half an hour before you got here to lower his anxiety."

"Good enough," continued Hunter. "Like I said, don't worry if it sounds crazy. Moser and I can sort that out later. Just tell us everything that happened that night—three nights ago, wasn't it?"

"My first night," whispered Leasing.

He looked nervously at the three older brothers—Mihaloff, Kaufman and Cook.

"I don't understand. Your first night?"

"On the job," said Leasing in a coarse whisper. "My first night as a Watchman. Old man Miller was supposed to... supposed to walk the floor with me."

Hunter looked over at Brother Mihaloff, but it was Brother Kaufman—the one with the round, shiny head and fierce eyes who answered his unspoken question.

"Brother Leasing was recently accepted into the Order of Watchmen. The Order of Watchmen are unique to our Detroit Masonic Temple, brother. Most Masonic Temples are too small for there to be a need for Watchmen. There are other large temples around the world, of course, but they do not share our tradition," said Brother Kaufman.

"Why only here?" asked Moser.

"Let's stay on topic," said Brother Mihaloff irritably. "The biggest Masonic event in history is taking place in this building inside of two weeks. We have spent millions rebuilding the Unfinished Theater to hold over five hundred VIP Masons coming in for the event from all over the world. We have no time for digressions. It is urgent that we stay on topic. We have less than fourteen days to resolve this matter. So, I repeat—stay on topic."

Moser turned his head to lock eyes with the old man. When Hank Moser drew a bead on a man, they generally turned away in discomfort. Brother Mihaloff did not.

Moser nodded. That didn't mean he forgot. Moser never forgot. And Hunter had never seen him forgive.

"And who is old man Miller?" resumed Hunter after an uncomfortable silence.

"He was the Temple Watchmaster," said Brother Kaufman.

"What exactly is that?" asked Moser, scratching the stubble on his chin.

"Later," said Brother Mihaloff.

There was something about the man's attitude that annoyed Hunter. No matter what he said, it came out like he was telling you to sit down and shut up. What was he so on edge about? Why the undertone of aggression? He and Moser were there at their request. They had answered the Masonic summons. Not exactly answering a Grand Hailing Sign of Distress, more like showing up because they'd been ordered to by the court. So why the attitude? Brothers Kaufman and Cook were more restrained, but they didn't look all that happy that he and Moser were there. They had that "you're not wanted here" thing going on like it was his idea to butt into their problem. He wanted to remind them that they invited him, not the other way around. But then again, maybe Kaufman and Cook didn't find out until tonight. Maybe just Mihaloff had invited him and Moser. Hunter could sense an undertone of anxiety and impatience in the way Mihaloff kept twisting his Masonic ring around and around, as though trying to screw it off his finger. Maybe it was all his idea to have them here. Hunter looked over again at Cook. Now there was an odd one. Big man, maybe six and a half feet tall. Bulky chest and shoulders for a man in his late sixties or early seventies. Like an advertisement for senior weight lifters.

He remembered suddenly last night's dream about the dead, but still alive Major Albert Magnus Hillis, suspended in the air eight feet off the floor, connected to the army of automatons by a spiderweb of glassine tubules. Pulsing with aethyric ectoplasm that flashed through his memory. The one that caused him to shoot straight up to a sitting position and open his mouth to scream. But he'd looked wildly around the room before realizing it was just a nightmare. Realized he was alone in his motel room. Realized he was safe, but didn't quite believe it.

He'd gotten up, gotten dressed and paced the room, trying to burn off the nervous energy. He'd taken the ghost box out of its case for the third time last night and tried again to figure out how it worked. Again, he gave up in frustration, knowing that he had been trying to distract himself from the desperate idea that if he tried to make a run for it, that It would be waiting for him in the parking lot.

Maybe he was reading too much into the way the three brothers were acting because he was still feeling wound up by the nightmare. Maybe he'd brought last night's fears with him into tonight's meeting. But Moser seemed to feel it, too. These men were well and truly frightened.

On top of all that, there was the building itself. Not just the dark paneled, depressing room they were sitting in with a man who believed a statue had tried to murder him. Maybe it was the entire place. The entire Detroit Masonic Temple. Over fourteen hundred rooms and fourteen stories of concrete, steel and neo-Gothic architecture. No. That was a ridiculous thought. But there were stories layered upon stories of haunted buildings in his files. Every ghost hunter ran into them. Buildings that just didn't feel right. If you dug down deep enough, there were always terrible things that had occurred within their walls. Terrible events that stained them and couldn't be wiped away. Like those discolorations you painted over, but seeped through again.

Hunter pulled himself back together.

"This Watchmaster, this old man Miller, you said he was showing you the rounds last night?" he asked Leasing.

"That's right."

"And did he see what happened?"

Leasing looked uneasily at the three senior Masons.

"Brother Leasing," said Hunter sharply, "there's no need to look for their permission. Just tell me the truth and get on with it. Did he see what happened?"

Without looking, Hunter could guess the reactions of Brothers

Mihaloff, Kaufman and Cook. But he didn't care anymore. What could they do, kick him out of the Masons? For what?

"Tell him," said Brother Mihaloff.

"Not because he says so," said Hunter irritably. "Because I'm asking you and you want me to know."

Brother Mihaloff bristled, but Hunter held out a hand to shut him up.

"Go on," he said to Leasing.

The doctor pushed his chair back a little further from the table, opened a latched leather duffel, drew out a small black case and placed it on his lap.

"We were walking the floors," said Leasing. "It's tradition. First month, you walk the floors with the Watchmaster. Been that way forever. Anyway, we were up on the fifth floor when it happened. I was walking with the old man in the middle like we're supposed to, staying away from the walls, eyes straight ahead. He was in front and me following right behind him."

Leasing's voice was sliding back into that I'm there now, re-living what I want to forget quality that Hunter had heard so many times before from victims of paranormal experiences. He had an urge to interrupt him and tell him not to go there when he suddenly was sure that he could feel the darkness outside the building listening in. It must be the Masonic Temple itself, Hunter thought. It was the biggest Masonic Temple in the world. He'd looked it up while Moser was driving, searching for any information on hauntings and paranormal events reported there over the years. From the images he'd found, it certainly looked like a place where malevolent spirits would gather. The Haunted Masonic Temple. The name seemed to fit, which led him to wonder why Leasing and the other Watchmen were told to stay away from the walls. He'd have to research that. Maybe Molly could find something he'd missed. If she would talk to him.

"We were down the hall with the two monk statues," continued Leasing in a voice hoarse with repressed terror, "the ones holding the Book of Life that's in a lot of the brochures. One on each side. The Guardians of the Arch, Watchmaster Miller said they were called."

Hunter could see the blank look of despair behind Leasing's eyes when he said old man Miller's name again, heard the tremor in his voice and saw—in spite of the obvious pain—his neck muscles tighten.

With Leasing's bloodshot eyes staring wide and straight past him like he wasn't there, Hunter risked a look at Dr. Smith. The doctor was watching Leasing closely. Without looking down, he opened the black case and reached inside.

"There was this crash, this boom, like a wrecking ball slammed into the wall behind the statue," said Leasing.

He rubbed the tip of his right index finger against the fleshy part of his thumb, as though sharpening one against the other.

"It scared the hell out of me, so I kind of jumped back—from the shock, I guess—and I heard Miller yell something, but I can't remember what. I was looking right at the one statue of the monk. The one with the hood down low over his face. Looks like he's praying. Miller was still yelling and pointing past me. I turned around to see what he was pointing at and, uh, I, I…"

"Finish it up," said Moser. "We're all brothers here. Get it over with and you can go home."

Moser had a way about him, Hunter thought. Like a good father. His Kentucky voice was firm, reassuring, and it didn't take too many words to get to what he was trying to say.

"Well, okay. It was the other statue. The one where the monk is staring straight at you, like he's wanting to know your business. Only it came to life and reached out and grabbed me by the neck and started talking to me. Shaking me. I couldn't get away; I couldn't move. You ever been so scared that you shut down and there's nothing you can do about it, but just stand there and watch it happen? That's how it felt. Like I was scared out of my mind so bad I was drooling, but I couldn't move even one damned finger."

"What happened next?" asked Hunter, showing no reaction at all.

Like it was perfectly normal to ask a question like that.

Leasing looked like he would vomit.

"It pulled me close, and it spoke to me. The statue spoke to me."

"You said that. What did it say?"

Leasing's entire body started to shake, as though he was having a fit.

Dr. Smith stretched out his hand and placed it on Leasing's forearm to calm him down.

"Take a deep breath, Mike. Relax," he said. "Just a little more to get out, but we're done here. You need a little more rest."

"Wait a minute—" began Hunter.

But there was no need. Leasing wasn't through.

"It told me Hiram Abiff was coming. Like in the ritual. And it looked at me. I'm not crazy, I'm not. Its stone eyes moved. It could see me, I swear it. And it said it again. I tell you it told me that Hiram Abiff was coming."

"That's enough," said Dr. Smith. He said it with a hard edge. Not fooling around. "You can finish this later."

The doctor held Leasing's eyes while Hunter saw him withdraw a syringe from the case.

"Maybe," said Hunter, "we could talk to Brother Miller the Watchmaster instead. You look like you should take it easy for a bit."

The room went totally still. The doctor shot a concerned glance at Brother Mihaloff. Brothers Kaufman and Cook glared at him.

"Something wrong?" asked Moser.

"Something wrong?" screamed Leasing.

He stood up and shook a fist at Hunter.

"Something wrong?" he shouted again.

Hunter slid his chair back, and he saw Moser tense. Brother Michael Leasing looked like he was getting ready to punch somebody.

"Stop this," shouted Brother Mihaloff, but he stayed seated. The voice of authority.

It didn't work.

"I'll tell you what's wrong," said Leasing and at the same time he knocked his chair backward and swept the water pitcher and glasses off the table.

The doctor made a grab for him, but he shoved him to the floor. Brothers Mihaloff, Kaufman and Cook were out of their chairs and moving toward him. Hunter and Moser stood up and backed away. Let the others who know Leasing calm him down. If Moser got involved, someone always got hurt, Hunter thought. But recently that was true of him, too.

Brother Cook got around the table first and grabbed one of Leasing's arms while the doctor scrambled to his feet and searched frantically for the syringe the agitated young man had knocked away.

"Miller's dead, that's what's wrong."

Leasing's face turned a bright shade of red as he screamed it out.

"I saw the floor fall away behind him and he started sliding back into hell. Black mountains on fire. Big dark flying things coming up for him. He was sliding back and there wasn't anything I could do. It was so fast, so fast, then one of those things caught him in midair and—"

Brother Cook spun Leasing around, grabbed him by his shirt front, lifted him straight up into the air and then began shaking him.

"That's enough," he said, loud enough to burst an eardrum. "I said that's enough."

By that time, Dr. Smith had his syringe ready and plunged it straight into Leasing's neck and immediately depressed the plunger. The younger Mason kicked at him, but the doctor was expecting it and let it slide past. He withdrew the syringe while Brother Kaufman went to the aid of Brother Cook by grabbing Leasing's feet so they could haul him back to the table and lay him out while they restrained him.

"Brother Leasing," shouted Brother Mihaloff. "Control yourself. This is lodge business and you will get a grip on yourself."

That man, thought Hunter, is used to giving orders.

Leasing continued to struggle for a few moments, and then, gradually, his histrionics passed and he lay on the table sobbing while Kaufman and Cook still held him down. Finally, Dr. Smith told them to let him go.

"Get me something to put under his head," he told the two of them.

"Hell, it was hell," said Leasing.

He was rocking his head back and forth as he lay pinned on the table.

"Won't take long," said the doctor to Brother Mihaloff. "Worked up as he is, it's racing through his system."

"Is there anything we can do to help?" Hunter asked Brother Mihaloff.

"You've done enough," said Brother Cook with an angry edge to his voice.

"There's no reason for that," snapped Brother Mihaloff. To Hunter and Moser he said, "No, thank you. I think we're through here for the night."

Hunter looked down at his watch. Ten thirty. At least they'd be out before midnight, and that would give him a chance to see Molly. For once, he wouldn't have to cancel out at the last minute. Too bad he couldn't tell her what happened tonight. Masonic secrets stayed Masonic secrets.

"Do you need help moving him to someplace more comfortable?" said Moser.

"We can handle it," said the doctor.

On the table, Mike Leasing had passed out.

"Okay," said Hunter. "When it's convenient, would you like us to talk to Brother Miller?"

Again, the momentary silence.

Brother Mihaloff took his cell phone out of his pocket and turned it on. They had all turned their cell phones off before they closed the door and started talking to avoid interruptions. The doctor and the other two brothers looked nervously at Brother Mihaloff, who was frowning.

"I'm afraid that won't be possible," said Brother Mihaloff.

"I understand," said Hunter.

"I'm afraid you don't," said the older man. "You see, we can't find Brother Miller."

Hunter exchanged a look with Moser.

"Missing? When?"

Brother Mihaloff held up a hand.

"Sorry. Let me check this message from my daughter."

They all waited while he held the phone to his ear. The blood seemed to drain out of his face as he listened, and he suddenly held the phone away from his head as though it had bitten him.

"My God," he breathed.

He pointed at brothers Kaufmann and Cook.

"You two take care of finding Brother Michael a bed and watch over him. Something has happened to my daughter. Doctor, could you please come with me to my house? I'm afraid I will need your services."

Kaufman and Cook asked no questions but got moving. They lifted Leasing's sleeping body in the air and began backing toward the door.

"Brother Hunter, would you and Brother Moser come with us? I may need your help as well. Please."

Moser spoke for them both.

"If you need us, we're there."

"Good. We'll take my car."

"If you don't mind, Moser and I will take mine," said Hunter.

From the look on Brother Mihaloff's face, he'd thought they might need what they'd packed in the trunk.

24

"What the hell happened here?" said Hunter.

"I don't know. Looks like something ripped the garage door off with its bare hands," said Moser.

"Enid, you have a way with words," said Hunter.

"Yep."

"What have we gotten ourselves into?"

"Hell if I know, but it doesn't look good. I'd say Brother Mihaloff has been holding out on us."

"Well, if he's anything like my Uncle Bartok, we need to go for the firepower early."

"Shotguns?"

"Suits me," said Hunter.

The Mihaloff farmhouse was a turn of the century gabled Victorian with an expansive wrap-around porch and twin peaks jutting up toward the starless night sky like guard houses. Off to the side stood a steel building large enough to hold a private jet. The paved private driveway leading to the house was nearly half a mile long. Brother Mihaloff definitely had money.

The two cars idled in the cold, Hunter's headlights pointing to where the garage door used to be. Mihaloff's headlights were pointing at the dark symbol painted on the front door. Mihaloff was looking at something on his phone while Hunter and Moser waited for instructions from him.

"What's he doing?" asked Hunter.

"Everything's connected to his phone," said Moser. "Probably checking the inside security cams before he makes a move."

"Lights are out in the house. What could he see on the security cameras?"

"You ever hear of infrared? Still, something's like a stone in my shoe I can't find."

"Don't go Jed Clampett on me."

Moser gave him a quick grin.

"I just can't reason a man as cold-blooded as him. He's going through his phone, taking his time to make sure he gets it all before he makes a move. Why? If that was my daughter had called and was in trouble, I think I'd be a bit upset. Like he was back at the Detroit Temple. Got one of his brethren there in that room telling us about a statue trying to choke him and he's got that 'hurry it up, I'm late for a meeting look' about him. Then there's him and the others not wanting that man Leasing to say anything about what happened to Miller. Maybe I'm thinking too much, but it's like a little rock in my shoe. I can't find it, but it bothers me."

"Yeah," said Hunter. "I've been wondering if his daughter really is inside. Or maybe he thinks there's something inside that he's afraid of. What do you think? I don't know what to make of him or this deal at the Masonic Temple."

Moser ignored the question. "I checked in with Kenneth and Ashley," he said. "Everything's good there. I keep feeling we ought to make a move against that fella Mr. Chirac before he comes after them or us both. We been re-conning him for so long I'll be retired before we learn enough about him to do something about it. I just don't know if we have time for waiting."

"If we could just find out more about him, we might have a chance. But you're right. We have to re-think this whole thing. I keep expecting to read Kenneth's and Ashley's obituary online. I felt guilty going to Atlanta to look for the ship fragment, but I would have felt guilty if I'd stayed. I wish Bartok were here to tell us what to do."

"Hey, let's talk about something else," said Moser suddenly. "Have you seen that one before?" he asked, pointing at the symbol on the door.

Hunter studied it. Frowned. Moser was pointing at a barely visible large symbol painted on the front door. The porch light was off so that the occult representation was only visible in the headlight beams of Mihaloff's car. Even then, it was hard to see. The door was dark colored, and the symbol looked like it had been painted on with black paint. He could make out most of it, but he'd need a closer look.

"Maybe, but there's more occult symbols out there than Facebook users. Hard to keep up with them all."

"Serious?"

"No. It looks like an ownership or a possession symbol. Enochian or something one of the Crowley crackheads would put together. Maybe both. A lot of crossovers going on now."

"Anything we need to worry about?"

"Who knows," said Hunter. "But there's only one way to find out, and that's to get a closer look. Hard to see the details from here."

"You thinking this is tied in somehow to that statue strangling Leasing back at the lodge?"

"I don't know. But I think you're right that Brother Mihaloff is sure as hell holding something back. I'd like to find out what that is, and I'd like to get a closer look at that thing on the door before we go inside the house, though."

Even though they were waiting in the car with a backseat full of firearms, Hunter still had the feeling that if they'd arrived earlier, they would have been in serious trouble. It was just a premonition, but he took it seriously. Since his trip below Townsend Mountain with his Uncle Bartok, he'd changed. He had strange dreams that he hoped to God weren't prescient. And sometimes, like when he and Moser had gone below into the Atlanta underground looking for the fragment from the other ship, he seemed more alive to danger. No wonder his great grandmother had said that no Hunter could go beneath Townsend Mountain more than twice in their lifetime. Their minds couldn't take that much influence. He'd only been down once, and he was feeling the strain. Somehow, he felt changed; he felt a closer link to the supernatural world.

"Let's get to it," said Moser. "If there was anybody aiming at us, they would have shot us while we sat here talking."

"Then what do we need the shotguns for?"

"Because I ain't always right. And maybe whatever ripped that door off the garage might still be here or might come back."

That would be bad, thought Hunter. That would be terrible.

Moser handed him the Mossberg and kept the Winchester for himself. As they climbed out of the car into the chill night air, they saw that Brother Mihaloff had brought some firepower of his own. What looked like a Colt .45 was dangling from his left hand. He looked over at Moser and Hunter's shotguns and gave them a quick nod.

"I take it you boys know how to use those?"

"We do," said Moser.

Hunter remembered that terrible night when his Uncle Bartok had asked Moser whether he loved his weapon. Over the days that followed, he'd learned that the two things that Enid Moser cherished most were his guns and his dogs. It was the night Hunter had first learned of the dark secrets buried beneath the ruined Hillis Estate his family and the Mosers had guarded for over a hundred years. That was the night he'd emptied Moser's pistol into the thing that Bartok had become. Since then, Hunter had developed a strange affection for firepower.

"Good enough. You two stay out here and cover my back. I'll go in first."

Brother Mihaloff turned toward the house again, but Moser grabbed his arm.

"What?"

"That ain't going to happen," said Moser.

"My daughter," said Mihaloff in a low growl, "is in there."

"If you're not going to pull the trigger," said Moser. "Get that pistol out of my gut."

Dr. Smith had backed up against Mihaloff's car and his right hand gripped the door handle. Hunter swiveled his shotgun in Brother Mihaloff's direction. He hadn't been in the Masons long enough to know if you got kicked out of the lodge for shooting a brother Mason, but he would back Moser's play. Mihaloff slowly lowered the pistol.

"What's your problem?"

"You ever thought it might be a trap?"

"I've checked the inside of the house. It's clear. Checked the perimeter. Clear. I'm going in."

"Moser's right," said Hunter.

Mihaloff eyed him like he was going to turn the Colt in his direction.

"That symbol on the door. I take it that's new?"

"Sure as hell wasn't here when I went to meet you two at the lodge. Maybe teenagers. What's your point?"

"That's bullshit," said Moser. "The nearest house is a couple miles back. I don't know what your problem is or what's going on here, but you ought to damn well tell us before we have to go inside. And that thing on the door don't look right. Hunter here thinks it might be a possession spell or something."

"That would be the trap," said Hunter.

"We're wasting time. I don't care what it is. My daughter is in there."

"You don't want to enter the house before we physically break that symbol."

"Why?"

"Because whoever put that there will own you."

"I think we should call the others," came the doctor's voice, suddenly urgent.

He'd let go of the car handle and walked over to rejoin them.

"It's the third sign," he said.

"Shut up, Ralph," said Mihaloff.

"You know what it means," pleaded the doctor.

"It means we talk later. Right now, I want to find Rebecca."

"Whoa," said Moser. "What's this third sign thing all about?"

"I said later," said Mihaloff. "How do we break this symbol and get on with it?"

His attention was fixed on Hunter, ignoring the doctor completely.

"Blast of triple aught buck?" suggested Moser.

"It's my door," protested Mihaloff.

"Hit the circle that wraps around it first," said Hunter. "Then blast away at anything that's left. Hope the door's solid."

"Reinforced steel," said Mihaloff.

"You expecting a war?" asked Moser.

"I like to be prepared."

"Frank," said the doctor to Mihaloff, "we're not safe out here in the open. We need help."

Dr. Smith looked nervously around at the invasive darkness. Tried to remember the thirty-four acres of open fields and trees that were the Mihaloff farm. The steel buildings, the wide creek. Enough darkness surrounded them that anything could be hidden out there. He remembered the first sign given them by the old man and shivered.

The unliving shall call my name.

He remembered the second sign.

The gates of Hell will open.

And the third.

The sign of the Whore will appear.

And the fourth.

The Blazing Star of Freemasonry will be recovered.

Was Brother Mihaloff blind?

"We need help," repeated the doctor.

"We have help," Mihaloff said, tilting his head toward Hunter and Moser.

"Not safe from what?" asked Moser.

Impatiently, Mihaloff turned and fired his Colt at the arcane symbol painted on the door.

He did it with a practiced, contemptuous motion, Hunter noticed. The way a man did when he was used to hitting what he aimed at. At that moment, he thought again about how little he knew about Brother Mihaloff. Hunter and Moser came to the Detroit Masonic Temple to help, because that's what Masons did when summoned. To listen to a man's testimony and see if it was possible that it happened the way he said it did. And to keep whatever they learned secret under Masonic oath. That was what they were supposed to be doing.

But why? Really, why?

With fifteen books on ghosts and the paranormal published, Hunter was the go-to guy when strange things happened in Michigan. He'd gotten used to that and between the speaking fees and the book sales, he'd made a good living over the years. But he'd never heard of a verified incident of a statue coming to life and listening to Brother Mike Leasing had only creeped him out, not convinced him that the event really happened. It made sense he'd been contacted to discreetly investigate Brother Leasing's claims. He'd researched some bizarre phenomena. But all of his years investigating the paranormal got turned on their head when he saw what happened to Brother Mihaloff's front door.

At the moment the .45 slug hit the reinforced steel, a brilliant flash of scarlet flared from the point of impact and traveled along the symbol lines like a cutting torch. It hissed and crackled like a splenetic snake. Where it passed, the flame left a track of glowing molten metal. Burning along the constricting circle, firing its way through the inverted pentagram and then through the sigils. And the smell was as bad as a zombie funeral pyre.

"That ain't good," said Moser.

"Wish we had a bucket of holy water," said Hunter.

Hunter had read a lot over the years about ritual magic, but never believed in it. Maybe he would have to revise that opinion.

Brother Frank Mihaloff could not take his eyes off the unearthly burning. His rugged features, the broad forehead, prominent cheekbones and thick white beard gave him the assured look of a man who could not be rocked by life's circumstances. And yet, there he stood, looking in shocked awe at something impossible burning into his own front door.

"Safe to get a closer look?" asked Moser when it had burned out.

"One way to find out," said Hunter.

"Don't do it," said the doctor.

Mihaloff grabbed his shoulder, pushed him off to the side, and spoke to him in a low, urgent voice. Neither Hunter nor Moser could hear what they were saying, so the two of them advanced up the curving sidewalk to the front porch by themselves.

Three brick steps up and they stopped. The remains of the symbol still hissed and seethed like an alchemical Ouroboros, devouring itself with an insatiable hunger. Hunter had never read or heard or seen anything like it in his life. How safe was it now? There was no way really to know. He was as shocked as anyone when it burst into flames. The only reason he wanted to break it before entering was because of his experience with Aeyrik, the scaled living door that sealed in the army of mechanical automatons and the maniacal creature named Albert Magnus Hillis. Disrupt the patterns, his Uncle Bartok had told him. Disrupting patterns broke occult power.

Tonight was a night where he could really appreciate the old man's knowledge of the dangerously arcane, if only he hadn't shot him to death last year.

Moser took two steps forward and slammed the butt of his Winchester shotgun against the still-glowing remnant. The force of the impact drove it clean through, leaving a two-foot glowing hole. With a quick flip, the Kentuckian reversed the shotgun and pointed it at the opening.

"Ready?" he said to Hunter.

"Maybe."

"Best move," said Moser, "while the two of them is still arguing. I'm getting to where I don't trust either of them."

Hunter looked at the doorknob. Another trap? Well, if he stopped to think about it, almost anything could be cursed. But his brain was just stalling. If Mihaloff was telling them the truth, his daughter might be inside. Maybe hurt. Still…

"You have a rag?" he asked Moser.

"Why?"

"I don't have to touch the doorknob in case that's a problem."

Behind them, he could hear Mihaloff and Dr. Smith still arguing.

Moser pulled a rag out of coat pocket and tossed it to him.

"Here we go," said Hunter. "Anything tries to eat me, you blow its head off."

"Let's do it."

Hunter opened the door with his left hand, keeping the Mossberg to his right shoulder, barrel pointing at the door opening by turning sideways so he could get through. If there was anything on the other side, the Mossberg would take care of it. Not enough room for the big twelve-gauge to miss. The door swung inward smoothly except for the scraping sound from the fallen metal fragments of obliterated symbol sliding along the tiled marble floor behind the door. Hunter got a good view of the size of the place and would have been impressed if he wasn't terrified.

"Move out of the way," said Mihaloff gruffly, as he came up from behind. "My house."

Moser stepped aside for Brother Mihaloff and his medical man to pass by him and into the vestibule. He noticed that the doctor now also carried a pistol. It looked small enough to be a .22 caliber and seemed kind of beside the point, considering what the rest of them were carrying.

They were the only noise inside the house. Hunter cocked his head to first one side and then the other, trying to get a feel for the place. It felt empty, but that wasn't for shit.

Mihaloff brought up his phone with one hand and held his .45 steady with the other. Hunter saw the little device plugged into its side and understood. It was a state-of-the-art Seek Thermal unit that turned Mihaloff's phone into a thermal imaging camera. The screen came to life and Mihaloff scanned the hallway, part of the living room and dining room. The inside of the farmhouse looked like it had been ripped up by a cyclone. Furniture was tossed and smashed into sharp-edged fragments, torn apart fabric and stuffing puffs were everywhere. The walls were punched in like someone had gone to work on them with a sledgehammer.

Hunter and Dr. Smith were with Mihaloff. Moser held the door facing outward to cover their way out and anything else's way in. Hunter wasn't sure whether he would rather guard the front door or be inside poking around. Now, neither option seemed that great.

"What in God's name happened here?" said the doctor, and the state of his nerves was apparent in the way he said it.

"She'll be in the panic room. That's where I'm going," said Mihaloff. "Ralph, I'll need you with me."

"Somebody tore this place to pieces," said the doctor.

"Wait a minute," said Hunter, and he walked to look at a section of the living room wall. After he studied it using a small pocket flashlight on the end of his key chain, he said, "I'd say some thing is the right word. Look at these claw marks."

"No time. We have to find Rebecca."

Hunter risked a glance in Moser's direction and wondered what the big man was thinking. At least with Moser covering the way they came in, they'd be safe. Now, if he just knew for sure that whatever ripped the house apart was gone, he'd feel a little better. When Mihaloff started walking, the doctor stayed close to him, and Hunter followed. The pocket light pushed back the shadows. They'd gone halfway into the house when Mihaloff stopped.

"Oh my God," he said.

He was looking down at the carpeting in front of an inset door with a keypad halfway up the wall next to it.

"What?" Hunter asked.

Dr. Smith pointed down at the floor.

"Blood," he said.

Swinging the beam of his flashlight down, Hunter dropped to one knee and shone the light directly on the discoloration.

"Not," he said, "human blood."

"What?" said a surprised Mihaloff.

"It's green," said the doctor.

"Rebecca," shouted Mihaloff.

He frantically tapped numbers into the keypad next to the door.

"Enid," called Hunter. "This way, now."

As the door to the panic room swung open, Hunter heard the hurried footsteps of Enid Moser pounding his way.

25

"Unholy," she screamed.

Her blood-smeared face whipped side to side and Hunter thought for a brief second it would spin around like that kid in the Exorcist and she would projectile vomit all over him.

"Hold her down," shouted the doctor.

"What's wrong with her?" asked Hunter.

"Keep her still, damn it."

"Shit, she tried to bite me."

"Rebecca," said her father, "it's all right now, I'm here."

And then she bit her father hard on the forearm. He screamed and tried to pull away and when he did, a bloody piece of his forearm and shirt stayed stuck between her teeth.

"Moser," yelled Hunter. "Get your ass down here."

At Wayne State Engineering school, they didn't have courses on how to hold down a crazy woman, and although Mike Leasing had been a bit of a warmup, Hunter thought if they didn't get her under control quick she would tear them apart. Dr. Smith was struggling to inject her with a sedative like he did Leasing, but her left hand got loose, grabbed a pair of surgical scissors and stuck them in his upper thigh. His scream was epic, like an Apache battle cry. Her father, Brother Mihaloff, had run to the sink and was pouring cold water on his arm where there was a hole torn in both his shirt and his forearm.

He swore as he opened a cabinet, yanked out a box of sterile bandages and a tube of triple antibiotic.

Hunter was pressing both of her shoulders down on the bed while twisting and yanking away every time her snapping teeth got too close. He didn't look her in the eyes as she whipped about, and he didn't know why. He just didn't.

It was the sweat that did it.

Like trying to hold on to a greased pig, as Enid's cousin Kenneth would have said. She was out from under him, off the bed, and then punched him in the throat with the hand that wasn't bandaged.

He'd never been punched in the throat before, and the pain and gagging reflex took him down. When he fell backwards, something slammed into his back and then his head whacked the floor with a resounding thump. He rolled and his hands shot to his throat reflexively as he coughed and choked. She was standing over him in a flash, looking down at him like she was ready to finish him, when she suddenly flew backward as Enid Moser yanked her hair. His forearm clamped around her neck. Within a few seconds, her head fell forward, and she was out cold.

The big man took her over to the cot and lowered her gently onto it. After smoothing her hair, he looked up and saw Mihaloff pouring peroxide on his arm and Dr. Smith taking off his pants. The scissors lay on the floor, the blades and finger holes smeared with blood.

"That for her?" asked Moser, pointing at the syringe the doctor had tossed onto a linen covered stainless steel table on rollers.

"What?" asked the doctor. He winced as he stepped out of the pants and hobbled over to the medicine cabinet.

"I said, is that for her?" Moser asked again.

"Yes, it's for her," shouted the doctor.

Moser raised an eyebrow.

"Sorry, it's just… just she stabbed me."

Satisfied, Moser picked up the syringe and delivered the sedative.

"You boys okay?" he asked Hunter and Mihaloff.

"No, I'm not okay," snapped Mihaloff. "She bit me. My own daughter damned well bit me."

Hunter was getting up, one hand still holding his throat.

"You'll make it," said Moser. "I'm going to find some boards and start nailing shut windows in case we get more visitors. Think one of you can cover me while I do?"

Mihaloff was struggling to bandage his arm. Red blood seeped through the gauze as he did.

"Help me do this," he said, "and I'll go with you. I know where the tools and boards are." He gritted his teeth together with pain. "Hurts like a son of a bitch."

"I can go, too," croaked Hunter.

"Bring your Colt," said Moser.

****

"What the living hell?" said Hunter.

The four men were gathered around the computer security monitor, watching the re-run of what had happened before they arrived. Rebecca was unconscious, stretched out on the cot in the first aid room. The men vacillated somewhere between exhaustion and high alert. Dr. Smith had cleaned and bandaged his leg, re-checked the bite on Mihaloff's arm, and passed out the pain pills.

They watched the action on the monitor a second time, and it still felt like they were seeing a sci-fi horror flick. A shootout between Brother Mihaloff's daughter and a squat, horned monster followed by a faceless witch was not what Hunter and Moser were expecting to see.

"Why is the face of the woman pixilated?" Hunter asked without waiting for an answer to his first question.

The lights were dimmed to eliminate room glare against the screen. Each of them had rolled a chair over to form a semicircle around the monitor. With the electronic glow shadowing their faces, they looked ghoulish. The doctor's thin fingers tugged nervously at the tear in his pant leg, where Rebecca had stabbed him. Mihaloff's hand alternately squeezed his forearm above where his daughter had bitten him and below it near to his wrist. He swore under his breath and clenched his teeth.

"Electronic interference," suggested the doctor. "As for the animal,

I don't know. Maybe a baboon. They can be vicious and big."

"What about the horns on the top of its head?" asked Moser.

"Maybe they were glued there by the woman? There are a lot of sick people out there."

"You going to stick with that story?" asked Moser.

"No," said the doctor. "I just don't know what else it could be."

"Uh-huh," said Moser.

"And I'm on pain medication."

"You want to tell us why that symbol was painted on your front door?" Hunter asked Brother Mihaloff.

Brother Mihaloff ignored him and started the video sequence again. The creature did not seem to interest him, only the image of his daughter shooting it and being clawed by it. The woman who came for the creature, however, was a different matter. He stopped the playback at the moment her pixilated face came into view. After staring at her face for a moment as though trying to force it to resolve itself into a normal face, he moved it forward again until she pointed at the camera and the screen flashed to white, static distorted light.

"Black magic," he said with the horror of it transforming his voice into a harsh whisper.

"There's probably a better explanation than that," said Hunter irritably. "Same with the blurry face. There are ways to do that with electronics."

Mihaloff looked over at him and scowled.

"And the creature with the horns?"

There were lots of ways the entire thing could have been faked, but Hunter had seen the claw marks on the wall. He'd seen the refrigerator lying at the bottom of the basement stairs after apparently having been thrown through the downstairs door. He could come up with elaborate explanations, but they didn't feel right. It would have been incredibly costly. And it didn't explain what had happened to Rebecca's arm. That was taking it too far. The whole thing seemed real, but he wasn't ready to go there yet.

"I don't know what happened," admitted Hunter with a yawn. "I'm tired and we need to look at this whole thing in the morning. But whichever way this went down, someone had to have a big reason for doing it. Are you ready to talk about the symbol painted on your front door? And I hate to ask this, but does this have anything to do with what happened to Mike Leasing?"

It came out harsher than he'd intended, but he was damn well tired, and his neck still hurt like hell from where Mihaloff's daughter had punched him in the throat. On top of that, it was humiliating, and he felt like Mihaloff and the doctor were keeping both of them in the dark. His Uncle Bartok had done the same thing to him and that had turned into the goat rodeo from hell.

"My daughter is lying in there injured," said Mihaloff angrily. "Your questions can wait."

"I'm afraid not," said Moser laconically, "unless you'd like to handle this on your own and I don't think you want to do that. I think you're scared shitless, brother, and that ain't a good sign."

"And you're not afraid?" asked the doctor.

Moser thought about that for a minute, then said, "We've seen a lot worse. You'll just have to trust me on that one."

There was an uncomfortable silence before Hunter spoke again.

"Why did you bring us to Detroit?" he asked Mihaloff. "Start there. We would come back this way once we found out you had Bartok's papers, but what exactly was so important that you'd essentially use the Grand Hailing Sign with the Worshipful Master of our Lodge?"

"I can't tell you that yet."

"Moser," said Hunter as he stood up, "let's go. I've had it."

He was done. If he had known what he was getting into beneath Townsend Mountain last year, Bartok might still be alive. Granny Hillis might still be alive, too, and so many others. He and Moser weren't going in blind again. Bartok had been his mentor until they'd had their falling out. Less than a year ago, the old man had called him back and asked him to return to the Hillis mansion deep in the Kentucky hills. Something important had come up. Something so desperately important that Bartok felt it overrode their earlier disagreements. He was, Hunter suspected, very ill and felt that time was growing short. He had called Hunter back to reveal to him the monstrous secrets beneath Townsend Mountain.

Together they had entered the entrance to a massive underground cave system where he had shown Hunter the army of mechanical men and the body of Albert Magnum Hillis, suspended in the air with his arms cut off at the elbows, his legs cut off at the knees and saw the glassine tubes that connected the body to the army of automatons. All this had been hidden below for over one hundred and fifty years and still Albert Magnus Hillis hung there, the silver implants in his eyes shining, and the man himself hideously alive. And when Hillis had stuck a tube into Bartok's neck and pumped contagion into the old man, Bartok mutated and Hunter had to kill him. The memories still gave him terrifying nightmares. Sometimes even while awake, he could see and hear the hissing, writhing mass of alien tentacles that shot from his uncle's stomach. He had enough to handle with Mr. Chirac's blood feud against himself and Moser, Kenneth, and Ashley. He just didn't need this.

"Wait," said Brother Mihaloff as he reached out with his good arm and grasped Hunter's arm. "Sit down, please."

"Give me a reason."

Brother Mihaloff glanced over at the doctor. The doctor seemed reticent to say anything, but then relented with a sigh and said, "Go ahead. We don't have a choice. We must have a Tyler and Bartok chose him. Time is short. The unveiling…"

With a quick glance at the blank white screen, Mihaloff looked at Hunter and Moser, considering how to begin.

"Just say it and get it over with," said Moser.

"All right," said Mihaloff.

Slowly, Hunter returned to his seat.

"Ralph," said Brother Mihaloff quietly, "can you please make certain the door to the First Aid room is closed? This is not for Rebecca's ears." When he saw Hunter's surprised look, he explained, "Masonic business…"

When the doctor returned and told him that his daughter was still sleeping and that he'd closed the door to her room, Brother Mihaloff continued.

"You realize that there are appendant bodies in Freemasonry, such as the Shriners, the Scottish Rite, York Rite, and so on?"

Hunter nodded.

"These are all very public."

Brother Mihaloff was silent for a short time as he let that sink into Hunter and Moser. The doctor watched the other men nervously.

Mihaloff changed the monitor, one of twelve, back to hallway surveillance and stared at the empty upstairs hallway where they'd found blood on the carpet. Then he started again.

"Would you like to know the greatest secret in Masonry, Brother Hunter? The only real secret in Masonry? Have you ever had the desire to get past the image of grown men dressed up in white aprons and gloves taking part in stupidly arcane rituals while extolling them to the rest of the world as sublime? All the while, the Craft speaks of the need for more light. Did you ever wonder what light Masonry was speaking of? Seriously, Mr. Hunter, has the overwhelming pretentiousness of our organization ever made you want to scream for simple answers to the question of what's the big deal in Freemasonry?"

"I've been a Mason for less than three months," said Hunter, oddly embarrassed to say it.

"I know what you mean," said Moser. "Not too often when you hear a brother say it right out loud, but I know what you mean."

"Good. But there is, behind all the embarrassment of adult males in the twenty-first century play acting as occult initiates, a real secret. I don't mean an allegory. I mean the only secret behind Freemasonry. A secret that men the like of Dr. Albert Mackey and Albert Pike could only dream of while they prattled about as pretend eclectic pagans. I mean the greatest secret of mankind. Hidden in the main by Masons, who never even knew they were hiding it. Only a handful of men over the centuries have ever known the actual truth. Dr. Smith and I and the Brothers Kaufman and Cook and a Frenchman who is currently out of the country, are the modern day guardians of this secret. Your uncle Bartok was the other. We comprise the Order of the Temple Guardians and we are a wholly unknown appendant body of Freemasonry."

"What exactly does all this mean?" said Hunter impatiently. "Can you just lay it out for us? We already have enough secrets to deal with in following up on my uncle Bartok's work. That's why we came here in the first place. I understand that the Temple Guardians are a secret, appendant organization of Freemasonry. And you say that my uncle Bartok was a member of your organization and that you all having been guarding a secret, but what does that have to do with me and Moser? Why did you bring us to Detroit in the first place? We have other things to do. That's why it's so important for me to have the rest of Bartok's papers."

Brother Mihaloff looked at him in surprise.

"Then you really don't know? Bartok never told you anything about the Temple Guardians?"

"My uncle Bartok never told me a lot of things. He was the most secretive bastard God ever created."

"Good thing he was," said the doctor. "I will miss him more than my father."

"But with his death," continued Mihaloff, "we have a dilemma. We have, for the first time in thirty years, a hole in the ranks of the Temple Guardians. A job opening, you might say. And it is an ironclad rule in our order that the Tyler chooses his own successor. And your uncle Bartok chose you."

26

"Me?" asked Hunter.

"You," said Mihaloff. "Which, if you accept, resolves my practical difficulty. You see, I can't explain what this is all about unless you are a member of the Temple Guardians. What happened to the statue and what has happened here are both under Masonic secrecy. But if you accept the position of Tyler to the Temple Guardians—and you were chosen as his successor by your uncle Bartok himself—then I am free to tell you everything. In fact, at that point, I truly must tell you everything on my honor as a man and a Mason. The Tyler is the keeper of all writings relating to this. The Tyler is charged with protecting the secrets of our order and the honor of our Craft. He guards, if you will, the door to our Inner Lodge, and by that, I mean morally, spiritually, and physically. You will have all the authority to protect our Order. None of us can overrule you."

"What about Moser?"

Brother Mihaloff turned to the doctor.

"Every Tyler," said the doctor, "has both the obligation and the need to choose a second. The second is effectively the Tyler's successor in the event of the Tyler's death because he had been chosen in advance. You were chosen by your uncle as his second."

"Well?" said Brother Mihaloff to Moser.

"You say Bartok was the Tyler until he died?"

"Yes."

Hunter was thinking the same thing. He had killed his uncle, and now whatever terrible secret it was the Masons were hiding was now therefore his responsibility. His uncle's death made it so.

"I've never heard of the Temple Guardians," said Hunter cautiously.

"Nor would you ever," said Brother Mihaloff. "We are a secret society within a secret society. We are a lodge within a lodge within a lodge. Our secret is real. Why else do you think I had this underground bunker constructed?"

"Meant to ask you about that later," said Moser.

"So, for you to tell us what's really going on here, we need to join the Temple Guardians? Is that about it?"

Both Brother Mihaloff and Dr. Smith nodded. This was, Hunter thought, getting crazier by the minute.

"There's no ritual," explained Brother Mihaloff. "There are no dues. No regalia. Just your Masonic oath that you will keep the secrets of our order. The word of a Master Mason to his brothers. It is a commitment we all guard with our life. Your uncle Bartok did the same. The secret of our Order is the most disturbing, and perhaps the most important mystery you will ever be exposed to in your life. It is, in fact, the most important secret in all of history. You need not believe me, but if you join our Order, you will soon enough see for yourself. Have I your Masonic oath that you accept the positions of Tyler and second?"

"Well, shit," said Moser. "What do you say, Hunter?"

It was the paranormal investigator in his head that would not let it go. A statue had tried to strangle one of the night watchmen. That same night, the watchman manically maintained that the entire fifth floor hallway had opened up into the pit of Hell and he'd watched his mentor slide down into it and be carried off by a flying bat-like creature. And after that, of course, the daughter of the man who had requested his and Moser's presence at the Detroit Masonic Temple to investigate the event was attacked by a deformed creature the same night Hunter and Moser were hearing the story of the strangling statue and the doorway to Hell. And the occult symbol painted on the home's front door. He really knew that symbol from somewhere. He just couldn't pin down where. And Mihaloff had just told him that this brotherhood of the Temple Guardians had possession of still more of his uncle Bartok's arcane papers. And there was the matter of the witch.

"I'm in," he said.

"Two for one," said Moser.

"Give me your word, your true Masonic oath, that you will keep the secrets of the Temple Guardians, so help you, God."

"I do so confirm," said Moser.

"I do so confirm as well," said Hunter.

"So mote it be," said Brother Mihaloff and the doctor in unison.

"Sorry," Brother Mihaloff added after a moment's embarrassed pause. "Force of habit. But I do so confirm in the presence of Dr. Ralph Smith, secretary of the Temple Guardians, that your oath of commitment is accepted and you, Ian Hunter, are our new Tyler. You, Mr. Enid Moser, are now the Tyler's second."

"That's it?" asked Hunter.

"Yes," said Brother Mihaloff.

"Feels too easy," said Hunter.

"It will get a lot harder when you learn the secrets of our order, I assure you."

"Which are?"

From down the hallway came a soft moan.

"I'll get that," said the doctor, and he started off toward the first aid room.

"You think she's okay?" asked Hunter.

"He's an excellent physician, and Rebecca's a tough woman," said Brother Mihaloff. "So, yes, she's in excellent hands and she will be fine. But you were asking about the secrets of our order."

Both Hunter and Moser nodded their agreement.

When the doctor returned, Brother Mihaloff began again.

"Outside, I believe you heard the doctor mention the signs."

"What was all that about?" asked Moser.

"There are four signs our order has always watched for per our codex."

"Signs of what?" pressed Moser.

"The first sign is this: the unliving shall speak his name. The second is that the gates of Hell shall open. The third is that the Sign of the Witch shall appear. And the fourth is that the Blazing Star of Freemasonry shall return to the universal lodge of our Craft. The last is the most important. If the first three appear, but the last does not, then the world as we know it will drown in evil."

Hunter looked at Moser, but neither of them knew what to say.

"Uh-huh," Moser finally said.

"You see why we called for you," said the doctor. "It's not just because Bartok appointed you Tyler. We had to know if the first and second signs were real. We didn't know about the third sign on the door yet. All these years, and none of us could really guess even what the first three signs were about. Or when and where would they appear. And no one could really explain them to us, not even Bartok, who was the most learned of all Masons. And now, with him gone, when Brother Leasing came to us with his story, you can understand our desperation. Was Brother Leasing hallucinating, or did it really happen? Did the statue, which would be considered the unliving, really say his name?"

"Whose name?" asked Hunter.

"Why, the name of Hiram Abiff," said the doctor. "You see the problem, don't you? For hundreds of years, we, the Temple Guardians, have watched for these signs. None has ever appeared. But with Brother Leasing claiming the statue grabbed him and told him Hiram Abiff was coming and the fact that Watchmaster Miller disappeared into what Brother Leasing claimed was Hell itself, well, we just had to know if it was real or if he was hallucinating."

"Those bruises on his neck seemed genuine enough," said Hunter. "No hallucination did that."

Dr. Smith looked expectantly at Moser.

The big man stretched his arms over his head and, as he lowered them again, said, "You were worried that he might fake it to cover something else up, right?"

"Like what?" asked Hunter.

"Like the murder of old man Miller," said Moser thoughtfully.

"An unpleasant thought," said Brother Mihaloff, "but a real consideration, I admit. It was Brother Cook who said that, however unlikely a possibility it was, we must consider it. Brother Cook is a former police detective. You must understand that after hundreds of years with no one in the Temple Guardians, neither hearing nor seeing any clue relating to the signs we were waiting for, that we were more willing to consider foul play than paranormal intervention."

"And the Sign of the Witch, that's what was on your front door when we got here?" asked Moser.

"We are afraid so," said Brother Mihaloff. "The last sign to come is the return of the Blazing Star of Freemasonry to our Order. We will know soon enough when the Frenchman calls. He is an archaeologist, and it is he that is tasked with retrieving it. Both he and Bartok had been seeking it for decades."

As the explanation unfolded, Hunter felt his skin tingle as though he were standing too close to a Tesla coil. What had they gotten themselves into?

"What are all these signs supposed to lead up to?" he asked, although he dreaded hearing the answer.

"The return of Hiram Abiff," said Brother Mihaloff.

"What does that mean?" asked Hunter.

"You recall the legend and its place in the Masonic ritual?"

"I do," said Hunter. "But Hiram Abiff is an allegory, not a real person."

He turned to Moser for support. The old man nodded and gave him the thumbs up.

Brother Mihaloff shook his head.

"Hiram Abiff was a flesh and blood man, not an allegory, Brother Hunter. That is the great secret of our order. The rituals of Blue Lodge Freemasonry revolve around his death and resurrection, but it is not only a metaphor for life lessons, I assure you. It is the re-creation of an actual event in history that happened to a man named Hiram Abiff. And although he was born before the construction of Solomon's Temple, he still lives today, over three thousand years later. I see by your faces you think I am crazy. You will judge for yourselves soon enough when you meet the man. Please reserve judgment on our sanity until that moment. Hidden away in the Detroit Masonic Temple are the writings of your uncle Bartok and all the Tylers before him collected about the history of Hiram Abiff. Don't ask what is in them because I don't know. Only the Tyler may read them, but I believe that what is in those papers is related to why this house was attacked tonight. If what Brother Leasing has told us about the statue asking for Hiram Abiff is what really happened. If what Brother Leasing claimed is true, then what our Order has waited and watched for all these centuries is actually happening. The time for Hiram Abiff to return is here."

Hunter looked at Moser. They were, he thought, deep into the crazies.

Too little sleep and too many weird places compressed into one night. He didn't know which place was the creepiest at night, the Detroit Masonic Temple, or Brother Mihaloff's underground bunker. Remembering the claw marks upstairs and the green bloodstains, he decided it had to be the underground bunker.

"So where is this Hiram Abiff?" asked Hunter.

For the first time since he and Moser had listened to Mike Leasing's story in that dark room at the Masonic Temple, Hunter felt the tension in his back and shoulders loosen.

"No one knows. To preserve his life, he went into hiding after World War II and kept his location secreted from the entire world, including us, so that he would be safe until the day of his return. Can you imagine that day coming? The Christians claim Jesus died, was resurrected and returned to heaven and will one day return to earth. That is, of course, what my daughter believes. They have no evidence of this at all, of course, other than old manuscripts written by those of their own faith, but we, as Freemasons, we will reveal living evidence for the beliefs of Freemasons all over the world and those of centuries past."

"So, if you don't know where he is, how do you know for sure that he exists?"

"Because," said Dr. Smith, "we have all met him."

Hunter looked over at Moser. If he could have done it without Brother Mihaloff and the doctor noticing, he would have pointed his index finger at his temple and made circles.

"What, were you blindfolded on the way to see him so you wouldn't know where he was?"

For the first time that night, Brother Mihaloff smiled.

"Nothing so mundane as that," he said. "But now that you are of our Order, you shall see for yourselves. You will see for yourself the true Light of Masonry. You shall meet the secret worth protecting by Freemasons and the Knights Templar over the centuries. You will meet a man who was alive during the crucifixion of Jesus. A man who spoke and interacted with Mohamed traveled to India and knew the Buddha. Think of it, Brother Hunter. You've studied with your uncle Bartok, conducted your own paranormal investigations, written books to debunk stories of life after death, werewolves and vampires. Can you think of anything you've discovered that will compare to this?"

"If it's true, then I'd have to say no."

Again, the paranormal investigator inside Hunter came to life. Was it possible? Was this really possible?

It was then that Dr. Smith put in, "And if this is truly the time for him to reveal himself, then he will also bring forth a gift for Masonry to share with the world. Once and for all, the true Light of Masonry will shine upon this world undimmed."

"What gift?" asked Moser.

"He will bring as his gift the cure for cancer and so much more. We have been testing it on a controlled basis for quite some time, and it is real."

Hunter raised an eyebrow.

"You're serious about this?"

"I am. Hiram Abiff is our perfect example of the four Masonic virtues of temperance, fortitude, prudence and justice. He exemplifies the perfect ashlar; he is a good and true man."

"Well, shit," Moser said again.

27

"This has been an awful, awful night," said Brother Mihaloff a short while later. "I was so afraid for Rebecca when I got the call. But she's safe now, and Ralph said she's going to be just fine if she rests. Thank you so much for you and your friend Mr. Moser coming."

Moser was upstairs again, patrolling the main floor.

"Glad to be here for you," said Hunter, and he meant it. After months of wasted effort trying to find a crystal fragment from the alien ship, it was good to get something done the right way. Neither he nor Moser were built for detective work. "It's kind of right up our alley. The main thing, though, is that she's going to get better."

"Yes, that is most definitely the main thing. I know she's a grown woman, but… she's still my little girl in so many ways."

It was four o'clock in the morning, and Dr. Smith slept in the bedroom closest to that where Rebecca was staying. They were seated on the rolling canvas camouflage chairs near the monitor banks. Both men looked worn and haggard.

"She and I are the last surviving members of our family. My wife died of cancer a while back."

"I'm sorry to hear that."

"Thank you. I had a son, but he died, too."

Hunter kept quiet. It seemed like the thing to do.

"He died in a fire. A… terrible way to go."

The older man stroked his snow-white beard as though remembering the event.

"Your house burned?" asked Hunter.

"What? Oh no, no. He was in an institution at the time."

Seeing the look on Hunter's face, Brother Mihaloff added reluctantly, "He was in prison."

"I'm sorry," Hunter said, trying hard to conceal his shock.

"So am I."

Brother Mihaloff got a faraway look in his eyes. If it wasn't for his aquiline nose and prominent forehead, Hunter decided, the man really would look Kris Kringle. No, that wasn't right. Brother Mihaloff was one of those men who seemed to have been born serious. Hunter had met men like him before. His own uncle Bartok, in fact, was a man like that. Both Brother Mihaloff and Uncle Bartok were men with a mission. They seemed never to have had a childhood. Both men were Freemasons, both hid many secrets, and both were formidable alpha achievers. But there was a price for that and a mandate, too. Formidable men did great things unless they made poor decisions. Bartok had said something like that when they were beneath Townsend Mountain, when they stood before Aeryk, the alien door that led to the cave of Major Albert Magnus Hillis.

"Do you have children?" asked Brother Mihaloff.

"No," said Hunter.

"Ever married?"

"No. Just never found the right woman or the time, I guess. Or maybe I just never made the time. Met some women I would have liked to have seen more of while I was ghost hunting and investigating the paranormal, though."

"Ghost hunting groupies?"

"Yeah, well, kind of, especially when I did stints on cable. It added a little glamor to my otherwise sterile, technical life."

"I don't understand," said Brother Mihaloff.

Hunter thought he looked genuinely interested, so he took a chance and explained.

"Mostly what I do is analyze the sites of hauntings on a data basis. It would be a lot more interesting to people if I were confronting ghosts live on national television, so that everyone could really get into it without having to be there. But that's not what I do. I developed a cloud-based interface for…"

Now it was Hunter's turn to drift off.

"You were saying?" prodded Brother Mihaloff.

"I almost remembered something that seemed important, but it slipped away."

"My apologies. I didn't mean to break your train of thought."

"Anyway, when I wasn't out doing paranormal measurements, I was writing. I've been pretty much of a loner most of my life. My mom and dad, maybe Bartok told you, died in a car crash when I was young, and Uncle Bartok took me in and raised me. So, I was an only child. No big deal, it's just that, especially around my uncle, there weren't many other children I was in contact with. And the things that Bartok and I were interested in weren't exactly mainstream activities, if you get my meaning. Anyway, I'd like to get married and have kids, I think."

Brother Mihaloff glanced toward the hallway leading to where Rebecca slept.

"I was never happier than when I was married," said Brother Mihaloff.

"It must have been hard losing your wife," said Hunter.

He didn't know what else to say.

"You have no idea," continued Brother Mihaloff. "She was the best part of my life. I can see her in Rebecca, which is doubly hard in its own way. Both of them were full of life, ready to take on any challenge; I married a special woman, Hunter, and she gave me a special daughter. My son, though, was another matter. It was as if he was born with something missing. We never understood what was wrong with him. To say that he was born without a sense of morality would be, I think, missing the point. Or maybe understating the point. Although the doctors found nothing physically wrong with him, there was something wrong with him. He was a huge, hulking boy—physically very gifted. But he was born without a sense of compassion. He wasn't autistic. Several of the psychologists who evaluated him said he was a sociopath. It was an easy diagnosis for them to make. Yet, he loved Rebecca. She was very much younger than him. My wife and I never thought we would have another child. But we did. Sometimes there's a sense of jealousy among children born so far apart. But our son accepted Rebecca immediately. I can't explain it. It was just so obvious that it made the diagnosis of him as a sociopath seem ridiculous. Sociopaths can't experience that type of feeling. Wouldn't you agree, Hunter?"

Hunter fidgeted. He didn't know how to answer the question and hoped that it was rhetorical. Finally, when it was clear that Brother Mihaloff was waiting for an answer, he said, "I really don't know. Psychology isn't my strong suit. I mean, some days I wish it was. People are so hard to comprehend sometimes."

"I understand what you mean. We are both technical men, you and me. I think sometimes that distances us from other people. When my wife died of cancer, many years after my son's death, I wondered if, since she died of brain cancer, that maybe he would have as well. Maybe an undetected tumor was influencing his behavior for the worse. I will never know, and maybe you can understand how that has haunted me all these years. And now... I believe that the technology Hiram Abiff is gifting the world could have saved both my son and my wife. Rebecca blames me, you know, for the death of her mother. She knows in her heart that even if I was home with her at the time of her death, there would've been nothing I could have done. But what eats at me, and what eats at her, is that if I was at home with her, she wouldn't have died alone."

"I don't know what to say," said Hunter.

"Please don't worry, there really is nothing to say. But perhaps now you have a better understanding of why the technology Hiram is bringing is so important to me personally."

"Yes, I do."

"And I hope it will bring some healing to our relationship—for Rebecca and me, that is—by my having a small part in the cure's unveiling for the disease that took her mother away from her."

Without thinking, Hunter said, "Maybe your son had some kind of brain cancer. Something that might have affected his behavior. Has Rebecca been checked?"

As soon as the words were out of his mouth, Hunter regretted them. Could he be more insensitive? To his surprise, Brother Mihaloff did not seem to notice the inappropriateness of the question.

"I've asked that question myself a million times, Hunter. And Rebecca has been checked. She didn't like it, but she endured it."

Moser had told him it was the way of Masons. Hunter had thought it was more hyperbole. Masons felt safe to talk to one another, because they were all brothers. "I wasn't so much for having friends," Moser had told him. "But when I became a Mason, that all changed. I found a group of men I could trust. When men trust one another, they talk to each other a lot different from when they be with men they ain't sure about." Now Hunter was learning a little more about that himself—to think he had only met this man the day before.

"I guess the testing methods weren't as accurate back then."

"No, not so much."

It didn't occur to Hunter at that moment, but later he would wonder why he didn't catch the problem with what Brother Mihaloff had mentioned earlier. The idea of a prison—a building of concrete and steel—burning to the ground should have stood out as unlikely.

"But at least you still have Rebecca," said Hunter.

"Yes, I have that. And she's a special young woman, Hunter. Our beliefs are radically far apart. She's angry that I let her mother die alone. I'm angry that she thinks that happened out of careless neglect on my part. But such are the ways of family. I hope that with the bringing forth of Hiram Abiff and his gift, she will more clearly understand my beliefs."

"I don't understand."

A pained look crossed Brother Mihaloff's face.

"She's a Christian," he said.

He was embarrassed when he said it, like he was saying she was mentally challenged.

"Oh," said Hunter.

"Yes. Worse, she's an evangelical Christian. In that way, she's like her mother was. When she believes something, she believes it wholeheartedly. I suppose she's also like me in that way. When I was raised a Mason, I truly believed in Freemasonry, Hunter. I believed in the fatherhood of God and the brotherhood of man. I still do, actually. I believe all men should meet on the level. I believe in the Masonic virtues of temperance, fortitude, prudence, and justice. I believe, if you will, in Freemasonry itself. The only thing over the years I began to sincerely doubt was the ritual of a Master Mason.

"Despite all the proclamations of how beautiful, wonderful and meaningful the raising of Hiram Abiff was in our Master Mason ritual, I thought it was more than irrelevant. I'd found it embarrassing. No matter how fervidly my fellow Masons proclaimed the symbolic beauty of that ritual, I thought of it as pandering to our need for carnival dressing and ritual. It was a marvelous story told in ritual the first time around, but after seeing it reenacted over and repeatedly, I saw it as a distraction from doing Masonic work. In its own way, it was as mythical as the resurrection of Jesus Christ. I wanted something more from Freemasonry. Not myths and legends with no basis in the real world, but something that exalted the scientific method."

Hunter leaned forward to listen more closely.

"Can you explain that to me?"

Brother Mihaloff actually seemed pleased by the question.

"Of course. The more I studied, the more I realized that Christianity, Judaism and Islam were all based on nothing but stories. There was no tangible evidence of the truth of the events described in any of them. We have no original documents for any of these belief systems. Each of them go out of their way to describe how faithful their holy books are to the original autographs. Disbelief in the accuracy of these documents is viewed as heresy. I understand the right of individuals, Hunter, to believe whatever they want, but to believe things that have no real evidentiary basis borders on insanity in this age of intellectual rigor. No one has ever seen anything like the events described in any of these documents. I will not call them scriptures, whether they are of the Christian faith, the Jewish faith or the Muslim faith, because, to me, they are all fake documents. They are, in a word, the fake news of the ancient world.

"There are many other faiths in the world as well, Hunter, besides the Big Three, but they all have the same problem. They are based on unprovable stories. They are all validated by fanatical followers who can't be believed because they are biased.

"But now, for the first time in history, we—that is the Temple Guardians of which you and Moser are now brothers—will bring through to the physical presentation to all of humanity evidence that the Great Architect of the Universe as described in Freemasonry is real. There is no one alive to verify Jewish claims of Moses and the burning bush, there is no one alive today to validate that Jesus in fact rose from the dead, and there is no one alive today to verify or validate that Mohamed was any kind of prophet at all. But the entire world will validate that Hiram Abiff has been alive for over three thousand years. And he will bring with him not only the cure for cancer and other diseases, but he will also bring with him documents he sequestered over the past hundreds and thousands of years. You recall the great library of Alexandria, do you not, Hunter? What if I told you that Hiram Abiff saved over forty-five hundred of the manuscripts contained there? How would you feel about that, my brother?"

"Is this true?" asked Hunter. "You understand my skepticism, don't you? I mean, what you are talking about is fantastic."

Hunter's cell phone rang like a fire alarm.

Hunter slid the answer icon over the screen and heard Moser's voice.

"Everything okay, Enid?" asked Hunter.

"Like a grave up here," answered Moser.

"You need me to spell you up there?" asked Hunter.

"No, I can handle this, but Hunter, whatever done tore this place up is real. This was no set-up job. I've been finding stuff up here you won't believe."

"I'm on my way up."

"No, stay where you are. I don't need anybody else up here messing the place up and leaving tracks, if you know what I mean. There is a story here if I can just follow it."

"Okay, but if you need me, call me."

"Roger that."

Hunter looked at the phone as though he wasn't sure what it was. He wondered exactly what Moser meant, although he knew he would tell him in due time. The old man had skills he didn't, and Hunter was glad of it. Moser knew more about danger than Hunter knew about math, and that was saying something. The video of the creatures attacking Rebecca was terrifying, but Hunter had a hard time believing it was real. If you really thought about it, believing that video was as hard as believing it was a setup job.

"Everything okay upstairs?" asked Brother Mihaloff.

"Fine. Moser just wanted to let me know things were okay.

Listening to you, I almost forgot he was up there. You were saying?"

"I was saying," said Brother Mihaloff, "that Grandmaster Hiram Abiff will bring through with him over forty-five hundred manuscripts from the library at Alexandria. You were no doubt thinking I was crazy."

"Shocked is a better word," said Hunter. "My understanding was that the entire Library of Alexandria was burned to the ground in a series of fires over the centuries."

Brother Mihaloff stood up from his chair and stretched.

"I'm going to get a cup of coffee. I'm too old for all-night vigils. But when it involves my Rebecca, I make exceptions. Would you like a cup as well?"

"Thought you'd never ask."

When they'd returned to their chairs, Brother Mihaloff continued.

"There's a lot of confusion regarding the Great Library at Alexandria, Brother Hunter. Scholars are a messy lot. Many are as opinionated as fanatics. In fact, as a friend of mine says, a scholar is, but a disguised, obsessive-compulsive opinionist. Analysis and rigor are only their friends if they allow them to opine.

"Part of the confusion, of course, relates to the intermingling in the common mind of the two libraries: which comprised the manuscripts housed in the Serapeum Temple and the Cesarion Temple. It is hard to discuss, of course, the destruction of the actual library of Alexandria without specifying which library you are discussing, you understand. Of course, the Serapeum Temple and the Cesarion Temples were public buildings—if they could be called libraries at all—and not likely the repository of the over three quarters of a million scrolls relating to art, literature, science, mathematics and music. The great library, however, was a different institution all together, and it was rarely identified correctly by scholars, many are even today ignorant of its true name.

"Some scholars blame the Caesars for the destruction of the great temple. They base this idea on accounts by Plutarch. I would not face the weather for a golf outing on anything written by Plutarch, Hunter. I have never given credence to his credibility. More likely, the great library of Alexandria was in actuality destroyed by the Caliph Omar. However, there is little support for this idea in academic circles because university professors these days live in fear of being called

Islamaphobes any time they question Islamic culture. The same used to be true when delving into issues of Christian history. And yes, before you bring up the point, it has been true for such a long time in Jewish history as well. All religions are exercises in self-protection, if you think of it, Brother Hunter. But Hiram Abiff will set all of that right. Imagine that day, Hunter. With the return of our great Grandmaster, so many of the lies of past cultures will be ripped away. So many people will be freed from the self-imposed blinders they have worn throughout their lives. My daughter will be one of those people.

"My daughter attends church three days every week. She believes, really believes, in the coming Armageddon. She believes in the literal coming of the four Horsemen of the Apocalypse. She believes in Satan and Jesus, angels and archangels. She believes the earth was literally created in six days and on the seventh day of that divine week, that God himself took a day off. She believes that when the apostle Paul was walking down the Damascus Road, Jesus spoke to him from heaven and then blinded him. You see my problem, don't you?"

Hunter thought about it for a minute. Yes, he could definitely see a problem.

"Is it you are about to unveil to the world a man who claims to be three thousand years old, and that act will deny the Jewish, Islamic and Christian scriptures and provide evidence to back up his claims, thereby destroying every tenet of her faith?"

Brother Mihaloff nodded.

"You are every bit as clever as your uncle Bartok said."

"I wish," said Hunter.

"But there is more," said brother Mihaloff. "My daughter will see the return of Hiram Abiff as the coming of the Beast of the Apocalypse."

Hunter blinked.

"The Beast of the Apocalypse?"

"Yes. Because of her belief in the fairy tales of the Bible, she will believe that indeed. Don't you see? To her, Hiram Abiff will validate the Book of Revelations. And that, I worry, will drive a wedge between us. My daughter's faith is everything to her, Hunter, and I'm afraid I will then lose her."

Hunter felt the weight of brother Mihaloff's despair cloak him like a heavy cape. He really was not sure what to think about everything brother Mihaloff had told him concerning Hiram Abiff, but he could see where he was going. This man had lost his son in a terrible fire, his wife to brain cancer and the thought of losing his daughter Rebecca by shattering everything she believed was almost more than the old man could bear. Hunter did not know what he could say that would be of any comfort to Brother Mihaloff.

"Please forgive me for asking this, but has it occurred to you that there are dark forces at work trying to prevent you from bringing Hiram Abiff out from the shadows?"

"Yes."

"Do you have any idea who could be behind it?"

"No. But I assume it to be religious fanatics."

"I never believed in black magic," said Hunter. "But if that video of the monster and that witch are real, then your daughter and you seem to be in a lot of danger."

Brother Mihaloff stared at him intently.

"Do you really have any doubts?"

Hunter really did not, and he found that as disturbing as anything he'd seen beneath Townsend Mountain. Whatever the creature in the video was, he had seen nothing like it. It was like a creature from a graphic novel. And graphic novels were not supposed to be real.

"No, I hate to say this, but given what we saw upstairs combined with the video, and the wounds on Rebecca's arm, I'm going to have to say I believe that whatever it was, it was most definitely real. And whoever that witch is, brother, she's serious."

"When I find out who she is, I'm going to kill her with my bare hands," said brother Mihaloff.

Hunter wasn't so sure that the witch could be killed with Brother Mihaloff's bare hands, big though they were. They were all in uncharted territory here, and he was willing to bet that even the old man knew that.

"But," said Brother Mihaloff after a moment's silence when he'd control his rage, "first I'd like Brothers Kaufman and Cook to show you what is possible. It will be something that you will never forget. Brother Moser and I will watch over Rebecca while you're gone. Will you do that for me as our new Tyler?"

As Hunter nodded his agreement, he felt a premonition of dread.

28

The next morning, while Rebecca still slept in the first aid cot, Moser and Brother Mihaloff stood watch. Hunter drove to downtown Detroit to the Masonic Research Clinic and met Brother Kaufman and Cook.

As the three of them entered the facility, Hunter told them how impressed he was with the size of it.

"This entire building is ours?" asked Hunter as the glass and chrome doors slid back to let them through.

Brother Kaufman nodded.

"We have only twenty-two patients at a time. The rest are research staff and laboratories. It's amazing, really, and totally beyond my ability to understand, but it's the results that count."

"You're not a scientist?"

Actually, with his bald head, angular face and aquiline nose, Brother Kaufman looked more like a movie Nosferatu than a scientist. Or, with a hunchback, he could have passed for Igor in the Frankenstein movie.

"Him?" asked Brother Cook with a stifled laugh. "Don't you recognize him? George was a movie actor before he retired. He was Uncle Fester in the Addams Family."

In response to Hunter's wide-eyed stare, Brother Kaufman said, "Don't listen to him. He's just jealous. I made documentary films. Nothing big, really. Endangered wildlife films, films about the damage industry are doing to the rain forest, that sort of thing."

"Anything I'd remember?"

"If you have to ask," said Brother Kaufman, "then, no."

Brother Cook volunteered that was a retired police detective.

Now I've got it, thought Hunter. He looks like that guy from the television show "The Shield." It was at that moment that Hunter realized he was enjoying the other two Masons' company. They weren't so bad when they weren't under stress. And they were treating him as a Brother Mason, not an interloper. He really was their brother now. He was their Tyler, and like Brother Mihaloff, they seemed deeply respectful of his office. Despite his initial misgivings at the way they treated him the first night they'd met, he found he was actually liking them.

Brother Kaufmann waved at the elderly man at the front desk, who nodded in return and then went back to staring at his computer screen.

"That's Brother Hedgeway," said Brother Kaufmann. "He'll be ninety-three years young next week. He used to be a fencing instructor until arthritis caused him to slow down and volunteer his time here at the Clinic."

"Huh," said Hunter.

"Down this way," continued Brother Kaufmann.

They went through a set of windowless doors that opened outward as they approached. Hunter looked back at the elderly man, who looked up and smiled.

"Computer controlled?" Hunter asked as they entered what appeared to be a small waiting room.

"Everything here is computer controlled," replied Brother Cook.

"Is this a second lobby?"

"Security scan," said Brother Cook.

"Someone is scanning us?"

"You bet. Facial recognition software checking us out. Your info, including several photos, were forwarded over by Brother Mihaloff, who personally gave the okay for you to enter and observe."

"Do we sit down and wait?" asked Hunter, pointing to a couch and six chairs. A television was mounted high in one corner, and a news channel was playing, but the sound was off.

"No," said Brother Cook. "This won't take long. We have three levels of security to protect what we've been doing here. The third and most important one you won't even notice."

That caused Hunter to look over in surprise.

"That's sounds pretty sophisticated."

"You should see our lockdown procedures."

The far door opened, and it was then that Hunter realized there wasn't even a knob or handle on their side of the door. A short man stepped out, his brown hair cut like Moe from the Three Stooges, and a long, thick mustache that made him look like a demented gun fighter. If not for the spotless white, rumpled lab coat, the illusion would have been complete. He stood, blocking the door from closing. Hunter tried to see past him.

"Hello, Doc," said the Brothers Kaufman and Cook.

"Hello, brothers. I take it this is Mr. Hunter."

"Absolutely," said Hunter as he extended his hand.

For a short man, the doctor had a handshake that Hunter thought would have belonged to the heavily muscled Brother Cook.

"I'm Dr. Rambert," he said.

"We call him Doc Rambo," said Brother Kaufman. "He strikes terror into the little perverted hearts of disease bacteria. Isn't that right?"

"Among other things," said the doctor. "I understand you boys would like Mr. Hunter to meet a few of our patients?"

A solemn nod from Brother Kaufman.

"Do you have a strong stomach, Mr. Hunter? And please understand that I don't ask idly."

Hunter glanced toward the two brothers, who just nodded, a more serious expression on their faces, and then back to the doctor.

"Probably average," he said. "Why?"

"Because you are only going to see three patients today, one of whom is burned very badly. Have you ever seen a burn victim, Mr. Hunter?"

The queasy feeling in his stomach wasn't pleasant. It was like an early warning system going off in his body.

"How bad?"

"Very. But you will only see her for less than a minute. It will be very stressful, I assure you, but I believe it will make the point. You'll be on the other side of triple panes of glass—we have to be very careful of infection."

"Her?" gulped Hunter.

"Yes," said the doctor. "Brittney Thomas. Aged ten. I wish I could prepare you for what you are about to see, but all I can give you is this."

From his pocket, the doctor pulled out a paper bag, like those Hunter had seen used for airsick airline passengers. Just seeing it made him feel worse, but he took the bag and clutched it against his chest.

"If you are particularly prone to anxiety or panic attacks, I can give you a sedative first."

He felt anxious just listening to the doctor.

"If you are not, though, I advise against it. It's important you learn what we're dealing with here. Are you all right with that?"

No, he thought, but he nodded that yes, he was.

"Good. Here are your masks, suits, gloves, and footwear. Put them on now. I'll be doing the same."

It made him feel like a cable repairman getting dressed to go into a customer's house. Thinking of that kept him from thinking worse thoughts.

****

The doctor and Brothers Kaufman and Cook waited outside the bathroom, where Hunter vomited for the third time.

That face. That poor girl's disfigured face. It was worse than seeing Albert Magnus Hillis hanging ten feet above the ground, his arms cut off at the elbows and his legs cut off above the knees with all the stumps connected to the pulsing blue-white ethereal fluid that flowed through them like rivers of ghosts. His eyes, which were only pieces of a silver embedded in his sockets. But the girl, the girl, was worse still.

His throat felt acid-raw, and his chest and gut hurt from heaving up the contents of his stomach. The stink made him want to vomit still again. He'd washed his face and scrubbed off bits of something ugly off the surface of the sink. The suit, masks, gloves and footwear were in the Biohazard container, but he could still taste the horror of throwing up in his mask. That poor girl. Three seconds after he'd seen her, he was running toward the designated bathroom, wearing a mask full of vomit. The mask lay forgotten on the floor.

What kind of monsters were they to show him this? He would berate Brother Mihaloff when he saw him. How could the doctors and nurses bear to work in this… this… place? For the love of God, how could they stand it?

But the girl. It was for the girl, he suddenly realized, and felt shame redden his face. Compulsively, he scrubbed his face again, until he felt it burn.

Thank God she was asleep when they'd let him see her. He couldn't imagine how she would have felt if she'd seen the horror in the face. She was in constant pain and always in danger of infection. Infection, hell, she was always in danger of dying. Or living the way she was. It seemed almost cruel to keep her alive. He threw that thought right out of his consciousness. This was all about her. Brother Mihaloff had wanted him to see that. He told himself to toughen up, then staggered to the door. He hated facing the others again after how he'd reacted.

He opened the door, then leaned on the frame.

"Not an easy thing," said Dr. Rambert, with a sad, knowing look on his face.

Brother Cook handed him a bottled water. Hunter shook his head.

"I can't."

"Drink it," said the doctor. "You're dehydrated. Just sip it, though; don't drink it all at once or you'll be sick again."

This time, Hunter took it and did as the doctor ordered.

"You did better than I did the first time," said Brother Kaufman. "This next part will be a lot easier."

"I—"

"Trust me. Now comes the part that makes it all worthwhile. Doc, lead on."

Brother Cook held his arm for the first few steps.

"You okay to walk now?"

"I think so, if we take it slow."

"You still look a little green."

"I'll make it."

A few minutes later, they were in an entirely new corridor, although Hunter wasn't sure how they'd gotten there—he'd been too busy looking at the floor to make sure he didn't fall.

Dr. Rambert knocked on a door, heard an answer from inside, then swung it open. He stepped inside and invited Hunter to step in after. The other two men followed behind him and closed the door after them. A young boy sat up in a bed, hunched over a game controller. He looked to be about fifteen, with wild red hair and freckles. He wore jeans and a blue T-shirt. No socks and tennis shoes. A typical, apparently healthy teenager. Hunter breathed a sigh of relief.

"Caleb, do you think you can pause that long enough to meet a new friend of mine?"

The boy protested, played on for a minute and then paused the game. He looked over at Hunter and smiled.

"I'm killing it," he said proudly.

"This is Mr. Hunter. He's a writer."

"Cool."

"Not always," said Hunter. "Nice to meet you."

"Yeah."

"You already know these other two men."

"Hey," said the boy. "Do you want to play?"

"Nope," said Brother Cook. "You'd just wipe me off the board."

"Me, too," smiled Brother Kaufman.

Caleb gave them a disdainful look.

"There's no board," he said.

Both men shrugged.

"See?" said Brother Cook.

"Whatever."

"Manners," said Dr. Rambert. "Please stand and shake Mr. Hunter's hand so you can get back to your game."

"What do you write?" asked Caleb, looking up with a slight look of curiosity on his face.

"Ghost hunting books," said Hunter.

"Really? Cool."

"Caleb," prompted Dr. Rambert.

The young man bounded off the bed and shook Hunter's hand enthusiastically.

"Can I get one of your books?"

"Sure, I'll even autograph it for you. I'll send it to the doctor to give to you."

"Can I get back to my game?" asked Caleb.

The doctor nodded, and the four men turned and left the boy to his enthusiastic button pushing.

When they were out in the hallway, Hunter asked, "What's wrong with him?"

"Nothing," said the doctor.

"I'm sorry?"

"Nothing now. Six months ago, he was a double amputee. A car accident took his legs."

Hunter felt his breath catch in his throat.

"What?"

"With the Hiram therapy, his legs regrew."

"Is there somewhere I can sit down?"

"Wait until you meet Bonnie," said Dr. Rambert with a slight smile.

But Hunter couldn't think that far ahead. He was still reeling from the idea that the teenager he had just seen what had once been a double amputee. It was too much for his mind to take in. People just could not re-grow legs. It was impossible.

"What is the Hiram therapy?"

"You must ask Brother Mihaloff that question, Mr. Hunter."

"I will, then. This is fantastic."

Dr. Rambert shrugged.

"Can you give me even a hint about what the Hiram therapy is?" said Hunter.

"Well, no. I can't."

Hunter stared at the man.

"I'm sorry?"

"I mean, it makes little sense to me either," said Dr. Rambert. "I'm assuming you're familiar with the way some species, such as the skink, can regrow a lost tail. Well, I don't really understand that either. I know it happens, but the mechanism is still beyond us.

Truthfully, we've dreamed of this possibility for decades in science. You could say we're getting closer, and we've had some successes in the laboratory sporadically, but this? The Hiram therapy is hard for me to grasp."

"I don't know what to say," said Hunter.

"All I can tell you," said Dr. Rambert, "is that it is amazing. More amazing still, to me, is that the Hiram therapy stimulates the brain to direct the body to accomplish its instructions. I assume that one day we will understand it, or at least I hope we will. But come, let's go check in on Bonnie. I can't say more to you until you've seen her, but her results are even more amazing."

The doctor led Hunter and Brothers Kaufman and Cook to another room. Once again, he knocked on the door, and when he heard someone inside say, "Come in," he led the three of them in to meet its occupant. She was a young woman in her early twenties, with thin blond hair hanging down to her shoulders. She had pale skin and bright blue eyes. Her face was thin, but her lips were wide, and she was smiling, revealing perfect teeth.

"Hello Dr. Rambert," she said.

She was sitting in a recliner near the window, which faced out onto a row of rooftops. In her lap was a book, and she had been reading before they interrupted her.

"Hello yourself," said Dr. Rambert. "I hope I'm not disturbing you, Bonnie."

"No, I'm always glad to have company. Especially if it is you. Dr. Rambert," she told the others, " he is my knight in shining lab coat."

Her smile was infectious. Whatever malady had troubled her before coming to the clinic was certainly long gone. She looked so healthy that Hunter had a hard time imagining that she had once been ill. What miraculous disease had the implant cured her of? Cancer? Diabetes?

"I brought some friends with me," said the doctor. "We're just making the rounds. I think you've met Brothers Kaufman and Cook, haven't you?"

"Did you think I would forget them?" she said.

"We should hope not," said Brother Cook.

Bonnie laughed. It was a lovely, magical sound, thought Hunter.

The sound of it almost made him forget the first little girl. Almost. He didn't believe he would ever truly be able to forget her. But the pure joy in Bonnie's face was a welcome relief to behold.

"Well, this young man," said Dr. Rambert, "is Mr. Hunter. He's a friend of Brother Mihaloff."

"Nice to meet you, Mr. Hunter," she said with a smile.

Hunter smiled back at her.

"I'm happy to meet you too, Bonnie," said Hunter.

"Well," said the doctor, "we'd best be on our way, Bonnie. Mr. Hunter is getting a tour of the facility, and there is much left for him to see."

As they closed the door behind them, Hunter remembered again the teenage boy who had regrown legs. He was about to ask the doctor what Bonnie had been cured of, when Dr. Rambert shook his head, held up a hand and led them away from the door and down the hall. He said nothing until they had reentered the same room that Hunter and the others had started their journey from.

"Take a seat, Mr. Hunter," said the doctor.

"I'm better now; I can take it standing up."

"I think not," said the doctor with a grim smile.

Not knowing what else to do, Hunter took a seat in an easy chair near the wall-mounted television. Brother Kaufman and Brother Cook did the same.

"Cancer?" said Hunter.

"No, Bonnie was the victim of a brain aneurysm. It's only in the last so many years that we've had much luck with brain aneurysms," said the doctor. "There was little we could do for Bonnie. Intracranial pressure crushed a third of her brain."

"That's awful," said Hunter.

The doctor took a breath, and then continued.

"We installed the Hiram device that is at the core of the Hiram therapy, hoping that it would help her recover from surgery. We weren't able to perform surgery on her, because she died before we could do so. Unfortunately, we had not even had time to activate the Hiram device."

"I don't understand," said Hunter.

He could feel the eyes of the other Masons on him.

Dr. Rambert looked down at the floor, seemed to choose his words carefully, and then continued the story.

"It was an act of frustration, Hunter. Our surgeon activated it after Bonnie was legally dead."

Hunter breathed a sigh of relief.

"So, she was legally dead, but not technically dead. That's what you mean, isn't it?"

"No, Hunter. She was really and truly technically dead. Death is a fluid term in that we can't actually consider all parts of the body dead if you understand what I mean. But I can tell you this: she was technically dead. And one third of her brain had been crushed. If she had lived, she would have been a vegetable."

Dead? Hunter thought. Not possible. No, this was better—no, this was worse than Caleb's legs growing back. This was beyond reason. Dead, with a crushed brain, and now she was sitting up reading a book? What was he supposed to think? Was the implant able to regrow the human brain? Was the implant able to bring someone back from the dead?

"It's hard to wrap your head around, isn't it, Hunter?" said Brother Kaufman.

Hunter gaped at him. Hard to wrap your head around? What the hell was the man thinking? She'd been dead. Was this science or magic?

"Brother, I don't think my head can ever wrap around this. Are you all telling me that the Hiram device brought her back from the dead?"

"As I indicated earlier," said the doctor, "death is a scientifically imprecise term. It's more likely that our understanding of death will have to evolve."

"I'll say," said Hunter.

Then a disquieting question occurred to him. He really didn't want to hear the answer, but just had to ask.

"So, after these patients are cured, you then remove the Hiram device?"

It was Dr. Rambert's turn to stare back in disbelief. The thought had either never occurred to him, or he wouldn't let himself consider it.

"Why on earth would we do that, Hunter? Once these Hiram devices are put in place, it would be criminal to remove them. Our job is to save lives, not destroy them. Think what would happen to all the children we've helped if we hadn't inserted it. And remember Brittney, Mr. Hunter. Remember her ravaged face? If she is restored, how could you think of returning her to what she looks like now?"

Hunter felt like vomiting again.

****

As they left the building, Hunter's mind was having a hard time absorbing all that he had seen. Brother Kaufman grabbed him by the shoulder just before they stepped out onto the sidewalk and asked him, "Now, Brother, do you see the wonderful importance of what the Temple Guardians have been doing for all these centuries?"

Back from the dead. Now he understood their attitude toward him at their first meeting. They were fearful that he would screw things up in such a way that the unveiling of Hiram Abiff would be held up and their medical miracle device along with that. It would be the greatest moment in the history of Freemasonry. The day that Freemasonry saved the world. No, he wasn't going to slow it up. He was going to do everything he could to make sure it happened on schedule. It would be the greatest event in world history. Or would it? Bringing back the dead? What was he thinking?

Dark days, he thought, dark magic.

"I think I need a drink," Hunter said. "And I don't even drink."

"That girl, the burn victim you saw," said Brother Cook, "she's going to be okay. The sign of Hiram will cure her. Think about it, Hunter. The world is going to change. The world will never be the same. Disease and death are about to lose their sting."

Hunter was so exhausted from analyzing the possibilities that by the time they drove onto the freeway that would take them away from Detroit, he leaned against the passenger-side window and fell fast asleep. But he dreamed of a device called The Sign of Hiram.

29

"What do you think?" asked Brother Mihaloff. "Will he be a true Tyler?"

The three of them were seated in the writing room on the second floor of the Masonic Temple. Although brother Kaufman often referred to the writing room as Mark Twain's office, he did not understand what Mark Twain's writing office looked like, even if the great American writer had one. It just seemed like the place where Mark Twain would have written. The ashtray centered in the middle of a barren library desk was empty. A Masonic docent had once confided to him his theory on the relationship between cigar smoking and quality writing. It was his opinion that when men quit smoking cigars, that men also ceased to write great fiction. It was a romantic notion, thought brother Kaufman, but it was also his opinion that what the world today needed was more romantic notions.

"I think so," said Brother Cook, rubbing his bald head as he spoke.

"As do I," said Brother Kaufman. "His uncle Bartok appointed him, and that's good enough for me."

"I agree," said Brother Mihaloff. "However, I have certain reservations."

Brother Kaufman arched an eyebrow.

"Such as what?"

Brother Cook leaned forward to catch whatever nuances there

might be in Mihaloff's voice.

"You think he's too young?" asked Brother Cook.

"No," sighed brother Mihaloff, "it's not that. A man's age or lack of it should never be used when rendering such an important judgment. It is not his age that concerns me."

"What then?"

Brother Mihaloff spread his hands wide.

"It's his lack of... fire. He does not seem to be a man of much passion."

"He's careful," said Brother Kaufman. "Bartok was like that as well."

"Besides," said Brother Cook, "it is already done. We have come so far already. There is no turning back. And there is no reason for turning back. The coming of our Grandmaster Abiff is truly the culmination of all Masonic history. It is still difficult for me to believe. Who could have thought we would live to see this day? All the centuries where our forbearers taught that the legend of Hiram Abiff was just a metaphor will be put aside. In just a few days, Freemasons around the world shall learn the truth; that the rituals of Freemasonry were not just metaphorical. They are real. These are great days, brothers."

The three men sat in silent awe at the roles they and the earlier Temple Guardians were playing in this greatest of all mystery dramas. The man who was the Great Architect of the Universe had rebuilt his Temple each time it was destroyed, was returning to accomplish this glorious task yet one more time. All would come about as it had been ordained.

"Gentleman," came a rich and sibilant voice from the doorway.

All three heads turned to see the arrival of the Frenchman. The fourth member of the Temple Guardians had arrived.

"I bring you good news," he said.

"Ah, Brother Chirac," said Brother Mihaloff, standing to his full height, "May I dare hope you have accomplished your mission?"

When the newly arrived Brother Chirac smiled broadly, the other Temple Guardians stood as well. It was to be a day of grand celebration. Brother Chirac stepped completely into the room and closed the door behind him. He wore an elegantly cut suit of the new décor, élégant popular among the Quebec elite, highlighted by a tie that rippled with the quiet discretion of polished muscovite. From an inside pocket, he withdrew an exquisite Luxuo cigar case of blackened gold, intricately engraved with the suis generis shape of the Davidoff cigarette and cigar boxes.

"We are alone, oui?" he asked.

"Certainly," said Brother Mihaloff.

"Ah, gentleman, then may I share with you our victoire convaincante—our convincing victory—over and against the powerful odds arrayed against us. We have located and are transporting even as we meet the fabled Blazing Star of Freemasonry to my home, where the lovely Eva Morgan will accept its care until the day our très bien Grandmaster Hiram Abiff steps onto the world stage."

The four men were quiet for several moments as each contemplated the meaning of this. The Blazing Star had been missing from Freemasonry for most of its recorded history. For Brother Chirac to have both located and retrieved it was an accomplishment that would be discussed and retold for generations yet to come.

"Brother Ralph will be so pleased to learn of this," said Brother Cook. "He has spent most of his adult life researching the Blazing Star's place in Masonic Symbolism. If his other duties had not prohibited him from traveling with you, it would've been his greatest pleasure to search for it with you. It would have made him feel like the Indiana Jones of Freemasonry."

Brother Chirac smiled a quick little smile.

"To paraphrase a degenerate Irish poet— and is it not so that all Irish poets are degenerates— '... a perfect cigar is a perfect pleasure. It is exquisite and leaves one unsatisfied. What more can one want?' M. Wilde's hidden cleverness is itself a degenerate pleasure. He skewers that which he does not understand. For it is a truth of immense consequence that no great cigar leaves a man unsatisfied. To that end gentleman, although it is true that one's pleasure may not supplant another, I pray that the cigars I have with me will at the very least remove from both yours and brother Smith's heart, the unfulfilled yearnings of exotic adventure. You were all, every one of you, my brothers, in my heart as I searched the world over for our lost Blazing Star."

"English may not be your first language," said Brother Mihaloff, "but you surely can make it sing."

****

The open stained-glass windows had cleared the room of cigar smoke, leaving behind only a rich cedar and wine smell. Outside, the diminishing night sounds of a city gorged like a leech with government money were like chaotic white noise.

Brother Mihaloff was returning his cell phone to his pocket.

"Our own Dr. Ralph Smith is not only impressed with the results of Dr. Rambert's work, I think he is as close to ecstatic as I've ever heard him," said Brother Mihaloff. "I'm telling you, Emile, he can't quit using the word miracle."

Brother Emile Chirac nodded his head in agreement.

"As a collector of curiosities and artifacts, I have little knowledge of medicine. But I wholeheartedly agree with his opinion. As a layman, I did not understand that the human brain played such a large role in regulating bodily health. You understand it is the Frenchman in me saying that the medical health of the body depends on the joy of the heart. Romance, a friend of mine used to say, cures all ills."

"Try being a police detective for a couple of years," said Brother Cook, "and you just might change your mind about that."

"I am sorry, Brother Cook, but a Frenchman, even a cynic such as myself, will never devalue the role of the heart."

"Try being an actor for a couple of years," said Brother Kaufman, "and see if that's enough to change your mind."

"Enough," said Brother Mihaloff. He raised his half-empty glass of wine in salute. "To the future," he said with a shout.

Brothers Kaufman and Cook raised their glasses as well, and shouted, "To the future."

Brother Emile Chirac only parted his lips in a predatory smile. Tomorrow, he knew, would be the first screen test of his brother's creatures' aptitude for Skype. Although he had little use for the medium, and therefore little knowledge of it, it was still his opinion that the dead would show poorly on webcams.

"Perhaps," said Brother Chirac, "we should toast as well to our new Tyler. I am so pleased that he accepted the position."

Brother Kaufman hiked his stockinged feet onto a coffee table and let out a contented sigh before he spoke.

"Brother Mihaloff is worried he's too skeptical to do the job correctly."

"That is not what I said," said Brother Mihaloff.

"It's what you meant," said Brother Kaufman.

"Yes, indeed. He is young," said Brother Chirac. "But the years will cure that, don't you agree?"

With a tired nod, Brother Mihaloff agreed. He got up and walked to the window overlooking the streets below. The city of Detroit and Freemasonry, he had long thought, were tied together. It was his belief that for a short but golden time, Freemasonry's beating heart was in Detroit. The very building they were in was a testimony to that idea. Wherever Freemasonry truly started, it was Detroiters who had built the biggest and most impressive Masonic Temple in the world. And who could disagree that the principles of Freemasonry were responsible for the explosive growth of Detroit itself? No rational person could dispute that. Detroit's success was entirely based on the principles of Freemasonry. The Masonic ideal of the Fatherhood of God and the Brotherhood of man was united in Detroiters to lead the world forward into a future of peace and prosperity.

"Of what are you thinking, my friend?" asked Brother Chirac as he and the others joined Brother Mihaloff at the window.

"I wish Brother Prince Hall was here to meet Grandmaster Hiram Abiff when he comes through the Empty Chair. Nowadays, our poor city," he ran a hand over the view of the tormented streets below, "is trapped in a national dialogue where racial tension is used as a whip as it was in the times before the Civil War. Grandmaster Hiram Abiff will see that the world puts all that behind them. With the power of the Blazing Star at his command, he will bring all the racial hatred in the world to heel."

"Indeed," said Brother Chirac.

Brother Mihaloff continued thinking out loud.

"We've talked so much about what his coming rule will mean. All good governance is based on the principles of Freemasonry. No, on the realized principles of Freemasonry. Grandmaster Hiram Abiff will make Masonic principles the law."

"Amen to that, brother," said Brother Cook. "Law enforcement could surely use a helping hand. Lord help anyone who tries to dick around with Hiram Abiff."

"And with the Sign of Hiram implanted beneath the skin of everyone's foreheads, disease will finally be conquered," added Brother Kaufman. "You should have seen the look on our new Tyler, Brother Hunter, when he saw those who had been healed by the Sign of Hiram. Yes, he is a skeptic. Yes, he is a famous skeptic. But when he left the Masonic Research Clinic, he left there a believer."

It is always good, thought Brother Chirac, for the new world dictator to have believers rather than followers.

"Can you believe this, brothers?" said Brother Mihaloff. The tremor in his voice was like the excitement of a teenager on his first date. "In a few hours, we will Skype conference call Grandmaster Hiram Abiff. It will be his first video teleconference. Eva Morgan has set everything up. All of us together on one video conference call. Think about it. A three-thousand-year-old man on a video conference call."

For the first time in years, Brother Mihaloff seemed genuinely happy.

That will change soon enough, thought Brother Chirac.

30

"Hello?"

Hunter had been summoned to the meeting that afternoon and Dr. Smith was now there as well, meaning they had a full house minus the Frenchman. The latter had business to attend to regarding the Blazing Star. Hunter was intrigued by the Blazing Star, which was the most famous symbol in Freemasonry after the Square and Compass, but there was so much going on that he filed it away for things to discuss later.

"Yes, we can hear you, but we can't see you on the screen," said Brother Kaufman, who had assumed control of the computer video hookup via Skype as he was, after all, an actor and a film director. "Is your camera on?"

"I believe so," said Hiram Abiff.

On the fifty-two-inch screen wall mounted at the end of the conference table, Hiram's face appeared and moved forward to fill almost the entire screen. After a moment's bug-eyed staring, Hiram's gigantic face was replaced with a gigantic finger tapping on the screen. Finally, after giving up, he leaned back and shrugged at the camera.

"Wait," said Brother Kaufman. "It's working now. We can see you just fine—can you still hear us?"

Hiram waited patiently but seemed just a little confused.

"I see your lips moving," he said, "but I can't hear you."

Hunter shook his head in amazement. This was a Kafkaesque farce. It was a high-tech burlesque. He was about to insert himself into the problem when a young woman put her head between Hiram and the camera. Hiram slid back in his chair to give her some space, and a moment later, she pulled back.

"Who was that gorgeous woman?" asked Hunter.

"I heard that," said a woman's voice to the speakers.

"Young and impetuous," muttered Brother Cook.

"That," said brother Mihaloff, "was Eva Morgan. She is the most gifted spiritual teacher of our age. Aren't you Eva?"

The young woman's face appeared on the screen again.

"You flatterer," she said.

Hunter had to consciously close his mouth. Eva Morgan looked to be Eurasian. She had the almond-shaped eyes and the gorgeous, rich, thick black hair and bud-shaped mouth of a truly sensuous woman. She reminded him of the villainous Tia Carrere in the movie True Lies. Rebecca was beautiful, but Eva Morgan was in a class of her own. He was disappointed when she pulled back again and was replaced with the face of Hiram Abiff.

"Eva is so much more talented with electronic things than I," said Hiram.

On the screen, Hunter could see the occasional age spots on the old man's forehead. Random wisps of thin white hair populated his nearly bald head. The wire-rimmed spectacles made his eyes seem slightly larger than they were. At the corner of his eyes just past the edge of the spectacles, Hunter saw the crows-feet wrinkles so common among the elderly. Hiram Abiff was not a distinctive-looking man. He did not have an air of gravitas about him. He did not project an eternal wisdom. He looked like the kindly owner of a small-town bakery called in for a video interview. Slightly uncomfortable with the technology. Not sure how to hold his head to get the best camera results. But willing to take part, because it made the others happy. Looking at him, thought Hunter, he seemed about seventy-four years old. Certainly not a man in his 80s. Definitely not a three-thousand-year-old man. The unreality of sitting around a conference table on Skype calling a man who looked like anyone's grandfather, but who was actually the founder of all Freemasonry worldwide, was a little more than his head could take after what he'd seen on the video cameras in Brother Mihaloff's house, and the healings at the Detroit Masonic research clinic. He needed more time for this all to sink in.

"This," said Brother Mihaloff, "is our new Tyler. He is, as you already know, the nephew of Brother Bartok. His second, Brother Enid Moser, cannot attend today as he is at my house protecting my daughter. These are grim times, Grandmaster."

"Indeed," said Hiram. "Brother Tyler?"

"Worshipful Master," said Hunter automatically.

Hiram cocked an eyebrow.

Brother Mihaloff leaned over and whispered to Hunter, "Worshipful Grandmaster."

"I'm sorry," said Hunter. "I meant Worshipful Grandmaster."

A smile from Hiram Abiff.

"Do you understand your duties?"

"To protect the Temple Guardians and their Worshipful Grandmaster from harm."

"And?" prompted Hiram.

Hunter turned to Brother Mihaloff. Again, the brother whispered the proper answer.

"From Cowans and Eavesdroppers."

"And from all Cowans and Eavesdroppers."

"What is the penalty," continued Hiram, "for a man ascertained to be an eavesdropper?"

This time, Brother Mihaloff immediately whispered the answer to Hunter.

"He shall '… be placed under the eaves of the house in rainy weather, till the water runs in at the shoulders and out at his heels.'"

Hunter repeated the penalty to Hiram, then nervously waited for the next question. Brother Mihaloff had said nothing about an exam.

"Good, very good," said Hiram. "And will you do your duty to protect both your Worshipful Grandmaster and the Temple Guardians from harm?"

"I do so confirm," said Hunter.

"Then, let us proceed to business," said Hiram Abiff.

Hunter missed the next few sentences uttered by Brother Mihaloff.

"What have you to report about the attack on Brother Mihaloff's house?" asked Hiram.

No one answered. Hunter looked from one man to the other around the table, wondering who would speak up.

"Brother Tyler," repeated Hiram. "What have you to report?"

"Me?"

"You are the Tyler," Hiram said. "Do your duty to protect both your Worshipful Grandmaster and the Temple Guardians. Explain to us what you have learned. Why was brother Mihaloff's house attacked?"

Well, what had he learned?

"Nothing yet, Worshipful Grandmaster," said Hunter like a Marine reporting to his drill sergeant.

"You have learned nothing? Nothing at all?"

"Worshipful Grandmaster, it has been less than twenty-four hours," said Hunter defensively. Hunter gaped at the men gathered around the table. No one had prepared him for this. He did not know he was supposed to have a report ready. The whole thing was ridiculous.

"You are new to our order," said Hiram in a voice that was both menacing and solemn all at once. "But our standards are high. Only the most competent are chosen to be Knights of the Temple Guardians. Do not assume that because your uncle Bartok, who was the finest Mason our order has ever produced, was your blood relative that you are not required to meet those standards. All the men surrounding you at your table are the finest in their field. Have you not researched them? These are your brothers. Do you not know them?"

Hunter felt the desire to sink into his chair. Hiram Abiff had more than an authority voice he had the authority voice.

"No Worshipful Grandmaster," said Hunter, "I do not."

"Then accept my word for this, Brother Tyler. In the New World, we're creating the skills, the experience, and the abilities of these your brothers are the foundation stones upon which we shall build. Upon my return, all governments of the world will operate the same as Masonic lodges. There will be no more communism, socialism or capitalism. There will be no dictators, no presidents, and no monarchs. Each government will become a Masonic Lodge. The blueprint for these governmental lodges is enshrined in the constitutions of our craft. Brother Cook will oversee Masonic justice. Brother Smith will oversee the administration and implementation of the Sign of Hiram. Kaufman will be in charge of the political rituals of the world. A person without ritual, Brother Tyler, is a lost person indeed.

"And what of Brother Mihaloff, you ask? It will be his great blessing to oversee the teaching and education of the masses for the true meaning of Masonic symbolism and ritual. The opportunity is wonderful and terrible at the same time. It will, of course, mean the end of all religion.

"Part of Brother Mihaloff's duties will be to reveal the accurate history of the major world religions. I knew the prophets of the Old Testament, I knew Jesus and I knew Mohammed. I spoke face-to-face with each of them. And yes, I knew the Buddha. The true history of these men and their beliefs has been sabotaged down through the ages. But I, Worshipful Grandmaster Hiram Abiff, have sworn to set that right. I have collected all knowledge concerning faith throughout history and it will be my gift to all mankind. Brother Mihaloff will be my apostle whose responsibility it is to share those truths with the world. Civilization cannot stand another religious war.

"The Frenchman, who I see is not present, will restore the genuine history of our craft so that all may see its glory. And you, Brother Tyler," said the old man on the screen, "shall have the most demanding responsibility of all."

Well, shit, as Moser would say. Hunter had seen none of this coming. The men around the table seemed supportive of every word that Hiram spoke. Could his own uncle Bartok have known of this and accepted Hiram's edicts? He didn't think so, but then, he had spent little time with Bartok for nearly twenty years. Could he have really believed in this insanity? Even if Hiram was three thousand years old, that did not mean that he knew everything and had the right ideas. Masonic world governments? Chances were zero anyone would go along with that.

"And what is that?" asked a nervous Hunter.

"Why," said Hiram Abiff with what Hunter thought was an evil little smile, "it will fall upon you and your sword to divide those with true ideas from those who believe falsehoods. Like the Tyler in a standard Masonic Lodge, you will allow neither Cowans nor eavesdroppers. Only those who accept Masonic law may take part in the benefits of the Grand Lodge."

"The benefits?"

"Yes, the benefits. Only free and accepted Masons may benefit from the Sign of Hiram. Those who do not embrace Freemasonry will be left to the foibles of modern medicine. Modern medicine, as I'm sure you know, Brother Tyler, has still not cured the common cold. Modern medicine has not cured cancer. Under the general heading of autoimmune diseases, modern medicine places all diseases that they don't know about. They ignore and leave in the dustbins of time the learnings of Paracelsus. The wisdom of Jesus of Nazareth. They believe in their arrogance that Edgar Cayce healed no one. That he was a fraud and a con man. Meanwhile, they comfort their patients, who entrust their health to them, with the idea that someday, sometime in the future, a medical cure will miraculously appear. In the meantime, they practice the fine art of imparting dignity to the ill. They brighten their hospitals with cheery colors to encourage recovery. Their nurses have become skilled in the art of concealing the awkward aspects of hospital life. I read an article recently which discussed the manufacturer of less obvious bedpans. Bedpans, you see, make everyone uncomfortable. I believe the thrust of the author's writing was that bedpans should neither be seen nor heard. So, when I return, we shall go about offering true health to the entire world, with the sole exception of those who reject Freemasonry."

Wow, thought Hunter. This was worse than the commercial years ago that showed Presidential candidate Mitt Romney pushing grandmother off the health care cliff. Or was that Paul Ryan? But this was worse, far worse. How was it that Brother Mihaloff and the others did not seem terrified by what Hiram Abiff was saying?

"Wait a minute, Worshipful Grandmaster," said Hunter. "What if world governments refused to go along with what you say?"

Hiram scowled. The lenses of his glasses seemed suddenly to reflect a soft blue light from somewhere in the room from which he was broadcasting.

"I believe I have already explained that they will not take part in the health benefits of the Sign of Hiram."

"I meant," said Hunter quickly, "what if they go to war against you to acquire the Sign of Hiram?"

"Ah," said Hiram. "That would be a terrible mistake."

The other men around the table went Stepford on him. They did not move, they said nothing, and for a moment Hunter wondered if they were still breathing.

"Brother Tyler," said Hiram, "when I return, there will no longer be war. The Blazing Star of Freemasonry wields power too awful to contemplate. The first nation to reject Freemasonry will be an example to all the nations of the world. They may reject Freemasonry, but after the first demonstration, I guarantee you that no nation and certainly no misguided groups of individuals will dare to attack Freemasonry. Pray, Brother Tyler, that if a nation does so, if a nation dares attack us, that it is a small nation. Because, believe me when I say that nothing but a crater in the ground will be where once that country stood."

Well then, thought Hunter, I'm so far over my head now I'll have to dig for months just to see the bottom of my coffin.

"Now," continued Hiram, "because our novice Brother Tyler has nothing to report on the attack against brother Mihaloff's residence, and if he is through with his questions, we will move on to discuss the arrangements for my entrance onto the world stage. Brother Kaufman?"

"Worshipful Grandmaster Abiff," said Brother Kaufman. "A complete replica of the Romanesque Lodge has been built on the stage of the now finished Hiram Abiff Theater. What was once the unfinished theater and a rude embarrassment to all Freemasons, is now completely refinished and re-furnished as the finest small theater in the world. Master artisans from all over the world have worked together to create and infuse your return with both beauty and grandeur. The hotel rooms here in the Detroit Masonic Temple have been brought completely up to date. All eighty rooms are now sold out to leading Freemasons from around the globe. The rest are staying in Detroit luxury hotels. We are on schedule down to the last jot and tittle."

The pride in Brother Kaufman's voice surprised Hunter. It hit him then that what he'd originally seen as a group of fearful older men was something different altogether. The only thing these men were afraid of was what Brother Mihaloff had talked to him about earlier. They were afraid—not fearful—but afraid that powerful dark forces were at work to stop the return of their Grandmaster. After the things that

Hunter just heard, however, he would like it for things to slow down so he could learn, truly learn, what he had gotten himself into. What these men were talking about seemed incredibly close to treason. Were they talking about overthrowing the United States government? Worse, were they talking about overthrowing the governments of the world? Did Hiram Abiff really have that much power?

A harrowing thought brought Hunter up short. Was that what this group was? Was he now with a group of terrorists harboring a three-thousand-year-old weapon of mass destruction? Did he need a lawyer? Wait, did he need a really big lawyer?

"Excellent," said the old man on the screen. "Have all the brethren arrived?"

"Yes," said Brother Kaufman. "They are all here, and all eager to learn the revelation of the great Masonic secret. And all are here, Worshipful Grandmaster, under Masonic oath. Their excitement is like an electric current coursing through the entire Detroit Masonic Temple. This building is once again alive with Masonic light."

Wow, thought Hunter. Brother Kaufman sounds like the Tin Man when he was ushered into the presence of the Wizard of Oz. Eric Hoffman would recognize Brother Mihaloff on sight. A genuine believer. A totally true believer.

"Tyler," snapped Hiram Abiff. "These details are of little use to you now in the discharge of your responsibilities. Your time will be better spent learning who wishes to stop my return and in guaranteeing the safety of your brother Temple guardians. To do otherwise would be monumental negligence, and I do not tolerate negligence."

Still fuming from the rebuke, Hunter let the door swing softly shut behind him, careful not to let it hit him in the ass on the way out.

Pompous prick, thought Hunter. The pompous three-thousand-year-old prick.

****

In the town of Borgo, where Hiram Abiff sat in front of the laptop she had brought him, Eva Morgan stroked the back of the old man's neck. The demons would remain quiet for only a short while longer. She could not quiet the things that inhabited Hiram's body indefinitely. But for a while, he seemed almost like a human being.

31

When Hunter told Moser the broad strokes about what he'd seen and heard in the Masonic Research Clinic and the Skype call with the Grandmaster, Moser wanted to know the details. It was hard to organize in his head to explain it. It was the greatest medical discovery in all recorded antiquity. It was the weirdest Skype call in history. He'd been so shocked by what they'd showed him at the Masonic Research Clinic and what he'd heard on the subsequent conference call, he never even pressed the point of how the Sign of Hiram worked. Hunter wondered if he was suffering from some kind of new information overload. Some of it is bad, some of it is great, but just too much of it. Especially Hiram Abiff's Masonic New World Order.

They were sitting in the main room of the bunker at the table near the computer console. It was still broad daylight outside, but neither of them was letting down their guard. It would be hard to do considering what they'd seen the night before on the video replays, and after listening to Brother Mihaloff tell them that Hiram Abiff was real. He was about to bring his friend up to date when Moser held up a hand.

"You hear that?" said Moser.

"Yep," said Hunter. "I think she's awake."

"Considering the way she woke up last time, I'd say we need to go check on her."

"Right behind you, old man. My throat still hurts just thinking about it."

They opened the door to the first aid room and saw her standing near the bed and shivering. She was holding a pistol in her good hand, down by her side. Moser moved quickly and yanked it out of her grip. Since she'd stabbed her doctor, bitten her father and throat punched Hunter, the old man wasn't taking any chances.

"Give me back my pistol," she said in an icy voice.

She was dressed in the same clothes she'd been wearing the night before, minus the sleeve Dr. Smith had cut away from her injured arm. The sedative was wearing off, but not completely, judging by the way she had to grab the metal support railing on the side of the wall. She looked like a wild woman, with dark brown hair matted together in some places and sticking out like she'd been shocked in others. Her eyes were slightly unfocused, but her face was hard with determination.

"Not a chance," said Moser. "Lay back down and get some rest. You got torn up pretty bad last night."

"I need that pistol," she said.

Her eyes grew more focused, and her voice had an element of command.

"Enid's right, Rebecca," said Hunter. "You're in no shape to do anything but rest. Dr. Smith will be back later to check on you."

She looked at him with sudden suspicion.

"Who are you?" she asked. "I don't know you. Or your friend."

"We're friends of your father," said Hunter.

"You're Masons?" she cut in.

Hunter and Moser exchanged a glance. The way she said Masons made it sound like she really meant vomit.

"Yes," said Hunter. "We're Masons."

"Give me my pistol."

"Not happening," said Moser. "Rest is what you need."

Rebecca collapsed backward into a sitting position on the bed. She wiped her forehead with the back of her good hand and took in a long, steadying breath.

"We saw the video footage of what happened," said Hunter before he thought better of it. Way to keep her calm.

Moser shot him a look.

"Nice shooting," said Moser. "But we can talk about that later, miss. Can you get her a sedative and a pain pill, Hunter? And a cup of water?"

The young woman glared at Moser.

"Sorry," he said. "You got kind of wild last night."

Hunter had a mental image of her trying to cut them with the broken end of an eight-ounce drinking glass.

"I had a good reason," she snapped back.

"Yes, ma'am. While Hunter's getting your medications, do you want a couple of warm washcloths to clean yourself up? We would have done it for you while you were sleeping, but we didn't want to wake you. Your father got you some clean clothes over there."

Rebecca followed his extended finger to where a change of clothes was stacked on a cabinet. She shuddered suddenly, violently at a flash memory of the events of the night before.

"Are you okay?" asked Moser as he stepped toward her.

Hunter came back with the pills and a paper cup.

"I'm okay," she said. "Really. I was trying to not to think about what happened, but it came back to me suddenly."

"What can we do?" asked Hunter.

"And it's a no about the gun," said Moser.

She gave Moser a weak smile, and Hunter thought if you washed away all the blood and put some clean clothes on her, she'd be a pretty woman.

"I need you to call someone for me. Right now."

"Uh—" was the first and only word of response from Moser. He looked at Hunter for help.

"I don't think your father wants anyone else involved," said Hunter.

"Then I'll do it myself," she said and levered herself up with one arm.

He held up his hands.

"Okay, okay. Who do you want us to call?"

"Pastor Howard. He needs to know about this. Ask him to come now. He'll know what to do. Tell him to bring the church elders."

"How about we just start with the Pastor?" asked Hunter. "The fewer people we involve in this, the better."

He wasn't even sure what a church elder was. Probably the most senior church members—the ones they had to roll in on wheelchairs. He'd only been to church a few times in his life, but he remembered a lot of people being rolled up the ramp. The people were old, their songs were old and the church itself already had a worn-out smell like the furniture in an abandoned house.

She started to object, but Moser held up a finger.

"One thing at a time, Miss Rebecca. One person at a time. Things like what happened to you last night need a lot of thinking on before we take our next step."

"We?" she asked.

"After what we saw in that video, none of us ain't going nowhere."

Hunter nodded in agreement. He was thinking about the horned creature in the video capture. It occurred to him that Moser was right. This had to be kept under control. He tried to imagine a new website called www.hornedcreatures.com and decided he'd rather not think about it. Or a new YouTube channel called The Woman and the Beast. The thought made him uneasy. Like he'd put his hand in oily water trying to find something he'd lost and instead felt something scaly brush across his palm. What was it he almost remembered?

"I came home to protect my father," Rebecca said suddenly.

"From what?" asked Hunter.

She was quiet for a moment and then, ignoring Hunter completely, she told Moser the phone number to call for Pastor Howard.

"You should use the wall phone," she said, pointing to the right of the door. "Cell phones don't always work down here. Depends on the carrier and maybe the day of the week."

"Good enough," said Moser.

He made the call while Hunter tried to look at the young woman without seeming to, passed on the message to a gruff sounding man, listened for a few seconds, and then hung up.

"He's on his way," he reported. "Kind of rough-sounding guy for a preacher."

"Couple years in jail will do that to you," said Rebecca.

****

While Moser prowled the house above the bunker with his best friend, the Winchester always at his side, Hunter sat in front of a desk in the bunker's study and stared at the two important things before him. First was the coffee cup full of hot black coffee. It was a heavy ceramic mug with the raised silver symbol of the Masonic square and compass on it. Hunter felt a genuine sense of pride in being a Mason. His father, who had died while Hunter was young, was a Mason. His uncle Bartok was a Mason. Bartok had once told him that one of their long dead relatives had been in the same lodge George Washington was raised in. There was an indefinable sense of history associated with being a Mason that was hard to ignore. With both his father and his Uncle Bartok dead, it gave him a connection to them both. They had gone through the same rituals he had. And he had spoken the same oaths, took part in the same rituals of admission they had and recognized the same Masonic symbols that he and Moser did. From Entered Apprentice to Fellowcraft to Master Mason, all men followed the same journey. And when complete, they all stood on the same level, which meant to him he and his family were all the same in the eyes of their fraternity. That, he had to admit, gave him some comfort.

The second thing of interest was the chest that contained the ghost box, which he and Moser had carried with them all over the country in their quest for the missing piece of the alien crystal that powered their ships and one of which Magnus Hillis had used in his construction of the ghost box. That crystal no longer held power. Hunter didn't want to leave it in the trunk. He never let it out of his sight for long. In one of Bartok's letters, he had instructed Hunter to see a woman named Mrs. Hathaway in Atlanta who had more information on the topic for him, but she had passed away shortly before they arrived. After much waiting and persistent finagling, he and Moser had been informed that all the papers Bartok had left with her for safekeeping had been forwarded to the Detroit Masonic Lodge, where his uncle was a life member.

"You going to drink that coffee or just sit there staring at that trunk?"

Moser had come up behind him so quietly that Hunter hadn't heard him. For a big, older man, the Kentuckian still could spook a cat.

"Just thinking," he said and spun the chair to face Moser. "This sounded pretty simple when we were asked to come here, but it's looking more insane every minute. Night watchman supposedly choked by a statue. Floor opens up to Hell and the other night watchmen slides down into flames and gets carried away by winged monsters. That and Brother Mihaloff's daughter attacked and torn up by an animal with horns on its head, plain as day. I could handle most of that after what we dealt with in Kentucky, but this idea that Hiram Abiff is real and a couple thousand years old makes me wonder about Old Man Mihaloff's medications. But it is absolutely damned hard to argue with what I saw at the clinic today. And the thing about the four signs reminds me of Biblical signs of the Apocalypse or something out of the Four Horsemen."

"I'm not sure I'm buying into that," said Moser. "Hiram Abiff is just a symbol, not a real person. That's what I've always heard and read. Checked it out on the Internet a few times. Still, if Hiram isn't alive, which I doubt as much as them using a real Bigfoot in those beef jerky commercials, so why would Brother Mihaloff offer to introduce you to him?"

"Old man, I just don't know. There's no record of Hiram Abiff as a real person—unless you want to count the occasional misspelled and misapplied mention of a guy with a similar name in the Bible."

"Same as I was taught. But these boys here in Detroit are a peculiar bunch. When Brother Mihaloff gives you the other papers from Bartok, we'll see what's what. Bartok never missed much, and I'll bet there are a lot of answers there. What did you think of the night watchman's story about the statue?"

"Probably the same as you," said Hunter. "There's no evidence it really happened except for the bruise-necklace wrapped around Leasing's neck. That looked pretty convincing, except it didn't prove it was done by a psychotic statue. He might have done it himself somehow if he was crazy enough. People go over the edge to get attention. Everybody wants to be important. They'll put their whole life on Facebook to get some validation. They'll sell their dignity for YouTube subscribers and their self-respect if it gets them more Twitter followers. You can imagine how much his online profile would skyrocket if he could convince people he was strangled by a statue. Prison inmates have more dignity than online people. Unless they're both prison inmates and online people. But I digress.

"The thing is, he just didn't seem like a fake to me, Enid. It was the way he looked. He looked legitimately freaked out, as in scared out of his mind. That other story about the hallway floor dropping out from underneath the other watchman and him being carried off by monsters into the pits of hell can't exactly be verified evidentially, either. And all we have is Mihaloff's word that the other watchman is missing. Kind of convenient, don't you think?"

"I do. And I like the word evidentially. Sounds scientific."

Hunter grinned. His throat still hurt like hell, and he was almost too tired to think straight, but it was still funny.

"But what happened here," he waved a hand around the room and pointed upstairs, "now this is something else entirely. And I think you were on the right to track about a linkage. I think Brother Mihaloff confirmed that. By the way, do I have to keep calling him Brother Mihaloff all the time, or do we only do that in a lodge?"

Moser looked toward the closed doors behind which Pastor Mark Howard was counseling Rebecca. He'd been in there the better part of the hour with no signs of coming out soon.

"Think she's telling him the whole thing?" he asked.

"I don't know," said Hunter, "if I was her, I'd be damned careful about mentioning this to anyone. It'd be like putting a neon sign on the top of your head that says 'Look Everybody, I'm Crazy.'"

"There's that," said Moser. "About calling the other Mason's brother all the time, it is a custom in most lodges, but that's about it. Mostly a way of saying you recognize them as your equal. You know, on the level and all that. But outside the lodge, it's mostly optional. Personally, I'm done with calling anybody brother today. I feel like we've been dragged through a stinking pile of horseshit. Upstairs looks like wild gorillas tore the place apart, and I'm not happy to be here if what really did the damage comes back and visits this place. So, when that old man returns, I want some more answers or there's going to be trouble."

"I like the way you say trouble. It sounds scientific."

"Yeah, don't it though? Lot of fireworks last night when that round hit the symbol on the front door. You expect that?"

"Truthfully? I didn't know what would happen. It was a gut call. I don't believe in magic, and I really don't like the idea of magic, real sorcery or witchcraft or whatever the hell it is. Bartok made me learn a lot about it, but it was theoretical. Like training to fight an imaginary enemy in a video game. I mean, face it. All video combat games are against imaginary characters. They don't really exist. Same with sorcerers, magicians and witches. At least, that's what I thought at the time he was teaching me. I thought it was all superstition. I got the theory. People like to dress up and pretend they're something they aren't. They like to think they have access to power that they don't really have access to. And they like to be different. Like their secret rituals and words of power. Kind of like Masons, when you think about it.

"Some groups shy away from the magical power stuff because it's by and large stupid. Others go all in for enlightenment, like Reiki masters and Hermetic practitioners and other people with too much time on their hands. This stuff's been around forever, Moser. It's like religion. Like the church people who dress up in robes and have their rituals and their own kind of magic. Or science, where all you have to say is scientists say that... and then you just fill in the blanks and it is considered sacred from that point on. And the masses just eat it up because the priests of science say so. Sorcery and magic were always like that to me. It is because somebody says it is."

The voice from behind them was so unexpected that Hunter almost fell off his chair.

"Are you trying to hurt my feelings?"

Pastor Howard was only five feet behind them and looking at Hunter with a wounded expression.

"You surely walk quiet for a preacher," said Moser.

"Did you hear him coming?" asked Hunter.

"Yep. But you were on such a roll with that speech of yours, I just let you go on for a bit."

Pastor Howard was every bit as tall as Moser, which put him at about six three. But where Moser was long and rangy, he was bulky. Lot of weightlifting going on in prison, thought Hunter. He hoped the pastor hadn't heard him making fun of online prison inmates.

Pastor Howard was thick about the chest, and with arms so well-muscled his sport coat stretched to contain his biceps. Hunter was feeling like he might need to work out a little more himself. Maybe more than that. The Pastor walked the rest of the way over, and Hunter realized he liked the man's squared-up looks. It was the solid chin and jawline that did it. The wide forehead and bright blue eyes. He looked like a man who could knock your lights out with one straight punch but not hold a grudge.

"I didn't mean to sneak up on you. I was trying to walk quietly so Rebecca could get back to sleep. Her medications should do the job, but she might put up a fight. There's not much passive about that young woman. Thank you, by the way, for keeping her handgun away from her, though she'll find another one around here as soon as she wakes up again. They're stashed all over this place and the upstairs, too. Her father prepared early for the apocalypse."

"Yeah, we've noticed," said Hunter, "interesting family."

"Mr. Hunter, you have no idea. I've known the Mihaloffs since Rebecca joined my church. Her mother passed away before I met Rebecca—brain cancer. Not a pleasant way to die, but I suppose there aren't many pleasant ways to die when you think about it. Now, if you don't mind, I have Rebecca's permission to view the security system video from last night. Can you show it to me, please?"

"I don't think we can do that without Brother—I mean Frank's permission. Maybe you could ask him first," said Hunter.

"Never mind," said Pastor Howard. "I'll just go wake Rebecca and have her show it to me."

He turned and started walking back toward the first aid room.

"Hold on," said Moser. "No need for that. He's right, Hunter. If he wants to see it, she can show it to him."

"Blessed," said Pastor Howard as he turned back, "are those who know when they're beaten and give in."

This guy will be trouble, thought Hunter.

****

"Stop right there," said the minister.

Hunter stopped the video feed the way Frank Mihaloff had

showed him. The three of them had watched it together, sitting at the console seated on folding chairs. Pastor Howard had shown little reaction to the horned beast wrecking the house and tearing after Rebecca, but when it came to the part where the woman with the blurred-out face was cradling the creature in her arms and looking straight into the camera, his face blanched and he took in a sharp breath.

"What is it?" asked Moser.

The minister leaned in toward the screen and then recoiled slightly, as though he didn't want to get too close.

"I know it's strange that her face is so badly pixilated you can't see it," said Hunter. "We don't know what caused that. Electronic distortion is our best guess. Hides her entire face. No way we know of to fix it, either. I know some AV engineers in the area who might be able to crack it if Frank gives the go-ahead."

Now it felt odd calling Brother Mihaloff by his first name. Hunter would have to think about the whole thing after he got enough sleep to remember his own name.

Pastor Howard was staring at him with a look of surprise and wonder on his face.

"What?" asked Hunter.

With a distracted motion, the minister reached into his sport coat and retrieved a card case. He took out two cards and gave one to each of them.

"My cell number is on these," he said. "You can call me anytime, day or night, although I think you'll be more likely to call at night."

"Did you see something in that video we missed?" asked Moser. "You seem kind of upset."

"Rebecca is a special woman. I'd like your word," said Pastor Howard, "that you'll watch over her as this thing unfolds. Can you do that for me?"

"As what unfolds?"

Moser didn't like the long way around on anything, thought Hunter.

"She's unusual. Quite special. Did you know that in seminary I was taught that not only was the canon of scripture closed, but there was no need for the spiritual gifts anymore, so that meant that they were therefore gone? Over. Done with."

"My apologies, pastor, but what in the hell are you driving at?"

It wasn't like Moser to swear at a pastor, but being up all night wasn't doing much for his good humor.

After rolling his chair around so he was looking directly at Moser, the pastor continued.

"Rebecca has dreams. Rebecca has visions. We're United Methodists, Mr. Moser. Not charismatics. You know what charismatics are, don't you? Good. Do you, Mr. Hunter? Wonderful. I did a lot of stupid and sometimes terrible things when I was younger. Jesus was kind enough to forgive my mistakes and even the things I did deliberately, so I have a new life in Him and I'm grateful for that. I'm grateful for my congregation. But I'm still working things out as a pastor. Pastors are like schoolteachers. We like the quiet students—the ones who do their assignments, make a few mistakes and then try hard to correct those mistakes. Congregants and students are alike in that way. We pastors like the quiet ones. They're less work. They're easier to counsel. But the special ones, the ones that make too much noise... those are a lot harder to handle."

"It's like this. Rebecca has what most would think of as prophetic dreams and visions, and experiences what some in the faith would call words of knowledge. For years she's brought them to me to discuss. At first, I admit I thought she just needed moderated mental health counseling. No such thing as the gifts of prophetic dreams and visions and words of knowledge, since the canon of scripture is closed to us Methodists. They have to be hypnopompic hallucinations or schizophrenia or PTSD or whatever flavor of the month the psychologists and psychiatrists want to call it. DSM-5 is out now, so it may have a new name. I'm afraid to look after they soft pedaled pedophilia as more of a lifestyle issue than a mental disorder. So, I'm ashamed to say that at first, I encouraged Rebecca to seek psychological counseling. But the problem didn't go away. Then came the psychiatrists and the drugs. God help me, I was an ignorant bastard."

"Did her prophetic visions have anything to do with statues coming to life or horned beasts or—"

The pastor cut Hunter off with a wave of his hand.

"The answer is yes to all the above."

Grabbing his shotgun from where it was lying on the console next to him, Moser took two or three hesitant steps toward the first aid room. Then he looked back at the minister.

"I think I'll stay a little closer to make sure nothing happens to her."

"It won't make a difference," said Pastor Howard, "until deep dark."

"Well, shit," said Moser, and he returned to his seat.

"Let me see if I've got this straight," said Hunter. "Rebecca foresaw all of this happening in a dream?"

"She did. I'm still struggling with accepting her gifts, you understand. As a minister of the United Methodist Church, I must say I'm confused about almost everything on this topic. I'm not supposed to be, you understand, but I'm struggling with the church's restrictions and admonitions on the topic. We're better with gender issues than spiritual gifts. But to get to the thing that confuses me more than all of that, do I understand that neither you nor Mr. Moser can see the woman's face in the video capture?"

"Pixilation," repeated Hunter. "Not sure what caused it, but that's what makes it impossible to see."

"But I can see her quite clearly and so could Rebecca. Can you not even see the number 666 on the woman's forehead?"

Not good, thought Hunter. Not good at all.

"None of us, including Brother Mihaloff or Dr. Smith, could see her face at all and no way in hell we missed that series of numbers. Are you telling me that looking at that computer screen, you see the woman's face clearly and you also see the number of the beast on her forehead?"

"I am. No hype. No—if you'll excuse the word—bullshit. I can see her face as clearly as I see your own. And you can't?"

"No."

No one said anything for half a minute.

"Protect her," said the pastor.

"We'll try," said Hunter.

"Keep your guns ready and with you," said Pastor Howard. "She thinks her father is protecting the Antichrist. She's adamant about it. So, while you're at it, you might hit up the Catholics for some holy water."

32

"Do I know you?" asked Mike Leasing. "Wait, you're... you're that woman."

After he'd calmed down, Brother Kaufman had driven him back to his apartment and dropped him off with instructions that if he felt he needed anything, he should call Dr. Smith. He'd been left with anti-anxiety pills and other pills to help him sleep. It was ten o'clock at night now and he'd been ready to take a sleeping pill so that he could drowse off when his doorbell rang. He'd opened it to find himself face to face with a beautiful woman with long, black hair. A woman he thought he recognized, but whose name he couldn't remember. It was the stress, he thought. It made it difficult for him to think. No matter how hard he tried, the horrible images of Brother Miller slipping down into the flaming darkness kept coming back.

"I'm Eva Morgan," said the woman. "Brother Mihaloff asked me to check in on you and make sure you were feeling better."

"Oh," he said. "Now I remember. You're the woman who rents the Masonic auditorium to give speeches on esoteric things. You're like a celebrity to Masons everywhere."

"Of course, but you exaggerate. May I come in?"

"Oh, yes, surely."

Mike Leasing stood to one side and felt her brush by him as she stepped into his apartment. He felt an electric tingle rush through his body as she walked by. She was wearing a high collared black cape and walked with an exotic sultriness as she stepped into the center of the room.

"I'm sorry," Mike blurted. "I've been gone for a bit and haven't had time to clean up."

His living room was a mess. The first beautiful woman who'd ever come into his apartment and it had to look like a bomb had gone off. There were magazines scattered on the couch and two empty microwave dinners on the coffee table. He'd tossed his shoes on the battered old recliner as he worried that the whole apartment smelled of stale socks.

"Let me clear you off a place to sit," he said, and picked up his shoes, walked to the closet and threw them in, slamming the door after them as though locking them away. "Can I get you something to drink? Would you like me to take your... cape?"

"Do you have wine?" she asked.

Mike looked desperately toward the kitchen.

"Beer," he blurted out. "I have beer. No wine, though. Would you like a beer?"

"No thank you," she said.

Ignoring his question about her cape, she walked to the recliner, looked at it for a moment with a curious expression, and then sat down, tucking her cape beneath her.

"Um... thank you for coming," he said. "I'm fine, really."

She shrugged and looked like she was going to get up and leave.

"But I'm really glad you came. I could use the company. Really. It will calm my nerves."

Eva Morgan was stunning in every way. Mike had always admired her pictures in the lobby. She was the pin-up girl of his dreams. And here she was, in his apartment. Wait until he told his friends. It never occurred to him to think it peculiar that she came to visit him so late at night.

"Then I'm pleased I came. Brother Mihaloff was worried about you, and when he explained to me what you had seen, well, I thought you might need company."

Mike cleared the microwave dinner containers from the coffee table, picked up the magazines from the couch and took the whole mess to the kitchen and disposed of them in the wastebasket. As he came back into the room, he asked her if she was sure she didn't want a beer.

"I am allergic to beer," she said.

"Oh, sorry," he said as he sat down.

"It must have been horrible seeing what you saw."

Mike drew in a deep breath.

"It… it was," he said. "Brother Mihaloff and the others worry that I'm crazy."

"And you?"

"Me? I wish I was crazy. But I saw it. I saw the floor open up and saw old man Miller — Watchmaster Miller, I mean—I saw him slip back into… into…"

"Hell?" prompted Eva.

"What? Wait… yes, I guess that's it. I saw him slip right back into Hell. And this creature, this black flying thing, grabbed him up in its claws and took him down… into the… pits, I guess. There was this smell, this sulfur smell. It was so strong it makes me almost gag to remember it. But I'm not crazy."

"No," she said, shaking her head gently, "you are not."

Mike Leasing stared at her in disbelief.

"You mean you believe me?" he leaned forward in excitement. Then doubt clouded his features. "Why?"

She smiled at him. Her lips were so red and so full. Her eyes were wide and bright.

"I look at you," she said in a voice that was almost a purr, "and I see a very brave man. Brave men have no need of lies. So, when you tell me, I believe you."

"They brought these two men in to interview me," said Mike in a voice colored with bitterness. "Brother Frank said they were ghost hunters. Paranormal investigators. Supposed to know if I was telling the truth. Like I'd make something like that up."

"Who were they?" she asked.

She smiled a seductive smile. An inviting smile. Mike Leasing badly wanted to please her.

"One was named Hunter, and he was the young one. The other was an older guy. I think his name was… Mosher. No, wait, it was

Moser. He was a tough one. Didn't look like a ghost hunter to me."

Her nails were painted bright red, the same shade as her lipstick, and she drummed them on her right knee.

"The younger guy was Brother Bartok's nephew."

Eva's eyes widened in surprise.

Eager to please her, Mike added, "Brother Bartok Hunter. He was a big deal in the Masons until he died."

"I see," she said it as though tasting the words. "And Brother Mihaloff thought to involve him in such a sensitive matter?"

Mike Leasing felt slightly dizzy. Eva Morgan looked better than any movie star.

"But his nephew is a Mason, too—even though he's a ghost hunter. The whole thing with him and the other guy being there was under Masonic oath. So, he and the old guy will say nothing."

It never occurred to him he was discussing Masonic business with a woman who was not a Mason.

"Moser?" she asked. "What do you know about him?"

He couldn't stop himself from answering. Didn't want to disappoint her.

"Nothing. Never heard of him before. I guess he's a ghost hunter, too."

"I see. You understand, don't you Michael, that these are... the most important secrets within Masonry?"

"Absolutely. What?"

"And you are now a treasured secret as well. In the ages to come, you will be known as the harbinger of Hiram Abiff."

"I will? Wait—what does that mean? I'm not sure what you're talking about."

He didn't want to disappoint her by his ignorance. Didn't want her to leave. Having her in his apartment felt like the most important moment in his life, and he didn't want to ruin it, but he didn't understand what she was saying.

"What you saw," she said, and stood up, "was the most important event in Masonic history. The light within Freemasonry that all Masons yearn for—do you understand?"

"Yes," he blurted. "Well, not exactly, but if you explain it to me, I will."

Eva Morgan stretched her arms over her head like a cat, and then brought one down to her side and she stood. The other she extended toward Mike in an invitation to rise, which he did quickly.

"Give me your hand," she said.

He extended it eagerly, and she took it in her own. Her hand felt hot to the touch and again, a tingling jolt of pleasure rippled through him.

"The greatest secret in Freemasonry is that Hiram Abiff is not a metaphor. He is a real, flesh and blood man who the Freemasons and the Knights Templar before them have hidden in their midst. They have kept him safe for the day of his return."

The sheer pleasure of holding her hand, looking directly into her beautiful eyes and listening to the sound of her voice, made the act of understanding seem insignificant.

"The events you witnessed the other night were the signs that your brethren all around the world have been expectantly waiting for all these long millennia. And you were the one to be present at their advent. It must have been a terrifying sight, my young man, but it marked you as unique, as special. The ghost hunters should never have been allowed to hear your story. Can we trust them to be silent, to keep your great secret? Brother Mihaloff was concerned that he had made a mistake. He even doubted you."

"But—"

Eva tugged him closer. He felt her lush body press against his. She placed a finger against his lips to silence him.

"I told him they could trust you. I spoke on your behalf and said that you would covenant your silence. I told him you and I would seal that covenant so that you could be trusted to take the secret to your grave. Will you agree to covenant with me?"

Mike felt his body tremble in anticipation.

"Anything. I'll do anything to convince you. What do I have to do?"

She smiled a delicious, tantalizing smile.

"We will, as they say, seal it with a kiss. Will you do that for me?"

His eyes widened in surprise.

"Yes, definitely. You bet. I'll—"

Eva pulled him in so close that Mike could hardly breathe and kissed him. He felt her tongue in his mouth and groaned in pleasure. She pulled back and looked at him with hungry eyes.

"May I have another?" she asked.

Before he could answer, she leaned toward him again, and her mouth pressed against his. Mike eagerly pressed his tongue past her lips and reached his hand around her back to pull him tight against him, but went rigid when he felt a suction against his lips like an octopus had fastened a tentacled sucker over his lower face. The excruciating pain was so intense that he tried to force his hand between their bodies to push himself away. He tried to scream, but it was lost in a rush of pain as Eva Morgan's mouth opened further and the force against his face increased until her mouth covered his entire head as it was sucked into her open maw. His body spasmed as its length was pulled into the oily blackness that was her true essence.

33

"You're looking better," said Moser.

"Getting the blood washed out of my hair helped," replied Rebecca.

"Ain't that the truth?"

Her arm was still wrapped in bandages, but at least they were clean bandages. Dr. Smith had stopped by and changed them. He wasn't happy about her not going to a hospital, but he had his instructions from Brother Mihaloff. There was a point to Mihaloff's method, of course. Hospital personnel would ask questions and answers that detailed an attack by a horned beast and a witch would just get ugly. Moser thought lying low in a private bunker with a medical room combined with regular visits from a Masonic doctor was, in fact, a better idea.

"You hungry?" he asked.

"I know where the food is. I grew up hanging out in this bunker. Dad told us we could last out a nuclear war here. Or a zombie apocalypse."

She seemed like she was going to smile a little when she said it, but then her face tightened and she headed for the food pantry.

"I've got two good hands to your one, Miss Rebecca. Why don't you let me help?"

Rebecca turned and stared at him a moment and then did smile when she said, "Miss Rebecca? I haven't been called that since I was five years old."

"Old men like me hang on to the ways of speaking we were taught when we was young. You should hear old Kenneth speak."

"Who?"

"Never mind. Here, let me give you a hand."

"MRE's are over in that cupboard," she said.

"Got a preference?" he asked.

"The cheese omelet. And I'll make the coffee. I really need it."

The bunker layout accommodated a fifteen by fifteen eating area, with enough chairs to seat six people, but it was easily expandable to allow four more. The kitchen and sink were a design marvel shaped like an oval with a butcher-block table and an overhead rack of utensils.

"Never seen a bunker this nice," said Moser.

"No? Dad wants to be able to live through any disaster, but doesn't want to eat from a Coleman stove propped on a card table. That's a quote he used to drum into our heads every time he got a chance. And you can't miss the subtle design elements like the Masonic tiled black and white checkerboard floor, can you? Or the compass and square marble carvings on either side of the main door. Or the trestle board paintings on the wall over the couch. But the Keurig coffee maker is good, and if you'll squeeze that omelet onto this paper plate I'm sliding your way, I'll be grateful."

Moser had lots of experience ripping open the foil pouches that contained MREs, or meals-ready-to-eat as civilians would say, and in the past, he hadn't always had a plate to squeeze them on. They were actually a miracle of modern technology, some with a practical shelf life of three to five years. Others claimed twenty-five years. He looked over at her and saw that, even one handed, she had the coffee going. And was bringing out real silverware to eat with and ceramic mugs for the coffee. Not a woman to complain, he thought. That rip down her arm and hand must still hurt like hell, but not a feel-sorry-for-me word out of her. And she liked Army omelets and could take care of herself. A good woman.

"You want me to heat it up in the microwave?" he asked her.

"Are you a city boy?"

"No, ma'am."

"Good. I grew up eating those things and I like them the way they are."

"That coffee ready? Smells like it," said Moser.

She brought two cups of black coffee over to the table, went back to get her silverware and paper towels for napkins. When they were both seated and sipping coffee, Moser thought the place was damned homey for a bunker and told her so.

"It saved my life last night."

"Amen," said Moser.

He waited for her to take her third bite, just the way Bartok had told him to do years ago, and then said, "That was damned fine shooting last night. But your father is a closed-mouth old mule, and I'd like to know what's going on here before somebody else gets hurt. Hard to help when you are wearing a blindfold, if you know what I mean."

She took another bite and chewed without looking up.

Moser hoped she would open up. This entire trip to Detroit was getting on his nerves, maybe even reminding him of his last trip to southeastern Michigan. The last trip had been to find the device called the ghost box. Then they'd found out about the screaming haint that haunted the Hillis family and had to take care of that, too. Once they found who had the ghost box, they had to deal with that Mr. Chirac and his thug, Ricci. All this before they used the ghost box to drain the power out of the army of mechanical automatons hidden in the caves beneath Townsend Mountain. And put the madstone back where it belonged. He couldn't forget that. It was, as the now dead Detective Alvarez would have said, a deadly goat rodeo. This thing with the Detroit Masonic Temple, the witch and her beast, and Brother Mihaloff's story about Hiram Abiff all seemed to add up to more big trouble, like last time. When they were through here, Moser thought he'd quit coming to Michigan altogether.

"Why do you want to know? I mean, really? I'm sure my father already told you I'm crazy because I'm a born-again Christian who has prophetic dreams, sees visions and prays too much. And he probably added that if I spent less time with the Bible and more with eligible young men, I'd be married by now. Or, what would make him even happier would be if I took a job in private industry instead of starting up and working in nonprofits."

Moser stared back at her without flinching. She had a temper, all right. Granny Hillis would have liked to have met her. A hard man, Enid Moser, nonetheless still mourned the loss of that old woman.

"I have heard none of that, Miss Rebecca from your daddy."

"Did he tell you I took a bite out of his arm while I was in shock, which gives him yet another reason for trying to get me to a psychiatrist again?"

"You don't seem crazy to me. You eat like a normal person. And he didn't say any of that. Truly."

"Ask if Dr. Smith agrees with you next time you see him. He's probably still limping from the scissors I stuck in his leg."

He couldn't help it. Moser burst out with a big, country laugh.

"What's so funny?" asked Rebecca.

Moser saw the way she gripped her fork and laughed again.

"You're thinking of sticking me with that fork, ain't you?" he asked.

She got madder. Her cheeks reddened.

When she noticed her one good hand squeezing the fork, she looked up at him and laughed, too.

"That close," she said when she'd caught her breath. "You were that close."

"Figured," said Moser. "I grew up in the country with sisters. Chances of getting stabbed with anything sharp or having a bucket thrown over your head while they tried to clang it with a wooden spoon were higher than you'd think."

"I wish I'd had brothers or sisters to grow up with. Both or either would have been great. I had a brother, but he died while I was young."

"I'm sorry to hear that."

She got up from the table, put her plate in the wastebasket and her fork in a compact dishwasher.

"You want more coffee while I'm up?"

"Please," said Moser.

"Where's your sidekick?" she asked while pouring him another cup and taking it over to him.

"Sleeping. That man can't think right without sleep. Learned that the hard way last time I was up here in Michigan."

"He's Bartok's nephew?" she asked.

Moser, for once on a rare occasion, showed his surprise.

"How'd you know that?"

"I knew Bartok through my father. Bartok actually told me a bit about you, too, Mister Enid Moser. I didn't connect you and Hunter to Bartok at first because of the pain and the painkillers." She rubbed her uninjured hand across the back of her head and winced. When she pulled her hand away, then looked down at it. It was clear of blood.

She looked down at her bandaged arm, then stroked it with her good hand.

"So, you knew Bartok. Well, shit—pardon the language, Miss Rebecca. That old man never mentioned you or your father to me."

"He was good with secrets," she said with a wistful smile.

"You don't know the half of it," said Moser.

Some nights he would swim in the lake of nightmares, where the water was always dark and brackish. Far out on its dark surface, he would see moonlight recoiling from its oily black ripples, unable to penetrate its depths. The surface would boil like viscous tar in a kettle, and from it would burst the hideous silver-eyed face of that monster Albert Magnus Hillis. Moser would wake up screaming and reaching for his beloved Winchester.

"Yeah," said Moser, "he sure was good with secrets. But that didn't always turn out so good."

"How about you?" she asked him, turning those big brown eyes of hers so that they stared right into his.

"Me? I don't like secrets much. I really don't. But there are some things too dangerous to pass around until they've been defused, if you know what I mean."

"Like a bomb?"

"Yep. Some secrets you don't want to detonate in public."

"I have a secret," she said.

Moser waited her out to let her tell it in her own time. He was just about to give up and ask her when she spoke.

"Did you know Bartok told me if I was in trouble and he wasn't there to help that I should call you?"

Moser was shocked.

"Like I said, Miss Rebecca, he never even mentioned you."

"He gave me your phone number. I still have it, but here you are, so I guess I don't need to call."

"Just say your piece."

It amazed Moser that he didn't question what she said. There was just something about her, bad temper and all, that he felt like he could trust.

"All right. My father and I have fought for a long time about his obsession with Freemasonry. It wasn't just the fact that he was at a Masonic lodge meeting the night my mother died, although that drove the wedge deeper. It was that I called him out on the lie that is at the center of Freemasonry."

This, thought Moser uncomfortably, was headed straight into awkward country.

"And that is?"

"The death and resurrection of Hiram Abiff. Oh, don't worry, Mr. Moser. My father didn't reveal any Masonic secrets to me. He didn't have to. The entire Masonic ritual, every part, is all over the Internet. And, the Masons have gone YouTube, or didn't you know? I didn't have to pry it out of him or go through secret Masonic papers. Masonry has suffered the same fate as the Hermetic Order of the Golden Dawn when Aleister Crowley put their secret rituals into book form and made them available to the public. The horror of it—their secrets became available for all to see, and that just took the fun right out of it. But not for the Masons, no, not for the Masons. They've rather taken to social media. They've made their rituals into a morality play for our time with their own YouTube channels."

She stopped for a moment to let him take it all in.

"You do remember, don't you Miss Rebecca, that I'm a Mason?" he asked.

"I do. And you've probably been told since you were raised at your lodge—that is what they call it, isn't it? Raised?"

Moser gave her a quick, reluctant nod.

"You've probably been told," she continued, "that all the ritual and beliefs were a metaphor, haven't you?"

Another nod.

"What if I told you they weren't? What if I told you that whatever

Freemasonry started out as, its beliefs and rituals were taken over by occultists?"

"With all due respect, Miss Rebecca, Hunter and I are Masons, and we damned sure ain't occultists. And to tell you the truth, I'm not even sure I know what an occultist is. You mean like black magic and such?"

"What if I told you," she said without slowing down, "that Masonry started out with good Christian intentions, but somewhere along the way it broke free of its moorings? It lost its way so badly that it re-wrote its own rituals to conceal a secret so depraved that almost none of its members know about it? And that those who do are blind to its evil."

"This would be where you tell me about the Masons hiding the anti-Christ?"

"So, Pastor Howard told you?"

"Yes, he did. And it sounds kind of way out there. Why in the world would you think such a thing? I've been a Mason since I was a young man and I can guarantee that I've never met one Mason who would even, well, would even believe anyone would think such a thing was possible. My Baptist minister is a Mason, and you don't get more Christian than that. Masonry's goal is to make good men better, not to make good men evil. But we always get tagged with the weirdest damned conspiracies. Excuse my language."

Her pretty face was lit with the intensity of a true believer, but Moser wasn't a man easy to persuade.

"What if I could prove it to you?" she asked.

"Prove what? Listen, Miss Rebecca, it's about time to kick that sleeping dog Hunter out of bed. He's smarter than I am. All I'm hearing is you believe this and you believe that, but I'm not hearing one good solid reason for what you're saying."

Suddenly, Moser really wanted to go wake up Hunter and let him handle Rebecca Mihaloff.

"Why do you think that woman was here last night and who do you think she was?"

"I give up. Who was she?"

"She bore the mark of the Beast on her forehead."

Here we go again, thought Moser.

"Only you and your pastor saw that," he said. "Me, Hunter, your father and Dr. Smith couldn't see diddly."

She gave him a measured look, like she was sizing him up. Then she held up her bandaged arm for him to see.

"You saw the horned creature in the video. You saw it rip my arm open, and you saw me bleed. You saw me shoot it dead. That was real. You saw the blood outside the bunker entrance. This bunker is the only reason I'm alive. If I were you, I would think less that I'm crazy and more time wondering why you couldn't see that woman's face when Pastor Howard and I could."

Moser thought about that. Maybe she had a point.

"Well, shit," he said. "What are you saying?"

"I'm saying that occultists have not only insinuated themselves into Freemasonry, but that they also changed the nature of it. Before the seventeen hundreds, there was no Hiram Abiff included in Masonic rituals. A small group of men changed all that."

Moser looked at her suspiciously. He wasn't used to having young women lecture him on the history of Freemasonry.

"And how exactly do you know all that?"

"I dreamed it," she said.

"You mind telling me about this dream?"

So she told him, in great detail, about the meeting from her dreams that changed Freemasonry forever.

34

Piccadilly, London 1721

The oil lamp radiated a soft yellow glow from the table lamp and in the hearth, the logs burned brightly, giving the room a cheery warmth that the three men gathered around the wooden table did not feel. Outside, the moonless night pressed against the stone cottage, a suffocating darkness, cold and damp.

"Draft coming from under the door," muttered John Theophilus Desaguliers.

"I tell you it is not," replied their host, the venerated James Anderson. "It's unseasonably bitter, it is."

"I tell you there's a draft from somewhere," maintained Desaguliers. "I can feel it in my ministerial bones."

"Bah," said the third member of the party. "You're an old man at thirty-eight years, John. Shall I get you a shawl to wrap around your shoulders?"

"There's a draft I tell you. Can't you feel it, or does that blubber you call prosperity act like a second jacket?"

Edward Lycenius was indeed a plump specimen of the English mercantile class. The income from his vast cotton holdings insured that he never missed a meal. He tapped his broad girth fondly and smiled back at his friend.

"Did I neglect to tell you of the fine goose that adorned my table earlier this evening? The stuffing, ah the stuffing. And the pudding, ah the pudding."

"Gentleman," said Anderson, rapping his knuckles on the table. "We have earnest business ahead of us tonight. Our commission is complete, save for we three attaching our seals to our work, attesting that it is our own. Any last doubts we have must be convicted. Any last fears must be slain, or we must retire from the battlefield."

Lycenius sipped from his goblet, savored the sweet alcohol, and sighed.

"Come, come, James—both John and I know the severity of our charge, yet must we act like hooded criminals being walked to the hangman's platform?"

Here, he pointed to a tilted stack of papers and smiled again.

"Have you not a celebratory bone in that gangling body of yours? We are about to commit to ritual the greatest secret ever held, yet you are acting as though we have committed an offense and are afraid of being caught. What fears have we to slay regarding this work of ours? How can we retire from the battlefield by betraying our benefactor?"

Anderson pulled at his collar absently and frowned. "I dislike that word, betray. And what fear must I confront? It is the judgment of God. What we are putting forth, if false, rings blasphemous and, if true, bodes much darker. Why must the story be hidden in this twisted ritual? Tell me that, if you can."

Desaguliers held up a hand and squinted with concentration.

"What?" asked Lycenius.

"A sound."

"The wind," assured the plump man, and took another sip.

"There is no wind," said Anderson.

"There is always wind."

"There it is again," said Desaguliers. "Only a dog howling. I thought it might be someone approaching. My mind is so fraught with anxiety that I imagine what I fear."

"And what do you fear most?" asked Lycenius.

"Hell," replied the clergyman simply.

"Amen," said Anderson.

"Will I never understand the two of you? Must you always be so dour? You act as though you're preparing for a funeral."

They sat in silence as the oil lamp's flame flickered above the wick. Even Lycenius grew more somber. He understood their dilemma, their doubts. Their undertaking would be considered glorious by some, yet mad by most. The guarding of a sacred truth passed down for over a two and a half millennium, as he and the others now saw it, but blasphemous by most. It was a turn in the road from what they thought they would be preparing. Just a simple updating of the Masonic Constitutions, which were the rules and regulations governing Freemasonry. All that had changed, however, when they had met him. The man who had outlived death.

Three months they had labored in recording the ritual as passed on to them by the subject of the documents, then re-writing parts of the same to make them simpler. It was Lycenius' contention that the language must be plain enough for plain-speaking men. If they were laboring for any other man, they would have presented their work for his valuation before proceeding further. But their benefactor was no common man. He was a man who had outlived death.

So, they set to work again.

****

Both Anderson and Desaguliers fretted the language not be so plain it lacked the quintessential qualities of both beauty and elegance. Metaphors, they maintained, were the provenance of poetry. Plain language, said Desaguliers, could yet be lyrical if thoughtfully elevated through prayer. Edwards, the other member of their little group, had been the most difficult to please.

"It is an affront to our Savior," he said at every opportunity. "And it is not what we were originally charged to accomplish."

"It is a metaphor for our Savior's resurrection," assured Desaguliers.

Edwards was not convinced. And he had laid his finger on what troubled them all to a greater or lesser degree. They had gone far beyond their charge, but that was not what vexed them.

In fact, it was the essence of what they wrote that disturbed them. They now wrote what they thought of as the New Constitutions of Freemasonry, but it was not exactly what they had been commissioned to write. But Worshipful Master Oliver Laud and his strange companion showed them the true reason behind the mystery of why they must create a new ritual. It was to conceal the secret of the man named Hiram Abiff in the Masonic ritual to prepare future Masons for the day when the truth would be revealed. The day when Hiram Abiff would leave the shadows and step into the daylight of life.

It was not what they had ever imagined they would write. They had been charged with re-writing the charges and regulations of the Craft. Their work was perfunctory and uninspired save for the wine selection always provided by Lycenius to, as he said, mellow their labors. It was, in fact, dreary work of the sort most would surmise suited the duties and proclivities of churchmen such as Anderson and Desaguliers. Edward Johnson had the most severe disposition of their group, but his methodical nature was that of a dependable man. Lycenius had been chosen as the fourth member of the group, he supposed, to prevent the others from creating too tedious a final document regarding the matter. To his thinking they were as complimentary a quartet that could be desired. They would fulfill their draconian obligations without exceeding them.

One night changed all that.

It was the night they were introduced to him.

The man himself. The man who had outlived death.

Worshipful Master Oliver Laud and another who would not identify himself had visited Anderson's cottage one night when he, Anderson, Edwards and Desaguliers were engrossed in their work. The rolling-clacking sound of horses pulling a carriage came as a surprise. The subsequent knock on the cabin's rough wooden door had been more surprising still, coming so late in the evening. Admitting their night's unexpected guests was the beginning of an almost epiphanous evening.

The Worshipful Master had shoulders like an oxen's yoke, a planar face and the eyes- wide-open look of a man who took troubles as they came at him. The other was of much slighter build, dressed in a simple wool cape wrapped around his shoulders, a workingman's coat of thick brown fiber and worn boots that had seen many miles of wear. An odd man to walk in, even with Lord Laud. There was about him an air of vacancy, so milk-and-water that as the night moved on, Lycenius easily forgot the man was present at all. Until the Worshipful Master introduced him.

Lycenius would never forget that moment. As he remembered it, the flame of the table lamp froze. The flames in the hearth did the same. The Worshipful Master ceased to move. His cheeks no longer blew in and out. His eyelids did not open and close. Both Anderson and Desaguliers stopped in place. Johnson seemed dead where he stood. Anderson's hand stopped halfway in midair as he reached to take the Worshipful Master's cloak. Desaguliers' greeting froze in mid-word. Lycenius looked at each of them in terrified wonderment.

Lord Laud's associate turned to face him. He stared incuriously, as though waiting for Lycenius to speak.

"What witchcraft is this?" asked Lycenius.

"Never confuse the grace of the Divine with sorcery," said the man in a flat, almost gentle voice.

Lycenius had not known what to say.

"They will waver," said the man. "They are the Pharisees of this age. They worship doctrine and ignore the Divine's coming kingdom."

By a trick of the light, his eyes glowed a soft blue as he stared at Lycenius.

"Who are you?"

He looked back at his three friends and again over at Lord Laud. No-one moved. The flames were still stiffened in place and he realized he could hear nothing except the sound of the man's voice and his own. An eerie silence filled the spaces between their speech.

"I am the man who will build the third and last temple in Jerusalem, as prophesied in the book of Revelation."

Lycenius was so astonished that he could think of nothing to say.

"All will be revealed to you this night. This very evening, you will be privileged to a great secret, one that your fraternity has held close at their highest level for generations. Only a few know this secret, but now you will shroud this Arcanum in myth and legend so that when the great day comes and the Jews return to their Holy Land, the temple will be rebuilt by my guiding hand and then, as foretold, your

Savior will return."

Still, Lycenius remained speechless.

"I know of the grievous loss you have suffered. No man should suffer the loss of their wife and child without hope to see them again."

"How do you know of this?"

The memory brought tears to Lycenius's eyes. The cholera had taken them both and caused him to agonize why it would be that a merciful God would allow such a thing to happen.

"I know that and more."

"Who are you?" repeated Lycenius.

"I am he who built the first temple, was murdered and, by the Divine's mercy, resurrected by the grip and word of King Solomon to live again and rebuild the final Temple. I have lived for over two and a half thousand years, and I cannot die again until I have fulfilled in whole the Divine's prophetic plan."

Lycenius felt as though he could not breathe.

"When the Temple is built, your Lord will return and claim victory and his enemies will be helpless beneath his feet. Then the dead will rise to life, and you will be reunited with your family. This is why your brethren have protected the secret of my existence. You and yours will now write my story to prepare the way. Because of your faith, Freemasonry will prosper and grow to spread around the world and when the time comes to reveal my truth, all Masons everywhere will hear that truth, and will rise to their feet to fight for the rebuilding of the Temple with me as its true architect. My story has been wrapped in silence within Masonic lodges for generations, but because of the ritual you will create, on that day we will at last reveal it to the world."

"Is this truly real?" asked Lycenius. "Or am I in the grip of delirium?"

"Will you stand with me tonight? Will you carry my story forward in ritual throughout all of Masonry? Will you act in courage should your companions flag?"

Dumbstruck, Lycenius could only nod, his mind filled with the thought of seeing his dead wife and child again.

"Who are you?" he asked again.

"My name," said the shadowed man, "is Hiram Abiff."

The doubts came later.

****

Was Hiram Abiff really chosen by God, or was he a demon?

There was no longer a middle ground on which to dither.

The three friends looked over and stared at the fire. Each knew the others were remembering the night as well.

"Aren't we a grim gathering?" asked Lycenius. The cheer seemed to leach out from him, leaving him wan and older than moments before. "Perhaps the coming of Edward will brighten tonight if only he is in good humor."

Anderson and Desaguliers looked back at each other, searching each other out. Something they were holding back. Something they had not told him. Somber men by nature, this yet puzzled him.

"What is it?" asked Lycenius. "Out with it, will you?"

"Did you know Edward was dead?" said Desaguliers finally.

The heavyset man lurched forward in his chair, aghast at the idea that Edward, whom he considered too piteously pious to die, was no longer among the living.

"When?" he asked. "How?"

As he asked these questions, part of his mind was reeling at the remembrance that Edward Johnson, a man renowned through the Craft of Masonry and a friend to each of them at that table, had been the one man in the room that night to raise his voice against not only altering their Masonic rituals, but introducing the story of the resurrected man and the Lost Word of Masonry. Johnson yielded to no man on matters of faith, and he had stood up for his faith in the very face of the man himself. Johnson was a Christian first and a Mason second.

Anderson began, of all things, to silently weep at Lycenius's questions. It was left to Desaguliers to speak.

"They found him last night at his writing desk, his quill in his hand, but the ink bottle knocked to one side. His forehead lay in the puddle of ink. We have been thinking of how to broach it without distressing you."

"But he was only twenty and four years old," protested Lycenius. "And," as an afterthought, "it is always distressing to hear of a friend's death, no matter the age."

"I should be clear on this," said Desaguliers, clearing his throat, "neither his hand nor his head were attached to anything else."

****

The cold, wet cloth on his face revived him. He had fainted forward. Anderson had reached out and prevented his head from striking the table. Desaguliers was slapping the top of his hand, telling him to come alive again. It was all too much. Johnson was dead. Johnson was dead and Lycenius awoke knowing in his heart who had killed him.

"Wine," he gasped. "More wine."

As Anderson reached out with more to drink, Lycenius seized it from him and gulped it.

"We didn't want to tell you," said Desaguliers. "We were afraid."

And they were right to be afraid. Their friend Edward was refusing to affix his seal to the finished compilation. He would not allow them to present the finished rituals, and in fact had urged them to bring the entire matter forward to the King.

"We must be careful what we say and do," agreed Anderson. "There must be no hint of our suspicions to a soul or we, too, may be found with our heads separated from our body. What course of action is there left to us? We are Christian men. Our lodges are Christian lodges. How can we present this abomination in good faith?"

They did not discuss further what had happened to Johnson. They were certain it was the work of Hiram Abiff. And that certainty forbade them from discussing it.

"We were to write a charter," said Lycenius, "declaring an applicant to Masonry only need believe in their own god, not the God of Christianity. It was to enlighten the lodge, to open wide the doors to admit men of faith everywhere. And the continued life of this man Hiram Abiff was to be an allegory for God's faithfulness to true

Masons."

His words came out as a plea for mercy.

"Have I not said there are many rooms in my Father's house? If it were not so, I would have told you," quoted Desaguliers. "A room for each faith in His house. Where is the wrong in that? What action is left to us now, except to declare that in our new constitution?"

Again, they fell silent.

Lycenius wondered how he had so easily been used by Hiram Abiff. He was supposed to urge the others on when they showed signs of doubt. Urge them to agree and submit the document, quelling their doubts and reassuring them of the rightness of their actions. He would see his dead wife and child again eventually if he did as he was told. As coldness crept over him, he realized that the price of his agreement was that hope of being with his family again. But Hiram Abiff was not the guarantor of souls, of that he was now certain. Johnson's death had made that clear.

"May we not do both?"

"I do not see how," said Anderson.

Lycenius sat back in his chair to think. Minutes passed as the two clergymen waited for him to unveil his thoughts.

"We must form a new lodge," he said at last.

"But we have no authority to do so," said Desaguliers.

"We will do this on our own authority," continued Lycenius. "It will be a lodge of four to guard our secret knowledge and to protect each other. We must keep alive our knowledge of how this change in Masonry actually began. Should one of us pass away, the others must find a suitable man of honor to replace him and carry on until the wrong we are forced to do is rectified. Hence, we must seek out a replacement for poor Johnson. We will learn what we can of Hiram Abiff, working discreetly lest we end up as dead as Johnson. And we will submit our newly created ritual work for approval in the meantime. That will, perhaps, keep us safe from him. It may yet keep us alive, so that we may defeat him. What say you to that?"

Anderson shook his head vigorously in dissent.

"What if he kills us all in a single night? Who will carry on our work?"

"A Tyler. We must add a Tyler," said Desaguliers.

"Can you explain your reasoning?" asked Lycenius.

"Because, as a Tyler protects the door to a lodge or meeting place, so this new Tyler will protect our secrets. We will have two secret lodges—one within the other. The Tyler will guard the entrance to both. To our lodge and the Arcanum of secrets. Whatever we learn about Hiram Abiff, we will give to him. He will take no directions from us, but operate as his own man. If foul play should befall the others, he will carry on. He must choose a replacement in advance so that when he himself dies, that second shall assume his place. Only the Tyler will know where the results of our inquiries will be kept. He must reveal to none of the others until there is enough evidence to act upon."

"You have been thinking about this," said Lycenius.

"We have both long considered what you suggest," said Anderson, nodding at Desaguliers. "It is a dangerous path, but if we proffer these new rituals, we must yet guard against their impact. If Hiram Abiff be true to his own words, we have done no wrong. If we learn he is not, we must then act against him. So, you contribute the idea of a secret lodge within our Craft. We contribute to the idea of a hidden Tyler, who holds all the power to act with or without our agreeance."

This time, they all heard dogs howling outside.

"We will walk forth this day in danger," said Desaguliers.

Lycenius banished the image of his wife from his mind.

"So be it," he said.

"By what name shall we call ourselves?" asked Anderson.

Dead men, thought Lycenius.

"The Temple Guardians," he said.

35

"Well, that's just great," said Hunter.

Moser and Rebecca turned to see Hunter buttoning his shirt with one hand and typing on his phone with the other.

"What?" said Moser.

"Molly won't answer the phone. I forgot I was supposed to meet up with her after our meeting at the Detroit Temple. Forgot to text her to let her know something had come up. I called her and got her voicemail. I texted her and apologized and she texted back that I always apologized after I stood her up and she was done being stood up. I can't believe I forgot. Well, considering what happened, I can believe I forgot, but I should have remembered, anyway. I am so screwed. And we need her help."

Molly Collins was a research librarian at the Detroit Public Library. They'd met when Hunter was researching Detroit haunted houses for a book he was writing. After hours of trying to understand their filing system, he'd gone looking for help and found her.

"Give her some time," said Moser. "We got work to do."

"You don't know Molly. She's got a temper."

Moser and Rebecca exchanged a glance.

"There's just no way she's going to let it go. I walked out on her when Bartok called last year before… you know, my trip down south. I just climbed out of bed, got dressed, and left."

Realizing the way it sounded, he looked up in embarrassment.

"Wait, I mean we weren't..."

"Can't you just shut up and finish putting your clothes on?" said Moser. "We got to talk. Rebecca here knows a few things that I think you need to hear if she's willing to talk about them."

"Let me try her one more time."

Moser shook his head.

"I miss my dog," he told Rebecca. "You could tell it to get to work and it would start tracking."

"What happened to him?" asked Rebecca.

A faraway look came into the Kentucky man's eyes.

"He got seriously ugly," Moser finally said.

He remembered the change. The tentacles. The parallel rows of teeth that were as sharp as the edge of sheet aluminum. The eyes. All of them. He shuddered, then got up to get another cup of coffee.

"Molly," Hunter was saying with his back turned to them. "Look, I'm sorry, I'm sorry, I'm sorry. I know you'll listen to this. It was an emergency. I need you to look into whatever you can find about the occult history of the Detroit Masonic Lodge. It's the biggest lodge in the world—there's got to be something out there. Ghosts, deaths, strange sounds, eerie lights, and anything else you can think of. You know, the usual. People that went inexplicably missing, strange smells and especially anything involving statues inside the building and outside, too. I'm sorry again, but please help. It's important. Not a word to anyone, either. No one other than you can know about this. I can't explain now. Shit."

Hunter shoved his phone in his pants pocket.

"Hung up?" asked Moser.

"No. Ran out of time on the voicemail. She'll probably delete it before she listens to it."

"Who is Molly?" asked Rebecca.

"Girlfriend," said Moser.

"Sort of," said Hunter.

"Oh," said Rebecca.

"I just don't see her very much."

"Can we get on with it?" said Moser. "Tuck your shirt in your pants, get some coffee and sit down. We got to talk. Your love life is lower down the pole."

While Hunter went for the coffeepot, running his fingers through his hair and tucking his shirt in while he muttered to himself, Moser studied Rebecca.

"Can we please get to it?" said Moser. "If you tell both of us what you told me and throw in what you haven't told me, maybe we can make sense of everything."

"Are you a Christian?" she asked Hunter suddenly.

He stopped the coffee in midair.

"I'm sorry, but what has that got to do with anything?"

"If you're not, I don't think you'll live through this. I can't say for sure, but that's what I think."

With a glance first at Moser, and then back to her, Hunter shrugged and then brought the cup the rest of the way to his lips and this time took a much longer drink. When he'd put the cup down on the table, he took the phone out of his pants pocket again and checked for messages.

"Did you hear me?" she asked.

Hunter scowled, put the phone on the table, then told her, "Rebecca, I appreciate the fact that Moser thinks you know something that might be helpful, and I really mean that. And I'm grateful you think that my being a Christian might keep me alive, but can we just start with what you know, move on to what you think, and then take a look at all that together? I trained to be an engineer and then moved on to debunking the paranormal and writing books about it. I'm big on facts, measurements and science. Ask Enid. I'm open-minded, but I like to look at the facts first. I need to approach this whole thing using the scientific method. All I've got so far is the video of what happened last night, the way the house was torn up, what looks like claw marks on some of the walls and your injuries and statements to go on. I think there's a lot more you could tell me before we get to the religious significance of what's going on. Can we agree to start with just that? Can you tell me what you know before we get into the Bible?"

He watched her jaw tighten as if a wire had been jerked at the back of her head, then she gradually let it go. Apparently, she'd had to deal with comments like his before. Hunter had interviewed other religious people for his books, and they fell into two categories—proselytizers and fanatics. It was hard to tell them apart looking at them, but about five minutes into the interview, the first group's network marketing mentality took over. Those were the proselytizers who treated any personal interaction as an opportunity to sign up a new believer. They couldn't help themselves.

And they didn't give out tracts anymore, they sent salvation updates by text. Or daily Bible quotes which miraculously appeared in his email box next to the emails, saying how fortunate he was that the former president of Nigeria would like to deposit fifteen million dollars into his personal checking account. If he would just be kind enough to send his bank account information and social security information along as well. The religious proselytizers meant well—sort of— but they just wouldn't quit.

The fanatics were a whole different matter. Every paranormal event he had ever investigated where there were religious fanatics involved—the Holy Rollers were the worst—were instant migraines. No matter what the facts revealed, the religious fanatics thought everything that occurred involved either Judgment, Hell, or the End Times. The Antichrist was also always a popular topic among religious fanatics who had experienced a paranormal event. Hunter thought she looked too normal to fit into either of the primary categories, but it was hard to tell with born again Christians. They came in all shapes and sizes. Altogether, except for the bandages on her arm, stabbing the doctor in the thigh with scissors, biting a chunk out of her father's arm and punching him in the throat, she looked normal enough. Looks really could, he thought, be deceiving.

"Okay," she said. "But it won't make much sense to a non-believer."

"But we'll start with the facts, right?"

"I said okay."

"Good enough," said Hunter.

He looked down at his phone, sighed, and looked back up at Rebecca.

"Molly's not the forgiving type," he said. "Anyway, your father hasn't given us much. But I have to tell you the idea of a witch and her monster sidekick is not what I thought we'd be getting into when we said we'd help your dad."

Hunter could see her face tighten with a sudden decision.

"Go home," she said. "Go see your girlfriend. Don't call, just go. If you don't get away from this, you'll never see her again. And yes, I saw that in a vision, too."

"Excuse me?"

"I said go home. You're not equipped for this fight. You're on the wrong side."

She looked directly at Moser, studying him.

"And you are too," she told him. "You're on his side now."

"Your father's?" asked Moser.

"More than that. Don't you understand? You and my father and his friends are protecting something evil. I can see it in your faces. No, I can discern it in your spirits."

I should have guessed, thought Hunter. She's a fanatic. In his experience, spiritual discernment was as reliable as acne medication.

"Can we slow down a little, Rebecca? You said you'd concentrate on the facts."

"Start with the dreams," said Moser. "Please."

"What for? You're just going to hear what I've got to say, then think I'm crazy and decide that there's got to be a rational explanation. I already shared one with Mr. Moser here, and he looked at me like I should be shipped off to an asylum. Well, here's a fact for you—the world differs from what you think, Mr. Hunter. You debunk everything. Since I knew you were Bartok's nephew, I read some of your books. I told Mr. Moser here that. I knew your uncle well enough to wish he was still alive. He understood the difference between fake science and reality. You make your living writing about ghosts, and you don't even believe in them, do you?"

Her cheeks were flushed red, and Hunter again remembered her punching him in the throat. He pushed his chair back in case she went commando again. But a part of him was angry he couldn't tell her that not only did he believe in ghosts now, that he'd seen one the year before and he wasn't likely to forget it. The screaming haint of a little girl still gave him the creeps when he thought about it, but it was something he could never write about without telling the story of Albert Magnus Hillis and the spirit driven automatonic soldiers beneath Townsend Mountain. They were two topics he could never write about or talk about. She had no idea what he believed in.

Moser saved by him speaking up before he could unload on her.

"Miss Rebecca, I can tell you for a fact that Hunter and me both believe in spirits, and more than that. We've seen things that no one else still alive has ever seen. I give you my word. We lost Bartok and my granny within weeks of each other over what happened back then, and that set us straight on a few things."

"Then tell me about it," she said. "Tell me so I know just how open-minded you are. Show me why I should trust you."

This caused both men to look uncomfortable. The alien ship buried beneath the ground. Bartok metamorphosing. The madstone. The ghost box. The burned bodies. The death of Detective Alvarez. Mr. Chirac. Too much to remember. Too awful to talk about with a stranger.

"We can't, Rebecca. It's… confidential," said Hunter. "Telling it to you would betray too many people without their permission."

His face was that of a little boy who'd come up with a good reason for why it was too early to go to bed.

She waited him out. Eyes staring straight into his. The force of her direct personality hitting him like a request from Marlin Brando in The Godfather. A demand he dare not refuse.

"It's a long story. We don't have time for it."

Still, she stared at him.

"Then I don't have the time to tell you what I know about last night."

"We just can't."

"Why not?" asked Moser. "We can trust her to keep it quiet. She just told me one of her dreams and, no, it don't sound crazy; it sounded like she was right there where the dream was happening while she was telling it to me. Besides, what happened to us at the Mountain ain't under Masonic oath anymore, anyway. It ain't under Masonic oath since Bartok went ahead and told you, and he's dead now. And Miss Hillis would be okay with it, I'm guessing. We could call her and Kenneth and get their okay, if'n you want. Or you can just tell her. With Bartok gone, you're kind of the keeper of his secrets, Ian. He appointed you, remember? It's your call, but who's she going to tell? Can you keep a secret, Miss Rebecca?"

"I can," she said.

"How do we know that?" asked Hunter. "It's been our family's secret for over a century and you think we should tell her because she looks honest? Last night, she stabbed her own doctor. How can she keep a secret as big as ours if she can't keep herself under control?"

Even as the words came out of his mouth, Hunter knew he'd made a big mistake. Rebecca Mihaloff was not a woman to provoke.

"Control? Control? Could you face what I faced last night, wake up with your arm ripped open, your own blood all over you, and then be in complete control of yourself? Do you have any understanding at all of the meaning of terror? I'd be dead if it wasn't for the fact that my father is so obsessed with survival that he built his own version of Fort Knox beneath this house. You and my father came after the damage was done. Just like when my mother died, he was busy with yet another Masonic Lodge meeting. Terrified? You bet I was terrified when I woke up. You didn't see that thing. And the woman, you're so blind, the whole lot of you are so blind you couldn't even see her face in the recorded video and you couldn't see the mark of the beast on her forehead. You're blind. You're all blind."

"Rebecca—" Hunter began.

"Don't Rebecca me," she snapped. "You have the empathy of cardboard."

Now that hurt, he thought.

But maybe today it was true. The stress of being sucked into this mess was hard on his head. After surviving the night he'd shot his uncle Bartok, he felt like he'd run out of emotional sensitivity. However many times he tried to wipe it from his memory, he could still see Bartok's mutated body jump and shake with each round. Hunter couldn't stop pulling the trigger until the writhing mass of tentacles quit moving. And in the background of that memory was... the creature that was Albert Magnus Hillis.

"I'm sorry, Rebecca. I wasn't thinking."

"Sorry? You say that a lot, don't you?"

Hunter looked down at his empty coffee cup and said nothing. There wasn't anything else he could think of to say. Maybe if he kept his big mouth shut, he wouldn't make it any worse.

"And another thing," she continued. "Thanks for the lecture on the scientific method. That helped a lot."

Hunter opened his mouth and started speaking before he could stop himself.

"Look, Rebecca, I deal with all sorts of people who aren't technical. I just wanted to stick to the facts and—"

"Not technical? You self-righteous demagogue. I have a Doctorate in Biochemistry. Do you really want to lecture me on not being technical?"

Now it was Hunter who turned red.

"Moser, would you mind shooting me before I say something else stupid?"

"How about gum instead?" asked Moser.

"What?"

Moser reached into his pocket, rummaged around until he found a pack again, withdrew a piece, and extended it toward Hunter.

"It'll keep your jaws busy, so you got to stop and think before you say something you can't take back."

After staring at the gum in Moser's extended hand for a minute, Hunter shrugged and took it.

"Okay, Dr. Mihaloff. Can we start again?"

"Tell me your story and we can," she said, trying to fold her arms over her chest, then seeing how the bandaged arm made that awkward, she instead rested both arms on the table.

"You really okay with this?" he asked Moser.

"Do it."

He started at the beginning, telling her of Bartok's call in the middle of the night, then detailing what his uncle revealed to him at the bottom of the stone stairway hidden beneath the grave of Major Albert Magnus Hillis.

36

Rebecca listened to the story of alien ships powered by the spirits of the dead, of Bartok being infected in the underground cave and his transmutation into a hideous monster, of Hunter shooting and killing him. She kept her face blank when Hunter told her about the ghost box and the enraged, demonic haint of a little girl mistakenly freed by Michael Hillis and her revenge on the descendants of those who had raped and murdered her. When he told her about the death of Detective Alvarez and how he and Moser and Michael's wife had put the ghost of the little girl back in the grave, she saw he was near tears. She tilted her head to one side thoughtfully when he told her about Granny Hillis, who had saved them all.

"That's about it," said Hunter. "I know it's hard to believe, but every word is the truth. Moser was there; he saw it all."

"That little girl's ghost killed my brother Rake," said Moser. "And those things underground killed my other two brothers, Johnny and Tyree. That's how real it was."

It was hard for her to take it all in without calling them crazy. Harder still to think of something to say. She didn't think she could have taken it all in, even if she wasn't on pain medication.

"Well?" asked Hunter.

Finally, she said, "Well, either you're both insane, or I owe you an apology. So that's really how Bartok died? You shot him to death?"

Hunter winced.

"Six rounds. He did the right thing," said Moser. "If Hunter hadn't shot him, I would have. You don't want to know what he was turning into, Miss Rebecca."

"It was awful," said Hunter. "It still gives me nightmares."

"I think I would rather remember him the way I last saw him," she said.

"Tell her about the dark man and the ghost box," said Moser.

Hunter hesitated for a moment, then told her about Emile Chirac, the man with the ghost box who had made a contract with Michael Hillis to trade it for the madstone Granny Hillis had given to her younger brother Becker. Becker had put it in the grave of the little girl to keep her tortured ghost still. With a quick look up at Rebecca to see if she thought he was crazy, he continued by telling her that Granny Hillis said that Mr. Chirac was a demon with a human countenance.

She studied him for a long time. Her expression gave no clue what she was thinking.

"That's it in the trunk," said Hunter. "There on the floor."

Rebecca frowned and followed his extended finger.

"Open it," she said.

"Look, I don't think that's such a good idea. It's more delicate than it looks. Inside are—"

"I'll do it," said Moser. "We been carrying this thing all across the country, Hunter, and you tinkered with it in every hotel we stayed in along the way. Miss Rebecca here ain't about to hit it with a sledgehammer."

Moser unlatched the brass locks to the trunk, lifted the lid and removed an inch-thick foam cover to reveal the bizarre machinery within. It was made of shiny dark wood with brass valves and glass covered gages and looked to be from another era. Rebecca got up and walked over to examine it with a look of amazement on her face.

"This is the device that brought the dark man through from the other side?" she asked.

The fingers of her uninjured hand ran over the surface as she closed her eyes. Hunter fidgeted, as though it might come to life beneath her touch. Irrationally, he wondered if she were having a vision of what had occurred the year before, when it had taken the life of Granny Hillis as she freed the spirits trapped in the underground automatonic soldiers. Hunter had only known the old woman a few days, but he missed her dearly, as she had treated him kindly and had given him a genuine look into the world of spirits that even Bartok had not.

Suddenly, Rebecca pulled her hand from the ghost box as though she'd been shocked.

"What is it?" asked Moser.

Her eyes were wide as she stared at Moser and Hunter.

"Yes, I believe you. I surely do."

****

Clearing his throat first, Hunter asked a question, as though desperate to change the subject. "You knew my Uncle Bartok?"

"She already told me she did," said Moser. "When you were busy stretched out on the bed looking at the inside of your eyelids."

"Huh. So how did you know him?" asked Hunter.

It was clear Hunter wanted to move away from the stuff of his nightmares toward something concrete. He seemed so earnest, so genuine, that it caused her to take a mental step back. This man really needed to run away from the coming confrontation as fast as he could. He and his friend Moser seemed like men that could take care of themselves—Moser especially—but this was not that kind of fight. Whatever they faced below Townsend Mountain was nothing to compare with what was coming now. She was certain of that. Maybe she should get right to the heart of it and get it over with before they got hurt. She knew what her father was hiding. They really did not.

"That's not important now," she said. "What is important is that as bizarre as your story is—and it is bizarre—what you have stepped into here is much harder to believe and much more dangerous. What were you thinking, joining forces with my father? He asks you to join an obscure organization that you know nothing at all about and you agree before you even ask serious questions. What kind of scientific method is that, Mr. Hunter? Wait, before you answer that, how much do either of you know about my father? I don't think either of you knew much about him before you came here. Am I correct? And yet you join because he asks you to?"

The two men exchanged uncomfortable glances.

"He's a brother Mason, Miss Rebecca," said Moser. "A Brother asks for your help, and as long as it's not illegal or immoral, you give it."

"I'm new to being a Mason," put in Hunter, "but that's the way I see it, too."

"This is worse than immoral," she said, her cheeks reddening. "It is an unholy thing you have agreed to."

Before Hunter could ask her for facts to back up what she was saying, Rebecca moved on.

"I know, Hunter, that you've already dismissed what I just said as delusional, but in your story about Townsend Mountain, isn't it true that you initially rejected what Bartok told you about what was underground?"

"I thought he was crazy," said Hunter, lowering his head, looking at his hands as he said it. "I really did."

"You're sitting in an underground bunker right now. Look around. Why do you think my father built all of this?"

"Zombie apocalypse?" asked Hunter.

His hopeful grin disappeared when she stared him down.

"Armageddon," she said. "That's what he built this for. You're looking at me like I'm simple again. I'm not. The secret to Armageddon, Mr. Hunter, is the man you agreed to protect. He died a long time ago. He is, in fact, already dead. But he walks with the living. Yes, he looks like any other man, but he returned from the grave without a soul. And he grows in power every day."

The look Hunter gave her jolted her. She hated it that this man suddenly thought of her as a deranged zealot. She decided to go at it a different way, to try to help him understand. It was difficult for her to work out why it was important, but she wanted him to get it. The fact that he looked remarkably like her deceased fiancé was probably a consideration, but she dismissed that out of hand. He might look like Austen, but he wasn't Austen. And Austen had died because she didn't believe in her visions.

"My mother died while my father was at a lodge meeting. He

never forgave himself, and even for me, it was a hard thing to do. He is a remarkable man, Hunter. Brilliant. Do you know what he does for a living? He runs a medical microelectronics company called LifeTech C.I. I see you've heard of it. It's a multinational firm with all sorts of divisions. Since my mother's death, he's devoted himself to finding a cure for brain cancer — for all cancers. People have attempted to do that for decades and failed. Progress in the fight against cancer has been a prolonged battle. He threw himself into it. My father was a driven man before her death, but after that he became obsessive. We were estranged for a long time after my mother's passing. I tried to rebuild the bridge between us. I forgave him. It was a very, very difficult to do, but I did. He, however, could think of nothing but finding the cure. A few days ago, he contacted me for the first time in two years and asked me to come here so that he could show me something that he claimed was the most important medical discovery of our lifetime. He claimed he had the cure for cancer. That's why I came here, Hunter. To stop him. And I think, no I know, that he sold his soul to achieve it."

Before he could think it through, Hunter blurted, "Look, I've seen what they can do with that technology. It's the most amazing thing I've ever seen in my life. Children are being healed. Burn victims, amputees and… more."

He'd hesitated before saying, "the dead are being brought back to life." It was a technicality, he was sure. Clinically dead, but not really dead. It was like Dr. Rambert had told him—it's hard to define dead. Not all parts of the body died at the same time. Still…

"You've seen this?" said a startled Rebecca. "Where? When?"

"Maybe I should wait until I ask your father about this," said Hunter.

"Maybe you should man up and just tell me."

Hunter looked over at Moser, who shrugged.

"If we've already trusted her with Townsend Mountain, maybe we should tell her everything. With what she's been through already, I don't see no reason we should be keeping her in the dark. Truth to tell, I think we're going to need her help before this is all said and done. She already faced up to the devil creature what attacked her, and that's good enough for me. Besides, she's a better shot than you, and I'd feel safer with her on our side."

"What about the Masonic oath and all that?"

"Well," drawled Moser, "I think we're a little beyond that now, aren't we? But Miss Rebecca, I think you're going to have to keep what you know about us and what we share with you from your father. Can you do that?"

"I will," she said.

"You okay with this, Hunter?"

Hunter looked at them with a suspicious eye. He knew co-conspirators when he saw them.

"No, I'm not okay with this, but yes, I'd rather have her on our side than not. Is that good enough for you?"

"For now," said Rebecca.

Hunter mulled this over, but he was already corralled. And the truth was, he was good with that. He barely knew Rebecca, but he already trusted her more than her father. Despite his new position as the Tyler of the Temple Guardians, he still did not fully trust the man. It was the way everything had happened so quickly.

"It was," he said, "at the Masonic Research Clinic in Detroit. What I saw, it bordered on miraculous."

"Or demonic," snapped Rebecca.

Hunter gaped at her.

"These cures were affected by a medical device being installed into the patients, Rebecca. This wasn't voodoo I was looking at, it was medical science. Why are you so upset about that?" asked Hunter. "From everything I've seen so far, it's the greatest medical discovery of the century."

"Everything comes with a price," she said.

"I don't understand."

"If you were a Christian, you would."

"That's just... ridiculous."

He'd been about to say batshit crazy, but miraculously, he stopped himself in time.

"Is it? Do you know how they do it? No? Then let me tell you—a nanochip implanted here."

She tapped her forehead.

"The human brain has an amazing ability to heal the body," she continued. "I'm not talking about the placebo effect. I'm saying that it actually controls the production of chemicals in our bodies. We just have never known how to manipulate that. This chip, this nanochip, is one part of the solution, but my father and his teams actually cracked the communications protocol to send signals to the brain via this chip that will instruct the brain to produce the chemicals needed to kill the cancer cells.

"He wants it installed in everyone, because not only cancer but many other diseases can be cured this way. It provides a real time monitor and early warning system. My father is also very politically connected, Mr. Hunter. He has the ear of the president himself and leaders of Congress. An executive order has been drafted that will demand it be implanted in every citizen. And other foreign governments will follow when they learn the benefits. Health care costs will drop dramatically. Lives will be saved. Lifespans extended. Its use will spread throughout the world. His breakthrough is not in the news yet, but will be soon."

"How do you know all of this?"

"I saw it in a vision, Hunter, and it was a true vision."

Hunter stood up and began to pace. Moser's eyes were fixed on hers.

Finally, Hunter stopped pacing and stared at her.

"And, again, why is that bad? Why would a Christian, of all people, object to people being saved from such horrible diseases? Your own mother died from one of them. Why are you against this? I should think you would be ecstatic. That's what I hate about religion. It's irrational. You're turning something wonderful into something terrible to support your obscure, cult-like view."

He remained standing across from where she sat, looking like at her like he was about to burst into another tirade.

"The Mark of the Beast. Isn't that right, Miss Rebecca?" asked Moser.

"Oh, for crying out loud, Moser. People see the mark of the Beast in everything these days. It's so common out there that the Mark of the Beast has become an Internet meme."

"Think about it," said Moser. "Chew on it for a while."

Hunter paced around the room again, then came back down and sat in his chair.

"You have to know how this sounds," said Hunter.

"'And he causeth all, both small and great, rich and poor, free and bond, to receive a mark in their right hand, or in their foreheads, and that no man might buy or sell, save he that had the mark, or the name of the beast, or the number of his name. Here is wisdom. Let him that hath understanding count the number of the beast: for it is the number of a man; and his number is Six hundred threescore and six.'"

"Don't quote the Bible to me, Rebecca," said Hunter. "Just don't. It irritates the piss out of me."

"Have my father show you his microscopic implant, Hunter. Tell him you're impressed by the idea, and you have to see it."

"Why? Why would I do that?"

"Because," she said, "it's shaped exactly the same as the symbol that was marked on our front door the night the woman and her beast came. I didn't see it, but I know it."

"Rebecca, I saw that symbol. It was not 666. Not the symbol of the Beast. Triple sixes are hard to miss."

"Are you sure? Look at the picture on your phone again, then analyze it. Moser told me you took a photo. Use what your uncle Bartok taught you. You'll figure it out. Study the symbolic gematria until you understand it. It is the number of the Beast, and my father's dream is to have it implanted beneath the forehead of every person on this earth."

"This is bullshit," said Hunter.

"When he calls—"

"Did he tell you he was going to call? Is there some way you know that for a fact or was that a dream, too?"

"It was," she whispered. "He's going to introduce you to the Devil."

"Well, I'm sorry, I just don't believe in prophetic dreams or the Devil."

His phone rang.

"What you see will amaze and bewilder you," she warned. "Don't be seduced by it. Satan can appear as an angel of light. He'll tell you what you want to hear. Guard your soul, Hunter," she said. "God willing, we'll talk again."

37

Detroit is never pretty, thought Hunter. Especially at night.

It was the kind of thought you weren't allowed to express anymore or you'd have Facebook gangs and Twitter tirades aimed your way fast. You had to say Detroit was experiencing a cultural Renaissance or coming back stronger than before or that it was diverse and beautiful. But Hunter thought that when people had to tell you what to think about a city, it wasn't worth thinking about.

But what was worth thinking about was that tonight, if Brother Mihaloff wasn't crazy, he, Ian Hunter, professional ghost hunter and now Tyler of the Temple Guardians, was about to meet a three-thousand-year old man. A man who had outlived death.

He pulled into a parking spot reserved for Masonic activities. The Detroit Masonic Temple towered over him. When he'd first read about it on his tablet computer, he wondered why anyone in their right mind would build the largest anything in Detroit. He craned his head over the steering wheel and turned his head sideways to look up through the windshield at it. Fourteen stories straight up highlighted by the searchlights that made it stand out like a monument against the swirling blackness of the night sky.

He sat back in his seat again and realized that there was something about the Detroit Masonic Temple that really bothered him, but he wasn't sure what. Maybe it was the fact that he was still fuming over Molly's texted reply to his continued begging to forgive him and tell her how desperately he needed her help. She'd answered him with two words that were both simple and straightforward—fuck off. Nowhere to go with that, except straight down. Maybe he was taking his feelings out on Detroit. But the building... there was something. Hunter just couldn't figure out what it was about it that bothered him.

The only thing he'd found online were rumors that the architect for the building supposedly leaped to his death from the same temple he was looking at. It was, as were so many of these things, a thoroughly debunked rumor. In fact, the man died in 1948, long after rumors of his suicide still circulated.

Brother Mihaloff was waiting inside for him, and although he didn't want to keep him waiting, he needed to think. The whole situation starting with the supposed strangling of Brother Michael Leasing by a statue, Brother Mihaloff's shocking phone call from his daughter and the carnage they'd found at the man's house was giving him a headache. Uncle Bartok had done it to him again, this time reaching up from the grave to present him with one more bizarre and unsolvable set of problems. Townsend Mountain had been bad enough, but at least then he'd seen the evidence with his own eyes and Bartok had explained what it meant. With Brother Mihaloff, he had heard Mike Leasing's story and seen the video from the attack on his daughter Rebecca, but he had witnessed nothing yet. When he walked into the Detroit Masonic Temple, that would all change.

Tonight, Brother Mihaloff was going to introduce him to the source of the mystery that Freemasonry had supposedly been guarding for hundreds of years—Hiram Abiff himself. A man who he claimed had actually been alive for over three thousand years. But that meeting would not answer how the woman in the video had known about the Hiram Abiff papers in the first place, or who told her they might be at the Mihaloff house. As with everything associated with Bartok, he always had to start with more questions than answers.

He wished Moser were with him, but even Moser had to occasionally sleep. Brothers Cook and Kaufman were guarding Rebecca, although from what he'd seen of her in action, it was more likely she would end up guarding them if something happened. And if something did go wrong, Moser would be up and in action immediately. His friend actually slept with his guns. And he'd told Moser it was going to be a long night with a lot of questions answered before the night was through. He didn't plan on returning until morning.

Another thing that bothered him as he sat in the parking lot with car idling was the fact that Rebecca knew in advance that her father would call him to come to the temple to meet Hiram Abiff, or, as Rebecca called him, the Antichrist. She could have overheard her father talking about the phone call in advance, but Hunter himself hadn't known it was going to happen. It could have been based on her subconscious assumption that her father would call. That was the most likely explanation. Precognition was widely accepted by people of all persuasions, but Hunter's reading of the literature, coupled by his varied run-ins with people claiming to have the ability, had left him with the opinion that it was all explainable.

He just needed a place to start so he could deal with this whole mess. As an engineer, he was taught to start out with clearly defined objectives for a project before undertaking any planning. But with the kind of things his uncle Bartok had been involved with, there was no place to start until you'd fumbled around in the dark trying to find out what the hell was going on.

Where was the right place to start with this? Was it the incident with Mike Leasing or the attack on Brother Mihaloff's house? Or both? If he could find the thread that bound them together, he could unravel both mysteries by pulling on the right thread.

For five more minutes he stewed, then gave up, turned off the car and headed inside the Masonic temple. The best he could figure was that he would start in the middle. Meet the supposedly three-thousand-year-old man—if there was one—and work backward from there, anyway. If Molly ever called him back and agreed to research the paranormal history of the Detroit Masonic Temple, that would make it easier, but if not, he'd go forward without her. He'd have to. Maybe Ashley Hillis could help. She was good with research, but he didn't want her involved with something like this if there was any chance at all of her getting hurt. She'd been through enough last year. Then again, she had Kenneth Hillis with her for protection, and Kenneth, too, was a brother Mason. It was getting so, he thought, half the men he knew were fellow Masons.

As he stepped inside the lobby, he felt as if he was entering it for the first time. The last time he'd come here, he'd been more focused on getting Bartok's papers and trying to figure out why he and Moser had been summoned through his lodge by Brother Mihaloff. This time, he was keenly aware of the awe-inspiring splendor of the Detroit Masonic Temple Lobby. It was a luxuriously designed building with stunning architecture and accouterments. Hunter couldn't believe he'd walked through it last time without being impressed. Then again, he could.

When he was thinking, he focused on his thoughts almost to exclusion. That was part of the problem he'd had with Molly. That kind of approach was never good for relationships. She'd been patient, she'd been tolerant, but his focus on exposing what passed for the supernatural had been close to an obsession with him. He realized for the first time he was like his uncle Bartok. No matter that he and his uncle had been at odds over the issue for twenty years. They were both totally immersed in a topic when they were investigating it. No wonder Molly had kept her distance from him over the last year.

He noticed a life-sized billboard of a beautiful, dark-haired woman that announced her as the Prophetess of the Universal Religion. Catchy, thought Hunter.

Hunter was so busy with his thoughts, he almost ran right into Brother Mihaloff, who stood like a master of ceremonies in the center of the lobby waiting for him. He wore a tailored black suit, a white shirt, and a burgundy tie. His own khakis, broadcloth shirt, and Hemingway jacket seemed too casual by comparison.

"Welcome," said Brother Mihaloff, "to the most amazing night of your life, Brother Tyler."

He smiled and stuck out his hand. Hunter was taken aback, but recovered quickly and shook the man's hand. It was like they were meeting for the first time.

"Thanks, I guess."

"There will be no guessing by the time the night is through, Brother Hunter. Believe me, no more guessing. Come, let us begin the journey."

He'd never seen Brother Mihaloff smile before, and it was oddly discomforting. The image of him as a game show master of ceremonies was out of place, considering what had happened at the man's house the night before. And the story Mike Leasing had told before that happened caused him to look around the building in apprehension.

"Who is that? She looks familiar," said Hunter, pointing at the poster.

"Ah. Eva Morgan. She is the woman who helped Worshipful Grandmaster Hiram navigate his computer. A wonderfully intelligent and entrancing woman. She holds monthly meetings in our auditorium that are broadcast around the world. Thousands of people come to hear her speak. She spreads the light that we seek in Masonry to everyone willing to listen and pays us a goodly sum for renting our facilities. We think of her as being equal in stature to Madame H.P. Blavatsky. You, of course, know who H.P. Blavatsky was. And Eva is quite trending on television and her social media stats are somewhere between those of Taylor Swift and Justin Bieber, whoever they are—so one of the younger brothers tells me, that is."

"Well, if you're going to have a prophetess," said Hunter, "it's good to have one that looks like her."

Hunter removed his phone from his pocket and took a picture of the billboard. Partly because the woman was stunningly beautiful and partly because he wanted more information about what was going on in this particular Masonic temple. Research was good when it came to the paranormal.

"Enough sightseeing, I guess—lead the way."

"Follow me, brother," said Brother Mihaloff, and he led him to an ornately crafted hallway.

"Where are we going?"

"To the Romanesque Room. A lovely example of Gothic architecture at its finest."

"Is construction still going on in the Unfinished Theater?" asked Hunter.

Without looking back, Brother Mihaloff said, "It is finished already; but we have crews seeing to the final details. When all that is finished, will be the moving of the Temple Chairs. But do not concern yourself with it. Tonight, focus on the Romanesque Room and your face-to-face meeting with the man himself—Hiram Abiff."

The three-thousand-year old man, thought Hunter. Was this really possible? He'd seen strange things buried beneath Townsend

Mountain. And that man Chirac had been over a hundred and fifty years old, but three thousand? That was really pushing it. Still, he hoped that seeing Hiram in person instead of on a computer screen would lay a lot of his doubts to rest about the man's authenticity.

"Will the fifth temple guardian be here?" asked Hunter as they continued down another hallway.

"What? The Frenchman? No, he is unavoidably out of the country again, but he will fly back for the glorious event, though. He would not miss it for the world. And remember, brother, he is tasked to return the Blazing Star of Freemasonry to us. If he is successful, as he almost always is, all will be well."

When he got back to the bunker, Hunter was going to have to learn more about the Blazing Star of Freemasonry. He wasn't sure, he realized, what it was exactly. He could go to Bartok's house, which, since he was dead, was his house now. Bartok's arcane collection of books about all things Masonic and the occult must have something about it. But for now, Hunter was reluctant to go, because it brought back memories of him killing his uncle. It just didn't seem right to move into the house of a man you'd murdered—especially if he was a relative.

They came to the double doors Brother Mihaloff was looking for. He stepped forward and swung them inward. They opened up into a room that was both oddly grim yet stately. The ceiling was arched and each of the two long walls leading toward the seat of the Worshipful Master in the east of the lodge room were graced by four ornately decorated arches that ran the length of the room. Beneath the arches, four delicately long brass sconce lights shone an effulgent light toward the ceiling. The carpet was an industrial beige and showed the wear of heavy usage over the room's long life. The walls were creamy white and a perfect complement to the wooden arches. Beneath each of the sidewall arches was a long leather cushioned bench. The floor was raised along the walls a good six inches above the main floor where Masons met on the level.

"A severe but beautiful room," said Brother Mihaloff. "Come inside and be welcome. Close the door and lock it behind you, will you please? We must not be disturbed."

As he did so, a confused Hunter asked, "But how will Hiram Abiff get in if I lock the door?"

Without thinking, Hunter looked up at the balcony over the Senior Warden's chair, looking for any sign of motion.

"Don't bother looking for him. He is not here. We are going to him."

"Then why are we here?" asked Hunter.

For the second time that night, Brother Mihaloff unnerved him by smiling at him.

"Because here is where the doorway is."

"He's in an adjacent room?"

"If you will stop asking questions, Brother Tyler, I will show you the answer."

Hunter held up his hand, palm toward Brother Mihaloff.

"Whoa. I've been down this road before. Last time I agreed to go into something blindly I ended up in a world of trouble. I'm not doing that again. I'll meet you halfway, though. Give me the broad strokes, and I'll go along the rest of the way to get to the fine print."

The muscles in the elder Brother's face tensed for a moment and Hunter thought he was going to see where Rebecca got her temper. Then he seemed to relax, letting out a slow breath.

"I forget that this must all seem strange to you because it is all new and, frankly, must be overwhelming. You have joined our Brotherhood at the culmination of a long journey in which the other Brothers of the Temple Guardians have been involved for a very long time. But I tell you, Brother Tyler, that the events of the next week will change the world. You have come at a propitious moment indeed."

Feeling far less confident than he tried to appear, Hunter waited him out.

"To your question—follow me."

There were four officer chairs in the lodge room. The chair of the Senior Deacon at the entrance wall, the Junior Deacon's chair midway to the right wall and the Worshipful Master's chair at the far wall. The chair in the middle of the left wall was precisely placed at Masonic north.

"You may have heard many variations of what this chair is called, but the true story is that it is the Chair of Hiram Abiff. It is called by most lodges the 'Empty Chair.' Not all lodges have the empty chair, Hunter, but it is a tradition we proudly continue, because it is integral to the Temple Guardians, of which you are now Tyler. We hold it sacred because it is the chair that Hiram will sit in when he is revealed to the world. But for now, it is the doorway. For generations, the north has been dark, but with the return of Hiram Abiff, it will be considered the direction of light."

It was a standard form Masonic station chair. Like any other officer's chair, it was extremely solid. The legs, arms and frame were cut from four-by-four dark walnut wood. The seat was brown leather. Four large Egyptian ankhs that looked like huge eye bolts were at each point of the solid marble square elevation beneath the chair.

"I don't get it. I see the chair, but no Hiram Abiff."

Leaning in toward Hunter, Brother Mihaloff's dark brown eyes fixed on him with the wild intensity of a zealot. Maybe that runs in the family, too, thought Hunter.

"You wanted to see Hiram Abiff, didn't you? Let's go see him together, right this minute."

While Hunter struggled with what to say, Mihaloff bent down near the left side of the chair, removed a thick wooden panel, and pointed to a lever tucked away inside of the chair itself.

"When I pull that lever, we will walk through the opening. There will then be an open pathway to another lodge where Hiram Abiff awaits. When the chair folds back on our side, the same thing happens to a chair on the other side, giving us passage. We call the pathway the Borgo Pass. Brother Hiram chose the name himself. When we have passed through it, you will learn for yourself the true secret at the heart of Masonry. The same secret that the Knights Templar before us died to protect. Both chairs will close back up when we reach the other side, or when one minute of our time has passed."

"One minute? That's cutting it a little short, isn't it? Is he in another lodge room in the building? He has to be if it only takes that long to get there. Why didn't we all go to the same place instead of going through all of this rigmarole?"

"Oh, no, Hunter. Hiram Abiff is in an entirely different city. To protect his location from prying eyes, we don't even know the name, but he has given it the name of Borgo."

Hunter waved his hands in frustration and almost turned away and left, but instead he said, "Okay, that's just plain crazy. What's behind the chair, an express train? Excuse my irritation, but this is exactly the same kind of mishmash monstrosity I always find myself in whenever I get involved with anything my uncle Bartok started."

"I understand, Brother Hunter, but if you'll follow me, you will see the proof for yourself. Remember, we have only one minute to cross before the chairs close on both sides and we will be trapped in a void that is worse than death itself."

Brother Mihaloff bent again and depressed the lever. Immediately, part of the wall behind it recessed, leaving a rectangular opening which opened into a darkness that Hunter could swear absorbed light.

"Thirty-two steps and we'll be there. Thirty-two steps to find the light all our brother Masons have sought since our beginning."

With that, Brother Mihaloff stepped through the opening.

I've been through worse openings, he thought, remembering the living, breathing door his grandmother had called Aeyrik and which he had cut through in a blind rage with the artifact Bartok had given him. Can't be worse than that, he thought as he followed Brother Mihaloff.

But he was wrong.

38

The moment he took his first step into the Borgo Pass, Hunter knew he had entered a place where the living did not belong. Outside of the gray-black protective membrane of the passageway leading straight ahead of him, he could feel the angry energy and mad, pulsating hunger frustrated at being kept back by whatever power maintained it. After momentarily freezing and looking at the rectangle of light behind him, he turned and followed Brother Mihaloff. The Worshipful Master of the Temple Guardians strode straight ahead, never looking back, walking with strong, purposeful steps.

Sweat broke out over Hunter's entire body. What had he done? What insane energy was pulling him forward? Why wasn't Brother Mihaloff running in fear through the Pass? Somewhere not so deep inside him, he knew that to be trapped in the Borgo Pass with the doors closed was the annihilation of his life, his reason and his very essence—just as Brother Mihaloff had told him—so why wasn't the man as terrified as he?

How many steps so far? Twenty? Twenty-five? He'd forgotten to count. Thirty-two were what Brother Mihaloff had said. Off to his right, he glimpsed a red electric whip lashing down with blinding speed and he heard a screech of raw agony and delight. He kept walking faster, blotting out the images that surrounded them on all sides beyond the membrane. Red, bat like creatures flapped into view and clawed at the tunnel's membrane. Brother Mihaloff seemed not to notice or not to care or to hear the awful insanity of the screeches that shook the walls of the passageway.

What kind of horror show is this? wondered Hunter.

Up ahead, an indeterminable distance away, he saw a rectangle of soft white light. He closed his mind, focusing in only on that doorway. Couldn't Mihaloff walk faster? Shouldn't they be running as fast as they could drive themselves? What if one of the things clawing at the membrane ripped an opening and came after them?

And then they were through, stepping into a replica of the room they had just left. The anticlimax was enough to stop his heart.

Hunter shakily followed Brother Mihaloff as he walked purposely toward the center of the room, where an old man in a long-sleeved white dress shirt stood waiting for them. A round wooden table was placed next to him, and three chairs were set in place around it. Behind him, Hunter heard the gears of the entrance-controlling chair sliding back into place to seal the opening. When it finished with a soft click, Hunter finally took a breath. What Brother Mihaloff had described as the passageway between two lodges, Hunter now thought of as a walk through Hell.

****

"Welcome, Brothers," said the old man. "Welcome to the Borgo Masonic Temple."

The words came out as an exhalation. Within the words of welcome, Hunter could hear a cacophony of voices pleading, demanding, ordering, and yet seductive. He shook his head to clear the sounds away. Had he heard that, or was hearing his own fears from last night? Or was it that his time beneath Townsend Mountain had unhinged him? Bartok said that a man could only go beneath the mountain twice if he was to keep his sanity. Even then, he must never venture into the caves of Major Albert Magnus Hillis alone. Had he really just heard so many voices speaking the words of Hiram Abiff? It only took a quick glance at Brother Mihaloff to convince him he had not. Brother Mihaloff acted nothing but normal. Lack of sleep and stress, thought Hunter, and last year's descent into the world of alien madness beneath Townsend Mountain had him on edge. He was hearing things. Besides, Hiram Abiff didn't appear to be anyone to be afraid of.

He was instead a kindly looking old man cut from the stereotypes of America's past, just as Hunter had seen him on the Skype call earlier. Wire-rimmed glasses perched on the bridge of his nose; there was a slight bend to his posture and a face that reminded Hunter of an old cowboy dressed for a go-to-meeting event. He was four or five inches shorter than Hunter, just enough for him to see the shiny top of his head. A horseshoe of white hair circled it.

It would have been a very normal scene, except that in his mind Hunter could still hear the screams of the damned as Brother Mihaloff and he stepped their way through the Borgo Pass. He could still see the red electric lashes and the flayed skin. And still, he could smell the odor of sulfur and the sound of many voices speaking through Hiram's mouth. And there was something about that which disturbed him even more. A vague memory of something Bartok had read to him when he was a teenager… "Our name is Legion," he replied, "for we are many." In that moment, in the Borgo Masonic Temple, that quote was more terrifying than his first sight of Albert Magnus Hillis's body hanging in Townsend's Cave.

Brother Mihaloff stepped forward enthusiastically and hugged the old man, patting him affectionately on the back as he did so. Watching this simple act of friendship caused Hunter's stomach to churn. His reaction was worse because it seemed to have no real evidentiary basis. Hiram Abiff was just an old man. Looking more closely, Hunter could even see the faint fuzz on the old man's chin that passed for a shadow beard. A perfectly normal old man. Except, according to Brother Mihaloff, he was three thousand years old. And you had to walk through Hell to find him.

"It's good to see you, Brother Frank," said the old man.

Then Hiram Abiff looked directly at Hunter. It caused Hunter's stomach to tighten. He couldn't explain why; maybe he was still wired from the trip through the Borgo Pass.

"And you are our new Tyler?" asked the old man.

"Yes. My name is Ian Hunter, Worshipful Master Abiff," Hunter said in a strained voice. He wasn't sure he had used the right title to address the old man. Masonic etiquette was as difficult to remember as a genealogy chart. But he charged ahead to conceal his nervousness.

"I am the new Tyler, replacing my uncle Bartok after his death," he said, and, by sheer force of habit, he stuck out his hand for Hiram to shake. He froze when he realized what he had done and stared down at his extended hand in horror. The tremors were obvious to both he and Hiram, although the old man showed no reaction. Brother Mihaloff seemed lost in a fugue moment; unaware of the tension in the Borgo Lodge Room. The thought of Hiram Abiff touching him made Hunter suppress a shiver. Three-thousand-year-old skin touching his own. This old man should be dead, thought Hunter. He should be dead and buried. Why wasn't he in a grave rotting like the rest of humanity before him?

The old man smiled a slight smile, like a hungry cat preparing to play with a soon to be dead mouse. But the instant their palms touched, Hunter was gripped by a sense of vertigo so debilitating he rocked backward in shock. The old man was staring into his eyes as it happened, and Hunter saw, or thought he saw, a blue glow emanate outward from them. It was over the instant the old man let go of his hand.

"You may address me," the old man said with a slight bow, "as Worshipful Grandmaster Master Hiram Abiff."

Hunter stopped and glanced around the lodge room.

"I'm sorry I misspoke your title. But is it true?" Hunter blurted out, "that you are over three thousand years old?"

"I am."

"Can you prove it?"

"Brother Tyler," snapped Brother Mihaloff, as he raised his hand in admonition. "We are guests here."

Hunter's first reaction was to apologize, but the whole situation was so bizarre he couldn't let it drop. Why didn't Brother Mihaloff realize that? How could anyone walk through that passageway they called the Borgo Pass and not know how horribly wrong this place was? The old man stared at him. Then he raised his palm toward Brother Mihaloff to silence him, but continued to focus on Hunter. The lodge lights began to slowly dim.

Disorienting terror suddenly flooded Hunter's body. Brother Mihaloff's mouth was still open and his eyes were wide and unblinking. His right was still extended toward Hunter. That was bad enough, but as the seconds passed, Brother Mihaloff stayed frozen in place. What was happening? wondered Hunter.

Thirty-two steps from darkness to light my ass.

Brother Mihaloff's mouth opened even wider.

Hunter's mind went completely blank when he saw something moving within the dark opening of Brother Mihaloff's mouth. Two orange-yellow eye slits blinked at him from the back of his throat, and then, something dark and slick began to slide past his teeth and emerge into the dim light. It was a glistening black snake's head, and it slid out a ghastly discolored forked tongue to probe the air in front of it. It was impossibly large—the thickness of a man's forehead—and it dropped onto the lodge floor with a wet slapping sound that caused Hunter to recoil and reach beneath the back flap of his jacket for his Smith and Wesson MP Shield. When his hand met empty air, he realized he'd left his pistol in the car. The serpent was now raised up on its tail like a cobra preparing to strike. Its body was now as thick as Hunter's leg. Brother Mihaloff stood like a statue. Hunter felt the perspiration form on his forehead as the snake hissed and opened its jaws.

"You asked for proof, Mr. Hunter," came the old man's voice. "Can a man cause this with less than three thousand years of the black arts?"

The snake's glistening black tongue extended out as though tasting the air.

The lodge room suddenly felt like an execution chamber.

The realization that he was weaponless, isolated, and in the presence of things dark and deadly pressed in on him. The surrounding air seemed alive with threatening energy. There was nowhere for him to hide and his protector, Brother Mihaloff, was more statue than human. Hunter's nervous system went into overdrive, and he could hardly process what he was seeing.

"Your uncle was a thorn in my side, Mr. Hunter," said Hiram. "But he is now dead, and I am still standing. And you killed him, I understand. Such a fine young man you are, to murder your own flesh and blood. And now you have taken his highest office, young Caesar; you are now Tyler of the Temple Guardians. Where is your sword, young Guardian? Where is your second? Are you so unseasoned that you leave your weapon and ally behind when you venture out? What manner of Tyler are you? Here you are surrounded by night terrors eons old, faced by the power of Hell itself, wrapped in darkness and wondering what will become of you. Was it not the slug-eyed Plutarch who wrote 'We do not ask thee to free from punishment those whom thou hast determined to slay, but to free from suspense those whom thou hast determined to save.' Would you not like to be freed from suspense, Mr. Hunter? You are not the man your uncle was. Your uncle was not foolish enough to venture into my little town of Borgo. No, indeed. Your uncle was not foolish enough to end up as snake food."

Hiram Abiff still looked like a little old man, but he was a little old man with a giant snake next to him. And without having to think it through, Hunter knew Hiram was right. Bartok would never have been so stupid as to walk through the Borgo Pass.

"Yet, little ant, people are sometimes sentimental about their blood relatives. They value them more than they are truly worth. Did Bartok so value you, Mr. Hunter? Did he so badly estimate your mettle? Do you have my journal?"

The charismatic emphasis on each of his words was mesmerizing. Hunter felt unaccountably insignificant in the presence of Hiram Abiff, whose glowing blue glasses seemed to hold him helpless in their pulsating glow. The snake was too awful to look at, and when it lowered itself to the floor and wriggled toward Brother Mihaloff, Hunter gave out a sigh of relief. As it wound itself in a fluid circle in and out between and around the Mason's legs, Hunter felt both twinges of revulsion and relief.

"Who are you?" he stammered.

"I am the Apocalypse, Mr. Hunter. I am the eater of souls, the master of Legion, the—"

Hiram Abiff suddenly screamed as his head ballooned outward until it was three times as big. His neck stretched out like it was made of rubber. Hiram's fingers grasped onto his elongated throat as though to keep it from breaking free of his body. He twisted and writhed in agony. Hunter clamped his hands over his ears as the room filled with whispers saying over and again, "Legion, we are legion."

The snake unwound from Brother Mihaloff's legs and slithered over to where Hiram continued his manic dance and screams.

Your uncle was not foolish enough to venture into my little town of Borgo, no indeed.

Well, I'm not stupid enough to stay, thought Hunter.

He looked back toward the Empty Masonic Chair they had entered through. It was closed, but he had seen where Brother Mihaloff had accessed the activation switch in the other chair. He was maybe fifteen steps away, and he was going to go for it. Fast or slow? he wondered. After only a few moments of thought, he decided to slow down. He was shaking so badly he didn't know if he could move quickly. The snake was locked on Hiram Abiff's screaming gyrations, and Brother Mihaloff was still stationary. Hunter took a step back toward the chair. Then another. He saw the snake arch up and look down at Hiram Abiff, who was on his knees with his hands still wrapped tightly around his neck, as though forcing his own windpipe closed.

Hunter kept walking backward while Hiram's insane self-struggle continued. He had no idea what was happening and didn't even want to know. The only important thing was getting the hell out of there. If he wasn't careful and the snake heard him, he would be snake meat, but he hoped that even the snake's ears were not good enough to hear over the racket Hiram was making.

Danger suffused the air like poisonous incense. Hunter knew without knowing how that if he didn't get back to the safety of his own world, that he would die here and no one would ever know what happened to him.

His foot struck the carpet lip on which the chair rested, and he almost fell but caught himself on the chair arm. No choice now. The snake might have heard him. He had to turn his back on Hiram Abiff to get to the switch that opened the membranous tunnel through the Borgo Pass. As he turned, he imagined he could feel the snake's teeth sinking into his neck. He felt the powerful jaws crushing his neck bones. Felt death descending on his shoulders and wrapping its enveloping black opalescent wings over him.

But he ignored his panic-induced imaginations and kneeled down on the right side of the Empty Chair. Even in the dim light, he could see that the facing on the side of the chair differed from what he had seen in the Detroit Temple. Panic seized him again. There was no switch panel with the Masonic Eye to slide aside and reveal the activation mechanism. Instead, there was only a raised piece of wood with no carvings fronting it. Hunter could feel the room close in around as he desperately tried to manipulate the raised wooden square, but it would not move. He tried pressing against it, but nothing happened. A quick glance over his shoulder told him that behind him, chaos raged as Hiram still squeezed at his own throat while he twisted and squirmed. The snake was transfixed by the drama.

Hunter felt the cold realization that there was no way out. He was trapped. He looked at the far end of the lodge at the double door, but knew he could not get by the snake. Didn't even want to try.

Your uncle was not foolish enough to venture into my little town of Borgo, no indeed.

Frantically, he looked around the lodge for something, anything to use as a weapon.

The Tyler's sword for every lodge was always kept on the outside of the lodge double doors. Again, he'd have to get by the writhing, hissing, demonic serpent to get to it and that just wasn't happening. Every lodge had the Worshipful Master's gavel—a big hammer—and it would be in the East of the Lodge. Stupid idea. Stupid. Stupid. What if he made a run to get it and it just wasn't there? Again, he'd be snake food before he had a second chance at survival.

Without warning, Hunter heard a loud thud and looked to see Hiram Abiff lying on his back near the Masonic altar. He looked dead. Hunter hoped he was dead. The snake lowered its head as though to sniff the body. Hunter had a moment of sheer brilliance that he would never afterward understand. He realized that the two chairs—one in the Detroit lodge and the one Borgo—were facing different directions. The Empty Chair in Borgo was in the South, not the North. It was like a mirror image. Everything a perfect duplicate, except in reverse. He scrambled around to the other side, found the raised Masonic Eye, and slid it aside to reveal the latch that would send the chair tilting completely back and down to open the door to the Borgo Pass. One firm push and it moved out of the way. He leaned over, reached inside, and pulled the lever. When the soft click of activation came, Hunter jumped to his feet and got ready to run through the tunnel. Then he remembered Brother Mihaloff. Nobody, he thought, should be left behind in Borgo.

As Hunter turned toward Brother Mihaloff, he realized that since Hiram Abiff had fallen to the floor, the room had gone completely silent. With a mounting sense of apprehension, he looked toward where Hiram Abiff lay on the floor. The old man was now up on one elbow, looking directly at Hunter with hate-filled eyes. This was it, thought Hunter. He'd turned back and now it was too late. But just as he thought it, the snake rose up to its full height and struck downward at Hiram with blinding speed. The old man dropped to the floor again, slapping up one hand to catch it by the throat just below its gaping jaws.

"You dare attack me?" screamed the old man.

Hunter wasn't waiting around to hear what happened next. He grabbed Brother Mihaloff, and with a grunt of effort, threw him over one shoulder and ran through the opening to the nest of terrors that Brother Mihaloff called the Borgo Pass. He didn't know how long he'd stood there, but what he remembered as he ran from the cacophonous battle behind him was that the Freemason had told him the two chairs would lay back in the open position for only one minute. Hunter ran as fast and hard as he could. He took in huge gulps of air as he pushed ahead and refused to look at the demented horrors that pushed against the membranous fabric of the Pass. Red and black light flickered around as he moved deeper into the Pass, but he did not look to either side. He had to get to the other door and close it permanently. Those things could never be allowed into his world.

Up ahead, he saw the other doorway open. How many steps he'd taken he didn't know. Brother Mihaloff said only thirty-two steps all total, but Hunter didn't pay attention to that. He just had to get the two of them out of the pass. Everything else could be sorted out later. He heard nothing but screeching and howling from behind him, but whether that was from Hiram and the snake attacking each other or the creatures pressed against the membrane, he didn't know. All he knew was that there seemed to be only three steps from the door to freedom when he saw the chair start to rise. Hunter would not be trapped in the Borgo Pass. He could not. He ran forward and literally threw Brother Mihaloff through the diminishing door, then dove straight through after him. The top edge of the chair slammed against his shin and he cried out, but he made it through and landed on the floor on top of Brother Mihaloff, who hit the Detroit Lodge floor only a foot from where the chair now stood. The door to the Borgo Pass was closed.

Hunter struggled to his feet and looked wildly around the empty lodge room. Brother Mihaloff lay unconscious on the floor. Whatever Hiram Abiff had done to him, it was enough that he could be thrown, smashed down on the floor, and still be unconscious. What the hell was going on?

He saw a standing spear behind him, off to the side of the Senior Warden's chair, ran over and bent down to examine the hinge that released the opening behind the chair. There was no way he was going to let Hiram or the snake come in after them. He checked the sides of the chair, but the line along the edge of it was too narrow to wedge anything in to keep the door from opening again. He got on his knees and looked at the chair's front seam. His shin hurt like hell, but he ignored it. The overpowering fear that his life and soul were at risk would not permit him to feel pain. Finally, he found a section of the front seam that looked wider than the others. But it was on the wrong side of the chair, he realized. The chair would tilt backward. How could he stop that? No time, no time, he thought. He jammed the tip of the spear into the narrow seam and piled all his weight against it. He couldn't leave it sticking out, though, so he pulled backward and snapped the wooden pole off just two inches above the spear point. Next, he hustled behind the chair and wedged the wooden pole between the solid wood back of the chair and the wall behind it. No way it was going to tilt backward with the pole pushing back against it. At least, he hoped it wouldn't.

What, he asked himself again, was going on? And what the hell was Hiram Abiff? How was it that Brother Mihaloff didn't notice that Hiram Abiff was like the Devil himself? Did the brother Mason truly not know that his own body contained a big black snake? His mind could barely comprehend what had just happened. All he could really understand was that he had to keep Hiram Abiff and that hideous serpent from ever coming through the Borgo Pass and into his own world. The attack by the snake and Hiram Abiff was completely insane. Why did the snake attack Hiram Abiff? Too many questions, but too much adrenaline running through his system to come up with answers.

Brother Mihaloff still lay on the floor where Hunter and thrown him. He wondered suddenly if he was still alive. Bending down again, he felt for a pulse on the neck and, after a tense few seconds, found one. Thank God, he thought. But when he woke up from his trance, what would he tell him had happened? The truth? Not a chance. If the rest of the Temple Guardians knew he knew, his gut told him he and Moser wouldn't last long.

Besides, Brother Mihaloff would never believe him. Hiram Abiff seemed to have him under some kind of spell. That was the only explanation he could come up with. Magic. Black magic. That's what it had to be. Until the attack on Brother Mihaloff's home, Hunter hadn't even believed in magic. He'd seen what Granny Hillis could do, but that was different. Somehow natural, even if unexplainable.

No, he would have to lie to him. He would have to come up with some kind of believable story and stall for time. Something that would explain why he'd wedged the Empty Chair closed. What the hell else could he tell him? That in the Borgo lodge Hiram Abiff had caused a giant snake to come out of his mouth? No. No way. And there was the fact that the man's jaws seemed to have returned to normal. They should have been broken apart. Magic. More Black Magic. They were in deep now, way too deep. Moser would think he was crazy when he told him what had happened. No, wait. Not Moser. Moser would believe him. But Rebecca? He thought about it as he looked at the unconscious body of her father. Rebecca might believe him, too. After all, she thought Hiram Abiff was the Antichrist. Yes, she would believe him. But what could they do about it? And could she accept the fact that Hiram had caused a giant black snake to come out of her father's mouth?

Could any of them trust Brothers Mihaloff, Kaufmann and Cook? No, they couldn't. They all believed Hiram Abiff was the second Masonic coming. Brother Mihaloff began to stir.

Time to lie like a son of a bitch. If he didn't, his gut feeling was that he and Moser wouldn't make through the week. He had to distract him.

Hunter grasped Brother Mihaloff's extended hand and helped him to his feet, then walked him to the double doorway that led out of the Romanesque room. The old man had regained enough of his faculties to ask, "What happened to me?"

"Even for a tough guy like you," said Hunter nervously, "there's a limit. You need to get some sleep every now and then."

"I feel disoriented."

"I'll help you walk. By the way, the Empty Chair device is very clever. Where did it come from?"

"From our French Brother," slurred Brother Mihaloff.

39

Detroit, Michigan, USA
   1919

Stanley Jones paced back and forth in front of papers scattered across a long oak table, muttering as though incanting to ignite them. It was only the two of them waiting for midnight to arrive. The Great Baphomet leaned back in the leather chair parked on the other side of the table and opened his mouth as though to snore, then thought better of it and instead swallowed another preparation of mescaline and a very special flower from Tibet, specially prepared in the basement of the very same bookstore where they waited. As Jones's black leather shoes slapped the hardwood floors, The Great Baphomet glanced over at the grandfather clock, which read fifteen minutes before midnight. Carved within the highest scrolling near the top, he saw the Scottish Rite double eagle.

"Did you know," he said slowly to Jones, "that vapid men produce vapid symbolism and that vapid symbolism insignificantly placed is the end of art?"

Abruptly, Jones stopped his frantic pacing and turned to gape at the Great Baphomet.

"You're bloody stoned out of your mind, you self-indulgent sod. It is the man himself I've got coming here to see us and you can't even sit up straight. Weave your magic on him and we will own the Freemasons. At least you razored your head before his coming. And I swear if you'd waxed those two tufts on your shiny medicine ball sized head into horns again, I would have hanged myself in the window if it wouldn't get you off."

Jones waved his hands in front of his face as though he wanted to make sure, absolutely sure, that they were still attached on a night where so much could go wrong. The wind raced and shrieked down the empty street outside like a chaointe banshee searching for the sick and dying. He glanced nervously at the wide bookstore window and shivered. Angry at his reaction, he again turned on the man in the chair.

"Sit up, will you?" he continued. "At least make the attempt to be prepossessing."

"Ah," said the Great Baphomet, "you presuppose that I wish to prepossess."

A shadow moved by the window and although Crowley, the Great Baphomet, noticed it and stiffened, Jones kept up his badgering rant. Eventually, he tired of it and attempted a honey trap.

"Bertha Almira will be so very excited if this goes well tonight. She will forget Ryerson is even alive. Status and power, eh? She loves to climb and loves to submit. A powerful, statused man can be an irresistible aphrodisiac to a woman who fancies herself the Scarlet Whore of Babylon."

"Fah," said Crowley as he suddenly jerked up straight. "And be quiet. Can you not feel how the pluck of the dark harp's strings music the night?"

Jones looked around the bookstore in bewilderment. Shelves of Crowley's unsold books, racks of his pamphlets and unsold copies of The Equinox indicted the erratic brilliance of the man. But what was he talking about? Music the night? What drug was he on now?

The pallid light of the single electric lamp holding down a stack of papers on the great table could not disperse the gathered gloom which clung oppressively to the rafters above the balcony. Jones suddenly felt a desperate need for more light. Everything about Crowley, he thought, could use more light.

"What did you say? Music the night? And did you ever consider that the rank odor of hashish on your clothes might be potent enough to permeate your brain and dissolve your thoughts?"

Crowley stood up in a fluid motion. What did that mean, a fluid motion? Very hard to explain, actually. Not moving like a panther. Much too heavy and sloppy to move like a carnivorous cat. Not even a house cat. More like a fat gorilla jumping up. Ready to beat its chest and roar. Yet when he turned his gaze on Jones, it was delicious witchcraft. He felt—.

There came a rap at the door.

The electric lamp fluttered, dimmed, bounced like a kerosene flame caught in the wind. The fluctuating darkness of the room came closer. A brutish wind seemed to race across Grand River Avenue and throw itself against the bookstore's windows, rattling them as though testing their defenses.

"They bring the violence of the night against us," said Crowley.

"What? Who?" said Jones, glancing nervously at the curtained front door.

"By the pricking of my thumbs, something—"

"Oh, shut up, will you," hissed Jones. "I'm going to open the door before they get annoyed and leave."

Jones had taken two hesitant steps toward the door when he heard Crowley call after him.

"Magical child of mine, ward yourself."

With one incredulous look backward, Jones stopped, then clenched his teeth and proceeded again toward the door. Its handle was so cold, he gasped. His senses were failing him because Crowley was literally driving him nuts. He steeled himself, grabbed the handle again, twisted it counterclockwise, and opened the door.

A jagged cut of blue-white lightning lit the street, revealing Martin Keyes, the Sovereign Grand Inspector General, who was considering their request. In the brief stormlight, his face seemed long and harsh. He was a man of average height, with a jaw like a boxer and the build of a footballer scarcely hidden beneath his jacket. He had always struck Jones as a man with a grim purpose, and never more so than on that night. The rain suddenly sprayed down over the city like water bullets. They punched against the store's canvas awnings. Jones quickly stepped aside to let the man inside. It wasn't until Keyes had entered the bookstore that he saw the man who followed behind him.

The second man had been shielded by Keyes's bulk, since he was nearly half a head shorter and with a slack-shouldered build. He had the look of an older man more comfortable with a ledger book than a hammer, and Jones wondered if he were the Order's treasurer. He stopped inside the threshold to wipe his wire-rimmed glasses with his handkerchief. Poor sod, thought Jones, can barely see, and that was a bad handicap to carry with you when you strolled the streets of Detroit at night.

"Well, that was in the nick of time," said Jones. "May I take your hats and coats?"

Both men unbuttoned their raincoats, then removed their hats and held on to them.

"Thank you, but that will not be necessary. We will not be staying long," said Keyes.

"Oh?"

"We have only a brief message to deliver."

"I see," said Jones.

He did not like the tone. Not at all.

"May we come in and sit?"

Outside on the grimly deserted street, rain continued to pound the night. Perhaps, Jones thought, it is to wash away our carefully laid plans.

"Certainly. Please take your choice of chairs and settle in. We were just discussing the rich possibilities between our organizations. Detroit will become the Paris of the West, rich in art and culture, vitally alive with the awakening realization of man's unlimited potential."

Keyes sat. The other man stood where he was.

Jones's eyes flitted to Crowley's, and he was surprised not to see his usual contempt for Masonic dignitaries, but what looked like fear. Never before had Jones seen the man afraid of anything. He would have to proceed carefully. Something was terribly wrong. Why would his friend and mentor be mortified by Martin Keyes? They had met only once in their discussions of subsuming the Scottish Rite under the Order of Thelema. Keyes had shown neither animosity nor support. Neither approval nor disapproval. He was a man who kept his own counsel. And the Lodge's bookkeeper was not a concern. Did Keyes's coming have an ominous meaning of which he was unaware?

"Would you like something to drink?" he asked Keyes. "And pardon my thoughtlessness, but I forgot to ask the name of your friend."

"He is only here to observe."

"I see. We have a fine selection of whiskeys and—"

"We have no desire to drink with you."

Stepping over to a crystal container near Crowley, Jones poured himself a drink. He made to pour one for Crowley, but his friend held up a hand. Not a drink? What was this? The man would drink to celebrate a plugged up crapper. Not a drink? And his hand. Crowley's hand had trembled when he held it up.

Jones took a long, slow gulp of the smoky liquid.

"It is my understanding," said Keyes, "that you—" and here he looked directly at Crowley— "proposed to replace the 'pomposities and banalities of our ragbag system of rituals'—as you so elegantly described them— with something of your own devising. Do I understand the matter correctly?"

That was in fact the way Jones had heard Crowley describe the Masonic system when under the influence of drugs or alcohol or both. He closed his eyes and waited for Crowley to say something to putty over the fast cracking situation. When the great man did not respond, he opened his eyes again and saw the innocuous little man that had tagged along with Keyes staring at him.

"As offensive as that is, however, it is not relevant."

"And what is?" croaked the Great Baphomet.

"That you will no longer either associate yourself with Freemasonry, nor meddle in its affairs. You respect neither God nor man, both of which are requisite for our noble Craft. You have the character of an open sewer, the self-conceit only a complete wastrel can lay claim to and the delusion that you are an important personage because you labor so very hard to corrupt corruption. Far worse than these, you slander the living God and for that, neither you nor yours are welcome."

Crowley's fist hit the table like a blacksmith's hammer.

"You dare affront the Beast?" he shouted.

"I do," said Keyes.

"Do you not know what power I wield?"

There was fire in his eyes now, Jones saw. The entire plan was falling down around them, but it would be worth it to hear Crowley rage at them. Thunder crashed outside like two trains colliding head-on, but that paled beside the Master of Magick's rampaging wrath.

From the corner of his eye, Jones saw the small man stand staring at him. The lenses of his wire rims reflected the desk lamp's light in a peculiar soft blue. But Crowley was in full bore mania, shouting with a voice vibrating with such timbre that it seemed he used the very room as a speaking horn.

"I am the painter of dead souls. I will rip and ravage and rape your rituals and remake them as I—"

There was a bright bark of sound and a flash of blue light from the little man that collided with Crowley and shot him fifteen feet across the room to crash him into a wall mounted blackboard, which split in two at the impact. Crowley's head bounced forward and back with a sickening slap and his eyes rolled up. Jones blinked, then blinked again at the sight of Crowley dangling three feet off the floor as though hung on a nail head.

The old man walked directly toward Crowley; his face was expressionless, but the edges of his glasses glowed an intense pale blue. Keyes sat where he was, a grim expectancy on his face. It was the antiseptic stare of the 33rd degree Mason that terrified Jones the most. How could any sane man look upon what had just happened and not feel the dread-soaked horror that he felt even now? Did Keyes not see what his companion had just done? But, of course, he had. What was this game, then? Were both he and Crowley to die here? And for what crime? For speaking ill of Freemasonry? No, there was something much worse here at work. Jones was certain of it. But what could he do?

He had a sudden, precipitant idea and began to chant softly yet quickly, sometimes stumbling over the words while weaving his fingers together to form a magical ward to protect both he and Crowley from this... whatever he was. But it was the magical intent that mattered, wasn't it? Or was it the visualization that was more important? Concentration and will, that was it. And he was a full-blown Magus after all and would crush this bespectacled intruder.

The old man stopped and turned to face him. Jones's mouth

suddenly felt very, very parched. His fingers continued to wiggle and weave as he held them out in front of him, but he could not, try as he might, speak another word. His will dissipated and he could neither concentrate nor visualize. The old man seemed slightly annoyed at his mumblings and finger weavings. The entire lenses of his glasses began to glow softly.

Without knowing why, but realizing his life was at stake, Jones shut his mouth, dropped to his knees as though kicked from behind and put his arms behind his back and then clasped his hands together as he leaned forward and touched his forehead to the floor. The surrounding air seemed to prickle with energy. Jones began to whimper. The hardwood slats felt hard and cold against his forehead. Who was this man? he wondered. What was this man? Jones squeezed his eyelids so tightly closed that it hurt. For the first time in his life, he did not want to know what was going to happen next.

Jones felt the air change, and lifted his head slightly from the floor, turned, and saw the old man continue walking toward Crowley, who was still pressed up against the wall by an invisible force. The Great Baphomet's flabby face inexplicably flapped outward slightly at the edges as though something were pressing against it.

When Mr. Keyes's banal associate was within a few feet of Crowley, he dropped to the floor like a sack of flour and lay there moaning. The old man took another step closer to Crowley and stopped again. Jones heard a soft unzipping noise, and realized to his horror what was happening as he saw the yellowish stinking stream splash on Crowley's chest. Jones lifted his head completely off the floor, sat back on his heels, and gawked.

What he saw just could not be happening. As the warm smell of urine diffused through the bookstore, the utter insanity of it all bewildered him. How could this be happening in a metropolitan city located in the heartland of America? It was… it was very much like, he realized with surprise, something that Crowley would enjoy doing to someone else. But now, wide-eyed and laid out on the floor covered in another man's urine, it was a very different experience for the Great Baphomet.

As the old man finished up, turned and approached him again, Jones quickly abased himself, forcing his forehead even harder against the wooden floor. Hands behind his back again, he closed his eyes as before and, for the second time in one night, he kept his mouth shut.

When Jones heard the door open and close shut again and Mr. Keyes and his hideous associate were gone, he lifted his head and looked nervously around the room. Crowley lay on the floor, stretched flat on his back in a stupor. Blood oozed from the back of his head. The bookstore was quiet. He realized that the moment the door had closed, the furious storm stilled—and that was more terrifying than anything. On the table, unmoved by the violent rush of energy that had tossed Crowley across the room like he weighed nothing, the desk lamp glowed a steady, eerie light. In the overhead darkness, the fuming shadows were quiet.

What had just happened?

Who was the sinister old man who had unleashed such horrifying magic?

Crowley groaned as a bubble of pale red spittle ballooned from one corner of his mouth.

Jones rose shakily to his feet, his mind racing with fearful doubts, and went slowly over to Crowley. He looked down on the prostrate form and felt like vomiting. The smell of urine seemed a living presence, and its awful, pungent odor held him helpless to move again. In his terrified state, he thought that his friend and mentor had been marked. To move closer seemed impossible. It was as though the man had been marked by a predator, in the way that big, carnivorous cats marked their territory. Crowley groaned again, and his now bloodshot eyes fluttered open.

"The horror," he said weakly. "The dark beauty of it."

Not knowing what else to say, Jones said, "I'll get you some towels and a change of clothes—from the basement. And rubbing alcohol to wipe away the… the odor."

He was still afraid to bend down and closer, afraid to inspect his friend's injuries.

"No," shouted Crowley, his eyes popping completely open. He tried to say something else, but a choking, strangled coughing fit overcame him.

Still, Jones did not bend down to comfort his prostrate friend. Somehow, he knew with an awful surety that to do so would mean his own corruption. Finally, the fit subsided and Crowley sat up. It was a painful process, wherein his hand slipped out from under him, and he fell backward, but he made the effort again, more careful this time until he was able to get to his knees. He looked at Jones for help, extending a hand upward. Jones hurriedly took a step back. Crowley's eyes widened, then comprehension lit his eyes.

"Did you hear what he told me?" he asked.

"He's a filthy pig," said Jones. "Surely you said some of those things, but you were drunk or maybe in a haze. The man has no manners at all. He had no right to call you—"

"Not him," said Crowley. "The other. The other. Did you hear him?"

Now Jones was worried. Perhaps a concussion. Perhaps the force of colliding with the wall had shattered Crowley's already tenuous hold on reality.

"He said nothing. Not a word. Not the whole bloody time he was here. You have a concussion. Or a swelling of the brain. You're lucky to be alive. I don't know how he did it—"

"Be still. The day is upon us. He spoke to me."

"I'm telling you, your brain was injured. He did not say a single word."

Crowley tapped the side of his head and then winced.

"In here," he said. "He spoke to me in here. In the most hallowed sepulcher of my cranium."

"I need another drink," said Jones.

The Great Baphomet began to laugh. The sound was straight out of an asylum's worst inmate's cell. Jones felt a drop of sweat trickle down from his left sideburn and continue down his cheek as he sloshed whiskey into his glass, then gulped it down straight. He coughed, slapped his chest, and then leaned his free hand on the table.

"We should get you to a doctor," he said to Crowley. "Or get a doctor to you."

"No."

Crowley said it with a mesmeric force. His eyes were mad.

"But you're bleeding. Look at your hand where you touched the back of your head."

With a joyous leer spreading across his face, the Great Baphomet licked the blood from his palms.

"You're mad. Let me at least get towels for you to wipe that... that filthy smell off you."

"Piss do you mean? Why never, man. It is his gift, his gift to me, and I am honored to receive the sacramental offering of his fluids."

Jones poured himself another drink and swallowed it faster than the last. His throat must have been numb because he did not cough or gag. He relished the speed with which the whiskey's warmth flooded his body.

"You're delirious," he said. "You've had a terrible blow to your head and you think you're hearing the voice of Aiwass again, but you're not. You need a doctor. I'm going to get some towels. I can't stand the smell."

The room swirled around him as he leaned away from the table. Was he delirious as well? Or inebriated? He'd tossed those last two drinks back awfully fast.

"Get me a jar instead. A clean glass jar," giggled the madman. "We must squeeze every drop of his blessed fluid from this shirt."

"What? Why would we do that? Really, you are insane. You've had a head injury and can't think straight."

"Oh, no. I heard him in my head. The Masons are about to build a new Temple here in Detroit. The largest in the entire world. He told me. They have formed a committee and are selecting a…"

Here he drifted off and Jones feared his eyes would roll back in his head and he would fall back to the floor in a coma. But still, he could not force himself to approach him and help him lie down.

"… an architect. Yes, an architect. And I must design two statues for its hallways. One will be a monk grasping the Book of the Law, his law. The Law of Thelema. The other will deliver the message when the time is right."

"And we need the piss for what?" asked a dubious Jones.

"For the magical ritual, of course."

"We need that old man's piss for a magical ritual? I need another drink. Why? And I repeat my drunken self. Why? Why?"

Crowley leered at him.

"To make the statue come alive, of course."

"Why in the living hell buried beneath Hades would we need to make a living statue?"

"So that it can be the harbinger of the end. And we must go to see a man about a set of chairs."

"A set of chairs? Are you totally mad? Wait, of course you are. How gauche of me to ask. And where may we find this man?"

"Why, on 666 Blood Road, of course. There we will see a very special collector of functional Arcanum. A very special collector indeed."

"Go on, you blithering bedlamite."

Crowley, who sometimes delighted in being called the Great Beast, leaned back on his heels and howled like a wild animal.

Definitely, thought Jones, another drink is in order.

40

Hunter's legs shook. Sweat popped out the pores of his body and he could smell the stink of his own fear. What the hell was Hiram Abiff? And how did that snake come out of Brother Mihaloff's mouth? No way that macabre thing could have even fit inside of Brother Mihaloff's body. And what was the membranous tunnel called the Borgo Pass? Worse, what surrounded it? It was like a scene from one of Dante Alighieri's books and not the one called Paradiso. No, the Borgo Pass was Inferno material.

He looked at Brother Mihaloff again with wild-eyed, manic fear. Was Rebecca's father even human? What if he suspected Hunter knew and disgorged another occult reptile?

No. No way in hell would Hunter let that happen. Brother Mihaloff could never suspect he knew. He'd swear it never happened before an IRS judge if it meant keeping the truth of what he knew from Brother Mihaloff. On second thought, he didn't even know if Brother Mihaloff knew he was carrying a monster around in his body. On third thought... on third thought, he had to fight the urge to run screaming out into the night. Bartok trained him himself, didn't he? But in the face of what he had just seen, Hunter didn't know if that counted for much. No matter how crazy he felt, he had to distract Brother Mihaloff long enough for him to figure out what to do.

"You ever passed out before?" Hunter asked, stalling for time.

Considering the huge black snake that slithered out of his mouth, Brother Mihaloff was most definitely under a spell. And what he knew, the person who had spellbound him would know. What was it Bartok had called the spell? A host spell. When he'd told Hunter about such things, Hunter's mind had been off somewhere else—probably on girls. Even for someone as introverted as he'd been, a fifteen-year-old boy was still a fifteen-year-old boy.

"I... what?"

"Listen to you. You're still shaking it off. While we were talking to Hiram, you passed out at the table. You need to sleep. It's been a hell of a week for you."

The important thing, if he remembered it right, was that the spellbound host could never suspect that you knew. That covered the possibility that they were sentient enough to know they were enslaved and would strike out at anyone suspicious of their status and, if they weren't aware of their situation, it would keep them from a mind-fracturing revelation.

"I-I don't remember..." said Brother Mihaloff.

Hunter steered him away from seeing the broken spear tip holding the chair in place.

The man's confused expression was real. Bartok had told Hunter about such things years ago. The spellbound regained their faculties slowly and their memories were blurred, sometimes even absent. They were easily led and were like patients coming awake after hypnogogic anesthesia. Their memories deliberately scrubbed clean of the painful realities of their ordeal. Hunter felt bad for lying to the man, but he knew that Brother Mihaloff must not find out what he had seen. Besides, how could Hunter make him believe that a huge black snake had slid out of his mouth? That would be far worse than the trauma inflicted on Brother Leasing because of what he had seen. But above and beyond all of that was the horror of Hiram Abiff himself. That Brother Mihaloff could not recognize the dangers of Hiram told Hunter that Brother Mihaloff and perhaps even Brothers Kaufman and Cook were all spellbound. Great. Was it possible that they were bound to tell everything they know to the Master of the Borgo Lodge? If they were, Hunter, Moser and Rebecca were in terrible danger. He would have to maintain the lie that nothing happened in their meeting with Hiram except pleasant conversation. He'd gotten some experience with that last year, while lying to Detective Alvarez to keep himself from being arrested for shooting his uncle.

"Come on," said Hunter. "Let me help you to your office."

He kept looking back over his shoulder at the spear tip he'd wedged into the line between the empty chair and the floor, expecting it at any moment to explode upward into the air as Hiram Abiff broke past the temporary safety measure.

"It's hard to believe, isn't it?" wheezed Brother Mihaloff. "You and I are among a handful of people who have met Hiram Abiff and are still alive. Think how many teeming millions have died since his resurrection and yet, in defiance of all reason, he still lives."

Oh, please God, just shut up, thought Hunter. Don't you know Hiram Abiff is a monster?

As the old man spoke, he stroked his white beard distractedly, as though the fragment of an elusive memory was close at hand, but just out of reach. Could he remember, thought Hunter, the slimy snake scales slithering across his lips? The thought of this so repulsed him he almost stepped back from the man.

"I'm having a difficult time processing all of this," Hunter told him after a minute's awkward silence. "It's hard to take it all in at once, you know. Hiram looked like any other seventy-year-old man I've ever seen. But he claims to be over three thousand years old. It's… it's mind boggling."

Difficult time processing all of this? Hell yes. Especially the part where he had to pretend he hadn't seen that enormous snake coming out of Brother Mihaloff's mouth. And three thousand years old? A monster can amass a lot of black magic in three thousand years.

"Claims?" said a suddenly angry and coherent Brother Mihaloff. "He claims nothing. He is over three thousand years old. Get those kinds of thoughts out of your head, Brother Hunter. You're our Tyler now. You guard the door between us and the rest of Freemasonry. You guard we, the Temple Guardians, from falsehood. To do that effectively, you have to know and believe in what you're guarding. There's no room for doubt. As our Tyler, you are the keeper and protector of all records relating to Hiram. If you have doubts, go through the records. Read the thoughts of your predecessors. We, the Temple Guardians, have kept the secret of Hiram Abiff since the infancy of Freemasonry. We are not gullible fools, Hunter. Every generation of Temple Guardians has lived this question and answered it in the affirmative. No Tyler has ever disproved the claims of Hiram Abiff. In fact, they have affirmed them."

Feisty for a spellbound, Hunter thought. Had to be careful of him. This old man was used to being in charge. Like his daughter, he had a temper, and it came out when someone questioned what he was saying.

"Including my uncle Bartok?" he asked.

This was, to him, the most important thing for his own sanity. Did Bartok know that Hiram Abiff was a monster, or had he been fooled like the other members of the Temple Guardians? No, not Bartok. He would have been hard at work trying to destroy Hiram once was he knew what he was. Bartok did not tolerate evil.

Brother Mihaloff turned his stern gaze away from him and stared up at the symbol that was on the wall opposite the doors of the Romanesque lodge. The letter "G" was inscribed in the center of a compass and square. There were some debates about the meaning of the "G." Some held that it represented the word God. Others that it stood for the Great Architect of the Universe. Others for Geometry. Whatever it truly stood for, Hunter thought, all Masons revered its significance. Masonry was like a religion; it sometimes required belief in what you either did not know or did not understand.

"It's the pressure," said Brother Mihaloff. He seemed to be more clearheaded as he spoke. "I'm sorry, Brother Hunter. And you're right —I'm exhausted. What happened at my house to Rebecca was terrible enough, but when I add to it the introduction of Hiram, not only to the world of Freemasonry but to the world, I feel overwhelmed. The stress is both wonderful and terrible. The knowledge sometimes lifts me up and other times I feel crushed by the weight of it.

"We have thousands of Masons in transit. Over half are already here in Detroit. There are over five million Masons in the world, and only six who know the true facts about the mystery of Hiram Abiff. The entire grand meeting of Freemasonry to take place here in a few days' time is in reality a gathering of venerable Masonic Worshipful Masters and Grandmasters coming together to hear a presentation on a topic of which they know nothing about. We are about to prepare the world by first shocking the most prominent members of Freemasonry itself. Imagine, we will unveil the cure for cancer and then we will introduce the man whose imagination and direction made it all possible. Hunter, had we achieved this earlier, my wife would still be alive today."

For the second time in as many days, Brother Mihaloff let slip his mask and Hunter could see the grief that tormented the man beneath it. If only he knew what had crawled out of his mouth a while ago, thought Hunter. Then he'd really be grief stricken.

"Many people would still be alive today if you'd been able to do that, but think of the future," said Hunter. "Think of all the people who can be saved."

Or not, he thought. What if he's bringing all these Masons to the Detroit Masonic Temple to spellbind them, too? What if he would turn them all into things that weren't human? Or what if he would make them into incubators for monsters?

But Brother Mihaloff had to be still human; he felt grief. Or seemed to.

He struggled to imagine what it would be like to lose the woman you loved to a terrible disease like brain cancer. Hunter had never been married. The longest lasting relationship he'd ever had was Molly, and after he'd bolted off without a word to Kentucky last year to see his Uncle Bartok, that relationship seemed pretty well over. She wasn't even returning his phone calls. The problem was, the things he and Moser were involved in were always things that couldn't be talked about with outsiders. The Hunters, Bartok had said, always had secrets to protect, and they almost always were bad. That sometimes even meant hiding them from people who cared about you. Molly had a right to be upset with him. And now, he and Enid had to keep more secrets from those whose society they'd joined.

"But we can't go backward," said Brother Mihaloff. "We have to keep our eyes on the future, although sometimes it's hard not to look back. But, to the present…"

Brother Mihaloff reached into one pocket and took out a ring of keys, which he handed to Hunter.

"As Tyler of the Temple Guardians, you now have the keys to everything in the Detroit Masonic Temple. The Watchmen report to you. As far as the rest of the world knows, the Temple Guardians are an association of Brothers come together for the sole purpose of tending to the affairs of the largest and most distinguished Masonic

Temple in the world—they care that we see there is always money to pay the bills. For years, the Temple owed a staggering amount in back taxes. Now that the Temple is solvent again, the mundane part of our charter is to make sure that it never happens again. You do not understand what secrets hide in this temple, Hunter. The world cannot afford to lose such things due to petty things as mismanagement of funds. So, as Tyler for the Temple Guardians, you are also Tyler for this entire building. Both the legacy and property of this temple are yours to protect when in the days to come it is renamed The Temple of Hiram Abiff. He will live and preside here."

Hunter looked back into the lodge room at the empty benches and stations. His gaze settled on the altar in the middle of the floor and then moved up to the balconies. To think that in a matter of days, all of Freemasonry would change, and the world along with it. If Brother Mihaloff had his way, Hiram Abiff would become the most well-known person in the entire world and the most powerful. He had to stop that from happening.

"What will we call him?" he asked.

"He will be Worshipful Grandmaster Hiram Abiff, the Master of All Freemasonry. Our craft will finally be unified. It will bring together all Freemasons around the world under his leadership."

From his tone of hushed reverence alone, it was plain that Brother Mihaloff was a true believer. He believed Hiram Abiff was the savior of the world. A man of greater influence and power than anyone who had ever lived. Whatever the three-thousand-year-old man said would be gospel to him. In his eyes, there burned the flames of true zealotry. Hunter had to be very careful. He didn't know why, but he could feel it. That was an easy self-deception, he thought. He knew why. The other members of the Temple Guardians were spellbound. And he knew for sure that to understand how to stop Hiram, he needed to see the assembled writings of past Tylers. If Brother Mihaloff got suspicious of his motives, they would shut him out. Then he would be cut off from all the records he would need to understand what was truly going on.

"I think Moser and I need to come back and investigate the statue that attacked Brother Leasing. Hiram—Grandmaster Worshipful Brother Hiram—should not come through until we make sure everything in the Temple is safe. I'm also worried about the attendees who attend his introduction. We must guarantee their safety. Moser and I will bring back equipment to determine whether the whole statue strangling him incident was in his head or really happened. If it really happened, we might need to postpone the unveiling."

"Impossible," snapped Brother Mihaloff. "There are too many people arriving here, too many preparations have been made and Grandmaster Hiram himself would not stand for it. He has been waiting for three thousand years to be revealed to the world."

"So far you've had one of the Watchman nearly strangled to death here and your own house attacked. There has to be a connection. What was that about the signs again? I'm the Tyler and I want to know, and I don't want to read through centuries of documentation to find out when you can tell me the answer right now. You asked for our help. We've given it to you freely. You trusted my uncle Bartok's judgment enough to accept me as your new Tyler; now is the time for you to extend that trust to include honesty. What was the doctor talking about when he mentioned the four signs at your house?"

Again, Brother Mihaloff looked at the letter G in the center of the conjoined square and compass. During Lodge business, the symbol was lit. Tonight, with Brother Mihaloff and Hunter the only two present, it was mysteriously unlit—mysteriously, that was, because the business they were discussing applied to the very future of not only Freemasonry, but humanity. Strange that the Masonic symbol of the Divine was not invoked, thought Hunter, on this of all nights.

"Let me give you something first," said Brother Mihaloff. "It only just arrived today but was addressed to your uncle Bartok. I have it locked away in my office in a hidden safe."

"Fine," said Hunter.

Although he thought at first that Brother Mihaloff was stalling, he was surprised to find the man talkative as they walked down the beautifully paneled hallways to his office.

"Look at these halls," he said. "A beautiful but dying testimony to the wonderful works men can accomplish when they unite both their wills and their hands in the execution of a grand design. That's what the world of Freemasonry has been lacking in these times, Hunter—a grand design. The Detroit Masonic temple is the largest in the world. In the entire world. Think of that. Is there anywhere more appropriate to introduce Hiram Abiff than to a humanity drowning in darkness?"

Even as Brother Mihaloff opened the door to his office, Hunter could not rid his thoughts of the terrible, glowing eyes of the old man. But he had to hide what he thought, or he would be pushed aside and unable to stop what would happen. He could go to the authorities, but which authorities? And who would listen to him? Who could he tell that a sect within the Freemasons was hiding the existence of a three thousand year old demonic monster who looked like a man? They would lock him in an asylum. He needed more time to figure this out and to do that, he needed more information. He had to play along for now. He had to pretend that he hadn't seen Hiram Abiff for what he really was.

"Come in and sit down, Hunter. Make yourself comfortable while I get the package."

The walls were elegantly wainscoted, as though architected for royalty. Brother Mihaloff's desk was a large walnut old world executive piece that could have come from a room in the White House. Paintings of famous Masons were hung around the room, including a reproduction of George Washington in full Masonic regalia. Hunter sat in a brass tacked brown leather chair and watched as Brother Mihaloff went to a bookshelf on one wall, pulled out two books and twisted something, then walked to the other side of the room and repeated the actions. On the floor, a marble square with the engraved symbol of the square and compass raised silently to a forty-five-degree angle. The old man reached into the opening and withdrew a large brown envelope wrapped in string. He then reached inside the opening again, pressed an invisible button, and withdrew his hand. Without a sound, the marble square lowered again until it was flush with the royal blue carpeting.

Brother Mihaloff walked over to where Hunter sat and extended the package toward him.

"It was addressed to your uncle Bartok, and as his sole heir and Tyler of the Temple Guardians, I entrust it to your care. If it relates at all to his researches and records concerning Hiram Abiff, it must be added, when you have evaluated the contents, to the other records. Copies will be made, and the documents distributed among the archived papers. One safe in this building contains the actual documents, and the other two contain complete copies."

The package weighed about the same as a trade paperback book and had roughly the same measurements.

"Thank you," said Hunter.

He looked at the postage mark and saw that it had been mailed two months ago. There were several failed deliveries, as though it had been mailed to several wrong addresses before finding its way at last to the Temple.

"The keys will admit you to the Temple any time, day or night. The security code is on that piece of paper taped to the key ring. On the reverse side, you'll find your personal identification code and another for Mr. Moser. The phone number is for the security company, in case you need assistance."

"I'll take good care of them."

"I'm confident that you will. And I have one more thing to give you before we discuss the incident with Brother Leasing."

Hunter could barely keep still. That Hiram Abiff could break through the empty chair and come after them was like a weight pressing against his chest.

Unaware of what Hunter was thinking, Brother Mihaloff, now recovered, went to a freestanding walnut hutch beneath the reproduction of George Washington in Masonic garb and pulled open a sizable drawer. From it, he removed a long, polished cherry wood case and carried it over to where Hunter sat.

"It is the imprimatur of your office. It has been passed down from the very first Tyler of the Temple Guardians to each successor of the office. Its last caretaker was your Uncle Bartok."

After laying the package on the chair next to him, Hunter accepted the long box with a feeling of wonder. He laid it across his knees and reached for the gold latches that held it shut, but stopped.

"May I open it?" he asked.

"It is your duty to open it. You are the Tyler, and although when you accepted the position you could not by any means know the gravity of it, the sword inside and all it represents will soon impress upon you the importance of your responsibility. You are the guardian of truth. Your duty is to protect us from error. Inside the case you will find a letter from your Uncle Bartok explaining your responsibilities in greater detail, but for now you realize that the sword of the Tyler separates truth from falsehood, light from darkness, and good from evil. Use it wisely, Hunter, but never hesitate to bring it forth when it is needed."

Hunter nodded, but was thinking he'd need a better weapon than this symbolic sword to stop Hiram Abiff. He didn't know when he had decided, but he was committed to the task.

Hiram Abiff, however, would shortly have an army of Freemasons protecting him and proclaiming him the new king of Freemasonry. How many Masons were there in the world? Five million? Great. They would be spellbound like Brother Mihaloff and not one of them could ask how human flesh could endure for so long as three-thousand-years. None of them could consider the idea that Hiram Abiff was not human. With only his gut instinct to back him up, Hunter had already decided that even if Hiram once was human, he wasn't anymore. That old man might look human, but he was demonic. The Borgo Pass established that beyond a doubt. Only a demon could have crafted such a horror.

With the lid open and tilted back, the overhead light shone on the sword blade and lit it with the radiance of sunlight reflecting off a pool of liquid silver. Lower in the case was a sheathed dagger.

"It's magnificent," said Hunter.

At the center of the hilt was the symbol of the square and compass, with the letter "G" prominent in the middle. Hunter lifted it by the pommel and was surprised by the weight. He slid his fingers down over the hilt and relished the feel of the leather. On the pommel, engraved in silver, was the Blazing Star of Freemasonry. The blade was thirty-six inches of polished, honed steel. Hunter looked down its length to the sharp point and placed the entire weapon back into the case before he nearly cut off a thumb examining it. But as he tilted it to one side, the light's reflection lessened, and he saw the scrollings etched into the side of the blade. They were the same symbols etched onto the knife his uncle Bartok had given him beneath Townsend Mountain to cut through Aeyrik, the living door that guarded the alien ship. This was the sword that Bartok had kept stuck into a stone in his den. My protection, he had called it from the day Hunter first saw it. The sharp-edged ward that keeps this home safe. And now it was his.

A magical sword, he thought. But no owner's manual to tell me how to use it. I wish Bartok were still alive.

And it was true. If only he hadn't killed him within days after they'd reconciled.

"Yes, isn't it, though?" said Brother Mihaloff. "A weapon from the old days and the old ways, yet still lethal. A symbol, yet a deadly symbol. The dagger, however, is another matter altogether. You can leave the package here and the sword, but bring the dagger."

It wasn't the suggestion, but the way Brother Mihaloff said it, that gave Hunter pause.

"No," he said, "I won't let either of them out of my sight."

"Your first action as a true Tyler," smiled Brother Mihaloff. "They are your responsibility now, your burden, and one day, perhaps, your deliverance. Come, follow me."

The feeling of pride that came with that statement surprised Hunter. Brother Mihaloff did not seem to be the type of man who gave approval easily. While the other man waited for him to get organized, Hunter withdrew the dagger from his case and slid it into his belt. He then situated the package inside the case and closed the lid, which would not close. After removing the package and setting it on the chair next to him again, he closed the case lid and stood up. He retrieved the package and tucked it into his inside pocket.

"Ready," he said.

Their destination was a suit of armor several halls and two floors down, with a shield bearing the Templar Cross through a crown and their motto. It stood in front of a dark paneled wall like a guardian.

"*In hoc signo vinces*," read Brother Mihaloff.

"In this sign, you will conquer," Hunter translated.

"You read Latin?"

"In the world of the paranormal and the occult, brother, it's either that or Google translator," said Hunter.

"I see," said Brother Mihaloff. "I'll stick with Google. But there are some things even it cannot divine."

With that, he placed a hand on either side of the shield and twisted it first to the right, then twice to the left, then three times to the right, and one last time to the left. The wall behind the knight opened inward into darkness.

"Interesting lock," said Hunter.

As long as it wasn't another occult tunnel like the Borgo Pass, Hunter thought he could handle it. Secret passageways were normal in the world of paranormal investigation. He had once investigated an abbey with a network of tunnels beneath it. They were stone arch reinforced throughout, and nearly six feet in height at their apex. Legends of spectral figures seen floating about the abbey in the middle of the night turned out to be a group of university students dressed in luminescent togas who entered and exited the abbey via a long-forgotten door.

Brother Mihaloff entered the opening and gestured for Hunter to follow. Once inside, Brother Mihaloff pushed on a square and compass on the wall. The door swung shut, shrouding them in darkness, but the second the door clicked back into place, recessed ceiling lights sprung to life.

"This way."

They were in a square room with no exits. The floor was the tiled black-and-white pattern that was so familiar to Hunter as a Masonic pattern, but the room was void of furniture. The only unusual element to the room was that it was totally empty. Brother Mihaloff led him to what Hunter thought was the East wall and extended a hand toward it.

"Yours to open," he said.

Hunter looked from Brother Mihaloff to the wall in puzzlement, then noticed a thin, short line cut into it.

"The dagger?" he asked, pointing at the slot.

"Yes. Your uncle Bartok's design. He was, as you are now, charged with protecting all items of importance belonging to our order. And, I must say, that never was a man more suited to the task. He had an amazing and complex mind. I do not understand how this lock works any more than I can explain the Tyler's sword you carry. We, the other members of the Temple Guardians, protected the secret of Hiram Abiff. Your uncle protected the order itself, as you do now."

"Against what?" asked Hunter.

"Behind this wall lie many centuries' worth of secrets, brother, beginning with the writings of a Templar monk named Archambaud and continuing in an unbroken line straight through to your uncle Bartok. Secrets such as these are, to the enemy, worth killing for. But open the door and see for yourself."

He withdrew the sheathed dagger from his belt and stood up. With a silent prayer for continued sanity, he slid the blade into the slot and heard a soft thrum, like the muted reverb from a sixties band. A soft click when it was finished followed this, and the panel swung inward.

"An amazing bit of electromagnetic machinery," said Brother Mihaloff. "That door weighs more than your car. The walls of this room are reinforced, like my shelter. And you can see why now, can't you?"

Hunter was not book-crazed, but as a writer of books about the paranormal, he could not help but be impressed with what he saw housed in the room. Journals under protective glass, cassette tapes, paintings of men from ages gone by, and the photographs. Each one by itself priceless because of their documentation of the astonishing life of Hiram Abiff. There were swords and shields, maces and pistols, knives and helmets. Newspaper clippings gone yellow with age and even a microfiche reader. A place for a researcher to get lost for hours on end.

"Which, to your question from earlier this evening, explains our… unease over Brother Leasing. Hiram, and by extension the Temple Guardians, has many powerful enemies. There are the Christians, the Jews and the Muslims, of course. The Buddhists don't as of yet have an interest, nor the Hindus. But the Vatican would surely do anything to prevent the world from ever knowing about Hiram, up to and including killing not only him, but all of us. There are fanatics among the Catholics who think the Inquisition should still go on. The Protestants have their own pious zealots who would burn us at the stake, as they did so many innocents in the Salem witch trials. And none of this includes the brain dead, zombie-like jihadi Muslims of the world. You see the danger?"

"I'm beginning to," said Hunter uncomfortably. But he knew already that the real danger was Hiram Abiff.

"Then there are the governments whose power is open and intractable. Should they know of our plans, the entire Masonic temple would be cut off, surrounded by armed guards, rail guns and black helicopters. The unveiling of Hiram Abiff will be world-altering, and politicians and their military do not approve of change. We must catch them unawares."

What was perhaps most disturbing about the way Brother Mihaloff delivered his message was that he was talking in a normal tone of voice. He did not seem to be a wild-eyed fanatic looking for converts. Instead, he came across as a man who didn't care if he was believed or not. He was just reciting the facts.

"You're perhaps frightened by my concerns, Hunter, thinking about all the things that could go wrong. But remember—Hiram Abiff has remained under our protection and the protection of the Knights Templar before us for over three thousand years after Hugh de Payens and his knights found him buried beneath the second temple. In all of that time, no one has discovered our secret. No one."

"It makes little sense," said Hunter. "I can't understand how he could remain hidden for over all that time. It makes a little more sense that he was safer under the protection of the Freemasons, but how did he survive before that?"

Their voices echoed around the hidden library. Hunter could see artifacts on the wall, stacked on shelves, and laid out on tables. Some he knew from his years of research—others, he couldn't begin to understand what they were. The room was fifty feet by fifty feet and twenty feet tall. Suspended ceiling fans rotated at the rate of once every minute, as though they were operating in slow motion. The hum of dehumidifiers filled the air like invisible insects. The doubts that plagued him crowded his thoughts.

"According to the account of the Knights Templar, he lay buried beneath the rubble of the second Jerusalem temple for over one thousand years. Hugh de Payens and his men found Hiram, chained in place a to a rock wall. Other men were shackled in the same way, but starvation and thirst had taken them. Hiram was forced to hear his companions die one at a time until he was eventually the last man alive. The torches had gone out. He was chained in the dark for over a thousand years. Think about that Hunter. Alone in the dark for over a thousand years and still sane. From that point until the King of France ordered their destruction, the Knights Templar protected him."

Hunter shuddered.

"And before that?" he asked.

"He wandered the earth," said Brother Mihaloff sadly, "looking for more light to guide him in our fallen world. He never stayed in one place too long because someone might discover that while those around him died, Hiram Abiff lived. He could have no close friends. Those were the days when people suspected of black magic were stoned to death and back then, who would not have interpreted his longevity as proof that he should be killed. Who could he confide in? Who would shelter him knowing that if others found out his true story that they, too, would be stoned—especially if they ever found out what he knew?"

It was as if the combined mass of the facts about Hiram Abiff was crushing his ability to think. His uncle Bartok had reared in him the knowledge and history of occult societies, but before Bartok banned him and before Hunter had developed opinions of his own, the depth of the old man's knowledge of esoteric things had seemed fascinating to him. The Illuminati, the Rosicrucians and other secret societies intrigued him in the way that fortune and glory had intrigued Indiana Jones. The story of Hiram Abiff was more fantastic than anything he had ever heard from Bartok, but something about it bothered him. Who had chained him to a rock wall beneath the Temple of Jerusalem and why? Was he chained there by men who saw the danger of what he was? And how had they been able to overcome him?

For the second time in his life, he wondered how he had again gotten involved in such a hideous mess. The answer was simple, though—it was what the old man would have wanted him to do. Bartok was like a monk devoted to protecting the world from dark things. His view of the world did not fit into the way the world was in modern times. He had been the only man Hunter knew who still used a handkerchief, and the only man Hunter knew who actually used a sword cane. While Brother Mihaloff waited for an answer to his question though, another thought nagged at him. Had his uncle suspected who or what Hiram Abiff was? That was the unanswered question that he had to know the answer to.

"Well? You see what I mean?" said a suddenly impatient Brother Mihaloff.

"No one would take him in," Hunter said. "Yes, I see that. I can't imagine why he didn't kill himself."

"What did you say?"

"The sheer frustration and depression at being an outcast would have been enough to break most people's minds. And he was brought back from the dead. How could anyone go through that and still have their psyche intact?"

"Funny, I hadn't thought of that," said Brother Mihaloff. "All of these years, and none of us in the Temple Guardians have ever discussed that. I think you have promise as a Tyler, Brother Hunter."

A sense of urgency pressed Hunter. Thousands of Masons from around the world were converging on the Detroit Masonic Temple. The day they would be introduced to Hiram Abiff, whoever or whatever he was. The idea caused him a sense of unease that he couldn't push aside. He had to learn more.

"Can we call it quits for the night?" asked Hunter. "I need to go see a friend of mine who I hope can provide me with research on statues coming to life so I can understand what happened to Brother Leasing. And tomorrow night, I'll need to bring Moser here and set up some equipment to see if I can find out what caused it."

Brother Mihaloff eyed him suspiciously, then nodded in recognition of what Hunter's new role was.

"Certainly," he said. "I'll tell the others."

"No," said Hunter. "No one is to know about this except myself, you and Moser."

"Why?" asked Brother Mihaloff, seeming genuinely interested.

"I don't want to say just yet," said Hunter.

"I don't like it."

"It's my duty as Tyler," said Hunter, "to protect you and the others, if what I think is going on proves out. If it does, you and your family are in danger. Our greatest danger is from within. Do you understand?"

Brother Mihaloff looked like he wanted to push the point, to demand to know what he was getting at, but he kept himself under control. That one of their inner circle might be responsible for the attacks clearly set him back.

"We'd better close up," he said. "I will check in on Rebecca and the others."

"I'll call them from the road as well," said Hunter. "First, I have to visit my researcher, Molly Collins, and I need to get on this right now."

On the way out, Hunter risked a look inside the Romanesque room to see if the spear was still wedged into place. As he opened the door a crack, he heard a sound like a cork popping on a champagne bottle. He was just in time to see the spear tip shoot straight up into the air, then fall spear point first onto the floor. Hunter locked the doors with trembling hands, then ran for his car like the devil was after him.

41

Hunter strained to keep himself under control as he left the Detroit Masonic Temple's parking lot and turned onto Temple Street. What he was thinking was crazy. A steady rain had started up and streetlights were a smeared blur. His windshield wipers seemed to drag across the windshield the way his thoughts struggled to slide past his elusive fears. It was hard to choose between Brother Mihaloff and his daughter. Brother Mihaloff thought Hiram Abiff was the Messiah, and his daughter Rebecca thought Hiram was the Antichrist. Brother Mihaloff was blinded by the cure for cancer Hiram had gifted him. Rebecca would point to the implants used to achieve this healing as a sign of the Apocalypse. The sign of the beast.

Bartok, you old bastard, he thought, whatever is in these papers better help.

The package lay next to him on the seat. He'd packed the sword away in the trunk. If he got pulled over, he'd have a hard time explaining why he was driving around with an enormous sword in his car. By the time he got out of jail, the potholes on Detroit City streets might be fixed, and that was a long way out in the future.

Through his rain-spotted rear window, the Masonic Temple looked like a fortress. A fortress against what? wondered Hunter.

He'd checked in with Moser and heard that everything was okay there. Rebecca was chafing at being confined to the bunker, but

Brothers Kaufmann and Cook were adamant about her staying there until her father gave the okay for her to leave.

"Not making the lady happy," said Moser.

"I bet, but at least she's safe there," said Hunter. "Listen, I will drop by Molly's and ask her in person for her help on this. She won't like it, but I'll beg if I have to. There has to be something in the Temple's past that will explain the statue's attack. I Googled and Binged it to death with no luck. I don't know how to dig around like she does. Maybe we'll get lucky, and she'll try to help us. I'm worried about this whole thing, Enid, seriously worried."

"Save it until you get here," said Moser.

That was the thing with phones and email. You never knew who was listening in.

"That will give me enough space to organize my thoughts," said Hunter. "If Molly comes on board, we might figure out what we're dealing with here before the lights go out. How's Rebecca doing?"

"Doing fine. You want to talk to her? Sore still, but for someone who was clawed up like she was, I'd say she was doing fine."

Hunter wanted to tell Moser about Bartok's papers, but didn't want to mention that over the phone, either.

"Good. I've got a lot to look into tonight. Are you guys covered if I have to work till the small hours?"

"We're good," said Moser. "And Kenneth is keeping an eye out for Mr. Chirac. Bringing up Darryl and Eddie Moser to lend a hand. They're good boys."

"Keep your head down."

Moser's cell clicked off.

Keep your head down. What a stupid thing to say. Then Hunter remembered the beasts that were captured on Brother Mihaloff's home security system. He should have told Moser to keep his weapons close. But that would be redundant. Moser always kept his weapons close. He remembered Moser's version of the line from the Godfather movie—keep your friends close and your shotgun closer. Hunter felt the same way since he'd had to kill his uncle Bartok. He kept his weapons close, too. Although there were some things, like the little girl's screaming haint from the year before, that really weren't impressed with firepower.

****

Molly lived in Allen Park, which was a twenty-minute drive down 1-75 South. He glanced in the mirror as he drove away from the city. It was always good leaving Detroit. Even in the rearview mirror, he could see the pollution being pumped into the city's night sky. It's never good, he thought, when the clouds coming out of the smokestacks were orange. Currently, the city was the darling of feel-good crowd joiners, but Hunter knew that beneath the bright banners and fresh paint paid for by people who didn't even live in the city, there still beat a heart of darkness.

The poor had been swept away from the city to be homeless somewhere else. Poor people were too depressing to be allowed to ruin Detroit's image. Hunter wondered idly where they'd sent them. He'd watched while demolition crews got rid of the blighted buildings where the poor could hide out their lives. Detroit was to be remade into a shining city on a hill, but the poor had to be gotten rid of first. It was easier when you demolished their homes. If they had nowhere to live, they'd have to move on. Basic strategy of effective pest eradication. Wipe out their homes and they had to find another city to tarnish. Fuck Detroit, thought Hunter. I'd rather have a dirty city with a clean heart.

But now, the city would be home to the presentation of the Masonic world's new leader—its Twitter rage. Stories about Hiram Abiff might break the Internet, something the Kardashians dreamed of but could never pull off. Hunter wondered if Hiram would need a press secretary to field all the media opportunities. Hiram Abiff courtesy of the Freemasons. Masonic membership ought to go through the roof. The cure for cancer, another fine quality Masonic product. Hiram Abiff, the year's most interesting old man. Hell, history's most interesting man ever. Thousands of years old, steeped in the knowledge of the ages, and yet he still had room in his three-thousand-year-old skull to absorb and improve upon modern technology. Oprah might do a special on him. He might be given all the Nobel prizes available in a single year.

Hunter felt sick.

He wanted to see Molly to counterbalance his negative perspective of Rebecca Mihaloff. That was the problem with discussing things with a crazy religious woman; even after you'd dismissed them as nut cases, the conspiracy side of your brain couldn't let go of that "what if" question. Like, what if Rebecca was right? What if those beautiful brown eyes of hers weren't the eyes of a religious fanatic? What if Hiram Abiff was, in fact, the real Antichrist?

Hunter wondered whether, if Molly dumped him for good, Rebecca would go out to dinner with him before the Apocalypse came thundering down on the world.

I think I need a cold shower, he thought. It's been a long time since my last night with Molly.

Just a few days to stop the unveiling of Hiram Abiff from happening, if it could be stopped. In his gut, Hunter was completely convinced that there was nothing any of them could do to prevent it. They could shoot him as he exited the Borgo Pass and entered the Masonic lodge, but he'd already been killed once. Hunter had a feeling bullets wouldn't stop him. Just like the screaming haint, only worse.

The Southfield Road exit came up quickly, and he slowed and took the turn. He took Southfield Road north for only four minutes before entering the semi-quaint city of Allen Park. Towns like Allen Park would always be semi-quaint to him, which meant that they tried so hard to be quaint that they were disqualified from ever being quaint. Taking a loop at the point where the road divided, he did a Michigan U-turn onto the southbound side and then turned right onto Park Avenue. He would be at her house in less than five minutes. Reflexively, he slowed down.

The dashboard computer screen told him it was twenty minutes before midnight.

He glanced at the package on the passenger's seat. Whatever it contained was from Bartok. It could contain Bartok's thoughts on Hiram Abiff. At the very least, it could contain his observations and thoughts about the old man. Maybe his theories as to what Hiram Abiff really was, or, better still, what Hunter could do about him.

Maybe he should keep driving. Why was he going to see Molly, anyway? She wouldn't help him. Those days were gone. What did he really need from her? Help. He needed help to find out the actual history of the Detroit Masonic Temple to see if it could be used in stopping Hiram Abiff.

The public history was available online. But the paranormal or occult linkages were not. If what he suspected caused the statue to attack Brother Leasing was true—if it really did happen—then there had to have been serious occult doings in the Detroit Masonic Temple in decades gone by. Hunter just did not understand where to search for the information. But Molly was a researcher at the Detroit Public Library. She knew where to find the things he would never find. Not everything was on the Internet.

But despite the situation and his needs, Hunter just couldn't do it. He couldn't get turned down again. She'd made her point. They were done. He turned a corner just three blocks from her house, then turned back again and ignored his pride and his shame both and knock on her front door and ask for help. It was the right thing to do. It was what he wanted to do. He felt good about the decision.

Maybe they were through, but she was still a friend. He could still ask one more time for help. When he was three houses away, the sight of another car in her driveway changed his mind yet again. He drove slowly by, noting that the car was a black Mustang. Not Molly's type of car at all. A muscle car. Definitely a guy's car. The lights were out in the house. It didn't take long to figure it out. He kept driving until he was out of the subdivision and back onto Southfield road.

Okay, he thought, that's annoying.

He got a coffee at a Tim Horton's and parked.

Shit, he thought. She could have told him.

Oh, she could have said, I've got a new man in my life. You should just stay away now.

That was really the problem. He'd never been around much.

Looking at the City of Lincoln Park, he decided he liked its look better than Detroit and Allen Park combined. A regular town. A town that worked for a living, Moser would have said.

He took a sip of coffee, nearly burned his lips and thought if he didn't have the brains to let the coffee cool, he would have a hell of a time figuring out Hiram Abiff. After a quick look around the parking lot to see that his was the only car, he undid the wrapping on the package and opened it. Inside was another layer of paper binding, but the words on its surface said that it was the property of My Dear

Nephew Ian Hunter, to be opened only by him and no one else. Inside, that layer of wrapping was yet another layer of paper wrapping and an envelope addressed to him. For a few minutes, he just sat and stared at it, afraid to break the unique wax seal affixed to it by Bartok. Then he broke it, slit open the envelope and withdrew a single piece of stationery from within.

After unfolding it, he turned on the interior light and read the contents written in Bartok's precise penmanship. He felt himself grow pale.

My dear Ian,

If you are reading this, my elaborate life has ended, and I must ask you to carry on my battles for me.

You are now caretaker for the horrors that dwell beneath Townsend Mountain. Remember what I taught you. It will not be enough, but it will show you the way. Albert Magnus Hillis and his army of spirit powered automatons must be contained until you or our descendants discover a way to destroy them.

Containing the Hillis monstrosity is burden enough for any man to bear. Having done so myself for most of my adult life, I know that to be true. You know by now that sometimes the price of protecting others is distancing yourself from them. There may be people who keep close ties in times of war, but I must tell you that given the nature of the wars we Hunters engage in, I could not do both. At a dinner table supping with friends, all the while we spoke of mundane things, I could still see the metallic silver eyes of Albert Magnus Hillis staring at me. Once, while walking with a lady friend through the park, she enjoyed the soft sound of wind trembling the trees. Myself, in the chambers of my mind, I heard the mindless screams of Albert Magnus Hillis.

You might expect another apology from me for being so distant over the years, but in fact, I don't have the time or focus to gift you with an answer. As the days go by, you will understand this. There are some men and women who must choose to battle the darkness that others can neither see nor arm themselves against. I detest drama, but the struggle we Hunters are engaged in was set in place long ago. Forgive me, Ian, if I could protect you from this responsibility, I would, but I know of no way to do that.

There is another, more deadly burden I must now ask you to bear, nephew, and it will take you into a world of secrets so dark and terrible that you cannot face it alone. The Mosers, of course, can assist you, but never if it means relaxing their guard over what lies beneath Townsend Mountain. I think you will most likely reach out to Enid Moser, and that will be a good choice.

I must be quick here. My hands ache with each word I write. I pray you will never have to bear the insistent, unrelenting pain of arthritis. But if you do, it will mean that you have survived, and for that I should at least be grateful.

Of all the people I have known who can help you face the darkness known as Hiram Abiff, there is only one that I myself would turn to. Her name is Rebecca Mihaloff, and she is the daughter of Brother Frank Mihaloff, the Worshipful Master of an appendant body of Freemasons known as The Temple Guardians. Without intending to, the Temple Guardians, of which I am a member, believe they are guarding humanity's greatest mystery and future hope. For many years, so did I, but I am an intense man and I applied that intensity to the challenge of Hiram Abiff.

You know that I have never been prone to hyperbole. So, believe me, Ian, when I tell you I discovered that this man, if he is indeed a man, is the greatest danger to the human race there has ever been. You must stop him.

The Temple Guardians will appoint you Tyler upon my imminent death. I have a disease inflicted by an enemy and known in the esoteric world as "burnt blood." There is no cure. But when I am gone, you must accept the appointment as Tyler of the Temple Guardians. This is only possible if you have become a Freemason. I have prevailed on Enid Moser to encourage you in the matter. You must listen to him, Ian. Join the Freemasons and accept the appointment of Tyler that they will offer you. You must do this in order to gain access to the information you will need to unlock the secrets of Hiram Abiff. But be careful. The other Temple Guardians are true believers that Hiram Abiff is the savior of mankind, waiting to be unveiled to the world.

They await four signs to precipitate his entrance onto the world stage. The first will be "the unliving will speak his name." Like so many of his lies, no one knows yet what that means. The second is that the doors of hell will open and afford a view of its horrors. The third will be the Sign of the Woman, who is his acolyte. This means that his coming is soon approaching. The fourth and last sign is perhaps the only one of these ruses that is real. The fourth sign is that the Blazing Star of Freemasonry will be returned to the Craft. It has been lost for generations, Ian, and it is a terrible artifact which I labor to acquire before the Frenchman, who also seeks it.

Keep your own counsel. You cannot trust any of the Temple Guardians. They are blinded by the existence of Hiram. But above all, do not trust the Frenchman. Never trust the Frenchman.

You will learn about the woman to be feared as well. She is the devil's own,

Ian. Beware of her. It is she, I suspect, of cursing me with "burnt blood."

This is all that I can tell you just now. The rest will be in the other papers I bequeathed to you. I leave all to you. All my learning, all my wealth, all my belongs and the destiny of the Hunter family. I pray I will find the Blazing Star of Freemasonry and destroy it before it is too late. It is the artifact that Hiram Abiff and his Scarlett Woman will need to turn their evil loose on the world.

I have hidden away, in the safest of places, the journal that will reveal to you the truth. It is called the "Confessions of Mr. Hyde," written over a century ago by Robert Louis Stevenson. Read it carefully, Ian. Not only your life and soul are at stake, but the life and soul of the world itself.

It was signed simply *Bartok*.

Hunter's hands shook. He re-folded the letter, slid it back into the envelope, and started the car.

"I have hidden away in the safest of places the journal that will reveal to you the truth."

Where the hell could that be? In his house? It seemed the logical place, since it was a warren of secret hiding places, but also the place where anyone looking for the journal would think to look first. Still, he could think of nowhere else Bartok could mean.

He pounded his hands on the steering wheel in frustration. For once, couldn't Bartok have just come right and said where something was? Did he always have to be so secretive?

Then his eyes fell on the sword case. He stopped pounding on the steering wheel and stared at it. Was what he was thinking possible? He turned off the car engine and pulled the case onto his lap. It was wide enough that it almost filled the front seat. He ran his hands across the rich feeling leather, then slid his hands down and unlocked the latches. Even in the dim light, the sword seemed to shine with an eldritch light. The rich fabric of the velvet lining was soft to his probing touch. From the car's console, he removed a pocketknife, and probed the edges of the velvet. He carefully levered up the edges until he could lift it free. There, beneath the lining, he saw a thin, yellowed handwritten journal. His breath hitched in his throat as he removed it and laid it on top of the sword. The title was The Confessions of Mr. Hyde.

With trembling hands, he turned on the overhead light, then opened the slender volume and read. He desperately wanted to drink his coffee but couldn't trust himself not to spill it on the pages. Looking around the parking lot to make sure again that his was the only car, he read through the entire journal. When he was through, he read it again, then returned it to its hiding place in the case and put the velvet lining back into place. He felt like he was moving on automatic pilot. The terror he'd felt while reading its contents was growing inside him like a wildfire in an open field. Hunter knew now who they were facing, and he wanted to drive over to the Mihaloff residence, pick up Moser and Rebecca and drive them as far away from Detroit as they could possibly get. But an inner certainty told him that there was nowhere on earth far enough from Hiram Abiff's reach to be safe.

He didn't know how Hiram had caused the incident in the Masonic Temple with Brother Mike Leasing, but he had to find out. The answer, he thought, might tell him something useful. It might reveal something they could use against Hiram Abiff. And he had to go see Molly and beg for her help. So, he propped the sword case next to him on the passenger seat, and, as an afterthought, buckled the seat belt around it to hold it in place.

He parked in front of Molly's house, put Bartok's letter inside his jacket pocket, placed the package on the passenger side floor mat, locked the car behind him and walked up the steps to Molly's front door. The confession of Mr. Hyde was not something he could show her. He could not. The less she knew, the better—for her own safety.

****

Hunter knocked twice, then rang the doorbell.

"Do you know what time it is?" asked the beefy man, who answered to the door.

The man who answered was half a foot taller than Hunter, dressed in jeans and a T-shirt that stretched tight across his broad chest. His hair was cut short, like a serviceman or maybe a cop.

"I'm sorry it's late, but I need to talk to Molly. I apologize if I woke you up."

"What's your name?" asked the man, his eyes narrowing. "Tell me it's not Hunter."

The door was chained and opened only a few inches.

"I'm Hunter. I just need to talk to her for a few minutes. Then I'll go. It's not about anything personal."

The man grimaced, slid back the chain, and opened the door, forcing Hunter to step back a step on the concrete porch. Hunter thought he was about to get his nose broken. But as the brute's hand clutched the edge of the door, he saw something on one of the man's right fingers.

"Yeah, well, she doesn't want to see you. Are you going to turn around and get back in your car, or do I have to carry you there and stuff you in?"

Hunter took another step back and slowly gave the Grand Hailing sign known to Masons around the world and then the plea of the Poor Widow's Son.

"Brother," he concluded, "I desperately need your help."

****

Sitting in an armchair in the living room, Hunter could hear the discussion in the next room.

"This is bullshit, Ron," said Molly, her voice rising in anger. "Just because you two are Masons, doesn't mean I have to talk to him. It's past midnight if you didn't notice. This is bullshit."

Ron spoke more softly, and Hunter didn't hear what he said.

"He could try using the phone," said Molly. "I don't want him showing up at my—at our—front door at all hours of the night."

Softer, reassuring words from Ron.

"This is ridiculous," said Molly.

Hunter heard Ron talking again, but all he could understand was the word important.

"All right, all right, but I want you in the room with me."

A few moments of silence that Hunter didn't want to think about. Then the two of them stepped into the room.

"Ron's a police officer, you know," said Molly, folding her arms across her chest.

She was wearing a white robe. Her hair was mussed as though she'd just woken up. Hunter thought she'd done that deliberately. Holly's hair always looked like she'd just brushed it when she got out of bed. She'd told him once that she was born tangle free.

"He looks like it."

In the light of the single living room lamp, Ron looked like a solid rock of a man with a much more tolerant disposition than Hunter would have guessed from their initial confrontation at the front door.

"Maybe we should get to this," said Ron.

"Sure," said Hunter. "Look, I don't know how to go about this, Ron. I made a Masonic oath not to tell anyone about what I have to say. But I have to tell Molly, or she will not dig up what I need to know. But the oath I made was in an appendant body of Masonry, not in the Blue Lodge."

"Could you drop the Masonic bullshit and just spit it out?" said Molly.

"You mean like Scottish Rite?" asked Ron.

"Maybe Molly's right," said Hunter. "I'm just going to get right to this. Ron, I don't know you, but we're under the Grand Hailing Sign, so I'm going to trust you on this. Molly, you knew about my uncle Bartok. I know you never met him, but you didn't like him on principle. I was angry at him and so you were, too. Ron, you didn't know him, but—"

"Bartok? Actually," said Ron, "I met him a couple times at Masonic functions."

"Really?" said Hunter.

Hunter had been in bed with Molly in a motel room south of the city when he'd gotten the call from Bartok last year. He'd told her he had to go. It was a call from Bartok. It was important. She'd just got up, got dressed and left without saying a word. Now the thought crossed his mind that maybe she was already leaving him, anyway. He squashed the desire to ask her how long she'd known Ron. Was she already sleeping with him before that night? It wasn't like they were engaged or anything, but it had just never occurred to him.

As though she'd picked up on where his thoughts were going, Molly looked away.

"Yeah, he was a pretty impressive guy. Really, really intelligent. The first time I met him, he was giving a talk about the origin of Masonic rituals and traditions. Second time I think he was giving a talk here at the Allen Park lodge about... Masonic Symbolism. Spoke without notes for two or three hours. I don't know how he fitted everything into one brain. We asked him questions for an hour or two after that and there wasn't anything he couldn't answer. That's what I remember. He was your uncle? You're a lucky guy."

"He's dead now. Heart problems."

As in, he was infected and turning into a monster, so I shot him three or four times in the heart, then emptied the rest of the rounds into his face.

"Too bad," said Ron.

"Look, Ian, I'm sorry about your uncle," said Molly. "He was a good man. I know it was hard, but what does Bartok have to do with why you show up here past midnight?"

She would always look beautiful to Hunter, but the fact was that tonight he just didn't care. Moser had been right when he called Molly his "sort of" girlfriend. And although he really hated it, Ron seemed okay.

Hiram Abiff was coming.

"I've got a letter he wrote me, that I want you to read. Ron, you first, so you'll see why I need help as a Masonic brother, and you'll understand why I've got nowhere else to go."

He withdrew Bartok's letter from his pocket and handed it to Ron, while Molly looked on in annoyance. Whatever he did involving the paranormal seemed to irritate her.

Ron read the front, then the back. It took him a long time. He either sweated easily or the letter was cranking up his stress.

"What is this?" he asked.

"Just what it says."

"Let me see that," said Molly.

"Was he in his right mind when he wrote this?" asked Ron.

"He was in his right mind right up to the day he died," said Hunter.

Actually, he was in his right mind, right until the alien claw drilled into his neck and pumped ectoplasmic fluid into his body. After that, Bartok went downhill quickly.

"So, you think this is real?" asked Ron.

"I do."

Molly finished reading the letter and put it on her lap.

"May I keep this?" she asked in a peculiar tone of voice.

"No. Now I need to tell you both what started this."

"Can I get some coffee?" asked Ron. "I think I need to wake up."

Hunter almost told him he knew where the coffee was and he'd get it going for them all but thought that was a bad idea.

"Me too," said Molly.

"I'll hold off on starting until you're back," said Hunter.

"I like him," said Hunter when Ron left the room.

"Shut up. Just shut up."

He knew that thin set to her mouth when she was angry. Knew the way she squared her shoulders back.

"Bigger than I thought."

"His pistol is in the other room."

"Got you."

"He's here," she said. "He's not running around the country chasing Bigfoot and ghost stories all the time. He doesn't believe in aliens or demon possession or this kind of craziness. He's normal."

I could fix that, thought Hunter.

"I know what you're thinking," she said.

Just then, Ron returned with a tray of coffee cups, creams, and sugar and sweetener packets. He'd also added a plate of Oreo cookies. Not only was Ron a cop, but a great cook.

"Thanks, Ron," Hunter said. "I was sitting in the parking lot of the Lincoln Park Tim Horton's looking at Bartok's letter and some other papers, but after two sips and the first letter, I forgot I had coffee."

"So, talk," said Molly.

"A couple of days ago, the Worshipful Master of our Lodge sent my friend Moser and me to meet with a group of Masons that look after the financial and physical well-being of the Detroit Masonic Temple."

"Why?" Molly interrupted.

It was her way that she asked the questions he was about to answer. It was always that way between the two of them.

"There had been an incident with two of the night Watchmen. That's Watchmen with a capital W, I think. According to the story we were told, while two of the men were walking the halls, a statue came to life and grabbed one by the throat and told him to bring Hiram

Abiff. I interviewed him two nights later and saw the bruising around his neck. They were tough to look at and harder to believe."

"Did you talk to the other man?" asked Ron.

"No. I couldn't. According to the brother telling the story, when he got free of the statue and turned around, he saw the floor drop like it was on a hinge and the other man fell back into it."

"Into what?" asked Molly.

Hunter didn't want to go into it, but it had to be said.

"He told us that the other man slid down into a pit of flames and flying monstrosities and then the floor closed back up."

Neither Ron nor Molly spoke. They just stared at him like he was crazy.

"I know," said Hunter. "But that was his story. That's what they called me in to investigate. The Masons who brought us in wanted to know whether I had ever heard of anything similar or whether I thought it was possible."

"Not too likely, if you ask me," said Ron. "Somebody was putting something up somebody's nose."

He mimed coke-sniffing until Molly cuffed him.

"But," said Hunter, "according to the Brothers, the other man is missing."

"I don't like the sound of this at all," said Molly. "What does this have to do with Bartok's letter?"

"My problem," said Hunter, ignoring her question, "is that I need to see if there are any connections between serious occult groups and the Detroit Masonic Temple, and I have no idea how to find out, Molly. I've Googled and Binged it until I was blind, but there's nothing. I found a rumor that the man who designed and oversaw the construction of the Temple committed suicide by jumping off the top, but it turned out to be an urban legend. No such thing ever happened. Can you help me? I'll investigate the place where it occurred tonight with Moser, but I don't think we will come up with a thing. You can't pick up magical activity with an EMF detector or a thermal imager."

"Like on the ghost hunter shows," said Ron brightly.

"Yes, like on the ghost hunter shows."

Hunter didn't want to tell them anything about Hiram Abiff. He had a feeling that anyone who learned about that would be in danger from the witch and her creatures. All he really needed was information.

"I could check on the missing guy if you give me a name," said Ron.

"Can you do it without attracting attention?" asked Hunter. "I can't have anyone, and I mean anyone, know that I've talked to you about this. I'm sorry I've told you anything, but I thought I had to, so you'd know it's serious."

"Wait," said Molly. "What does this have to do with Bartok's letter?"

Hunter was about to say that no, that was all, but realized that keeping things from here had always been a problem between them. But he didn't want either her or Ron to suffer for what they knew.

"I'd like to keep the two of you out of this," said Hunter. "I don't want either of you to get hurt."

"Tell me why you think it's dangerous," said Ron. "Who are you afraid of?"

Hunter shook his head.

"It's not who, Ron, it's what."

Ron and Molly just stared him, again. Hunter to a deep breath, and then continued.

"There's this woman," he said awkwardly. "She's... special."

"I can't believe this," snapped Molly. "You came here to talk about another a woman? Is she the woman in the letter? Are you crazy?"

"It's not like that," said Hunter. "Not like that at all. I just met this woman two days ago."

"Well, that makes it all better. Thanks for clarifying that. Would you like us to help you ask her out?"

"Molly," said Ron. "Let him talk."

Hunter looked at him gratefully. He liked Ron.

"She has prescient dreams or visions. I've never met anyone like her."

"Well, good for you," said Molly. "And quit stalling me. Is she the woman in Bartok's letter or not?"

Ron put his hand on her forearm and squeezed gently.

"You mean like she sees the future?" asked Ron.

"Yes. Maybe. I'm hoping it's yes, though, because Moser and I are over our collective heads on this one. The thing is, she's Christian and…"

"Wait," said Molly. "You're trying to hook up with a Christian? What the hell has happened to you?"

Ron held up his hands, palms out.

Hunter kept going.

"Yes, she's the woman in the letter. Not the Scarlett Woman, but the woman Bartok said to go to for help. I've met her. Two nights ago, a creature trying to kill her attacked her. It ripped her house apart and clawed her arm badly before she shot it. She would have been ripped to pieces if she didn't escape into the house's panic room. It's on video. The Mihaloffs have a video security system."

The room went silent. Ron stared at him like he thought he was crazy. Molly was embarrassed for him. Hunter looked down at his watch.

"I think you'd better leave," said Ron, getting to his feet. He looked at Molly, then clenched his hands and stood up like he was ready to shove Hunter toward the door. "I've heard enough. I knew and respected your Uncle Bartok, but this is just too weird. We don't need to be involved in this. Grand Hailing Sign of Distress doesn't cover crazy; you know what I mean."

Hunter looked up at him.

"Wait," said he said, "I know how this sounds, but —"

"Get out," said Ron. "Now. Bartok was a good man, but it sounds to me like he had mental problems before he died, so the best thing you can do is burn your letter and forget all about it. Don't embarrass your family or Freemasonry. You're a Brother so I'm going to cut you some slack, but if you don't leave now, you're not going to like what happens next, and I mean that."

After a moment's hesitation, Hunter stood. He felt a smoldering frustration catch fire somewhere deep inside.

"You ever see a dead girl come back to life and burn a man to death?"

He took a step toward Ron. Something in the way Hunter looked caused Ron to pull back, the way a man does when he thinks he might catch an unknown disease.

"Well, I have. You ever hear the fevered whisperings of the dead as they try to pass from one world to the next? Well, I heard that as I watched an old granny woman shepherd them on by with a power that was I don't know what. You ever see a hundred and fifty year old man with metal for eyes scream lunatic gibberings while looking at you like he wants to eat you? Brother, you just don't know how to scare a man who's seen what I've seen."

Ron held up his palms to stop Hunter from saying anything else, but Hunter had already turned and was walking out the door. As he opened the car door, his mind returned to the journal titled The Confessions of Mr. Hyde.

42

Bournemouth, England 1881

"Are you well?" the shadowed man asked.

"I'm recovering," said the writer.

In fact, he was still unwell. The fevered palsy came and went unpredictably. He had lost enough weight that his wife was increasingly overwrought. His vision came and went, and yet the doctors could offer no explanation. Beneath his nightshirt, his arms were pustules with red, inflamed boils. The night before, he had slept little owing to the racking spasms that racked his body. But it would not be seemly to let this man know the details of his infirmities.

"You asked to know my story," said the man without acknowledging his reply, "or rather, to know more of my story. I would ask, before I speak further for your Masonic oath, that it will remain between us. Can you, dear sir, provide me with such reassurance? Forgive my asking, but you are a writer, and writers must publish or wither away."

Stevenson had indeed been tormented by publishing what he already knew of the man's story many times, but as a member of the Masonic Temple Guardians, he knew he could not do that. The penalty would be a long and painful death.

"I so affirm it," he said.

Neither spoke for a while. Outside, the anemic moon scarcely illumed the gray-black skies. The hour was late, and the rabble of street noise was as saturnine as the confining quiescence of a locked cell. His wife and adopted son had long since succumbed to slumber.

"In all these many centuries," said the man sitting in the shadowed corner opposite Stevenson's bed, "I have told only three other men my dilemma. All are sadly long dead and gone. I have carried a great and terrifying burden for longer than you can conceive in your ghastliest imaginings."

Stevenson tightened his chest and throat to stop a sudden coughing spasm, but he could not restrain it for long. It came out as a series of short, restrained barks that he finally stifled by pressing his palm over his mouth. He grasped the edge of his bedsheets and wiped the spittle from his pointed beard.

"My apologies," he said. "During the cold months, my lungs struggle."

"Shall I come back another night?"

"No," said Stevenson.

The edge of desperation in his voice was hard to conceal. This was a story he very much wanted to hear. Although he could not, would not write the story, he knew he would somehow use it in his fiction.

"Very well. Have you ever pondered the existence of the soul?"

"I beg your pardon?"

The dark shadows in the corner blurred, and, for a moment, Stevenson was seized with the disturbing thought that this visitor was only shadows masquerading as a man.

"The soul, the human soul. The incorporeal essence of good, tainted with the sin nature of the flesh. Do you apprehend? Have you not wondered that the two coexist in the same body?"

The other. Yes, the other. Myself and the other fellow.

Yes, he knew the twin nature well. There were days, most usually in the autumn, when propelled by an unaccounted urgency, he hunted through his own thoughts looking for the other. Myself and the other fellow. The twin fellows that shared his brain and his body. He was healthy and strong in the warm months. He came from a line of lighthouse engineers. It was men's work if ever there was. That was his true self, of course. But came the colder months, the other overcame his true self, and he was certain that his body changed into the body of someone else. His constitution suffered, and he became so different that he was even afflicted with weak lungs. Then it became not his own body, but that of the other.

Yes, he knew the truth of it and worse.

Within his own very nature, he was both hunter and hunted.

Myself and the other fellow.

Like the differing poles of a magnet. One, yet opposite.

"Ah, I see that you have," continued the man in the shadows.

Oh, he had indeed considered the worriment.

One evening when the gaslights hissed above the cobbled streets of Bournemouth, he had seen from his window this very man now seated in the shadows do something abhorrent. It was so ghastly, ubiquitous yet cruel that it would not leave his mind. He could scarcely recognize him at first as his body had contorted—or was merely an illusion caused by the ruminative fog clouds that gathered so low to the ground that night—so that Hiram looked deformed and hunched over as he knocked the girl aside with a blow to the side of her head and continued walking down the lane. Stevenson had heard the sharp sound of the blow and knew it had cracked the girl's skull. The man of shadows simply walked away as though nothing at all had occurred. Were it not for the girl's limp form laying prostrate on the stones, one would not have guessed what occurred. He had run to her, praying he could revive her, filled with revulsion at what he had seen, yet part of him wondering at the man's lack of remorse. Was he truly a man or the other fellow that was not only capable of such unrestraint, but a man for whom it was typical? Stevenson shuddered at the confused memory.

"But what, my brother, if you had no nature at all within your heart? What if your flesh were an empty house swept clean of all the furniture? The owner of the house gone, and the doors to your home flung open so that any passing visitor could simply step in and take possession? Any spirit could come in and sup. Any spirit or legion of spirits at all—no matter how foul— and you would be powerless to bar the way as you, the owner, were no longer in residence."

Stevenson pressed back hard against the pillow in horror and heard, he thought, rather than felt his heart pounding hard against the restraint of his ribs. Did Hiram know he had witnessed the incident with the girl? Was this Byzantine approach intended to terrify him into silence?

"I cannot begin to contemplate such circumstances," he said.

"For nearly three thousand years, I have done nothing but contemplate it," said the shadows.

Hiram's words resounded through the room's darkness as a cacophony of disconsonant cracked bells, as though they had been spoken by a thousand tortured spirits. A man or being such as him, thought a subdued and abject Stevenson, should not exist at all. How could God allow him to walk the earth, or was Hiram beneath God's feet already by being on earth?

"I was a power in this world until my fall, writer."

There was a sibilance to the way the shadowed man drew out his words. The image of a black-eyed slithering snake with its glistening forked tongue sliding in and out elicited from him a shiver.

"Someday you will change the world," said Stevenson.

Inexplicably, he felt bile threaten to bubble its way up his throat. The fever must be returning, he thought. I am not well.

"Do you know how much power a man can accumulate in nearly three thousand years? Can you imagine the wrath of that man betrayed?"

Before the writer could answer, he saw two bright blue eyes grow in the darkness. He felt the bed shake slightly, and then it rose slowly from the floor. What in God's name? His head began to whip back and forth wildly, and his body palsied. The two glowing eyes glared piteously at him from the darkness.

"I will tell no one," whimpered Stevenson. "No one. On my Masonic oath, I swear it. I swear it."

The bed, now three feet in the air, slowly lowered to the floor. Hiram's blue eyes vanished, and all was darkness in the corner again. Stevenson's fingers gripped the bed sheets so hard his hands ached.

"Betrayal is a form of pride," said the disembodied voice. "Once I, too, was guilty of pride. I was a man charged by King Solomon to oversee the building of his temple to his God. It was honor enough for any man. The King himself praised me. All revered me for my skill and dedication to building the temple as God's prophet David had revealed it. The honor of my commission was more than any man could desire. I was a lion among architects. And yet, someone… something whispered in my ear that with my great genius, I could improve upon the divine design. Madness. Madness."

The last words exploded from the shadows.

"Who?" the writer could hardly believe he dared to ask the question. "Who whispered in your ear?"

Silence filled the room and Stevenson felt the air condensing into a cloying miasma. It became more difficult to breathe, as though the man's disapproval poisoned the very air.

"I do not know his name. I do not know if I will ever know his name. Yet he was the same who, when I was murdered for my transgression of altering the temple's design by my fellow masons, brought me back to life, though I was dead and buried. But I was brought back empty of a soul. For thousands of years, I have had to contemplate my death and rising as a hollow man."

After nearly three thousand years, thought a cowered Stevenson, a man's sanity could become malformed and demonic.

"Come Robert, you believe that I have lived so long, but cannot believe that I was murdered and resurrected? You reject God—say no protest. A man who has lived as long as I can see more than mortal men. You reject God and embrace logic and therefore, your ideas can never rise above machines and chemicals. The great Paracelsus, whom I knew well, would have whipped you himself for the sheer pleasure of seeing you suffer for so limiting your own thoughts. He was a beastly intellect and loved nothing more than breaking a fool. You are a Mason, and a man must believe in God to be a Mason, but it is because you do not that I speak to you. A man, even a man such as I, must have a confessor. And who better than a dying atheist, and you indeed have the smell of fatality about you. A deist is only a man too weak to submit to faith. And therefore, I tell you this historical truth— I was murdered and brought back to life in the body, but with no soul."

The blue eyes sprang to life in the corner. Stevenson shrank back in desperation, but they faded as quickly as they had appeared.

"No soul. Can a man with no soul be found in any way guilty of anything? When his body is an empty house seized at any moment by demonic forces who come to live and invite still more evil? I have committed hideous deeds the thought of which would make your skin peel away from your body. But I am guilty of nothing, for it was not I but the evil that possessed me that bears the mark of shameful guilt. You have thought long on man's warring impulses, I know. I have thought longer. I have done many things, but I am neither evil nor good, do you see? A man with no soul has no moral character and can therefore bear no guilt. Do I intrigue you with this truth?"

"I—"

"Have you tasted the flesh of another man?"

The voice rasped like a different man's voice. No, not another man, but something far worse. Stevenson closed his eyes.

"It is sweet. Have you dissected a living man in search of his soul? No? I see how remorseless horror grips you, Robert. My mind understands your revulsion, but I myself have no soul with which to embrace it. For three millennia, I have been a hostel for terrible, hungry spirits. They come without announcement, no matter where I tried to conceal myself. When they come, I debase myself with whatever corruptions they seek. But I am a man with no soul and therefore bear no guilt."

"Please," begged Stevenson, "tell me no more. I can bear no more."

Another silence while he kept his eyes closed, afraid even to think.

"You reek of disease," said Hiram Abiff.

Stevenson opened his eyes and recoiled at what he beheld. The luminous, terrible eyes were growing, growing and were at the moment the size of a full grown man. He screamed and felt his throat constrict with a coughing fit. He closed his eyes again and began to weep.

He heard footsteps approaching by the hallway and his eyes shot open. She must not enter the room and see the horror of it. But the room was empty. Fanny came through the door crying, "My dear, are you all right?"

He thought quickly.

"Why did you wake me? I was dreaming a fine bogey tale."

She began to weep.

Later, he wrote that fine bogey tale of the horror of a soulless man overtaking the body of a good man. It lessened the night terrors, but not completely. He never spoke of the true events of that night to anyone. But, not so many years later, when he read about the alarming murders in Whitechapel, Robert Louis Stevenson realized that something had to be done. Hiram Abiff was protected under Masonic oath, but he did what he could without violating that oath. He recorded what he knew under the title The Confessions of Mr. Hyde.

43

"Are they gone?" asked Hunter. "Check the surveillance feeds. We have to talk."

Moser studied the screens for a minute. It was three o'clock in the morning.

"Gone," he said. "Kaufman and Cook both."

The door to Rebecca's room opened, and she stepped briskly toward him. She did not look happy. She should have been sleeping, Hunter thought. Didn't zealots ever sleep? Her face had that "I'm not happy" look. But he couldn't bring himself to tell her what had happened. The image of the snake emerging from her father's mouth was too much for him to handle.

Hunter ignored the look. No time for agonizing.

"Do you have pistols with sound suppressors?" he asked her.

"I'd like to talk to you about what you told Mr. Cook and Mr. Kaufmann," she said, ignoring his question completely.

"Never mind that," said Hunter irritably. "I lied to them. Told them everything was wonderful and what an honor it was to meet the great Hiram Abiff just to get rid of them. It was all bullshit. Do you have pistols with sound suppressors or not?"

"What has come over you?"

"I met him, that's what. I met Hiram Abiff, and he scares the hell out of me. And I went through something worse than under

Townsend Mountain to get to him," he said to Moser.

"No shit?" said Moser.

"No shit. Then I spent some time in an all-night diner's parking lot reading Bartok's notes and observations about Hiram. That's why I need the guns—because Rebecca was at least partially right. Enid, can you get pistols with sound suppressors?"

"How fast?"

"I need them today. Enough for the two of us. We need to get back to the place where I met him. We need to go in gunned up."

"You want to tell me what this is all about?" asked Moser.

"I want to go back into the Detroit Masonic Temple."

"And…" said Moser.

"I have to see where he's at. If he's in a city at all. Could be someplace…. else."

"Like what?"

"Like not of this earth," said Rebecca.

"She's right," Hunter told Moser, "but Rebecca, if you start bringing religious crap into this now, my head's just going to blow up and get blood all over this survival bunker. So, can you just watch the screens for a minute while Moser and I go to my car and get a few things I left there so the Brothers Cook and Kaufmann wouldn't see them?"

"What few things?" she asked.

"Papers from my uncle Bartok and a big sword. Will you do it?"

"Hurry up," she said.

Hunter stuffed his Colt in his jacket pocket and headed toward the two thousand pound door to the regular world.

"Hold on," said Moser. "I'll go first. Rebecca has set us on speed dial. She sees something, she'll let us know, and this old shotgun will clear the room quick enough. If she has a cell signal."

"That's reassuring," said Hunter.

The massive door swung open to let them out and closed behind them, locking Rebecca in. They went up the stairs cautiously to the next floor and, just as they approached the second security door, it swung inward to let them back into the house and, like the door to the bunker itself, closed with a powerful shudder.

"Unusual house," said Moser. "Wouldn't mind having one like it myself, private bunker and all."

"I hate it here," said Hunter. "Place gives me the major creeps."

"Hold on," said Moser as he raised the barrel of his shotgun.

"You hear something?" Hunter whispered.

Moser cocked his head to one side.

"Don't think so, but just being careful."

"Okay."

Hunter took a few steps forward, stopped, and turned around.

"You see something you don't like," he told Moser, "just shoot it. We can interrogate it later."

"Got you covered."

Moser rubbed the back of his free hand over his iron gray mustache, then wrapped it back around the Winchester's stock.

With a look around the darkened room, Hunter headed toward his car. The night air was brisk, the sky clouded over like it was mulling over soaking them before they even got the trunk lid open. He stopped ten feet from the vehicle with a thoughtful look on his face.

"Change of plans. Let's go get Rebecca and take her with us."

Moser gave him the Moser stare, the one that made him look like an iconic tough cowboy, then asked, "You know what you're doing this time?"

"Oh yeah," said Hunter. "Do I ever."

****

"My father," said Rebecca, "will kill you when he finds out about this."

"Probably," said Hunter.

"I'm going with definitely," said Moser.

Hunter pulled his phone out of his pocket, pushed the speed dial, and rang Brother Mihaloff. The voice that answered was thick with sleep.

"Hello?"

"It's me, Hunter, and yes, everything is all right. Sorry to wake you, but wanted to keep you up on what I'm doing. Working out the way you were hoping, but I'm following every loose end."

"Great, but why did you—"

"Just wanted you to know we're on the way to meet with my researcher Molly Collins again," lied Hunter, "and I've got Rebecca in tow to make sure she's safe. I figured if those horned creatures come back, we'd better be prepared and I didn't want Rebecca alone. Got Moser with me to watch over her every second. We're stopping in at Bartok's house—mine now, I guess—to examine some of his reference books."

"What? You took her from—"

"We took a medical kit too," said Hunter. "We need Rebecca's help, and she's the only one that's seen the beast, so she's our best chance of identifying what leads the researcher has found to date. Sorry it's so late, but I want you to know about our every move. I'm going to keep her safe and protect the coming Grandmaster."

It had a nice sound to it. Yes. The coming Grandmaster. He didn't even have a hard time lying about what was going on. The announcement of Hiram Abiff to the entire Masonic world was getting too close for comfort. He'd lie to the Pope if he had to.

"I... I..."

"I'll call you if we find something important," said Hunter, then he tapped the end call button.

"That took guts," said Moser. "It won't hold, but we can run with it for now."

"You better have a good plan," said Rebecca.

At first, she wasn't going to come along, but when Hunter had let her read Bartok's letter, she was suddenly primed for action. She and Moser packed up a medical kit full of her antibiotics and pain pills, scissors, bandages, ointments, and gels. Then she packed a suitcase with everything she'd need in case she was gone for a few days. Moser helped her on with her shoulder holster and coat and loaded her pockets with rounds. Getting her in the passenger's side door of the truck was like a Houdini trick in reverse, with Moser on the bench behind the passenger seat and Hunter cramming her gently in enough to close the door without re-opening her wound.

Then they loaded the ghost box back into the trunk and were ready to go.

As he slid into the driver's seat, he looked over at her and asked, "Are you good?"

"Let's get out of here," she said without looking at him. "I don't know if I'll like what we're doing, but anything is better than sitting in that bunker waiting for the monsters to come to us."

Moser seat belted the ghost box crate in tight.

****

Four ten in the morning and the sky rolled by like a fog of black and gray with no moon in sight.

"Shit, this looks grim," said Hunter as they rolled over the free bridge to Grosse Ile, a small island south of Detroit, right across the river from the towns of Wyandotte and Trenton.

"Do you have to swear every time you're under stress?" asked Rebecca.

"Well… no. It just helps sometimes."

"I'd prefer you didn't."

Hunter looked up in the rear-view mirror to see Moser shrug.

"And don't look back to Mr. Moser for approval. Just say you'll try not to do it so much."

He didn't want to seem like a pushover, so Hunter pretended to think it over.

"Or I'll shoot you," she said.

"Yeah, okay," he said with a smile. "And you're right. It feels good to be out of the bunker and away from the Detroit Masonic Temple. I've had enough creepy for one night."

"So, we're going to Bartok's house?" asked Moser.

"My house now, Enid," said Hunter. "I just couldn't bring myself to go there before now. And then I got to thinking—there's a reason Bartok had his house on an island."

"What's that?" asked Moser as they left the bridge, turned right and looped back under to ride the edge of the island.

"Running water, I suppose," said Rebecca.

"That's right," said Hunter, and peered at the post numbers on the side of the road. His eyes were tired, and his mind was full of Freemasons and the horrors of the Borgo Pass. He'd left the driver's side window cracked so the chill night air would help keep his eyes open.

"I thought that was for vampires," said Moser.

"You keep an eye out for Creek Road—it cuts off to the right a little after the number thirteen hundred and nine stone marker, and I'll tell you what I know."

"Deal."

"Water drains their power when they're surrounded by it," said Rebecca. "That's the theory behind the lore, anyway. No spell may be sent at those surrounded by water and none may be sent from those surrounded by water. It's like Las Vegas that way."

"That's a different way to look at it, I guess," said Hunter.

"And what did Bartok tell you?"

"Bartok told me if you deduct what Wiccans say from what they think, you'll be richer than if you add the two together."

"You need some sleep, brother," said Moser. "That made as much sense as a toilet without a handle."

"Here," said Rebecca suddenly. "Stone marker thirteen hundred and nine."

"Got it."

Hunter brought the car to a stop five feet away from a black, eight-foot-high spiked fence. It reminded him of a cemetery fence.

"I'd feel better about this if it was sunrise," he said.

"What's the code?" asked Moser. "I'll punch it in. Anything's better than being squashed back here. Sorry Miss Rebecca. Just my knees seem to age faster than the rest of me."

"No code," said Hunter

Hunter withdrew a little black box and aimed it at the electronic key lock cemented into an obelisk of fieldstones as tall as the truck by the side of the gate. After a loud click, the gates swung inward. Easing the vehicle into drive again, he drove slowly along a stone cobbled road. Rebecca twisted around in the seat and was rewarded by seeing the gates swing closed behind them. The road was a curving swath cut through trees that looked to be as old as the island itself.

"We're coming in the back way," said Hunter. "The front of the house faces the river. When we leave, we take the boat if we want."

"This I got to see," said Moser.

"Not my boat. Well, now it is, thanks to Bartok."

"Are we almost there?" asked Rebecca.

The truck was inching along at ten miles an hour, the headlights shining like twin spotlights on the dense tree line set back only five feet from the rough road.

"Couldn't Bartok afford a paved road?" asked Rebecca.

After the next turn, she gasped in surprise. A bank of lawn security lighting flared and lit a five-hundred-foot long expanse of grass and the three storied, turreted brownstone terrace house at the end of the road. Enid and Rebecca raised their hands to protect their eyes from the overwhelming brightness.

"Like opening night," said Hunter. "Stays on for half an hour after it detects motion."

"Dumbass," said Moser.

"It's beautiful," said Rebecca.

"Sandstone taken right from the Hummelstown Brownstone Company. But we can talk about that later if we're still alive. Here's the most important part coming up."

Hunter drove straight to a dark paneled section of the back wall where the driveway widened. There was a separate garage off to the right, but he ignored it.

"The garage is that way," said Moser.

"One of them," said Hunter and he kept heading straight toward the house.

"Slow down," said Rebecca.

"What're you up to?" asked Moser.

"Watch. Here it comes."

Rebecca braced herself against the dashboard. Hunter could feel Moser's fingers digging into the back of his headrest.

The section of panel suddenly shot sideways thirty seconds before they would have impacted it. Hunter pressed down on the brake just as they slid into a large open space, and the retractable door slammed shut behind them. An overhead light came on and Hunter turned the ignition key to off.

"Slick, right?" he asked Moser.

"If I could reach you with my good hand, I'd dent your head," said Rebecca.

"I'd let you do it," said Moser. "In fact, I'd help you do it. Now, can we please get out of this truck? And yep, never saw that one whenever I was here to visit your uncle. He always had a few surprises."

Hunter got out of the car, went around and helped Rebecca out after she put up a quick but insincere fight about being able to do it by herself—which she could have if her coat pockets weren't packed with ammo and her suitcase wasn't on her lap. When she had got out the door and on her feet, a grateful Moser climbed out after her.

"Damned if I don't know how an accordion feels," he grumbled.

"What's with the fast entrance garage trick?" asked Rebecca as she absently rubbed her bandaged arm.

"Bartok always told me it was in case something was hard on his tail and he needed to get inside quickly without getting out of the car. That's the way he put it, too. Something, not someone. I always liked it because it was cool."

"Can we go inside now and get some sleep?" asked Rebecca.

"Absolutely," said Hunter.

He was ready to sleep an extra day or two just to catch up.

By the time they'd shouldered up the bags, Rebecca had gotten to the end of her patience and went to the door at the end of the room and opened it.

"Some security system," she said as the door opened inward.

She was about to say something else, but at that moment, she saw the metal grillwork that sealed them into the garage.

"Yes, it is," said Hunter.

"Would you just shut up and open the gate?"

"Yes, ma'am," said Hunter as he pulled out the remote unit and aimed it at the gate. A frame of blue light flashed to life around the door frame. He took out his keys, walked past Rebecca, inserted an odd looking one into the key slot and twisted it to the left. With a loud click, the lock disengaged. Hunter withdrew the key and pushed the door inward. "After you," he said to Rebecca as he stepped out of the way, and she brushed past.

Motion activated dimmed lights came on in the entryway leading to the kitchen as she glanced around the inside of the house.

"Nice," she said.

Moser and Hunter followed her in with the bags full of weapons and guns, which they unloaded onto the kitchen table and counters.

"One more thing," he said.

Without looking over his shoulder, he knew Moser would be holding his Winchester, listening to and examining the surrounding space. It was something she probably wouldn't have liked him to do, but Moser was different. She seemed to have taken a liking to the Southerner and already trusted him. It would be awhile, if ever, when she extended that confidence to him. Hunter was used to people thinking he was odd, though, because he really was. He scooped up the package full of papers and the sword case and carried them into the house, closing the iron gate behind them. He placed it on the kitchen table next to a bag of guns he and Moser had brought along from Kentucky.

"Mr. Moser," he said, "since according to Bartok's will I officially own this place, I can say this is the first time I've had a place to call home since the day you burned down my last one."

"Well, I'll do my best not to torch this one."

"What's your plan?" asked Rebecca. "My arm hurts and I need sleep."

Hunter looked around at the emptiness. It wasn't the lack of furniture that caused him to think of the place as empty. It was the lack of his Uncle Bartok.

44

"Two things first," said Hunter. "I say we change the dressing on your bandage, make sure you've taken all your meds, then we turn the living room into our sleeping quarters tonight, go to sleep for five hours and then we'll be ready to go after coffee. I can't think without sleep."

"That's it?" asked Rebecca. "How about you telling us what happened when you went with my father earlier tonight?"

"Not now," said Hunter.

"That's about all he's capable of till he gets some sleep," said Moser.

"Fine. No questions, no talk, just sleep, then start fresh in the morning."

"Good," said Hunter.

"What's in the big box?" asked Rebecca. "And what are those you brought in?"

"What about the sleep part?"

"I won't be able to sleep until I know," she said.

"This is a big place," said Moser. "How about if I prowl it while you two talk? That way I can sleep with only one eye open instead of two. Plus, I miss Mr. Bartok and I'd kind of like to look around this old house."

"Be careful," said Hunter.

He didn't know why he said it, but it was something in the back of his mind that must have prompted it. Moser was always careful. Since Bartok's death, he and Moser had traveled to Atlanta to follow up on some things in Bartok's notes that needed tying up. From there, they'd returned to Townsend Mountain for Moser to spend more time with his relatives, the ones who'd been left behind by the deaths of his brothers. While there, Hunter had joined the Freemasons with Moser vouching for him. It seemed the thing to do. And it cemented the friendship between the two men and with Hunter's own family history. As far back as he could trace, the Hunters and the Mosers had always been Masons. Moser was the closest thing to a family Hunter had left. As the older man walked down the hallway, Hunter was suddenly afraid for him. He felt danger in the air like a faraway electric hum. A quick glance at Rebecca and he felt the same sense of danger. What was he forgetting that made him so paranoid?

Hiram Abiff was coming. And whatever Hiram Abiff was, Hunter was afraid.

Rebecca noticed Hunter's eyes locked onto the hallway down which Moser had gone.

"He's older than I thought he would be," said Rebecca.

"Yeah," said Hunter. "I really don't know how old he is."

"You're worried about him?"

"I'm worried about all of us."

"Why?"

"Because I've seen that thing called Hiram Abiff."

"So have I," said Rebecca.

"What? Oh, right. In your dreams."

"Yes."

"Here, help me move this couch. Just lean up against the back and push with your hip. Ready? One, two, three."

He left the living room and returned to the kitchen to fetch their bags. It took him three trips.

"You don't approve of my dreams."

"Not now, Rebecca. I'm tired. I'm confused and I'm afraid."

While he spoke, he rearranged the end table and another couch on his own.

"Pullout bed," he explained as he tossed the cushions aside and yanked at the base.

"Why didn't you go with him?" she said, nodding toward the hallway.

Hunter secured the bed.

"Just a minute," he said. "There are blankets, bed sheets, and pillows in the hallway closet. I'll be right back."

He looked back over his shoulder as he walked and said, "Take that pistol out of your holster and keep it ready, will you? I think we're safe here, but your dad's house looked pretty safe, too."

Moser met him in the hallway. His Winchester was tucked under his right arm. He looked tired.

"Hard house to clear," he said. "Too many windows. Too many side doors."

"Too many memories," said Hunter.

"That too," said Moser.

"C'mon, let's get the beds squared away."

They walked back into the living room, and both men stopped cold. Hunter dropped the bedsheets, pillows, and blankets onto the floor. Moser raised the barrel of his shotgun, thought about it, and then lowered it again. Rebecca stood in the middle of the floor, facing them. The barrel of her revolver was pressed hard against the underside of her chin. Her eyes were rolled back into her head.

"Rebecca?" called Hunter softly.

He felt Moser's hand on his shoulder.

"I don't think she's here," said Moser.

He pointed toward the living room window.

What Hunter had thought was moonlight shining in through the window was actually a blue, white mist. Within that outline, he could see a faint image of Rebecca staring back at him, her arms outstretched, her lips moving, but no sound coming from her ghostly pale lips. He shivered as the cold realization that he was staring at her trapped spirit forced its way into his mind.

"What do we do?" asked Moser quietly.

"I don't know," said Hunter.

"Ever seen anything like it?" asked Moser.

The phantasm was floating two feet off the living room floor, a translucent specter through which Hunter could see soft moonlight highlighting the endless lawn. He turned back to look at Rebecca's physical form, noticing that her finger had found the trigger. An urgent gurgling came from between her compressed lips. Drops of dark blood slid down from the corner of her mouth. What the hell was happening? Was he seeing a forced astral projection? It wasn't possible, no, just not possible.

"No, but—"

"We don't have time," said Moser. "She's in serious trouble and I don't think she's got much time left."

"Let me think," said Hunter. "This just isn't possible, Enid, not in this house."

"Why?"

"This entire place is protected. It's warded. Someone has hexed her, and that's impossible."

"What's that?" asked Moser, pointing at something that Hunter couldn't see.

"What's what?"

"That."

And that's when Hunter saw it. A thin cobweb of light running between Rebecca's body and the wispy spirit.

"Astral cord."

"So, someone or something pulled her spirit out of her body?"

"Yeah, I think so."

Hunter took his phone out of his pocket, plugged in the thermal attachment module and took six shots from different positions in the room from Rebecca's body, the silver cord and her suspended spirit. Light flashes lit the room in eerie displays of impossibility. Hunter could hardly think about it, though. The adrenaline surge made it difficult to keep his hands from shaking.

The thought that he was doing something completely useless kept pushing at him, but it was the only thing he knew to do. He felt like a photographer at a crime scene, except the victim was still alive but dying as he took the pictures. He switched to infrared mode and snapped the next set of photos. It was a long shot, but he needed information, and this was the only way he could think of to get it.

"You about done?" asked Moser.

"Yes. Let me bring up the pictures."

He felt bad the moment he said it. There was Rebecca's body, standing three feet to one side of him in the darkened living room. And there was her spirit, floating three feet away from him on the other side. Nothing he knew from his years of investigating the paranormal or the occult that could help her, he thought in frustration. As he thumbed through the photo images he'd taken, he stopped and enlarged one of them.

"Hunter," said Moser.

"Just a minute," said Hunter. "It looks like a heat trail that stretches outward from the window."

"Look at me," said Moser.

"Wait, I think I—"

"There are a lot of things moving near the edge of the lawn."

Hunter looked up in horror at the window behind Rebecca's floating, pleading spirit. Moser was right. In the distance, there was movement. It looked like an army of darkness slowly and methodically moving across the lawn in an ominous black cloud.

"Shit," said Hunter.

"I thought you said this house was protected," said Moser.

"That's what Bartok told me."

"Your uncle Bartok is dead. Maybe the protection died with him. Damnation, maybe he was the protection. Can we move her?" asked Moser, nodding toward Rebecca.

"If that silver cord breaks, she's dead. If we move her, it'll break."

"Shit," said Moser. "Are you sure the wards are on?"

Hunter could feel the sweat building on the back of his neck. He looked at Rebecca's floating spirit, her arms stretched toward him, pleading for help. He'd heard of ghosts sobbing—had run into a few instances of it himself that he hadn't been able to disprove—but he had never heard of ghost tears. Yet he was certain that Rebecca was crying, and down her phantom cheeks, he could see them glisten.

"What?"

"The wards, do you think they're turned off because Bartok's dead?"

"How the hell would I know?" asked Hunter. "I haven't been to this house in twenty years. I thought Bartok's wards were always on. I don't even know where they are. Hell, I don't even know what they look like. Unless the stone..."

Moser yanked him around and glared at him.

"That young woman there needs you. Think of something. It's what you do. Did Bartok leave something for you? Anything?"

"No. Nothing. A bunch of papers. Everything in this house, but —"

"Nothing?"

"I told you—wait. Stay here. Don't let her move."

Hunter ran to the kitchen table, moved aside the packet of papers, and fumbled with the latches on the sword case. Finally, they snapped open, and he lifted the lid. Silver light flooded out from the blade's reflection. He looked at the sword, then at the dagger. The sword was bigger. The last time he'd seen it, it was sticking out of the big rock in Bartok's den. The sword had to be inserted into the stone for the wards to work.

"What're you going to do with that?" asked Moser when Hunter returned with the sword.

"Put it back where it belongs, so maybe the wards will work."

"Well, get to it. Look out there."

Hunter followed Moser's eyes. The roiling mob of black shapes was much closer.

"It's looks like an army of them. I think it's those horned things hit the Mihaloff house. Should we make a run for it?" asked Moser. "Load her and her ghost in the truck and try to outrun them?"

"She'll die if we move her," said Hunter. "Or worse."

Moser nodded.

"What if I get in the truck and run it straight at them?" said Moser.

"Are you crazy?" said Hunter.

"I don't plan on dying. I'll cut to the side at the last second and lead them away from the house. If they're chasing after me, you might have time to save her. If you can figure it out, call me and I'll drive back here and come in through that fancy garage door of yours fast as I can get here."

"Don't do it. You won't have a chance," said Hunter.

"Give me a reason. Tell me you can get those wards up."

"I'm not positive it will work."

"Time's up then. I'm taking them down the road. If it works, it'll buy you time."

"Too late," said Hunter.

Standing outside the window was a black cloaked form, surrounded by hundreds of green yellow eyes. Hunter raised the sword and Moser lifted his Winchester. The dark hood didn't conceal the figure's face. It was simply an oval of flat darker blackness staring back at them.

"Don't shoot," said Hunter. "If you break the perimeter, they'll come pouring in."

"I don't think the glass is going to stop them."

"Not the glass. The threshold."

To Hunter's horror, the etheric body of Rebecca spun toward the dark cloaked figure as though turned by an unseen hand.

"Can that thing pull her through?" asked Moser quietly.

For a moment, Hunter couldn't deal with the paralyzing fear. He didn't know how. He simply didn't know if that woman wrapped in darkness could pull Rebecca's spirit through the window glass. Had he ever come across such a thing? Had he ever read anything about it? The figure outside the window moved to within a foot of the window. The dark beasts crowding in around her began to spread out. He could hear huffing and growling, and the window fogged with their angry breaths.

"They're surrounding the place," said Moser. He kept his finger on the trigger, the barrel pointed directly at the cowled figure's chest.

The air in the room was tainted by the smell of fear and tension. Fainter than gun smoke, but more explosive than gunpowder. A static charge clung to the two men, and Hunter thought that a false move by them could ignite a disaster. He barely knew Rebecca, but he could not stand the sight of her catatonic physical form and her floating etheric body by a silvery astral cord, that if broken, would mean her death. They had been talking just minutes ago. She was fine when he left the room, but when he returned, she was under siege. The thing on the other side of the glass was trying to take her soul.

Every house had a threshold, though most were weak. But a house owned by a man like Bartok was a much stronger barrier. But was it enough?

"Every house has a beating heart, Ian," his mentor had told him.

"It is the room where the owner is most strongly invested. That is what powers a home's threshold. The owner's life energy enables it."

"You remember that mirror in the hallway?" whispered Hunter.

The figure on the other side of the window raised both arms in a darkly dramatic gesture, palms facing the glass. Hunter could feel the malice radiating from her like the heat from a fire.

"I remember it."

"Rip it off the wall and bring it here with the back facing toward the witch."

Moser walked backward, his Winchester still aimed at the thing in the window. The witch. Hunter could not believe he had called her that. A real witch. Not a new age Wiccan or people superimposing their desperate personal failings on a patchwork religion created by that creepy fraud, Gerald Gardiner. A real witch. Her cowled face turned to follow Moser as he backed out of the room and disappeared into the hall. Why couldn't he see her face? Was it a spell? Was it magic? She turned back to look at him as though she had heard his thoughts. Her arms were held motionless above her head as though she were about to conduct an orchestra.

"Hang in there, Rebecca," he said softly. "Helps on the way."

Moser came back holding the mirror, its back facing the window. Hunter leaned toward him and whispered in his ear.

"One of us," he said, "is going to have to go to the window, spin that mirror around quickly and then slide it in between Rebecca's spirit and that witch. We're going to reflect her own energy back at her. Maybe it will break the spell over Rebecca. If it works, hold it there while I make a run for Bartok's study and turn on the wards."

"You got that figured?"

"I think so."

After a quick side-wise look at Rebecca's physical form standing rigid and her eyes rolled back with the whites showing, Moser let the Winchester hang from his shoulder strap and walked toward the window with the backward mirror. Hunter was amazed at the way he walked straight to where the witch stood without showing fear.

"Don't look in her eyes," Hunter said.

But Enid Moser had been dealing with night horrors a lot longer than Hunter. His eyes looked straight at her center. Hunter felt his heart beating harder and faster as Moser stood right next to Rebecca's ghost-like spirit form. The witch had cocked her head toward him, then turned her attention back to Rebecca and brought her hands toward the windowpanes. Before they touched the glass, though, Moser flipped the mirror so that it was facing the window and slid in between Rebecca and the figure in black. There was a flash of scarlet-white light and a shriek of rage. Moser stood there with his head tucked against his shoulder, holding the mirror in place like a crucifix. Then a bullwhip snap and before Hunter's unbelieving eyes, he saw Rebecca's spirit form shoot back across the room and merge with her body. She dropped straight to the floor with a thud. Hunter recoiled as her revolver hit the floor next, but it didn't fire.

"Hold it there," said Hunter.

"Hurry," said Moser. "I feel like I'm holding it up against a windstorm."

Hunter wanted to go over to the young woman and make sure she was okay, but there was no time. If he didn't get to Bartok's study soon, none of them would be alive like morning.

Keeping the sword close, but not so close he'd cut off part of his leg while he ran, he took off through the kitchen, down the hallway past four ragged breaks in the plaster where Moser had ripped the mirror off the wall, up the stairway to the second floor, then took a dogleg right down another hallway and opened the door to Bartok's study. He looked to the left and right, ignoring the bookshelves, stacks of books and manuscripts on the floor, the desks and globe lamps but didn't see what he was looking for. In twenty years, Bartok would have moved at least once, he thought with frustration.

Old man, where did you move it to? he screamed inside his head.

Bartok's study was large, but not large enough to hide a three-foot boulder mounted on a four-foot square marble pedestal. Then it hit him. He stepped around the door he'd just opened and there it was, beneath a Renaissance portrait of King Arthur and the Knights of the Round Table. Hunter glanced at the sword. At that moment, it was truly beautiful and lit with the glory of its calling. All his life, Hunter had thought it was a trick, that the sword was not really Excalibur, King Arthur's sword, but just a fake to make a point. Bartok was big on the lessons of symbolism, but Hunter had never understood the point of inserting the sword's blade into the stone's slot. Tonight, he hoped that he finally did.

He found the narrow slot where he needed to insert it. And he prayed it would operate the same type of machinery that Bartok had used to guard the Library of the Temple Guardians.

Old man, he thought, this better work.

Without another thought, he slid it into the crevice. Just before the sword enter the stone, he saw a sparkle of purple light from inside, but as he pushed the blade in all the way, it disappeared. When the guard touched the stone, there was a loud click, a scream from the living room and a surge of invisible energy surged out from the stone. Hunter jumped back and almost fell. Every muscle in his body quivered like he'd been shot with a Taser. His vision blurred and then clarified, then blurred again and returned to normal.

It worked. He could feel it. The room, the very house itself, came alive with a subtle energy.

"It's on," he shouted.

When Moser didn't shout back an answer, he remembered the scream. He scooped up Bartok's dagger and ran toward the living room. He could hear Rebecca saying, "You're okay, you're okay. Let me look at it. You've got to sit down before you fall down."

Something was wrong with Moser. Hunter hustled back down the stairway and into the hallway leading to the living room.

As he stepped into it, he saw Rebecca trying to steer his friend to the couch.

"Go get towels and the medical kit," she said without looking back at him. "And a pitcher of water if you can find one."

Hunter froze. There was so much blood. Moser's face was covered with it. His hands. His coat.

"Get moving," snapped Rebecca with barely repressed fury. "Do you want him to bleed to death while you're just standing there?"

"I'll be fine," said Moser. "Scalp wound, and I cut my hands."

Broken glass from the mirror was scattered all around the floor. The mirror's frame was split and lay on top of the blood smeared glass. But the living room window was intact.

"Move," shouted Rebecca.

Hunter grabbed the first aid kit from the kitchen table and took it to Rebecca.

"On the couch," she said without looking at him.

With a quick glance at the living room to make sure the witch was still gone, he turned and went back for the towels and a pitcher of water. He looked in the nearest linen closet and found that it was stacked with white towels and washcloths. He grabbed both.

Not a good color choice for cleaning up blood, he thought.

But he took them into the living room and stacked them on the couch next to the first aid kit. He heard Rebecca asking Moser, "How many fingers am I holding up?" as he went into the kitchen.

How had the witch known where they were? They'd told no one. They weren't followed—he was sure of that. Unless… unless there was a tracking device on the truck. Easy enough to check, he thought. And then he remembered with a sick feeling in his stomach that he'd told Brother Mihaloff. The spellbound.

"Hurry up," shouted Rebecca. "What's taking you so long?"

Ouch, thought Hunter.

The corner cabinet above Bartok's Swedish stove had a crystal water pitcher on its second shelf. He took it down, rinsed it in the sink —what was he thinking? Rinsing wasn't going to disinfect it. He turned on the water, felt the temperature with his wrist and when it was lukewarm, he closed the valves and took it to Rebecca, who glared at him. It was hard to believe that only ten minutes ago she had been standing rigid with her eyes rolled back, her spirit being pulled from her against her will by a black-hearted witch. No matter how upset she seemed now, Hunter was just glad to see her alive in one piece.

"Go get garbage bags for the towels," she snapped.

Brother Mihaloff's daughter, like her father, had no problems giving orders.

"Are you okay?" he asked Moser.

"Go get the garbage bags, young man. I'm fine. Nothing that some well-placed butterfly stitches won't fix. Go on. Get going."

"What happened?" asked Hunter.

"Do I have to get them myself?" asked Rebecca, with a knife edge to her voice.

After a few minutes rummaging around in a broom closet inside the mudroom, he came back with a box of thirty-gallon black garbage bags. Moser was lying on the couch, which seemed a foot too short for him. Rebecca had his head elevated with two cushions, and she was cleaning his face with one washcloth. He saw she had already butterfly-stitched a long cut just below the hairline. Just as he was about to ask her what happened again, she pointed at the bloody towels and facecloths stacked on the floor.

"In the bag," she said.

He was about to demand an answer, then he gave up and started putting the bloody wads into a garbage bag. It went on like that for a while. Her telling him what to do and him following orders. Somewhere along the line, he'd realized how shaken up she was and how important it was for her to feel in control again. There was no way for him to imagine what it had been like for her, and part of him never wanted to know.

Not everything is good to know, Bartok had once said.

The longer he followed in Bartok's footsteps, the truer that was sounding.

His two companions looked the worse for wear. Rebecca's face was a few shades paler, and her cheekbones seemed more prominent. Her eyes were sunken; she kept swiping her hair out of her eyes while she worked on Moser's hands. Her hair glistened with blood. He wondered for an irrational moment if the blood came from a small hole in her head where her soul was ripped from her body by that terrifying woman floating outside in the darkness. Whoever or whatever she was, she had to be one hell of a powerful practitioner.

He'd never believed such things as what he'd just seen were possible. Whenever Bartok had discussed such topics, Hunter had mentally tuned out. Before Townsend Mountain, he did not believe in anything that couldn't be measured and discussed rationally. That belief and his confrontations with Bartok were what had spurred him on to debunk the paranormal. His obsession with the topic had propelled him to write two bestsellers and a slew of other popular books on the topics. Now, he wasn't sure what he believed.

Witches, he thought. Now I believe in witches, too. What next?

That's when he remembered Hiram Abiff.

They were linked in some horrible way. The witch and Hiram Abiff. Bartok had said as much in his letter. Hunter remembered the old man's glowing eyes and shuddered. He remembered the tunnel

Brother Mihaloff had called the Borgo Pass and thought he should have never, ever came back to Michigan.

"I said, are you there? Do you feel dizzy? How many fingers am I holding up?"

It was Rebecca's voice. At first, he thought she was talking to Moser, but then realized she was talking to him.

"I'm fine," he said. "I was just thinking. How is Moser? How are you?"

"Trust me," said Moser, "I'm going to feel like hell in the morning, but I'm fine. Miss Rebecca gave me one of her pain pills. Good thing I had my head hunched next to my shoulder when that mirror blew apart. Otherwise, I'd have pieces of glass sticking out where I've got eyes, and maybe my throat cut open. Never saw what happened to the witch woman and her monsters, but she didn't like that mirror, that's for sure. Soon as I shoved it between her and Rebecca, well, Rebecca's spirit snapped back into her body. Seen nothing like it."

"How's your hands?"

"They hurt like hell and I'm not going to be much of a trigger-puller for a bit."

"Pain pill seems to have started to work," said Rebecca. "It was his forehead bled so much. Glass shard cut the palm of his right hand and one was sticking clean through his left hand by half an inch."

Hunter felt sick just hearing about it. He hated the thought of being cut. He had fifty-five stitches along the inside of his right leg where he'd fallen from a tree as a kid and caught it on a nail head sticking out enough from the trunk to rip through his flesh.

"How are you?" he asked.

Moser looked cleaner than her.

"Don't worry about me," she said. "I'll be fine."

But she wouldn't be. That was easy enough to see. Rebecca Mihaloff would never be the same. Her eyes looked almost vacant, as though her spirit had returned, but she was afraid at any moment it could be ripped away from her again. She looked vulnerable.

"Do you want me to wipe some of the blood off you?"

She arched one eyebrow and said, "I think not."

Vulnerable, but heading toward furious again.

"Sorry. I didn't mean anything by it. I just meant... do you know where you're cut? Can I do anything for you?"

She eyed him coldly.

"No," she said. "But if I need more towels or garbage bags, don't worry, I'll ask."

"Did I do something wrong?"

"Do you have a bathroom here where I can clean myself up?"

"It's down that hall," said Hunter. "Third door on the right. I'll walk you there."

"Thank you," she said. "I'll find it myself."

She walked over and picked up her bag with her good hand, slung it over her shoulder, retrieved her revolver, and disappeared down the hallway. A few seconds later, he heard the bathroom door click shut.

"What the hell did I do?" asked Hunter.

"Well," said Moser. "It was your idea to bring her here. Not your best plan, I have to say."

45

That night, after she'd finally fallen asleep, Rebecca dreamed again of the monster that was coming and how he had come to be.

****

Outside Damascus, Syria A.D. 35

It was too late to kill him.

The flash of light, the voice like angry thunder crashing down from the heavens. The mystery of what it said confused Hiram. Was it about him? Was it a voice at all? He had seen the short bald-headed man suddenly afflicted by jerky spasms, then lost sight of him as he tried to block first his eyes from the brilliant white light and then his ears from the thunder-crack voice that blasted the little group into silence. Hiram was actually within hailing distance when the coruscation lit up the world around them all.

The ground was hard and rough as a sanding stone as first his hip and shoulder, then his face and hands hit. His eyes blinked yellow white stars. The worst pain was as the ground raked his knuckles bloody raw and when a stone the size of an egg and split his lip and broke two of his front teeth. Tenebrous reverberations tormented his ears. He felt the taste of blood in his mouth and the warmth of it spreading across the backs of his hands. After rolling onto his back, he stared up at the darkening sky and closed his eyes. When the blood filled his mouth, he turned his head to one side and spit onto the parched ground. His vision was still blurred and shaky as he got to his knees and stared at the small group of men he had been shadowing.

Only one of them mattered. The one who must be stopped. That one was dazed, rolling back and forth on the ground with his limbs shaking and a thin white froth clinging to his lips. The others backed away from their companion, fear twisting and contorting their features. They stared wide-eyed at the man rolling on the ground before them as though he was possessed, then glance nervously upward as though expecting a new catastrophe to descend upon them.

"Who are you, Lord?" asked the prostrate man in an awestruck voice.

Hiram Abiff edged closer to hear the response. The surrounding land was empty. The others looked skyward again, waiting for an answer. They were so agitated they didn't hear him approach. The day was warm, and the air was still. He could feel blood well up from the abrasions on his knuckles and slide down his fingers. A vicious dust devil wind sprang up and spun like an out of balance top as the short bald man was helped to his feet by the others.

"What is it?" asked one man. "What is wrong?"

The balding man stood bowlegged, twisting in a circle and holding his outstretched hands toward the sky as though trying to catch raindrops.

You are mine now, thought Hiram.

"Let me help," said Hiram, walking up to them and extending his bloody right hand to tap one man on the shoulder. "What is wrong with him?"

The two traveling companions turned to look at him, confused, as though they could not understand him. And they could not. Hiram's mouth was swollen and bruised; blood dripped over his lower lip as if he had just returned from battle.

Suddenly, the afflicted man stopped spinning, dropped his hands, and stared straight at Hiram. "I am blind," he said as he pointed a finger at Hiram.

His eyes were covered with slick black scales and shown an iridescent black green. Hiram stepped back in shock.

"I am blind," repeated the afflicted man, "but still I can see evil."

"It cannot be so," said Hiram.

"May the Lord rebuke you," said the man.

There came another flash of white light and Hiram found himself lifted off the ground and flying backward through the air until he was impaled on the broken limb of a tall tree.

As the others walked away with the blind man, oblivious to what had just occurred, Hiram grasped the broken end of the branch protruding from his stomach and screamed. The pain of it vibrated throughout his body as blood and entrails dripped down the hem of his robe and fell unseen to the earth below. Hiram was beyond seeing. All that his mind could process was the unendurable pain.

****

He hung there all night, sweating and squirming and begging those who passed by him for help. At first, they would avert their eyes and quicken their pace toward Damascus. Later, with dusk still a few hours away, they came back in straggling groups cloaked in frightened whisperings to stone him as he twisted and dodged to avoid the rocks they threw at him. The rough branch was tilted upward so there was no escape from it. He screamed and howled like an angry hyena as the stones crushed his eye socket, then cracked and disfigured his skull. They kept their distance in the beginning of the barrage, calling him a devil and a blasphemy on the land. The barrage of rocks battered him beyond recognition. The pain drove him to madness. His skin felt cracked and dry from the blood oozing from his wounds. When his body reformed around the penetrating branch, the flow of coppery smelling fluid would begin again.

The mob, which had gathered around him in a semicircle to stone him to death, recoiled in horror. As his vision returned, he saw them rip their robes and pull their hair.

"He is no man," said a man with wild brown hair. "He is a demon."

No, thought Hiram, I am a man with no soul. A man with no soul and infested with demons. Since being brought back from death, he was nothing but an empty shell where any demon could rush in and take command. But from the midst of his writhing agony, a thought took hold. He would take the invading spirits and never let them go. He would take hold of them and subjugate them. He would become the Lord of Demons and inflict pain and suffering on those who stoned and ridiculed him.

With dusk drawing closer, they whispered to one another.

"He cannot die," said a stocky man. "He has no life to lose."

"Abomination, he is an abomination," said another.

"Fire purifies," said a hunched over one-eyed man.

Broken pieces of dried branches jutted out from the larger branch on which he was impaled. He could not slide past them. His hands were slick with blood. When he tried yet again to pull himself over, he spun to one side and hung upside down, screaming in agony as the rough, weathered bark tore at his insides. Blood flowed downward to cover his face and eyes and blind him.

"Mercy," he cried. "Mercy, in the name of all that is holy."

Just as the blood reached his lower eyelids, he saw them approaching with bundles of branches and pitch-soaked torches.

46

Moser was the second to open his eyes. He blinked at them once, twice, and then a third time from behind his raised hand. The frayed, bloodstained bandages on his hand dangled between his eyes. When he moved his hand away, he could see Rebecca Mihaloff sitting on a brass studded leather chair, staring out and across the lawn. Her hair was a tangled mess and her pale face looked haunted. In her lap was her pistol. Hunter lay asleep on the floor under a pile of blankets.

"You been up all night?" Moser asked her.

She nodded, but said nothing.

"What happened to him?" he asked, pointing at Hunter.

Without looking back, she said, "I couldn't sleep, and he couldn't stay awake."

It figured, thought Moser.

Both of his hands hurt like hell. Rebecca had cleaned and bandaged them, as well as any nurse. But they still hurt and would for a while. He gently flexed his hands one at a time and decided he could still pull a trigger when it needed to be done.

"You want some coffee?" he asked.

He was up on one elbow now, looking at her, trying to establish a connection. Being attacked in her own house by the witch and her horned monster was bad enough, but after what happened last night, well, he didn't know how she could just hang on. Moser had seen terrifying things in his life, but seeing her suspended in midair by that witch last night had been among the worst. As he stared at her, he wondered what would have happened to her if that luminescent astral cord spirit had snapped. But Hunter had made the right call. Putting the mirror between the witch and Rebecca had saved her life. Beyond that, it was hard to say. Had he saved her soul, too? Maybe, thought the Kentuckian, but it was hard to say.

Rebecca turned to him suddenly, and he saw the tear streaks down her face.

"Have you ever been terrified?" she asked.

"I have," he said, and sat the rest of the up and swung his legs over the side of the bed.

"No, I mean really terrified. As in, scared out of your mind."

"I have," he repeated. "Growing up around Townsend Mountain, we had Mr. Bartok. He taught us Mosers right early in life. Between working for him and my stints in the military, it's hard to remember a year I wasn't shaking in my boots, and I do mean as in, scared out of my mind."

"You know what I mean," she snapped back at him.

He stood and stretched.

"I reckon I do, Miss Rebecca. Being scared of losing a person's soul differs from being afraid of dying, but I've been there too. You're just going to have to trust me on that. But God will not let you just slip away from him, if you'll pardon this old man saying so."

Time passed as she looked at him, watching to see, he supposed, if he had enough spine behind what he said to look right back at her. The sound of Hunter's snoring broke the spell, and he grinned.

"The Hunters are a noisy bunch, ain't they?"

For a moment, he saw her eyes light up, and he thought that temper of hers was going to catch fire, but she shook her head in disgust and looked back out the window.

"You know," he said, "he saved your life last night."

"He's the one who brought me here in the first place," she said.

"I know you're angry, Miss Rebecca. Guess I would be, too, but did you really think you could live the rest of your life hiding out in your daddy's underground bunker?"

She opened her mouth to snap back at him, then seemed to think better of it. Better to be mad than lost, his cousin Kenneth would say. Granny Hillis would say that Kenneth was a better hog wrestler than a talker.

"How are your hands?" she asked.

"Well," he said after making a show of inspecting them, "I had a right fine nurse take care of them. Long as I can pull a trigger, I'm going to be all right."

"You have to be able to hold the gun, too," she pointed out.

"Between you, me, and Hunter, we've only got three good hands."

"Is he much of a shot?" she asked as another snore rumbled out from beneath the covers.

"Not really," said Moser, "but he's getting better. Got a good teacher, you know?"

"That would be you?"

"Yep."

"Why don't I make that coffee?" she said. "I've got one less injured hand than you do."

"Thank you much. I'm going to go find the head while you do that. And, Miss Rebecca?"

"Yes?"

"Keep that pistol of yours with you, will you? You're a better shot than that young man making all the noise."

Following his own advice, he took his Winchester into the bathroom with him.

****

"I was afraid that if I fell asleep, she'd take control of me again," she said.

"Hunter was worried about that, too," Moser replied. "Bartok taught us to watch what we were thinking when we went to sleep. My daddy said the same. You have to understand we were a long ride away from Townsend Mountain. Had to be. Closer you got, the more... uncomfortable it got. And Bartok's rule was you never slept on the mountain proper. One of my cousins couldn't listen any better than a block of wood, and decided he was going to do it anyway to show how ignorant me and the family was."

"What happened?" she asked after a perfunctory sip of her coffee.

They were sitting at the kitchen table drinking coffee and eating dehydrated pears from one of Moser's MRE packets. The brownies were already gone, and she'd eaten half a western omelet.

"He seemed all right, for the first week, Miss Rebecca. When Bartok heard about it on the second day, he told my daddy to keep a close watch on him."

"And?"

"At night, he'd wake up screaming. We had to tie him to the bed. That just kept him in one place. He screamed until his voice was gone. We tried giving him sleeping pills from the drugstore. It didn't stop nothing. Daddy tried liquoring him up right before bedtime. Sorry, Miss Rebecca, but he couldn't think of nothing else. So, he was drunk and screaming. Said there was these alien robots trying to get into his head; they had these drill bits and were trying to break through his skull. That's pretty much all we could understand. We tried keeping him awake, but you can guess how that worked out."

"What did you end up doing?" she asked.

Moser didn't answer at first.

"Enid?" she asked again.

"Don't pay this old man no attention, Miss Rebecca. I don't think I'm remembering this right. It was a long time ago."

"Did you kill him, like Hunter did Bartok?"

Outside, it was a good morning, Moser thought. He could see the river from where they sat. Scattered white clouds, the kind Granny Hillis said was God's sky flowers, floated high in the sky. And the sun a buttery yellow ball, taking its sweet time as it worked its way up toward noon.

"Mr. Bartok came down to see what could be done. You got to understand that in that short time, my cousin had already begun to change. We had to tie up the dogs because they were going crazy, too. They started barking and howling so they couldn't be shut up. They smelled him, don't you know? Daddy and Mr. Bartok sent them away. Mr. Bartok, thank the Lord, had brought down some powerful tranquilizers, the kind they give horses, I think, and after a shot of that he was out and quiet. Mind you, even tied down, it took four of us to keep him still so he could put the needle in. But we eventually got it done."

"Tell me what happened to him," she said.

This time, there was steel in her voice. She wasn't going to let it go. Even though he was afraid her hearing about it would make it worse for her, she was a strong young woman. Maybe hearing what happened would actually help her.

"Mr. Bartok and my daddy decided they had to put him up in one of the cabins further away from the mountain. I think they'd pretty well decided they were out of options and didn't want us younger ones to see what was going to happen as he got worse. They had him in la la land from the meds when they took him from the house. It was in the early afternoon 'cause they didn't want to do it at night when he was at his worst. Daddy made us stay inside, but that didn't stop us from looking out the window. They made it to about thirty feet from the van when this black bear came barreling out from the tree line. Mr. Bartok and my daddy neither one had time to think. I can still see it in my head, the look on their faces when they saw this big-assed creature on a flat-out run at them and roaring as it came. A black bear can cover ground quick, Miss Rebecca. They can move along at thirty miles an hour or so.

"It crashed into Bartok, knocked him over like he was a bowling pin and my daddy tripped over his own two feet trying to get out of the way. It wasn't pretty what happened next. That thing had my cousin by the throat and was dragging him along like he was taking home dinner to the young-ins. Daddy had a rifle in the car—daddy had a rifle close by pretty much wherever he was. He had it out of the truck, stock up to his shoulder and was ready to fire when Mr. Bartok pushed the barrel aside and down. From where I was at the window, it looked like my daddy was going to knock Mr. Bartok's lights out. But he didn't even lift his fists to take a punch. He knew Mr. Bartok was right.

"Kind of a hard lesson for kids our age, but we got the message. Stay away from the bad places at night. Our brains is easier to get to after the sun goes down. That's all I'm trying to say. When we're going up against the bad things, we got to be careful about going to sleep. So, you were right to be worried."

Rebecca looked away from him, toward the water. In the morning light, her eyes were ringed by dark circles. Her skin was pale, and her shoulders slumped forward with exhaustion. Minutes passed by them without a word. Moser looked over into the other room where Hunter was still sleeping and wished he'd hurry and wake up. Talking to a young woman like her was a two-man job.

"Are you saying this is a bad place?" she gestured around the Bartok house with her bandaged hand.

She had turned away from the water and was looking right at him again. He thought, or maybe he hoped, he saw more determination in the way she'd sat straighter.

"This here place? Nope. You got to remember this was where Bartok lived."

"All right, but I wasn't sleeping when it happened. I was on full alert and armed. I don't even know how it happened. One second, I'm looking around the room for cushions we can use as pillows, and the next minute, she owns me. Explain that."

"You want to wait for Hunter to wake up and let him tell it?"

"No," she snapped. "He's too condescending."

Moser had to think about that one.

"I suppose you got a point there, but give him time. He's still… adjusting. Mr. Bartok is a hard act to follow."

"So, you explain it to me instead or I don't think I'll ever sleep another night. How did she do that? How was she able to do that?"

"Sorcery, probably. Black magic. Whatever you want to call it. I don't pretend to understand that kind of stuff. Never studied up on it and even if I had, I probably still wouldn't have understood it. Mostly I can't stand the idea of it. But that ain't what this is all about, is it? Being caught by it makes you feel unclean, or weak, or casting about trying to figure out if you're spiritually weak. You're probably thinking that if you were spiritually strong, she couldn't have trapped you. Well, that's horseshit, if you'll pardon the language. It's got nothing to do with nothing. Would you figure you was weak if she shot you with a Colt .45? Would you figure if you were spiritually strong the bullet would just bounce off? What you got to get in your headstrong young head, Missy, is that a weapon is a weapon. If it's a knife, or hypnosis, or a shotgun, or magic. You don't have to be strong to pull a trigger. You don't have to be strong to cut with a knife. And if you don't know that somebody that is lying in wait for you has a weapon, you ain't too likely to be ready for it. Does that help?"

"Maybe," she said, and set her lips in a firm line.

"You know what this Sergeant told me once?"

"No."

"He said, 'Moser, why don't you just shut up and reload?' I didn't like hearing it, but he was right. Maybe you don't like hearing it now, but it's what you need to do."

"I'd like to slap you and watch your head spin," she said.

"That's the spirit," he said, and winked. "More coffee?"

****

"This place ain't changed much since my first visit," said Moser.

He saw her looking over her shoulder back at Hunter, who was now at the breakfast table, caffeinating himself into a state of wakefulness as he pored over an old leather journal. Even half-awake, the intensity of his focus was obvious. The young man seemed to know only two speeds—total immersion and watchfulness. Moser wondered if Bartok was like that in his younger years.

"What?" asked Rebecca.

"Take this staircase," said Moser. "Looks the same as the first day I came here to see Mr. Bartok. We're standing here in the… the…"

"Vestibule," she said.

"Right. The vestibule. To the left, you can see the living room with the fireplace and the rest. We got this marble tiled hallway that goes all the way back to the poolroom with the gigantic windows, looking out on the back lawn."

Rebecca stopped, grabbed his arm, and looked up at him.

"Are you thinking of going into real estate or something?"

The smile that cracked across Moser's craggy face was genuine.

"Nope, I'm just leading up to the important point."

"And that is?" she asked.

"So, the first time I was here, Miss Rebecca, old Mr. Bartok asked me what I saw, and I said what I just told you. In return, he says to me, 'Enid Moser, you are too blind to be carrying a weapon. You see the rooms and the furniture, but what do you really see?' So, I ask him what in the name of Renfro Valley is he talking about. He says, 'Close your eyes,' and I did. Then he asks, 'how many stairs lead up and how many lead down?'"

He gestured at the horseshoe stairway that led up to the second floor wrap around balcony.

"I told him thirty-two. It seemed to me there was about fifteen or sixteen steps going up and then down again on the other side. Thirty-two total stairs meant sixteen up and sixteen down. Thirty-two is an important Masonic number, so I went with that. He tells me, 'look again, my friend, for there are sixteen going up and fifteen going down. It is always harder to go up than it is to go down.' So, I can't help myself, Miss Rebecca. Every time I come back to this house, I always count the stairs. It's a habit with me now. Not much I can do about it, I guess, but I'd sure like to let it go now that he's gone."

Since Rebecca knew Bartok, she didn't find it hard to believe he would go to such lengths to make an esoteric point. But it was the first time she'd ever been to the house and wondered what other eccentricities there were to be found. She wondered, in fact, whether Enid Moser was wrong in his analysis of the witch's attack. Bartok was a man of the mysteries in many senses of the phrase. His family heritage was split between two entirely disparate worlds- Kentucky and Detroit. It would be hard to find a more unlikely heritage than that. She really knew very little about him personally except that he had an encyclopedic knowledge of the occult and mystery teachings, and most especially of Masonic history, symbols, origins, teachings, and rituals. Her father, who looked up to very few people, respected both Bartok's knowledge and his wisdom.

"What you're looking to see for yourself, I reckon, is what saved you last night from that evil witch. We'll take the left-hand part of the stairway and head on up. Look here and see that the forward facing part of each stair has the Masonic black and white tile pattern you can find on many lodge floors. So, follow me up and we can see the ward Hunter was talking about. I don't understand how the hell they work—pardon my language, Miss Rebecca—but maybe you or Hunter will know better than me. Come on."

Men of Moser's culture always went up the stairs first and had the woman follow, to demonstrate their respect for the woman. When it came to going through a door or entering a house, they would hold the door open, and allow the woman the choice of going in first or going in second. "Southern men," Bartok had once explained to her, "don't want a lady to worry that they're looking up her skirt while she's going up the stairs."

As she followed him up, she wondered if the reason she was vulnerable to attack was that, despite what Moser had said, this was formerly Bartok's home. In other words, a Freemason's home. For too many Freemasons, Freemasonry was an occult religion. She had never asked Bartok about his faith, but as she walked up the stairs, paintings of the Masonic trestle boards by George Stewart were evidenced everywhere along the walls. There wasn't a cross to be seen. Her father's house was a Freemason's house, too. Masonic symbols were embedded in the woodwork like magical symbols. Twice she had been attacked by the witch, and both times she was in a house devoted to Freemasonry. She decided she would call Pastor Howard, tell him everything that had happened, and ask his opinion. And she would ask him to come to the house and pray with her. The creature called Hiram Abiff was demonic, and Freemasons had protected him for centuries. Because of that, there was no help to be found from them. She needed the help of the Divine, not help from grown men who dressed up in aprons and thought themselves above the Word of God.

As they stepped onto the second floor, Rebecca looked down and tried to see Hunter at the breakfast table, but he was out of her line of sight. It was just as well, she thought. Hunter was the worst of the bunch. He was irritatingly clueless about the dangers they faced. A ghost hunting engineer who wrote book after book, debunking the world's spiritual dangers. In her experience, fighting the forces of evil took more than a thermal imaging camera and an EVP recorder. And the shotguns he and Moser carried could work against the physical dangers like the horned beast that had attacked her, but against the witch who summoned it, shotguns would be no defense at all.

"First time I came here," continued Moser, "I spent half my time looking around for secret passages. This mahogany wainscoting here has all these Masonic emblems in carved relief that seemed to me that if I'd pushed against them, they'd swing open into secret hiding places.

But I never could find one that did. Well, anyway, follow me down this hallway."

He was right, thought Rebecca. Bartok's house seemed custom made for secret hiding places and hidden passageways. The sconces mounted on the walls head high... she wondered if one or more of them could be pulled downward like levers. This is a house, she thought, of secrets. She just needed to know which levers to pull to open them up.

When they got to the third door down the hallway, Moser stopped and moved aside so she could enter first.

"Dr. Bartok's study," he said.

It had the look of a university professor's office. The thick red and gold trimmed tapestry window curtains were closed, and despite the bright early morning outside, the room was in darkness. She ran a hand over the wall past the doorway and flicked the switch. The frosted globe desk lamp placed at one corner of Bartok's huge round desk flared to soft light. It was a heavy antique desk in the shape of a horseshoe, and behind it stood a monastic, straight-back chair. Books and journals were scattered across the surface of the desk. An elegant black ink pen stood embraced by a green-blue wave swirl of sparkling glass like a mermaid's pen holder.

"You got to turn around to see the stone," said Moser. "You walked right by it on the way in."

Rebecca turned around and saw that she had walked past it without seeing it. There was nothing to it, really. Just a big gray, ugly rock with a sword hilt sticking out of it. She walked back to where it stood against the wall and examined it.

"I thought there would be symbols carved into it," she said. "Or at least magical injunctions. It's just a big rock."

Moser came in to stand beside her.

"That sword handle sticking out of it makes it look like a thing from the movie, the one with that special sword for King Arthur."

"Excalibur?" asked Rebecca.

"Yeah, that one. Anyway, I asked Bartok if that's what it was, and he laughed so hard I thought he'd rip a gut muscle. But he wouldn't tell me anything more about it."

"Do you really think that rock drove the witch and her monsters away?"

"Seems like it," said Moser.

"Is it like a holy relic?"

"I don't know. Like I said, Bartok wouldn't tell me anything about it."

"How does it work?"

"You got me," said Moser.

"I think it's like an electronic pest control device," said a haggard voice from the hallway. "You know, the ones that give off ultrasonic sounds to drive mice crazy? I think it's like that. Whatever it gives off, it drives them away because they can't stand to be near it."

Hunter walked in and when he saw the look on Rebecca's face, he held up his hands defensively.

"I didn't mean to interrupt," he said.

"What is this thing, really?" she asked in a way that seemed oddly confrontational, even to her.

"I don't have a clue."

"Don't either of you know anything about this at all?"

She turned so she was facing both Hunter and Moser and glared at them.

"You brought me here," she continued, "because you thought it would be safe. If you don't know what this rock is that's protecting the place, how do you know you can depend on it? What powers it? How long is it good for? Is it like a battery that wears down and needs to be re-charged?"

The two men looked at each other, then down at the ground and then up again.

"We don't have a clue," said Moser, and Hunter seconded him.

"I could guess," said Hunter, "but that's all it would be is a guess. My uncle Bartok is dead, Rebecca. He's the one who understood all this stuff. I was the kid who was always trying to debunk everything. We didn't agree about much of anything until after he died. What I mean is that while he was alive, I just didn't appreciate him enough."

Rebecca grimaced, then walked around the desk and pulled apart the heavy drapes that blocked the sunlight.

"I have to see the sun," she said.

The desk's globe lamp's glow was lost in the brilliant sunlight that flooded the room.

"Ouch," said Hunter as he shielded his eyes.

None of them spoke for an uncomfortable few moments. Rebecca stared at the rock. Moser stared at Rebecca. Hunter avoided both of their eyes. He felt a terrifying vulnerability come over him. He had witnessed what neither of the others had. The memories sickened him.

"Hard night," said Moser, flexing his fingers. "You up to talking now? We need to know what went on when you and Rebecca's father met with Hiram Abiff."

"I'm going to sit down," said Hunter.

Rebecca sat behind Bartok's desk. Moser and Hunter each sat in one of the desk chairs that faced her.

"Well?" asked Rebecca.

How could he tell them about the trip through the Borgo Pass? He hesitated, and Moser prompted him.

"I'm guessing it's bad," said Moser. "Just start at the beginning and keep going. Don't think about it, just tell it."

Hunter nodded, but looked at Rebecca and said, "I need to ask you a question first."

He reached into his inside pocket and drew out his phone. With a slide of his thumb across the screen, he brought up his photo album and clicked on the photo of the magical symbol that they had found on the front door of the Mihaloffs house. After looking at it for a long minute, he gave up and slid the phone across the desk to her.

"I've looked at that symbol a hundred times and I still can't see the sign of the Beast in it. Can you please show me? Slide your finger across the screen if you want because I took the picture from a few different angles. No matter what angle I look at it from, though, I just don't see it. Please."

At first, she didn't look down at the phone. Instead, she turned to look at Moser. He stared back at her, then nodded. With an exasperated sigh, she looked down at the picture on its screen. It was so obvious to her. How could Hunter not see it? Obviously, despite his education and experience, he had no spiritual sight. She slid her finger across the screen again to view it from a different angle. She did it again and then again, then froze with her thumb held in place against the screen.

"What is it?" asked Hunter.

Her face paled, and her mouth hung open. She gasped and then slid the phone back toward him.

"What?"

"Call Pastor Mark," she said in a strained voice.

"Why?" asked Moser. "What's wrong, Miss Rebecca?"

Rebecca's face seemed to have drained of all color. Her eyes were wide with horror and she pointed at the phone.

"It's her. Look at the picture on the phone."

Her finger trembled as she pointed at the phone.

Nervous and confused, Hunter picked up the phone and brought the screen back to life. The picture he'd taken of the billboard in the Detroit Masonic Temple's lobby stared back at him.

"I don't—"

"It's her," whispered Rebecca. "It's the witch."

Moser scooted closer to Hunter to get a look at the screen.

"Who is that? Where did you take the picture?"

"It's—" he checked the screen again. "It's Eva Morgan. That's what Brother Mihaloff said her name was. It was in the lobby of the Detroit Temple. She gives lectures there once a month. He called her the 'modern-day Madame Blavatsky.'"

"The witch," said Rebecca, her voice rocketing up in volume. "She's the one I saw on the security monitor back at Dad's house that night. Call Pastor Mark."

"Well… shit," said Moser.

Hunter found his wallet and pulled out the pastor's card.

Before he dialed the number, he said, "Your father knows her, Rebecca, and I told your father we were coming here."

While Moser tried to calm her down, Hunter made the call.

When the Pastor finally answered, Hunter said, "Pastor Mark? It's me, Ian Hunter. I think we may need that holy water sooner than rather later."

PART THREE

47

"I was hoping you wouldn't call," said Pastor Mark.

"I was hoping I wouldn't have to," said Hunter.

He wasn't smiling when he said it.

The four of them were sitting in the living room. Hunter and Moser had cleaned things up, folded up the foldout beds and returned things to the way they were before they'd turned the space into a makeshift rest area. They left the bloodstains on the carpet where Moser's hands had bled out on them. The pastor had gotten there in under an hour. He was dressed the same way as when they'd first met—a denim shirt, corduroy jacket, jeans, and loafers.

"You don't have to do this," said Hunter. "Moser and I can—"

"Back off," said Rebecca, and she held out a hand palm out.

Hunter flinched and scooted over further toward the opposite arm of the couch. He looked at Moser, who sat in the chair next to where the pastor sat, but the old Kentuckian only shrugged. Why in the hell Rebecca was always so angry at him was beginning to get on his nerves. Religious people could be very weird.

"This is where it happened?" asked Pastor Mark.

"Yes," said Hunter.

Rebecca glared at him, then looked directly at her pastor.

"Yes, this is where it happened."

"Tell me about it," said the pastor, his voice tinged with the dread.

The curtains were pulled back, and sunlight warmed the living room like a giant spotlight. In the glare, Hunter had a hard time believing they'd been attacked by a witch last night. He shivered and saw from the corner of his eye that Moser was watching him.

Rebecca recited everything she could remember. Her voice was strong and even, without a hint of hysteria. It was almost too objective, thought Hunter. It was almost impersonal, as though she were talking about something that happened to someone else. He saw her hands folded in her lap, her eyes locked on those of Pastor Mark, as though daring him to call her a liar. The pastor kept a blank, nonjudgmental stare, and Hunter wondered if he'd learned to do that in prison. But when Rebecca told him the part about the mirror Moser used to drive away the witch, and Hunter sliding his sword into Bartok's ward stone, Pastor Mark flinched.

"What is it?" asked Hunter.

The pastor ran his hand reflexively over his chin and looked away from the group. His jaw was set as his eyes stared out across the empty yard.

"Pastor?" asked Rebecca nervously.

He stared a little while longer, then looked back at her.

"Just processing everything," he said. "Hard to believe."

"Every word of what she's told you is true," said Hunter.

"I have no doubt," said the minister. "Rebecca, God bless her, always tells the truth."

"And there's more," said Hunter. "It gets worse."

Rebecca and Moser stared at him.

"You've done a lot of paranormal investigations, haven't you, Mr. Hunter?" asked the pastor. "In fact, you're rather famous for it, aren't you? I was reading one of your books on the subject today when you called."

"They kind of pale when confronted with the real thing," said Hunter.

"Indeed, they do. Have you ever investigated prisons?"

Rebecca looked distraught over the direction the discussion was going. Moser raised an eyebrow at the pastor, but, as usual, waited to hear the man out before saying anything.

"Once," said Hunter.

"It was closed, I imagine."

"Yes."

"It's when the prisons are active that you can find the worst happenings. In fact, I believe active prisons are the most active locations in the world for… hauntings and demonic possession. You wouldn't have any way to know that, I realize, but I assure you it's true. I can say that from personal experience."

"What—" began Rebecca.

Her pastor held up one meaty hand to stop her.

"You'll see why it's important soon enough, Rebecca. I have something to tell you and both Mr. Hunter and Mr. Moser need to hear this, too, because it somehow it ties in with what's been happening to you. Can you all bear with me?"

When the three of them had nodded their heads in agreement, Pastor Mark continued. Rogue dirty clouds thrust themselves in front of the sun, and the front lawn turned an astringent gray, pale as bone dust.

"The places are few in the world where so many people compromised by evil are restrained as they are in prison. So much evil contained by concrete and iron bars. Not much good happens there and what evil is done in such places is rarely discussed with members of the outside world. One night, as an example, has stayed with me. There was an inmate named Ozzie the Razor—I won't tell you his real name, but he was accused of helping his cellmate to escape. It was a ridiculous charge. There was no way for him to have escaped from his locked cell, even if he had the help of ten inmates. To make matters worse, the other inmate — his name was Ray—had a very low IQ. He wasn't the brightest inmate on the cell block. Houdini, he was not. Do you understand, Mr. Hunter?"

"Yes," nodded Hunter. "I think I have the picture."

"The guards and the warden put serious… pressure on Ozzie to come clean and tell them how it had been done. They were… brutally efficient about it. But Ozzie could never help them. There just was no way out of that cell. Despite the statewide manhunt that ensued, Ray was never found. Not a trace of him. And no one has heard from him since. Despite the massive resources of the state and federal justice machinery, despite all thoughts to the contrary, Raymond Bates escaped from the very same prison where I did my time, and then vanished into the societal woodwork. Except that as an inmate at that same penitentiary, I can tell you it just wasn't possible.

"Many dark stories circulated among the guards and other inmates as to what happened to Ray, including the rumor that Ozzie dismembered and ate Ray, and the other that a gang of inmates who were devil worshipers sacrificed him, drank his blood, burned his body in the furnace room and blended his ashes with motor oil."

"Remind me never to do time in prison," said Moser.

"Me, too," said Hunter.

He looked at Rebecca and then at her pastor. Both seemed haunted. Rebecca was easier to understand. He'd seen what she'd gone through. But there was something about the look on Pastor Mark's face that was close to the drawn horror in her face. What had he seen?

"There came a time when I became Ozzie's new bunk mate. After the stories I'd heard about what had happened to Ray, I was… uneasy about this. I slept with my eyes open a lot, if you know what I mean. Ozzie didn't look like a psychopathic, cannibalistic maniac, but prison is prison. Prison is boredom, violence and degradation. Just not in that order. Prison can also be the accumulation of evil, as it was where I was imprisoned. Do you understand, Mr. Hunter?"

"No."

"Good. I hope you never do. The air in that prison reeked of depravity. So, you can imagine how I felt when, one blizzard raged November night, Ozzie the Razor told me what really happened. In the weeks leading up to that night, I had tormented myself trying to guess whether it was possible for Ozzie to, using a razor or shiv, to destroy Ray's body without leaving a trace. It was driving me crazy, but what else did I have to think about, bunked with a man known as Ozzie the Razor? I was ecstatic to learn that Ozzie did not work in the kitchen, and I think you can see why. Body disposal and kitchen work should never, ever go together."

Here Pastor Mark paused for a while, as though the horror of that thought was overtaking him again. Hunter looked at Moser and Rebecca and saw that neither one of them wanted to hear where this was going.

"One night, the night of a blizzard, I learned worse thoughts. Noises magnify in prison. Ozzie was restless. He hadn't slept well for days. I heard him say the word demon in his sleep. It terrified me, Mr. Hunter. His voice was ragged and torn and he was so agitated I thought he was experiencing a seizure. I was considering going over and shaking his shoulder to wake him up, but in prison such things are always bad ideas. So, I watched. He woke finally and choked back a scream.

"'It's coming for me. God help me, it's coming for me soon,' he said.

"His face was wild with terror, and I will never forget his ghastly visage. He looked right at me and asked if could I help him. The demon was coming for him. He was shaking so badly it was difficult to understand him. He had to repeat the words three times for me to get what he was talking about. I didn't know what to say, Hunter. I was as scared as he was. But he knew I was a Christian. That I was saved.

"'Please, Father,' he said.

"I wanted to tell him I wasn't a priest, that I was just a believer, but he was terrified that I couldn't say the words. I was a believer, and I could pray for him was what I finally told him.

"'Make the sign of the cross on me,' he said.

"Hunter, I didn't know how to make the sign of the cross, the way the Catholic priests did. He cried when I told him that. I told him I was not Catholic, but that I would pray for him, and I did. I prayed for many things after my conversion, but this was the first time that I'd prayed for a demon to leave a man be. There is not much space in a shared prison cell, but I felt the walls squeeze in even closer as I kneeled and prayed for Ozzie.

"The temperature in the cell dropped, the way you see it happen on the ghost hunter shows, which should not have surprised me, except that in my life up until then, I had never seen a ghost hunting show. I knew nothing about such things at all. But the cold was real and, one other thing, I knew we were not alone. I heard loathsome murmurations tugging at my mind—I could actually feel them, Hunter, I swear. They were like fingers of terror grasping at my identity, tugging and pulling my thoughts apart.

"Something dark had entered the cell while I was on my knees praying with my eyes closed tightly and my entire body shivering like our cell had become a freezer. Above and about us in the cell's darkness, I heard wings flapping and tiny, vicious jaws snapping angrily open and closed. Small. About the size of my hands. But evil. I could feel them. Reptilian and evil. You understand why I didn't open my eyes, don't you?

"Ozzie and I were both under some form of malevolent spiritual and physical assault. If I opened my eyes, I knew, I really knew that there were things fluttering about my head that would dive in and pluck them out. My mind was flooded with awful, disgusting thoughts that, as much of a sinner as I knew myself to be, were not my own. Images of rape and murder and torture ran across the movie theater of my mind. I didn't open my eyes to see what it was. I pressed them tightly closed because I was terrified to see what was there with us.

"Prison holds many types of terrors for its inmates, Mr. Hunter. In my experience, though, a prisoner keeps his eyes open at all times because you always want to know if someone is coming for you. As much as you can, you keep your back to the wall. You look no one in the eye. You stay aware that they are there, where they are, and who's connected to them. That's how you stay alive.

"But that night, I kept my eyes closed because I didn't want to see what was there. It's easy enough to see, isn't it? It's easy enough to understand, isn't it? I was afraid to see what was in the room with us. In order to keep that terror away from us both, I prayed to God for safety until the sweat dripped off my forehead so quickly I must have lost a couple of pounds right there, right then.

"Do you want to know why I shave my head, Mr. Hunter? It's not a prison thing. No, here's why—while I was praying, I felt claws, little fingered claws plucking at my hair and trying to pull it out by the roots. Oh, I see by your face you think I was delusional, that perhaps there was a bat in the cell, or maybe more than one. Flying about my thick, demented skull, flapping its wings the way bats do when chasing insects, becoming confused and getting tangled up in my hair. You think that's why I shaved my head bald, so that it could never happen again?"

The sun continued its downward trek across the arc of the afternoon sky. The room filled with a discomforting silence.

"That's not what I was thinking," said Hunter.

But Pastor Mark pressed on as though Hunter were no longer there.

"But eventually—I don't really know how long it took—the thing, the whatever monstrous thing it was, seemed to melt away in the presence of my prayers."

Pastor Mark was looking out and across the expanse of lawn and not really seeing it. He was seeing, Hunter and Moser both knew, an event in his past that still haunted his daylight hours. After a minute, he continued.

"I asked Ozzie to tell no one about what happened that night. He told me he'd kept his eyes wide open in terror while I kept mine closed tight in prayer. He told many people what happened that night and they told still others until what I'd done was famous throughout the prison. Other inmates began approaching me, asking for me to pray for them. You can't imagine what it's like for a Christian in prison. None of you can. We're objects of ridicule. Considered weak. Automatic punks—prey, in the language of the outside world.

"Suddenly, I was left alone. The verbal and physical harassments ceased. It wasn't because I became an overnight evangelical rock star in the prison cells. It happened differently than that. Ozzie, you see, had a friend. A very large friend that inmates and guards both stayed clear of. I never found out what he was in for, but one day Ozzie told me this man was assaulted by five gang members with shivs — knives—who wanted to take him down. He killed all five of them with his bare hands. Apparently, it was caught on camera. It was... gruesome, from what I'm told. I don't know how, but one of the gangs got hold of the video. I never saw it, but it was recapped several times for me.

"How I got left alone was that this big man—who barely spoke to anyone—came up to me after I helped his friend Ozzie. The entire cafeteria went quiet, and the guards went on high alert. Whenever this big man did something, everyone paid attention because somebody always got hurt. I thought I was pretty well dead when I saw that he was walking straight for me. Being noticed is never good in prison. Being singled out can be a death sentence. But he kept coming and my nerves started screaming for me to run for my fool life. I was, however, too scared to move.

"When he finally stopped in front of me and said loud enough for everybody to hear 'thanks for helping my friend,' I thought I was going to pass out. He said nothing more. He just went back to where he was sitting, and that was the last of it. That minor exchange made my life in prison a lot better. As far as the others were concerned, I was under this giant's protection."

Pastor Mark rubbed the back of his neck, and once again stared out the window.

"What happened to Ozzie?" asked Moser.

"He got a back door parole," said the pastor.

"Pardon?"

"He fell down the stairs to the yard and broke his neck."

"For real?" asked Moser.

"A bunch more inmates died mysteriously after that. It wasn't good to kill the big man's friend was the lesson most of us took from that. But a month before he died, Ozzie told me the big man had been receiving visits from a man who seemed to come and go as he pleased around the prison. He'd be seen at night when there was no way to come and go about the cell block.

"I asked Ozzie what he was talking about. I told him that wasn't possible. Somebody was seeing things, that was all. But, of course, that wasn't all. I got requests to bless the cells near where Ozzie's friend was held. I didn't want to go at first. I'm not the exorcist type, not then and less now. Cell blessing seemed somehow hypocritical to me back then. I was saved, I was sure of that, but I wasn't a minister, much less a priest. These men, though, they were desperate. They were hard men, and they were desperate. So how could I refuse them? Would Jesus have refused them? Hunter, I didn't know what the Lord would do. I had a head full of rocks back in that place. I really didn't want to do anything. Just like the night I prayed for Ozzie, I was afraid.

"But I did it. Somehow, the guards were in on it. They let me in, but asked me to bless them in return. One or two of them had seen the dark man, as they called him. I went in that night and blessed both the guards and the entire row of cells in the name of Jesus and begged for his protection. I went straight down the row and the inmates quietly thanked me. These were violent men, unaccustomed to saying thank you to anyone, but that night they did.

"When I came to the last cell in the row, I realized I was at the big man's cell, and I began to shake. I looked down at the hallway floor. I didn't want to see the man in his cell. I was afraid, Hunter. I was at the end of a row of prison cells where convicted murderers cowered in their cells against an imaginary person they called the dark man. Did I really believe in such a thing as I was praying against?

"'Red eyes,' one convict had whispered to me. 'The dark man has red eyes.'

"A demon who came and went through prison walls as though they weren't there. A demon with red eyes. A man or dark figure that some of them called El Diablo. I stood there for the longest time, unable to look up. I stood there, my head hung forward, and I prayed for strength. A man like me, a man who had done what I'd done… I had no right to pray for protection. Even as I had these thoughts, I knew that not only did I have that right, but that the real reason I prayed was that I was terrified. When I looked up, I saw that the big man was standing on the other side of the bars, staring at me, his dark eyes like pools of nothing.

"You want something?" he asked.

"His voice was deep and rough in the darkness, but it was not challenging. It had more of a resigned curiosity.

"'Some men on this block have seen a… a dark man here at night sometimes. They think they're in danger. Maybe you, too.'

"He said nothing for three or four minutes, I think. Prisoners, men like him, have a formidable friendship with both solitude and silence. He was like that. He rarely spoke. And his silence was… heavy… unforgiving.

"'They are afraid of the devil?' he finally asked.

"I could only stutter. 'The devil. El Diablo.' What could I say? I didn't want to admit to myself that it might be the truth.

"'I figured,' he said. 'But the deal's done. He'll be coming soon to take me out of here.'

"'But,' I said. 'You can't. You can't.'

"He went quiet again. We stood for the longest time in complete silence. My mind was locked on the way he said it. Like he said, he'd just bought a pair of socks. My muscles felt locked in place. I couldn't move. The tension held me in place like banded steel. Did this man really believe the devil was coming to set him free? What had been the price?

"'When you get out of here,' he finally said. 'Don't do nothing to put you back in. It was good what did you did for Ozzie, but you can't save everybody. Some people ain't worth saving.'

"'I don't believe that,' I whispered. I could hardly recognize my own voice. It was so hoarse with terror.

"'Don't come back,' he said. 'This place ain't right. He's going to burn it the day after you leave. That was a part of my deal. The day after you leave.'

"He stepped back into the darkness of his cell and disappeared. It was the last I ever saw of him.

"I should have stayed and fought for his soul, Mr. Hunter, but I turned away and walked out as fast as I could, thinking if I looked back something would rip my head right off of my neck."

"Well, shit," said Moser.

"The day after I was set free, the prison burned. Concrete and steel burned like paper. Every person inside died. It shouldn't have been possible, but it happened. You can look it up online and watch some of it on YouTube if you don't believe me."

Rebecca looked both horrified and confused.

"It sounds horrible, Pastor, but what does it have to do with what happened here last night?"

"For one thing, it should explain why it is I can believe your story. For the next part, I'll wait until Hunter here tells us all what happened to him at the Masonic Temple last night."

How, Hunter wondered, did the Reverend know something happened at the Masonic Temple?

After taking a few minutes to get his thoughts in order, Hunter told them his story.

48

Hunter told them about the Empty Chair and its magical unlocking mechanism that opened a passageway between the Detroit Masonic Temple and the town Rebecca's father called Borgo. Outside, the sun was relentlessly sliding away from the oncoming darkness. He could not help but feel that their chances of survival were also sliding down toward hopelessness. He wondered how often his uncle Bartok had sat on the same couch talking with colleagues as the night crept up on them.

"It's hard to describe," he said. "I followed your father through the empty chair gate. He said it was thirty-two steps from side to the other and not to get caught between, because something horrible would happen to me if I got distracted and both doors closed. The way he said it, I would be relegated to worse than oblivion. But as I walked through the darkness, there was a horrible red-black light that filtered through the skin and on the other side, I could see… things moving about in a terrifying aether, where I could hear or feel crackling flames lick against that skin. I'm trying not to be overly dramatic about this, but it was like walking through hell. There were red whips snapping against beings who screamed at the contact. Things that flitted and flew and clawed to get through. I saw impossibly long snakes wrap their bodies around the thin tunnel wall and squeeze. There were crunching noises like something was biting into bone and I kept hearing a howling far away, but it was always getting closer."

He visibly shuddered as he said this last.

"We got it," said Moser. "It was a terrible place to be walking through. Not a place to dawdle."

"Yes," said Hunter. "That describes it."

"Please," said Pastor Mark, "continue."

The thought of telling what happened to Brother Frank Mihaloff in front of his daughter filled Hunter with dread. He looked over at her and hesitated.

"I can take it," she said. "Whatever it is, I can take it."

If only that were true, thought Hunter.

He took a deep breath and told them about his meeting with the creature called Hiram Abiff. As he spoke, he avoided looking at Rebecca. It was too much for him. This will destroy her sanity, he thought. So instead, he stared at Pastor Mark while he re-told the story.

When Hunter was through with his recounting of the events at the Detroit Masonic Temple, Rebecca looked stricken, and Hunter thought she would cry.

Let it out, thought Hunter. Sometimes a good cry cleans the mind, so it's safe to think again.

Instead, she tightened her jaw, looked around at the three men and said, "This creature has possessed my father. I will see him burn in Hell."

"Rebecca," said Pastor Mark, "please. I have more to tell you all."

His voice was stern and tinged with a dark element of dread.

"But—"

"Please," he said again.

"What is it?" asked Moser.

The big Kentuckian leaned forward in his chair with his bandaged hands resting on his knees. He hadn't shaved since the night before, and it gave him the look of a rugged frontiersman.

"I saw you running out of the Masonic lodge," said Pastor Mark. "I was there. I couldn't sleep thinking about what happened to Rebecca, and couldn't shake the fear that it was something to do with her father and Freemasonry. So I drove there and parked a block away, turned off the lights and just sat there looking at that ominous building as if I stared at it long enough, it would reveal its secrets. I was about to leave, Hunter, when I saw you run out the door like the devil was chasing after you."

"Didn't even see you," said Hunter.

"Now I know why you were running. But as you left, I saw a man emerge from the dark shadows of one of the Temple's corners. He was a big man. When he moved into the light a little more to stare after you, I recognized him."

"Wait," said Hunter. "You mean someone was watching me?"

"Yes," said Pastor Mark. "Or maybe he was waiting for you to leave. But I recognized him. The light was poor, but considering the circumstances under which I met him in prison, I will never forget him."

"It was the big man from prison?" asked a shocked Moser.

"The man suborned by the devil?" asked Rebecca.

"The man suborned by a devil," said Pastor Mark. "Yes, it was him. It was Ricci. Older now, but it was definitely him."

"Wait," said Hunter, his voice suddenly like an alarm bell. "What did you say his name was?"

"Ricci."

There was silence in the room as Hunter's face progressed from alarm to fear.

"Not possible. Not possible. Chirac's thug," said Hunter. "Oh, my God, Moser. Mr. Chirac is the Frenchman. The fifth member of the Temple Guardians."

Uncharacteristically, an agitated Moser stood and paced.

"Got to call Kenneth and warn him," he said.

Hunter stood and joined him.

"Now we've got to go back to that other lodge and find out where it is located."

"Why?" asked Moser.

"We have to stop him from coming through into our world. Think about this—if Hiram Abiff has got Mr. Chirac and Ricci helping him, we are all in trouble. There's nothing good can come from anyone who's tied in with that dark man."

Rebecca and the pastor exchanged glances.

"Who," she asked, "is Mr. Chirac?"

"You remember the man I told you came through the ghost box from the other side into the cave beneath Townsend Mountain and butchered Colonel Albert Magnum Hillis near the end of the Civil War?"

A look of horrified realization twisted across Rebecca's face.

****

"I'm going with you," said Rebecca.

"No, you're not," said Hunter.

They'd moved to the kitchen table for coffee and whatever else they could scrounge up.

"Double that," said Moser. "You're injured."

He nodded toward her still bandaged arm and hand.

"So are you," she said, pointing at his bandaged hands.

"Moser's bigger," said Hunter.

"He's what?"

"I mean, he's a soldier. He's got combat experience."

"And you," she asked, "what's your combat experience? You shot and killed your Uncle, is that it?"

Pastor Mark looked up from rummaging through the cupboards and raised an eyebrow toward Hunter.

"Going on four o'clock," said Moser. "We best sort this out and get on with it. Hunter, you got some kind of plan?"

Hunter was still staring at Rebecca, shocked by what she'd said.

"It's what he would have wanted me to do," he told her.

"We were discussing combat readiness," she said, turning a kitchen chair around and sitting down on it, "and I don't think you're up to going back through that tunnel, the Borgo Pass, as you called it. You look scared."

"I am scared," said Hunter, slamming his hand on the kitchen table. "You should be, too. This Hiram Abiff, whatever he is, is awful. I saw him in person, and I'm telling you that if you're not scared, you're crazy. Anybody that can make a six-foot snake come out of somebody's mouth is someone I'm flat out terrified of."

"That's my father you're talking about," she said.

It was like a verbal whip slashing across the table, but Hunter wasn't having any of it. The situation was beyond serious; it was flat our horrifying, and he was tired of being her patsy.

"And that's my uncle you're talking about."

"Slow down, you two," said Moser. "Doesn't help to take each other apart. You got a plan, Hunter?"

Pastor Mark wandered over with a box of Ritz Crackers he'd found in a cabinet.

"A plan for what?"

"For putting a stop to this," said Moser. "If I've got this right, Rebecca's father and Mr. Chirac are going to be bringing this abomination into the Detroit Temple in just a few days. I think once he's here, he will not have any interest in going back. Not when us Freemasons crown him king of the world. With him bringing the cure for cancer and all these other diseases, like you said, Miss Rebecca, I think people would lynch us if we tried to get rid of him after he got here. So, Hunter, however many of us go back through the Borgo Pass to find where he is, are you sure we can get back here—just in case, that is, he ain't from this world?"

Suddenly he felt that Bartok's death had appointed him a lifetime guardian of the sane world, and it wasn't a job he wanted to accept. The others were more qualified than he was to deal with Hiram Abiff. Moser was the guardian of Townsend Mountain, with a military background that went back to his teenage years. He'd probably lied about his age to join up with the Army early. Mark was a pastor, armed with a prayer arsenal and prison education in playing rough. Rebecca towered over the rest of them with her spiritual gifts and was well trained in defending herself from her survivalist father.

Yet they were looking at him, as if he'd know what to do. He thought about that. That's what he now was, the Tyler of the Temple Guardians. The responsibility of protecting Freemasonry from the terrible mistake of accepting Hiram Abiff was now his. But what exactly was Hiram Abiff, and why had he been hiding out from the world for over three thousand years? And why now? Why was he re-entering the normal world now? And Mr. Chirac was the Temple Guardian tasked with bringing back the Blazing Star of Freemasonry? Just what the hell was going on?

"Okay," said Hunter, "to your last question first. I just don't know the answer."

"Gut feel?" asked Moser.

"My gut feeling is that we can get out. But my gut feeling is also that if Hiram Abiff knows we're there snooping around, well, then things are just going to get ugly and uglier. And if that happens, we're in real trouble. And all that assumes we don't run into Mr. Chirac."

"Why?"

It was Pastor Mark who asked the question. Without knowing why, Hunter looked over at Rebecca before answering.

"It's because we don't really know anything about who or what or why Hiram Abiff is. Ghosts I know about—the theory of ghosts, the lore and mythology of ghosts. I know the scientific techniques the best ghost hunters used to monitor paranormal activity. All of it is at least comprehensible because I understand the topic. But with Hiram Abiff, I don't really know what he is. Even Google and Bing know pretty much nothing. They know the role Hiram Abiff has in Blue Lodge Freemasonry rituals, but that's it. There's no credible history about Hiram Abiff. Pastor, there's a lot of bullshit out there about Hiram Abiff—he was the first Freemason, he was the Grandmaster of Freemasonry, et cetera, but that's what it is—pardon the language, it's just bullshit. And there really is no Hiram Abiff in the Bible. That's bullshit, too."

"Do you have to keep swearing?" asked Rebecca. "The scriptures say that—"

"And don't start that, don't even start that," said Hunter. "I'm pissed off enough as it is. This whole thing is insane. That little old man lives in the back bedroom of Hell and made a gigantic snake come out of your father's mouth, Rebecca. I'm scared and I'm smart enough to know it, so just give me a break, will you?"

The sun was edging still lower in the afternoon sky. Hunter felt the overpowering need to go home. This would always be more Bartok's place than his, he knew, but he was already home. He could feel all the secrets and the unfinished business that Bartok had left behind after his death weighing on him. He had barely had time to process his uncle's death after the events at Townsend Mountain, the ghost of the little girl and their dealings with Mr. Chirac. It had been off to Atlanta to recover journals that would supposedly lead them to the Blazing Star of Freemasonry, which, according to Bartok, was a fragment of the crystalline heart from a strange craft lost for tens of thousands of years. But they had failed. Someone had already beaten them to it. Someone named Mr. Emile Chirac. While he and Moser were off following Bartok's paper trail, Mr. Chirac had retrieved the object, whatever it really was. Hunter wished he knew why it was so important. Why was its return so important to the coming of Hiram Abiff?

"You done?" asked Moser.

Hunter took a deep breath, then let it out slowly.

"I'm sorry, Rebecca," he said.

He waited for her to say something.

Finally, she said, "I take you at your word." It came out with difficulty. She added, "And I'm sorry about Bartok."

Hunter nodded and looked over at Pastor Mark.

"This," the pastor said, "is a difficult time for us all. Please continue."

"All right," said Hunter. "The biggest problem is that we just don't know enough, like I said. Not only is there virtually no information extant on who Hiram Abiff is, we also don't know what he is, and we don't have a lot of time to dig out the answers. However, what we can say is that there is black magic involved and demonic forces are at work. One trip through the Borgo Pass, and if a person isn't spellbound like Rebecca's father seems to be, then the demonic involvement is absolutely clear. But if we knew at least where this place called Borgo really was, then maybe we could stop or at least slow down Hiram Abiff's return. All we really have is the journal— wait, Enid, could you please go up to Bartok's study and retrieve the sword case? I left it upstairs. You should all see the journal tucked inside."

"Journal?" asked Rebecca. "What journal?"

"It's called the Confessions of Mr. Hyde, but it will make more sense when you see it. I don't know if everything in it is true or if it's just the imaginings of Robert Louis Stevenson's mind, but it's really the most we have."

"On it," said Moser, and got up and headed out the door and upstairs.

When he was gone, Rebecca stared at Hunter and said, "But we know what's going on. All you have to do is read the Book of Revelations and you'll know, too."

"She's right," said Pastor Mark. "I think you need to read it."

"Already have," said Hunter. "Bartok made me read it ten or twelve times. Drilled it into my head. I remember the story and it just doesn't match what's going on here. I understand what the two of you are getting at, but I'm telling you, something is off with this whole situation."

"Just like the woman's picture on the screen where you couldn't see her face," said Rebecca. "You are spiritually blind."

"Rebecca," cautioned Pastor Mark.

"It's true," said Rebecca. "He's blind to what's occurring, so he can't know what he's fighting. If he doesn't see the truth, he'll get us all killed."

Moser came back with the sword case at that moment and passed it to Hunter.

"You two at it again?" he asked.

Rebecca looked away.

Hunter put the case on the big table, opened it, and pried away the velvet lining. From the inside of the case, he pulled out the journal. His mouth was pressed into a thin line as he handed it over to Rebecca.

"Read it," he said, "and then we'll talk."

With that, he got up and left the room, heading for Bartok's study.

****

The desk was too big and important for him, he thought. He didn't have the gravitas that Bartok did. Hunter made his living debunking the paranormal right until the night Bartok had summoned him to Townsend Mountain to learn the family secrets. When he learned what was hidden beneath the mountain in the giant cave, his life had changed forever. Suddenly, the famous paranormal investigator and debunker had seen the evidence firsthand for ghosts and aliens.

Hell of a night, he thought.

Bartok was the master of esoteric knowledge. He had tried to train Hunter when he was younger, but Hunter just couldn't accept the lessons. There were no such things as ghosts and goblins, witches and sorcerers. Now, with Bartok dead, Hunter was still the pupil, and a pupil who had taken the wrong road in life, researching and debunking the paranormal. He'd made a good living at it and was considered one of the leading ghost hunters in the country. His books weren't best sellers, but they sold well and provided him with a good income. The problem was, there were ghosts and aliens and goblins and witches and probably a lot more and a lot worse out there—like Hiram Abiff and his scarlet woman. And was it possible, as Rebecca believed, that Hiram Abiff could even be the Antichrist?

He'd been sitting in Bartok's chair—his chair now—when his cell phone rang. The number wasn't one he recognized, but he answered anyway.

"Hunter," he said.

"We have to talk," said a familiar voice.

"Who is this?"

"It's me, Ron. Molly's Ron."

Ouch, thought Hunter.

"What can I do for you?" he asked, his voice not quite concealing his irritation.

"I checked out what you told me about Watchmaster Miller—just in case you weren't crazy."

Hunter sat up straighter in the chair. "And?" he asked.

"I can't find him. He's missing. His neighbors haven't seen him in days, he's missed appointments. His Masonic brothers are worried about him. I checked the hospitals, his sister, who is his only remaining relative, and I even checked the funeral homes. Nothing. It's like he's dropped straight off the earth, Hunter. And his mailbox is stuffed full of mail. I'm worried about him. And I can't get hold of Brother Mike Leasing either. That doesn't feel good, either. Can we meet? Truce this time. Sorry about the other night, but well, it was late, and I was tired, and you sounded out of your mind and you just happened to be Molly's ex-boyfriend."

Despite the situation, Hunter managed a small, bitter smile.

"I can work with that," he said.

"When and where?" asked Ron.

"I could actually use someone to cover my back," said Hunter, "while I check something out. I'll have a few friends along with me, including Brother Frank Mihaloff's daughter and her minister. And a friend of my uncle Bartok's. Four of us and you. This will go down around midnight, say eleven o'clock we meet and then go to the Detroit Masonic Temple?"

"Why don't we just meet there?" asked Ron.

"Because I'm not sure it's safe in the parking lot."

****

When Hunter re-entered the kitchen, the change in atmospherics was immediately apparent. Rebecca was still reading or re-reading The Confessions of Mr. Hyde. Pastor Mark was looking up at him with a mixture of sympathy and impending doom, and Moser was now the one most seriously pissed off. Now they knew everything he knew—well, almost everything.

"I just got a call from Molly's new boyfriend," he told them. "He did some checking around and learned that Watchmaster Miller—the old man who Mike Leasing thought was dropped into the pits of Hell when the Temple floors opened up—well, he's totally disappeared and Ron's worried. Mike Leasing's dropped off the planet, too. So, I asked Ron to meet up with us tonight to cover our backs when Moser and I go back through the Borgo Pass to see if we can find out where Hiram is."

"Is he a Brother?" asked Moser.

"Yes, he is."

"Good."

"Maybe," put in Pastor Mark. "If the Temple Guardians are under the influence, so to speak, how do you know other Freemasons aren't?"

It was a good question. How far did the influence, the spellbinding of Hiram Abiff and the witch extend throughout Freemasonry?

The answer was, he thought, that neither he nor anyone else in the world knew. How far and how powerful could a magical spell be? Was there any limit to how much Hiram and the witch could control?

He tried his best to remember what his uncle Bartok taught him about magic, sorcery, and spells. There were rules, he thought. Time limitations, distance limitations and geography limitations. Which were the most important? Was there one single constraint that ruled the others? There were knowledge limitations.

What about the occult symbols that were used? Freaks like Aleister Crowley and his ilk preferred the Egyptian languages and rituals for periods of their career, but then moved on to find others. The more arcane, the better. From the Egyptians to the Tibetans, from the Tibetans to the Mayans. On and on, their search for powerful spells went. Hunter had never considered the implications of this before. The reality of magic was a new concept to him. The idea a person could be spellbound was disturbing.

"Pastor, if we start thinking like that, how do I know that you and Rebecca aren't under his magical influence as well? What about Moser?"

"Bullshit," said Moser. "Sorry, pastor."

The pastor waved the comment away.

Rebecca finally laid the Confessions of Mr. Hyde on the table.

"Do you believe this?" she asked Hunter.

The question surprised him. For once, she didn't seem to be angry with him. She seemed to really mean it.

"I don't know."

"Don't equivocate," she snapped. "Just come out and tell us what you think."

So much for anger control, he thought.

"All right, I think I believe it. My only caveat is that Robert Louis Stevenson was prone to fevered illnesses. The whole thing could be just a hallucination of his when he was sick. And he was known for terrible nightmares. Some of them happened to him while he was awake. He was a writer, we also have to remember. He had a wild and untamed imagination. So, the other explanation might be that this," he pointed at the journal, "could be a draft of a story. Perhaps an early, discarded version of Dr. Jekyll and Mr. Hyde."

"But you don't think so," she pressed.

Hunter struggled with the question. Logic wouldn't help him here.

It was yet another gut call.

"No," he said finally, "I don't think so. I think it explains a lot."

"Good," she said. "I agree. We're dealing with a demonic force. A resurrected man brought back from the dead by a powerful demon. A resurrected man without a soul. Demons may have the power to resurrect the dead, but they have no power to bring back a man's soul. And remember in the Gospel of Luke where it says, 'When an unclean spirit goes out of a man, he goes through dry places, seeking rest; and finding none, he says, 'I will return to my house from which I came.' And when he comes, he finds it swept and put in order. Then he goes and takes with him seven other spirits more wicked than himself, and they enter and dwell there; and the last state of that man is worse than the first.'"

"I thought we agreed no Bible quotes," said Hunter.

"Back from the dead," muttered Moser. "Well, shit."

"I'm not sure Bible quotes or our guns will protect us when we go to Borgo to see where Hiram is. If what the journal says is true, men have tried to kill him before with no luck," said Hunter. "The best we can do is sneak in, find out what we can about where this place really is and then sneak back out."

"God will protect us," said Pastor Mark.

"He hasn't stopped Hiram yet," said Hunter under his breath. "But we have to try. If we don't know where he is, though, I don't know what we can do about stopping him. So, I say we go in, see what we can learn and get out fast. Your father," he said to Rebecca, "said that once a month he goes through the Borgo Pass to meet with him, and since we've done that once, we should be safe, maybe. Nobody but us coming and going. There's no way to be sure, but with the limited amount of time we have left, we have to take the chance."

"I'm going," said Rebecca. "After what I've read, I'm going."

"Me, too," said Pastor Mark.

"You know I'm with you," said Moser.

"We have to be careful to move quickly. Anyone trapped in that portal between two places is toast," said Hunter. "That's one thing your father told us that I believe."

He stopped after he said that and looked up at the ceiling. Rebecca was about to say something more, but Moser held up his hand to stop her. Hunter was thinking. The young man had an idea, and that was what they needed. Hunter had come through for them in their fight against Mr. Chirac and the haint. Moser was hoping for a repeat.

Finally, he asked, "What is it?"

Hunter seemed not to hear him.

"Hey, over here, what is it? You got something?"

"Maybe."

"Well, give, damn it. Sorry Miss Rebecca, Pastor."

Neither paid attention to him. They were looking at Hunter hopefully.

"Maybe. I don't think I buy this idea that your father only goes through there once a month. That just doesn't seem right."

He looked up at the wall clock to check the time. Four o'clock. The afternoon had gone dark, as though a storm were coming. Gray-black clouds huddled over the Detroit River, and Hunter felt a chill go through him like a passing spirit. It was going to be a dark and stormy night, and he wondered if he would ever see daylight again.

"Did you get any holy water?" asked Pastor Mark. "I think we're going to need it."

Hunter looked up to see if he was joking.

"The Catholic church doesn't pass it out for things like this," he said. "I've tried over the years, believe me."

"Got any other spiritual-type weapons?" asked Moser.

"Prayer," said Rebecca.

"There's that," said Hunter. "We could use a lot of that. Pastor, can you bless Yale locks?"

"Are you serious?"

"Yes, I am."

"Well, what in the world for?"

49

"There's something I forgot to tell you," said Hunter.

"Tell me," said Pastor Mark.

Hunter noticed that Pastor Mark didn't show fear. His years in prison might have had something to do with that.

"When we got back to the Detroit Temple through the Borgo Pass, I took one of the spears from the Senior Warden's station, jammed the tip in the small space in the floor near the base of the chair and wedged it in to prevent the chair from opening again in case Hiram or that damned snake was following us. Then I broke the staff and jammed it against the base of the chair, hoping that would help hold it in place."

"And?" said Moser.

"And when I was leaving, I looked inside the Romanesque room to make sure it was still secure. When I had the door half open, I looked through and saw the spear tip shoot up in the air and the last part of the staff break in two. I slammed the door shut and ran for it, as you saw, pastor. I was thinking this time we run a heavy-duty lock through the base of the chair and the floor ring next to it. If you blessed it, maybe it would help."

"Huh," said Pastor Mark. "I'm not sure it works that way, but under the circumstances, I'll try it."

"Let me get this straight," said Moser. "You wedged that spear point in there good. When you checked back to see if it was still there, you saw it shoot up like a bottle rocket. So that gate is open now? That means that thing Hiram Abiff can come dancing through if it wants to?"

"I was afraid to go back in and hammer it into place," said Hunter. His cheeks colored when he said it, and he looked away. "I just slammed the lodge room door closed, locked it, and ran for my car. Detroit's bad enough at night, but what I saw in the Borgo Pass and Borgo itself were a lot worse. My legs took off running so fast it was like they were on a different circuit that bypassed my brain entirely."

"At least you got my father out alive," said Rebecca.

It was hard to tell if she was thanking him or being sarcastic. But her father was her father. Family was family, spellbound or not. It was hard for Ian to remember what it was like when he first realized his uncle Bartok really was infected with alien fluids, and was changing right before his eyes. There was the moment he realized Bartok was really gone, that his body looked the same, but Bartok, Master of the Esoteric Arts, was somewhere else. His body was little more than a shell.

"What?" asked Rebecca.

"Nothing."

"Tell her," said Moser.

The old Kentuckian kept flexing his fingers open, then closed. Hunter knew that meant he was afraid they'd scab up and get stiff, which was not good for a shooter. Moser was tough enough to handle the pain and the slippery fresh blood when the scabs cracked. He had a lot of field experience. It was the fact that Brother Mihaloff was… contaminated that bothered him. Same as it bothered Hunter.

"It's not your father's fault," Hunter said carefully.

"No?" said Rebecca as she stood abruptly from the table. "It's all this Masonic esoteric occult nonsense that put him in a position to be spellbound. Do you honestly think if he had not been involved in Freemasonry that he would still have been exposed to this Hiram Abiff creature? Do you?"

There was a certain truth to what she said. From its relatively straightforward beginning as a craft of stonemasons, Freemasonry had been transformed into something entirely different. Its rituals had attracted occultists of all stripes and denominations from McGregor

Mathers, to Aleister Crowley, to Manley Hall, and other crackpots. Most Masons did not understand the infiltration of occultists into their ranks. Rituals, thought Hunter, it was the damn rituals that drew them. What was it about a ritual that was such a draw? And what type of people felt the need to dress up and act out rituals?

"I think he did not understand what he was getting into. As I understand it, there are only five or six Freemasons in a generation that know about Hiram. And from what I've seen of his power, I can't imagine anyone being able to stand up against him."

Rebecca whirled to look down on her pastor.

"Do you see why I say he shouldn't go? He has gifted the enemy—our enemy—by accepting his power. He will get us all killed, or worse."

The kitchen and dining area, large though it was, suddenly seemed tiny. Hunter was on his feet, too, hands on the table, face red and leaning forward.

"It's called logic, Rebecca," he shouted. "L-O-G-I-C. I'm telling you that your father had no way of knowing what Hiram Abiff was. What's so hard to grasp about that? Why does he have to be guilty? Sure, we have to stop Hiram Abiff and the witch, but we also have to save your father and probably Brothers Kaufmann and Cook. And Pastor Mark is right—we don't know how many others are affected. But if we stop Hiram Abiff, I think it will break the spell."

"You see what I mean?" Rebecca shouted back. "You think it will? Based on what? Isn't it more logical that destroying Hiram will break the spell?"

"Yeah, okay," said Hunter thoughtfully, all the anger drained away at the thought. He turned his head to look out over the river. He rubbed his hand over the two-day-old bristle that covered his chin. His newfound fear of Hiram Abiff had blocked the danger posed by the witch. "Who is this witch?" he asked. "Really?"

"Pastor Mark," said Moser. "Something I have to show you outside. Just thought of it."

Moser stood slowly, twisting the kinks out of his neck as he did so.

"What is it?" asked the pastor.

"Easier to show you."

"Okay. You two okay without us?"

He felt Moser's fingers dig into his bicep, then allowed himself to be led away.

"Oh," he said.

****

"Well," said Hunter, "that was convenient."

The kitchen clock read five-thirty. Outside, the light was leaving, and the darkness was moving in. It was happening while they sat and discussed what was going on, what to do and thought about why it had to be them, to stave off the threat of Hiram Abiff. And he wondered what exactly was the threat Hiram Abiff posed. The coming of the Apocalypse? That worked if you were Christian, but if you weren't, well then, what was there really to fear?

"Rebecca—" he started.

"I do not accept your leadership," she said. "I just can't. I won't be led into battle by an unbeliever. Surely you can see that?"

"This is such bullshit," said Hunter. "And don't tell me not to swear. I'm tired of all this. Whatever gave you the idea that I want to be the leader of this little group? I'd rather we call in the Pope or Mother Teresa or..."

"She's dead."

"What? Who?"

"Mother Teresa is dead. I'd think you'd know that."

"No, I thought she was still alive. When did she die? Wait—never mind. The point is, I don't want to lead anybody. Moser and me—"

"Moser and I," she put in. "You can't even keep your grammar straight. Are you always like this under stress? How are you going to keep it together the next time you face Hiram Abiff?"

It was the disdain with which she stared at him that offended him the most. Who was she to judge him?

"I'm the guy who..." he said, waving his arms at the house about him, "who owns this place."

Rebecca crossed her arms over her chest, then asked him, "Do you really feel you earned it?"

"This is so—you are so—I'm not the problem here."

"Then who is? Are you calling me the problem?"

"I'm calling Hiram Abiff the problem. Who do you think I'm calling the problem? And you called him the problem first."

"Nothing. I'm going to see Moser and Pastor Mark. They have a clue."

She turned and headed for the front door. Her dark hair swung behind her as she walked away. He would never understand why women got so angry at him. Molly was the same way. She talked to him like he was clueless or doing something deliberately stupid. He just didn't get it. Why didn't they just tell him what they were thinking? How could they communicate without talking? Hunter just didn't get their innuendos at all.

If he hadn't taken over as Tyler for Bartok, he wouldn't be involved in this whole mess. Now they had to deal with both Mr. Chirac and Hiram Abiff.

On an impulse, he called down the hallway after Rebecca, "What was that supposed to mean?"

Instead of an answer, he heard the door slam shut behind her.

Beautiful women, he thought, were not always nice. With a nod to the inevitable, he picked his Colt off the table, slid it into his shoulder holster, and headed up to Bartok's study. In the back of his mind, he was halfway hoping the ward stone would protect him from Rebecca's anger. He had always thought of Christian women as providing first aid to wounded puppies and feeding the poor. It never occurred to him they could be so down and out prissy. He suddenly remembered Molly and how upset she'd been with him. Maybe, he thought, I'm the problem. Maybe I get so wrapped up in this esoteric bullshit that I don't pay enough attention to the people standing right in front of me. Maybe if I did that, Molly would still be with me.

He wrestled with those thoughts for a minute, but let it go when he wondered for the first time how the two empty chairs—one in the Romanesque Room in the Detroit Temple and the other in the Borgo Temple — communicated with each other. How did one chair know when the other was opening? The method wasn't mechanical or electrical, that was for damned sure. It had to be a magical connection. There must be something within the chairs themselves, some kind of a magical device that connected them. He'd look for that tonight.

Tomorrow, he'd call Molly and ask if she'd do him one last favor by researching magical connections. It would be hard seeing Ron later tonight. Something peculiar about having him along—Ron being her new boyfriend and all, but the man seemed all right. Maybe everything was for the best. Maybe they'd end up being friends.

50

"Can I help you?" asked Ron.

It was an hour past dusk, but the streetlights in Molly's neighborhood had not come on. The street was instead engulfed in a rich, moonless dark. In the vestibule light cast by the open front door onto the porch, Ron could see a beautiful woman with long, black hair standing on the front porch. She wore a high-collared coat.

"I'm here to see Molly. Is she home?"

Her voice was rich and seductive. A woman, thought Ron, who was used to getting her way. But Molly was in the back bedroom of the house getting dressed. She was getting ready to attend an informal gathering of library researchers, who met twice a month at a local burger and beer joint.

"She is, but she's getting ready to go out, so she won't be long. Can I tell her your name?"

"Eva Morgan. I'm here to pick up some research she has for Mr. Hunter. I won't take up much of her time."

"Just a minute while I go tell her you're here. Would you care to come inside?"

"Thank you so very much."

Ron could not help but watch her mouth as it formed the words. She had full lips painted bright red, a model's wide eyes, strong cheekbones and a delicate chin. Her perfume was a rich, heady aroma that made him feel slightly dizzy. Eurasian, thought Ron without meaning to. She's the best of both worlds. He saw her glance at the pistol tucked into his shoulder holster, and then she arched an eyebrow.

"Sorry," he said. "I'm a cop. Just got off duty. Excuse me. Have a seat, will you? TV remote is on the couch. Watch whatever you want. I'll go get her."

He looked at his watch and saw that he had plenty of time to make it to Hunter's house.

"I won't be a minute," he said and headed to the back of the house to tell Molly she had company.

He still remembered the details of her beautiful face and the strange aroma of her perfume when he almost plowed straight into Molly.

"Hey," said Molly. "You look like you're walking on autopilot."

Ron stopped, blinked, and then shook his head. He felt like he did when he first got out of bed.

"I was thinking," he said. "No, maybe my blood sugar is low."

"You need something to eat."

"Just trying to remember something. My brain feels kind of fuzzy… wait, I know what it is. Your friend Eva is here to pick up some research you did for her."

"Who?"

"Eva… Morgan."

"Dear, I don't know anyone named Eva Morgan."

"I let her in to wait for you," said Ron.

"Why did you do that? She's here now? Where?"

"I left her in the living room. She said she was your friend."

Molly straightened her blue denim shirt, checked herself out in the hallway mirror and then headed toward the living room, building up a head of steam. She didn't know anyone named Eva Morgan.

Behind her, Ron said in a thick voice, "Wait for me." When he said it, it had that don't leave me here alone sound to it, which was strange because she had never seen Ron afraid of anything. He was missing the fear gene.

As she got near the bend in the hallway leading to the living room, lights in the house went out and she stopped where she was.

"What the hell?" she said.

Her voice came out thin and whispery.

"Ron, are you there?"

"Right behind you."

She barely controlled the urge to scream when he laid his hand on her shoulder.

"Just a sec," he said.

The sudden, soft blue glow of his phone seemed too bright. She saw his thumb slide across the screen as he activated his flashlight app. The LED beam lit the hallway in a little white flare of light. The house was eerily quiet. Molly felt suddenly vulnerable.

"Streetlights were out," said Ron. "Maybe a downed wire somewhere."

Being in the dark had never bothered Molly. Her parents had lived in a part of northern Michigan where the electricity was notoriously unreliable. Whenever the power went out, her mother had a seemingly unending supply of candles. In the wintertime, they had a supply of wood for the fireplace. Power outages rarely bothered her, but this one did. There was the faint odor of drying herbs in the air.

"Maybe," she said, and then remembered that someone named Eva Morgan was supposed to be waiting for her in the living room.

"Come on, follow me," said Ron and he held the light from his cell phone up like a torch in front of his face as he walked by her. He stopped when he reached the corner, and, to her surprise, turned off the phone light.

A faint scarlet glow spilled from the living room into the hallway now.

"What is it?" she asked when she came up behind him.

When Ron didn't answer, she slid past him to look down the remaining short hallway into the living room. Sitting on her couch with her legs crossed was a woman wearing a high-necked black and scarlet opera cape. Molly walked the short distance to the living room and heard Ron behind her. The effulgent scarlet light came from everywhere and nowhere. It made no sense.

"Who are you and why are you here?" she asked the woman.

She felt an occult energy pulse the room like an astral strobe light.

"You must be Molly," said the stranger, rising from the couch.

She smiled, but did not extend her hand. Molly thought that she did not need to. She knew who was the predator and who was the prey. The rustling of her high-collared cape and the eerie scarlet light surrounding her caused Molly to think of a Tarot card priestess she had seen once when browsing through New Age bookstores with Hunter.

"I don't know you."

Molly was right to the point.

"I work with Ian Hunter. He sent me to pick up the journal you discovered."

Eva smiled the most insincere smile Molly had ever seen in her life. It was as though it really didn't matter what she said. She would get what she came to get with little effort. So, whoever this woman was, she was certain Ian Hunter hadn't sent her. She wasn't Hunter's type.

"Ron, are you listening to me?"

She turned to see Ron staring straight ahead, his eyes fixed on the woman. Getting more irritated and spooked by the minute, Molly held her hand up before his face and snapped her fingers just two inches in front of his line of sight.

"What's with you?" she asked when he didn't respond.

"He can't hear you," said the woman. "You and I are the only two important people in this room."

Something in the woman's tone caused Molly to shiver. She wished again that Hunter was with her. The temperature in the room dropped.

"Look at me when I'm speaking to you," snapped the woman.

But Molly was afraid to turn around. The sight of Ron transfixed, like he was under some kind of spell, terrified her.

"I said look at me," she hissed.

Molly shook her head from side to side. Suddenly, the scarlet light coalesced around her like red-hot steel bands, pressing her arms tight against her sides. She was lifted straight up in the air and spun viciously around to face in the woman's direction. Molly screamed in pain and terror. "Help me," she screamed at Ron, but he continued to stare zombie-like at the woman that Molly now knew was not a woman.

"Please," said Molly in a choked voice. "What do you want? Just tell me."

Eva Morgan perched on the couch arm and looked up at her.

"I want the volume titled The Confessions of Mr. Hyde, Molly. Although, I will also take any other writings you may have collected for Mr. Hunter relating to Hiram Abiff."

"Who?"

After a moment's thought, while Molly hung in the air and whimpered, Eva Morgan got up from the couch and walked over to where Ron stood. Molly tried not to watch, but couldn't help herself. The scarlet bands cut off her circulation, slowing the flow of blood to her head. They also compressed her ribs, making it difficult to breathe. Her fear of this woman and what she could do was making it hard for her to think. When Eva Morgan opened her mouth and licked Ron's cheek with a long, red and black forked tongue, the contents of Molly's stomach seemed to explode upward, then shoot out her mouth spraying vomit across the coffee table and carpet. She felt like she was going to black out, but instead, she dry-heaved. The smell of vomit was overpowering. She couldn't lift her arms or free her hands to wipe it away from her lips and chin because the bands of scarlet light wrapped around her like a boa constrictor.

"What a lying, foul creature you are," hissed Eva. "I could grow to like you, but if you don't tell me where the journal is, I will strip your skin and pour salt on the raw flesh beneath."

"I can't breathe," coughed Molly. "Please."

Eva lifted a hand, and the pressure from the scarlet energy bands lessened slightly. Molly drew in quick, ragged rasps of breath.

"Kitchen table," she gasped.

While Molly struggled painfully to breathe, Eva walked past Ron, who stood still as a wax figure, and into the kitchen. After a few moments, she returned with a sheaf of papers in her hands.

"Is this everything? Tell me truly, sister, if you wish to live. These are not the Confessions of Mr. Hyde. They are photocopies from a diary instead."

Molly, her vision fading, nodded her head.

"Yes. Yes, that's all."

With a slight wave of her hand, Eva untangled the magical bands and Molly dropped to the floor and lay there gasping next to Ron's still figure.

Eva looked back at Molly and Ron.

"I will not harm you further," she said.

A stunned Molly looked back at her and managed, "Thank you."

"But they will."

Eva Morgan stepped out onto the front porch, pulling the screen door open wide.

There was nothing for Molly to see for a moment, and then the first horned goblins squeezed through the door. She screamed and turned away. The first thing she saw was Ron's pistol at eye level. She stood, undid the protective strap that held the pistol in place, and yanked it free. With a quick turn, she faced the creature, flipped the safety and pulled the trigger while aiming at its massive head. Instantly one of its rheumy, yellow-green eyes exploded into a pulpy mass. Its massive, clawed hands swung up to cover the eye socket while it howled in rage. Molly pulled the trigger again and shot it in the throat twice, thankful for every hour she'd spent at the range. The wire-haired creature spun in place, gripping its throat to staunch the flow of fluids leaking from its neck. She pulled the trigger again and shot it in the chest just as another of the beasts shoved it aside and charged full speed at her.

In a panic, she swung her gun arm back to deal with the second threat, but was not quick enough. Its wide-open jaws snapped closed with incredible speed and force around her forearm, severing it. As Molly screamed, the beast leaped at her and bit again, this time biting off most of her left thigh, sending her spinning into Ron, who fell into the corner of the hallway wall and split his scalp open with a rush of blood. But he didn't feel the pain because Molly's screams ripped through his re-awakening mind. He struggled back to his feet, no longer under the witch's spell, but still disoriented. Blood poured down his forehead, blurring his sight, but what he could see overloaded his brain with horror, revulsion and an adrenaline rush more powerful than anything he had felt in his entire life. Automatically, he reached for his pistol, but couldn't find it. Molly was lying in a pool of blood with a hulking, a hairy beast chewing on her neck and shaking her like dogs do to a rat.

He swung his head around looking for his weapon, but a horned, clawed hand ripped across his face, ripping away skin and cartilage and leaving a bloody, pulped mess in its wake.

He was dead before the feeding began.

Eva Morgan stood in the doorway, tapping the papers she held in one hand against the other as she watched.

Hungry, she thought. Goblins are always hungry.

When the feeding was done and her creatures were back with her standing on the front lawn, Eva extended her hand and a whirling mass of violet fire shot across the yard and blasted through the living room window. As the fireball ignited and the house burst into flames, Eva Morgan opened a portal for her and her remaining creatures to return to Borgo.

51

"Got a minute?"

It was Pastor Mark, standing in the doorway to Bartok's study. It occurred to Hunter that Pastor Mark was a rough-looking man. He must have weighed two hundred and fifty pounds if he was an ounce, and most of that looked like a weightlifter's muscle. A good man, thought Hunter, to have on your side in a fight. What was it that this man had done to be sent to a prison where Mr. Chirac's thug Ricci was an inmate? Murder? If it was something that bad, how could he have gone from murderer to being a minister? He was about to ask when he realized he hadn't answered the pastor's question.

"Sure. Come on in."

"Nice desk."

"Thanks, but it's Bartok's desk. I just inherited everything he owned. Funny, before the will was read, I never even considered that I'd be in it."

"Why not?"

"Long story," said Hunter, waving off the topic. "But you had something you wanted to talk about?"

"Rebecca. We need to talk about Rebecca."

"I don't know what it is about me that seems to set her off, Pastor. Why is she always mad at me? Is it because I brought her here and she was attacked? If that's it, then I've already apologized to her more times than I did to my ex-girlfriend."

Pastor Mark looked at him for a long time. So long that Hunter felt uncomfortable.

"You need to slow down a bit," said the pastor. "This will be complicated, and I think you will only get it if you listen carefully. You up for that?"

Hunter swiveled in the big leather chair and looked outside and up at the sky.

"It's headed toward dark," he said. "I'm worried we're running out of time."

And he meant it.

"Better than going forward with unresolved issues that come back to split us apart when we need each other the most, and believe me, Hunter, we need Rebecca."

"I'm afraid for her," said Hunter. "I don't want anything to happen to her or you either, for that matter. You're both innocent bystanders."

The pastor grinned at him.

"Really? Innocent? I'm an ex-con, Hunter. A lot of us will tell you we were innocent, or that we were set up, but not all of us, and I'm one of those. I deserved what I got."

"I mean you don't have to get involved any further—either one of you. What I saw happen to Rebecca last night was evil beyond anything I've thought possible. I-I really thought we would lose her. She may not like me, but I couldn't live with either of you being hurt. This doesn't have to be your fight. It's bad enough Moser and I are in it."

Hunter had to look away from the pastor, and again his eyes went to the gradually darkening sky outside. Midnight was when he and Moser would hit the Borgo Pass. They'd go in armed with silenced weapons, leaving the pastor and Rebecca behind. It was bad to split up, he thought, but somebody had to stay behind that knew what was going on in case he and Moser didn't make it back.

"Pay attention to me," snapped Pastor Mark, and the tone of his voice brought Hunter back.

"What?"

"You're acting like an idiot. Rebecca is a better shot than you, one handed or not. And this is her fight, not just because of her father, but because of the spiritual forces we're fighting here. I know you're the big-time ghost hunter, but listen to me, Hunter, this goes way beyond ghosts. You act like the Antichrist is just another tormented spirit. It's not. Maybe you've watched too much TV to be impressed by the end of the world, but I hope not.

"Video games, movies, graphic novels and most other media have dumbed us all down, my friend, and I'm not preaching to you. I'm not trying to convert you. What I'm really trying to do is tell you that what's coming is absolutely horrifying, and the Antichrist is the main attraction. What's coming is horrifying death and destruction, and you are just not equipped to fight it. That's why Rebecca and I will go through what you call the Borgo Pass. You and Moser will stay behind and guard the Empty Chair and defend us if something tries to follow us back through when we return."

Hunter stiffened his back and stared at the minister. Who the hell was he to say where he could and could not go?

"I will not. I'm the Tyler of the Temple Guardians now. I'm the one responsible for making this right."

"And who confirmed you as the Tyler?"

"Rebecca's father," said Hunter, feeling like he'd won the exchange.

"The one with the big black snake crawling out of his mouth?"

There was no response adequate to answer that, so Hunter put his hands down on the desk and breathed out a prolonged sigh.

"No, don't say anything yet—just listen," said the pastor. "You feel Rebecca is angry at you?"

"I know she is," said Hunter. "Her disdain for me radiates off her in waves."

"Don't make me get up and punch you in the head. You just don't know enough to understand what's going on with her. She was engaged once, Hunter, to a man who looked like your twin. I kid you not. He would be the same age as you now if he'd lived that long."

"Pardon?"

"Rebecca has to do this. She's the one who knows, really knows, what we're fighting. She's seen him in her visions. Do you remember me telling you about the time she confided her visions to me, and I sent her packing to a psychiatrist to get medications? Well, my response caused her to dismiss the vision she'd had about stopping her fiancé from going to Detroit that night. That will weigh on my conscience for the rest of my life.

"He was stabbed in Detroit that very night. A man on a street corner waved him down. Looked to be lost and poor and confused. Her fiancé—Austen, I think—pulled the car over to the curb and rolled down his window. He asked if the man needed help. You can guess where this is going, can't you? Man on the sidewalk said he was lost and could Austen please help him with directions. In Detroit. Rebecca's fiancé, a born again Christian who had very much spent his life ministering to the poor, got out of his car and went to the man to offer his help. He even took out his wallet to give him money. While he did that, the man stabbed him two times in the stomach, and when Austen fell forward, the guy cut his throat. He took off with the wallet but left the car running and ran away on foot. Again, I tell you are close to being his identical twin. Do you understand what I'm telling you? Somewhere inside her, Rebecca does not want to see her fiancé killed twice."

"But I'm not her fiancé," said Hunter irritably.

"You're too smart a man to answer like that," said the pastor. "That's not all there is to it. Last night she saw in a dream that if either you or Moser enter that hideous tunnel again that you both will die."

"Look, I'm sorry her dead fiancé is my doppelgänger—or was my doppelgänger—but I can't stay out of this. And I don't believe in dreams or visions. I'm the Tyler of the Temple Guardians. Bartok expected me to follow in his footsteps and take care of this."

"So?"

"What do you mean, so? I've got a responsibility to follow this through. Not only to Bartok, but to the rest of the world, too. You haven't seen this creature, this Hiram Abiff. I have. I've felt the danger, seen the evil."

"What did you do to Mr. Chirac, Hunter?"

"Do? You mean the switch with the bones and the madstone?"

"No, I mean, did you and Mr. Moser take him on and finish him? Or were you afraid?"

A minute passed without a response from Hunter. The two men eyed each other, neither willing to back down and break the silence.

But before the pastor could continue, he put in, "Look, you haven't met Mr. Chirac. Neither have me nor Moser. All we have to go on is what Granny and Ashley Hillis told us. We can't find any information anywhere about him except in the journals of Bradley Hunter, one of my ancestors."

"And?"

"And according to Granny Hillis, Mr. Chirac is a demon, returned to the world with a physical body. Neither Moser nor I even know what he looks like, and I really don't want to take on someone she thought was a demon unless we know how to take it down. Maybe an exorcism would do the job, but we don't even know where he is. Moser and I drove to check out the place—or reconnoiter, as Moser calls it—and his entire street was no longer there. He lived on 666 Blood Road, and there's never been a road named Blood Road in that area. And the 666... later we took Ashley and Kenneth—he is a cousin of Moser—and went looking everywhere we could to find the place. We followed Ashley's directions, but the street just wasn't there. So not only had Mr. Chirac vanished, but so did his entire house and the street he lived on. So, if you think Moser and me are chickenshits, you're welcome to that opinion."

There was really no way he could explain the twin horrors of Magnum Hillis and Mr. Chirac. How could he ever hope that the pastor would believe him without seeing for himself the horrors that lurked beneath Townsend Mountain? The way he was looking at him, Hunter doubted that Pastor Mark believed what he just said. And Mr. Chirac was almost impossible to explain.

Finally, Pastor Mark said, "You really don't believe in demons, do you, Mr. Hunter? That's why you haven't taken on Mr. Chirac. You say you don't know what he is, and because of that, you and Moser haven't made a move on him. Is that about it?"

Hunter couldn't bring himself to say it. He just nodded. But before the pastor could continue, he said, "You've never seen Mr. Chirac. Moser and I haven't, either, but Ashley Hillis told me enough to scare the hell out of me."

"You don't really believe that, do you? I think you're afraid to recognize what he is. And that's why you have to stay out of this one, Hunter. From everything Moser has told me about what happened with the events at Townsend Mountain and what followed, you took two decisive actions that were instrumental in both of you staying alive. First, you shot your uncle when he turned into something... monstrous. Second, you figured out a very clever way for Ashley Hillis to return the madstone to Mr. Chirac without him being able to use it.

"So, you can shoot when it's necessary and you have a very inventive brain. Neither of those two things gives you the background to deal with the dark forces surrounding Hiram. Nothing in your engineering bag of tricks will help you fight him. This is a spiritual problem. Be on the side of God to join the fight. Demons on one side, those of God on the other. Unbelievers on one side, believers on the other. That's what you have to recognize to be in this fight."

"That's what I've got a Colt for," Hunter said, pointing his chin at his holster.

"And that," said Rebecca from the doorway, "is precisely why you can't go into the Borgo Pass again."

****

Neither Hunter nor Pastor Mark had heard her approach. Moser was standing behind her, looking straight over her head. Rebecca had a Bible tucked in the crook of one arm and what looked a .38 revolver in a pancake holster on her opposite hip. It was an oddly sexual pose that, for a moment, took Hunter's mind off the matter of Hiram Abiff.

"This is not a physical battle, Hunter," she added. "It doesn't matter how good a shot you are or how smart you are. We're dealing with spiritual evil here, and the only thing that counts is faith in the Lord. Buddha can't help you, science can't help you and Allah cannot help you. Only Jesus can."

Hunter covered his face with his hands and shook his head. Rebecca Mihaloff would drive him crazy. He was about to tell her to keep her religion to herself when he felt a buzz in his pocket. He took out his phone and saw that he had a text message from Molly. He'd thought they were through the last time he'd seen her and Ron, so he wondered what she was texting him for. He thumbed the phone's screen to life to see what she wanted.

He did his best to ignore Rebecca. The text message and attachment made that easy. He felt the blood drain from his face. Finally, he understood the mystery behind what had happened to Brother Mike Leasing. Rebecca droned on in the background as though he was paying attention to her.

"I know this is hard for you to hear," she was saying. "I know it's not what you want to hear, but it's the only truth that will literally save you, Mr. Hunter. I'm not trying to proselytize you, I'm trying to keep you intact and alive. This is spiritual warfare, and you're just not equipped for it. Can you understand that?"

"Moser?" asked Hunter, ignoring her completely.

"Your call," said Moser. "But I got a feeling about this. I think she's right. Been weighing on me and I don't like it. Aliens and screaming ghosts is one thing. I think you and I are up to that if we have to be, but evil like this is purely a different matter. Wherever this town of Borgo is, I don't think either you or me are the right ones to go in. Don't get me wrong, I think Rebecca here and the pastor going in is purely stupid, too. I think we should just take an ax and knock that chair-gate to pieces and burn them. That's what I think. You?"

Hunter looked up from his phone and saw Rebecca staring at him with her arms folded across her chest. He noticed for the first time that she had her rich brown hair pulled back into a ponytail. Such a beautiful woman, he thought. Yet such a stern face. He used to think some religious people were perennially grim-faced because of the Heaven or Hell thing. But seeing the concern in her face—concern for him—he wondered if it was because they knew so much and were afraid for so many. No matter, really, because the text Molly had sent him changed everything.

"I'll stay and guard your exit," said Hunter to Rebecca as he read it. "What about you, old man?"

The attachment in Molly's text message contained eight pages of typewritten text she'd apparently shot pictures of with her phone and a preface that gave him the key points. What is said gave him acid indigestion. He looked at Moser, who was fuming at the idea of playing rear guard while Rebecca and Pastor Mark did their scouting for them.

"I'm tired of talking about this stuff so much, but I'm staying with you. Rebecca and the pastor here will go in for us. I got that. I don't like it, but, like I said, I'm tired of talking. Let's just get to it."

"A good choice, Mr. Moser," said Rebecca.

"I don't know about good, but let's get moving."

"Ron will be here shortly," said Hunter. "What about him?"

This time, it was Pastor Mark who spoke up.

"He must stay with you and Moser. Only Rebecca and I will go in. We know more about what we're going to be up against."

"All right, but there's something you should know first. While we were talking, I got a text from Molly. She sent me a scanned copy of a short diary kept by Charles Stanley Jones."

"Who is that?" demanded Rebecca.

"He was, for a time, second in command to Aleister Crowley. It's brief, but in it he tells the story of an older man with glowing blue eyes that came to visit him one night, back in 1919."

"The Aleister Crowley?" asked Pastor Mark.

"Yes, the Aleister Crowley. It seems he was supposed to be meeting with a man representing Scottish Rite Freemasonry regarding Crowley's efforts to merge his organization with theirs. Some kind of trade that I don't exactly understand. But I think you should read it. I've gone through the bullet points Molly included with the text, which give the broad overview of what happened, but you should read this for yourselves. It's the key to what happened to Mike Leasing and Watchmaster Miller. And it shows some of what Hiram Abiff is capable of—but from the other manuscript that Bartok left us, we get an even clearer picture of what he's capable of doing."

There was an apprehensive silence around the room as he handed his phone to Rebecca.

Twenty minutes later, the others had finished reading the file Molly had sent him. Moser's face was tight with anger. Pastor Mark shook his head in frustration. Only Rebecca seemed to take it in stride. Hunter was having a hard time figuring her out. She was a tough, well-educated woman whose moods seemed to cycle between wild west confrontational and level-headed.

"Did you see any of what Jones writes about in your... dreams or visions or whatever?" he asked.

She didn't like the question; he could see that by the way she pressed her lips together and the way she narrowed her eyes.

"I'm not a psychic, Hunter. I don't interpret dreams, read the future in Tarot cards or do water dousing. But I will tell you this—when my father introduces Hiram Abiff to all the world, with the cure for cancer and other diseases as a gift, almost everybody will buy into him as they applaud him as the new leader of humanity. They will hang on his every word. He will perform miracles and signs for them. They will worship him and then he will drown us all in rivers of blood."

"You don't get invited to a lot of parties, do you?" said Hunter.

"I do not."

"Sorry. Look, I'm not trying to upset you, it's just that I know little about what you experienced. I was hoping to learn more about Hiram Abiff if you had experienced a… vision, or whatever happens to you."

It wasn't true. It still irritated him that the sudden shift in their relationship had occurred almost without warning. She was now the expert. He was the one feeling his way around in the dark. And outside, the edge of night was at hand. Hunter didn't have to swivel his chair and look out the window behind him. After the events at Townsend Mountain, he could feel the approach of night the way animals sensed predators were stalking them. Something dark and powerful and without mercy.

"It doesn't work that way," she said. "I only see what the Lord wants me to see."

"Can we get down to it now?" asked Moser. "What are you taking in with you, Miss Rebecca?"

"Two silenced .38 revolvers and plenty of ammunition. Shoulder slung automatic rifle. Headlamps and back up flashlights. And my phone. Pastor Mark, how about you? Do you have a choice of weapons?"

The pastor took a deep breath before he said, "I've done time, Rebecca. I can't carry a weapon."

"That's crazy," said Hunter. "You've not seen him. You can't go in unarmed. And Rebecca, I'd give the pastor an automatic rifle, too. Hell, if you can find a couple of grenades, I'd take them, too."

Rebecca gave him a grim smile.

"Got that covered," she said.

Hunter winced.

"I can't do that," said Pastor Mark. "I just can't. If I'm caught with weapons, whether it's in Detroit or Borgo—wherever that is—I'll be sent back to prison."

"Miss Rebecca," said Moser, "why don't you at least pack an extra handgun for him? Then, if things go south, you can hand it off to the pastor."

"Good idea, Mr. Moser. Let's start packing. And Hunter, can you draw us the layout of the Borgo Temple?"

"I can do better than that. The Detroit Masonic Temple has a website with 3D views of each of the lodge rooms. The Borgo Temple is laid out exactly the same as the Romanesque Room. But is there anything else you want me and Moser to do? I don't know about Moser here, but I'm starting to feel like I'm dead weight."

"Think of a way," she said with some bitterness, "to save my father."

"I'll try," he said, although he did not understand how to free Brother Mihaloff from the spell the witch had him under.

"And Hunter?"

"Yes?"

"Pray for us, will you?"

"I don't know how," said Hunter.

It bothered him to say it. But it would have bothered him to leave it unsaid.

"You asked if I'd dreamed about Hiram Abiff?" she said in a tense voice.

"Yes?"

"Sometimes they are from a long time ago."

He looked at her. He didn't understand.

So, she told him about one of her dreams.

52

The Sea of Galilee, A.D. 36

Ignoring the hot but indifferent sun, Hiram Abiff looked straight ahead as he walked to the edge of the sea and continued briskly, confident of his ability to walk on water this time. When his foot sunk beneath the icy touch of the surface to plant itself firmly on the sandy bottom, he closed his eyes and concentrated as he walked forward.

Rise, he thought. I am the master of this world and I do what I will.

The water rose to his knees, his thighs, his groin and his waist, but he kept going.

I am the master of this world and I do what I will.

It was lapping at his chin when he screamed out his frustration, shook his fists against the sky, then turned around and walked, dripping wet, back to the shore. From somewhere off to his right, he heard a pack of wild dogs yipping, probably fighting one another over a kill. Like me, he thought, they fight over the dead. He walked twenty paces from the water's edge and found a flat, dry spot to sit down.

It was his fourteenth aborted attempt. He was convinced that it was a matter of focus. If the Galilean had done it, he could do it. Focus. It had to be focus. Many had claimed to know the secret, but none had accomplished the feat. Even good silver could not buy good magic. A month ago, he was convinced that he could open the eyes of the blind, heal the ears of the deaf and loosen the tongues of mutes. He had performed none of these miracles. But he could curse the healthy with white leprosy spots.

"Do it again, do it again," shouted a high-pitched voice.

He looked up and at the top of the hill that rose not twenty feet away from there; he saw a small group of children. They ran, stumbled and fell down its sides to assemble in front of him and clap their hands with joy. The youngest, a dark-skinned boy whose eyes were bright with excitement, squealed with laughter.

It was at that moment that a raging spirit entered Hiram. Then another lusting for chaos and a third that was crazed and tormented, and they overwhelmed his thoughts by their sheer malevolence. Seizing control of him, they saw through his eyes, crushed his own thoughts and focused his attention on the children before him. His mind filled with spilled blood as he reached down into the bag he had left on the sand and pulled from it his ax.

53

"Ron's still not answering his phone," said Hunter.

"Did you try Molly?" asked Moser.

"Three times with no answer."

"Well, shit, maybe he's stuck in traffic?"

"Maybe. I don't like this, though. This whole thing feels off. I'm having a hard time with this not being spiritually qualified bit."

"I don't like it," said Moser.

They were sitting in Bartok's study—Hunter still had a hard time with it being his study—trying to get hold of either Ron or Molly and getting nowhere. Hunter sat behind the desk, cell phone in hand, and Moser reclined in the guest chair.

"You think I should leave a note on the front door?"

"No, I don't," said Moser. "You left them both voicemails, and that's enough. No need to leave a note on the front door—you never know who might end up reading it, if you get my drift."

Before Hunter could answer, pastor Mark poked his big bald in the room.

"You boys ready? Any word from that policeman?"

Hunter got up from his chair as Moser unwound from his. Without thinking about it, they touched the pistols hanging from their shoulders.

"You got coats to put over those, so we don't have to go walking into the Detroit Temple with firearms hanging from your shoulders?" asked the pastor.

"What? Oh, right. You bet," said Moser as he put on a huge red and black flannel shirt.

Reaching back to pick up his tan corduroy sport coat lying on a short bookshelf behind him, Hunter threw it over his shoulder as the three of them left the room and headed downstairs. Rebecca was waiting at the bottom of the stairs, looking for all the world like Rambo's little sister. Her brown hair was pulled back in a tight ponytail, and she wore a thick Camo hunting jacket with enough pockets to hide a small armory. She wasn't smiling, but she looked righteous. Posture straight, chin up, eyes bright and her bandaged hand sticking out from beneath her cuff. She was going into the Borgo Pass and out the other side to do what she was born to do—confront evil and beat it down.

Pastor Mark looked resigned to his fate. Solid, strong. A man who didn't like where they were going, but would go anyway. Wider and bulkier than Moser, but just as determined once he set his mind to something.

Hunter was different. He was so conflicted about what they were doing that it was in danger of turning into full-blown paranoia. Something just didn't feel right about not being able to get hold of either Ron or Molly.

But it was already eleven-thirty at night and Ron had neither called nor shown up, so he'd have to catch up with them later. Two things about Ron not showing up and neither of them answering their phone bothered him like nothing else. The first was the night Rebecca's father's house was attacked. The second was the night that Bartok's house—make that his house now—was attacked. In both cases, how did the woman know where they would be? The answer always linked backward to the same person, and that was Brother Frank Mihaloff. And he had given Molly's name to Brother Mihaloff. Looking back, he saw it for the senseless, idiotic action that it was. He was trying to deflect Brother Mihaloff from knowing where the three of them would be. So, he'd given Brother Frank her name to sound authentic—just in case the old man checked up on them. And now, both Molly and Ron were missing. Had he, without thinking, endangered their lives?

"Hey, you with us?" asked Moser.

"Just thinking."

Rebecca and Pastor Mark were already leaning against the SUV. The outside lights lit the grounds like daylight for the full length of the property. Moser had turned all the arrays on to make sure nothing came up on them unawares.

"Keys?" she said, holding out her hand.

"You know, this is my vehicle," said Hunter as he handed them over.

As she turned and unlocked the door with the remote, she said over her shoulder, "I just want to get a feel for how it drives."

"I don't get it," said Hunter as he and Moser climbed in the back.

"No way to know which one of us will be too injured to drive, so I want to get a feel for the way this beast moves in case I end up being the one healthy enough to drive," said Rebecca.

When she'd climbed in and shut the door behind her, Pastor Mark said, "She might be pulling your leg on that."

"Uh-huh," said Moser.

****

The drive to the Detroit Masonic Temple took just under an hour because of the construction that never seemed to end along I-75. No matter how many times they re-built or resurfaced the freeway, the potholes always reappeared bigger than ever, like acne scars on the face of the once beautiful highways. The congealed darkness hovering over the city disturbed Hunter. He remembered the scene from Ghostbusters when Gozer the Traveler returned. Dark clouds pressing against the apex of the building where Sigourney Weaver lived. The movie was rightfully made in New York. If it was made in Detroit, thought Hunter, almost everybody would have died except the monster.

As they got out of the car, Hunter's sense of dread deepened. The Detroit Masonic Temple towered over them, its front lit by spotlights as though they were entering a theater where the end of their life would play out. The four of them stopped and stared at it, and Hunter wondered if they all felt that same sense of impending doom. From the corner of his eye, he saw Rebecca pull out her nine-millimeter and check the slide, then return it to her holster hidden beneath her windbreaker.

"Let's do it," said Moser.

Hunter led the way. Pastor Mark swung his head back and forth, looking for Ricci. The night air was cool and moist. Clouds blocked the moon's eye from following their progress. Despite the werewolf sightings and legends he'd investigated over the years with no concrete results, the full moon still caused the hackles on the back of his neck to rise. After Townsend Mountain, nothing seemed safe anymore when darkness blanketed the world.

The steps leading to the massive front doors caused him to pause, but when Moser elbowed him, he got moving again. The door moved back silently in the dimly lit lobby. At the end of the long open space, he saw the life-sized poster of Eva Morgan. Rebecca pushed him aside and headed straight for it.

"Rebecca—" he began.

"Save it," said Pastor Mark. "Don't slow her down. We have God's work to do tonight."

"Amen," said Moser.

He followed the other three and stopped with them to get a closeup of the witch-woman's face. He looked nervously about, as though she might come suddenly flying out of the shadows.

"Well?" asked Pastor Mark.

"It's her," said Rebecca.

"How did this happen?" asked Moser. "How did our Craft became so infested with evil?"

"Pride," said Rebecca, and then, "which way, Hunter?"

"Follow me," he said.

Their soft-soled shoes made little sound as they followed him down the labyrinth of hallways to the double doors of the Romanesque Room. He took out the keys to unlock the doors, but then stopped, turned to Rebecca and Pastor Mark and asked, "Are you sure about this?"

"We're sure," they said, almost in unison.

"Open the door," she said.

Hunter took a deep breath, unlocked the doors and slowly, fearfully, swung them inward. He saw as he did so that Rebecca had screwed in her silencer. How the hell, he wondered again, did we get into this situation? Moser had his own silenced pistol out and hanging at his side.

****

"Let's do it," said Pastor Mark.

"Over this way," said Hunter, and he led them to the Empty Chair.

The silence of the Romanesque Room made the air seem heavy and thick.

"This it?" asked the preacher.

Hunter nodded.

"You have to see how this works, so that once you're on the other side, you'll know how to get back. He stepped to the side of the chair, showed them how to move aside the plate and then, using the flashlight app on his phone, lit up the inner space to show them the lever inside. He moved aside to let them inspect it.

"Rebecca," said the pastor, " look at this."

She took the flashlight from Hunter and looked inside.

"Did you know about this?" she asked and pointed her finger into the cavity. She was kneeling down and looking directly inside the base of the chair.

Pastor Mark stepped out of the way as Hunter moved in next to her and went to one knee. His shoulder pressed against hers as he leaned in, and he felt the brush of her thick hair against his cheek. She was a heady blend of gun oil and clover.

"I need to get closer," said Hunter, and immediately felt awkward at having said it.

Rebecca reached over, wrapped her hand around the base of his neck, and pulled him in.

"There," she said, pointing into the opening, "just under the lever."

Hunter should have expected what he saw beneath the lever. He'd been so stressed at escaping from Borgo that he'd forgot the question of how the chairs communicated. It was an obvious point, but it didn't occur to him. But when he saw what Rebecca was pointing at, he smiled.

"What? Why are you smiling?"

"It's how the whole thing works," said Hunter.

"And?"

"It's her symbol. See how it's connected to the chair lever by that silver filament? I bet there's one just like it in its twin over in Borgo, wherever it is. Wait, there's more of the filaments. It's like a spider web. I wonder…"

"Hunter?"

"Yes?" he said without looking up.

"Get out of my way. We need to get moving."

"Wait."

He held up his hand like a traffic policeman.

"What?" said Rebecca as she stood and waited for him to move.

"I… I don't know. Something. Maybe. I need to—"

"You need to get out of my way, Hunter. I know you don't like it, but we're going in."

The need to push back against being pushed around was getting strong. The idea of Rebecca and the pastor going in made him both mad and frustrated. It made him mad because although they believed all the religious stuff they spouted, Hunter thought—no, knew—it would be of no use against Hiram Abiff. What he'd seen and what he'd read made that clear to him. He didn't need anyone else's opinion. Hiram Abiff scared the hell out of him. The Confessions of Mr. Hyde was difficult to believe, but terrifying. The section from Charles Stanley Jones's diary that Molly had forwarded to him, though, was particularly creepy. He and other investigators of the paranormal and the occult believed that most of the writings about Aleister Crowley were popular myth, but there was something about Hiram Abiff urinating on this supposed magical master that was deeply disturbing.

He felt Moser's rough hand settle on his shoulder.

"It's time," the old man said.

Reluctantly, Hunter stood. Once Rebecca and the pastor were through the gate, he would look more closely at the magical circuitry and try to understand it. Some part of him knew it was important.

"Wish us Godspeed," said Pastor Mark.

"I do," said Hunter.

"Open it up," said Rebecca with a touch of impatience.

Hunter nodded, bent down to pull the lever, but stopped and stood up again. He felt dizzy and disoriented, and then the world disappeared for him. He turned and faced Rebecca.

"What?" she asked, and her sigh of exasperation was evident.

She was about to say something else, but stopped and stared in disbelief at Hunter. His eyes had gone completely white. His pupils and corneas had disappeared. She took a step back and raised her pistol.

"Rebecca," Hunter said, in a voice that was not his own. "When you enter the tunnel between worlds, do not hesitate or stare at what surrounds you. The demonic dead will try to capture your eyes if you look at them. Therefore, walk quickly and with your heart and mind set firmly on the door that leads to the other side. When you enter the other world, do not leave the room you step into. Leave the man where he has fallen. Save the woman. God be with you both."

"What in—" she began, but saw that Hunter's eyes had returned to normal. Tears streamed from the corner of her eyes.

Pastor Mark stared in disbelief at what had just happened, his mouth agape. But Moser just nodded as though he'd expected it.

"What are you crying about?" asked a bewildered Hunter.

Rebecca stepped over and kissed him on the cheek.

"What's that all about?" he asked.

"Nothing," she said. "Open the gate."

A confused Hunter bent, looked back at her again, and then pulled the lever. The Empty Chair leaned back and opened into darkness.

****

Rebecca watched in astonishment as Hunter's eyes turned completely white. And then he spoke.

"Rebecca," Hunter said, in a voice that was not his own. "When you enter the tunnel between worlds, do not hesitate or stare at what surrounds you. The demonic dead will try to capture your eyes if you look at them. Therefore, walk quickly and with your heart and mind set firmly on the door that leads to the other side. When you enter the other world, do not leave the room you step into. Leave the dead man where he has fallen. Save the woman. God be with you both."

She began to cry. The voice coming out of Hunter's voice was that of her dead fiancé, Austen. She said a silent prayer of thanks to God and, when Hunter's eyes returned to normal, gathered her courage, stepped over to Hunter and kissed him on the cheek. She wiped away her tears as he stared blankly at her.

"What's that all about?" he asked.

"Nothing," she said. "Open the gate."

A confused Hunter bent, looked back at her again, and then pulled the lever. The empty chair leaned back and opened into darkness.

Pastor Mark took a step toward it, but Rebecca put his hand on his arm to hold him back.

"I'll go first," she said.

He was about to object, but stepped aside and let her pass. She walked directly into the darkness without looking back at the others, and Pastor Mark followed.

****

They'd gone a few steps into the blackness when the first electric red and purple whiplash snapped nearby on the other side of the membranous tunnel. Her hand spasmed around the grip of her nine millimeter Smith and Wesson MP Shield, but she did not stop. Behind her, she heard Pastor Mark gasp. She'd lost track of the steps; she just kept moving. Their feet made no noise as they moved ahead, or perhaps it was that the screams of the damned all around them made it impossible to hear anything else. Jagged, weeping, explosive crying as though someone's child were being ripped away from them. What was this place? Hunter was right. This passageway went straight through Hell, and if it ripped, they would drop into the angry, hungry flames that licked upward toward their feet. Hunter, who thought everything had a logical explanation if only you researched and thought about it long enough. Hunter, who looked so much like Austen, but was not him. At least tonight he would be safe. The world she and the pastor were entering this dark evening was not for unbelievers. She could feel demonic eyes locked on them as they moved forward.

Sixteen steps, maybe eighteen steps.

The walls of the membranous tunnel shook as a giant claw slapped against it. Rebecca lost her balance and would have fallen if Pastor Mark hadn't reached out and grabbed her arm. An internal warning alarm drove her to keep moving without even looking back. No matter what she saw or what she heard, she kept moving. Austen's voice speaking to her through Hunter stayed fixed in her mind: Do not hesitate or stare at what surrounds you.

Suddenly, straight ahead of her, she saw a door opening into a rectangle of dim light. Pistol up, both hands tight around the grip and a slight bend to her knees, Rebecca stepped through the opening and was hit in the face with a spray of blood, and her ears rocked with screams and the roar of wild animals.

54

"I am not," said Mr. Chirac, "in the habit of making house calls."

Hiram Abiff sat at a wooden table in the middle of the Borgo Masonic Lodge, in the space where, in a normal Masonic Temple, would be the altar to the Great Architect of the Universe. He wore a red and black fleece-lined coat as though, like so many elderly people, he was cold. Mr. Chirac postulated that the ancient creature's body was, in fact, always cold in this created world, empty of genuine hope. Like Hiram himself, it was without a soul. Five lit candles on brass stands formed a pentagon around the table where Hiram sat and glared up at him with solid black eyes.

"A lovely arrangement," said Mr. Chirac with an elegantly sarcastic grimace and a nod to the configuration of the candle stands. "Perhaps a candelabrum would have been more appropriate, but, as is sometimes said, *chaque artiste a d'abord été un amateur, n'est-ce pas?*"

"Do not vex me," said Hiram in a flat, menacing voice. "You come as called."

He adjusted his wire-rimmed glasses with his right thumb and forefinger, both of the nails of which, Mr. Chirac duly noted with disapproval, were sharpened to knife-like points.

"I come by invitation and under the guarantee of hospitality by my brother," said Mr. Chirac.

In the soft candlelight, his black silk suit shone with a comfortably rich luster. He'd taken great pains to select a tie and shirt suitable for the occasion. His bloodstone ring glowed a soft pink, to match the hue of those inset into his platinum cuff links. There was no need, he thought, for a pocket handkerchief to lighten the mood, as he was only meeting to negotiate a bargain with his demonic brother. And family or not, it was his long held opinion that a civilized man did not negotiate while sporting inappropriate accouterments.

"You have violated that sanction," warned Hiram, "by bringing one uninvited."

Mr. Chirac sighed, but decided the nuance was lost on this dull, yet dangerous cretin.

"I have matched familiar with familiar," he said, "as is our custom under the binding covenants."

The hulking Ricci stood behind him and was off to one side. Long ago Mr. Chirac had given up on the ephemeral desire to find a gentleman's attire suitable to the brutish menace. Gorillas, he opined, were notoriously at odds with sartorial expectancy.

Hiram rose slowly from his chair and walked toward them. The man was perhaps a head shorter than Mr. Chirac, but still there was an aura of chaotic menace about him. Inside this Nephilim-created creature, reflected Mr. Chirac, lurked the condensed evil of a plethora of corroded lives. The creature's shiny bald head passed by the Frenchman as he approached Ricci to appraise him. Ricci looked down at him, turned his gaze to Mr. Chirac, who only shrugged, then returned to staring straight ahead impassively. The old man was facing Ricci's chest.

"I wish to examine him," he said.

"Carefully," cautioned Mr. Chirac, "very carefully."

The old man reached up and unbuttoned the top three buttons of Ricci's shirt. Mr. Chirac arched a curious eyebrow. Hiram glanced up at Ricci's scarred face as though looking for a reaction, but the bulky man continued to stare straight ahead. As the old man opened his shirt and scrutinized the thick rope-like scars across his hairy chest, Mr. Chirac glanced languidly around at the shadowed corners huddled around the lodge room. His ring thrummed as his eyes fell on the back wall of the lodge where there was clearly a deeper darkness. As with most Masonic lodges, there were passageways behind passageways behind passageways. And what lurked in those passageways was the entity Mr. Chirac had come to bargain with. Hiram Abiff was only the gatekeeper, but a formidable one at that.

When Hiram opened Ricci's shirt to reveal the blue-violet metal sigil embedded in the skin over the big man's heart, he tilted his head backward and screamed with a sound like a train dragging a crumpled car down its tracks. Mr. Chirac pulled his pocket watch from inside his suit jacket and glanced at the time, then returned it to his pocket. An insolent thought prompted him to consider tapping his foot to measure the passing moments, but he refrained.

"You have not the authority for this sign," shrieked Hiram. The frames of his glasses glowed a faint blue. "No authority," he repeated with a menacing growl. "How is this possible?"

Mr. Chirac did not respond, because, as Oscar Wilde said, "Bad artists always admire each other's work."

"You will answer," commanded Hiram.

"You may enter, my dear," said Mr. Chirac, as he ignored Hiram and turned his head toward the Worshipful Master's chair in the East. "Your perfume is itself a sufficient invitation."

From the corner of his eye, Chirac saw a blast of blue-black fire hurtling at him, propelled by a howl of demonic rage by Hiram Abiff. The woman, whose seductive fragrance contrasted with the hellfire erupting from Hiram, remained hidden in the shadows.

"Enough," bellowed a voice from a dark assemblage of roiling shadows now gathered at the exact center of the lodge room's ceiling, and, at that precise moment, Hiram's hellfire froze in midair, only three inches from Mr. Chirac's face.

"You may release him, Ricci," said Mr. Chirac.

Ricci had hold of Hiram Abiff by the head after knocking off the old man's glasses, and had pressed his thumbs against the old man's eyes until they exploded inward. He stood there, with his thumbs still jammed into his eye sockets for no longer than three seconds, withdrew his thumbs, snapped Hiram's neck to one side and then returned to where he had been standing a moment ago.

"Was that truly necessary?" asked Mr. Chirac.

Ricci, his stare never drifting away from the broken-necked Hiram, simply shrugged as he removed a coarse cloth from his pants pocket and wiped his thumbs clean.

"Straighten his neck, if you please," said Mr. Chirac irritably. "I will not negotiate leaning sideways."

The big man took a step toward Hiram, whose head expanded to twice its size as he opened his mouth and shrieked.

"Or not," said Mr. Chirac.

Hiram reached up with both hands and snapped his own head back into place. The bones immediately reconnected with a sickening suction sound. The old man's eyes were empty sockets as he raised one hand, and the glasses leaped from the floor and slapped back into his palm. Mr. Chirac noticed the curious fact that the old man's eyes were now imaged in the lenses. As he placed them over his eye sockets, the images were pulled back into the empty sockets and became new eyeballs.

"*Mieux vaut prévenir que guérir,*" thought Mr. Chirac, which, when loosely translated, was to say that it is better to prevent than to heal.

Out from behind the Worshipful Master's chair stepped a woman of rare and appreciable beauty, so refined that she distracted from the descent of the Nephilim darkness, which now formed an oily gathering near the end of Hiram's table. Her hair was the color of polished teak and fell about her shoulders like rivulets of black rain. She wore a long black robe with a high collar clasped tight against her neck by a necklace with a golden emblem that Mr. Chirac knew only too well.

"Again, I ask you, brother, how did you come through into a new body?" rasped the Nephilim darkness.

"What we enunciate between us will be between we two and we two alone," said Mr. Chirac.

The candles flared with the Nephilim darkness's rage, then dimmed again.

"Send him back through," the Nephilim said of Ricci.

"I think not," smiled Mr. Chirac.

"Dare you test my power in this, my own created world?" bellowed the Nephilim.

The room thrummed with a pulsating effulgence of blackness. At its core hovered the oily boiling emptiness. The air sparked with random bursts of electricity as the Nephilim darkness seethed.

Once again, Mr. Chirac withdrew his pocket watch, glanced at it to ascertain the time, and then shook his head as he put it away.

"Dare you test mine, brother?" he said.

Hiram Abiff stood at the right side of the demonic presence. The woman stood to its left, and, although Mr. Chirac knew that there was a certain relevance to such positioning, he had an alchemical reaction progressing through a delicate stage in his home laboratory, and wished to move the proceedings along. The operation was known as fermentation, and was the fourth step in his efforts to create a Bezoar stone, which was also known as a madstone. He ventured this complex alchemical transformation to replace the stone he lost to Granny Hillis the preceding year. Her stone now resided in a large briefcase, firmly placed between the ribs of a little girl who died horribly years earlier.

If that madstone was removed from the coffin, it would release a screaming haint, which even Mr. Chirac hesitated to attempt. Hence his attempts to create his own. The fermentation stage of his work would proceed for several days longer until the planetary alignments were fortuitous. He would then proceed to the distillation stage, which was the stage during which the madstone would form if he had executed the proceeding steps completely. It was his tenth attempt, the earlier nine being unsuccessful. Hence, he was growing impatient with his brother Nephilim. Only a madstone of sufficient power would keep at bay the spirits that came every night, attempting to drag him back to the hellish world from which he had come. And, although technically the fermentation stage of his alchemical operation could proceed unattended for much longer, he was eager to return to his home laboratory to observe it. Besides, Lily must be fed, and she grew fractious when her feeding schedule was not adhered to fastidiously.

The explosive rage Mr. Chirac felt building inside Hiram was a powerful confluence of dark energies waiting to detonate. The woman seemed calm and even somewhat amused. Ricci showed neither emotion nor interest. Mr. Chirac raised his left hand and the bloodstone ring glowed with a scarlet effulgence.

"Sleep," he said, his voice acidulous, yet cold as chrome.

The woman's head dropped suddenly forward. Hiram's head did the same. Mr. Chirac's bloodstone ring dimmed.

"Ricci," said Mr. Chirac, "make them comfortable on the floor."

Mr. Chirac felt his brother Nephilim's gaze burning into him like a psychotic blowtorch. Even the most glorious spirits, he thought with a rueful smile, had all the subtlety of road flares.

After stepping to where Hiram stood as though sleeping, Ricci palm struck him in the chest and the soon-to-be master of the entire Masonic world hit the lodge floor with a solid thunk.

"Gentler with the woman," said Mr. Chirac patiently.

Ricci raised an inquiring eyebrow.

Mr. Chirac sighed.

"She is not of the same substance as the Abiff creature. If you fracture her face, it will temporarily impede her functionality, which will make our contract more difficult to execute. Besides, as we say. *Si vous voulez vous venger d'un homme, envoyez-lui une très belle femme.*"

"Again?" asked Ricci.

"If you desire revenge on a man, send him a really beautiful woman," replied Mr. Chirac with an exasperated shrug.

Ricci picked up the woman, held her out before him, and let her drop. Before the back of her head hit the floor, he extended the toe of his shoe to catch it.

Mr. Chirac shook his head.

"And your man?" growled the Nephilim darkness. "I demand reciprocity."

"I require at least one witness to our arrangement and my dear Lily lacks the sensitivities to do well in this... environment. My manservant Ricci is the acceptable substitute to protect my interests."

"Your interests are of no importance to me," snapped the Nephilim darkness.

Mr. Chirac paused before speaking, examining his manicured fingernails in the candlelight.

"Do you apprehend the sometimes hideous opprobrium of arguing with the disembodied?"

"I will—" began the Nephilim darkness.

"If you could, you would have already, dear brother. We are, after all, family, and verbal artifice is of little use to either of us. But in all of history, I am the only one among our kind to return to the world of men and their oh so succulent women with a new body to walk the very earth we were cast out from, so if you might dispense with your arrogance you may find what I have to say of some value to you. And, as we both are aware, your power has not a fulcrum to leverage it against one such as I am now, and therefore it is an odious misuse of your time to attempt to remonstrate against me because only I, as you well know, can help you regain the corporeal existence you desire above all else. We were equals in the netherworld of eternal darkness, but no longer. All of our kind lust for flesh, for with flesh we gain power. It is our curse and yet we can never satiate it. As the Marquis de Sade so eloquently explained, 'Lust's passion will be served; it demands, it militates, it tyrannizes.' All this you know, brother, for you have birthed her from your lust and arrogance."

Mr. Chirac pointed a single elegant forefinger at the unconscious woman.

A roar like a thousand tempests crashing on a single craggy shore exploded into the room. Ricci, who expected the tirade, waited until the blasts of wind and furious noise dissipated, and then removed his index fingers from his ears.

"Once you had," continued Mr. Chirac, unimpressed by the Nephilim's rage, "a glorious, beautiful, and powerful body. You towered over the humans as an astonishing being, gifted with the divine right of an eternal king. Now, you are reduced to an impotent vapor pulling the strings of your mortified puppet." Here he cocked his finger at the prostrate Hiram. "So I ask again—what is your offer?"

"Have you found it?" asked the darkness after a tense moment.

"Show yourself," said Mr. Chirac. "I grow tired of your darkness. Black was never, truly, never your most flattering color."

A dangerous silence filled the room, but then the oily blackness shimmered as though bright blue diamond dust had been thrown against its surface. The scintillating brilliance radiated through a multicolored array of color and suddenly, from its midst, stepped the translucent image of a twelve foot tall man, who towered over both Mr. Chirac and Ricci. His rich, golden hair hung down over his shoulders and his fine-featured face was a chiseled handsomeness, stunning to behold. The visually overpowering muscularity of his body was awe-inspiring.

"Had you considered dressing before appearing in your form?" asked Mr. Chirac. "Surely there is a loincloth to avail you in this sterile world of yours."

The Nephilim stood like a giant Greek statue, perfect in its artistry.

"I ask again," it said, "have you found it?"

"Yes, and Ricci has arranged its delivery to a place of my choosing," said Mr. Chirac. "The Blazing Star of Freemasonry will then be in my possession."

Silence again.

"You will bring it to me at that very instant," boomed the Nephilim's voice.

"Do you know," said Mr. Chirac distractedly, "that this body of mine has not aged even a single day in the last one hundred and fifty years?"

"How? How did you accomplish this? I demand again to know how you brought yourself back through with a living body. All these years I have demanded an answer from you, and you have yet to reveal it to me. Is this a way to treat your true family, brother?"

A low buzzing filled the lodge room as a cloud of flies rushed out from behind the Senior Deacon's chair and landed on Hiram Abiff's head. Mr. Chirac shook his head reproachfully as the green-black insects inched toward the old man's nose, their iridescent wings held tight to their body as they slid into his slitted nostrils.

"Enchanting," said Mr. Chirac. "Yet your boorish creature is an anarchistic maelstrom whose growing power concerns me," he added as he once again indicated the prostrate form of Hiram Abiff.

"You fear him?" asked the Nephilim.

There was an undertone of triumphant glee to the question.

Mr. Chirac removed his pocket watch once again and looked at the time.

"Your plan has many weaknesses," said Mr. Chirac without looking up, "and he is the worst among them. When he steps onto the world stage, you will lose control of your millennia old homunculus. Even now, he cannot control the choleric souls of the ravenous demons that possess him. If we do not settle on a contract before midnight, I will leave you. If you do not have him under control by the day of his return to the world," here he once again indicated Hiram, "I will feed him to Lily."

"You may try," said the Nephilim darkness.

His voice rippled with ancient menace.

"You have been too long without a mortal form, brother, so I forgive your naivete. You are dissipated. In your current..." Mr. Chirac considered for a moment, then shrugged, "... predicament, you are, if you'll forgive me, less than terrifying. Father would be... disappointed."

An aberrant spidery red lightning shot across the lodge room's ceiling like fissures fracturing concrete during an earthquake. The floor shook, and the overhead chandelier rattled and swayed. One of its bolts snapped, and it dropped an inch. Another and it fell further and hung precariously. Suddenly it stopped. Mr. Chirac felt the re-gathering of the Nephilim substantiality.

"What do you require?" it asked in a tone that managed to convey both power and treachery.

Mr. Chirac clapped his hands only once. This was an extraordinary gesture of tribute for him, reserved only for family, for, as a matter of general principle, he most assuredly strongly disapproved of clapping, most especially in the practice of magical rituals. His feelings on the matter were on a par with his repellent loathing for those who spelled the word "magic" with an added "k."

"Ricci," he said suddenly, "I require a chair."

The dispassionate behemoth obliged his employer by retrieving one of the folding metal chairs clustered about the table in the center of the room and brought it to him. Mr. Chirac stared down at the seat as though truly seeing it for the first time. He tilted his head to one side and focused in on something tucked into the first metal joint beneath the seat.

"A hair," he said with controlled abhorrence. "Simply exquisite."

He lifted his chin and looked around the room at the four stations of the lodge. There was only one, however, that seemed to interest him and so he began walking toward the Worshipful Master's chair in the East.

"What do you require?" thundered the Nephilim darkness.

Mr. Chirac walked up the short flight of steps leading to the Worshipful Master's chair and, when he was standing just in front of it, he stared down at the seat, looking at it from different angles. He raised his hand and waved his bloodstone ring two inches above it, then repeated the same motions on the sides, the back and then finally the footstool.

"Intriguing," he whispered. Then, he turned and announced to the room, "I will sit here."

And he did so.

Ricci had returned to where he stood originally and was now a perfectly motionless statue. He evinced no interest in the towering Nephilim.

"A satisfactory throne," pronounced Mr. Chirac. "Attend."

From within his suit jacket, he removed an unsealed vellum envelope and laid it on the Worshipful Master's stand before him.

"Within this envelope, my brother," he said to the Nephilim darkness, "is our contract."

"I have neither true hands to hold it, eyes to read it, nor fingers to hold a pen, as you are so well aware."

"So, just so," said Mr. Chirac. "Ricci, will you please assist my truculent brethren?"

Ricci shrugged, walked past the fallen woman and the abhorrent Hiram Abiff, retrieved the document from his employer and carried it over to stand before the giant. He stared at the chest of the magnificent image with all the interest, Mr. Chirac would later reflect, of a lumberjack watching urine drip from a felled oak tree.

"Ricci will now read aloud the concordat between us, which will, when signed, or, in your case, imprinted with your essence, to represent the complete accord between us. Before he begins, however, I will highlight the key elements of our covenant. First, I must, as the party of the first part, acquire, take possession of the Blazing Star of Freemasonry and pass it to that woman..." here he took up the Worshipful Master's gavel and pointed it at the witch still lying on the floor. "... and prepare for her the ritual to follow in harvesting the energy of the Freemasons' thoughts by means of said Blazing Star, which she will then use it to perform said ritual to the exacting expectations delineated in said instructions. Attend, si vous plait. This will be no mere invocation. The Hermetic energies involved will be staggering. She must make no missteps or the results will be disastrous.

"If all proceeds successfully as you have planned, and your emissary," another pointing of the gavel at Hiram, "can re-enter the world of humanity via the Freemasons, then he will be introduced to the assembled body of Freemasonry in the Detroit Masonic Temple and, at which point Ricci, from his hiding place, will shoot him in the head so that he may then resurrect himself to the undying bewilderment and awe of all in attendance. Are these elements acceptable to you?"

The Nephilim darkness was silent.

"You must return me to the world as well," it said at last. "I must have my freedom. That must be part of our agreement."

"If only I had the device that returned me to the world to accomplish that," said Mr. Chirac, "I would of a certainty offer my services, but alas, other parties have acquired it since we last communed. If only there were someone or something—" he glanced at fallen the woman, "to retrieve it for me."

"Take it from them," hissed the darkness. "Rip it from their hands, break their bodies apart, and cast the pieces aside."

"That would, of course, be an enchanting way to spend an otherwise wasted evening, brother, but I have covenanted not to do so, nor to harm the individuals who have possession of it. Such agreements," said Mr. Chirac as he turned his attention to Ricci, "are always binding."

"Then I will send the woman," said the darkness. "Tell me who has possession of this device."

"Soon," said Mr. Chirac. "First, you must commit to our agreement."

"If you were not already damned—"

"I repeat, are the elements of my side of the covenant acceptable to you?"

"You will control the Temple Guardians?" asked the darkness.

"No, I will not."

A hiss escaped the Nephilim as it transformed back into a swirling occult tourbillion.

"That remains," said Mr. Chirac with studied calm, "the sole responsibility of your woman and the eminent Brother Frank Mihaloff, who is already, might I remind you, under the spell of both your woman and your creature. If they encounter... obstacles, then she may seek me out and I will provide assistance. Since Hiram may not pass into the mortal world until all is ready, however, I assume she will continue as your liaison with the Temple Guardians and the rest of Freemasonry. So, decide now. Do not undervalue my offer."

After another moment of silence, then Nephilim darkness agreed.

"But for my side of the contract?"

"Ah, you are wise beyond wisdom. Ricci will now read our covenant in its entirety," said Mr. Chirac.

When the big man had completed his reading, he returned the document to its envelope, walked it back, and handed it to Mr. Chirac. He then returned to his position and stood as though nothing had happened.

Mr. Chirac stopped for a moment to direct a scowl at Ricci, then looked back toward the darkness. "It is the device, dear brother, which I could use to bring you through to again to the land of the living if you are successful in establishing your creature Hiram as the new Grandmaster of all Freemasons. But I caution you that if your venture is unsuccessful, our mutually binding contract will be null and void. From our former days of glory, to our banishment, until now I am still the only one of our kind to return to the mortal world, and that is only because of the ghost box. If you do not have your servitors first procure it and then return it to me, then I cannot bring you through to the mortal world again."

"No."

"Yes. Without the device and the harvested power of the Blazing Star of Freemasonry, it will be impossible to bring you through, no matter how strong your will. And... you must find a host spirit to accompany you through the void or the device cannot accomplish its task without destroying you in the process. Might I suggest the spirit of the late and lamented Aleister Crowley?"

"You lie."

Mr. Chirac did not pretend outrage at the observation. Instead, he used a gesture to indicate his body.

"Does this, dear brother, look like the body I once owned? Did you really think that extraterrestrial technology could surpass a barrier erected by the Divine Being to keep us from returning to physical form? Even in the tortured terrain of the incorporeal, there are in fact boundaries. So it is, that even such as we must become body thieves if we are to acquire what we desire."

"Why him? Why the one called Crowley?"

Displeasure twisted Mr. Chirac's face.

"You know the answer to that question," he said. "Additionally, your Hiram has controlled him once before, which will make the operation more likely to succeed. Now, do you agree to our covenant?"

Another silence.

Then, a reluctant "I do."

"So, just so," said Mr. Chirac. "Regarding the device implants, Brother Mihaloff has perhaps a million of them ready to be... inserted. Clinical trials have proceeded impeccably, and he has secured the approval of the Surgeon General. President Usman, of course, is deeply conflicted by this matter, as by accepting their use to cure disease, he is a traitor to at least three and perhaps more of the world's major religions, including his own, but since the comprehensive testing has in fact validated that these implants can cure cancer, he must decide in favor of his new religion or politics—the expediency of curing cancer will, in fact, insure his re-election. In this regard, your Hiram has performed admirably in the device's creation. It is a peculiar judgment on the world, think you not, that a creature such as he with neither moral compass nor soul is so ingenious in the matters of science and yet beyond callous towards human life. Perhaps, it is his very lack of soul and therefore morality that paves the way for his successes in the ways of science. Yet what good is the scientific method to one condemned to eternal Hell?"

To Mr. Chirac's consternation, the Nephilim actually replied to this thought.

"They are dogs rolling in their own urine."

"I see," said Mr. Chirac. "Thank you so much for that insight. One cannot acquire too many non sequiturs. But to return to the matter at hand—the implants are a marvelous blend of science and magic. But I must inquire as to the success of the program that your female was to oversee."

"It is done."

Mr. Chirac straightened his cuffs and shook his head. "They provide the means of their own demise," he said.

"You do not approve?"

"Approval is a bourgeois game. However, again, I must tell you I do fear that your plan is both excessively Byzantine and pretentious. It is also somewhat inopportune. Has it occurred to you to wait an appropriate amount of time before launching an attempt to control the entire mortal world? Do you not consider it premature to launch your assault against humanity on the first day you re-enter their world? And with all your machinations in motion, why do you persist in allowing your creatures to hunt for that useless journal? Are you truly so mortified by the possibility of it being found and the world learning the truth about who Hiram Abiff really is?

"As the finish line approaches, dear brother," he continued, "a runner does not to stop to look for his wallet. There are only days in which to prepare for your creature's presentation to the world as the Grandmaster of all Freemasonry and yet you have your woman hunting after Brother Mihaloff's daughter and the granddaughter of Enzo Corvasce in case one of them has the thing. A manuscript titled *The Confessions of Mr. Hyde* would not ignite a serious investigation in any event. Have you not more important things to manage? And with the… program she has overseen the creation of, is it really necessary? Are we really reduced to using… software…"—his displeasure at the word was evident—"to harness occult energies?"

A scornful clucking issued from the darkness.

"You have always pulled back from war and the planning of its tactics," it said. "Tactics require a fanatic's obsession with each and every detail. You have always preferred cunning, treachery, and betrayal to swords and spears."

"I prefer," said Mr. Chirac, "subtlety to a battle hammer. I prefer my enemies to immolate each other by their own hubris."

"You disdain the blood that flows from battle. So little have you changed."

"I prefer to sip it, not bathe in it, brother."

"I," said the Nephilim darkness, "demand the battlefield, the power birthed by victory. When Hiram triumphantly steps again into their world, and you have brought me through as his master, we will subdue them all."

"Again brother, I cannot bring you back through to the mortal world—no one can do that without the ghost box and only then if you ride along with another spirit of the damned. Your labyrinthine plot will amount to nothing if one of your creatures cannot return the ghost box to me. I ask you one last time—will you commit to your obligations as described in our agreement?"

"I do so commit."

"So mote it be, then," said Mr. Chirac. "Ricci, present the contract for my brother to impress."

Ricci walked forward again and held up the document before the Nephilim darkness. After a long moment, a single drop of dark, viscous ectoplasm fell to the area of the document marked "Consenting Signature." A puff of smoke rose from the spot where it struck.

"Wonderful," said Mr. Chirac as he rose from his seat. "I would stay for a celebratory flute of champagne, but I have alchemical labors to attend to this so-fine night. Ricci, the chair, if you please."

Ricci stepped over the chair known in Freemasonry as the Empty Chair, bent down, then slid aside a panel and depressed a lever. The entire chair tilted and disappeared backward to reveal a square hole beneath it and stairs descending into darkness. As Mr. Chirac arrived at the entrance, the Nephilim called after him.

"What?" the Nephilim darkness said without prelude and asking about Ricci, "is your creature?"

A curious smile crossed Mr. Chirac's face.

"Something your creatures should fear," he said.

But Mr. Chirac knew that Hiram Abiff's power was growing, although his brother was blind to it. Soon, it would be too strong for even his brother to control. The woman was a different and more mysterious story. And, with that parting thought still on his mind, both Mr. Chirac and his hulking manservant disappeared down the stairs and into the Borgo Pass.

55

Mr. Chirac was alone in his laboratory. The soft whir of the electric fan, which drew away the toxic fumes from his experiments, was the only noise other than his own soft, steady breathing. He leaned forward on the large granite table that was his laboratory workbench. Its cold, hard surface had been always a delight to him. It was made for stability; it was designed for stability. It was a joy to behold and a joy to use. It was dependable. But what lay on that granite table, halfway between his furnace and a selection of crucibles, was an abomination. It was an abomination shaped like a small chicken egg. It had a jelly-like consistency. A putrescent odor.

Mr. Chirac drummed his fingertips and frowned. It was, of course, true, that many alchemists suffered from mental disorders because of their unfortunate lack of knowledge concerning how to properly handle deadly lab chemicals. In a way, many alchemists suffered from their own version of mad hatter's disease. They were careless in their use of mercury. They did not understand what hydrogen cyanide was. And arsenic, by any other name, was still a deadly poison. Therefore, unfortunately, their advice and proscriptions could not always be trusted.

Another man would have reached out to either Dennis William Hauck or one of his many notable students for alchemical advice; but Mr. Chirac was not just any other man. He had centuries of experience in the alchemical arts, and he would not be denied success; nor did he require advice.

Yet, was there something wrong with his method? No, surely not. In his astrological assignments? Out of the question. He was the most knowledgeable man alive in such arts. The *Great Arcanum* operation was trivial to him. When other, lesser magicians were fumbling with the *Clavicula Salomonis*, he was busy completing his first creation of a Philosopher's Stone. His first Magnum opus. So how could his exemplary attempt at creating a simple Bezoar Stone be such an unparalleled disaster? He would attempt the operation again and again until he had mastered the problem, of course, but what was he missing? That was the conundrum he wrestled with on a night where every soul living in Detroit, Michigan, could feel that something evil was winging its way toward their ruined city.

Hiram Abiff was coming.

Fah, thought Mr. Chirac.

The real threat to humanity would be the arrival of his brother. For millennia, he and his brother had railed against their captivity in the cacophonous world of demons, where the air was always rent with unremitting, unending wails and screams of agony. A world to which they had been consigned by the Divine and where electric whips of scorching hot lightning bolts flailed the captive spirits daily. It was a world where the smell of burned sulfur suffused the air. It was a world where the demons could never be exorcised, because it was, in truth, the world they called home. The red and black scabrous things that skittered through desolate landscapes of fire and boiling pitch were the reigning monarchs of that which could never die. It was the infernal world to which he, his brother and all the Nephilim had been eternally consigned as their curse for violating the commands of the Divine.

Trapped in that hellish place, he and his brother burned with rage. They had unsuccessfully combined their great intellects in the search for a way to escape. It was his brother who had conceived the idea to resurrect a mortal man in such a way that it might be put to use in creating a way for the Nephilim to break free. This was possible because the Nephilim could, in fact, manifest briefly in the mortal world, but at a great cost. Manifesting in the real world without a body drained the vital energies of the Nephilim and could lead to their utter dissolution if they grew careless. But Mr. Chirac's brother was the most powerful of all the Nephilim. He was also the most ambitious, the most brilliant and aggressive planner of all the Nephilim that had ever walked the earth. When he had walked the earth, no mortal woman had been able to resist his charismatic charm, his brilliance, his muscular intellect. They looked at him as a god come to earth. His brother had then been in his glory. Even afterward, in the confines of their imprisonment, hearing the wailing of the damned echo all around them, his brother's mind was fixed on returning to the mortal world. To walk it again as their king. It was this overpowering need to relive that life that drove him to create Hiram Abiff, the soulless homunculus, to do the work of returning him to the world.

Even after Hiram's nearly three thousand years researching all the lore and the legends of the world to find a way to bring his brother and the others back, the creature had found no answer. During that time, the creature known as Hiram Abiff had grown more and more powerful as it absorbed more and more demonic spirits and began to master integrating them into its own being. Now, Hiram was perhaps more powerful than his brother had ever dreamed it could be. But his brother had never feared anyone or anything save the Divine itself.

Mr. Chirac drummed his fingers on the laboratory marble table top again. Was it possible that his brother's soulless homunculus might know the alchemical secrets behind successfully creating a madstone? It was an unbearably offensive thought. Indeed, thought Mr. Chirac, it was galling to think that Hiram Abiff might know more of alchemy than he himself. That could not be tolerated. He would have to dispatch Lily to deal with the creature when the time was right. For now, he must concentrate on the mystery of why he, Mr. Chirac, could not create a true madstone. That was the problem that was driving him to frustration, to irritability, to… rage? No, not rage. He would solve this problem.

There was a knock at the door, and Mr. Chirac looked up sharply. As he did so, he considered the aluminum stand from which hung packets of blood for use in his experiments. Blood, he thought. Perhaps the packaged blood did not possess the proper vital fluids. A madstone was formed inside a deer, while the deer was living. Yes, that was so. Living energy gave the blood of a deer the necessities required to make a magical madstone. Living blood, he thought. Harvested from the living at the moment of exposure to the philosophic mercury. Indeed. Yes, indeed.

Another knock.

"I do not wish to be disturbed, Ricci," he said irritably. "Unless it concerns the Blazing Star."

"It's here, but you might have a problem with its condition."

Mr. Chirac felt a chill take hold of his body. Its condition? His field of vision seemed to narrow as he considered what that might mean.

"Come in, Ricci," he said, when he had sufficiently recovered.

A brace of soft light flooded the far end of the room as Ricci opened the thick-planked door and stepped in, carrying a wooden crate. With his shoulder, he pushed the door closed behind him and then walked toward his principal.

"The concern?" asked Mr. Chirac.

"Where?"

"Put it..."

Mr. Chirac looked at the room where every table save one was covered with glassware and reagent jars and various alchemical paraphernalia.

"On the table nearest the Soxhlet extractors," said Mr. Chirac.

Ricci cocked an eyebrow.

Mr. Chirac pointed with an elegant finger toward an empty table.

"Near the tall glass columns on the heating mantle," he said.

As Ricci positioned the box on the table nearest the designated glassware, Mr. Chirac drew in a sharp breath. The back right corner of the box was splintered. A dark rage boiled up from inside him.

"How?" said Mr. Chirac.

Before Ricci could answer, Mr. Chirac held up his hand in an imperious gesture.

"You have detained the delivery man? A Mr. Brimblewood, if I remember correctly."

"Like you asked."

"Mr. Brimblewood's services were recommended by whom, again?"

"That guy you dealt with on the gypsy mirror thing. You asked me to get a name from him."

"His name, Ricci," said an exasperated Mr. Chirac.

"Meridian. Krikor Meridian."

"Ah. So, just so. Then you were correct in saying after meeting him that no good can come from a grown man named Krikor. My judgment was weakened by my good manners, of which you have none and therefore your judgment was the more accurate. We will no longer deal with Mr. Meridian. Mr. Brimblewood, however, is another matter. Please bring him here so that I might discuss the matter with him."

"His truck?"

"You may dispose of that later tonight."

"Okay."

Ricci turned and walked back toward the exit. As he was closing the laboratory door behind him, the sound of Mr. Chirac's voice stopped him.

"Oh, Ricci."

"Yeah?"

"Be sure to bring some electrician's tape with you and some pliers."

Ricci stood silently in the door for a moment.

"Yes?"

"You want I should bring a bucket, too?"

Mr. Chirac showed his thin little smile and stroked one corner of his mustache.

"How very thoughtful of you, Ricci, but if you remember, this floor is equipped with drainage pans."

Ricci nodded and finished closing the door.

56

"Can't go in until midnight. Got to leave before two. Those are the rules," said Ricci.

When he turned, his massive bulk hid most of the walnut double doors. Eva Morgan could still see portions of the symbolic scrollings etched into the molding peeking past his left bicep.

"How very primitive," she murmured as Ricci's thickly calloused hands touched the brass door handles. "Did you select the moldings?"

Ricci's hand fell from the door handles and hung at his sides.

"Ma'am?" he said without turning to face her.

Eva stepped up close to him and placed her palms on his sculpted shoulders.

"You need a tailored suit," she whispered up at his right ear. "You'll break the seams if you flex. I tell you this because I adore primitive men. Explain to me why your master does not provide you with more suitable attire. What manner of beast is he?"

"It's midnight," he said.

The door handles turned by themselves, and the doors swung inward.

"Don't let him touch you," said Ricci as he stepped inside to introduce her.

"Why ever not?" she asked.

"It's an ownership thing."

****

"Why, it is Eva Morgan, the woman herself. It is such an honor and quite the delightful pleasure to have you here in my home as my guest, as opposed to the sterile environs in which we last met. I must tell you I shivered with anticipation when Ricci informed me you would enjoy my company to discuss the artifact, of which I am now the opportune custodian."

Mr. Chirac moved so quickly across the lamb-white carpeted floor to greet her that she forgot Ricci's proscription and extended her elegantly braceleted hand for him to kiss. The hint of a smile crossed his face as he bent over and touched his lips briefly to the back of her hand, raised up and then, looking directly into her gray eyes, bent forward slowly and kissed the same spot again, his lips remaining much longer this time. Eva felt a thrill move down her back, as though a chill drop of water slid down her spine. She thought how easy it would be to remove the long hairpin that held back her hair and push it into precisely the right spot on his neck to kill him. The thought of it warmed her. Of course, there would be the thuggish manservant Ricci to deal with, and, although she was not afraid of him, there was something about him that suggested he was more than she could see. Something much more dangerous than she needed to deal with just then.

She noticed the pale red stone set into the ring Mr. Chirac wore on his right hand. It was a soft scarlet color, refulgent with a tinge of gold reflected from the room's rich surroundings. The sight of it gave her an uneasy feeling. It was the color of thinned blood.

"Come, my dear," said Mr. Chirac, "allow me to escort you to a seat. There is nothing quite so bracing in this world for a man as the privilege to linger in the presence of an exquisitely beautiful woman."

Gas lights mounted on the walls, gamboled with spirited flames. As Mr. Chirac grasped her elbow with one hand and her fingers with his other to lower her into a leather chair, Eva took in the pink marble balustrade of the half balcony that surrounded the man's library and office. Behind her, she felt Ricci's presence as surely as if he had reached out and touched her. Mr. Chirac walked past a delicately embroidered burgundy and gold divan, and continued on to stand next to a gilded Louis XV design Bureau-plat writing desk with ormolu-mounted cabriolet legs. He rested one hand on its navy blue gilt-tooled leather writing surface affectionately. Eva looked around the room at the impressive mahogany bookshelves with beveled glass doors, golden candlesticks, and a pink marble fireplace mantel embellished with an acanthus leaf spray front piece. A circular limestone fountain with four outward facing cast iron dolphins was off to one side, situated in the middle of a black and white ceramic circle. She could only just hear the faint whisperings of the flowing water.

When she turned her head to take in the other side of the room, she froze. Chained to the base of a four-foot-tall marble obelisk lay a sleek, black panther. Its eyes were open and fixed on her own. Its wet, black nose flared as it breathed in her scent. Mr. Chirac had so engaged her attention when she entered the room that she had not noticed the deadly animal.

"Will you forgive my indiscretion for not introducing Lilly," said Mr. Chirac. "I frequently keep her in the room with me while I conduct my research or peruse through my prized manuscripts to relax from a particularly egregious day's work. Lily, this is Eva, a client. Eva, this is Lily—my only companion in this estranged life I live, save for Ricci."

"I see," said Eva. "And what do you call her?"

She pointed at the white marble statue of another panther chained to the obelisk that lay in a prone position just out of Lily's reach. It was singularly sculpted and looked so palpably alive that were it not for the lifeless eyes, she could imagine it turning its head to appraise her.

"A marvelous piece, is it not?" said Mr. Chirac. "Its very provenance is shrouded in mystery. I spent many years in artful exploration, seeking it out after I was first alerted to its existence by an Italian official. However, since I was unable to apprehend its true creator, I did not feel it appropriate to name her."

"Her?"

"Why yes, my dear. Does she not radiate the cunning, menacing femininity so feared in the wild? See how patiently she lies in wait, as does her companion Lilly. But I implore you not to test Lily's instinct of predation. White carpeting and red blood are an unfortunate combination."

He was smiling apologetically at her, after mentioning the lamentable results she could expect if she moved too close to the panther.

"But to the point of naming her, until the moment you stepped into this room, I decried my failure to intuit a name that would appropriately attribute the sensual danger she represents. Now, if you do not object, I shall give thought to naming her Eva."

As he held her gaze, Eva crossed one leg over the other, causing the slit in her dress to open and display her elegantly muscled legs. An inner smile of satisfaction flared to life as Mr. Chirac glanced down and stared for a long time before lifting his eyes to hers again.

"Yes," he said softly, "I think I will indeed name my white marble statue Eva. So, just so."

Eva compared Mr. Chirac to the brilliant but dispensable John Amrozi. Which of the two was the more dangerous? In his naivete, Amrozi could not comprehend the harm he could inflict on humanity with his programming skills, or of the catastrophe his labors could wreak when in the hands of beings such as Eva or, far worse, Hiram Abiff. Even now, as she sat in the home of Mr. Chirac, John Amrozi's creation lurked in every computer connected to the Web. At the precise moment Hiram had specified, it would evoke the identical thought in the mind of every person connected to the Internet, and she would harvest that power for Hiram. Unless, that is, she could find a way to capture it herself. To enslave humanity by the collected power of their own thoughts held a delicious irony, and with John Amrozi's Borgo virus and the artifact she was here to collect, Hiram Abiff would become the slave master of the world. She almost regretted slicing Amrozi's throat. But, as Hiram had assured her, John Amrozi would soon return. That thought chilled her. Did the returned dead remember who it was that had killed them?

"To business then," said Eva. "Have you the artifact?"

"It is, in fact, my business to acquire such things, yet there is the matter of the attendant paperwork. Such minutiae are what prompted the late C. S. Lewis to opine that his vision of Hell was that '... it is conceived and ordered (moved, seconded, carried, and minuted) in clean, carpeted, warmed and well-lighted offices, by quiet men with white collars and cut fingernails and smooth-shaven cheeks who do not need to raise their voices.' I find his work quite instructive, and although it is cadaverous in comparison to Proust, it is radiance personified when compared to Sartre."

How did Traverse Nations compare to this man? she mused. Traverse nation commanded a military budget that would dwarf many a nation's entire economy. He had the authority, the ruthlessness and the base insanity of a man tasked with the nearly unlimited power a nation could bestow when the stakes were high enough.

Yet there was a sensuous animal magnetism which radiated from the man who stood so indolently before her. It would have been an intriguing exploration to ferret out his secrets, she decided, but she had too little time.

"Do you think someone like myself is interested in your paperwork?" she asked and arched one eyebrow to emphasize the point. "I am here only to collect the artifact."

Mr. Chirac straightened and bowed slightly.

"Forgive me, Eva. I would hardly risk invoking your disapprobation. With your acquiescence, I shall retrieve the artifact and present it for your inspection."

Eva gave an approving nod, then, on impulse, ran the tip of her tongue over her lip as Mr. Chirac watched.

"So, just so," he said with a gleam in his dark eyes.

He left by a door on the far wall behind the dolphin fountain. After a minute or two had passed, Eva turned to glance at Ricci. She extended one nail painted bright red in his direction, then motioned for him to come to her.

Ricci stood motionless on one side of the double doors. He looked at her, but did not move. Anger smoldered in her when she saw, of all things, pity in his eyes.

"Come here."

"Mr. Chirac likes things to be where they were when he left the room," he said. "We have an agreement."

"I don't care what agreement you have with him; I demand you present yourself to me."

"He'll be back soon," said Ricci.

She studied the jagged scar that cut across his face and wondered how he had acquired it.

"I want to examine your scar more closely."

"No, you don't."

"Are you intimidated by my beauty?"

"No."

"What then?" she asked, attempting to restrain her temper.

"Just looking ahead," he said.

The artifact was all that really mattered, but it annoyed her that this hulking thug had the spine to defy her.

She heard the door open and turned to see Mr. Chirac carrying an elaborately carved jade box half as tall as himself. He walked as though it weighed no more than a chiffon pie. Ricci disappeared behind a white and gold enameled hutch that stood in front of a half wall, and returned carrying a wrought-iron table which he set in view of Mr. Chirac's desk. He then took the jade box from his master and lay it on the iron table.

"Thank you, Ricci," said Mr. Chirac.

When his manservant had returned to his position by the door, Mr. Chirac turned to her as he placed one manicured hand atop the shimmering green box.

"It is my custom," he said, "prior to displaying items resident in my collection, to provide my client with an oral provenance for the piece under discussion."

"I would much prefer that you just open the box so that I might see it."

Whether it was the faint downturn of his mouth or the narrowing of his eyes, she could not say, but a look of reproach crossed Mr. Chirac's face.

"My brother spoke very highly of you, which recommendation I will subsume in this matter. Yet I caution discretion. The provenance of this artifact is essential. To open the box carelessly would destroy its contents and instantly dissipate its matrices. The Blazing Star of Freemasonry, which is the artifact you seek, is, very simply put, a gathering of relational loci with the capacity to absorb and contain an infinite magnitude of energy. Beyond that, my lovely young woman, the Blazing Star of Freemasonry is fittingly invisible to the human eye. Though it is portrayed on a portentous number of lodge floors, the Blazing Star is neither a two-dimensional image nor a three-dimensional object."

"It is a magical locus?" asked Eva, her curiosity now engaged.

"It is instead a construct of uncountable loci. You are familiar, of course, with ley lines as conduits of occult energy, and with also the well-known fact that the interstices where such lines overlap are the locations known among those who conduct commerce at New Age stores as places of power. Many of the people involved in such esoteric matters believe that proper timing is also an element involved in identifying a place of power, but these ideas are only the prattling of Wiccans. Truly, there is no such thing as time in the power loci."

Eva resented being lectured, especially by a Freemason, and most especially this one, who seemed unaware of her power.

"If I may not open the box, then how will I be able to charge it with the energies harvested from the Borgo Moment?"

"You are perhaps referring to the moment when the computer virus Monsieur Abiff mentioned earlier will cause anyone staring at a computer screen to think the same thought?"

"I am."

"I see. I have written out the ritual on these linen papers," he waved a hand at a roll of off light brown papers wrapped with a fine ribbon of black velvet and tied at the top with an elaborate knot. "Please do not succumb to anxiety regarding the pronunciations of the beings whom you will summon to assist you in your work. I suspect they are well known to you as you are the *soror magisterium* of my dear friend Hiram, but if you have concerns, it is he who will instruct you. And now, my dear and most provocative lady, the time has come for you to append your signature to the *juridiquement le contrat ayant force obligatoire* I have drawn up for you. It stipulates, as a matter of course, the prompt return of the Blazing Star of Freemasonry to me three days hence at exactly the stroke of midnight."

"I will sign no papers," said Eva.

"How... awkward," said Mr. Chirac.

The Blazing Star of Freemasonry was on the iron table. The ritual instructions were on his desk. She would take what she needed. She was the Scarlett Whore of Babylon. She focused her magical will and began the summoning chant, but there was no surge of energy surrounding the space where she sat.

"The moment's decorum has declined," said Mr. Chirac sadly. "You see, you possess no magical powers in my home. After an unfortunate incident involving a... practitioner who took it upon herself to violate the hospitality of this, my very own residence, I reluctantly invoked measures to see that such discourtesy would not reoccur."

Eva took in a sharp breath when she realized that he was telling her the truth. However he had accomplished it, he had stripped her of her powers. She raged against the indignity of it. Still, the memory of the stiletto strapped to her inner thigh elicited a wicked smile from her.

"Ricci," said Mr. Chirac.

Before she could slide her hand toward the knife, she felt her breathing constrict from the pressure of two enormous hands wrapped tightly around her neck.

"Careful, Ricci," admonished Mr. Chirac. "I wish no disfigurements or bruising on her exquisite neck, and I would also appreciate her being able to draw a breath occasionally."

As she struggled to breathe, Mr. Chirac retrieved a wooden chair from a reading table near the bookshelves and sat down in front of her.

"Perhaps, even though from the neck down, your musculature is paralyzed and your windpipe is nearly closed, you wonder why I brought this so-fine chair here to sit in front of you. It is because I not only take umbrage at the mere mention of the word squat, I believe the practice itself is suitable only for degenerates and anarchists. Hence, this chair.

"Further, Mr. Abiff was well aware of this aspect of our arrangement. I suspect he shared this information with you, but that your rather imperious nature caused you to rebel against the precept."

As he spoke, Mr. Chirac leaned forward and slid his hand up and inside the slit that sliced up the front of her skirt. Eva shivered as he touched her. She struggled to breathe, and her face turned a deeper shade of red. He withdrew the stiletto from her thigh sheath and held it up before his face.

"I have a penchant," he said with a thin smile, "for weapons such as this."

He held the knife up to his nose and inhaled deeply, as though catching her scent, then turned and placed it on top of his desk.

"Now, Miss Morgan, I will very shortly ask Ricci to release you. There is much you do not know about me, which, although it does not excuse your indecorous temperament, will perhaps prevent future misadventures as your apprenticeship progresses to its final anabasis. This is a matter of commerce, yet I confess that I have taken a somewhat personal interest in your future as a result of meeting you. Please do not press against the limits of my hospitality. There is much in this house you should not wish to learn."

A low growl rumbled across the room as the black panther voiced its concerns.

Eva felt Ricci's massive hands release the pressure on her throat. She thought she heard him back away, but couldn't be sure. A wave of dizziness washed through her and for a moment she thought she would be sick. She blinked rapidly as her vision cleared.

"Would you like a glass of wine, perhaps?" asked Mr. Chirac.

"No. No thank you," she gasped.

"What is required is that you slice the tip of your left thumb and press it against the document. Please do not provoke me further by allowing a drop to fall on this so-lovely carpet of mine. Perhaps an aberrant thought will cross your mind as to the many other things you might attempt with your knife. I urge you to remember that there are many things much deadlier than a woman with a knife."

Again, the low growl of the panther.

"Lily so dislikes it when my guests displease me. Are we in agreement?"

No, Eva was not in agreement, but she nodded as though she was. It dawned on her that she had severely underestimated this man. Mr. Chirac retrieved her knife and passed it to her hilt first. His smile was wide and sincere. He handed her a single parchment with the agreement written in tightly scripted gold ink. She could not make it out. It was difficult for her to concentrate. The immense power of Ricci's fingers moments ago locked around her throat disoriented her. The caress of Mr. Chirac's hand on her inner thigh. The script itself blurred into a sheet of gold.

"By the pricking of my thumbs…" urged Mr. Chirac.

Without looking up at him, she stuck the point of the stiletto in the fleshy part of her left thumb, then returned it to its thigh sheath. With her right index finger and thumb, she leaned over the parchment and squeezed gently. A single drop of bright red welled up along the cut and then dripped onto the document. Mr. Chirac handed her a scarlet handkerchief. Eva pointedly ignored this gesture and instead inserted the tip of her finger into her mouth and sucked gently. All the while, she held his gaze with her own.

Finally, when she withdrew her finger, Mr. Chirac nodded approvingly and returned the handkerchief to his breast pocket.

"To business," he said. "There is much I must now relate to you and if you would be so kind as to listen without interruption, I will impart to you the elements that are critical to the success of your enterprise. Will you permit me such latitude?"

"I will," said Eva.

"So, just so. First, the requirements of the document you just signed are but two. You must return the Blazing Star to this very room within seventy-two hours after you cast your final spell and before midnight. And you must return it exactly as you received it. Should you fail, I will exact an appropriate penalty which will require you to assist me in such a task as I so designate.

"Now concerning Hiram. Your patron, Monsieur Abiff, has had much time to accumulate power since his return from death and has enjoyed many centuries to construct his plans. Yet, as I have learned in my somewhat shorter span of years, a plan of such complexity invariably creates weakness by its very nature. I quote Alan Perlis, who, in an indiscreet irrationality, said that 'Fools ignore complexity. Pragmatists suffer it. Some can avoid it. Geniuses remove it.' It is a melancholy actuality that the removal of complexity creates yet more complexity and still more weaknesses. Monsieur Abiff's plan is brilliantly conceived and, on the surface, quite simple, yet I am obligated to point out to you that each component of his plan must proceed correctly in order for the entire vision to be realized. This is the danger.

"I am reluctant to report that last year I was undone by the machinations of an old woman and her friends, who upended certain of my plans by a yet more-clever plan of their own. No one, it seems, is immune to the deleterious effects of confidant planning. If you fail in your efforts to acquire the power you seek to harvest and impart to him, chaos will descend upon him like a block of stone dropped from the sky. That power you seek to accumulate is necessary for him to persuade the world at large to accept a three-thousand-year old man as their savior.

"It is true, he will offer them a cure for cancer and other diseases that he has assembled from three millennia of knowledge, but to convince them to accept his leadership and displace the disparate faiths they hold dear, he will need the power which you will attempt to collect with this artifact. It is true that the President of the United States, his Surgeon General and the titular head of the Federal Food and Drug administration have, at the urgings of Brother Mihaloff, accepted already the plan to implant such devices in their citizens, but the people themselves would revolt if they saw Monsieur Abiff for who he really is. If for some yet unforeseen reason you fail, the result will be calamitous. Do you understand?"

"Yes," said Eva.

"When your benefactor was resurrected from death, he returned without a soul, as I'm sure you're aware. Ah... I see that you are unaware of this, but it is as it is. As an empty vessel, he was defenseless against the marauding, tormented spirits who possessed him at will. Ah, I see you are distressed. Shall I continue?"

Who was this man, and how did he know so much about Hiram? She felt an almost overpowering desire to leave, without or without the Blazing Star. But a terrible sense of unease now filled her. She wanted to hear more, but how could she trust a man whose manservant had nearly strangled her? How could she trust a man as dangerous as Mr. Chirac? A man who had stripped her magical powers from her without her knowledge. And yet he knew something, and that disturbed her.

"Continue," she said.

"As you wish. The possessions continued throughout the centuries. They twisted what was left of his mind. They used his body as their own and committed atrocity after atrocity. In your most wicked of dreams, you cannot conceive of the horrors they committed. The resurrected man with no soul became a repository of demons."

"How do you know all of this?" she whispered.

"That I am not to share with you. But to continue, as the centuries unfolded, Hiram began to… restrict the demons who possessed him. Gradually, he began to control the very malignant spirits who tormented him. He acquired their power. Do you see the ironic evolving complexity? Hiram is not a single entity, but many entities presenting as one. My brother still roams this earth and, even though disincarnate, should Hiram fail, his wrath would be upon you both. Should that happen, I invite you to come to me for sanctuary."

Mr. Chirac's face blurred for just an instant and Eva saw something violet-black blossom behind his eyes.

"And you could protect me from his… benefactor?" she asked. "And if so, how? His benefactor must be ancient and powerful."

"Mademoiselle," said Mr. Chirac, "the line between droll and gelastic is finer than you think. Let it not escape you that *le monde invisible est en guerre*—when you do choose to take sides, take care that your decision is still relevant."

57

Ashley Hillis sat before her computer, typing furiously to finish her latest book on schedule. It was titled "The Lansing Lycanthrope," and it was the third in her "Alpha Male Rogue Werewolf" series. She wasn't happy with it, but she had a timetable to keep or there would be hell to pay with her publisher. Werewolves were her favorite paranormal characters after the events in Sharkey's Park last year had frightened her off ghost stories. To her, ghosts were far too real and terrifying to write about now. Alpha werewolves were safer.

She was up late. It was past midnight, and she wasn't sure just how much time had passed since she didn't allow clocks in her home office and refused to look at the time in the lower right-hand corner of her computer. In fact, she'd covered up that portion of the screen with blue masking tape. There was just no way she could concentrate on her story if she kept looking at the time. Outside, the night was a rich blackness where spectral bundles of mist walked carefully across the lawn like secretive mummies fresh from their tombs. What an image, she thought. What an awful description. She was about to try a different metaphor for the night, but pushed it aside instead. She had a schedule to keep.

Her phone rang. Unknown number.

Ashley ignored it.

She was two-thirds of the way through her plot, and it was

514

bogging down. Each sentence was harder to write than the last. She was rushing it, she knew, but she could go back and edit it after she'd worked through the rest of the book. The pressure was giving her a headache.

The phone rang again, and once more she ignored it.

Who had her private cell phone number, anyway?

The phone rang seven times and then quit. Each ring was a needle pressing into her temple. Only five people, maybe six at most, had the number. Kenneth, Ian Hunter, Enid Moser, her new lawyer, her secretary, and her business manager. Wait, she thought, seven counting her agent. But she knew that even though her cell number was on a do not call list, there were always hackers who could get into anything. But she couldn't imagine a time share salesperson calling her this late at night. Yet the number was unlisted.

The phone rang still again. She let it ring. The sound made her shiver.

There was a knock at the door, and she said, "Come in."

"I'm sorry, Ashley," said Kenneth. "I heard the phone ringing and thought you'd fallen asleep at your desk. Everything all right?"

"I don't know," she said. "Only a couple of people know this number. The screen says the number is unavailable, so it isn't any of them calling."

She held up the phone so he could see.

"You want me to answer it, if they call again?" he asked.

"I can answer my own phone, Kenneth."

"I got it."

It was his way of saying "okay," or "I understand." After a year of living together in the same house, Ashely still hadn't learned to speak Southern, but at least she was beginning to understand it.

"You still working on that werewolf book?"

Ashley ran her hand through hair and sighed. After the events at Sharkey's Park, her hair and eyebrows had turned gray-white, but now, just a touch of color was starting to return. She doubted it would ever fully colorize again, and she didn't always want it to. Truth to tell, it gave her a highly distinctive look for her author photo on the back of her books.

"I'm trying to, if this phone will leave me alone."

"Well, I'll skedaddle out of here and let you get back to it."

The tall, lanky Kentuckian had just turned to leave the room when the phone rang again.

Ashley stared at it like it was going to come alive and bite her. One ring, two rings, three rings. She looked up at Kenneth, then back at the phone. Four rings, five rings. Impulsively, she reached over and picked it up. After another indecisive moment, she pushed the answer icon.

"Hello?" she said, like it was a question.

The voice at the other end was a deep, rough baritone.

"Mrs. Hillis?"

"Who is this?" she said, but she knew that voice, and it panicked her.

Kenneth raised an eyebrow.

"You know who it is. I need to talk to the old woman."

Ashley squeezed her eyes closed as though trying to block out an unwelcome vision. She didn't see Kenneth's forehead wrinkle in consternation. The man on the other end of the phone was Ricci, Mr. Chirac's brutish manservant or bodyguard, or whatever he was. Kenneth's grandmother had protected his secret from Mr. Chirac, and the man had stood up for Granny and Ashley in their showdown with Mr. Chirac, whom Granny called the Dark Man.

"She's... gone," she said.

"When will she be back? I need to talk to her. It's important."

Ashley opened her eyes and saw that Kenneth was standing next to her, deep concern evident in his face.

"She's permanently gone," she said.

"Dead?"

There was a hopeless agitation in Ricci's voice that was clear even across the wireless network.

"Yes."

"That's no good."

"No, not good at all. We miss her."

Silence on the other end of the phone.

"Is there something I can help you with?"

Kenneth made a hand motion to get her attention, and she saw him mouth the words, "Who is it?"

She put her hand over the receiver, leaned toward him and said,

"That man. That Ricci."

The look on Kenneth's face was not only surprise, but anger. Ashley held up her hand, quieting him down for the moment. Even when he'd backed Enid Moser down while Moser was holding a shotgun at her and the others, Kenneth hadn't shown anger—just calm, measured restraint. It went with the territory of being a wild hog wrestler. He was the exact opposite of her husband Michael, who had died—or rather been carried away into the world of the dead by a screaming haint. Michael had been rich, handsome, suave, and sophisticated. Kenneth was, well, a former hog wrestler and after that, he had been Granny Hillis's protector. Sometimes, she now knew, life took you down a few wrong paths before you finally met up with the right people.

"Who's there with you?"

"Kenneth Hillis. You remember he was with me when I last came to visit you."

"The tall guy with the shotgun?"

"Yes. Granny's nephew."

A grunt from the other end of the phone.

"Mr. Ricci, are you in trouble?"

"Mrs. Hillis, if that old woman's gone, we're all in trouble."

"What do you mean?"

Ricci went quiet for so long that Ashley thought he'd clicked off.

"Usually he just deals with dirtballs and they get what they should get. Sorry about your husband, I just meant—"

"I know what you meant," said Ashley.

"Anyway, now he's dealing with some things that are really, really bad."

"He's—"

"Don't say his name, Mrs. Hillis. I think he can tell when you say his name. He can't know I'm talking to you."

"Okay, I understand. But what do you mean by things?"

"They look like people, but they're not."

"What are you talking about?" asked Ashley nervously.

"They'll bring Hell to earth."

"Does this have something to do with the Detroit Masonic Temple?"

The connection came to her without thought. It was the look on Kenneth's face after he got off the phone with Hunter and the tremor in Ricci's voice that did it for her.

Kenneth laid his palm on her shoulder and mouthed, "Don't talk to him."

That made her mad. Kenneth was overly protective of her since that bizarre night they'd first met when he and Granny Hillis came to meet her and her lawyer, Henry Wendland. Henry died later that night, the night the screaming haint came calling. Kenneth had been the steady point in her life since then. But sometimes, in his desire to protect her, he crowded her.

"How'd you know about what's going on at the Temple?" Ricci asked.

She was right. There was a connection. Suddenly she realized that whatever was going on at the Detroit Masonic Temple was more exciting than what she was writing. From the corner of her eye, she saw Kenneth was about to blow a gasket because she was talking to Ricci and worried that maybe she would give away some Masonic secret about what was happening at the Temple. But she didn't know any Masonic secrets, and Kenneth had refused to tell her the details of what he and Hunter had discussed. But before she could see a way out of her dilemma, Ricci made it unnecessary.

"Never mind. Hunter, I should have known. He's part of the problem."

Kenneth was so agitated, he reached for the phone, but Ashley twisted out of the way.

"No," she said.

She was getting really agitated.

"No, what?" asked Ricci.

Ashley glared at Kenneth, but he wasn't backing down.

"Kenneth doesn't want me talking to you," she said.

"Put him on," said Ricci. "I need to talk to him, anyway."

"Why?"

"Just do it, Mrs. Hillis. I don't think we have much time."

This time, it was Ashley's turn to glare at Kenneth as she handed him the phone.

"Ask him. He's the one who wants to talk to you."

Kenneth looked at the phone like it was a live snake. He was thinking it over, she knew. It was the way he did things. Moved in on instinct, then slowed down to make sure he was doing the right thing. Then, if he was sure it was right, he moved fast and got it done. This thought irritated her. Moved fast and got it done? The longer she was around him, the more she even started to think like him. Finally, he put the phone to his ear.

"What?"

Ashley reached for the Excedrin bottle. She was getting a huge headache.

"Listen up for a minute. You don't like me. I get that. But if you can't throw that over for a minute, the world will get flushed right down the shitter. We can't let that happen. The guy I work for has gone too far. Even with the old woman dead, we got to do something."

"That old woman, as you call her, was my granny."

"She was your grandma? I liked that old woman. I wish she was still here."

Kenneth let that hang for a minute, and then drawled, "You turning good Samaritan on me, big boy?"

Ashley cringed at the sarcasm in Kenneth's voice.

"Are you as useless as you sound, or are you going to help?"

"Why should I help you?"

"That's enough, Kenneth," said Ashley, her face turning red with anger. "If it wasn't for Mr. Ricci, neither Granny Hillis nor I would have walked out of... would have walked out of that man's house alive. Did you forget that?"

She saw the remembrance of that night flash through his eyes and saw him suddenly look like he was embarrassed. He couldn't talk for a minute. She reached out, grabbed his free hand and squeezed. The sense of loss in his eyes made her want to stand and hug him.

"You still there?" asked Ricci.

"Yeah," said Kenneth in a suddenly thick voice. "I am."

"There's things coming for the ghost box. Keep Mrs. Hillis out of the way, okay?"

"Who's coming?"

The tense anger flushed back into Kenneth's face.

"Not who. They're not people, like I told her. They may look like people sometimes, but they're not. And they're dangerous. They walked right out of hell kind of dangerous."

"What're you talking about?"

"Your granny would know. Didn't you learn nothing from her?"

"You're hurting my hand, Kenneth," said Ashley in a strained voice.

He looked down at her like he was coming out of a daze.

"Sorry," he said, then loosened his grip on her hand.

Kenneth did know. He thought of the nights he'd spent listening to Granny on her front porch. That old woman knew more than any human being Kenneth had ever known. Things on this earth and beyond. Things of the heart and things of the mind. When his family was killed in a car crash and he returned to Kentucky, it was she who brought him back from the depths of depression. He'd leaned back on her front porch at night with his legs swinging over the edge and him chewing on a long weed as she talked about the things most city folk never heard of and never would. She was tough, and she didn't let him wallow in grief, but talked to him like he was a man. Told him of the things that lived beyond the night. Told him how sometimes they had to be put down and how hard it was to do it. Told him how there were things a man best not take on alone.

"What is it you need?" Kenneth asked.

"We need to meet. We can't do this over the phone."

"Where and when?"

Ricci gave him an address in downtown Detroit.

"When?"

"After dark, tomorrow. Maybe ten o'clock. That's the safest time for it. He don't get up till sunset, but he doesn't really get to it until after midnight. I got to be back before then."

"Serious?"

"Yeah. I don't get it, but I won't live long enough to understand."

"Huh."

"Helping you will get me killed."

"For real?"

"Worse than that. But I don't got a choice. I can't let the world go down. She's in the world."

Kenneth looked at Ashley, then said, "Who?"

"Mrs. Hillis will know. Tell them to keep her safe. Don't let me down on this."

"I don't even know—"

"One more thing. When you come to see me, don't leave Mrs. Hillis alone. Take her to stay with your friends. When you get back from seeing me, you'd better all stay together. Bad things coming. Don't let them get that ghost box. And make sure that other person Mrs. Hillis knows about is safe. Keep her from the bad things."

"You," said Kenneth, "got a funny way of talking."

But Ricci had already hung up.

Kenneth held the phone back out to Ashley.

"What in the hell were you two talking about?" asked a bewildered Ashley.

"I'm not sure I know exactly. That man's harder to understand than a screeching owl in the rain. He said there's a woman he was worried about that he was sure you knew who she was. I don't get that. Do you know who he was talking about?"

"Uh, no. How would I know? I only met him once..."

Ashley's voice drifted off as she tried to remember.

"Oh no," she said.

"What?"

"I think he's talking about his sister."

"Yep."

"Kenneth," she said, "you'd better call Hunter and find out what in the world is going on."

"Yep. I'm doing that sure as I'm from Kentucky, but there's more and I don't think you're going to like it."

So, he told her about the meeting and how, for her own safety, she couldn't be left alone anymore.

"You take Moser with you," she said. "I mean that, Kenneth. I'm not about to lose you."

"Well, Miss Ashley, I believe that's the nicest thing any woman ever said to me."

She punched him in the stomach, but it was like hitting a washboard.

58

"No," said Rebecca. "Just me and Mr. Moser."

"But—" protested Hunter.

"No buts," said Moser. "Do like the lady says."

Hunter stepped back and allowed Rebecca and Moser to pass.

"Up the stairs," said Rebecca.

Moser dutifully carried the young woman they had found in the Borgo Temple up the winding staircase to the second floor, with Rebecca following behind.

"I'll bring the medical supplies," said Pastor Mark.

Rebecca and Moser kept moving and then disappeared out of sight around the corner. Pastor Mark took the supplies from the medicine cabinet that Hunter led him to and followed behind. Hunter made sure all the doors were locked. He stared out the front window at the driveway, looking to see if anyone or anything was following. When he saw nothing, he held his hands in front of his face and saw to his amazement that they weren't shaking. What a night, he thought. What a night.

Who was the young woman they had found? Who was the man Jimmy she kept screaming about? And what was that about needing a phone to call the President? He had no answers to any of those questions, and he was tired of having no answers. He felt as lost as he had in the aftermath of what happened to him and Bartok and Moser

522

at Townsend Mountain. He had to figure out what to do. Everyone else seemed to know what they were doing except him. And he had to get some sleep. Absolutely needed sleep.

Upstairs, he could hear Rebecca giving directions. He wanted desperately to call Dr. Ralph Smith, but that would be disastrous. Brother Ralph Smith would undoubtedly tell brother Mihaloff whatever he found out. Hunter couldn't let that happen. As far as he knew, all the Temple Guardians were spellbound.

The witch—Eva Morgan—was unlike any witch he had ever heard or read about. What she had done to Rebecca fit none of the lore he knew about witchcraft. And her creatures were just flat out impossible. What were they?

Pastor Mark called down for him to bring more garbage bags and more towels. Hunter hustled away to do just that. This, he thought, was a night like no other.

****

"That was a lot of blood," said Hunter.

"Yes," said Pastor Mark. "Her shoulder was ripped up badly."

"We need a doctor for her," said Hunter.

"You know why we can't call a doctor," said pastor Mark, "there's too much at stake. And we don't know who to trust."

"I'm sorry," said Hunter. "I'm just worried she'll get an infection or worse."

"She gave her pain pills and an injection of antibiotics. But I know what you mean. I know nothing about medical things either."

"I'm glad I'm not the only one," said Hunter. "But if we get through this, I'm going to have to take some serious first-aid classes."

"What did you mean when you said 'or worse'," said pastor Mark.

Hunter shifted uncomfortably.

"Nothing."

"Tell me, Hunter."

"It's just… I'm worried she might be contaminated."

The minister thought about that, and a worried look crossed his face.

"Oh."

"It's not a general fear," said Hunter. "Or maybe it is. Like when someone is bitten by a werewolf. Or like what happened to my uncle at Townsend Mountain. I don't even know if that's possible, considering what attacked her. But we really don't know."

"Thanks, Hunter. You really know how to put a man's mind at rest."

Hunter nodded. The closest things he could think of to what Rebecca had described in the car were goblins. Maybe just something that looked like goblins. How the hell was he supposed to know?

"Maybe we should tie her down," said Hunter.

He thought back to when Enid Moser had done the same thing to his uncle Bartok. But that was different. Moser had known what was going to happen to his uncle Bartok. He had experience in the things that went on at Townsend Mountain. What none of them had experience with was what Rebecca and pastor Mark had described in the Borgo temple. Was it, in fact, possible that the young woman upstairs was contaminated? Better that they tie her down, than to find out too late that she was transforming into the same type of creature that had attacked her.

"Rebecca will know what to do," said Pastor Mark. "Like I told you before, she's a very special woman."

Hunter didn't know about that. So far, she reminded him of St. Augustine with Special Forces training.

"Maybe we should tie her down," repeated Hunter.

"Tie who down?" came Moser's voice as he walked around the corner and into the kitchen.

"Hunter thinks we should tie the wounded woman upstairs down in case she's contaminated."

"Well, what if she is," said Hunter. "Like the dogs and…"

Moser grabbed more paper towels, went to the sink and wetted them. Then he turned back to the other men and asked, "I got any blood on my face?"

"Some on your neck, maybe, unless that's dirt," said Pastor Mark. "Get closer so I can see better."

Enid walked toward them and then stopped only a few steps away from them.

"That better?" he asked.

"It's blood," said Hunter.

"Shit," said Moser. "Sorry, pastor. That woman up there can sure bleed." He stopped for a moment to scrub his neck, held up the paper towels to check if he got anything off, and then continued. "She was hurt bad enough, though. Noisy cuss, too. Did you hear her yelling about cutting somebody's nuts off named Traverse Nations? What the hell kind of name is that? Oh… sorry, pastor."

"We couldn't make out what she was saying down here," said pastor Mark. "I bet there's not a piece of plywood anywhere in this place. Everything is made with quality materials. And quit saying you're sorry, Moser. I did time in prison, remember? I've heard a few people swear in my life."

They were a haggard-looking group, Hunter thought. Pastor Mark's eyes drooped and his big shoulders slumped forward. Enid's thick head of hair was messed up and his jaw and chin were covered in a patchwork of black and white stubble. Hunter hadn't looked in a mirror yet, but he probably looked as bad as the others.

"Is Rebecca still with her?" asked Hunter.

"She's upstairs praying for her," said Moser.

"Ah," said Pastor Mark. "Praying for a healing."

"A healing?" said Hunter. "You mean like a faith healing? Did you see the extent of those wounds?"

"I did."

Hunter turned to look at Moser.

"What did you think?"

"They looked as bad as any I ever seen, and I've seen my share of wounds in my time. Unless Rebecca's prayers bring a miracle, I think she will lose the use of her arm."

"Maybe we should get her to a doctor," said Hunter. "I mean, I know we think it's dangerous, but this could be serious."

Moser and pastor Mark looked at each other first and then looked at him. The look of sadness in their eyes was hard for Hunter to see.

"I think," said Moser, "we done plowed this ground before. I don't want nothing bad to happen to that woman upstairs, but, and I truly do hate to say this, but I think if we take her into any kind of a medical facility, we are all going to be dead before too long. And maybe a lot worse. If that old man in that other world comes through to this world and controls enough Masons, I think there's going to be a war. And I don't mean no war between people. I mean, a war between people and something much worse. What do you think, pastor?"

"Based on what I saw in that other world, I'd say you're right, Mr. Moser. You can't even imagine what it was like there. Those monsters. Those creatures. That woman, that witch, that Eva Morgan. If we let them come through that door between worlds, it will be like giving the key to the city to the devil and his hordes. And from what you've told me, Hunter, we only have a few days to stop it. If we bring the authorities into this by taking her to a doctor, they'll gum up the works and before we get them believing what we've said, that door will open and out will step Hiram Abiff. And I don't even want to think about that."

Hunter didn't know what to say. Maybe there was nothing good that could be said. He felt lost. So much had come at them in such a short time.

"Hey," he said. "I forgot."

He took out his cell phone and in front of the questioning glances of the Moser and pastor Mark, he dialed Molly's number. One ring, two rings, three rings, and he knew then in his gut that Molly would never again answer her phone.

"Who you calling?" asked Moser.

"Molly."

The way he said it told Moser everything he needed to know.

"Don't call again," he said to Hunter.

Hunter nodded distractedly and then dialed Ron's number. One ring, two rings, three rings, and he knew it was all over for Ron, too.

"Were you calling that guy Ron?" asked Moser.

Hunter nodded.

"Don't call him again, either. If they're both dead, the police will be checking their phone records. If they contact you, say you were just trying to get hold of another Mason to meet for dinner and you gave up calling. They'll ask how you know Molly, and you'll have to say she's your ex-girlfriend. That'll get their antennae wiggling, but it ain't likely to go anywhere. Got it?"

Hunter shook his head yes, then set the phone on the table dejectedly, unable to face Moser's eyes. But as soon as he had, it rang. Hunter scooped it up like it was going to give him the winning lottery ticket.

"Hello? Molly? Ron?"

Moser saw his friend's face twist into a confused expression.

"Kenneth," said Hunter, "what are you calling this late for? Uh-huh. Yes. What?"

There was silence again as Hunter listened for a few minutes.

Then he said, "Maybe you'd better run this by Moser."

He held the phone out, and Moser snatched it out of his hand.

"Hello? Kenneth? Are you all right, boy? What? Tell me, brother."

This time, it was Moser who listened for a few minutes before speaking.

"Kenneth," he said into the phone, "don't go squirrely on me. You can't go alone. You got that, big man? I done lost too many friends and family already. I don't care how tough you are, you know better than to go meet that ex-con by yourself. What? Well, I know you're sweet on Ashley and she's thinking that fella Ricci is some kind of good guy underneath his scars and shit, but you got to remember who he works for. And how do you know he's showing up alone? Maybe he'll have that panther of his with him. What? Look, let me spot for you from the roof? I know you can handle it, you stubborn son of a bitch, but—hello? Hello? Aw, shit."

Moser handed the phone back to Hunter.

"That bad?"

"What the hell do you think? That stubborn cuss is worried about getting me hurt, but he's going to do it by himself? That dumbass. He's been like that all his life, the son of a bitch. No way to stop him, though."

"We could call Ashley," said Hunter. "Maybe she'll tell us where he's going."

"Nope. He wouldn't tell her. And she's on her way over here tomorrow. And from what he said, that man Ricci is trying to protect that woman Pastor Mark and Rebecca brought through that chair opening. He told Ashley the woman he's trying to protect was there with us in the Temple tonight. Maybe she'll tell us more when she gets here."

"Pardon my asking," said Pastor Mark, "but who is Ashley and who is Kenneth?"

Hunter explained that Ashley Hillis and Kenneth helped them stop the screaming haint last year.

"The what?" asked the pastor.

"A ghost," said Moser. "Hey Hunter, what are you thinking about?"

So lost in thought was he that he seemed not to hear Moser's question.

"Hunter?" prodded Pastor Mark, and he reached out and put a hand on Hunter's forearm to get his attention.

"No," said Hunter.

"I don't understand."

"I mean, I think Moser has the wrong woman. I think the woman that Ricci was talking about wasn't the woman you and Rebecca saved."

"What are you talking about?" said Moser.

"I think he was talking about Rebecca."

Stunned silence filled the room. Moser and Pastor Mark looked at each other in surprise, then turned back to Hunter.

"You're shitting me," said Moser.

"Oh my God," said pastor Mark.

"Brother Mihaloff told me that he had a son. A son who died in a fire. He said the boy had something wrong upstairs. That today we would call him a sociopath. And that he died in a prison fire."

Both Moser and pastor Mark looked toward the stairs. They stared upward in disbelief. They had both met Ricci under different circumstances, but neither could easily process the idea that Rebecca was his sister.

"But," said Moser to pastor Mark, "I thought you said Ricci was let go before the fire?"

Pastor Mark had to think about that.

"Someone," he said thoughtfully, "must've had the fix in and told Brother Mihaloff that his son died in the fire. That's the only way to explain it. And it makes sense. They probably didn't have any contact the entire time Ricci was in prison. So, someone fed Rebecca's father that story."

"Possibly," said Moser.

"More than possible," said Hunter. "Given the way Mr. Chirac deals with things, I'd say that's exactly what happened."

"I wonder if Rebecca knows?" said Moser.

"I'm betting not," said Hunter, "and I don't want to be the one to tell her. But I'm betting that he doesn't want her to know. Somehow Granny Hillis knew his secret and told Ricci about it that night when me, Moser, Ashley, and Kenneth went there last year to confront Mr. Chirac. She said she would keep the secret from Mr. Chirac if Ricci let her in that night."

"That brings us back," said Pastor Mark, "to who exactly that young woman upstairs that was wounded actually is."

"No way to know," said Moser. "She didn't have any identification with her, not even a driver's license."

"We will have to leave that a mystery for now," said Hunter. "I don't think there's any way to figure this out until she's awake and can tell us herself. But there are a few other things that occurred to me that just make little sense about this whole situation. If you think about it, Moser, for example, this whole thing for Hiram Abiff to be introduced into the world in this gigantic event really kicked into gear after the Temple Guardians found out that Uncle Bartok was dead. I'm wondering if there really could be a link between the two. I don't know that it is, but it's got me thinking.

"And I'm tired of operating in the dark. This is too much like what went on at Townsend Mountain last year. We didn't make any progress in solving that situation until we could sit down, collect all the information, and fit all the pieces together. Maybe that's what I need to do next—go upstairs to Uncle Bartok study and start fitting some pieces together. I think if I can organize everything we know, we can fill in a lot of blanks in this story. Maybe we can even figure out what to do after I've organized my thoughts. You guys mind?"

"Get to it," said Moser. "It's what you do best."

Finally, Hunter thought he was back on his game. Molly and Ron were probably dead. All the more reason to avenge them by putting a stop to this whole mess. He desperately hoped they had enough time to prevent Hiram Abiff from entering the world. There were a few other things he wanted to do before Armageddon started.

59

Hunter sorted through his uncle Bartok's books, took some down, and put them back. He wasn't sure that what he was looking for could be found in books. Bartok had a wide variety of books on the history and symbolism of Freemasonry, which looked interesting, but didn't seem like they would have anything concerning the origin of the Master Mason ritual wherein the legend of Hiram Abiff was revealed. So instead, he went to his tablet computer, which was on the desk, sat down and searched the Internet to find out when Hiram Abiff first appeared in Freemasonry. The date really wasn't critical to him, but he thought it would get him thinking along the right lines.

After searching the web, he found mention of Hiram Abiff in Prichard's Masonry Dissected. It was an early primitive form of the legend. But in the year 1738, Dr. James Anderson and his associates published the constitutions of 1738, revealing the high Hiramic legend in full form. Prior to this time, there was no mention at all of a personage titled Hiram Abiff. Hunter found this curious, but he put the fact aside for the time being to concentrate on all that he had learned in the last few days.

First, Brother Mihaloff had told him that the Temple Guardians had taken over where the Knights Templar had left off. He had said that the Knights Templar had found Hiram Abiff chained beneath the second Jerusalem Temple. Further, he claimed that Hiram Abiff had existed since the time of the first Jerusalem Temple, and that he was the chief architect in charge of implementing the designs for both. Whether or not this was true, Hunter had no idea. But he thought about the possibility.

What if Hiram Abiff had been a man alive at the time of the first Temple? The story was that after the destruction of the first Temple, that God had kept Hiram Abiff alive to build the second Temple. That made little sense to Hunter. Hiram would have been long dead by the time the first Temple was destroyed. And there was a long time in between the time before the second Temple was built. There was the story of Methuselah, who lived almost 1000 years, but no one who had been kept alive by God for 3000 years. And, as the chief architect in charge of implementing God's design for the Temple, Hiram was just following a design made by God. Any architect could have done the same.

Why was there any reason to consider Hiram different from the others? Surely, the Lord could have had any other architect follow the same plan. Yet he supposedly kept Hiram Abiff alive even while the Temple stood. It just made little sense.

In the months after, brother Mihaloff and the other members of the Temple Guardians found out that Bartok was dead, plans to take Hiram Abiff from wherever he was hiding to the Detroit Masonic Temple with grand fanfare. There, he and Brother Mihaloff would introduce his cure for cancer, which involved the implant in the forehead that Rebecca had told him about. The implant, according to Rebecca, was a replica on a miniature scale of the blood symbol that had been painted on the Mihaloff front door.

Next, there was the prophecy allegedly passed down through the Temple Guardians concerning the signs that would herald the return of Hiram Abiff. The unliving would speak his name. The doorway to hell would open up. The sign of the enemy would be seen. And the Blazing Star of Freemasonry would be returned to the Masonic brethren. The first three had been fulfilled and, according to Brother Mihaloff, the blazing Star of Freemasonry was in the hands of the fifth member of the Temple Guardians and would be returned on the day that Hiram Abiff entered the Detroit Masonic temple.

From what he had read in the PDF files from the diary of Charles Stanley Jones, he and Alistair Crowley had used their magic to create the first prophecy. At least they had used their magic to create the statue that tried to strangle Mike leasing. In addition, they had created the magical chairs in the Romanesque Lodge that were used to connect the world of Hiram Abiff to the real world.

Back to the statue. Although Crowley and Charles Stanley Jones had created the statue, someone had to have activated it recently. That somebody, Hunter guessed, was most likely the witch named Eva Morgan. No way to know for sure, but that was his best guess. Also, since the statue had been created by Crowley and Jones in the 1920s, Hiram Abiff's return had clearly been planned for nearly a century. Maybe longer, much longer. But the why and the meaning of all this was still unclear. He hoped the woman Rebecca and Pastor Mark had saved, if she survived, would know things that could clear this and other questions up. After all, she had been in the world on the other side of the Borgo Pass. What had she seen there? Why was she being attacked by the monsters in the Borgo Temple? And who was she?

Hunter realized at that moment that he was still tapping the ink pen on the desk; he had been so deep in thought he never even noticed. That's the problem with this whole mess, he thought. There's so much going on and my brain keeps taking off in different directions. I have to stick to one thing. What should that be? It came to him as though it had been waiting for him to ask that simple question since the whole affair started.

The symbol that had been burned on Brother Mihaloff's door. That he could get his head around. It was right up his alley. He was, after all, a famous—or semi famous-paranormal investigator. The problem was, he had never seen that symbol before. Even Bartok had never shown such a symbol to him. Maybe… maybe Bartok had, but he just hadn't paid attention. Hunter looked up again at the rows and rows of books stacked in the dark-colored bookshelves that lined the walls of Bartok's study.

"These are the books that hold my attention and have value to me," said Bartok. "If they don't hold my attention and have little scholarly value, then they don't belong in this study."

Then he would rub his mustache with his right index finger as though sharpening one against the other. So precise. It was the way Bartok's mind was constructed. And yet, he was not limited to dry, tightly constructed arguments. Bartok had a wonderful imagination, and he remembered hours and hours of discussion with his uncle.

He dearly missed that old man. It had never occurred to him in his entire life that one day Uncle Bartok would be dead. He wondered if one of the books on Bartok's shelves held the answer to what the symbol was and where it was from. Too many to read now. It would take weeks to go through them by himself. But these were not all of Bartok's books; they were just those he was most fond of reading. There was also the library, which was easily three times the size of Bartok's office. The Apocalypse would have come and gone twice by the time he searched the books in the library.

No, he was still looking for meaning and, truth to tell, that kind of thing wasn't his strong suit. He had to approach this differently. He had to approach this as an engineer. The reason he had been a successful paranormal debunker was because he had approached the topic as an engineer, not as a ghost hunter.

He brought out his cell phone and thumbed through the photo gallery until he brought up the image of the sigil hidden in the Empty Chair at the Masonic Temple. It was a black and red mandala violated by... by what? An overlaid symbol of a winged man with his chest broken wide open... and something dark and violent encircling him. Why hadn't he seen this before? Was it true what Rebecca had said about him? Could he really not see what this symbol really was because he was blinded by his own beliefs? That disturbed him.

Again, he realized he was off track. It wasn't only the symbol, it was the way it was wired into the chair and the pulsing lights behind it that looked like little Christmas tree lights. It was some kind of combination electrico-magical device. Who in the world had the genius to create such a thing? Did someone as drug addled as Aleister Crowley really have the focus to devise this symbol? Hunter looked at the symbol again after closing his eyes and re-opening them. The bizarre image of the man with wings and his chest torn open was gone. Now he saw the face of the old man. He saw the face of Hiram Abiff.

"Son of a bitch," said Hunter softly. "This is not damned well possible."

He was looking at a photo he'd taken with a camera. There couldn't be any magic in the photo itself, could there? How could it change like that? Unless... unless Rebecca was right. Unless what he saw was functionally limited by his own mind.

But understanding all of that wasn't what was important. He had to stop the creature called Hiram Abiff from entering the Detroit Masonic Temple. If he could interrupt the circuit, maybe he could do that. If there was no electro-magical connection between the two Empty Chairs, when one opened, the other would not get the message to open at the same time. Hunter thought about that possibility, but put it aside. If he tinkered with the device, he had a feeling either Mihaloff or Eva Morgan, or maybe even Hiram Abiff himself would fix it. That just would not do.

He thought some more and then grinned stupidly. How about if instead he installed the remote control device to open and close the circuit inside the chair in the Detroit Masonic Temple? Then, if the Temple Guardians activated the chair to open both sides, so that Hiram Abiff could come through and present himself in front of the assembled Freemasons, Hunter might activate the circuit again to close both doors with Hiram Abiff trapped inside. Brother Mihaloff had cautioned Hunter against going through the Borgo pass too slowly because of the danger of being trapped inside. He had told Hunter that anything trapped inside would be destroyed.

Another idea came to him. What if how it worked was that the Borgo pass itself was not there until the doors open? The doors opening would trigger the magical creation of the Borgo Pass. When the doors on both sides closed again, the pass would disappear and the hellish creatures outside the Borgo Pass would make short work of the poor soul trapped in between.

"You making any progress so far?" asked Moser.

Hunter didn't look up; he seemed lost in thought.

"You deaf? I asked if you was making any progress."

Without looking up, Hunter said, "I think I am. At least I was until you asked me that."

Moser walked into the room, looking as bad as Hunter felt. He pulled a chair from the other side of the desk away from Hunter to make enough room for his long legs and then sat down.

"What's going on with Rebecca and that woman?"

"She said not to disturb her," said Moser. "But when I walked by the door, I could still hear her in prayer."

"I didn't know people could pray that long."

Moser laughed and leaned his head back to look up at the vaulted ceiling. In the dim light coming from the hallway, combined with the backlight of Hunter's computer, Moser looked like Ichabod Crane, with long, rangy muscles and a scraggly face.

"We had a pastor once who claimed he could pray from morning till night."

"Seriously?"

"Nobody wanted to put him to the test," said Moser. "But for sure, that man could pray with a fervor."

"What's Rebecca praying for?" asked Hunter.

"She's praying for healing."

"From the look of that wound," said Hunter, "that woman needs a lot of prayer. And she really thinks prayer can heal people? I'm not mocking her, I'm just saying no one has ever recorded a scientifically verifiable healing."

Moser scratched his chin and then yawned.

"Looked bad to me, too, but Rebecca's faith is powerfully strong, Hunter. Most of you city people know little about faith healing. Usually it's stuff you read in magazines or see on television about somebody in the Philippines yanking out some evil hunk of junk from somebody's abdomen right on camera. I don't know how anyone could believe that, anyway. Folks that believe that kind of stuff just haven't been out and about much. People that live in cities have way too much fun making fun of hill people. I ain't talking about you, of course, Hunter, but college-educated people got a way of jumping to conclusions. No offense."

"None taken," said Hunter. "So, you really believe in this stuff?"

"I do."

"How come you never said anything about this kind of stuff?"

"Didn't think I had to," said Moser. "And the topic never came up before."

"Have you ever seen anything like a healing? I mean you personally, not something somebody just told you about."

Moser scowled. It was the first time Hunter had ever seen him scowl.

"You got something to say," said Moser, "just say it."

Hunter thought a minute before speaking. In his experience, topics like faith were always sensitive. People thought if you question their ideas on the topic or beliefs that you were calling them stupid or crazy. Either one of those two reactions was bad. But considering their current situation, Hunter felt he had to ask.

"Okay," he said. "I don't mean to offend you, and I'm surely not questioning what you believe or think you've seen, but I'd like to hear it for myself right from your own mouth. And, Moser, I mean this—if Rebecca can pray over that woman, and that woman is miraculously healed, then I'm going to be the first one to stand up and say it's not just possible, it's real."

Moser leaned back in the chair and closed his eyes. He stayed that way for so long Hunter thought he might be asleep. Neither of them had slept much since they'd arrived in Detroit. And they'd both been wired since their first meeting in the Detroit Masonic Temple. What a present, though—listening to Brother Mike Leasing's story. But he was so tired. He was thinking of leaning back in his own chair and closing his eyes for just a minute when Moser opened his eyes and started talking.

"You've asked me a couple of times how it was that me and the other Mosers were able to guard Townsend Mountain from the rest of the world without knowing what it was. How we could guard something that was said to be so evil that no one, including your uncle Bartok, would even tell us what it was—like we'd run away if we ever found out. Mosers never run away. Never. I expect you know that by now. So how you figure we could do that? Ask yourself."

Hunter was going to stand up and stretch, but he was just too tired to make the effort.

"I don't know," he said. "I couldn't have done it."

"Your family did. Think it through. Bartok died doing it. And you saved a lot of people when you did the same thing. So, our families have a long history of protecting the world from evil. You're new to the game, young man, but I'll tell you how the rest of us stayed our hands steady—it's because we'd seen some powerful good miracles in our lives. You saw one, too, when you saw what Granny Hillis did using your ghost box. You tell me here, you sitting here in your old uncle Bartok's chair, and he a man who saw more mysteries than any man should, you tell me if that wasn't the damnedest thing you ever saw. A miracle, wasn't it? Something impossible for regular folks. But that's what keeps people like the Mosers and the Hunter's going. We see a miracle like what with granny Hillis, and we know there's good out there that will save us from the evil.

"Now, I know why you got a problem with Rebecca, and it ain't an easy one for you to fess up to. Fact is, your whole head is full a cow manure when it comes to being a Christian. Don't worry, I ain't going to try and straighten you out. That's between you and the Lord. But what's between me and you is that as a Moser to a Hunter, I'm telling you, son, to keep your eyes and your ears open for miracles. You got to look for the hand of God everywhere in life. If you don't see it there, you got to pray that you do. People like you and me we just don't have enough in us to fight against pure evil without help, Hunter. It's more than there being no shame in asking for help. It's just plain stupid not to. So, when we go up against this Mr. Chirac and against Hiram Abiff, we need every bit of divine help we can get, son. They are a lot out of our league.

"To answer you directly, do I believe in faith healing? I do. More than that, I believe in God, and I believe that to be on the side of the good news, you got to be a child of God. So, there you have it. I already done prayed for Miss Rebecca and for that woman what we don't know who she is. You might think about doing the same. These are evil times, Hunter, and I believe they are going to get darker."

Enid Moser really was a man of few words. In fact, that was the longest discourse Hunter had ever heard issue forth from the old man. That should have scared Hunter, but it made him feel better. He hadn't realized how much he wanted miracles on his side. He didn't want to have to say out loud how terrified he was of both Hiram Abiff and Mr. Chirac. But it was a fact. He was terrified of them both. And the witch... she both terrified and disturbed him. She was like an occult hit woman.

"Okay," said Hunter. "I understand, but it's going to take my mind a long time to catch up with yours. I have an easier time believing in UFOs than I do in miracles."

"Don't worry, it ain't your mind I'm worried about catching up. It's in here."

Moser tapped his calloused hand against his chest.

"Huh," said Hunter.

"So, you were thinking," said Moser. "What you got?"

Hunter drew in a breath, thought for a moment, and then spoke.

"Look at this," he said, and slid his cell phone over for Moser to see.

Moser studied the image for a moment and then shook his head.

"What the hell is this thing?" said Moser.

"I think," said Hunter, "it's a communication device. When one door is open, it sends a signal for the other chair to open at the same time. Which is damned peculiar. I mean, think about it. There is no connecting cable to carry an electrical signal through the Borgo Pass. Instead, I think it's a magical signal being sent. Kind of a wireless magical signal, if you think about it."

"So, how exactly does that help us?"

"Well, I was thinking that if I can find a way to bypass the magical circuit, we could stop the chair at the other end from opening."

"And?"

"Yeah, I don't see a way for it to help us. Unless maybe once Hiram Abiff enters the Borgo Pass from the other side, we could interrupt the signal so that the door beneath the empty chair in the Detroit Masonic Temple doesn't open."

"Wouldn't that be too late?" asked Moser. "I mean, both doors would be open. And if I understand what you're saying, this device doesn't close the doors, it opens them. Aren't they kind of like on a timer, from what you said, so that both doors stay open a certain amount of time and then close at the same time?"

"That's what I think. They must be on some kind of a timer. In looking at this mess," Hunter pointed at the image on the smart phone, "I can't tell if there is a timer. Or maybe it's somewhere deeper beneath the mechanism. I'm just saying if we can trap Hiram Abiff in the Borgo Pass with the doors closed, he would be destroyed. That's what Brother Mihaloff told me, that anyone trapped in the Pass when the doors close would be obliterated."

"Kind of thin, don't you think?"

"Yeah, but it's all I've got now."

Both men were silent.

"Or," said Hunter, "if as soon as he came through into the Detroit side, we shoved him back in as the door was closing like you did by hitting that monster in the head and it fell back in, the door would close and he'd be screwed."

"Wouldn't the entire place be filled with like a thousand Freemasons?" Asked Moser. "Do you really think they would stand by while we did that?"

"I don't know," said Hunter. "But it's an idea."

"Uh-huh."

"Or maybe… You know, Brother Mihaloff said he's going to be enthroned in the Empty Chair. So, if I could ring this device," he pointed at the phone again, "to open up when he does, he would drop in and maybe I could activate the Detroit chair to close up without opening up the other chair on the other side of the Borgo pass."

Moser mulled that over.

"There' are a lot of holes in that, Hunter," said Moser. "But I'm guessing you already noticed that."

"I did," said Hunter.

Moser got up and stretched.

"It's a start," he said. "Why don't you sleep on it? We can kick this around again in the morning."

Hunter was about to answer when he heard a scream from down the hallway. Before he could even get out of his chair, Moser was off and running that way with his pistol already out.

60

Marla screamed and sat up straight. She was in a dark, unfamiliar room. Where was Jimmy? She opened her mouth to scream his name, but her survival instinct kept that urge in check. She slapped her pants pockets, looking for weapons. Her legs were bare; where the hell were her pants? Beneath her was a soft mattress. In a bed; she was in bed. But in bed where?

Her eyes began to adjust. She saw a thin line of moonlight shining in through a crack between two curtains. An open door, with a faint light coming from the hallway. And then, running footsteps. Getting closer to her. Coming on fast.

She scrambled off the side of the bed and headed for the bedroom door so she could hide behind it. Her heart raced as she tried not to think of what could be coming. She had to get out of sight. But she'd only taken a step toward her goal when someone moved in front of her, held up her hand and said softly, "Everything's okay. Don't worry."

Before she could respond, the woman's fist slammed up beneath her chin and cold-cocked her into unconsciousness.

****

"You two having a disagreement?" asked Moser.

"Help me get her off the floor, will you?" said Rebecca.

"Where to?"

"Back on the bed."

It was harder than they thought to get her back up on the bed and beneath the blankets. Sometimes, unconscious people were as hard to move as the dead. When they'd covered her up, Rebecca tucked the top sheet just beneath the woman's chin and patted her on the hand.

"I'm sorry," she said. "But you looked too crazy to be up and around."

"That's why you hit her?"

"You're smarter than that, Mr. Moser."

"Well, thank you for that, Miss Rebecca, but I still don't get why you hit her."

Rebecca led him into the hallway, then put her hand on his forearm.

"I have a feeling," she said.

"Ha," said Moser. "When you say a feeling, you mean…"

"I don't know what I mean. But I feel like something out there," she waved a hand towards the bedroom window, "is looking for her. Something or someone is hunting her. What I feel is that it's that witch."

Moser looked toward the bedroom window.

"I think you're right," he said. "Truth is, Miss Rebecca, I'm not all that sure that this ward stone thing of Mr. Bartok's will save us if that she devil comes calling again. Hunter said we should tie her up."

As he said it, he remembered the night he had to bind Bartok's hands and feet and then wire him to the floor. Not a good memory.

"For once," said Rebecca, "he got something right."

Hunter ran up to them.

"What's happening?" he asked.

"She woke up," said Moser, pointing towards the unconscious woman lying on the bed. "And Miss Rebecca put her back to sleep. She was pretty agitated, so Rebecca and me now agree with your earlier idea about tying her up."

Hunter blinked.

"I'll go get some rope," he said.

After Ian returned with some rope from Bartok's workshop, they tied her hands and feet together. Then Moser and Hunter ran the ropes underneath the bed and over top of the woman three times and tied the knot on the side.

"That should slow her down," said Hunter.

"I'm sorry we had to do it," said Rebecca, "but it's safer for her, and safer for us."

When Hunter looked at her quizzically, Moser said, "Miss Rebecca thinks the witch will be looking for her."

Hunter looked straight at Rebecca when he said, "You think if she's agitated, it will be easier for the witch to find her?"

Many years ago, Bartok had told him about something called… beaconing. According to him, agitated people's energy pulses like an airport runway beacon and he added that a skilled occult practitioner could easily find them by that signature pulsing, which was unique to human beings. The agitation, he'd explained, was unique to each individual, like a psychic footprint. Hunter had nodded and smiled and gone back to the book he was reading. He was fifteen then and already the rift was widening between the two of them. With each passing year, Hunter was learning just how much his uncle knew, and realizing how much he missed the old man.

"Yes, that's right," said Rebecca. "I think the more worked up she is, the easier she'll be to find."

"Do you think it's safe for us to get some sleep now?"

Rebecca nodded at him.

"I think so. I'll doze off in the chair next to her again," said Rebecca.

"I could do it," said Moser.

"No, I knocked her out, so I'll be the one," said Rebecca.

Hunter looked at Moser, Moser looked back at him, then both men shrugged at the same time.

"Let's go find Pastor Mark a place to sleep, too," said Moser.

****

Hunter was awakened from sleep by Moser shaking his shoulder. He opened his eyes slowly.

"Everything okay?" he asked groggily.

"She's awake," said Moser.

Rolling out of bed slowly, Hunter got to his feet. He'd slept in his clothes, and he felt as rumpled as they looked. His head felt like it was stuffed with cotton. The .45 revolver lay next to his pillow. Grabbing his holster from the nightstand, he slid his arm into his shoulder strap, then Velcro'd it into place.

They arrived at the bedroom where they left Rebecca and found that pastor Mark was already there, freshly showered and dressed. The young woman he and Rebecca had saved glared up at them from the bed. Rebecca sat in the chair next to her.

"Who are you people?" asked the woman.

Her voice was rough. If she had a gun, thought Hunter, she'd be pulling the trigger with the barrel aimed in their direction.

"I told you," said Rebecca, "we're friends."

"Then why am I tied down? And where is Jimmy?"

"Do you mean the young man who was in the Borgo Temple with you?" asked pastor Mark.

"Yes."

"He's—" began Rebecca.

"We believe he's dead," said Pastor Mark.

The look of rage on the young woman's face was so intense that Hunter took a step back involuntarily.

"I'll kill that bitch," said the woman.

"Who?" asked Hunter.

The woman's face turned from rage to bewilderment. The look of terrified remembering popped her eyes wide.

"Oh no, oh no," she said. "I need a phone. You can dial the number if you hold it to my ear. I have to report in now. He has to know or—"

She stopped as though realizing she'd said too much.

"Get me a phone now," she snapped.

"No," said Rebecca. "Not until we know who you are, and what was going on in that place we saved you from. Otherwise, you get nothing."

There was a finality in Rebecca's voice that brought the woman up short.

"You don't understand. You don't know what's at stake."

"Nothing until you tell us who you are and why you were there."

Pastor Mark looked uncomfortable with the direction things were going.

"Maybe we should—"

Rebecca cut him off.

"Not until we get answers first. Our lives are at stake, pastor."

"My name is—," said the woman.

"Don't lie to us," interrupted Rebecca. "Don't shake your head at me. You were going to lie."

"You don't understand," repeated the woman. There was desperation in her voice. "I don't think there's much time."

"We know there's not much time," said Hunter.

Rebecca glared at him. Too bad, he thought. We're all in this together, sister.

That seemed to stop the woman. She seemed to be thinking furiously. Wrinkles lined her forehead as she thought.

"I have to go to the bathroom," she said finally.

"No," said Rebecca as she shot Hunter a look. It was a stay-out-of-this-look. "Wet yourself or mess yourself if you want. We've got bigger problems than that, and if you want our help, you'll tell us who you are and why you were there in that place."

It was pathetic, thought Hunter, watching the woman's struggle to free herself. He felt sorry for her, even though he had no idea who she was. It was easy to understand Rebecca's tactics. The concern on her face was clear. She and Pastor Mark had saved her from a pack of hideous monsters, but none of them knew whether or not she was under the influence of Hiram Abiff and his witch. With the way Rebecca was approaching things, though, it might take a while for the woman to break. And what if she was legitimately trying to reach out to someone she knew could help? What then? Hunter was fed up with waiting for things to happen. He decided to try a different approach. The problem was, with the way magic supposedly worked, knowing someone's name allowed you to do them harm by casting spells on them. Hunter chewed his lip, thought about it while the woman glared at them, and then decided they were, in his view, running out of time.

"My name is Ian Hunter," he said, stepping forward.

"No," snapped Rebecca. Her face was red and her features were tight.

"We need your help," he said, as though she hadn't spoken. "We're afraid to talk to you because we're afraid you might be... spellbound. In other words, you might be under the influence of either Hiram Abiff or his witch."

Rebecca moved more quickly than Hunter could have imagined him. She had him by the front of his shirt and looked straight at him, rage burning in her eyes.

"Enough," she said.

But in an instant, Moser had his hands on hers and broke her grip.

"We're not going to go there," he said.

None of them saw the woman's eyes widen.

"Get your hands off of me," said Rebecca.

Moser had already done so, but didn't bother to say it.

"I will not have him put us all at risk."

"Miss Rebecca, if I thought Hunter here would do that, I'd escort him out of the room personally. Let him say his piece. We're in deep here, and we need to hear what he's got to say. I think we're running out of time."

"But she would have—"

"Would she?" asked Moser. "I know you saved her, but this isn't the way to go about this."

Rebecca looked at Pastor Mark.

"Are you just going to stand there?"

"I am, Rebecca. Let's take a deep breath and hear what Hunter's got to say."

"If any of you feel I'm putting you at risk, you're free to leave."

"And go where?" demanded Rebecca.

"That's exactly my point. I don't feel safe," said Hunter. "None of the rest of you do, either. Until we get some answers, we're trapped here, helpless to do anything. Look, I know you don't agree with me, Rebecca. I get that, but I have a feeling about this. Trust me for just a little while. Or, if you like, we can blindfold her and let me drive away with her, so she'll never know exactly where we are. That way, none of you are at risk, only me."

Rebecca bunched her fists like she was ready for a fight, stared daggers at him for a few moments, but finally, to Hunter's relief, she stomped over and sat down again in the chair. Hunter took a deep breath, then started again.

"Now that you know my name," he said, "may I ask yours? Just a first name will do."

The woman stared up at him uncertainly for a moment and, after seeming to resolve an internal struggle, nodded.

"My name is Marla."

Hunter smiled.

"Thank you for that, Marla. I'm going to ask you to tell me your story, but first I'm going to tell you ours. For your own peace of mind, you need to know that first."

He turned to Moser.

"May I borrow your knife? I'd like to cut Marla free so we can talk."

The big Kentuckian thought for a moment.

"You sure about this?"

"I am."

"I'll do it," said Moser.

He got out his pocketknife, walked over to the bed, and began sawing the rope. When he'd cut through the ropes holding her to the bed, he leaned down, lifted the sheet off and piled them at the end of the bed next to her feet.

"All of them?" he asked Hunter.

Hunter nodded.

"All of them," he said.

****

Marla rubbed her wrists, one at a time. They were raw from her attempts to slip her hands free. As she did so, she never took her eyes off of the man who'd said his name was Hunter, the man who'd set her free.

"Would you like a glass of water?" he asked.

"Yes."

"Pastor, would you get Marla a glass of water?"

"Pastor?" she'd asked.

"I'm a minister," said the big, bald man.

"Jimmy was a priest," she said.

She didn't know why she said it. She didn't know why Jimmy's death had hit her so hard. Maybe it was because he'd been the only sane person in the insane world of Borgo.

"I'm sorry," said Pastor Mark. "Were you close?"

"No," she said. "I only knew him for about a week. He was just..."

Her voice faded off, and she closed her eyes.

Pastor Mark came back with a glass of water while she processed her remembrances. She took the water from him and drank two small sips. Hunter watched her with concern. The tall, rough looking older man stared at her. Careful eyes, cool. A man, she thought, with military experience. The young woman who had come in, guns blazing, had gone back to lean against the door flame. The man Hunter had called Pastor was big, powerfully muscled and hard looking. With his bald head and big hands, he looked like a biker who'd lost his motorcycle jacket. What a crew, she thought.

Her muscles ached, but she was used to that kind of pain. A sudden thought made her jerk her right hand to her shoulder. Someone had dressed her in a large denim shirt and her fingers ran over the cloth, pressing experimentally on the fabric. There should have been a wound there. She should have felt pain. She remembered one of the creatures clawing her shoulder, cutting deep, scraping talons against bone.

"My shoulder," she said.

The three men stared at her blankly. The woman had a faraway look in her eyes.

"What?" asked Hunter.

"One of those things, those monsters clawed my shoulder, but I don't feel any pain."

Without a thought, she began unbuttoning buttons. When she finished, she took her shirt off and looked down at her shoulder. There were no wounds, not even a red mark. She felt like she was losing her mind. Had she dreamed everything? No, she hadn't. She definitely hadn't. But then where were the wounds?

She looked up and saw that Hunter had looked away. Why? she wondered. Then she realized she was only wearing a thin black bra. If the situation wasn't so bizarre, she would have laughed. Was he that shy? The pastor and the tall, lanky man stared at her. Their eyes were stretched wide with... what? Wonder. Their eyes were filled with wonder. After a few seconds of staring at her, they turned and looked at the woman. She nodded.

Hunter finally looked over at them and then at the woman.

"You did this?" he asked her incredulously.

The woman stepped away from the door frame.

"No. I did the praying. God did the work."

She smiled, then bowed her head.

"What happened to my shoulder?" Marla demanded.

It was the bald-headed minister who answered.

"I believe you have been healed. Don't waste your time questioning it, Marla. Just give thanks."

Marla stared at him like he was crazy. A faith healing? Not likely, but she didn't have time for that now.

"I have to make that call," she said, getting back on point.

Focus was everything. She had to contact the president. President Usman had to bring in the military.

"Ten minutes of your time," said Hunter, who had finally torn his eyes away from the woman near the door. "Let me tell you what's been happening to us. Can you give me that?"

The military. What good would bringing in the military accomplish? The government had brought in the military for years. And the president had sent her into Borgo knowing what she would be up against. Ten minutes, she decided she could definitely give Hunter ten minutes.

"Go," she said.

Hunter didn't know where the best place to start was for a story like theirs, so he started with the story of Mike Leasing.

"Everything has moved so fast that it's been hard to think," said Hunter. "Like I told you, me and..." he drifted off as he looked to Moser for whether or not to say his name.

"Moser. Enid Moser," said the tall, rough-looking man.

Hunter blew out a breath of relief. Having to remember not to call Moser and the others by name made it harder to tell the story straight. It was a complicated story that required a lot of explanation.

"Moser and I were sent up by our lodge—our Masonic lodge, that is—because we do paranormal investigations."

The dismissive look that Marla gave him made his insides clench together.

"Wait," he said, "not like that. We debunk paranormal events. I'm an engineer by trade and Moser is—"

"Ex-military," said Moser quickly.

Marla gave a brief smile, like she'd already known that. Men like Moser had a certain look, a certain bearing.

"So, we were called up here by—" he nodded at Rebecca, "—the father of the woman who saved you. One of the brothers, sorry, one of the Freemasons who worked as a night watchman, was nearly strangled by a statue..."

The time slipped away from Marla as she listened. When Hunter had talked, she'd switched her eyes from one of them to the other to see how they reacted to what he was saying. It was one of the many ways she had been trained to detect lying. Eye motions, reactions of people involved and others that hadn't really been worth learning. But she didn't see any sign of deceit. Hunter believed what he was telling her, and so did the others.

"... And that's why were at the Temple," he was saying, finishing up his story. "Rebecca and Pastor Mark—" Hunter looked over at the woman and the bald man. "I'm so sorry," he said.

The bald man shrugged, but the woman shook her head and looked away like she was thinking "dumbass" or "couldn't keep your mouth shut, could you?"

"Anyway, that's our story. We brought you back here because of the ward. None of us understand how it works, but it does, so we thought we'd all be safer here. It stopped the witch when she was trying to get Rebecca."

Marla wasn't sure how much time had passed. She'd been so caught up in what Hunter was saying. The idea that the Freemasons had been hiding Hiram Abiff for centuries was so insane, it was like something you'd see in the supermarket tabloids or cable news. Impossible. How could an organization like the Freemasons keep something so hideous secret for so long? One thing Marla knew was that conspiracies could only work if just a few people were involved. The more people involved, the sooner the whole thing fell apart. There were millions of Freemasons around the world. How could they keep a secret like this?

She felt the eyes of the others fixed on her, waiting for her response. There was nothing she could tell them without being court martialled. She was an operative of the federal government.

"Thank you for telling me all this, Mr. Hunter —"

"Just Hunter."

"Thank you for telling me all this, Hunter. I would have never guessed. I wish I could tell you my side of the story, but —"

Moser stepped in.

"But she can't," Moser said. "She's with the government and she's too stupid to see that they're most likely already compromised. She'll tell whoever she reports to, and they'll file an after-action report. They'll all huddle up and strategize and by the time they're through, it'll be too late."

Hunter was stunned.

"How do you know all that?" he asked.

"I can smell it on her," said Moser. "Worked with a lot of people just like her in the wars. Yes sir, no sir people who would let you go into battle knowing you'd die, considering it all part of some up top strategy that wasn't worth a piece of cow shit for those of us on the ground getting shot at. What are you?" he asked Marla. "CIA? Army intelligence or part of some black ops team?"

His mouth turned up in disgust as he spat out the question.

"This is a matter of national security, you cracker dumbass, and if you don't shut your mouth, you're going to find yourself in a world of trouble. Am I clear on that?"

The rage she projected came from watching Jimmy die, watching Hiram Abiff fry a squad of soldiers no more than twenty feet from her, the slag heap of melted metal that was Minus Eight, seeing that witch woman and her monsters coming pouring out of Traverse's mouth and the walking dead following them to the Borgo Masonic Temple. She'd roared it at Moser like he was personally responsible. She wanted to see him cringe. She wanted to see somebody cringe.

"And she's full of prideful arrogance and makes mistakes even a grunt wouldn't make. When she said national security, she just gave it all away. If I was her handler, I'd court martial her myself. She's going to get a whole mess of people killed, or worse. Doesn't understand that witch and Hiram Abiff probably already got her bosses under their influence and she to blind to see they're spellbound. When all the lights is out, people going to remember her as the woman who done let those monsters own the world."

Moser had the others' full attention, although they weren't sure why. None of them, with the exception of Hunter, had ever seen him rant and rave like he was doing. He didn't see the woman climbing out of bed, pulling the sheet off the bed and twisting it into a rope.

"The president thinks different," she said as she threw a section of it forward to loop it around Moser's neck. Except Moser had already moved out of the way and shoved his shotgun under her chin.

"Don't move anymore, Missy," he said in a low growl. "Double aught buck makes a terrible bad mess. And don't go all kung-fu on me. I may be old, but I'm still pretty quick. Got a few years of practice behind me. And besides, I was just riling you up, so you'd get talking. Godawful things coming our way, and we'll be stronger together than separated. You can slap me silly later if you still feel like it."

The red-hot anger didn't disappear all at once. She still wanted to hurt this man, just not so much. He was smiling, and that pissed her off. He'd said she was stupid, and that pissed her off, too. But she'd heard what he said. A part of her brain remembered President Usman saying, "After tonight, I will never speak to you again and do not attempt to contact me. Never. Just accomplish your mission and then disappear." She wasn't just expendable, she was erased. There would be no files on her, no record of her anywhere. He'd sent her to die. Worse, their scrubbing of her files meant they'd made it so that in the eyes of the world she'd never lived.

Her mother and father had been field operatives. There was no recognition of their service to their adopted country. And now her, thrown away the same way. Just accomplish your mission and disappear. Well, in that case, if she never lived, she never signed all those secret and confidential documents, either. There would be no record of them. She was now officially on her own.

"You still thinking?" asked Moser. "We're running out of time here, so you think you could hurry it up?"

"I hate you," Marla said.

"I'll grow on you," said the old man. "I'm like moss that way. But Hunter here pisses off every woman he meets sooner or later."

He jerked a thumb at Hunter, who winced.

"You got anything to eat?" she asked finally.

"Crackers and cans of beans," said Pastor Mark. "Hunter just moved in here, so we're low on supplies. I don't think he's had time to shop."

Marla looked back and up at Moser.

"You're right," she said. "He's already beginning to piss me off."

61

Crackers and baked beans and three dill pickle spears. These people would never win stars for entertaining. But she refilled her plate three times. Pastor Mark did the same. He looked like a three thousand a day calorie man.

They'd moved to the living room, where there were more places to sit while she told them her story. Outside, the day was bright and Marla had her first idea of just how big Hunter's home was. The lawn outside seemed to stretch forever. And then there were the wide, curving staircases that dominated the lobby. Hunter, she decided, must be rich.

"There she is," said Moser, and pointed out the front window.

Coming up the drive was a white SUV.

"Who?" asked Marla.

"Ashley Hillis," said Hunter. "She's the one I was telling you about. The one whose husband let loose the screaming haint."

Hunter said it matter-of-factly, which, to Marla, didn't make it sane.

"I don't know about her hearing what I have to say," she said.

"You will," said Moser, who then turned to look at Pastor Mark and Rebecca, who sat side by side on a small divan. "I think you'll like her, too."

When she was not on a mission, Marla kept to herself. She had a very select group of friends. None of them were work associates. Work associates could be dangerous. Instead, Marla's friends had wings, sharp beaks and viciously effective claws. Marla was a falconer. She related to raptors more easily than she did to people. Which was why the common interests and tight relationships with the others kept her separate from them. She was the outsider. And this woman coming up the driveway would be another stranger; another variable in an already complicated equation. But that wasn't the problem. The problem was that although Marla was still committed to her mission, she no longer had a defined mission.

"Are you sure she needs to be in on this?" asked Marla. "The more people that know about this, the more chance we can have leaks. And if one of those leaks gets to the wrong person…"

Although she'd addressed the question to Hunter, it was Rebecca who answered.

"We know all that," she said. "None of us are stupid. We need help is all and there aren't many people we can trust with these kinds of things. Moser vouches for her; that's good enough for me."

Marla realized she hadn't said Hunter vouched for her, and that was good enough. No, it was Moser. She'd noticed the tension between these two right away. She wondered for a few seconds what might have caused it, but then she put it away. It really didn't matter unless it affected her mission, and she'd cross that bridge when she came to it.

Her mission was clean and simple—kill the thing called Hiram Abiff ,and run his witch through a blender while she was at it. What to do with these people afterward wasn't yet clear. When everything was said and done, she didn't think President Usman would want people who knew what had happened hanging around. Loose ends, she remembered the saying, could get tangled up around your throat.

Hunter went to the front door and opened it as the SUV pulled in front of the house. Marla saw a white-haired woman exit the vehicle and head toward Hunter with an overnight bag over one shoulder and pulling a suitcase on rollers behind her with the opposite hand. She was a striking beauty who looked to be only twenty-six years old. But her hair and eyebrows were as white as bleached sheets. Marla gave Moser a questioning glance.

"It was that night in Sharkey's Park that done it to her," he said.

Marla didn't believe such a thing was possible, but seeing the woman, it was hard to dismiss.

The two of them, Hunter and Ashley, came in the front door. Hunter locked and bolted it behind them. They left the duffel bag and the suitcase in the vestibule, and entered the living room. Hunter made the introductions while Ashley took in the assembled group with a wary look in her eye.

Hunter said, "Well, now that everyone knows each other, or at least we know each other's names, we can get down to it."

Ashley took a chair, Hunter took another, then all eyes turned to Marla.

"Marla," said Hunter, "can you tell us what you've been through?"

That's when it hit her. What she really needed was people with a lot of pull and a lot of resources to bring to bear on this problem. And, a lot of authority people. Resources combined with authority got things done. This group of people seemed to have none. And Ashley, a paranormal romance writer, just didn't fit her bill at all as someone to partner with. Still, who could she reach out to other than these people? There was no one in the community she could trust enough to reach out to. She was by presidential command disappeared. Erased. For all her life as a field operative, the agency had supplied her resources. Now, she was persona non-gratis. At least these people seemed to have an inexhaustible supply of guns. Rebecca had even brought a phosphorous grenade into the Borgo Masonic Temple. Where in the hell had she gotten a phosphorous grenade?

And from what they were saying, time was running out, and Hiram Abiff would soon come through the Borgo Pass into the Detroit Masonic Temple to the applause of the whole Masonic world. Freemasons were connected. At least, Hunter and Moser were tied into that mammoth organization.

What also bothered her was that Hiram Abiff seemed immune to weapons. So, although guns made her feel better, would they be of any use? Traverse Nations and his predecessors had used the most advanced weaponry the United States military had in its arsenal to absolutely no effect against Hiram Abiff. Maybe a minister like the big bald man and a faith healer such as Rebecca could do some damage. Who knew?

"Marla?"

It was Hunter

"Okay," she said, "I'll tell you my side of the story. But I will not tell you who ordered me into the town of Borgo. Can you go with that?"

There was no hesitation by the rest of the group. They all nodded their heads almost in unison. Marla glanced over at Ashley Hillis.

"I might have white hair, too," she said, "after this is all said and done."

"You get used to it," said Ashley.

She took a breath and then told her story. Every detail. The look of intense amazement and terror on most of their faces did not surprise her. What did surprise her, though, was that neither Hunter, Moser or Ashley reacted the same way as the others. Ashley looked grim and angry. Moser showed not much in the way of a reaction at all. Hunter's face showed a dark intensity. When she was through telling her story, right up to where Rebecca and pastor Mark saved her, he leaned back in his chair and stared up at the ceiling lost in thought.

"And one thing I know for sure," she added for everyone's benefit, "when Hiram and his witch shut down Borgo, when they destroy that town, they're coming through to our world and bringing hell with them."

"Wait a minute," said Ashley.

Pastor Mark broke in and told her of the healing.

"Oh," said Ashley.

"Marla, that took some guts to go in there to face that old man and his witch," said Moser.

"More like blind obedience," said Marla. "With some stupidity thrown in. Orders are orders."

The group fell silent, and for that, Marla was grateful. She reached out, grabbed a bottle of water from the coffee table, unscrewed the cap and drank it all down. Her nerves jangled like she'd shoved her fingers into an electrical socket. But she felt more comfortable with these people than she did with anyone in the town of Borgo, except for Jimmy. She just couldn't figure out what to do with them. Out of the corner of her eye, she saw Rebecca Mihaloff looking at her. It irritated her, but she figured she was just on edge because of the situation.

Without Rebecca Mihaloff praying for her, she probably would not have a left arm. Goblin teeth and claws were not exactly antiseptic.

Rebecca nodded.

"You heard what I said about God being the one—"

"Yes, I got it. But thanks for praying for me."

Jimmy would have liked her saying that. It wasn't like her to care what people thought. And she wasn't sure why she cared what he thought. Especially since he was dead... Marla stood up from her chair so fast it was like she'd been shot in the air.

"We will need a plan, Miss Rebecca. This whole thing seems more up your alley. The rest of you agree?" said Moser.

Marla felt the anger rise in her, and she said, "Wait a minute. I appreciate the fact that Rebecca and the pastor saved my life, but this is a matter of national security, and I have the training. The rest of you don't. I think I ought to be the one with the plan, and that's not up for a vote."

Moser didn't seem fazed in the least by what she said. Hunter didn't even look up from his tablet computer. Ashley cocked an eyebrow. Rebecca glared at her, and Pastor Mark just shook his head. Moser had told her the pastor had done time in prison, and she had to admit he had that look of... not controlled violence, but of violence controlled.

"What is it you had in mind?" asked Ashley.

There was something about the way she asked it, like whatever it was Marla had to say, it wouldn't cut it. Well, if that's what she thought, then white hair or not, she was in for a big surprise.

"We need to gun up," Marla said. "You've got quite a stash here from what I've seen, but do you have more? If not, can you get more? And, I really hate to ask this, but can you get your hands on explosives?"

She was talking right at Moser, but she could see the shock on the rest of the group's faces. Except for Hunter, who was still scrolling through something on his tablet. Typical head up his ass engineer, she thought.

"Go on," said Moser.

Marla felt her energy coming back.

"I'm out of the loop permanently with my agency. They never

expected or wanted me to get out of that place. Everything about Borgo is classified at a level that top secret doesn't even apply to."

"What is it you're planning to do with all these explosives?" Moser asked.

Marla took a deep breath before answering.

"We have to blow up that chair and the entire room. We have to make sure that Hiram Abiff can never come through. We need a blast powerful enough to close it off."

Moser nodded thoughtfully, but then asked, "What makes you think he can't come through some other way? He made one passage to come through. If he can make one, he can probably make another."

"But we have to try," she retorted. "We can't let that monster into our world. Are you with me?"

"I think we should go back in and finish him face to face," said Rebecca. "Evil has to be confronted face to face. I'm sorry, Marla, but blowing up the Detroit Masonic Temple—even just a part of it—is not going to stop this evil."

"Pastor?"

It was Moser asking the question. The most levelheaded person in the room. Marla felt things slipping away from her.

"I just don't know," said Pastor Mark. "But at the very least, we should go to the Lord in prayer to seek an answer. I don't think we can figure out what to do any other way. This creature— this Hiram Abiff— seems to be immune to bullets, explosives, poisons and even, if I understand you correctly, Marla, to a nuclear weapon. I don't know what we can do to stop or destroy him by ourselves, with our admittedly limited resources. From everything you've told us, the United States military threw everything they had at him. And it did nothing. And I agree with Mr. Moser. I think if we block his way, he'll just make another way in. Here's something else: we have so much information between everything we've all seen, and all the information Mr. Hunter has gathered, plus what you've told us, that I'm having a hard time getting my head around everything all at once. Maybe there's another way we're not seeing because we have too much information."

Before Marla could say anything, Moser turned to Hunter.

"Hey, science boy," he said. "You got anything to say?"

Now Marla was really getting angry. These people had no idea what they were dealing with. She didn't care what they'd seen or what they found in the way of information, they had never seen Hiram Abiff in action the way she had. She was just about to tell them again that she was in charge and that if they didn't want to follow her orders, she would go it alone. But Hunter spoke first.

"Yes, I do."

"Talk on Brother," said Moser.

Hunter stood, stretched, and yawned in front of them.

"Sorry," he said, "I don't do well without sleep. But yes, I have an idea. I have a plan, I think. But if it's going to work, I'll need all of you to look at this differently."

Although she hated it, Marla was willing to give him that. But Rebecca shot to her feet.

"I told you," she said, "your ways are not right for what we're facing. You can't just engineer evil away. Science won't impress the antichrist and the Scarlet Whore of Babylon. They will use science against us. They've already duped my father and the rest of the Freemasons. He's offering an electro-chemical cure for cancer. And as far as they are concerned, that makes him wonderful, not evil. My father so badly denies God and wants to replace him with medical science. There's nothing wrong with medicine, but this isn't medicine. It's a gift brought by a demon. But they're too blind to see it. They don't believe in miracles.

"You saw with your own eyes what God did for Marla. Science isn't the only way. I have nothing against scientists. My father is a scientist. I am a scientist. But that can't blind us to the reality of evil or the greatness of God.

"You look at these things as though there is a practical answer to evil. There is not. I understand you cheated Mr. Chirac last year. But cheating the devil once is not the same as destroying him. Only God can do that. And until that time, you have to remember what it says in the Bible. What it says in First Peter, Chapter five, verse eight: 'Your enemy the devil prowls around like a roaring lion looking for someone to devour.' And that is the truth, Hunter. It will be that way until the Lord Jesus Christ returns. In James Chapter Four, verse seven, it says, 'Submit yourselves, then, to God. Resist the devil, and he will flee from you.'

"So I have a plan, too. And I believe it is a scripture based plan. We submit ourselves in prayer to God, asking for his blessing on what we are about to do. And then we resist the devil. And then he will flee."

"What?" asked a surprised Marla. "What the hell do you mean, resist the devil?"

If Rebecca seemed shocked by her swearing, she didn't seem to care.

"Face to face with Hiram Abiff—we ask the Lord to rebuke him."

The room fell silent.

"Jude chapter 1 verse nine," offered Pastor Mark to a stunned Marla. "'But even the archangel Michael, when he was disputing with the devil about the body of Moses, did not himself dare to condemn him for slander but said, 'The Lord rebuke you.'"

"What is this?" asked Marla. "Bible class? I know you're religious and all, and I sure as hell thank you for praying for my healing, but we need explosives to take care of this once and for all."

Marla felt like she was talking to a classroom of idiots. Rebuke away Hiram Abiff? Oh yeah, she'd like to see how that worked— but by remote video camera, not in person.

"Okay, I hear you, Rebecca," said Hunter. "And I hear you, too, Marla. Just five minutes is all I'm asking; ten tops. Just give me that, okay?"

Rebecca and Marla both glared at him. Out of the corner of her eye, Marla saw Ashley smile. Marla wanted to slap that smile right off of her face, and she bet Rebecca would be glad to help her.

"Get to it," said Moser. "We don't hurry this up, and I smell a fistfight coming on."

Hunter seemed to feel the tension in the room as well. He laid his tablet on the seat behind him, seemed to get his thoughts in order, and then started. Reluctantly, Rebecca sat back on the divan next to pastor Mark.

"All right," said Hunter, "here's the way I see it. Rebecca, you may not like my engineering approach to things, but I'm not even going to apologize for that. It's just the way my brain works. It's my training. So, we define our objective, which is to destroy Hiram Abiff and his witch. Second, we evaluate our resources as they are now. Whatever else we need comes later. Right now, our resources are us, and I think they'll be enough."

Marla wasn't happy with the way this was going. She needed to be the one in charge because that was the only way she could make sure that Hiram Abiff and that witch were completely and utterly put down for good. But she caught Moser's look from the corner of her eye. The old man actually winked at her. Marla really did not like being winked at.

"We need to compile and organize all the information we have from the confessions of Mr. Hyde and the short points from the diary of Charles Stanley Jones. Also, we need to organize all the information we have for what has happened to us—" here Hunter pointed at Rebecca, Pastor Mark and Moser. After a moment's confusion, he also pointed to himself— "and that's a lot of work."

He turned to face Ashley.

"Ashley," he asked, "are you in?"

She brightened when he asked the question. It was as though, Marla thought, she was just waiting for something useful to do.

"I'm in," she said.

"Good," said Hunter. "If we don't do this, and if we don't start it soon, we're likely to miss a critical piece of information that might allow us to stop Hiram Abiff. I don't want that to happen. Ashley is a writer, so she's perfect for the job.

"Next, Moser and Marla are the muscle."

"Don't forget Kenneth," said Ashley.

"Right," said Hunter. "And here's where I think that is critical. Right now, we're sitting in Bartok's old house. We feel safe because of the ward stone upstairs. It worked once. That's great. But I'm not all that comforted. I'm not worried about black magic spells, I'm not worried about those creatures attacking us here. What I am worried about, though, is the fact that Eva Morgan can spellbind people. She's using your father," here he turned to Rebecca, "and who knows how many others as human conscripts. I'm worried about somebody showing up on our doorstep with a bunch of guns, or an armored Humvee, or maybe even a rocket launcher. Do you get what I'm saying, Marla?"

Marla didn't answer, but she was thinking. Maybe Hunter wasn't so stupid after all. She should at least let him finish.

"But that's just half of the problem," said Hunter. "We can just dig in here and be safe for now, but that would not stop Hiram Abiff."

"So how do you plan to do that?" asked Marla.

"We have two protection issues. Wait, make that three. The first is here at the house. The second is when we're in transit anywhere. The third is that we're wide open when we're in the Detroit Masonic Temple. The Detroit Masonic Temple is where I think we can put a stop to Hiram Abiff."

"By blowing it up?" asked Marla.

"No. I think that would be a terrible idea for the reasons Moser here already brought up, because he'll just find another way out. If he comes there as planned, we will know his moves in advance. My idea, which I already mentioned to Moser briefly, is that we let everything go exactly as planned. Hiram Abiff is brought to the Borgo Pass and up through the Empty Chair into the unfinished theater. This stage is set up the same way the furniture is in a standard Lodge room. The Worshipful Master is in the East, senior deacon in the West etc., after introducing Hiram Abiff to the entire audience of Freemasons, then Hiram will be appointed the Grandmaster of all Freemasons worldwide. The Empty Chair is where he will go to sit. No longer will the Worshipful Master sit in the East. In the Detroit Masonic Temple, the empty chair will be elevated in the north higher than the Worshipful Master's chair has been in the East."

"That," said Marla, with real heat in her voice, "is the stupidest idea I have ever heard. Why in the hell would we want to do that? Why in the hell would we want him to come through the Pass into our world?"

"Let him talk," said Ashley Hillis. "What is it, Hunter?"

"Thanks, Ashley. This is where we get to the engineering solution, sort of. We're going to rig the chair, so that after Hiram Abiff sits down on it as the new Grandmaster of all the world's Freemasons, we activate the chair to dump him straight back into the Borgo Pass. I want to override the magical circuitry so that the chair at the other end does not open. This will trap him in between worlds. It's the one thing brother Mihaloff warned me not to do. He warned me not to dawdle and get trapped in the Borgo Pass with the doors closed. What he said was that anything trapped in the pass would be destroyed if the chair doors closed behind them.

"I don't think we have to shoot Hiram Abiff, I don't think we have to blow anything up, and I'm not against rebuking him, but only as his ass is flying backward in the Borgo pass with the doors slamming shut behind him."

No one said anything. Rebecca didn't like it, and Marla sure as hell didn't like it, and Pastor Mark seemed confused, Moser was nodding his head in agreement and Ashley Hillis was smiling. But Hunter was nervous and seemed to think the others didn't agree with his plan.

"You said he was immune to weapons," he said Marla. "And it's the only way I could think of to—"

"Would you just shut up for a minute?" said Marla. "What do you think, Moser?"

Marla noticed that Rebecca turned toward Moser.

"What do you need to get this done?" asked Moser.

Hunter breathed a sigh of relief.

"We need to buy some equipment, some tools—and that includes electronics — after that, we need to start building. Oh, one more thing. I'm going to contact Rebecca's father and tell him that for the next two nights we'll be guarding the Romanesque room. I'll say we'll be doing it to…"

"To protect it and the chair from the evil forces that attacked the Mihaloff residence," said Ashley Hillis.

"Always nice to have a writer around when you need one," said Moser.

"So, this chair," said Marla, "can be programmed to dump him backwards into the Borgo Pass, where he'll be ripped to pieces?"

"It can."

"How reliably?"

"I'm pretty good at this stuff, Marla," said Hunter with a smile.

"You'd better be," she said, "or a lot of people are going to wind up dead or worse."

62

"I'm going," said Marla.

"I need you," said Hunter.

"Get a blow-up doll," said Marla.

"What? Oh, please. I mean, I need you to be my bodyguard when I install my modifications beneath the chair. I don't want to get my head bitten off while I'm screwing things together. I'll need total concentration for what I'm doing. I need you to watch my back."

"This Ricci," said Marla, "he's hired muscle for Mr. Chirac?"

It was Ashley that answered.

"I don't think he's hired muscle," she said. "He's more like... a combination slave and familiar, if you get my drift."

"No," said Marla.

Hunter hated being between the two women. He was lucky, he thought, that Rebecca went outside to let off some steam. As long as she didn't start target practice in the backyard. What an odd combination of violence and spirituality she was.

"Let's just say he does what Mr. Chirac tells him to do most of the time, and no one knows why. What Pastor Mark told us about his time with Ricci in prison and also seeing him outside the Masonic temple is the only new information we have on him," added Ashley.

"I want to be there when Kenneth meets with him. Can you call him and set it up?"

"Not," Ashley said, "unless Hunter agrees to it. Hunter?"

"Moser?" asked Hunter. "What do you think?"

"Up to Kenneth," said Moser from the kitchen table, where he was cleaning his shotgun. "He's happiest working alone, but he's got Darryl and Eddie coming, so, like I say, it's up to him. Man like that Ricci, I'd say bring the extra firepower. But you don't want so many people he gets mad about it. Ashley, did he say for Kenneth to come alone?"

"Not exactly."

"Then give Kenneth a call and ask him. He don't know Miss Marla, but I'll stand up for her if need be."

Marla smiled appreciatively at Moser, then glared at Hunter.

"Let's get this straight," she said. "I don't work for you."

Hunter's patience was wearing thin. People that went assertive when they were frustrated were a pain in the ass at best, and useless at worst. He wondered which she would turn out to be.

"I really will only say this one time," he said. "You don't like my plan and have ideas of your own, then don't bother coming back to this house. And that goes for you, too," he said to Rebecca, who had just come back inside through the front door. "I'm not the guy in Die Hard and I'm not James Bond. I'm an engineer with enough paranormal experience to make me dangerous. And that's going to have to be good enough. I want you to help me, but I can't force you and I don't have time to argue, so I won't. Make up your mind right now. Get on board or leave. Front or back door. Either one's good."

He turned to face Pastor Mark.

"Pastor, are you any good with carpentry or metal work?"

It was as though he'd left Marla and Rebecca behind. As though if they would not follow his plan, he had no use for them. Nothing personal, just work to be done. His Uncle Bartok may not have liked the way he handled it, considering the stakes. There was a place and a reason for emotional conflict sometimes, he thought, but when there was a job to be done with a schedule, you just had to drop that crap and get to work, and that was what he was doing. Somehow, he knew that Hiram and the witch were responsible for Molly's and Ron's deaths, and Hunter wanted to make them pay for it. Guns were shit useless, as Moser would say. But engineering problem-solving methods were dependable, and right now he wanted to know that he had a chance of taking the evil team off the board.

"Passable," said the pastor.

"Good enough. Follow me downstairs to Bartok's workshop."

"Don't you think—" began Pastor Mark, pointing at Marla and Rebecca.

"No," said Hunter, "I don't." To Ashley, he said, "Don't worry about the quality of the narrative. Just the high points. Things that are factual are prime, the speculation—"

She cut him off with a wave of her hand.

"I know what you want, and I know how to do it. You focus on the device."

It was hard for Hunter to reconcile, even though it had been a year, her white hair with her youthful face.

"Got it," he grinned.

Finally, someone who could work instead of just giving off attitude.

"And thank you, Ashley," he said.

Marla was telling Moser to call Kenneth as he and Pastor Mark headed toward the basement stairs. That was a mistake, he thought. She would have gotten better results with Ashley calling him. Kenneth was partial to Ashley.

****

"Some basement," said Pastor Mark. "It's more like a…"

The pastor's voice echoed down between the empty spaces and resonated off the strange brass and glass mechanisms.

"Museum of obscure machinery?" offered Hunter. "A steampunker's dream?"

The pastor surveyed the laboratory glassware, the shelves of reagents, the marble countertops with what could only be explained as peculiarly shaped flasks on hot plates partially filled with a variety of purple and green fluids. There were sinks, giant fume hoods and next to a roll up desk the size of a Volkswagen Beetle, a medieval suit of armor sat upright in a straight-backed wooden chair. The basement stretched the entire length of the house and was lit with a burnished light by a variety of glowing hanging bulbs that looked to have been added at random intervals over the years.

"It's more a museum of the arcane," whispered the pastor.

"Oh, don't romanticize it," said Hunter. "Down here are only the tools of my uncle's trade. He believed in mystic technology, whatever that is."

"And you?" asked the pastor.

"I'm still trying to wrap my head around the world, Pastor, but I don't want that to impede taking action. In fact, I think I'm the wrong guy to make sense of the grand picture of what Hiram Abiff is and what his terrible plans are. I think I know a way to stop him, maybe even destroy him, and that's enough for me. Are you ready to get to work?"

"I am."

Footsteps behind them.

"Hunter?"

It was Ashley.

"Over here," Hunter called back.

Ashely came into view, her white sweater yellowed by the light.

"Kenneth," she said, "says bring her on. So, Marla's a go."

"I don't know if that's a good idea. I don't know if she'll be safe out there."

"Rebecca's going as her bodyguard."

Hunter clenched his fists and was about to say something when Pastor Mark beat him to it.

"Good," he said. "Rebecca can protect her."

"Can't they stick to a plan?" said Hunter. "Who's going to cover our backs while the three of us are putting things together?"

"Moser's staying with us," said Ashley.

"Good," said Pastor Mark. "Hunter and I have to get back to work. Thanks for letting us know, Ashley."

As Ashley disappeared back up the stairs, he added, "Is she any good with a gun?"

"Kenneth's seen to that," said Hunter. "But this is just stupid."

Couldn't Marla and Rebecca see Ricci was separating them?

"No stopping them," said Pastor Mark.

"But this is splitting us into two groups. We're stronger together."

"Hunter, you're preaching to the choir. So, what is it we're down here to do?"

For a moment, it looked like Hunter was going to scream. They were just ignoring him, but he knew his plan had the best chance of working. But…

"You're right," he said at last. "We need to get to work. Follow me."

He led the pastor over to a high school green fume hood with a glass sliding door that stood next to two others against one wall.

"Bartok had more hideaways built into this place than you'd believe," he said, as he slid to the glass door upward.

Inside was a marble top that must have weighed a few hundred pounds, a faucet with two handles to either side, a drain and three valves with metal hose barbs attached. One read air, the next read hydrogen, and the last was labeled vacuum. Hunter pressed against the label/knob of the one marked vacuum and waited. There was the sound of hidden machinery engaging, then slowly the entire fume hood swung inward to reveal a room lined with books and a wooden desk in the center with a giant magnifying glass attached to it by a large retractable metal clamp. Hunter stepped into the room and flipped a switch. The light was a soft yellow.

"UV filters," explained Hunter. "A lot of these books are very rare and ultraviolet light can damage them."

Pastor Mark followed him in, then closed the door behind them.

"The air in here is filtered," said Hunter.

"What are we looking for?" asked the pastor.

Hunter went over to a bookshelf and peered at the titles. He put on a pair of disposable gloves from a wooden box mounted on a brass stand. After he had them snugged into place, he pulled down a tall, four-inch-wide book and carried it over to the wooden table and laid it dead center. There were two rounded wooden strips that were set into a groove. He slid these apart until they were just under the outside edges on either side.

"Better for the spine this way," said Hunter, like a chef on a television show explaining each of the ingredients he was using to make a meal.

"What in the world is that?" asked Pastor Mark, pointing a finger at a bizarre, complex, multi-colored symbol.

"Don't touch it," said Hunter quickly. "Get a pair of gloves and put them on. And bring me those tipped tweezers, would you?"

When Pastor Mark returned with gloved hands and tweezers, Hunter thanked him, then pointed the tweezers at the multi-colored symbol.

"It's a power symbol from a European sub-cult of German occultists. This entire book is a collection of so-called magical sigils and signs from various practitioners and secret societies. But this isn't the one I'm interested in. That one is closer to the end of the book."

Using the tweezers, Hunter carefully began turning pages.

"Is that Egyptian?" asked Pastor Mark.

Hunter continued to turn as he replied.

"No, it's faux Egyptian. Occultists can't seem to resist symbols that look like they came from the Middle Kingdom. Anything to make their symbols seem taken from Ancient Egyptian wisdom. It's hard to find secret societies that start with something new. Instead, their founders churn out books with titles like 'Isis Unveiled' or 'Chariots of the Gods.' For some reason, they think of it as validating their lineage. Wait, here's the one I want."

With one hand, Hunter swung the giant magnifying glass over the symbol. With the other hand, he placed his cell phone just above the top edge of the book. He slid his finger over the screen, brought up his gallery of photos. After a few swipes, an enlarged a photo of the symbol from the Mihaloff's front door appeared.

"Look familiar?" he asked the Pastor.

"Kind of," said Pastor Mark.

"Same basic concept," said Hunter.

"How did you learn about all this?" asked the pastor.

Without looking up from comparing the two symbols, Hunter said, "From Uncle Bartok. And, for generations, my family has been involved in researching these kinds of things."

"Why?"

Hunter looked up from the magnifying glass with a thoughtful expression on his face.

"That goes back a way," he said, "but the short form answer is that my ancestors were all nuts."

"Do you really believe that?"

After a quick look around the basement, Hunter looked back at the pastor and nodded.

"Yeah, I do. At least I used to."

"But?"

"Ever since Townsend Mountain, I've been having second thoughts. Uncle Bartok used to say that we're all surrounded by an invisible war. Does that make sense?"

Pastor Mark shrugged. He supposed he understood. It was Biblical in a way, if he took the Bible literally, which, for the most part, he did. In fact, the Bible portrayed an epic, invisible war throughout mankind's history. Witches and demons and more were not just mentioned in the Bible, the invisible word manifest in the physical world was... part of the Bible. Were they truly, as Rebecca thought, in the end times? Was Hiram Abiff really the Antichrist? Was that what they had stumbled into?

"I guess," said the pastor. "It feels like this shouldn't be over my head, though. If we're all involved in spiritual warfare, it seems like it should be my department, if you get what I mean."

"I do," said Hunter, "but it's like these symbols we're looking at, and this whole mess with the Freemasons—none of its exactly in the Bible except for vague references in the Book of Revelations. Things like the sign of the Beast and all that. And I don't think Hiram Abiff is the Biblical Beast. I think he's evil as shit, but that's a different story. So, I don't see how your theological training is supposed to help."

"Rebecca thinks he is the Biblical Beast," said Pastor Mark.

"Thinks is the operative word. I don't think she's one hundred percent sure. And, like me, I think she's uncertain what Hiram Abiff or his witch even are. I've never come across literature defining creatures like either of them. That's what's the most disturbing thing to me, pastor. I mean, look around you. Think about it. Think of all the occult knowledge in this old house. And all I can come up with is this..."

His finger pointed at the large symbol in the old book laid out on the examining table beneath the microscope.

"Why is that symbol so important to the witch?" asked Pastor Mark.

"It's probably not," said Hunter.

"I don't get it."

"More important to us is its origin. Have you ever heard of the Monas Hieroglyphica? It's sometimes called the Hieroglyphic Monad. Created by Dr. John Dee, the Elizabethan occultist back in the mid fifteen hundreds, although as in all things occult, there are those who claim it is a more ancient symbol. In the occult," he said with a rueful smile, "ancient is always better. You never say older. Ancient is cooler."

"For a paranormal investigator, you have an odd way of looking at things."

"Healthy, is how I think of it," said Hunter. "People wrapped up in the occult, the mystical and/or religion—no offense meant—are wrapped up in a point of view, and that makes it hard to analyze events accurately."

"And how," asked pastor Mark, "do you analyze the witch who tried to steal Rebecca's soul, the creatures who attacked her in her home and the monsters we found on the other side of the Borgo Pass?"

No way out of this one, thought Hunter. The big, bald-headed man was right. Cool headed analysis sounded good in theory, but what about if the events you were analyzing violated the laws of science itself?

"I don't," said Hunter finally. "I just do the best I can. Like this symbol we're looking at. What I was saying before about the origin might be important. What's unusual about it is that it's somewhere between a magical sigil and a mandala."

"Can I sit down?" asked Pastor Mark. "My back hurts. I'm a little old for hustling down tunnels that lead through Hell."

"Grab a stool."

"Okay," said Pastor Mark as he grabbed a wooden stool, dusted it off with his hand, and dragged it over to the table. As he sat, he continued, "what about this guy Dr. John Dee and his Hieroglyphic Monad? What exactly is it?"

Hunter pointed out this symbol:

* * *

"This is the key element in the sigil we saw on Brother Mihaloff's door. It's repeated over and over in a variety of combinations. In fact, save for the random slashes, it is an artifact built on a visual honeycomb of Monads."

Pastor Mark rubbed his lower back and stretched.

"I don't get it," he said when he was through. "What is so all important about this… monad, as you call it? What's it supposed to be? A person?"

"Kind of quiet down here, isn't it?" asked Hunter suddenly. "When I was a kid, Bartok always had something going on. Experiments, watching movies—down there is a door that leads to a small movie theater, one level down. Taking notes, making journals. He traveled all over the world, you know? This house is so… empty without him."

"I'm sorry, Hunter."

"He always had people over, too. Whenever he was in town, if it was Tuesday, he'd invite the chess club over. And he was a member of the Philalethes Society—and before you ask, that's a Masonic research society."

For a moment, Hunter stared up at the ceiling, lost in thought.

"You were saying… about the Monad," prompted Pastor Mark.

Slowly, Hunter returned to the moment. The pastor thought he could see just a hint of wetness in the young man's eyes.

"The Monad. Yeah, well, according to some scholars of Dr. Dee's work, it's supposed to represent the knowledge that links all known worlds."

"Ambitious claim for what looks like a one-eyed stick figure," muttered the pastor.

"It is, but let me cut to the chase. Bartok believed it was more than that, but that Dr. Dee obscured it from uninitiated eyes by a simple ruse."

Pastor Mark arched an eyebrow and looked interested.

"And what was that ruse?"

"It's a two-dimensional figure, and in the real world of the occult, there is no power fulcrum that is less than four dimensional. It's a form of hermetic string theory."

"I don't get it," said the Pastor, "and I'm getting hungry again. Can you hurry it up?"

"Yeah, me too. Funny how stress makes you hungry, isn't it? Well, anyway, Bartok believed that the Monad, when created in the four occult dimensions, was a power gateway. He thought each point of the Monad represented a crystal interstice…"

"Hey, Hunter," said Pastor Mark, reaching up and shaking Hunter's arm. "You keep drifting off. What is it?"

"Transmutatio formalis, sed non essentialis… that's it. Two mysteries in one. I have it now. The Blazing Star of Freemasonry is the crystal from the other ship that Bartok had Moser and I looking for. Its structure is identical to the combined interstices of the Monads united in four dimensions."

Pastor Mark looked at him as though he were crazy.

"Hunter, do you need to lie down? You're babbling on like a rabid monkey."

The look on Hunter's face was wild and crazy, ebullient, and unexpectedly lit up by an enthusiastic burst of energy. He reached out and placed his palms on the minster's shoulders and leaned forward.

"I know the secret of the ghost box," he whispered. "The Blazing Star is the crystal that can power the ghost box again."

"And what good does that do us now?"

"Don't you see?" exclaimed Hunter. "It's the same crystal structure that creates the Borgo Pass. It's the same alien technology. My only worry was that even though I know the sigil is electro-magical in nature, that I couldn't understand what did what. But now that I know it is identical to that which I've been studying in the ghost box, I think I can make my plan work."

The ringing of his cell phone interrupted his explanation. What the hell? he thought. Ashley's name appeared on the screen. He answered the call and held the phone to his ear.

"Everything okay?" he asked. "Why are you calling instead of coming down here?"

"What is it?" asked Pastor Mark.

"It's Moser," answered Ashley. "I think he's having a heart attack."

63

A jagged bolt of lightning cut across the darkness, revealing a fast rushing collision of turbulent black clouds. The rain came rushing at them seconds later, pounding down on the SUV.

"Just gets better and better," said Kenneth, slapping his palm against the steering wheel to drive the point home.

"You're sure that's the building?" asked Marla from her seat next to him.

"Damn sure. It's the only one with the sign says Black Eagle bar."

"There are no lights on," said Rebecca from the back seat.

Kenneth twisted in his seat and turned his head slowly around to face her.

"I don't think," he said, "that if he's the go-to man for that Mr. Chirac, that he needs light, if you get what I mean."

"You mean you don't think he's human?" asked Marla.

"Don't know one way or the other. It just ain't good to be surprised in a dark building."

"We're three hours early," said Rebecca. "Maybe he's not there yet."

"He's there," said Kenneth.

"How do you know?"

"Because I can feel him, that's how."

They sat in silence for a few minutes, digesting that thought. Kenneth had met Ricci only once, and that was the night Ashley, Granny, Hunter, Moser and he had gone to deliver the little girl's bones to Mr. Chirac in return for the ghost box.

"How long do you think this will keep up?" asked Marla.

"According to my phone," said Rebecca, "it's not supposed to be happening at all."

"Figured that," said Kenneth.

"What do you mean?" asked Marla.

"I mean, this isn't going on it all. There is no rain in this area."

"Explain," said Marla.

"When Ashley and the rest of us went to see Mr. Chirac last year, the GPS couldn't even find the street. As in, it wasn't there."

"I don't like this," said Marla.

"Me either," said Rebecca.

"Yeah," said Kenneth, "but it is what it is."

They were parked five storefronts down from the Black Eagle bar. A couple of times around the block, moving at normal speed, and they had found nothing worth noticing. Delray, Michigan, reminded them of a ghost town. Closed down storefronts with iron gates pulled in front of them, shattered windows with boards nailed over them. Del Ray was a town that had done poorly over the last 30 years. The fires of United States Steel lit the skies with a violent shower of angry red sparks.

"I'm going in," said Kenneth. "If I'm not out in thirty minutes, drive away and Darrell and Eddie can make the call whether to come looking for me."

"Not happening," said Marla.

"I wasn't asking," said Kenneth. "This one ain't nothing to play with. If I get the two of you killed, well, that's just a no good for anybody."

"I can't speak for Rebecca here," said Marla, "but we make our own decisions. And don't think I'd go in looking after you. If I go in, I'm looking for answers, whether you're dead or alive. And if that man knows something, he's going to give it up to me."

Kenneth turned around, so he was toward the road. He glanced up in the rear-view mirror at Rebecca.

"That how you feel too?" he asked her.

Rebecca hesitated. Kenneth could see in her eyes that something was bothering her. She was staring at the Black Eagle with a look of apprehension.

"You listening to me?"

"I'm not supposed to go in there," she said.

"Pardon?"

"Nothing. Just go if you have to. Where are your cousins?"

"On two different rooftops," said Kenneth. "They dug in about an hour ago."

"What about the rain?" asked Marla.

Kenneth looked out the window and up at the sky. That didn't seem like it was going to stop anytime soon.

"They'll do what they have to do. Sat out in worse storms in this. Ain't going to help, though."

"No," said Marla.

Kenneth handed the keys over to Marla. He looked her square in the eyes and then said, "think about what I told you. Remember, I don't think we're dealing with a normal man."

"Got it."

"I hope to God you do."

Kenneth lifted the flap of his denim shirt and checked his pistol. He was carrying a .357 Magnum.

"You going to be able to draw that fast enough?" asked Marla.

He didn't answer; he just opened the car door, stepped into the night and closed the door behind him.

****

Within seconds, Kenneth Hillis was drenched. He kept his head down. With one hand, he held his shirt closed. Covering the distance would be the worst part, he thought. Water pooled in the street, and it didn't take long before he felt it seeping into his supposedly waterproof boots.

"Nice," he muttered to himself.

The only noise was the sound of the rain. Kenneth didn't like the situation much, but there was nothing to do about it. He thought of Ashley waiting for him to return to Ian Hunter's house. His two good friends, Moser and Hunter, would be there. Family, friends and a woman to love. A lot to give up if he was killed. But more to lose if he didn't follow through. If Ricci knew something, anything, Kenneth had to find it out. And there was the fact that Ashley trusted Ricci.

By the time he made it to the entrance of the Black Eagle bar, Kenneth felt like he'd been thrown headfirst into a raging river. Something not natural about this storm. Granny would know, but Granny was in heaven, best he could figure. There was a torn awning over the front door. It mercifully sluiced away some of the rain. Methodically, he lifted his wet shirt and checked his pistol again. It was a good piece, and he was fairly sure it would still fire.

The doorknob turned, and he gently pushed it open with one hand while aiming the gun inside with the other. The streetlight in front of the bar was out, most likely blown out by punks long ago. The room inside was draped in complete blackness. This was one night he surely wished he had night vision goggles. He keened to his ear but heard nothing. It was like stepping into a room that absorbed both light and sound.

Steady, he thought, stay steady.

He'd made it about four feet into the room without stepping into anything or knocking anything over, when a voice to his right said, "Nice gun."

"Kind of hard to see in here," he said sheepishly.

"I figured that," said the voice he now recognized as belonging to Ricci.

"I'm going to slide some night vision goggles over to you. Don't get shaky or trigger-happy with that thing. Here they come."

Kenneth heard the noise as the NVG's slid across the floor and it stopped against the toe of his boot. Keeping the gun aimed toward where the voice had been, he reached down, felt around for a moment, then picked up the night vision goggles.

"Damned thoughtful of you," he said as he put them on.

"The on button is on the top," said Ricci.

The room came suddenly into focus in the familiar pale yellow-green color for Kenneth. He saw Ricci standing five feet away from him. Ricci was as tall as Kenneth, but about twice his width and weight. The dark turtleneck sweater seemed stretched to the limit by Ricci's muscular neck. His hands hung at his sides, and they were empty. After a moment's thought, Kenneth returned his pistol to its holster. He didn't like doing it, but part of him told him it was the right thing to do. He swiveled his head to look around the room. It was littered with broken chairs and tables and what seemed to be a splintered hole the size of a basketball in between him and Ricci. At the back of the bar was a mirror, split sideways with one pie sized piece missing.

"I got some things to tell you, but first, how many did you bring with you besides the two on the rooftops?" said Ricci.

Well, thought Kenneth, there goes that.

"Two more. Total of four."

"Where they at?"

"The other two? They're waiting in the car."

"When are they coming in after you?"

"Thirty minutes," said Moser.

"Good enough. We'll be done in ten. I got a few things to tell you, but they'll be quick. Longer we're here, the more chance of dying. First thing I already told you—somebody's coming for the ghost box."

"Who?"

"She's a witch. Her name is Eva Morgan. She's not quite human."

"She already attacked the house. Went after Rebecca."

Ricci's face, normally passive, twisted with rage. Kenneth saw his hands ball up into fists.

"Don't worry, Moser and Hunter took care of that. Rebecca is fine. Hunter's got some kind of gizmo in his house that prevents her from showing up."

"Good. She's all I got. Should put that thing somewhere really, really safe. Tell that to Hunter. He'll know what to do. Next, that thing Hiram Abiff, when they introduce him to all those thousands of Masons, I'm going to be in a hidden passage, with a rifle, and when he sits down in that chair, I'm supposed to shoot him straight in the head."

"Why?"

"Ask Hunter. But according to Mr. Chirac, his head's going to heal up. Right in front of everybody. And the witch, she's got some kind of magic crystal that she's going to use in a ceremony to create the delusion that Hiram Abiff is the Masonic Savior. I don't know more than that."

"That's kind of a lot right there," said Kenneth. "What's the last thing?"

"I have to do what Mr. Chirac says. I can't always make up my own mind. I can't explain how he does it, but that's our deal. That's our contract."

"I don't get it. Why are you telling me that?"

"Because," said Ricci, "if he tells me to come after you, I'll come after you. So, if you see me coming, kill me."

"Brother, you seem like you'd be a hard man to kill."

"You have no idea," said Ricci.

"You got any suggestions?"

Ricci seemed to think for a minute.

"No," he said. "But if I was you, I'd get some bigger guns than that shooter you're carrying."

"I'll do it," said Kenneth.

"Then we're done. You leave and go take care of my sister. Tell Moser and Hunter the same things I told you, and then tell them to take care of my sister, too."

"Done," said Kenneth.

"How about leaving those night vision goggles behind?" said Ricci.

Reluctantly, Kenneth did as he was asked and was stepping outside into the noisy night rain when he heard Ricci call out behind him, "Watch out for the hunting packs."

Kenneth nodded and stepped out into the car-wash the city of Del Ray called night. What the hell, he thought as he sloshed back toward the car, was a hunting pack?

****

Marla saw him coming first.

"There he is," she said.

"I see him," said Rebecca.

"This is bullshit," said Marla. "Why did we come along if we're just sitting in the car?"

"There's a reason."

"Like what?"

"I don't know. But..."

"Are you okay?" asked Marla, noticing the blank look that came across Rebecca's face.

"Start the car," said Rebecca suddenly, and now her voice was ice. She pressed the switch to lower the rear window on the passenger side and stuck the silenced barrel of her Beretta out the window. "Run," she shouted at Kenneth.

Kenneth didn't look around to see what the problem was. He just started running through the puddles, water spraying up around his legs in plumes, as he sprinted for the SUV. Marla had it started up again and had her own pistol up in one hand.

"What is it?" asked Marla. "What is it you see?"

"They're coming," she said.

Marla swung her head back towards the driver-side window, lowered it and looked out. She had no idea what Rebecca was talking about, but from the tone of her voice, it wasn't good. All she could see were dark, empty storefronts, wet sidewalks, in the distant streaks of fire that shot up from Zug Island. No cars coming their way. Nothing moving on the street except Kenneth Hillis. He was ten feet away from the car when a manhole cover shot straight up into the air with a noise like a gunshot and something like a shiny jet-black skeleton climbed out of it, stood up straight and screeched. As Kenneth opened the front passenger door and jumped in, Rebecca fired off two shots and splintered the thing's head.

"Shit," Kenneth said, slammed the door shut behind him and got his own pistol. A ragged claw reached through the open window and raked Kenneth's forehead down to the bone before he had the .357 all the way out of its holster.

The barrel of Rebecca's pistol swung up just enough so he could see it, then she fired off another round and this one cut the thing's arm off at its bony elbow.

"Go," shouted Kenneth as he brought his left forearm up to cover the wound on his forehead and fired into the leering face of the creature who'd attacked him, as it fell back one-armed onto the street.

Marla jammed the accelerator pedal all the way to the floor and shot out into the street.

"If this is just Del Ray," said Marla, "I can't wait to see Detroit."

"More coming," shouted Rebecca.

"Where?" asked Kenneth.

"Don't know yet."

With a sound like a head-on collision, another manhole cover smacked down on the street, bounced up in the air and over the top of the SUV as it shot underneath the projectile's arc.

"Shit," said Kenneth. "That was too close."

Up ahead, two more manhole covers shot up in the air and two more creatures crawled out from them. More followed. Soon they formed a line of oily black skeletons blocking the street ahead.

"Going through," shouted Marla.

"Windshield wipers, dammit," said Kenneth.

"No time," said Marla. "I'll drive, you shoot."

Forty feet. Thirty feet. By the time they were less than twenty-five feet away, it was like a small army of skeleton demons blocking the road. Just as Kenneth poked his .357 Magnum out the window, Marla slammed her foot down on the brake pedal, yanking hard on the wheel at the same time and almost flipping the SUV straight up in the air. It shuddered and tilted over onto two wheels as she executed a movie perfect U-turn. Kenneth smelled burning tires and the ozone rich night as a lightning bolt shot straight up from the street in front of them and lit the raindrops like a Vegas waterfall.

"Hey," shouted Kenneth.

"Shut up," said Marla.

She slammed the gas pedal down to the floor again and, with smoke fuming off her tires, careened down West Jefferson toward Detroit.

"Rebecca," said Kenneth.

"Got 'em," she said as she climbed into the back of the SUV and flipped up the back window. She snapped a tripod into place, then aimed the suppressed barrel of a rifle out the window.

"Hell of a town when monsters pop up in the streets and there's not a cop in sight," yelled Kenneth.

Rebecca ignored him and fired off three single shots. Impossibly, the demon skeletons were gaining on them. She knew it couldn't be happening, even as she shot the head off another one. Where we the people in this town? Where was the traffic? It was like they were in a separate world. As she sighted and pulled the trigger again, she gave up thinking and kept on shooting as water sprayed up like geysers from popping manhole covers. Through the open hatch, she could hear the screams of rage as the creatures came leaping after them. The targets were hopping like skeletal apes, popping up from the exposed sewers and hitting the ground running. What were they? The thought that Hunter would know popped into her mind.

But before she'd finished the sentence, Kenneth had already fired twice and hit the floating apparition center mass. He saw her jerk in midair and almost drop.

"That's for Moser," he screamed and fired again, hoping to shoot her between the eyes. He would never know for sure, for at that exact moment, Marla stuck her nine millimeter in front of his face and fired past him at the thing coming straight for him from the sidewalk. Marla was the only one who hadn't screwed her suppressor into place.

"Damn, woman, would you mind saying something before you fire that thing?" howled Kenneth.

But Marla was busy steering the car like it was a cruise missile straight toward the witch.

"Rebecca," she shouted even louder than before, "witch, dead ahead."

A quick look in the rear-view mirror, and Marla saw Rebecca had already belted herself into place with rope around her waist looped through cargo eye hooks bolted tight to the vehicle's frame. She saw Rebecca twist herself around and slap the rifle on the roof after discarding the tripod.

"What?" yelled Kenneth.

Marla ignored him; she just focused on the witch, her pistol now on the console, both hands on the steering wheel. Eva Morgan floated twenty feet from the ground with a small army of skeletal creatures working themselves into a maniacal frenzy beneath her feet. Skeletal creatures exploded, which confused the crap out of Kenneth until he figured out that Rebecca must be mowing them down with whatever she was shooting. Kenneth leaned out the window again and started firing after using his speed re-loader to fill the empty chambers of his revolver. God bless whoever invented speed re-loaders, he thought, as he started firing.

He fired only at the witch. He was too busy to wonder where the hell the Del Ray police were hiding, or how she could dodge his rounds. She blurred to one side each time he fired, but on the fifth shot he aimed to the left of her and as she blurred that way, he saw her yank her hand like she'd been stung and knew he'd hit her. While she shook her hand in disbelief and pain, Kenneth took careful aim and put the next bullet into her forehead. To his shock and horror, he saw a long, serpentine black tongue shoot out of her mouth and speed his way, but before it could wrap itself around his neck, the night air seemed to shiver and then she and her monsters were gone.

The rain stopped, and he saw people walking the streets, who suddenly stopped and gawked at them.

"Rebecca," he shouted, "get back in the car."

But even as he called it out, he looked back and saw her sliding inside the vehicle with her rifle held close against her as she swung the rear window back into place. She disassembled her weapon, folded it and slid it into a duffle like she'd done it every day since high school. Kenneth was thinking she had.

Marla slowed down and was almost at a complete stop when Rebecca said, "Drive. Don't floor it, just drive normally. Everything is okay again."

A car shot across the intersection before them, and Marla had to swerve hard to the right to miss it and almost clocked an oncoming Chevrolet Volt.

"Better," said Rebecca after they'd gone another block and a half and people had quit staring after them. "Now let's get out of here using the side roads. With any luck, they won't shut them down."

They drove on in silence for a while, Marla dodging in and out of side streets, the GPS complaining that they'd gone the wrong way every thirty seconds until they were heading south on US 85. The overhead clouds were dark and restless, but there was no longer any sign of the earlier storm that had drenched them.

"What just happened?" asked Kenneth, turning to look at Rebecca.

She didn't look back at him; instead, she kept scanning the streets and sky around them.

"You expecting more?" asked Kenneth asked her.

"Call it," said Marla as she made a sharp turn off Fort Street and swung into the Lincoln Park CVS Pharmacy parking lot. "We going home, or are we hunting?"

Her pistol was now out of sight in the driver's side door pocket. She was feeling pumped again. She was back in control. Well, maybe not in complete control, but at least she wasn't still trapped in Borgo with Hiram Abiff.

"We regroup back at the house, right, Kenneth?" asked Rebecca.

"Let's do it," said Kenneth. "Right now, I ain't getting a good feeling about leaving Ashley alone."

Outside the car, the night rolled by like the wounded reality it was.

64

Enid Moser's eyes were completely black, and fluorescent scarlet worms wriggled across their surface like they had Bartok's a year ago on Townsend Mountain.

"Holy shit," said Hunter, his voice trembling as he spoke. "What happened?"

"We were talking, just talking," said Ashley, her voice trembling as bad as Hunter's, "and he froze mid-sentence and his eyes turned. He said, 'Get away Ashley, get away now.' That's when I yelled for you and when you didn't answer, I called."

"I think you can put the pistol down," said Pastor Mark, reaching forward to press her hand down.

"No," said Hunter. "Keep the pistol pointed right at his gut. Back up about six steps. Pastor, you do the same. Keep a forty-five degree vector between the two of you."

"Hunter, what are you—"

"Just do it," Hunter snapped.

Moser was sitting on the couch, his posture ramrod straight, staring straight at Hunter.

"What next?" asked Ashley.

"You remember what I told you happened to Bartok?"

There was a genuine agony in Hunter's voice. He was reliving the changes Bartok had gone through in his transformation. The physical strength, the speed and the tentacles bursting out of him as the shell that was once his body burst open.

"You mean...?"

"I do. He's changing. Like Bartok."

"Oh no," said Pastor Mark. "Are we going to have to..."

"I don't know," said Hunter.

The living room lights were off, and only the lawn spotlights' determined glow allowed Hunter to notice how his friend gripped the shotgun. Hunter had never seen this coming. And he could never have imagined it happening at a worse time.

"Old man," he said. "Are you in there?"

Moser continued to stare at him with alien eyes.

"Do you think he can hear you?" asked Pastor Mark.

"Hard to tell," said Hunter.

"He did," said Ashley. "Moser, you better not check out on us yet."

Moser opened his mouth and screamed an alien scream that Hunter remembered so well. Hunter stiffened and both Ashley's and Pastor Mark's faces went white.

"Don't you..." said Hunter.

"I couldn't even move my trigger finger," said Ashley.

"Same here," said Pastor Mark. "What the hell was that?"

"There are headlights coming down the driveway," said Ashley.

"I hope to God that it's Kenneth."

"I hope to God that it's Rebecca," said Pastor Mark.

"Me too," said Ashley.

Hunter stared at Moser's craggy face. The Sam Elliott looks. The strong cheekbones, the grizzled chin, the normally bright blue eyes. But now, Moser's eyes were completely alien. "When it comes time," his uncle Bartok had told him, "you'll be glad to kill me." Not this time, thought Hunter. Not happening twice. Enid Moser wasn't family, but he was the closest thing to a best friend Hunter had. What could he do?

Moser's shotgun raised.

"Careful," said Hunter. "Don't shoot yet."

Could Moser shoot him? Did the alien intelligence controlling his mind even know what a shotgun was?

The shotgun started shaking. It was as though Moser was

struggling to keep it pointed down, but the alien presence was fighting to lift it up. Hunter, Ashley, and Pastor Mark stood stock still. None of them dared to move.

"Hunter?" asked a nervous Ashley.

"I don't know," said Hunter.

He couldn't tell them to shoot Moser. But then, when he realized Moser was fighting to bring the shotgun to his own head, Hunter sprinted across the room and rammed into Moser, knocking his friend and the couch over backwards. Hunter had one hand on the barrel as they tumbled over and another on the stock. He'd missed in his attempt to pull Moser's hand away from the trigger guard. He'd knocked the wind out of himself as he hit the floor and blew a hole in a wood and glass curio cabinet.

"Shit," he yelled as a piece of glass sliced the side of his head. He would have felt the blood flow if Moser hadn't rolled away and clubbed him with the side of the Winchester.

He was on his knees weaving back and forth and the last thing he heard as he keeled over was Moser's voice yelling above the ringing in his ears, "You broke my damned finger."

And then he was out.

****

"How are you feeling?"

It was a woman's voice, soft and reassuring. Concerned, but calm.

"Huh?"

Hunter struggled back to consciousness. His head hurt mightily, and his back felt like someone had kicked him with a steel-toed size fourteen boot.

"At least you didn't get your head blown off or Moser's either," said a voice he recognized as Pastor Mark's. "Close, though."

"My head hurts," said Hunter, and then his eyes popped wide open. He tried to sit up, but his back muscles seized up in protest.

The room was in semi-darkness—the overhead light was off, and the room was only lit by the light coming in from the hallway. He was lying on a bed in one of the guest rooms, a thin linen coverlet pulled up to just beneath his armpits. Rebecca Mihaloff reached over and put a hand on his chest, then pushed him back down.

"Take a few minutes to get yourself together, Hunter. And don't touch the bandage on your head. Moser is in the next bedroom, resting fine. We splinted his finger, and although he's still sore, he's resting, too. He seems better now."

"He's not," said Hunter, with a trace of anger in his voice. "It's that place, reaching out to us to take one more from the families that guard it. That miserable, godforsaken place. It's like it's cursed us. Buried in concrete and still trying to kill us. How the hell did Magnus survive the cement being poured into his tunnel? And the draining of ectoplasm by the ghost box. He should be dead; he's got to be dead."

"You're babbling," said Rebecca.

"Help me sit up," said Hunter.

"Help me get his other arm," said Pastor Mark.

Between the two of them, they got a bewildered Hunter to sit straight up on the edge of the bed by propping one elbow against the headboard. He felt burned out and exhausted. Enid Moser was his best friend; he was like family to Hunter. He was the steadying influence that had seen Hunter through Bartok's last days.

The eyes, the eyes were lit with the purple-black twisting light of the alien influence. There was no going back. In all the records Hunter had scoured looking for information about the horrors below Townsend Mountain, not one person who had been infected had ever been cured. Not one person had ever survived. How long did Moser have left before he completely changed? What if he ended up like Bartok? Wired down to a bed with metal cables to hold him in place until the moment where the tentacles when first his body burst apart, and Hunter would have to shoot him dead. It would be just like uncle Bartok, Hunter thought. Shoot him till the pistol ran empty. Hunter felt his stomach go cold.

"Hunter?"

"What is it, Rebecca?"

"This is like what happened to your uncle Bartok, isn't it?"

"We're going to have to kill him, Rebecca."

"Whoa, hold on there a minute," said Pastor Mark. "We're not killing anybody."

"He's going to ask me to. Ask him yourself. He's strong. He's already figured this out. I can't believe I didn't. This can't have been the first time he felt it coming over him. He was fighting it, bringing the shotgun up under his chin so he could blow his head off. Stupid, stupid son of a bitch."

"God might have other plans for him," said Rebecca simply.

Hunter looked at her with sudden hope in his eyes.

"Can you—"

She shook her head. "God's not an ATM, Hunter. 'I will have mercy on whom I have mercy, and I will have compassion on whom I have compassion.' That's what he said to Moses. His plans are his plans, if you see what I mean. I've already prayed for him the way I prayed for Marla."

"And?"

"And nothing—nothing yet, I'm afraid."

"This is bullshit," said Hunter. "She was a total stranger. Why would He heal a total stranger instead of my best friend? Tell me that. Why? It's not fair. It's not right."

"Don't go there," said Pastor Mark. "We're accountable to Him, not the other way around. In Romans, the apostle Paul says, 'Does not the potter have the right to make out of the same lump of clay some pottery for—'"

"Stop it," shouted Hunter. "Just stop it. Don't quote the Bible to me while my friend is dying in the next room. You're worse than Baptist missionaries. You know what's going to happen to him before long? Those things, those filaments, will show up in his eyes more often and he'll start talking like he's an alien conqueror and how he's going to rip apart our bodies so he can devour our life force—"

"You stop it," snapped Rebecca. "Get a hold of yourself."

"Why? It's going to happen. Soon we'll see those lights crawling around just beneath the surface of his skin. Then his skin is going to turn yellow-green, and let me tell you we better have tied him down with cables by then or he's going to attack us with superhuman strength and start ripping us apart."

"Would you shut up?" came a woman's voice from the door.

It was Marla, standing in the doorway, her fists bunched.

"You realize he can hear you in the next room, don't you?"

"Oh no," said Hunter.

"Oh yes," said Marla. "Rebecca, Pastor, can one of you slap him senseless if he loses it again? That witch is doing everything but kick our asses into a blender and push the button. And Hunter, you're supposed to be the big brains here, but I'm not seeing anything out of you except chaos. Can you get yourself together, or do we have to tie you up and throw you in the closet until this is over?"

Hunter flushed with rage.

"You do not know what's happening to Moser," said Hunter.

"Oh, I think I do," said Marla.

She took a step into the room and flipped the light switch to the on position as she did. The bright light took everyone by surprise and Hunter, Rebecca, and pastor Mark held her hands up to protect their eyes.

"Your friend," continued Marla, "is turning into a monster. I get it. Where I just came from, in Borgo, Michigan, that would be considered a minor event. I'm sorry it's happening, he's sorry it's happening, you're sorry it's happening and everybody else's sorry it's happening. But from what he says, and what you say, there is no going back. He's prepared to die if he has to, and I like that in a man. Everybody here is on the firing line, including you. You haven't seen what I've seen, and I haven't seen what you've seen. Does that about cover it? Because we've got work to do. If you think your way can stop Hiram Abiff, if it can kill Hiram Abiff, then I say go talk to your friend and then get back to work."

"You are a—"

"I know. I'm an insensitive bitch, Hunter. But I just saw my friend Jimmy die. And me, Rebecca and Kenneth just got attacked by skeleton monsters, and your friend Moser is going to turn into a monster soon enough, and we're most likely going to kill him. I don't have room for any emotions, and I don't have any emotions left, anyway. You wanted to know who sent me to Borgo, didn't you? Well, I'll tell you now, it was the President of the United States. That fucker dimed me out. He sent me someplace he never thought I'd come back from. Well, I got news for him, and I've got news for the entire United States government.

"They kicked me off the team, and that's fine with me. Now I've got no use for them, anyway. They're all dickless wonders. I'm on a new team now. Your team, Hunter. And I want to see Hiram Abiff and that freak of a witch go down in flames. Me, Kenneth, Rebecca Ashley and Pastor Mark and your friend Moser talked it through while you were out cold. Everybody seems to think you're the smart one, so we're going to go with your plan. But we need you at one hundred percent. We'll all mourn everybody we've lost later. You good with that?"

Hunter turned to Rebecca.

"Don't push it," she said.

"What changed your mind?"

Rebecca looked over at Pastor Mark first, and then back at Hunter.

"Both the pastor and I think you're right. Hiram Abiff just doesn't match all the criteria for the Beast. He is just trying to convince everyone that he is, for some reason. And somehow, my father has fallen under the witch's influence, and I surely hope you can come up with the way to set him free of that."

Hunter looked at her, was about to tell her thanks for the support, but stopped with his mouth open.

"Hunter?" asked Pastor Mark. "What is it?"

"I... I had a thought."

His eyes took on a vacant, faraway look.

"What if," he said, "what if the implant, the neurotransmitter or whatever it is can cure Moser?"

Rebecca shot straight up out of her chair.

"No," she said with a fierce intensity.

"And then, take it out after it cures Moser of the alien influence," said Hunter.

"It's the mark of the Beast," said Rebecca.

"But you just said it wasn't," said Hunter. "I mean, you just said that Hiram Abiff is not the great beast of the Apocalypse. If he's not, then the implant is not really the sign of the beast."

"Later," snapped Marla. "There's not time enough for that now, Hunter. Build your contraption, then we take out Hiram and that witch. Then we take care of Moser. No time to do this any other way."

Rebecca started to object, but Marla said to her, "Later." First, it appeared Rebecca would explode. But when Marla placed a hand on her shoulder and said, "Please, we can talk about this later. We have to get moving," Rebecca slowly nodded her head in agreement.

"I need to see Moser first," said Hunter.

****

"That young woman surely knows how to tie a fella up," said Moser.

He was sitting up in the recliner in the far corner of the bedroom, next to an old-fashioned lampstand. That his eyes looked normal again immediately made Hunter feel better. Moser's wrists were double tied together, the same as his feet.

"What's going on?" asked Hunter. "How… how did this happen? Did I miss something?"

Moser chuckled ruefully.

"No—well, sort of. It's like this: there's only so long a fella can be near Townsend Mountain before it gets to him, and I was there longer than anyone before me. You remember what happened to the dogs, don't you?"

Hunter did. They'd changed.

"This is no way for you to go," said Hunter.

"You'll take care of business when the time is right."

"No. No, I can't do that. There has to be another way. The implant I was telling you about at Brother Mihaloff's clinic. Maybe it could fix you."

"No. Not going to happen, brother."

"Moser, just listen to me. They would take it out afterward. It wouldn't be in your head forever."

"You don't know that," said Moser. "Maybe it changes a man in ways he can't go back."

"Listen, you stubborn old shit—"

"No," bellowed Moser. "Ain't nothing left to talk about. Those things ain't right and you know it. Just get that shit out of your head and go build your machine so we can stop that thing from coming through. Hunter, get that straight. We are Masons. We make good men better. They don't cater to monsters."

They were all pushing on him, Hunter realized. All trying to get him angry enough to get to work on the device to put underneath the Empty Chair, including Moser himself. Compartmentalize; that's what Moser had always told him got him through combat. They were trying to get him to put his fear for Moser's safety away in a mental compartment so he could work. But Hunter couldn't and wouldn't do that. He could, however, use his fear and anger as fuel to drive him to work faster and smarter to stop Hiram Abiff and to save his friend. There had to be a way to do both.

"Are you listening to me?" demanded Moser.

"I am."

"Keep your mind on what you got to do."

Hunter nodded, stood, and turned around. Kenneth, Hillis and Ashely stood in the doorway. Kenneth looked like he didn't know what to do with himself. Ashley had her arm around his waist. She still looked pissed about the ugly new wound on his forehead beneath the bandage. Hunter was about to move past them when he heard Moser's voice behind him.

"Hunter," he said.

"Yeah."

"You can't figure everything out. Sometimes all you can do is all you can do. I know how I'm going to have to die, and I know where I'm going when I do. That's enough for me. You got that?"

"I do, old man."

"Then get to it."

Hunter nodded again and kept on going past Kenneth and Ashley. He was tired of just nodding at what everybody else had to say.

"You okay?" Ashley asked.

"Not yet," said Hunter.

The others were waiting in the hallway, too. It was getting to be a crowded old house.

"Pastor Mark," he said. "Can you help me out?"

"I'll go with you, too," said Kenneth. "I got to have something to do, or I'll go crazy."

"Let's go," said the minister.

As the three of them walked toward the stairs leading to the basement, Hunter realized for the first time that a man could be angry and grief stricken all at the same time.

65

"Careful," said Hunter. "Those things cost me seven thousand dollars apiece."

"Don't you worry, writer-man," said Kenneth. "They made in the States, or is they foreign?"

Kenneth wore a denim jacket that looked like it had been in too many bar fights and a black cowboy hat that looked brand new.

"Just shut up," said Hunter as he ran his hand through his hair. Sometimes, Kenneth sounded too hillbilly for his own good. "Pastor, is that lift gate giving you trouble?"

"I've got it," said the minister. "It helped when I clicked off the wheel locks."

They'd parked at a side loading entrance, so they could unload the electric power stackers Hunter had ordered. They each sported a seven-hundred-watt drive motor, a two-thousand-watt lift motor with four hours service per charge and two twelve-volt, seventy AH rechargeable batteries with built-in chargers. No problem with them doing the job since they could both handle fifteen hundred pounds without breaking an electrical sweat. They just had to get them to the Unfinished Theater and over to where the Empty Chair was already re-mounted.

"Hurry up," said Marla. "Too much line of sight and too little light around this rig. Tell me again why we had to do this coming up on midnight?"

The night was misty, and moonlight rolled off it like mercury sliding down black glass. Hunter could feel the danger in the air like an infrasonic hum. He looked over at Pastor Mark, who had a lug wrench slid through his belt, since he refused to carry a gun, because he didn't want to end up back in prison. Marla was carrying a short rifle that fired enormous bullets. The odd one out was Rebecca, who had a crossed holster set with Smith and Wesson nines. Her hand still wasn't the best and the pain of using the rifle the other night had cost her, so she'd gone with the pistols. The long, black trench coat and the low hanging pistols gave her a Matrix look. Hunter missed having Moser cover his back, but one look at the things crawling through his eyes had convinced Hunter that what Moser really needed was to be in a cage, but they'd settled on Marla tying him up again. Like Moser said, whoever Marla really was, she sure knew how to tie a fella up.

"All right, Kenneth," said Hunter, "if you and the pastor each take one of the stackers, I'll take the device and the toolbox, and we can head upstairs after Marla and Rebecca roll down the door and lock the place up tight."

"Not a chance," said Marla. "You roll down the doors and make it tight. Rebecca and I will cover you. Bodyguards only do one thing, Hunter. Bodyguard. If we take our eyes off of you to close up shop and something comes at you, who do you think will protect you?"

Hunter clearly hadn't considered that. But it made sense.

"Got it," he said.

He had his own .38 in a shoulder holster, but with any luck, it would stay there all night and just be for show. He thought about that when he'd pushed the button on the automated system that lowered the access doors. They were big enough to allow about anything smaller than a tank to enter. Tanks and guns. Weapons were easier to think about than what might come out from beneath the Empty Chair. The memory of Moser's shotgun stock smashing into the monster and driving it back into the Pass put the whole idea into perspective.

"What?" asked Kenneth, looking at Hunter curiously. "You got something to say?"

Hunter thought about that, then said, "No, I'm fine."

"Well, we'd best get moving. I take it we don't know exactly how long this will take."

"No," agreed Hunter, "we don't."

What he didn't say was, if it worked at all.

The door came down on the concrete with a soft thud, and the world outside of the loading dock disappeared. Hunter had the device he'd built, and the associated tools for installation arranged inside a work chest on wheels he'd picked up at one of the last remaining Sears stores on the planet. Tools, Moser had told him once, need to be bought in a store, not off the Internet.

All of them walking down the Masonic Temple hallways, beautifully adorned as they were, was like taking a repair crew into a morgue. The sound of the wheels rolling along the otherwise empty marble floor was eerily like he imagined it would be like to roll gurneys past dead bodies, bringing them still more corpses to swell their ranks.

"I'm sure glad you know where you're going," said Kenneth.

"It's only my fourth visit," confessed Hunter.

"Don't worry, if he gets lost, I know the way," said Rebecca.

"Really?" said Marla.

"My father's been bringing me here since I was old enough to walk," said Rebecca.

The talking made Hunter feel better as he led them down the hallway to the elevator that would take them to the top floor. If he understood it right, the Masons ran out of money before they finished the upper floors. The unfinished theater had remained unfinished since the nineteen twenties, until Brother Mihaloff and crew had fixed all of that.

They made a strange caravan, he thought, when they finally arrived at the freight elevator. Two armed women, ready for action, the preacher who couldn't carry a gun because of his criminal record, a hog wrestler and a ghost hunter/writer. Thank God Rebecca's father had been true to his word and the entire building was empty other than them. He couldn't imagine what anyone would think if they saw the gun-toting team. They would probably dial 911 faster than Hunter could get out an explanation. By the time Hunter and the others got out of jail, Hiram Abiff would already own the world.

"Can we fit all of this in?" asked Pastor Mark, looking dubiously at the size of the stackers and the workbench on wheels.

"If everybody holds their breath," said Hunter.

"Serious?" asked Kenneth.

"No. It's going to be a tight fit, but I think we've got it."

"You men load everything in, then get in yourselves and Marla and I will squeeze in last," said Rebecca.

Kenneth and Pastor Mark maneuvered in the electric stackers since they were the most complicated to get in, followed by Hunter and his workbench with the structure he and the Pastor had built balanced on top of it. Finally, when they were all inside, Marla stepped in, followed by Rebecca. Hunter noticed that, aggressive though Marla was, she automatically gave the final point position to Rebecca. That Rebecca had shot it out with monsters to save her and then nuked the place with a phosphorus grenade as they were leaving had evidently made a big impression on the government agent. That and the fact that Marla had gone to sleep torn up when they got her to Bartok's place, but then woke up healed after Rebecca prayed over her, seemed to have been enough to win Marla over. Hunter still didn't get that. He'd never, ever imagined such a thing to be possible.

The doors closed, and the elevator rose.

"Is it just me, or does this entire building seem sinister?" asked Hunter to no one in particular. "It's like being in a John Carpenter horror movie."

"It's just you," said Pastor Mark.

"I feel it, too," said Marla. "It reminds me of being in Borgo. Like there's something wrong. Or like something is going to happen."

"Like what?" asked Kenneth.

"I don't know. It's just... a premonition. A bad feeling."

"And we're only just passing the third floor," said Hunter. "I hope it doesn't get worse the higher up we go."

"It will," said Rebecca.

The grim tone of her voice kept them silent until they reached the very last floor. What they saw on each other's faces frightened them, though they tried not to show it. Seeing their looks, Hunter was glad he'd brought his revolver. It was his experience that pistols, shotguns and rifles were damned well useless against ghosts and evil spirits, but carrying a handgun made him feel better anyway. He didn't think either Hiram Abiff or Evan Morgan would go down, even with a forty-five round to the face. And that was a very disturbing thought indeed.

The motion stopped as the number ten lit up on the side panel. Rebecca stood to one side of the metal door as it slowly began to open, and Marla took the other side so they would have a convergent line of fire and be less likely to be shot. Kenneth and Pastor Mark scrunched down behind their respective stackers. Hunter didn't move. He wasn't sure if it was because he was protecting his device with his body or just frozen in place. But the feeling of impending disaster was, as Rebecca had implied, much worse on the tenth floor. There was, he felt, something or someone up here waiting for them.

But as the door slid up and revealed the dimly lit hallway, Hunter wished he'd brought a bank of halogen lights to drive away the shadows. He saw Rebecca and Marla sweeping the hallway with the flashlights mounted on their weapons, but there was nothing to see except an empty hallway. His hand was on the handle of his revolver.

"Stay here," Rebecca told him.

Almost as though they'd rehearsed the maneuver, the two women stepped out of the hallway and split up to put distance between them.

"You feeling kinda like a third thumb?" asked Kenneth in a low voice.

"Yeah," whispered Hunter.

And he was. He was out of his element, and he sorely missed Moser. He tried not to think of what was happening to his friend. The old man had warned him to concentrate on what he was doing, and he was trying. But he felt like he was trapped in a locked cell, watching the fuse burn down on a bundle of dynamite.

Hiram Abiff and Eva Morgan had to be stopped, but he had to save Moser. It occurred to him at that moment that maybe he was delusional. From what Marla had told them, there was probably no way to stop Hiram Abiff, and Moser would turn into a tentacled monster just like Bartok.

Those were the thoughts that tried to hold him down, to make him give up. He wondered if it was the Detroit Masonic Temple that caused him to despair, or if it was something that had invaded the Masonic domain. The witch. Maybe, he thought, it was the witch he was feeling. Maybe she had spellcast this entire floor.

"The hallways are clear," came Rebecca's voice from outside the elevator and down the hall.

I don't think so, thought Hunter.

Something.

Something was wrong. Something was on this floor that shouldn't be. He was sure of it.

"Did you check the Unfinished Theater?" he called out.

"Doors are locked, Hunter. We need the keys."

Reluctantly, he walked to the front of the elevator and handed Rebecca the keys. As she and Marla headed toward the locked doors, he followed.

"Don't even think about it," Marla called over her shoulder. "We'll come back for you guys when know the entire floor is clear."

Something.

Someone or something was on this floor that shouldn't be. He did not understand how he could feel it, but he could. Maybe an aftereffect of going under Townsend Mountain. He may have been more sensitive to the supernatural now. Maybe, he thought, I'm going to end up like Bartok and Moser. If that happened, he was going to quit looking in mirrors.

He looked over at Kenneth and saw he had his forty-five revolver out. His cowboy hat was pushed up, and he looked tense.

"You feel it, too, don't you?" asked Hunter.

"Something's not right," agreed Kenneth.

"You know what bothers me?" asked Hunter.

"Bullets might not stop whatever's here?"

"Yeah. I don't think shooting at the witch did you and the others any good last night. I think something else was at play."

"Like what?" asked Pastor Mark.

"Don't have a clue," said Hunter.

"Pastor, you feel that... bad vibe in the air."

"Yes. Hard to believe a couple of nights ago, my biggest worry was how to add another ten people to my congregation. Whether to go door-to-door to get the word out or schedule another meat loaf dinner open to the public. Now, I've seen one of my church members mauled by a monster, shot it out with monsters in another world called Borgo, and now I'm here with you guys waiting while two women gunmen are making sure it's safe for us to roll out this equipment. So, I can safely say I feel a bad vibe in the air. I don't take drugs, but I'm about ready for anti-anxiety medication. Prison felt safer than this."

Both Hunter and Kenneth stared at him.

"Well," said Kenneth, "that was a mouthful."

"Sometimes when I get nervous, it's hard to shut me up," said the Pastor.

Five minutes passed, with none of them saying a word. Waiting in a six feet deep by eight foot wide metal box was getting on their nerves.

"I'm going out to check on them," said Kenneth at last.

"They might shoot you by mistake," said Hunter.

Kenneth chewed on that.

"I hate this," he said.

"So do we."

Quiet again for another minute.

"All clear as best we can tell," came Rebecca's voice at last.

She stepped around the corner, her gun held loosely by her side.

"Best you can tell?" asked Kenneth.

"There are so many secret passages in this building you can never be sure," she said. "Half the Detroit Police force could hide on this floor and we'd never know."

"That's comforting," said Pastor Mark.

"Let's get this stuff out of here," said Hunter, and he pushed the work table out and into the hallway.

He was tired of talking.

Rolling the equipment down the marble tiled hallway, Hunter would have been impressed by the craftsmanship of the flute bronze wall sconces, the alternating black and white columns with their elegant entablature and the stunning gold and white archways except for the hollow dead sound the wheels of his car made reminded him of why they were here and how few people would know they were there if something should happen to them.

Rebecca held up a hand, and their little procession came to a sudden halt.

"You hear that?" she called to Marla.

"Yeah. You want me to check it out?"

Rebecca tilted her head to one side as the listening. She looked upward at the ceiling.

"You think there are passages up there?" said Hunter.

Hunter remembered what Rebecca had said earlier about the Detroit Masonic Temple being literally honeycombed with secret passages. That someone or something could be crawling overhead gave him the creeps.

"No," said Rebecca. "Leave that to me. You get them into the theater safely."

Her voice echoed up and down the hallway. The doors to the Unfinished Theater stood wide open, with Marla standing guard.

"Miss Rebecca," said Kenneth, "there ain't no reason for you to go alone. Show a lick of sense and let Marla or me go with you."

Rebecca gave him a stony stare.

"What is it with you and Moser, Kenneth? My name is Rebecca, not Miss Rebecca."

"Well, Miss Rebecca or just plain Rebecca, this hillbilly says that it ain't smart to go alone."

"Kenneth, we don't have that many people. Do like I'm saying. Let's get this over with."

"Rebecca, listen to him," said Pastor Mark.

"No, we need Hunter's device installed. I can take care of myself."

"But—"

She was already heading down the hallway and not looking back.

"I worry about her," said Pastor Mark.

Hunter was about to say something, but started pushing his work cart forward instead. He tried not to look at Rebecca as he did. There was something distracting about her and, truth to tell, in between being angry at her, he was getting rather fond of her.

"Hurry," said Marla.

He was the slowest of the three men, since he had to physically push his cart. Kenneth and the pastor's stackers were electrically powered. He could no longer hear Rebecca's footsteps, and that bothered him. She could take care of herself, he knew that. In fact, she could take care of herself in a dangerous situation better than he could. Hunter lacked formal weapons training and military experience, but Moser was an excellent teacher, and Hunter was a fast learner.

Still, some people seemed they were born into taking care of things, and Rebecca Mihaloff was one of those. If her father found out that Hunter had let her go alone tonight, there'd be hell to pay. While thinking that, it occurred to him that, according to what Kenneth told them earlier, there'd be hell to pay if Ricci found out they'd brought her into a dangerous situation, too. Why hadn't he thought this through?

But the option was between leaving her back at Bartok's where she was out of their sight, and where Moser might go alien at a moment's notice, or bringing her along. At least here they knew where she was. Except now. Now she was off on her own. Stupid, stupid move, thought Hunter.

"Which chair?" asked Marla, as the men maneuvered the equipment into place.

"Same one you came through last time," said Hunter.

When he saw the look on her face, he realized his mistake. She didn't know the way the Empty Chair worked or even that it was called an Empty Chair. He had talked little to her since Rebecca and Pastor Mark had saved her.

"The one to the right of the Worshipful Master's chair," he said.

She gave him another blank look.

"That one," he said, and pointed directly at the Empty Chair down on the stage.

The only way that the formerly Unfinished Theater was less than the main Masonic Theater was size. It was a newly minted version of the Masonic Theater on a miniature scale. It could only hold between seven hundred and seven hundred and fifty people at a time.

"Wasn't there a back loading door we could have come in through?" asked a clearly irritated Marla. "How are we supposed to get this equipment up on that stage?"

"But there's a double door to either side of the stage area that we can roll everything through. It winds around back behind the main platform. It'll work."

Marla grimaced.

She might be a field agent like Moser thought, but she clearly was used to details being planned out more thoroughly than this. Maybe I could learn some things from her, he thought. If I live that long.

The thought surprised him. But now he would have to deal with it. Odds were, they'd all be dead within the week. If things got rough tonight, it was just possible Moser would outlive them all. Now there, he thought, was a grimly sobering thought.

The cartwheels squeaked as he pushed it down the walkway that girded the circumference. It was like rolling equipment into a beautiful mortuary under the cover of darkness. Every sound echoed through the now finished auditorium and seemed to amplify before gradually fading away. The feeling of being watched was still strong. But no matter how hard he, Marla and the others looked, there was nothing to see except rows of red velvet, deep cushioned seats and the stage outfitted as a Masonic Lodge.

Hunter imagined what it would be like filled with Masons from around the world. People titled "Worshipful Master" this and "Worshipful Master" that. Decked out in their tuxedos, their Masonic jewels, their top hats and their aprons. He knew it would be livestreamed to lodges all around the world. This would be history in the making.

They moved backstage, the electric motors of Kenneth and Pastor Mark's stackers oddly comforting in the vacuum, whose only other sounds were echoes. Maneuvering between the props and boxes, they finally all made it to the stage, where all the lodge furniture was arranged exactly how it had been in the Romanesque Room.

"What now?" asked Kenneth.

Marla's eyes kept scanning the area. It's bothering her, too, thought Hunter. Something wasn't right.

"Before we do anything else," said Hunter. "I need to get a look at the wiring beneath the chair. Then," and he pulled out a set of wires and clips from his vest pocket, "I'll re-route the electro-magical pathway so it doesn't open the door on the other side of the Pass. Then we can install the device we built."

"You don't exactly know what you're doing," said Kenneth.

He said it; he didn't ask it. Kenneth was a lot like Moser for calling things as he saw them.

"Mostly," said Hunter, "but I've got a good idea. It will help a lot if I look at the wires again. Can you hold the lighted magnifying window for me while I make sure this is going to work?"

"Shouldn't you have figured it out before you bought all this equipment?"

"Give him a break, Kenneth," said Pastor Mark. "We've been

running short of time since this whole mess started. We're going to have to have a little faith to get through this."

Kenneth rubbed his rough couple of day's old beard with his even rougher hand.

"I can do that, I guess," he said.

"Why don't you men quit talking and get to work?" said Marla. "Rebecca's not back yet and I don't like that one bit."

After exchanging looks with Kenneth and the pastor, Hunter took out his lighted magnifying window from a drawer in his worktable and handed it to Kenneth. It was a square piece of magnifying glass in a frame of black plastic with LED lights mounted around the inside edge of the frame.

He walked over to the empty chair and kneeled down beside it. Then he slid open the wooden panel that revealed both the lever and, further back inside, the scarlet-red electromagical symbol. Although he knew it wasn't possible, Hunter was sure that he could hear it emanate a soft hum, like that of a tiny electric chair warming up for an execution. And that made him wonder where Rebecca was.

Marla must've been having similar thoughts.

"Pastor," she said, "can you cover for me while I go look for Rebecca?"

"I can do that," said Pastor Mark.

"No," snapped Hunter. "She has to take care of herself for now because we have to get this done and I need the coverage."

"Hunter," said the pastor, "it's been a bit, and we have heard nothing from her. I'm getting worried."

"Stay here," said Hunter firmly. "We have a job to do, and not much time to do it. I need you here."

He looked over and saw the Kentuckian staring at him. Kenneth Hillis was a lot like Enid Moser. They could generate that serious look at the drop of a hat. After a moment, though, Kenneth nodded.

"How do you want to do this?" said Kenneth.

"Hunter," said Marla, "you can have the plans, but you don't give the orders. I'm going after Rebecca to see if we have problems."

"I told you," said Hunter, "I need you to cover our backs. If we don't get this done quickly, it will not make any difference what happens to Rebecca, to you, to me or to anybody else. Stay or go, but quit bothering me. I have work to do."

Marla looked like she would shoot him, but Hunter turned back to the symbol recessed within the chair. He wasn't bluffing. He really believed that if they didn't get this done, there was no stopping Hiram Abiff. Everything Marla told them about her experience in Borgo only made that point more clearly. When he didn't hear her leaving the auditorium in search of Rebecca, he got back to work.

He was about to reach his hands in to see if he could pull the symbol out and forward without having to take apart the chair, when Kenneth asked, "What if it's booby-trapped?"

"Thanks, Kenneth," said Hunter. "I really needed that."

"Well, what if it is?"

"I don't know. I wouldn't even know how to tell the difference. Even though I think you're right, I just don't know how to be sure not to reroute and then clip the right wire."

Maybe he needed to take the entire side panel apart on the chair so that he could get a better look at what he was going to do. But what if taking off the panel set off a booby-trap? Screw it.

"Pastor Mark?"

"Yes?"

"Can you hand me that tool bag on my work chest?"

"Got it," said the pastor.

As he took the bag, he could feel Marla glaring at him. Too bad, he thought. Rebecca could take care of herself, he knew that. He cared what happened to her, but this was more important at the moment. Rebecca knew the risks. For what he was doing, though, Hunter really didn't know the risks. What if he opened a permanent gateway to the world of Borgo?

"That side piece you're looking at," said Kenneth, "just might slide off."

"Maybe. But if it doesn't, I'll get it off one way or the other."

"Now you're talking."

After feeling along the edges of the sideboard for hidden buttons, Hunter gave up and tried sliding it this way and the other. At first, it seemed like it was permanently fixed in place; he could get it to slide forward. It was like two pieces tied together by the same mechanism. He could slide the door that covered the smaller opening to forward and out completely.

"Nice," said Kenneth.

"Okay, now could you kneel here and then hold the magnifying window in front of the opening? The switch for the lights is on the bottom right there."

When Kenneth had it in place and the lights on, it opened up a whole new world beneath the chair for Hunter to stare at in confusion.

"Shit," he said. "The electromagical circuits operating this chair are way more complicated than I thought."

"You know which wire to cut and splice?" asked Kenneth.

Ignoring him, Hunter lay down on his side and stared into the opening at what he thought had been the core magical component—the sigil and its attached filament wiring. What he had not seen before was a series of four glowing, different colored crystals attached to each other and to the sigil. There was another sigil, it appeared, on the far side of the chair attached to the crystals as well as by a set of filaments. But most surprising of all was that each of the wire components was attached to a silver disc the size of a pie pan at the back of the chair.

Well, he thought, we are well and truly screwed now.

If he'd seen all of this the last time he looked beneath the chair, he would have never considered interrupting the circuits in such a crude manner. What were those crystals, anyway? he wondered. Some kind of power source? What if they were, and the silver disc was the energy transmitting unit that connected magically to the other chair? He leaned in a bit toward the magnifying window, but had to back away a little to get an undistorted view. When he got his angle just right, he saw them. Pictographs. Picture writing that he'd never seen before. He was somewhat of an expert on occult symbols—it went with the territory of being a paranormal investigator—but he had never seen anything remotely like them. Unless…

"What's going on?" asked Kenneth.

The thing was, he could see that all the filaments leading to the silver disc intersected in a header that was attached by a thin rod running through the center of the disc.

"I need to take the whole back side of this thing off," Hunter said.

"Why?"

"Don't ask him so many questions," said Pastor Mark. "I think we need to get this done and then go find Rebecca."

"No," said Hunter. "I need help with this. I think I've got the right concept about what we need to do, but I'm open to ideas. I don't want to overlook anything. So, Kenneth, I'll hold the magnifying window in place and you look. Focus on the silver disc at the back. I think that's kind of an occult transmitter which, when we flip the lever, it sends a signal to the other chair to open at the same time. My idea is to put in a wireless switch to interrupt that transmission by remote.

"Here," said Kenneth, handing him the magnifying window.

As Hunter took it, he looked up at Marla and saw that Pastor Mark had gone to stand with her. Both looked increasingly tense. Both looked ready for something bad to happen.

I wouldn't want her gunning for me, thought Hunter. Or him. The pastor was the kind of guy you noticed because of his size and his rough look. But since this whole thing began, he'd seemed to fade into the background of Hunter's perspective. It wasn't exactly that he wasn't there, just that he didn't seem to have as strong a personality as Rebecca, her father, Moser, and the others. Having survived the horrors of prison, he clearly had a strong mental spine, but maybe it was him not talking as much as everyone else. The more people talked, the more he seemed to back away. Hunter remembered their talk around the table at his house. Pastor Mark contributed, but was mostly silent unless he was telling them about Ricci. Maybe he'd learned that in prison. Less said, less trouble.

"I see what you're saying," said Kenneth. "Ain't no way to get to that disc thing without taking the back off. Doesn't seem to be a trip wire to set off. I got a little experience blowing things up, and I hope I ain't wrong, but I think we can take it off without setting off a trip wire."

Hunter heard footsteps behind him and looked up in alarm, but it was only Marla and Pastor Mark.

"Let me get a look at that," said Marla.

"What for?" asked Hunter.

"I heard you talking, and I know something about trip wires."

The two men stood up, and Hunter handed Marla the magnifying window. She knelt down, brushed her long dark hair to one side and peered through the glass.

"You want me to hold that for you?" asked Kenneth.

She ignored him and moved her head from side to side to get a better look.

"What the hell is this?"

"It's—"

"Don't bother," she said. "I wasn't looking for an answer. And I think you got lucky taking the side panel off without a problem."

She stood and brushed off her knees before continuing.

"I think there might be a pressure switch in play with this piece of furniture. Maybe two or three."

"Okay, but why? Why do you think that?"

Hunter realized he was getting irritated at her and couldn't figure out why.

"The idea of using electrical trip wires evolved over time. I think this device was built before then. It just doesn't look old enough. So, I think there might be an order to the way you have to take this thing apart. Each piece you slide out along a track releases one pressure spring or button. I've seen it before in early European explosive devices. Mechanical was big back then. Electric devices were still magic to most people."

The implications of this information silenced the men. What Marla said not only made sense, it stopped their progress dead. He was about to ask her what they should do next, when the sound of someone clapping caused them all to turn their heads toward the auditorium balcony. Marla's rifle came up as she turned to find the source of the interruption.

"I would not," came a man's distinctive, measured voice, "fire your weapon, my dear. It would only result in the unfortunate and untimely death of your friend, Rebecca, and, ultimately, the world as you know it."

Marla did not shoot, but she did not immediately lower her rifle, either.

Hunter stared in shock at the man, who stood in front of the balcony railing. Who was he and how had he gotten in with none of them seeing or hearing him? And did he really have Rebecca captive?

"You are, to my understanding, our new Tyler," said the man.

The acoustics in the Unfinished Temple were remarkable. The man sounded as though he were standing only ten feet away. He wore a black tuxedo with a brilliant white shirt, and in his front pocket he sported a scarlet handkerchief. From what Hunter could see, he looked remarkably like the old film star Clark Gable dressed for the theater, but he acted as though he were a producer come to examine the performance of his lead players.

"Who are you?" asked Hunter.

"Ah, the eternal question," said the man.

Behind him, Hunter heard the faint sound of Kenneth on the floor wriggling his way between the benches to conceal himself. Marla and Pastor Mark stood where they were. Like Hunter, they were unsure of their next moves.

"You are no doubt worried about your lady friend, which would explain why Mr. Hillis is so ill-concealed behind the benches. May I, with all respect, Mr. Hillis, recommend that when you attempt to conceal your considerable length behind a bench, you first determine that you have chosen one longer than yourself? Your work boots give you away.

"Rebecca Mihaloff is now in the hands of one of my most valued employees and he is not, I assure you, a man to provoke. If you return your equipment and stand where I can see you, I offer that she might be returned to you unharmed. Should you stay where you are... I can extend my assurances to you I do not tolerate fools, nor those they value. I have been bested only once, and that was by your grandmother. I admit to retaining a certain... pique regarding that incident, although I was grieved to learn of her untimely demise. As regards revenge, I am of accord with the German poet Heine. Are you familiar with his writings, Mr. Hunter?"

"No."

"I am," said Pastor Mark, to the surprise of everyone.

The man standing before the balcony railing tilted his head to one side, as though to get a better look at the pastor.

"And you are?"

"Don't tell him," said Hunter quickly, laying a restraining hand on pastor Mark's shoulder.

"Why?" asked the bewildered man.

"They can do things with your name," said Hunter.

"I would applaud your insight, Mr. Hunter, but I have already clapped twice this year and I am afraid that already surpasses my self-imposed quota, yet I plead extenuating circumstances."

"Why did you ask us about Heine?" asked pastor Mark.

From where Hunter stood, he could see the momentary glimpse of the man on the balcony.

"Because the thought of Mr. Hillis's grandmother—and I thank you for re-joining our little group, Mr. Hillis—causes me to experience the need, no, the desire, to achieve a degree of revenge, but she is unfortunately no longer with us. This awkward fact recalled the irony of an elegant quote from Mr. Heine, wherein he admonishes us that 'We should forgive our enemies, but not before they are hanged.'"

"Now I know who you are," said Kenneth, with a quiet snarl in his voice. "And you're lucky she's dead, or she'd put you down."

"There is a certain poetry to your dialect as well," said the man.

That's when Hunter got it.

"You're Mr. Chirac, aren't you?"

"M. Emile Chirac, at your service," said the man with a dignified bow.

Hunter saw the slight movement of Marla's rifle barrel as Mr. Chirac leaned forward and was grateful that she did not pull the trigger. Whatever this man wanted from them, he was, from what Granny told him, unlikely to die from a bullet. And wherever he was, Ricci would be close by. He didn't like that thought at all, although Ricci had met with Kenneth, and warned him that Mr. Chirac would send the witch for the ghost box again. A sudden panic seized him as Mr. Chirac straightened to his full height again. What if, as Mr. Chirac stood talking to him, the witch was attacking the house again while Moser lay bound and defenseless with only Ashley, Darryl and Eddie to protect him?

"I come," said Mr. Chirac, "with an offer which, I believe, will be mutually beneficial."

"Where's Rebecca?" said Marla, with a raw touch of anger in her voice.

Mr. Chirac paused and seemed to notice her for the first time, even though Marla was a hard woman to miss. Even from as far away as he was, Hunter noticed the way the man's eyes seemed to roam over her.

"What a pleasure it is to meet you in person, Miss Corvasce."

Hunter blinked. Did these two know each other?

"How do you know my last name?" asked Marla.

"Let us just say that a mutual acquaintance is quite choleric with you, and she is not a woman—although I use the term with a fair degree of liberal largess—to offend with impunity. It causes me pain to share this with you, but during our last conversation, she informed me that she wished to peel the skin from your body and dine on it while her creatures scrubbed your body with lye. It was an unpleasant image, and although I put forth a strong effort to calm her by proffering her a soothing lavender tea, I fear she was still obsessed with defiling your ever so attractive face when she left."

"What do you want?" said Kenneth, and Hunter could hear the anger in his friend's voice. But Hunter had a feeling that anger was not productive when dealing with Emile Chirac.

"You are a sensible man, Mr. Hillis, yet you have a direct nature which I find to be somewhat contrary to your Southern heritage. However, be that as it may, let us return to the reason I have come to visit this so beautifully renovated theater. The reason, clearly stated, is that I wish to make a binding arrangement with Mr. Hunter."

"We," said Hunter, waving his hand at the others, "are in this together. I won't discuss anything if I'm operating alone."

Mr. Chirac coughed politely into his hand.

"Your friends may listen to everything which I have to say to you, but I will not contract with a collection of people. Egalitarianism and collectivism are much too incestuous to tolerate. No, I bargain with only one person at a time, and believe me when I tell you, Mr. Hunter, that you will fail at what you are attempting to do tonight without my help and therefore require my assistance. I come in good faith to devise a binding arrangement. You and I are members of the same organization, my young friend. In fact, although our paths first crossed under socially awkward circumstances, you should know that I have also in the past, labored to protect your family. Your uncle Bartok was, in fact, my brother, as we were both members of the Temple Guardians. This is why I tried to stop the rather lovely Miss Morgan from infecting him with the scorched blood disease that would have taken his life had you not been forced to shoot him to death first."

Hunter felt like he'd been punched in the gut and leaned against the Empty Chair for support. The news that his uncle had been infected with a disease by Eva Morgan made him angry and sick at the same time. Between Townsend Mountain and the witch Eva Morgan, Bartok had never stood a chance. And he could not escape the feeling that neither could he.

"In his role as Tyler for the Temple Guardians, your uncle made a plethora of adversaries," continued Mr. Chirac, "and you, my young friend, have now donned the mantle of his responsibilities and his enemies are now yours. He was quite proud of you, did you not know? He believed you had, as he said, the aptitude to perform the role you have ascended to this very season.

"However, you have an unfortunate lack of experience in these matters and, if you will forgive my pointing this out, you have the occult experience of a washtub. Had you the temerity to remove the back panel of the Empty Chair, you would have unleashed the bone demon who is the guardian of the chair. Bone demons will eat through your skin and burrow into your osseus matter to eat the marrow, Mr. Hunter. It ends unpleasantly with the creature eating upward through your spine to dine on the succulence of your brain."

"How do you know?" asked Marla before Hunter could get the words out of his mouth.

"Why, my dear woman, it was I who designed both chairs."

66

Ignoring their collective shocked expressions, the elegantly dressed man pressed on.

"Here is my offer," said Mr. Chirac, with an astonishingly graceful wave of his hand. "I will make it possible for you to selectively interrupt the... circuitry of the chair, as you so inaptly call it, so that at your command it will open up the passageway between this world and Borgo, but will not open the chair on the other side. As I understand it, that is what you are attempting to accomplish in your own rather inelegant way, is it not?"

Hunter felt suddenly angry.

"How do you know that?"

Mr. Chirac ruefully shook his head.

"I have many resources, Mr. Hunter. Ricci is the only member of my staff you have met. Forgive me for saying that you would not enjoy meeting the others. My chef, for example, derives from a tribe of cannibals. He reacts poorly to those guests dissatisfied with his cuisine. He creates, despite that inconsequential failing, an exquisite cordon bleu.

"But I digress. You inquired how I am aware of your plans. Besides my vast network of sources, it is also a fact that the acoustics in this newly redone theater are marvelous, are they not? But one must be attentive. It was the rather unfortunate Walter Lippman who voiced the idea that '…the music is nothing if the audience is deaf.'"

"What the hell are you talking about?" asked a gruff Kenneth. "You keep talking and you know all we want is Rebecca back safe. If you got her, you better give her back pronto."

By an odd trick of the dim light, Mr. Chirac's eyes seemed to glow red for the briefest of moments.

Hunter held out a palm to slow Kenneth down.

"Hold on," he said. "Okay, you overheard us. You're willing to help us, but I know for damned sure that you always want something in return. Granny Hillis told me all about you."

The briefest of smiles, Hunter thought, but it was difficult to see details in the dim light… still, he felt it.

"Yes, indeed. The ghost box, Mr. Hunter. I wish its return. Is it not humiliating enough that the old woman bested me regarding her madstone? It would be the sheerest of prevarication if I pretended insouciance in that matter. So, indeed, I would like my ghost box returned as payment for my efforts with the Empty Chair. It is a well-balanced offer, I should think. The ghost box is useless to you. You have no grasp of its intricacies and were that of and by itself of sufficient import to make my argument, it has no energy source left to power it. It is therefore a useless historical artifact to you, but it is my historical artifact, and I will have it back."

"No."

In the dim theater, Mr. Chirac's form was not clear, but, only for a second, Hunter witnessed the optical illusion that fire sprang up along the edges of the man's suit collar.

"Do not press against my goodwill, Mr. Hunter. I extend this offer only once to you, and that as a Masonic courtesy."

"He's lying," said Kenneth. "He ain't no Mason."

Mr. Chirac took a step backward and placed both palms urgently over his heart.

"What, not a Mason? You wound me, Mr. Hillis. My paid in full lifetime membership is in my coat pocket. Shall I present it for your inspection?"

"Don't mean nothin," said Kenneth. "Paid up dues don't make a man a Mason."

"But I was raised on—"

"And it don't matter what day you was raised a Master Mason. A Mason is a Mason 'cause of what's in his heart, and that's all."

After a moment's pause, Hunter was surprised to see Mr. Chirac place one palm before his stomach, then one behind his back before he bowed in acknowledgment of what Kenneth had said. But when he straightened, any semblance of civility was gone, being replaced instead by an icy glare that Hunter could feel all the way on stage.

"Are you familiar with Sodom's Shackles, Mr. Hunter?" he asked in a tone that caused Hunter's terror meter to spike.

"No."

"Are any of you? And, Miss Corvasce, yes, you could aim and, in theory, hit me, but in reality, you and your comrades would die before you could pull the trigger."

Hunter turned, saw the look on Marla's face and then glanced back up at Mr. Chirac and once more back at Marla.

"Please don't, Marla," he said simply. "He has Rebecca."

In the pale light, he saw her jaw muscles loosen as she lowered her rifle.

"What do we do?" she asked Hunter.

"We listen."

"So, just so, Mr. Hunter. You listen. You will bring the ghost box to me here, tomorrow night at precisely midnight. By then, I will have arranged for the chair to function as you intend."

Hunter looked at Pastor Mark, who had remained quiet during the exchange. Fear, revulsion and terror crowded his wide face. '

"Pastor?" Hunter asked.

The preacher opened and closed his mouth as though trying to speak, but nothing came out except tightly bunched gasps as though something were stuck in his throat.

"Pastor?" asked Kenneth, his voice full of concern.

Marla never took her eyes off Mr. Chirac. Her thick, dark hair hung to one side and obscured most of her face, but what Hunter could see of the tilt of her chin and the forward leaning of her head reminded him of a tigress. Then he saw her eyes flick around the room and then back to the dark man. Looking for Rebecca, he thought. Trying to get a glimpse of her. Not knowing who was holding her for Mr. Chirac or where he or she was restraining her. It occurred to him that Rebecca was a very special woman to Marla, though she did not show it. Rebecca had prayed for her healing and her prayers had been answered. A woman like Marla would go a long way to protect her.

"I... I..." stuttered Pastor Mark.

"Ah, indeed," said Mr. Chirac with a touch of evil glee in his voice. "At last I remember you. You are an old friend, reverend. Yes, all the years of your youth spent rejecting your Savior and courting me and mine. Do you remember walking down that dark prison corridor all those years ago, fearing the Devil while he was instead secretly watching you? You perhaps glimpsed my shadow hovering in the corridors, methodically counting your sins like a cashier at a casino, or was it that I inhaled them like the delicate, yet cloying odors of the grave that no morturarian can ever seem to quite wash away after titivating a particularly loathsome cadaver. No? So, just so, yet you could feel my eyes upon you, could you not?

"Yes, I believe it is so. *Sacra bleu*, I have had a revelation—yes, at this very moment. The ghost hunter will yield to my requirements, if only because he lives in terror of the Abyss known as Hiram Abiff. I have, however, another matter of import to bring forth that desperately needs resolution.

"You and I must bargain for the life and wellbeing of your congregant."

"No," screamed Pastor Mark.

He did not stutter. He was not gasping for breath after screaming it. Seeing the blistering rage on his face, Hunter, for the first time, could see that the pastor might have done things in a rage that would require him to be locked away for the safety of those around him.

"*Mai oui,*" exclaimed Mr. Chirac. "You remember Sodom's Shackles? No? Are you as the young ghost hunter and his friends? Have you learned all you know about evil from the Internet? *Accorder une attention.* I have recently lost a valued indentured employee, whose service will be so sorely missed. He demonstrated poor judgment by inflaming my displeasure in an important matter. I should like you, or perhaps one of your friends, to join my employment as his replacement. It is, of course, a lifetime *devoir.* You, or your chosen surrogate, will present yourself to me three nights hence for my inspection."

From behind Pastor Mark, Kenneth's voice rang out.

"And why in the hell would he do that?"

Mr. Chirac inclined his head in Kenneth's direction.

"Because," he said in a soft growl, "if he refuses, I will not remove Sodom's Shackles from Rebecca's beautiful freckled wrists. Now I bid you good evening, and look for our meeting tomorrow night at midnight. My associate will return your lovely friend to you if only you stay where you are."

He turned and began walking toward the back balcony exit.

"Where's Rebecca, you bastard?" shouted Kenneth.

As Marla lowered her rifle for the second time that evening, Mr. Chirac disappeared into the darkness.

****

It was the little boy's teeth, small, and each filed to a point, that most unnerved Marla. She wanted to lift him up by the throat and shake him until he answered their questions. His voice was deep and gravelly, like that of a chain smoker, and that was all the more infuriating and yet terrifying. And Rebecca, poor Rebecca.

"So, if you hurt me," said the cretin, "she dies. Mr. Chirac don't like nobody messin' with his staff."

"What's your name?" asked Hunter.

"Ain't got none."

"What's he call you so we'll know what to call you?"

Hunter's voice was cold and measured. Marla had not seen this side of him before. He appeared to be on the verge of a psychotic break.

"Spike," shrugged the boy. "On account of my hair. You get it?"

The boy's hair was gelled into spikes. His eyes were yellowed, with red rings that circled round them like diseased eyeglasses.

"Tell me again about Rebecca," said Hunter.

"I don't like repeatin' myself," said the creature.

"Let me stomp his face in til he talks," said Kenneth.

He'd been pacing back and forth across the stage in a fury since the demon boy showed up with Rebecca.

Spike raised his right index finger and waved it back and forth in admonishment. Marla grabbed Kenneth's wrist just in time to prevent him from breaking it off. Rebecca was seated in the Junior Warden's chair across from them, staring straight ahead, a tear dripping down her cheek. Pastor Mark knelt down beside the chair; he was too mortified to say anything. He had guilty written across his face as surely as if he'd been convicted by a jury.

"Say it again," Hunter told the boy.

With a quick intake of breath, Spike huffed his cheeks, blew out the air and aimed eyes at Hunter.

"It's like this," he said. "Them bracelets can't come off until he says so or she'll die. He's got some kind of… a… thing he unlocks them with. I never seen it. Anyways, it's that or nothing. That rod that goes through her wrists makes her part of it, you know what I mean? She can't talk and she can't see nothing, but she can hear. She's easy, though, to take places. They don't stop her from walking none. Hurts like hell, I think. When his guy put that rod through her wrists to lock it together, they can't scream, but before their eyes go white like that, you can tell it's bad. This one guy, we tried tapping on his wrist to see if he could tap back an answer. We'd tap one, then two, then three. He never tapped back."

"What happened to him?" asked Hunter.

"His partner didn't take care of business, like Mr. Chirac's contract said to, so he died. You can only have them on for so long before you kick over. Then Ricci got the partner and put them on him and did the same thing. These things ain't good. You should do what he wants, so she don't die."

From across the room, Pastor Mark sobbed. Kenneth and Marla looked away from him.

Hunter asked, "Ricci put these on?"

"No," said the boy. "These he put on himself. He made Ricci hold her still, though."

"Will you get in trouble for answering these questions?"

The boy laughed a big man's laugh.

"Nah. He told me to answer them. He said it would make it worse for you. Seeing as how it's your fault and all for taking his ghost box."

"What is he?" asked Hunter.

"Now that," said the boy, "ain't worth dying for."

And with that, he turned on his heel and left them.

Out of sheer frustration, Marla pointed her rifle at him and tracked him with her scope until he was gone.

"That ain't no little boy," said Kenneth through clenched teeth.

"No," said Hunter, "It sure as hell isn't."

"Would a bullet in the back of the skull hurt him?" asked Marla.

"I've got no damned idea," said Hunter.

He turned to look at Rebecca and felt his heart go cold. She sat straight upright in the chair. Pastor Mark had pushed back her hair to wipe away her tears. Her hands were in her lap, separated one from the other with a red brass rod an eighth of an inch thick and a foot long. The ends were forced through her wrists and bolted on the outside by handcuffs made of the same red brass material, and they were three times the thickness of normal restraining cuffs with shiny black gears and symbols scratched into them like magical calligraphy. Around the point in her wrists where the rod punctured through her skin, dried blood had caked in thick, dark rings.

"I'm going to kill him," said Hunter. "If you can hear me, Rebecca, you'd better damn well know we're going to take him down. I have no idea how, but they've messed with you for the last time. First, we get you free, then we kill him. Right?"

He was looking at the others expectantly. "Right?" he asked again, this time louder.

"Damned straight, brother," said Kenneth.

Marla nodded. "I'm going to cut his head off," she said, looking straight at Hunter.

But it was Pastor Mark who said, "She's going to live, and he's going to die wearing these damned shackles because I'm going to put them on him."

"Amen, brother," said Kenneth.

Pastor Mark helped Rebecca to her feet.

"I know you can't speak with these things fastened to you, and you must be scared, but we're never going to leave you until this is done and you're safe."

With Sodom's Shackles fastened through her wrists, Rebecca could not even nod.

67

Somewhere past the sound of the demon's insistent whisperings, Rebecca could hear the sound of her friends. But her mind could not pull together what they were saying because the demon would not be silenced. It laughed in her ears. It seemed to pull her hair. She felt it try to rip away at her thoughts. Blinded to the outside world with a demon her only companion in agony, she felt terror such as she had never known. Why was the demon tormenting her? For pleasure or purpose? No, it was because of its nature. It was its evil heart, she finally decided, that drove the monster to these ends. It would never stop until her spirit was broken. If it would only quit long enough for her to get her thoughts together. But the demon knew she could not be allowed that luxury.

She was tired, oh so tired. But what would happen if she fell asleep?

Die. She would surely die.

No, no, no, said the demon's voice in her head. When the shackles are removed, you will kill everyone you see.

****

Marla followed Hunter down the hallway to the room where Moser was bound and kept. When Hunter entered the room, she kept a discreet distance. She liked the old man, but if he went alien on Hunter, she was going to shoot him until he was permanently down. After a long, long night, her pistol felt heavy in her hand, but after what she had lived through over the last week, she was damn well not putting it back in her holster.

"Marla," said Moser.

He sat up tall on a straight-back chair near the window. His eyes were normal; everything about Enid Moser seemed normal. What had Hunter had told her—once infected there was no going back?

"Old man," said Hunter, "it's good to see you looking better."

His affection for the old man, thought Marla, was genuine. They seemed unlikely friends, but surviving tough situations had a way of bonding together people from different worlds.

"Some," acknowledged Moser. "But you know, I ain't ever going to get any better. You're going to have to put me down, Hunter, soon enough. We just don't know exactly when."

"Don't say that," said Hunter. "Don't ever say that again. We can figure this out."

Marla knew that tone. Marla knew those words. She'd heard them enough in the field over the years. It translated to "I hate this, but there's not a fucking thing we can do about it." Moser seemed to interpret Hunter's words the same way.

"Look, Hunter," said Moser, "it ain't your fault and there ain't a thing in the world we can do about it."

The pain that those words caused Hunter was hard for her to take. Hunter wasn't like her, he wasn't like Rebecca and he wasn't like Kenneth or his cousin Moser. He clearly wasn't a gunslinger, and he seemed sometimes to be reluctant to stand up for himself and his ideas. But he was smart. She had to give him that. It was just that no amount of smarts could have prepared them for Mr. Chirac's demands. And no amount of smarts could have prepared them for Mr. Chirac's device—Sodom's Shackles. Even after the things she had witnessed in Borgo, the sight of the rod pushed through Rebecca's wrists was almost more than she could take. The woman who had saved her now needed their help in the worst way, yet none of them knew what to do.

Before being sent by President Usman to the town of Borgo, all that Marla knew about the occult was from horror movies. And she had only seen a handful of those. Her favorite was an English horror film called Dog Soldiers. Werewolves versus the Army. After visiting Borgo, she could relate to that. Except where were the soldiers when the night horrors attacked?

"I hear you," said Moser. "I ain't real fond of the situation myself. But the truth is, I done lived too long, too close to Townsend Mountain, and now I got to pay the price, same as your poor uncle Bartok. There's only so much of that energy a man can be exposed to before he turns. I served your uncle the longest of the Mosers that watched Townsend Mountain, and now it's come to claim me. You need to be ready to kill me, Hunter. You know that, don't you? I'd consider it an honor if you do the same for me as you done for your uncle. Besides, you're a better shot now—it won't take as many bullets."

Moser gave Marla a weak smile when he was done saying that, and, for that brief moment, his matter-of-fact effort at trying to put their fears at rest caused her to remember Jimmy stepping in front of her to save her life.

"That will not happen," said Hunter.

The edge in his voice caused Marla to turn and gape at him. He no longer looked confused. He no longer looked overwhelmed, trying to get a handle on things that were too complex or beyond rational thought. Now, Hunter looked straight-out angry.

"What are you talking about?" said Moser.

"I got a whole different idea."

"There ain't different ideas with the curse of Townsend Mountain."

"Yeah, well, I got one. That curse took my uncle Bartok, killed your brothers and now it's coming after you. Well, it will not claim you. Like I said, I've got a whole different idea."

He'd come to within three feet of where Moser sat strapped to the chair.

"Hunter," warned Marla, "stay back from that chair. If he's going to turn into something hideous with tentacles sprouting all out from him, you need to keep your distance."

"Stay out of this, Marla," said Hunter.

"Pay attention to what she says, young man," snapped Moser. "I know you're angry, and I ain't so happy about this myself, but use your head. Get back."

But Hunter didn't get back. Marla didn't like where this was going.

"You listen to my idea, Moser," said Hunter. "Because it's a good one. And I'm willing to bet your life on the fact that it will work."

"Exactly what the hell are you talking about?" asked Moser.

"I'm talking about the Sign of Hiram."

"What is that?" asked Marla. "Is that the implant thing you were talking about that they used at the clinic?"

"Bingo," said Hunter. "It restored burn victims and amputees. I'm betting that it can handle an alien DNA transformation."

"No," said Moser in a quiet voice that didn't leave any room for discussion.

"If you think I'm going to let you turn into a monster like Bartok and be forced to put you down, you've got another think coming, old man. And what is the big deal? It's an electronic chip in your forehead. Would you bitch like this if the doctors wanted to put a pacemaker in you? Or how about an insulin pump?"

"It's more than that and you know it," said Moser.

"No, I don't."

"You do. It's the sign of the devil."

Hunter slapped his forehead with his open palm.

"You're as bad as Rebecca. Hiram Abiff is a monster. He's not the devil. I'm not arguing against your religious beliefs or hers. That old man might practice magic, but he's not magic."

Marla spun him around by the shoulder and got right up in his face.

"Hunter, you may be really smart, but right now, you're being really stupid. You saw him for a few minutes. You saw a gigantic snake come out of Brot's mouth. You saw Hiram's head get big and then get small like a balloon fighting with itself. But I've seen one hell of a lot worse from him, and let me tell you, Moser's right. That old man is the devil."

"You're as superstitious as the rest of them."

"I don't care what you call it," said Marla. "That old man is truly evil. And he has powers you've never dreamed of. I don't think we've seen half of what he can do. But what I told you before is absolutely true. He made it so that nuclear weapons didn't work in Borgo. They shot him with rocket launchers. They poisoned him. They sprayed him with holy water. According to Traverse, when I first got there, they just finished using napalm on him. If you don't think that old man is anything other than a psychotic sorcerer, you're fucking nuts and we should untie Moser and tie you to that chair, because if you can't see the truth when it's right in front of your eyes, you're no good to any of us. In fact, if you can't recognize what our enemy really is, then you are too dangerous to be left running around free."

Another woman would be out of breath after saying all of that, but not Marla. Marla was so mad she could keep yelling at Hunter for as long as he could stand up on his own two feet.

"Marla," said Hunter patiently—or at least he hoped he sounded patient—, "you're missing the point. I'm not talking about the old man. Not really. I'm talking about the implant. The Sign of Hiram. That is a technology, not the Sign of the Beast of the Apocalypse. I'm not talking about the Book of Revelations. That's the mistake Pastor Mark and Rebecca are making. And I think they're playing right into Hiram's hands. He talks about rebuilding the third Temple of Jerusalem. I think when he does that, he's just making up his own street creds. I think he's playing off the Biblical story because if the other Freemasons accept him as the builder of the first two temples, then, to them, he has the force of God behind him. Don't you see that?"

"No," said Marla and Moser at the same time.

Hunter threw his hands up in the air and said, "That's because you're not listening. Haven't you ever seen the movie Army of Darkness? You know, where there is the scene with Bruce Campbell holding up the shotgun in front of people in a medieval village and telling them as he waves it in the air, 'This is my boomstick.' And they believe him. Even though they don't even know what a boomstick is. Except that it's a metal pipe that makes a big noise. Don't you see? Technology is technology. Technology is not magic. It may look like magic, but it's not. And I don't believe that the Sign of Hiram is in any way magic. I believe it is technology. And that being the case, even though it's invented by an evil son of a bitch, it's just a piece of electronic circuitry."

Marla and Moser seemed to think about that. To Marla, it made sense. To Moser, it sounded like bullshit.

"What about what Rebecca said about its design having the number of the Beast in it? How about that? I ain't having nothing to do with the Sign of the Beast."

"It's the same thing," said Hunter, "as Hiram using handpicked Biblical tales concerning the Jerusalem Temple as a cover to make him seem more legitimate."

"I don't get it," said Marla.

"Sure you do," said Hunter. "You and Moser just don't like it. But think about it—this man is supposed to be three thousand years old. He's had a lot of time to plan. Brother Mihaloff told me that for a lot of Hiram's existence, he had to keep moving so that no one would notice the fact that while everyone else died off, he still lived. So, eventually, he comes up with this plan."

"Go on," said Moser.

Marla saw Hunter's face light up. His old friend wasn't completely dismissing what he had to say.

"Okay," said Hunter. "Why is it that both the Knights Templar and the Freemasons were protecting Hiram? Was it because he was a really nice guy? I don't think so. In fact, I think Hiram Abiff did everything he could to conceal anything and everything about him, except those things that contributed to the idea that he was the lead architect for the Jewish temples. To the Knights Templar and the Freemasons, he could claim that God had kept him alive for this one great purpose—to rebuild the Jewish temples again and again whenever they were destroyed to glorify God's name. Who would be more likely to support that insane narrative than the Knights Templar? Or the Freemasons. Both built their legacies on the Old and New Testaments combined.

"So, moving forward, the first two temples were destroyed by the time that Christianity was getting up and rolling. Jesus even makes the prediction that the second Temple, which was around when he was teaching, would be left without one stone standing on another soon. So, two temples down, and, according to the Book of Revelations, there's one left to come. And God has made provision for this final Temple to be rebuilt by keeping His alleged servant Hiram Abiff around to finish the final job. Are you with me so far on this?

"But, apparently, the big Abiff screws up. For some reason, he appears to Harry Truman after President Truman has nuked the Japanese. The president's bodyguards go nuts, and Hiram murders them. Suddenly, the great Hiram has to go into hiding."

Despite themselves, both Marla and Moser were drawn into what Hunter was saying. It made sense. Whatever kind of horrible monsters Hiram Abiff and his witch Eva Morgan were, they were not the Beast of the Apocalypse and the Scarlet Whore of Babylon. They were just using the biblical stories to make believers of the people they hoped to dominate.

"So why are they doing all this?" asked Moser. "So, these two—this Hiram Abiff and Eva Morgan— are hoping to take over the world. I get that part. And they're figuring that people want to see the fulfillment of biblical stories, so they are more likely to believe and fall under the spell of Hiram and his girlfriend. Okay. But what's this all about? Just taking over the world? Don't you think there should be something more for all this deceit?"

"Like what?" asked Hunter.

"Wait," said Marla. "I think he means that there might be a reason they're doing this other than being the new world rulers. You think they might have a more complicated endgame. Is that it? Because I asked Jimmy if Hiram Abiff was brought back from the dead to do all this, then who did it?"

"Did what?" asked a confused Hunter.

"Who brought him back from the dead in the first place? If you're saying that it wasn't God who brought him back, then who?"

"The devil," said Moser.

"That's just the kind of bullshit propaganda that Hiram is using to run this game. Who says that he had to be brought back from the dead in the first place?"

"Here's something that really bothered me in Borgo," said Marla. "Traverse said they blew Hiram apart by shooting him until they ran out of bullets. And then he just kind of reassembled. In all the movies, and all the stories I've ever seen, read or heard about, when the resurrected dead are blown to pieces, they don't reassemble. Do you see what I'm saying, Hunter? How does he do that? What I'm asking really is how these little pieces of his body know to reassemble. Do all of his little body parts have brains that say, 'Wow, we've been split up by all of these bullets? We need to get back together again. Start crawling.'"

The look on Hunter's face was one part confusion, one part derision, and one part thoughtful. In the end, the thoughtful part won out. He snapped his fingers so loudly, it sounded like a twenty-two pistol had gone off in the room.

"That's it," he said. "I've been trying to remember that point since I found out about Hiram Abiff. You're right, Marla. You're absolutely right."

He was so excited, she thought that he was going to kiss her. But then he looked at Moser and did three quick fist pumps into the air.

"She is so fucking right. I've been trying to remember what Bartok said about different magical spells. I mean, that old man taught me so much that sometimes it's hard to find the information in my brain. Wait. I've got it. It's a construct spell."

Hunter smiled like he'd won the lottery. Then his smile drooped.

"Egregoric spell. Almost. It's an Egregoric construct spell. That's exactly what it is."

Now totally energized, Hunter whirled the other way to face Moser.

"That's it, old man. Bartok taught me about it a long time ago."

"What in God's name is it?" asked Moser.

"It's... do either of you know what an Egregor is? No? All right, here's a short definition— it's a thought form. A thought form that's sometimes alive."

"No shit?" said Moser.

"No shit," said Hunter. "But it's more than just that. The true essence of an Egregor is to be found in its patterns. That was a prospective unique to Bartok. Modern day magicians, sorcerers, psychologists and philosophers compare them to corporations or memes. They just say that to sound like they know what they're talking about. Comparing them to corporations or memes is just plain self-satisfying narcissism. Bartok not only really knew what Egregors are, he had, according to his notes—"

"Could you get to the point, Hunter?" interrupted Marla. "Can you just tell us what we need to know?"

"Sorry. Here's the deal." Hunter started pacing the room again as he talked. His nervous energy felt like a static charge in the room. "All right. Forget that question. The example still holds true. If you hold a magnet underneath the paper with iron filings on it, all the iron filings will line up according to where the lines of force are."

Hunter let that sink in their brains for a minute or two before proceeding; when it seemed like they'd gotten it, he continued talking.

"The energetic pattern of the magnet is responsible for patternizing the filings. In other words, the magnetic field is the construct around which the magnetic filings line up into patterns. It is effectively the egregor of the magnet. So, if Hiram Abiff's material substance keeps reforming, then there must be an Egregoric construct around which that substance realigns. Whether we say that Egregoric construct is a physical or energetic interaction as in the case of the magnet and its lines of force, or we claim it is a magical spell that keeps realigning the material substance of Hiram Abiff's body, the result is the same—if he's blown apart, if he's shot, if he's squashed and you take the big rock off of him, then he is going to re-form according to the energetic patterns of the Egregor. That's how he does it. That's why he's impervious to being killed. And he's not human, so he can't die the way we do. We have to disrupt his Egregoric patterns. There has to be a way to do that. That's how we kill him."

"I don't like this thing about the implant. It ain't right to put something in a person's head what was made by that monster."

"Would you rather become a monster?" asked Hunter.

"Shit," said Moser.

"Yeah," said Hunter.

Now Marla thought Hunter was in his own element. He had found and inserted another piece into the puzzle. All of those years of government money, as Traverse would have said, and no one had come up with the answers Hunter had. No, he wasn't so stupid after all.

"Hunter, but what the hell is Hiram Abiff, and where did he come from?"

Before he could give her an answer, she heard Ashley's scream echo like a bullet ricocheting its way down the hallway.

68

In his anger, Jubelum grasped the stone hammer's handle harder still, and then in a rage so intense red spots swirled momentarily before his eyes like scarlet stars birthing a swarm of angry comets, he swung the mallet upward and then down with crushing force against Hiram's skull. The bones made a wet snap and the Grandmaster of the temple's stone masons dropped to the ground. In the dim desert light, Jubelum could see the blood spreading like a dark stain beneath what was left of the master's head.

Jubela and Jubelo stepped out from the bushes and walked hesitantly toward him.

"What have you done?" said Jubela.

"What have we done?" said Jubelum.

"We have killed our Grandmaster," said Jubelo.

Somewhere far away in the twilight, where the desert lay down before the approaching night, a hyena howled.

"It was his due," said Jubela. "He would secretly defile the temple with that cursed offering to the Nephilim abominations."

The three had been spying on Grandmaster Abiff for months, because they suspected him of giving the Masonic word to foreigners. The Masonic word was how a Mason's wages were determined by the paymaster. One word for an Entered Apprentice, one for a Fellowcraft and the last and highest paying word was that known only by the

Master Masons. Only Grandmaster Hiram Abiff could give out that word, and it must be done by him in secret. Their discovery that the Grandmaster of all stonemasons was giving out the Master's word to foreigners, in violation of sacred law, had left them horrified. The three had gone looking for him, waylaid him by the side of a desert road and begun badgering and threatening him. They demanded that he acknowledge his guilt, but in his arrogance, he refused—even though they had seen his treasonous acts with their own eyes.

"We were in the right," agreed Jubelum, "but now we have no proof. Because of this, King Solomon himself will see us executed for having murdered his beloved Hiram."

"We must deliver his body at least to King Solomon," said Jubela, his voice quivering with fear. "It was an accident, we must tell him. A fall, yes, a fall. What fools would present to a king the body of the man they murdered? No, he will think us innocent."

"We must hide the body," said Jubelo. "It is impossible to deceive King Solomon. The Lord our God has gifted him with wisdom."

Jubela, Jubelo and Jubelum were brothers, often confused by others because of their looks and names. In conversation with others, Jubelum did most of the talking. It was less confusing that way. They had been granted apprenticeship in the stonemasons' lodge by an act of mercy years ago. A debt paid for a kindness showed by their father to another stonemason who had taken ill.

The construction of Solomon's temple was the greatest event of the time, and work for stonemasons was plenteous for those who knew the trade. Solomon's wealth was the stuff of legends, and he paid skilled craftsmen well. Jubela, Jubelo and Jubelum had worked their way up from Entered Apprentices of the trade to that of Fellowcrafts, or those stonemasons of medium skill. For that, they received medium wages. The best wages went to those few known as Master Masons. They would soon achieve that rank and the attendant wages. But then came the day when the three of them observed that there were foreigners—strange and exotic and with the strangest expressions. Faces that seemed to change ever so briefly when you looked away and then back at them quickly.

The three were loyal to their King Solomon and determined to learn the truth so they might inform the King. But they did not count on the arrogance of Hiram Abiff.

First, Jubela had confronted him, demanding the truth, and then shoved him when he became arrogant. Then Jubelo accosted him roughly. He had then laughed at them both. When Jubelum came upon him and demanded the same answers. Grandmaster Hiram had refused as before, but viciously dismissed them from the Stonemasons. They could no longer work at the craft, he sneered. Only those who submitted to Hiram Abiff could work as stonemasons.

But Jubelum carried his stone hammer in his apron.

Grandmaster Hiram Abiff, ruler of the lodge of stonemasons, would refuse no one anything ever again.

"We must hide the body," repeated Jubelo.

This they did by burying him west of Mount Moriah.

****

By the time an angry King Solomon and his men had found the body of Hiram Abiff, he had been in the grave for fifteen days.

The following evening, all three brothers had been captured by twelve stone masons. The King had ordered them to pursue and capture the three Fellowcrafts and learn the fate of Hiram Abiff. They found Jubela, Jubelo, and Jubelum near the grave where they had buried their master, terrified that they would be found out and afraid to leave the country since they had no permit to do so from King Solomon.

After the three confessed what they had done, they were then executed.

Jubela's throat was cut open, his tongue ripped from his mouth, and his body buried beneath the sands that bordered the sea. He had only accosted Grandmaster Hiram. Jubelo had done worse by cuffing the Grandmaster to hurt him enough to frighten him into confessing. They therefore cut open Jubelo's left breast while he still lived, took out his heart and other vital organs and scattered them on the rocks for the vultures to pick apart and devour. But the worst punishment was reserved for Jubelum, for he had murdered their Grandmaster Abiff, having struck him with the stone hammer.

****

It was midway between dusk and the hour of high night when King Solomon and his sixty guards returned. The twelve Fellowcrafts had dug away the dirt that covered the grave where Hiram lay buried and piled it to one side. They stood near the head of the grave, huddled by the small fire they had built to keep scavengers away from the decaying body. Each of the twelve men kept their head down, their eyes fixed on the dirt below their feet, waiting to be addressed by the king.

With a word from their commander, the guards dismounted and formed a large circular perimeter, spears pointed outward. The king dismounted next, and only after his feet touched the dry earth did the last member of his entourage do the same. He was a man wrapped in darkness, his face hidden in shadows immune from the sparking firelight. From the bag draped over one shoulder, he withdrew a black, pointed stick and held it down and to his side as he and the king approached the grave.

The king stopped two feet from the grave and stared down at it.

"Torch," he said.

A guard broke rank and brought a torch soaked in pitch and stuck it into the flames of the Fellowcrafts' fire. When it flared brightly, he turned, bowed, and extended it to the king. The monarch shook his head, and the guard stuck it into the earth near a corner of the grave. With a nod from his king, the guard returned to his post.

What the king saw at the bottom of the shallow grave flooded him with despair. The body had decayed at a preternatural rate. Putrefaction was well underway. Were it not for the soiled clothes, he would not have known it was a body. Without the skills of Hiram Abiff, he feared he could not accomplish the construction of the temple in his lifetime. He rent his robe and cried out. The Fellowcrafts cowered. The guards stiffened, but the black-cowled man beside him stood straight and still.

"Your servant sees, my lord, that the great Hiram has been dead many days."

The king closed his eyes to dismiss the sight.

"He no longer has the spark of life within his frame," hissed the cowled man. "Yet, with your permission…"

"We will not speak of this," said the king.

"My Lord," acknowledged the black-cowled figure.

"Never," said King Solomon.

"I require the Fellowcrafts," said the figure.

"All of them?"

"Just these twelve, my king."

After a curt nod, the King of all Israel turned and walked away with his head bent over in shame. He did not see the dark-cowled man's reptilian tongue shoot out and taste the odor coming from Hiram's grave. Satisfied, he turned and studied the twelve cowering Fellowcrafts.

The blood of ten men, he thought, should be enough to summon the demon known as the Nephilim darkness. The King will allow me to recreate Hiram from this dead body of his into a new form. A form of the Nephilim's making, yes. To finish, his task would be to create the first of the Nephilim's army of the dead.

69

"Can you see him?" asked the darkness.

Hiram could not speak, because the villagers had sewn his mouth shut. He writhed in agony, but the darkness that was always with him spoke to him. The smooth sibilance of its whispers was dark magic, and Hiram felt it wrapping him in a velvet cloth of susurrations.

It was midday, and the sun was a fiery blaze high over the lake. The tombs to his right were whitewashed bones, bleached glaring white by the relentless brilliance. It pained his eyes to stare through the rock opening, but he could not look away since he was walled in, chained and shackled to the cave wall. The villagers had left an opening at eye level, so they could look in and make sure he had not escaped.

He tried to scream, but the gut thread wound in and out of his lips clamped tight his lips. Sweat slid down past the thick shelf of his bristling eyebrows and dripped into his eyes. He blinked. Blinked again. Through the opening, he could see that a small boat was approaching the shore.

The taste of old blood coated his tongue.

The younger men of the village wanted to burn him. The older men objected vigorously that if he were burned, his demonic spirits would only take over a new body. After much fearful discussion, they chained him to the rock wall and built a new wall to encase him. Then they had chained him and had finally sewn his lips together so that he could not convince an unwary traveler to set him free. Instead, the women came and spat on him through the opening. It dried on his face and the flies feasted on it. As they covered his tightly closed eyes and walked along his brows, it felt as though his skin was alive with disease. He stood in his own excrement, and delirium fevered his brain.

They had talked of blinding him, of digging his eyes out with their own fingers and filling the sockets with ants. They had screamed and beaten him with thickly knotted sticks while he was thrashing against the rough rock wall. Three times they had killed him by brutal stonings. Each time they killed him and he came back, they cursed and beat him again with a manic frenzy.

"He cannot die," said one.

"He is already dead," said the eldest. "He will always be dead."

"He is an empty shell that day by day is home to more and more evil spirits," said an obese man. "Not even a prophet can cure him."

And so, they walled him in and left him.

****

There was another like him who roamed the tombs. The people of the village had tried to subdue him as well, but he was too fast and was so wild they left him alone. Hiram hated him for being free. Through the slender opening in his wall, Hiram saw them catch him only twice. They chained him each time, but he broke the links while screaming because of the demons biting at his insides. He was an empty man, Hiram saw, possessed by the unholy as he himself was. By day and by night, the wild man would run howling among the tombs, cutting himself with sharp stones and pulling out bloody chunks of his hair. Because of this, not only did the villagers leave him alone, they stayed as far away from him as possible. Even wild dogs ran from him.

The men in the boat stepped out and into the water and dragged it onto the beach. They stood aside and showed deference to one of their number. There was something about that man. If Hiram could only have leaned forward, he could have seen the man more clearly, but he was tightly chained and could only slide up and down along the rough wall. The man's face was turned away toward his companions, who were also leaving the boat. Off to their right, he saw pigs suffering under the heat. Some lay on the ground. Others wandered drunkenly toward the water. They were fit companions for the wild man.

The demonic spirits invaded him suddenly in a blinding burst of scarlet light. He felt them rush in through his closed mouth, their vaporous stink nauseating him, and their squirming choked him. The men from the boat were forgotten. The laughing darkness was forgotten as the ravenous spirits cracked his head against the rough stone wall, then forced him to his knees while dragging his face against the rock and scraping his face into a bloody mess. He tried to scream as the pain blistered him and he felt the blood seeping from his shredded face. His mind quaked with the delirious screams of the tormented spirits. He twisted his body and felt the stitches tear through his lips. The pain was unbearable as they finally ripped through completely, and he felt the blood smear his lips. The darkness smothered his mouth and whispered again into his ear.

An unholy spirit bit into his intestines and Hiram's entire body began to spasm. He straightened up again and his teeth clamped down and bit off half his tongue. Against his will, his mouth opened and closed, and then he gulped back the bloody mess and swallowed it.

As quickly as they had come, the demonic presences left him, and a consuming rage raced through him like a fire through dry weeds. He would never be free from them. They were free to torment him because he had no soul of his own. He was centuries old, and had yet an eternity of torment and torture ahead of him.

When the palsy passed, and he could feel his body healing, he straightened himself and lifted his eyes to the narrow brick opening. He saw, to his surprise, that the wild man of the tombs was rushing toward the leader of the men from the boat. They were now close enough to where he stood chained that he could see them more clearly and hear some of what they said.

The wild man fell on his knees in front of the leader and wept.

"Come out of the man, you unclean spirit," said the leader. And then he asked the wild man, "What is your name?"

The wild man looked up at him with strange eyes and said, "My name is Legion; for we are many."

To Hiram's horror, the demons were speaking to the leader. They begged him not to send them far away, saying, "Send us into the swine, that we may enter into them."

Could this man, whom the spirits feared, help him? Could this be the healer with power over spirits that everyone had been talking about before he was chained to this forsaken prison? Could this be He who forgave? Could this prophet let him die and stay dead?

A shadow fell across the opening.

"Hello," said the voice of darkness.

"No, no, go away. Leave me alone. Let me see Him."

Blood bubbled from his split lips as he spoke. His words were thickly confused by his torn and bloody tongue. The shadow pulled back from the opening so that Hiram could see the awful face of he who had pulled him back from death to a soulless life so very long ago. The dark angel of all his pain.

"Watch," said the darkness.

Suddenly, Hiram saw the unclean spirits rush out of the wild man and enter the herd of swine. They bucked, scrambled unsteadily to their feet and then ran off in a fit of violent squealing to the nearby cliffs and plunged to their death in the foaming, merciless sea.

"You wish to know if the man who freed that man from a legion of demonic spirits can heal you, too, Hiram? He can, he most certainly can. He can heal you and forgive all that you have been and done. So," said the angry darkness, "instead, here you will stay until he is dead for all to see."

Before Hiram could respond, the dark angel hammered a stone into the opening with its giant hand, and Hiram Abiff was once again plunged into darkness. His screams echoed in the claustrophobic stone prison, bouncing from stone to stone and back at him, bombarding him with his own madness.

70

It was too late to kill him.

The flash of light, the voice like angry thunder crashing down from the heavens. The mystery of what it said confused Hiram. Was it about him? Was it a voice at all? He had seen the short bald headed man suddenly afflicted by jerky spasms, then lost sight of him as he tried to block first his eyes from the brilliant white light and then his ears from a thunder-crack voice that blasted the little group into silence. Hiram was actually within hailing distance when a coruscation lit up the world.

The ground was hard and rough as a sanding stone as first his hip and shoulder, then his face and hands collided with it. His eyes blinked yellow-white stars. The worst pain was as the ground raked his knuckles bloody raw and when a stone the size of an egg split his lip and broke two of his front teeth. Tenebrous reverberations tormented his ears. He felt the taste of blood in his mouth and the warmth of it spreading across the backs of his hands.

After rolling onto his back, he stared up at the darkening sky and closed his eyes. When the blood filled his mouth, he turned his head to one side and spit the hematic mess onto the parched ground. His vision was blurred and shaky as he got to his knees and stared at the small group of men he had been shadowing.

Only one of them mattered. The one who must be stopped. That one was dazed, rolling back and forth on the ground with his limbs shaking and a thin white froth clinging to his lips. The others backed away from their companion, fear twisting and contorting their features. In turn, they would stare wide-eyed at the man rolling on the ground before them as though he was possessed, then glance nervously upward as though expecting a new catastrophe to descend upon them.

"Who are you, Lord?" asked the prostrate man in an awestruck voice.

Hiram Abiff edged closer to hear the response. The land around them was empty. The others looked skyward again, waiting for an answer. They were so agitated they didn't hear him approach. The day was warm, and the air was still. He could feel blood well up from the abrasions on his knuckles and slide down his fingers. A vicious dust devil wind sprang up and spun like an out-of-balance top as the short bald man was helped to his feet by the others.

"What is it?" asked one of the men. "What is wrong?"

The balding man stood bowlegged, twisting in a circle and holding out his outstretched hands toward the sky as though trying to catch raindrops.

You are mine now, thought Hiram.

"Let me help," said Hiram, walking up to them and extending his bloody right hand to tap one of the men on the shoulder. "What is wrong with him?"

The two traveling companions turned to look at him, confused, as though they could not understand him. And they could not. Hiram's mouth was swelling and bruising, blood dripped over his lower lip as if he had just returned from battle.

Suddenly, the afflicted man stopped spinning, dropped his hands and stared straight at Hiram. "I am blind," he said as he pointed a finger at Hiram.

His eyes were covered with slick black scales and shown an iridescent black green. Hiram stepped back in shock.

"I am blind," repeated the afflicted man, "but still I can see evil."

"It cannot be so," said Hiram.

"May the Lord rebuke you," said the man.

There came another flash of white light and Hiram found himself lifted off the ground and flying backward through the air until he was impaled on the broken limb of a tall tree.

As the others walked away with the blind man, oblivious to what had just occurred, Hiram grasped the broken end of the branch protruding from his stomach and screamed. The pain of it vibrated throughout his body as blood and entrails dripped down to the hem of his robe and fell unseen to the earth below. Hiram was beyond seeing. All that his mind could process was the unendurable pain.

****

He hung there all night, sweating and squirming and begging those who passed by him for help in getting down. At first, they would avert their eyes and quicken their pace toward Damascus itself. Later, with dusk still a few hours away, they came back in straggling groups cloaked in frightened whisperings to stone him as he twisted and dodged to avoid the rocks they threw at him. The rough branch was tilted upward so there was no escape from it. He screamed and howled like an angry hyena as the stones crushed first his eye socket, then cracked and disfigured his skull. They kept their distance from the beginning of the barrage, calling him a devil and a blasphemy on the land. The barrage of rocks battered him beyond recognition. The pain drove him to madness. The blood would ooze from his wounds, then dry up and his skin felt like a dry, cracked riverbed. When his body reformed around the penetrating branch, the flow of coppery smelling fluid would begin again.

The mob which had gathered around him in a semicircle to stone him to death recoiled in horror. As his vision returned, he saw them rip their robes, and pull their hair.

"He is no man," said a man with wild brown hair. "He is a demon."

No, thought Hiram, I am a man with no soul. A man with no soul and infested with demons. Since being brought back from death, he was nothing but an empty shell where any demon could rush in and take command. But from the midst of his writhing agony, a thought took hold. The Nephilim darkness was right. He could one day take hold of the invading spirits and never let them go. He would take hold of them and subjugate them. He would become the Lord of Demons and inflict pain and suffering on those who stoned and ridiculed him.

With dusk drawing closer, they began to whisper to one another.

"He cannot die," said a stocky man. "He has no life to lose."

"Abomination; he is an abomination," said another.

"Fire purifies," said a hunched over one-eyed man.

Broken pieces of dried branches jutted out from the larger branch on which he was impaled. He could not slide past them. His hands were slick with blood. When he tried yet again to pull himself over, he spun to one side and hung upside down, screaming in agony as the rough weathered bark tore at his insides. Blood began to flow downward to cover his face and eyes and blinded him.

"Mercy," he cried. "Mercy in the name of all that is holy."

Just as the blood reached his lower eyelids, he saw the crowd approaching him with bundles of branches and pitch-soaked torches.

71

It was the first true silence he had known in over three thousand years. No cacophony of demon voices ripped through his being and deafened him to his own thoughts. Finally, by the exertion of his own true magical will, he had conquered the demons within him. They were subsumed into the substance of his own being. He was no longer a soulless man inhabited and tormented by demons. Now, he was truly the master of the demons. He sat again on the porch steps of the Borgo Masonic Temple.

With his mind freed from the incessant distractions of the demonic gibbering in years, he was free to cast back into the memories of his horrid life. One repellent memory after another paraded before him like marchers and celebrants in the rituals of the Red Death. Backward he went, century after century, millennium after millennium. Back through his meeting with President Truman, back to his brief dealings with the reprobate Alastair Crowley, to his terrible mistake in revealing his secrets to Robert Louis Stevenson, whom he thought was dying, backward to the rewriting of the Masonic constitutions, his last talk with Jacques de Molay, to the early days of Christendom when he had suffered so much. He had no soul, but now, with his victory over the demons that inhabited him, he had the blessed silence to relive his life with his memories.

He remembered being sealed into the tomb by the Nephilim

darkness so that he could not see the one called Jesus heal the other poor creature inhabited by legions of demons. He remembered crying tears of blood for his loss. Hiram Abiff could not die. He could only suffer and inflict suffering.

There was nothing of his own death that Hiram could remember. He had been the chief architect of the Jerusalem Temple. He was master of all crafts. Brilliant in his designs. Many said his ideas and architectural creations rivaled that of which the Divine could produce. Even King Solomon agreed the Divine had gifted him with unrivaled genius. Hiram Abiff was a man among men. Yet, he was not of royal blood. He had no kingdom of his own to rule. Oh, King Solomon had given him wealth and property, prestige and concubines, but he would not grant him Royal status. He was too valuable as an architect.

Perhaps he would have been content to live his life as the King ordained, but the King himself had married foreign women and, gradually, had listened to their whisperings about foreign gods. Yet, he would have been content with his lot in life had not one of Solomon's concubines introduced him to the last living sorcerer of the Nephilim. She had given sons to these offspring of the fallen sons of God. When they had been decimated by the Divine's anger, she had turned for mercy to King Solomon. This was, of course, only natural, that she would seek mercy from the greatest among men. Before this, she was the wife of the greatest of the Nephilim.

When the Nephilim had been destroyed, they went neither to heaven nor hell, but were sentenced by the Divine to the realm of demons for eternity. In her rage, this woman swore an oath to bring back her Nephilim husband to the world of mortals. He alone knew the names of each Nephilim. Without these names, none could return. The Divine had placed a great barrier between the worlds of the demonic Nephilim and the world of mortals. But the Nephilim's pet sorcerer had a plan.

Hiram could remember this now. Before, he could only remember fragments of all that had occurred to him. But finally, after three thousand years, he had mastered and quieted the demons within him by subsuming them to himself. The Nephilim's plan was a magnificent architecture. It required a certain special location for the spell he would have his sorcerer perform. There was only one place on earth with the accumulated power necessary to act as a base for this spell. That location was the location of the Jewish Temple to God. Sacred ground. The spell needed to be cast on sacred ground. The Nephilim's Sorcerer of Darkness could not enter the sacred realms of the Temple alone. Even King Solomon himself could not authorize such a thing. The Temple was nearing completion, but not yet complete.

But the Nephilim darkness knew that Hiram could sneak the sorcerer in, and so the Nephilim darkness had come to him and whispered to him. Making promises, extending offerings, praising him and telling him that his great creative brilliance was lost on King Solomon. Wisdom, said the Nephilim, is not bound to appreciation. Ofttimes, great wisdom breeds great arrogance. And in his great arrogance, King Solomon was not willing to bestow royalty on the very man responsible for building the temple to his God.

Hiram listened.

Piercing the veil between worlds would be more difficult than building one hundred such temples as he was erecting in Jerusalem. Mighty magic was necessary. More than that, intimated the Nephilim, the most powerful magical tool in the world would be required. It was a crystalline structure not of this earth. It came to this world from a place beyond the second heaven, carried to earth by boats of silver light. The Nephilim sorcerer had sought and found a piece of this crystalline structure, which was known as the Blazing Star.

A secret chamber must be constructed within the Temple before its completion. A tunnel must be dug leading to the chamber. All the workers who took part in this work must be killed. An altar must be constructed within the chamber. On an altar must be placed the Blazing Star. On the day of the temple's sacrificial dedication, the sorcerer priest of the Nephilim must be led to the underground tunnel to the secret chamber. There, he must perform the ritual to harness the Blazing Star's energy to pierce the veil between worlds so that the Nephilim could return to the land of the living.

But Hiram's secret work had been revealed by three fellow craft, who had captured and killed him. The enraged Nephilim would not, however, accept defeat. His sorcerer had gone to Hiram's grave in the desert and resurrected him using a powerful magical spell. Hiram was returned from the grave, but without his soul. He was an empty vessel, and almost at once, the battle for his will began. Every roaming demonic spirit claimed his body as their home. He was forced to fight each new spirit to maintain control of his sanity, if indeed a man resurrected from the dead could ever claim rational thoughts. This battle, which began so soon after his return to the world, had continued every day of his existence.

The Nephilim tried again when the time seemed right after the destruction of the first Temple. They almost succeeded at the building of the second Jewish Temple, but instead, Hiram was captured by a horde of soldiers and chained beneath the ground in a deep cave. There he stayed in darkness, with neither food nor water, but his body required neither.

For a thousand years he stayed buried in those deep dark caves until the Knights Templar had discovered him. He provided them with gold beyond their wildest dreams, and they had provided him with freedom and protection.

There was much to do in Borgo before he left, but most of that would be executed by Eva Morgan. Hiram had already accomplished everything that the Nephilim darkness had required of him. Now was the time to think of only one thing—his return to the real world. This world, this Borgo, was just a magical construction of the Nephilim darkness. It was a pallid representation of the world that both he and the Nephilim longed to return to. But this thought caused Hiram to seethe inside. The Nephilim would return to a body. Hiram would remain a construct of Egregoric magic. Hiram would be the right hand of the Nephilim darkness when they both returned to the world. The right hand? After three thousand years of unabated suffering, he would return to be the Nephilim's right hand?

For three thousand years, the Nephilim darkness had exercised its great power to control Hiram. Despite being trapped in the insubstantial world of demons, it sometimes could gather the power to reach out and influence those it chose. It had done so to take advantage of Hiram. The Nephilim darkness cared for no one and nothing except for itself, and those Nephilim that remained trapped with it. It dreamed of setting them free and bringing them through to the mortal world so they could rule it once again, as they did so many thousands of years before. The price of realizing that grand dream had been Hiram's life.

Hiram had thought himself incapable of feeling emotion. He

thought that because he did not possess a soul, he could not possess feelings. Now he saw that was because he was constantly at war with demonic spirits trying to control him, he could not feel emotions. It was not that he was incapable— he could see that now. No, not incapable. Only, he had been overwhelmed by demonic assault. But he could feel. Oh yes, he could feel.

Emotions raced through his body, unhindered by demonic gibbering. Now he felt rage. Overpowering rage. Rage at the Nephilim. Rage at King Solomon. The concubine provided the necessary ingredients for the spell. Rage at that sorcerer. Rage at the Knights Templar. Rage at the Masons. Rage at the entire world. Most of all, he felt rage at the Nephilim.

He stood up. Darkness descended on Borgo. There was much to do.

And as he sensed the Nephilim darkness approaching, Hiram had an idea. It was an idea it had been incapable of producing over the last three thousand years. Oh yes, he had a stunning amount of knowledge. Wonderfully arcane knowledge. He'd realized now that in consuming and subsuming the demons who had tormented him, he had created something that could purchase his freedom. Yes, he had learned something with which to purchase his freedom.

"Hiram…"

"Yes, my master."

"I see that you have achieved self-mastery. This is a glorious day, Hiram. You are now ready to rejoin the world. You have yourself under control and can accomplish my plan without error. You have achieved true self-discipline. I applaud you."

The Nephilim darkness hovered over a pair of streetlamps that had just flared to life. In the distance, Hiram heard or sensed the movement of soldiers. And then, he smelled the approach of Eva Morgan. For the first time, he breathed in her scent the way before his death he had breathed in the aroma of morning flowers. From the corner of his eye, he saw her approach. She wore a midnight blue high collared cape that shimmered in the gaslight. Her rich, thick hair gathered around her neck like an elegant sable scarf.

Hiram turned again to look at his master.

"It is time," said the Nephilim.

"Long past time," said Hiram as he took one last glance at Eva Morgan.

Then, he opened his mouth and consumed the Nephilim darkness in one terrible inhalation. The Nephilim darkness struggled inside him. It fought and clawed and cursed. But Hiram Abiff had been consuming demons for a very, very long time.

When it was through, Eva Morgan approached and laid a hand on the back of Hiram's neck.

"You and I, my master, have worlds to conquer."

"We do indeed," he said. "Kneel before me. If you bite me, I will eat you for dessert."

Eva Morgan looked up at Hiram and smiled.

72

As Traverse Nations and Eva Morgan set about unlocking the cages beneath the state of the art Borgo science and military complex, Monsieur Emile Chirac gazed in horror at the mystery his occult scrying produced. His brother, his family and companion through eons of glory and then torment, was gone. Destroyed in a single instant. With a scream of white-hot rage, he brought both fists down on his etched glass scrying table and cursed. Far below the elegant Chirac residence on Blood Road, Ricci winced, then shook his head at Lily in her cage. "That ain't good for somebody," he said to the sleek panther.

Perched on a precarious ledge at the highest point of the Borgo Masonic Temple, Hiram Abiff glared down at the soon to be destroyed town where he had been imprisoned for seventy years. Molten. He would soon reduce it to molten slag. For the moment, though, he satiated his anger by listening to the screams now coming from the streets and houses as the reanimated dead searched for food.

Far away, in the White House, President Usman began to sweat profusely for a reason he couldn't identify. He worried if the red phone with no connecting wire was about to ring.

At the Detroit Masonic Temple, until late in the night, The Temple Guardians attended to the final logistics of what they had headlined "The Grand Masonic Event." Masonic dignitaries from around the world ate and dined on the finest food the Detroit Masonic Temple could offer while waiting for the grand unveiling that was to make Masonic history. Perhaps, as one suggested, hopefully, masculinity would once again be in fashion.

In Hunter's mansion, Rebecca sat still and straight in her chair, her eyes a milky white, her hair greasy and brushed back by Pastor Mark. Sodom's Shackles kept her in a submissive coma. Kenneth and Ashley watched her for any sign of awakening. "Mr. Ricci ain't going to like it," said Kenneth. "He asked us to watch over her."

"Then he should have done something about it," she snapped.

"He did," said Kenneth. "He warned us first."

Pastor Mark kneeled on the floor next to Rebecca and prayed even harder even than he had on the blackest of nights during his prison years.

In a back of the mansion, Hunter, Marla and Moser looked up in shock at the sound of Ashley screaming Hunter's name.

Parting the suffocating fog that rolled and billowed across the mansion's driveway like an errant cloud bank, the creamy white 1939 Packard touring limousine came to an abrupt halt before the front door as its headlights were extinguished. Its side lanterns glowed a soft, lambent yellow.

In just two days, Hiram Abiff and his witch would return to the mortal world, with the demons of hell screaming behind them in tow.

73

"Stay here," said Hunter. "Watch over Moser."

Before she could object, he was out the door and running down the hall.

"So, you got a boyfriend?" asked Moser as Hunter receded down the hallway.

"What did you say?" asked a stunned Marla.

She gave him a look that communicated that no matter how horrible it was that he was turning into an alien monster, she could make his life much worse before he died.

"Not for me, missy. I got other things on my mind. I'm just a little worried about my friend after I'm gone is all. Didn't mean to bother you none."

"Good," she said, and, while still keeping an eye on him, she moved quietly over to the door to look around the corner.

"His girlfriend just dumped him and hooked up with somebody else."

"Oh, well, from what Ashley heard on the radio, his girlfriend is dead—both him and her new boyfriend."

"Well, shit," said Moser.

****

"What is it?" gasped Hunter as he entered the living room where Rebecca and the others sat waiting for him.

"Out there," said Ashley. "A car just pulled up."

"A car?"

"Take a look."

She pointed toward the living room curtains, which were closed, but with a six-inch gap. Hunter wanted them closed after the witch attack, but Rebecca wouldn't tolerate it. She wanted them open at least enough to see out, so she could be forewarned when something came at them. But, for the moment, she sat motionless in the chair, the brass and glass engraved Shackles of Sodom restraining her. Drops of fresh blood appeared around the edges of where the red brass rod had punctured both wrists. Her eyes, milky white, still stared straight ahead, seeing nothing. Hunter quickly turned away to walk over to the gap in the curtain. He couldn't stand seeing Rebecca the way she was. It hurt and infuriated him in a way he did not tolerate well at all.

It took a moment for his eyes to adjust to the sight of the old white limousine idling in the circular driveway before the front door. It was like something out of a movie. It reflected the security lights, as if someone had just finished waxing and buffing it just before he'd stepped to the window.

Hunter was born and raised in Detroit. He knew a 1939 Packard Super Eight seven passenger touring limousine when he saw one. It was a car any red-blooded young man from the Motor City would never forget. As he stared out at it, the driver's window rolled down a few inches and a white flag poked out.

"What the hell is that?" asked Hunter.

Kenneth pulled the drapes apart a little further, stared for a moment, and then said, "I think it's a flag of truce."

"Well, that's a new one," said Hunter.

"Yeah, well, a better question is, who's inside?"

True. Who the hell was inside?

"Think it's safe?" said Hunter.

"No, but it might be necessary," answered Kenneth.

Hunter thought he knew who was inside, but this was the last thing he'd expected.

"Anybody want to go with me?" asked Hunter.

He turned and looked around the room at the others.

"I will not leave Rebecca's side," said Pastor Mark.

The minister looked stricken.

"I'll go," said Ashley.

"Not," said Kenneth.

"I will."

"You can both come," said Hunter. "The more people with me, the safer I'll feel."

"No," said Kenneth, and he turned to face Ashley with his chin square-ahead. "I ain't losing you."

"I'll go," said Ashley. "If it's who I think it is out there, he'll only talk to one of us at a time. And it's my ghost box he wants, so I'm the one who will talk to him."

This is a little awkward, thought Hunter.

"Ashley, that is pig farmer crazy," said Kenneth. "That man is dangerous and—"

"And I've faced him before, Kenneth Hillis. I know you want to protect me, and I appreciate that, but back off. I'm not afraid of him."

"Granny's dead and gone," said Kenneth. "You sure you can do this without her?"

The big man clearly did not want Ashley to leave the house unprotected and go face to face with Mr. Chirac.

"I am," she said.

"Woman, why can't—"

"Kenneth," Ashley said, "I'm done talking about this. But if you don't mind, I'd like you to poke that big sniper rifle that belongs to Miss Mihaloff out the window at the car soon as I leave the house. If something happens to me, you blow that car and him right to pieces."

She smiled a quick, bright smile, kissed him, then headed toward the door, her white hair floating behind her.

"I can't get used to her hair," said Hunter as he watched her go.

"There's a lot more than that about her to get used to," said Kenneth. "Trust me on that one, brother. You keep an eye on her while I go get that rifle from the kitchen table, will you?"

"You got it."

Hunter envied Kenneth more than a little. They'd met dealing with the screaming haint that Ashley's husband had awakened by removing Granny's madstone from its rib cage. Granny had told Kenneth before she disappeared into the Aether that he should look after Ashley. But Kenneth hadn't needed a lot of prodding on that front. Ashley Hillis, with her full head of hair turned white by her encounter with the haint, was still an intelligent and attractive woman. Before he could complete that thought, Kenneth was disappearing down the hallway with Rebecca's sniper rifle slung over one shoulder. Hunter knew he would be in the reading room next door with the barrel of the rifle sticking out the partially cracked window in a matter of seconds. When it came to Ashley Hillis, Kenneth didn't take any chances.

When one of the passenger doors of the limousine opened and no light came on inside, Hunter felt his heart sink when Ashley stepped into the vehicle and the door closed behind her, he took his forty-five out of his shoulder holster and checked to make sure that he had a full six rounds in the cylinder.

"What happened?" asked Pastor Mark.

"You keep an eye on Rebecca," said Hunter. "Kenneth and me will take care of Ashley. Sorry, I don't mean that the way it sounds. I just mean that, however much danger Ashley's in, Rebecca is in more."

****

"Why, Mrs. Hillis, what a pleasant surprise." said Mr. Chirac. "I was expecting Mr. Hunter."

"Why is the overhead dome light turned off?"

Mr. Chirac sat on one side of the car all the way toward the back. Ashley sat closest to the driver's side, but with her back toward him. There was, as she could see by the outside light that filtered through the openings in the velvet curtains, a wonderfully intricate oblong table between them. The curved half-couch she sat on was so soft and molded, she suspected she could go to sleep in minutes just sitting here if she chose to.

"Perhaps you would enjoy a sip of wine as we converse?"

"No, thank you."

"I pray you will not object to me partaking of a glass?"

"No, not at all."

Just being near the man, she felt an odd mixture of irritability, anger, fear, and anxiety. She had not seen the driver when she entered the limousine. She hoped it was Ricci. He had saved her from the loathsome Mr. Chirac once before, and if he was the driver, she had at least a prayer. They now knew, however, that Ricci was not the only employee of Mr. Chirac. Spike, the demon boy, had shown them that. And then, there was the matter of the cannibalistic chef that Mr. Chirac also employed. Who knew how many other unfortunates were enslaved to him? She shuddered to think about it.

"Would you like a cigar?"

"No, could we just get on with it?"

"*Certainement*, mademoiselle."

Ashley stewed while Mr. Chirac went through the typical bottle opening, airing the wine, sniffing the wine, tasting the wine, and finally, after all that, actually taking a drink. Mr. Chirac, being French, had spoiled the entire culture and its rituals for Ashley. Before meeting Chirac, French culture was marvelous to behold. After meeting Mr. Chirac, she considered French culture was decadent beyond redemption. Finally, after his elaborate wine tasting ritual, Ashley asked, "Why exactly are you here?"

Mr. Chirac grimaced. America was, to him, the land of hot dogs made of who knew what, of carbonated beverages, whose acidity burned away one's sense of refined taste, of deodorants that smelled considerably worse than perspiration and, finally, the land of action before reflection.

"I am here," said Mr. Chirac smoothly, "to show good faith."

It was Ashley's turn to grimace.

"I think not," she said firmly. "I think you want something from us, or you wouldn't be here."

Instead of commenting, Mr. Chirac simply reached inside his jacket—which Ashley noticed for the first time was made of a dark burgundy velvet—and withdrew a red brass key the length of his palm.

"I bring proof of my sincerity."

Without warning, Ashley heard Granny Hillis's voice as she counted out in her mind the proper rules of engagement when dealing with a demon. First, accept no food. Second, accept no drink, and third, accept no gifts. "If you do that, girl, you just might make it through the night," she had said.

"I can't accept that," she said.

Mr. Chirac raised an inquiring eyebrow.

"And why not?"

"I think you know why not."

For the briefest of moments, Mr. Chirac seemed irritated, although she could not quite say how she knew. His forehead did not wrinkle. His eyes did not narrow. His lips did not tighten. Even in the confines of the spacious limousine, she felt a sense of tension charge the air. She felt a sense of danger. Granny Hillis had told her that Mr. Chirac was a dangerous man. She had suggested to Hunter that he might be a demon. Ashley could stop herself from shivering.

"So, just so."

"What," she asked him, "were you offering this key to me for?"

Mr. Chirac leaned slightly forward at the waist and studied her.

"I hope, Mrs. Hillis," he said, "that our relationship is not colored by our first meetings. Your husband had done me a great wrong, and I felt compelled to pursue certain redressments for which I now have nothing but regret."

The night was too dark outside the limousine and the security flood lamps were too bright for her to see whether Kenneth had the sniper rifle pointing out a window. But she knew that he would. She knew her man. Kenneth Hillis would shoot his way through the Great Wall of China if that was what it took to save her. And even with Rebecca trapped by those hideous steampunk-like handcuffs and Enid Moser transforming into an alien monster, she knew that Hunter, Marla, and Pastor Mark would come running to her with their guns blazing. They were getting to be, she thought, quite the team.

These thoughts were important to her, because Ashley was afraid of Mr. Chirac, and she was woman enough to admit it. Whether he was a man or a demon, he was indeed someone to fear. Despite being afraid of him, she really, really wanted to tell him to go back to hell. But she took a deep breath and got her feelings back under control.

"We don't have a relationship," she said. "So, if you don't mind answering my question, what is the key for?"

Mr. Chirac stared at her for over a minute before answering. She had the feeling he was mentally drawing an "x" between her eyes.

"It is the key to Sodom's Shackles," he said. "Beneath the left wrist shackles, you will find the place to insert it. A turn to the left will open the shackles. A turn to the right will surely kill her."

"And why would you give me this key?"

"As I intimated, I'm proffering this key to you as a gesture of good faith. Our common enemy has grown stronger, and I believe we will need the assistance of Rebecca."

"Our common enemy?"

Hiram Abiff was who he was talking about, but Rebecca wanted to make him say it. It was important. She didn't know why. But it was important.

"Mrs. Hillis, must we go on like this? With the change in circumstances, time is not fleeting, it is flown. Hiram Abiff has transmorphed. Do you comprehend my meaning?"

"No."

Mr. Chirac poured himself a half glass of wine.

"There is a story, Mrs. Hillis, of a man in India who saw one fine evening a wounded mongoose limp past his window. He went to the door and opened it to get a better look. There, to his surprise, in the doorway stood the tiger who had mauled the unfortunate animal. Now, do you comprehend my meaning?"

"No."

After a quick shake of his head, Mr. Chirac downed the entire glass of wine.

"Please, Mrs. Hillis, I implore you to be more discerning. I am explaining to you that Hiram of Abiff was once one thing, but now is quite another. He was once dangerous—a mongoose can be dangerous, my dear. But now, he has become a tiger. A starving, diseased tiger."

Ashley drummed her fingernails on the table.

"How is that possible?"

Chirac looked away from her, then down at his own precisely

trimmed fingernails. His eyes rose to her breasts and stayed there for an uncomfortable moment before he finally brought them up to look into hers.

"It is possible, Mrs. Hillis, because he has devoured his master. Go tell this to your Mr. Hunter, and he will know that of which I am speaking."

"So, he's like the Highlander?"

"I beg your pardon?"

Opening her hands, palms up, Ashley stared at him. Was it possible this man had never watched a movie? Especially a movie as great as the Highlander?

"You know, the movie. A Highlander. Starring Christopher Lambert."

"I'm afraid, Mrs. Hillis, that your knowledge of American culture far exceeds mine. Could you perhaps be more precise?"

"In the movie, and it is a great movie, not just a good movie, but a great movie, Christopher Lambert plays a Highlander named Connor MacLeod. He belongs to a clan of immortal warriors."

"How... fascinating," murmured Mr. Chirac.

"In the movie, whenever one of these warriors kills the other on the clans of immortal warriors, they absorb the power of the one they've killed. This goes on and on until the last immortal warrior has absorbed all the power. All the power, do you understand?"

"Quite."

"Okay, is that how it is with Hiram Abiff?"

Cocking his head to one side, Mr. Chirac used the tip of his index finger to brush each side of his finely manicured mustache. Ashley thought the gesture made him look very much like an evil Clark Gable.

"Do you know," said Mr. Chirac, "that I believe you are correct? More correct than you know. The Hiram Abiff creature was returned from the grave, resurrected—if that is the proper term for what occurred— without a soul. Because he had no soul to contend for his newly restructured physical body, any evil spirit that found him could occupy him. In fact, the number of demonic spirits that could occupy him at any one given moment was Legion. You understand the implications, do you not? This creature, this Hiram, was created by a... shall we say, a family member."

"Nephilim?"

Burning rage flashed in Mr. Chirac's eyes and then vanished. In the limousine's darkness, a blazing hatred flared and then disappeared as though someone had opened the door to a furnace to reveal the burning flames inside, and then closed it quickly. *What manner of creature is he?* thought Ashley.

"Forgive me, Mrs. Hillis, but for a moment, both your knowledge and your insight startled me. Yes, Hiram Abiff has committed an unthinkable act. He committed an unforgivable act. Yet, because he devoured a Nephilim, he is immeasurably more powerful than ever he was. Now, he is attended by the witch. You apprehend the danger, yes? Together, they are formidable foes."

"How powerful are they?" asked Ashley.

"There is, my dear, no way to measure such things."

"Can they be stopped?"

"I do not know, Mrs. Hillis. No being such as Hiram Abiff has ever existed. With his ability to absorb demonic spirits, with his ability to translate both their life force and power into his own personal energy, we may very well not be able to stop him.

"However, you must tell your Mr. Hunter that I have fulfilled my part of my obligation. His machinery is now working. I have altered the path of the electro-magical lines of force in the device in the Empty Chair, so that the chair in the newly re-created Romanesque room functions as he desired to. I have left his remote control and other equipment as and where it was. I will leave, too, this key to Sodom's Shackles on his workbench. He must decide whether or not to employ it. It is my strongest recommendation, Mrs. Hillis, that he does so. Rifles and pistols are well suited for earthly battles, but for magical or spiritual warfare, bigger guns are not worth having. Purer hearts are."

Deals with this devil, she thought, *never turned out well.*

"I'll pass on the message," she said.

"Please do," said Mr. Chirac. "Now, the hour grows late, and I have much to do, so that I must reluctantly bid you adieu."

The passenger door opened of its own accord. Ashley, after an initial hesitation, stepped out onto the lawn. She stared back at Mr. Chirac as the door, once again, acting of its own volition, swung closed. She looked toward the front seat, but could see no driver. She did, however, see the steering wheel turn and heard a soft, metallic sound as the gearshift engaged, and then stood back as the driverless car motored silently away.

PART FOUR

74

It was four o'clock in the morning when Hunter, Marla, and Pastor Mark pulled into the parking lot of the Detroit Masonic Temple. They'd decided that no one went anywhere without at least one other person with them. The rest of the crew was left guarding the house and Rebecca and Enid. Everything was empty in the parking lot, and the city was just coming to life. Hunter idled the truck's engine looking around for trouble, but the Detroit Masonic Temple was void of life. He had to defeat Hiram Abiff, or all civilization as he knew it would fall under Hiram's thumb. Hiram would go to war with mankind, with the Freemasons as his standard bearers. All five million of them—and that would just be the beginning of his army.

"I see nothing, do you?" said Pastor Mark.

"No, but I wouldn't expect to, would you?" said Hunter.

"I don't trust it," said Marla.

"Come on," said Hunter, "let's get this over with. If there's any danger, all we can do is try to see it coming before it's too late."

He got out of the car, huffed a little bit at the cold air and waited for the others to do the same. They joined him where he waited at his car door, and Hunter led the way. Up the stairs to the door they went, and they waited at the silent door while Hunter unlocked it and let them in. They entered the building and waited while Hunter closed it behind them. Then, they walked across the immense expanse of opening, stopping for a second before the picture of Eva Morgan that dominated the entire entranceway.

"How can someone so beautiful be so evil?" said Hunter.

"Yeah, well, I don't know. Let's get moving," said Marla.

They took the freight elevator to the fourteenth floor, no one saying a single word on the way up. When the doors opened, Hunter withdrew his Colt and led the way. Marla had a sweeper—a sawed-off shotgun—and two pistols of Glock manufacture. The good pastor carried a wrench, still unable to bring himself to carry a firearm.

Hunter hit the lights, and the auditorium came into clear focus. It was as they had left it. The rows of chairs, the empty aisles and the overarching ceiling with its Masonic emblem of the Blazing Star of Freemasonry, and the insignias of the Square and Compass, the Double-headed Eagle of the Scottish Rite and the Triple Tau of the York Rite. They looked beautiful in the soft lights that came from hidden sconces. Yet, when Hunter saw them now, they only engendered a sense of dread in him. In two days, Hiram Abiff would come through the empty chair and the world as he knew it would end.

"Let's get to it," he said.

His voice echoed throughout the amphitheater and sounded strange to him. As they walked down the stage, he was on high alert, but he felt nothing. When they got up on the stage, they found his toolbox where he had left it when they left in a rush to get Rebecca home.

"Do you think he really fixed it?" said Pastor Mark.

"Only one way to find out," said Hunter.

He squatted down next to the empty chair and, with a look over his shoulder to see that Marla was covering him, took the cover off. With his phone's flashlight app activated, he shone it into the opening. He thought it looked okay, but he couldn't tell. All that talk about bone demons eating through his osseous had him coy about fiddling with the mechanism.

"Well?" said Marla.

Hunter stood up in frustration.

"I just don't know. And, truth to tell, I'm afraid to mess with it because of the curse."

"I've got the key to Sodom's Shackles from your workbench. Let's clean up and get gone," said Pastor Mark. "This place gives me the heebie-jeebies."

Marla and Pastor Mark each took hold of one of the electric power stackers and Hunter took hold of his workbench on wheels and they pushed them onto the elevators and pressed the down button. The doors slowly closed. Hunter looked out at the expanse of the auditorium like it was an alien planet. Empty, deserted and barren of all hope—and with no warning at all, a rheumy-eyed monster leaped around the edges of the door and stuck its clawed hands in and reached for Hunter.

He leaped back out of the way to avoid the slashing attack. The doors were two-thirds of the way closed, and this prevented the goblin from reaching all the way in. The goblin thrashed, trying to grab them. Marla fired a single blast from her shotgun into the goblin's face and he flew back. Green goblin blood sprayed out from the hole in the goblin. The roar of the shotgun was huge in the confined space of the elevator and came without warning.

He was replaced by two more goblins scrambling to get in. Their snarls of rage were deafening, and Ian had to scramble back even further to stay out of their grasp. Pastor Mark struggled to get forward and swing his wrench, but Marla fired her shotgun again, and the bark numbed their hearing and blew another hole in one goblin. Hunter dropped his Colt, and the remaining goblin wouldn't let him get near it by swiping at him viciously every timed he went near it. Pastor Mark swung his wrench and crushed its head.

"Get him out of the door, it's blocking it from closing," shouted Hunter, as he stooped and retrieved his Colt.

"You're in my line of fire," shouted Marla.

"What?" shouted Hunter.

"God in Heaven, those things—" shouted Pastor Mark.

"Goblins," yelled Marla. "I owe them one for Jimmy."

As Pastor Mark bent down to shove the dead goblin that he had cracked its skull, one more goblin came at him. He looked up just in time to see Hunter blast three shots at it and watch as it staggered back.

"Come on," Hunter shouted. "Get that thing out of the way of the door closing."

But it was too late. The door sensed that something was blocking it from closing, and it opened.

"No," shouted Marla.

Pastor Mark finished dragging the hoary thing out of the opening, clearing the way for the door to close.

"Get down," shouted Hunter as he pulled pastor Mark inside.

"Marla's shot gun boomed once, twice more, and it knocked two goblins that would otherwise have leaped into the opening on their backside. Hunter frantically jammed his finger against the close button. The doors reversed course just as they finished opening all the way and began to close.

"Cover me," said Marla as she reloaded the double barrel and shouldered her way to the front of the car.

She stepped outside and saw the witch that was causing the goblins to portal in. She fired once, twice, then let the shotgun swing back on a rope tied around her and pulled out the two semi-automatic Glocks and fired away with them both. The witch held up her palms, and the bullets stopped in mid-air. She smiled and said something—Marla would wonder what it was, but she was too deaf to hear—and Hunter shouted something to Marla. She turned then and dove into the elevator just before it closed. The witch cursed the bullets, and they reversed course and would have killed Marla had not the elevator doors closed at just that instant. They ricocheted off as the elevator began its descent.

Hunter's ears were ringing.

"Sweet Jesus," he yelled. "I can't hear myself think. That was close."

The elevator continued its slow descent.

"What if they're waiting for us when we get off?" shouted Pastor Mark.

"I've got more where that came from," yelled Marla, as she loaded another round of double-ought buckshot.

But Hunter had another worry on his mind. It worried him that when the elevator came to a stop and the doors opened, that the witch would be waiting for them. A quick check of the elevator revealed they were on the seventh floor and then the sixth.

Marla seemed in tune with his thoughts.

"How do you want to play this? I volunteer to be point on this one," she yelled.

Hunter thought about it. They were now on the fourth floor.

"Okay," he shouted back. "You've got the most guns and you're the better shot. Marla?"

"What?"

"Be careful. You, too, pastor."

Then they were on the first floor. Slowly, the door opened to a lobby full of people.

"Marla, put your guns away, quick," said Hunter.

He shoved past her to give her time to cover, sliding his Colt in his waistband beneath his coat. The entire lobby was full of people looking at him. He did the only thing he could think of on the spur of the moment.

"Hello, Brothers," he said.

A rousing chorus of "Hello, Brother" went up from the assembled throng.

"Just making a few last-minute changes to the Unfinished Theater," he explained.

"Carry on, Brother," came the response.

There were fifteen or sixteen of them and coming up the aisle fast was Eva Morgan, the witch. She slowed and stopped when she saw the crowd.

"Could I get a hand, Brothers? The little lady is having a hard time with the power pack."

Marla glared at him and was just about to say she could handle it just fine and she wasn't his 'little lady' when she saw the witch.

"Certainly, my Brother. Come on boys, let's give the folks a hand. What's your name?" said one Mason, extending his hand for Hunter to shake. "My name is Randy Sawalski."

"Ian, Ian Hunter," he said, grasping the extended hand.

The witch looked furious at being outsmarted. Marla gave her the finger, while pastor Mark just stood there, his hands clasping and unclasping on the massive wrench that he was carrying.

"My name is Marla," she said.

Pastor Mark just grunted, his eyes fixed on the witch, until she just disappeared. One minute she was there, the next minute she was not. He looked startled for just a second and then settled into a grim stare. While Randy and his friends finished their introductions, Hunter and Marla noticed the witch was gone, too.

"Where do you got to put all this stuff?" asked Randy.

"I've got a truck right in the parking lot," said Hunter.

When they had got it all loaded in the truck, Hunter thanked Randy and his friends, and got into the truck. Hunter backed out of his space, swung the truck around, set the phone for directions home, and then drove like the devil himself was after them.

"Man, that was close," he said after a little while.

"Too close," said Marla.

They drove on in silence just a little way to catch their breaths.

"Those things, where did they come from?" said Pastor Mark.

"From Borgo, that's where. The same place you and Rebecca saved me from. She just ported them in," said Marla.

Hunter asked, "I get how the witch could somehow make a portal into the Masonic Lodge, but how did she get into an island like Grosse Ile? I mean, I thought running water was supposed to stop them."

This time, it was Pastor Mark, who came up with the answer.

"That's just it. She opened a portal that put her right smack in the middle of the island. She didn't have to deal with the running water," he said.

"So, she can show up anywhere with her goblins at anytime?" said Hunter.

"I guess so," said Pastor Mark.

"Except to those places where there is a ward stone activated?"

"Yes."

"If she can come through anytime and anyplace," said Marla, "How come Hiram Abiff can't?"

"I don't know," said Hunter.

"Because he is restrained by a greater force. Possibly because of some punishment, and he can only leave when—"

"Jimmy said that there was a darker force at work in Borgo. He called it the Nephilim darkness."

"That would make sense," said Pastor Mark. "Something to restrain him. I wonder why, though."

"I don't know," said Hunter, "but for Mr. Chirac to voluntarily return the key to Sodom's Shackles, that means serious trouble somewhere. Hiram Abiff absorbed the Nephilim if you remember, according to Chirac, so he must be powerful enough to cause Mr. Chirac to worry and need our help."

Hunter drove down West Jefferson where there was some construction going on, but it was minor. He was amazed at how grim this section of Detroit was. There were actually hookers working the streets at 6:oo a.m. The buildings were either boarded up, caged off or left in a dilapidated state with their raggedy shells of buildings. Liquor stores seemed to be the only survivors in this grim array of buildings. Next came the dreary fronts of buildings with painted over windows covered by sliding steel grates. And then they were in the town of Del Ray, where destruction was a way of life. They drove on through the rotten neighborhoods in silence.

Finally, Hunter spoke.

"I think she didn't follow us because she knows we'll come back."

<h1 style="text-align:center">75</h1>

Pastor Mark ran into the house.

"Did you get it?" asked Ashley.

"Yes," said he said triumphantly.

Hunter and Marla followed him. Kenneth was in the other room, talking quietly with Enid.

The pastor knelt down before Rebecca, bowed his head, and said a silent prayer. Hunter and Marla both kept their eyes on Rebecca. She was seated on a couch, with the first rays of the morning sun shining on her, a study in the torture she was undergoing with Sodom's Shackles. Her hair was in disarray, she was hunched over, racked with pain and her eyes were rolled back in her head, so that they could see only the blood-shot whites of them.

When Pastor Mark was finished with his prayer, he looked up and inserted the key to Sodom's Shackles, and turned it a single click to the left, and when he did, the rod inserted through Rebecca's wrists disappeared. Next, the handcuffs themselves sprung open. The assembled crowd of people held their breath.

Rebecca fell forward and Pastor Mark caught her. She whimpered as Pastor Mark comforted her.

At least we have her back, thought Hunter. That's something we didn't have before.

Hunter's cell phone rang. He took it out of his cargo pants pocket and checked the number. Brother Frank Mihaloff. He let it go to voicemail; he was too worn out to deal with him and his problems.

"Who was it?" whispered Marla.

"A pain in the ass," said Hunter, and left it at that.

Ashley Hillis went over to Rebecca, moved Pastor Mark aside, and hugged her.

"There, there," she said, "everything's going to be okay now."

After a few minutes, Rebecca straightened up and said, "Everything will be okay when I get my hands on that miserable man and choke him to death."

Hunter looked at Marla and said, "She's back."

Kenneth Hillis poked his head around the corner and said, "Everything okay in here?"

"Everything is fine now. We got Rebecca back," said Ashley.

"Good to have you back, Miss Rebecca," he said, and went back to talking with Enid.

"Do you have any water?" said Rebecca.

"Yes," said Hunter, "I'll get it."

Hunter came back with a glass of water and gave it to her. She drank it down in one gulp.

"You do not understand what it was like," she said afterward. "A demon... a demon was torturing me."

"A demon?" asked Hunter.

"Yes, a demon," snapped Rebecca. "It was always at me—always telling me tales of blood and destruction. That my friends didn't care for me. That they wouldn't come and get me. It was awful."

"Well, we came and got you, Rebecca," said Ashley.

"But I held strong," said Rebecca.

"I know you did, and that's all that counts, isn't it?" said Ashley.

"I'm going to kill that man," said Rebecca.

Hunter thought that forgiveness was right out the window. He would like to get his hands on Mr. Chirac, too. But first, they had to stop Hiram Abiff and his witch.

Marla said, "Nice to have you back, Rebecca."

"I need some sleep," said Rebecca. "I've got to rest."

"Come on," said Ashley, "I'll walk you to your room."

Pastor Mark stood up and let them pass.

"Praise the Lord," he said. "Rebecca's back."

"We'll see," said Marla when Rebecca was out of sight.

"Wait a minute—what do you mean by that?" asked Hunter.

"I wonder if that's the real Rebecca or only an approximation of her."

She looked down at Sodom's Shackles.

"This was too easy. It doesn't seem odd to you?"

"No, not particularly," said Hunter, "why?"

"That's insane," said Pastor Mark. "Isn't it?"

"Pastor, all I'm saying," said Marla, "is that we should watch her, really carefully, to see if Chirac has anything else in mind for her. We've just got to pay attention."

The two men fell into an uncomfortable silence at that.

"What, do you think I'm wrong about being cautious?" said Marla.

"No, sweet Jesus, this complicates things," said Pastor Mark.

"You aren't kidding," said Hunter. "Man, can't this ever get easier instead of harder?"

Marla shrugged but said nothing as if to make it known that yes, it sucked, but there was nothing they could do about it.

"So, how do you want to do this?" she said.

"Well, one of us ought to stay with her at all times," said Hunter.

"Let me guess, you vote for me?"

"I can't stay with her at all times, and somebody's got to spell Kenneth with Enid."

"Pastor Mark," said Marla, "how about this? You watch her during the day, and I'll watch her at night. What do you say to that?"

The pastor looked uncomfortable for a minute, but agreed.

"But pastor?"

"Yes."

"If she is under some kind of spell, don't hesitate to kill her."

"My God, I can't kill her."

"I think Marla means," said Hunter, "in an extreme case."

He gave a look at Marla to quell her response.

"I just couldn't."

"It may come to that pastor—you or her," persisted Marla.

Before Hunter could step in, Pastor Mark said, "Then I would rather it be me."

"Suit yourself, pastor, but remember that one of us may have to do it for you and clean up two bodies instead of one," said Marla, and turned toward the kitchen.

"Is she serious?" said Pastor Mark to Hunter.

"I'm afraid so. I'd like to say we could talk reason with her, or knock Rebecca out, but people under the influence of spells aren't very rational. I'm sorry."

"Do you think she's under the influence of a spell?"

"I don't know. I've never dealt with someone under the influence of magic. I guess we could... hypnotize her and find out if someone else was living in her head."

"No," said Pastor Mark, shaking his head. "Rebecca would never agree with that."

"Why not?" said Hunter.

Just then Marla returned from the kitchen, and Ashley came down the stairs to rejoin them.

"She's tired, so I left her to get some rest," said Ashley.

"Good," said Marla. "We can talk about her."

"What do you mean?" said Ashley.

"Marla thinks that Mr. Chirac may have had a poisoned pill in Sodom's Shackles. That's why he gave the key up so easily," said Hunter.

Ashley looked from Marla to Hunter.

"What in the world is a poisoned pill?" she asked.

"Like he may have had a spirit in Sodom's Shackles that transferred over to her consciousness, right, Marla?" said Hunter.

"I've seen a full grow man disgorge a spirit that then turned into that witch Eva Morgan, so don't tell me I'm paranoid. I know I'm paranoid."

"So, what do we do?" asked Ashley.

Pastor Mark sat down on the couch and Ashley sat down next to him. Marla settled into a wing-backed chair. Only Hunter remained standing, and he paced.

Why did this have to be so complicated? he wondered.

"I think I could hypnotize her and find out," Hunter volunteered.

"I said she wouldn't go for that," objected Pastor Mark.

"We don't have any choice," said Marla. "We've got to find out immediately. I vote yes. Ashely?"

Ashley considered the options for a minute, then decided.

"I vote yes," she said, "and so does Kenneth."

"I vote no," said Pastor Mark.

"Noted," said Marla. "Hunter?"

"I vote yes, as well. With a caveat."

"What's that?" said Marla.

"You can't force people to go under a hypnotic trance," said Hunter. "Do you understand?"

"Yes," said Ashley.

"What are our options?" asked Marla.

"We exclude her from this point on," he said. "We cut her off from what we're doing entirely."

"She won't like that," said Pastor Mark.

"I'm sorry, but that's the way it's got to be. We have to find out if she's possessed or under some nefarious influence, courtesy of Sodom's Shackles."

"You can stop arguing about it. The answer is yes," said Rebecca from the top of the stairs.

All eyes turned upwards towards her. She stood there at the top of the stairs, all 5' 7' of her, her brown hair a tangled mess. Somehow, she looked frail, not her determined self.

"I couldn't sleep," she said. "It was bothering me, too. Where the demon went, I mean. I'm ready for anything that will get this out of my head. It's driving me crazy. I've got to know."

Hunter looked at the group of his seated friends. It wasn't hard to pick out who he wanted to be with him for the hypnosis session.

"Pastor Mark," he said, "I'll need you. Care to join me?"

"It would be my honor," he said.

****

The guest bedroom where Rebecca lay had the lights turned off, the door closed, and the curtains drawn. She had her eyes closed and was slowly drifting into a hypnotic trance. There were two chairs on either side of the bed. Hunter held one of her hands, and Pastor Mark held the other. Hunter had arranged a table at the foot of the bed with a metronome on top of it, slowly ticking away the time.

"Now Rebecca, take a deep breath in through the nose, and then exhale out through your mouth. Feel your body sinking deeply and relaxing, letting go of any tension that may be stored within the body and relax. Let your breathing become rhythmic and gentle. Feel the rise and fall of your chest as your breath goes in and out, in and out. Feeling relaxed, feeling tired, letting go. Relaxing into the moment. You are in a safe environment.

"Relax. Shine the spotlight of attention on your feet, searching for any inner tension. Tighten and tense your feet, release the tension. Now shine the spotlight of your attention on your calf muscles and repeat, tensing those muscles, then relax, letting go of all the inner tension. Move your attention to your thighs and then repeat, tensing and releasing your thigh muscles. Relax. Now shine the spotlight of your attention on the middle of your stomach, tighten and then relax your stomach muscles. Release the inner tension. Now shine the spotlight of your attention on your shoulders and arms. Tighten the muscles, then release. Feel the tension dissipate. Relax, drift away into the safe space within yourself, relax. Now shine the spotlight of your attention on the muscles of your face. Tighten and release those muscles. Let go of all the inner tensions. Relax. Relax.

"Inhale deeply, breathing in through the nose for a count of 1... 2... 3... 4 and hold the breath for a count of 1... 2... 3... 4 and now exhale through the mouth for a count of 1... 2... 3... 4. Repeat. Relax.

"Now, imagine you are standing at the top of some steps that wind down into a walled garden. From your vantage point, you can see a carefully tended garden with beautiful flowers. The fragrance from these flowers is heady, the scents linger in the air, so as you breathe in, you feel the wonder of nature. As you move down the steps, you move deeper and deeper into this journey, feeling more and more relaxed.

"Moving onto step.... five.... Feeling more and more relaxed.

"Four.... sinking deeper into a state of deep relaxation.

"Three....feeling deeply contented.

"Two.... feeling inner peace wash over you

"One.... letting go.

"Now you walk through the garden to a gate. You open the gate, and you walk for a while and you find yourself in a quiet, secluded cove where the sand is golden, and the sun is high in the sky. It bathes you in its luxuriant light. Relax.

"You feel very relaxed. You lie down in the warm sand. This feels good and reminds you of your childhood. The warmth from the sand emanates through your back. You are so very, very relaxed. You are at peace. You feel warm and protected.

"Now together we will count down slowly 10.... 9.... 8.... 7.... 6.... 5.... 4.... 3.... 2.... 1 you are floating in a warm, safe space."

With the hypnotic induction done, Hunter glanced over at Pastor Mark, who was looking like he was in a trance himself, until he looked up at Hunter and nodded. He nodded back. Now came the hard part. This was the first time he had done this. He had never gone looking for a demon in someone's head; he didn't know where to begin. This was harder than anything he had tried before. Might as well get right to the point.

"Rebecca?"

She didn't respond.

"Rebecca?"

Still no response.

"Rebecca, I want you to respond to me."

"Yes."

"Rebecca, what is your full name?"

"Rebecca Ann Mihaloff."

"Who is your father?"

"Frank Mihaloff."

"Relax."

Rebecca seemed relaxed. There was no point in delaying.

"Rebecca, are you alone in there?"

No answer.

"Rebecca, are you alone in there?"

Still no answer. This was strange. She lay still on the bed. Serene. Passive.

"Rebecca, are you being constrained from answering?"

This time she gave a strangled cry and uttered the word "yes."

"Relax, relax."

Hunter looked at Pastor Mark. He saw a man in shock that gradually melded to determination.

"Well," Hunter said, "I guess that answers that question."

"Yes, I guess it does," said Pastor Mark.

"Now what?" asked Hunter. "Should we wake her up?"

Pastor Mark considered the question seriously for a few minutes before answering. Hunter knew what agony he must have been going through. The man felt a personal responsibility for Rebecca's plight. When she had Sodom's Shackles put on her, he hadn't been there, and he felt it keenly.

"No. I'll pray for her."

"Yes, but what do we do then?" asked Hunter.

Pastor Mark looked him in the eye.

"I'll pray for her," he said seriously.

And he bowed his head in prayer. Five minutes passed, and Hunter felt slightly uncomfortable. Pastor Mark kept his head bowed. Fifteen minutes passed and Pastor Mark was still praying. By the time twenty-five minutes had passed, Hunter was having to go to the bathroom something fierce. Thirty minutes passed, and he really had to go to the bathroom. Pastor Mark still bowed his head in prayer. Beads of sweat appeared on his forehead. Hunter got up from his chair quietly and headed to the door. He would just be gone a little while, and he couldn't hold it any longer.

He made it to the door, opened it, and was surprised to see Marla and Ashley standing there.

"What—" began Ashley, but Hunter quickly held his finger to his lips as he quietly closed the door behind him and ran for the bathroom, signaling that he would be back shortly.

When he got back, Ashley and Marla were still there, and the door was still closed.

"Did he signal for me to come in?" asked Hunter.

"No," said Ashley. "What's going on in there?"

"He's praying for her while she's in a trance. And you were right, Marla. She's possessed by some... some... spirit that transferred over from Sodom's Shackles. I should have thought of that as a possibility after what I saw in Borgo. Good catch."

"I've seen that trick enough times in Borgo to make it stay in my mind forever," said Marla.

"He's been praying for her for an awfully long time," said Ashley.

"Yeah, I know."

"It's been like an hour."

"I don't know what to tell you. Hey, could you stay here and watch for a minute while I go check in on Enid and Kenneth? I'll just be a minute."

"Sure," said Ashley. "Marla, would you sit with me?"

"I'll be glad to," she said.

"Thanks," said Hunter.

He took off down the hallway, but hadn't made it ten steps when he heard a crash of breaking glass, and Rebecca screamed. Marla opened the door quickly and went inside with Ashley on her heels. By the time that Hunter made it to the room, he saw Rebecca sitting up in bed and Ashley comforting her. Marla was at the shattered window, looking out and down.

"What happened?" Hunter asked her.

She moved aside and shook her head. Hunter looked out the window and saw pastor Mark's body on the cement driveway. He couldn't believe it.

"Jesus," he breathed, and turned to Marla.

"Yeah, I know," she said.

He turned to Rebecca, who was sobbing against Ashley's shoulder.

"What happened?" he asked Ashley.

But Ashley didn't have a clue.

"Rebecca, what—"

She shoved aside Ashley's ministrations, and with tears running down her cheeks, said, "I'll tell you what happened. That thing inside of my head, Pastor Mark prayed it would leave me and take possession of him instead. Do you hear me? And then, when it did, he jumped out the window rather than let it live inside of him. That's what he did. He gave his life for mine."

And she turned to Ashley again and buried her face in her shoulder and sobbed.

Hunter looked at Marla with astonishment, his only emotion. He couldn't believe it. He looked out the window again, but there was the evidence of it. Pastor Mark's body was still sprawled there. Now they were down two good men, and Hunter wondered what he would do about it.

76

Hunter and Kenneth took Pastor Mark's body to the basement of the house while Marla and Ashley nailed boards up over the open window. The men had the grimmer job of it. They wrapped pastor Mark's body in a tarp and hauled him inside and down the stairs. Then they put his body in a freezer that intended for something else— God knew what, with Bartok's strange tastes. When they had him secured in the freezer, Kenneth looked at Hunter.

"I didn't know him very well. Hell, I only met him two days ago, but he seemed like a nice fella. Shame he had to die like this," said Kenneth.

Hunter nodded.

"It seems like a common fate among the good ones, Kenneth."

He was thinking of Enid Moser when he said it.

"Yeah, well, let's not make a habit of it. There's enough of us Mosers and Hunters have died because of that cussed place on Townsend Mountain, and now there's this, that poor pastor dying because of that miserable Mr. Chirac. I declare, when I get my hands on him..."

"I don't think you're getting your hands on him will do him in, Kenneth. I think we have to be cleverer than that."

The two men walked the length of the basement laboratory in silence, each with his own thoughts. As they went upstairs, a

681

particular grimness settled over them. They worried with their decreasing numbers, if they could defeat Hiram Abiff and his witch, Eva Morgan.

As they walked into the living room, they noticed that Ashley and Marla were grim. They looked defeated.

"Where's Rebecca?" said Hunter.

"She's in her room, crying her eyes out," said Ashley.

"I think she was pretty close to pastor Mark," said Marla.

"I'd better go see her," said Hunter.

"You'd better give her a little while," said Ashley.

"No time for that," said Hunter.

He knew they were running short of time and people. He was desperate for Rebecca's help. As he went up the steps, he considered how to approach Rebecca, but by the time he had made it to the second floor landing, he was no further ahead than when he started. There was no nice way of saying that Pastor Mark was dead, but they had to postpone grieving for him because they had a bigger problem to solve. He gathered his courage by the time he got to the door and knocked.

"Yes."

"Rebecca? It's Ian Hunter, can I come in?"

Standing there waiting for an answer wasn't getting him anywhere. He was about to try the door handle when it opened. Rebecca stood there on the other side, her eyes red from crying. She stepped aside to leave him room to enter and walked over and sat on the edge of the bed.

Suddenly, he knew it was all up to him. He was the most outstanding paranormal investigator to come out of Bartok's line, but he felt like he knew nothing.

He hesitantly walked in and said, "Rebecca, how are you doing?"

"About as well as you'd expect," she said with her eyes not meeting his.

This was bad. He walked over to the boarded-up window and pulled the chair over to the edge of the bed to sit at eye level with her. Still, she avoided looking at him.

"Rebecca, I'm sorry about Pastor Mark, I really am."

"Thank you. I've known and respected the pastor for seven years.

And all we can do with his body is put in a freezer downstairs."

"I'm truly sorry about that. It's all we can do right now."

"What do we tell the other church members? I'm sorry, but Pastor Mark can't come to the phone right now because he's dead?"

"Rebecca, I—"

"You don't know what it was like, Hunter, to have that thing living in your head. It was only for one night, but it tormented me the entire time. It kept saying repeatedly that my friends didn't care about me. That I had no real friends. That I should kill every one of you. That I should slaughter every one of you in your sleep. You know what that was like?"

"No, I don't. It must have been… horrible."

Hunter didn't know what else to say. He hadn't thought of how she had felt, any more than he thought of how Marla had felt escaping from Borgo. Or how Pastor Mark had felt when he hit the pavement, when he had burst out the window to seal the doom of the demon that infested his head. He hadn't even had time to think about how Enid Moser felt. That was the most damning of all. He had, it seemed, a broken team and there was nothing at all he could do to repair them. "I just want to say how sorry I was about the pastor."

Now Rebecca raised her eyes to his.

"Thank you," she said.

"If there's anything I can do, you have only to ask."

With that said, he turned and began to walk out of the room.

"Hunter?"

He stopped and turned around to face her.

"Yes?"

"I'll be down in a few minutes, and together we'll plot how to get our revenge on the bastards who did this."

Hunter gave a quick nod of his head, turned, and left the room.

****

The room that they kept Moser in was just down the hall. Hunter gave some thought to just saying goodbye later—having to kill Enid

683

Moser was harder than killing uncle Bartok. With Bartok, the change had been immediate and threatening and he had to react right then or die. Not knowing in advance had been a blessing in disguise. He didn't really believe that Bartok could change into an alien. The whole thing came as an egregious surprise. But with Enid, he knew with enough advance notice to make it too painful to contemplate. He would rather think of that anytime than right now, but it had to be dealt with.

When Hunter opened the door to Enid's room, it surprised him to see Kenneth Hillis snoozing in a chair facing Enid. But Enid was wide awake.

"Hey, Hunter. Come to see the old man, did you?"

Hunter stepped into the room and took a seat on the edge of the bed.

"You know Pastor Mark is dead, right?"

The old man shook and said affirmatively, "It's a damn shame," he said.

"Yeah. It is at that."

"But you got Rebecca back, I hear."

"We did. And thank God for that."

"Don't you worry about it none, Hunter. He died in a righteous cause. Ain't nothing else a man can ask for than that."

Hunter thought about that. Enid was right, and that gave him some measure of comfort.

"How are you doing, old man?"

"I'm doing fine and dandy, although I've had better days. Days when I wasn't roped up like a steer."

"I'm sorry about this, Enid. It's all we knew to do."

"Well, you could chain or cable me up."

Hunter thought about that and decided he liked it.

"Let's see what I can do. Bartok's got to have some chains or cables dangling around here somewhere."

"No rush, it's just I'd like to move around a little bit. You look like you got the world on your shoulders, boy."

"That obvious, huh?"

"Yep. Why don't you tell this old man about it, get it off your chest?"

Hunter wasn't too sure about sharing anything strategical with Enid, considering he might turn into alien any moment. But come to think of it, he was all roped up, so there couldn't be any harm to it, and he sure needed someone to talk to.

"I depend on you, Enid, and now you're gone."

"Well, I'm here for a little while anyway, so why don't you tell me the rest of what's bothering you?"

Hunter wondered if he was doing the right thing by sharing his burdens with Enid. Although, come to think about it, who else was he supposed to share them with?

"Pastor Mark's death has got me down. And Rebecca, she has not been taking this too well. First the witch, and then Sodom Shackles. And then there's the thing with you. And that's before we get to Hiram Abiff and Eva Morgan. And then there is Ricci. I don't know what side of the fence he is on. I suppose he's got to be on Chirac's side in the scheme of things."

"You sure got your hands full, don't you?"

"I do at that, old friend."

"So why don't you quit moping and tell me what you will do about it?"

"I don't know, Enid, I really don't know."

"Cut the crap, Hunter. You know what to do. You just don't like it."

"But there's more, Enid. You said that I should get this off my chest, so let me finish."

Enid grinned.

"All right, might as well get it all out now."

"The Brothers Mihaloff, Kaufman, Cook and Smith are all spellbound. The fifth member of the temple guardians is Chirac. So you can see how my head is a little twisted up."

"Yeah, I can see how that would be a mite difficult, but again I ask you, what are you going to do about it, Hunter?"

"Enid, all I've got to play this with is Kenneth, Ashley, Rebecca, and Marla."

"What about Darrell and Eddie Moser?"

"Oh yeah, I forgot about them."

"Hey, it's what you keep me around for."

"Score one for your side, Enid. What am I ever going to do without you, old man?"

"Just remember me at my finest," said Enid. "That's all I can ask of you, Hunter. Now enough of that kind of talk. Again, I ask you, what exactly are you going to do about this mess?"

"I have been thinking about that. It's in Mr. Chirac's interest that the chair works. Because now, he's afraid of Hiram, and I, for one, don't blame him."

"Go on," said Enid.

"All right, assuming that the chair actually works the way I intended it to, all we've got to do is wait for Hiram to take a seat in that chair, and then we dump him backwards."

"Tell me why you don't just do it while he's coming through. I mean, wouldn't it be simpler to just do it when the chair is activated in Borgo, wait for him to get inside it and not open the chair-door on the other side?"

"I already thought of that. The problem is we don't have any way of knowing when he's coming through. For all I know, with the other side being spellbound, he's already here, hiding out at Brother Frank Mihaloff's or at Brother Kaufman's or... well, you get the picture. We don't know exactly where he's at. You see what I mean? And the chair trick will only work once."

Enid took in a long breath and let it out slowly.

"I see what you mean."

"And we've got no way of knowing where Eva Morgan is. That one can come and go between Borgo and Detroit any time she wishes. And then there's Mr. Chirac. He wants either the ghost box or that I should give him one of ours to make up for a shortfall in his employees."

"One of our what? One of our people?"

"Yes, one of our people. But don't worry, I didn't make him a deal."

Enid was thinking. He grew silent and when Hunter tried to find out what he was thinking about, he shushed him. Finally, he spoke.

"Do you think that this Mr. Chirac would know where this Eva Morgan was?"

"I think so, yes. Why? What are you driving at?"

"And do you think he would know what she was up to—I mean,

at any specific time?"

"I would think he could find out. But again, why?"

Enid grinned.

"Well, because, Hunter, I've got the trade of a lifetime for him."

"What kind of trade?"

"I think I've got just the man for him."

And then Hunter got it.

"No," he whispered. "No way. Just no way."

"We've got two days before Hiram Abiff comes through the portal, right?"

"Yes."

"Now we just have to get hold of Mr. Chirac today or tonight and make the proposal to him."

"I won't do it, Enid. I won't."

"Kid, this change will come on me one way or the other. And I'd sure rather be placed with Mr. Chirac when it happens. The look on his face would almost make it worth dying for."

"I'm telling you, Enid, I just won't do it."

"This is the only way that you're going to pull this thing off, Hunter, so don't sass me. This is my one way to go out with dignity, and don't you dare take it away from me."

"I—"

"Listen to me, Hunter. It's the only way you will find out where Eva Morgan is in time."

Hunter put his head in his hands and began to whimper.

77

Hiram never slept.

At night, he wandered the world of Borgo unseen, but tonight, he waited inside the Borgo Masonic Temple for Eva Morgan. He paced impatiently around the room. Tomorrow night was the night which would be the fruition of all his plans. At last, he would be free of Borgo, and Borgo would be no more. Three thousand years he had endured for this day, and finally, it was his. He had devoured and mastered all the demons that had tormented him over the years. But of all the demons he had devoured, the sweetest tasting by far was that of the Nephilim darkness. The moment that he had opened his mouth and swallowed, it had been sublime.

He felt it still struggling to be free. Yet it was trapped with all the other demons and rotten evil spirits that had tormented him over the years. All their power was his to use. And it felt glorious.

Eva interrupted his thoughts by entering the doorway. In her human form, she was a lovely, lovely woman, even a seductive woman. But in her true form, she was a snake.

"Yes?" said Hiram.

"The cages in the viaduct's basement have all been unlocked, and we have unleashed the dead things."

"And Traverse?"

"He was the first casualty. He went down screaming."

Hiram nodded his head up and down.

"Excellent. Excellent."

"The rest of the night will be spent on the living in the complex. The dead things will hunt them down, and they will die horrible, delicious deaths."

Hiram laughed out loud, a frightening sound, an eerie sound. There was no mirth in that laughter at all.

"Come with me Marla, we shall observe."

"As you wish."

They walked down the steps of the Borgo Masonic Temple. All around there was the chaos of the dead chasing the dead, the screaming for help, somebody please help. Hiram and Eva ignored them and yet savored their fear. Occasionally, a group of soldiers that were among the living would attempt to stand their ground, firing round after round into the dead things, but soon they would go down under the assault of the already dead.

The already dead were hideous concoctions and monstrosities that were once human, but had transformed into wild beasts with sharp teeth and claws and unrecognizable things that were their faces. They were part wolf, part goblin things—they were Hiram's early experiments with making goblins.

Fog filled the night that the streetlights of Borgo barely penetrated. The cobbled streets and the shops were haunted by things in the darkness, with the creatures running wild in them and the terrified, screaming citizens. The viaduct that housed the military complex was barely visible through the mist, but Hiram could see the open doors that meant that was how the creatures had escaped. People must have run from them and, in their fright, forgotten to seal them afterward.

"You have prepared the ritual for the Blazing Star of Freemasonry?" asked Hiram.

"Yes, when I leave here tonight, I shall begin the ritual. We shall finally harvest the energy of it."

Just then, the creatures tackled a man not twenty feet from them. He tumbled to the ground in a jumble of arms and legs. The creatures ripped his arms off and began to chew. The man lay in a pool of spreading blood. A brave soldier stopped and fired a round off at him, just in time to be slammed from behind to the cement, and have his head ripped from his body. The blood sprayed everywhere as the goblin thing chomped down on his body.

Hiram Abiff and Marla, after pausing briefly to scrutinize that, continued their walk toward the viaduct. The frenzied killings that were going on all around them didn't distract from their conversations.

"You're sure nothing can go wrong?" asked Hiram.

"The Brother, Monsieur Emile Chirac, gave us a perfect rendition of the ritual to follow. I have only to return the Blazing Star within three days from the time I use it."

"Return it? Why whatever for? I doubt that Monsieur Chirac shall be alive much longer than three days. I see no need for that last of the Nephilim reborn to survive. Do you?"

Eva smiled a wicked smile.

"I would take the greatest of pleasure in killing him myself," she said. "But he is strong, so strong. And his familiar, Ricci, is powerful, too."

"But surely you can destroy them?"

"I was unprepared for them beforehand, but this time I shall be ready."

"Shall I take that as a yes, Eva dear?"

Eva didn't like that Hiram was so cavalier in his question. In fact, she out and out resented it. Truth be told, she chafed under Hiram. It was true he had the power, but that power was rightfully hers. She must bide her time and strike when he least expected it.

"Yes," she said.

As they walked through the viaduct doors, she fumed. Hiram would get his, soon.

"Eva?"

"What?"

"Don't you have things to attend to, such as making sure the ritual goes as planned?"

"As you wish."

"Eva?"

"Yes?"

"If the ritual does not go as planned, I promise that I shall have you for lunch."

His eyes flamed an electric blue midst all the chaos that surrounded him, and Eva felt the beginnings of fear—an emotion hitherto unknown to her. She bowed and then vanished through an open portal. It was the one thing that Hiram could not do, and Eva would not explain it to him. It irritated him, but not overmuch. He would observe her over time, and if she did not perform the way he liked, he would digest her slowly.

Continuing his walk through the doors, he had to sidestep one fleeing soldier. Soon afterwards, he had to make way for three goblin monsters that came tearing after the man.

Hiram smiled as he walked on through the viaduct complex to the main attraction.

78

Ricci stood at attention in front of Mr. Chirac's desk, an Olyphant Battle Horn affair that was deliciously tasteful in its beauty, stripped down to his waist, chained and his back flayed painfully open.

"Ricci, what am I to do with you? You disobeyed my orders and met with that hill person Kenneth Hillis," said Mr. Chirac.

He said the last few words with obvious disdain. Lily sat quietly growling at Mr. Chirac, her sleek, black fur beautiful in the dancing flames of the fireplace. Ricci stood mute before Mr. Chirac as he had a ball and strap across his mouth. Spike sat giggling nervously in a chair near the door, his feet swinging back and forth because his childlike frame could not touch the floor.

"I've treated you well enough, haven't I? You have all the food you could ask for. You're free to come and go except between the hours of sunset and midnight when I demand you attend to me. You have the freedom to finally strike back at the human excrement who held you under their thumb for so many, many years, and, might I say, put you in prison, yes?"

Mr. Chirac waited impatiently, drumming his fingers on his desk.

"Spike, remove the ball and strap from Ricci's mouth. I must have answers to my questions. And Spike?"

"Yeah?"

"If you do not immediately cease that incessant giggling, I shall cut your throat," said Mr. Chirac.

It took a moment for that to sink in, but when the diminutive Spike finally caught on, he leaped to his feet and fairly ran to Ricci. He began pulling a chair facing Mr. Chirac's desk over behind Ricci so he could stand on it and undo the strap affair.

"Spike, if you so much as lay a foot on that chair, I shall skin you alive."

Spike gulped and returned the chair to its former position. Next, he looked around and saw a stepstool which Mr. Chirac nodded at. Relieved that he would not risk his employer's ire, Spike carried the stepstool over to Ricci's front and looked for approval from his master. When Mr. Chirac irritably nodded his head, Spike climbed the step stool and disengaged the ball and strap. When he had the device off, he carried it away along with the step stool.

"Well, Ricci, what have you to say for yourself?"

The big man considered for a moment before answering.

"I warn you, you will only get one chance to tell me the truth, and I shall check with the Band of Truth."

Ricci remained stoic. His back hurt more than he cared to say. It was an agony to stand straight up before Mr. Chirac's desk. He felt faint, but he dared not show weakness in front of his employer. It had been two days since he had anything to eat or drink. Spike's expert hand had whipped him until he could barely think straight. The little man had taken to his task with glee.

But could he hold out against the Band of Truth? Ricci didn't think so.

Mr. Chirac had all the time in the world to torment him. He could whip and starve him, but Ricci didn't care. He would not give up his sister. He could use magic against him. But Ricci was obstinate. He would not, repeat not, give up his sister voluntarily. If he could kill himself, he would, if it came to that.

"Could I have some water?" he gasped.

"*Certainement.* Spike, some water for Ricci."

While Spike got the water, Mr. Chirac studied Ricci. He steepled his hands together in his customary fashion. Never before had he had a bondservant possessed of such pertinacity. What was he missing in deciphering the man? While Ricci carefully sipped his water to assuage his thirst, he considered. Had he not given him plenty of opportunity to exercise his vengeance on those he hated? He wondered. Right now, he could sorely use Ricci's strength and talents in his battle against Hiram Abiff. He was running out of time. Ricci would have to be brought back into the fold.

"I've decided to give you a *dire pour le sursis de l'exécution*, Ricci, if you will answer one question. But I warn you, you must answer it truthfully, agreed?"

Ricci merely nodded.

"I demand acquiescence."

"Yes," Ricci said, with great pain.

"*Bien*. Now Ricci, did you convey anything by word or action that would be detrimental to me or my plans? Be careful with your answer."

Ricci appeared to think for a moment and then shook his head no. To confirm this for Mr. Chirac, though, he said out loud, "No."

"You're certain, Ricci?"

"Yes," Ricci croaked.

How odd. Then what did he meet that mountain man for?

"Tell me one more thing, Ricci. For what in the world did you meet that man?"

"He wanted to tell me that the old woman had died."

Mr. Chirac was appalled.

"But I have felt her presence around here..."

Mr. Chirac thought for a moment. A presence could be detached from a body... was it possible that the old woman's ghost still watched him from the other side?

"Could I sit down—I'm feeling kind of faint."

Mr. Chirac appeared to think that over. And then he said, "Spike, take back Ricci to his room and take those blessed handcuffs and leg irons off. This is no way to treat a valued bondservant. Get some salve for his back, and Ricci?"

"Yes?"

"Have Spike bring you some food and then rest. I expect you to be ready to work at 6 o'clock sharp. Now go—I have things to attend to."

As he shuffled off with Spike at Ricci's side, Mr. Chirac contemplated his good fortune. The old woman was dead. Excellent.

That meant that the ghost hunter was that much more vulnerable.

79

"Here's what we've got," said Hunter to the assembled group.

Present were Rebecca, Marla, Kenneth Hillis, Ashley Hillis and Enid Moser. Enid was carried down by Hunter and Moser in the chair that they roped him to. They were assembled in the living room with the rest of the cast seated on the couch, and Rebecca and Marla were seated in chairs.

"We've got Hiram Abiff coming tomorrow night. This will be the main event in his quest to take over the world by first co-opting the Masons."

Everyone listened attentively. This was a matter of life and death for the world as they knew it, and they all were aware of it.

"I know this seems strange, but he's going to offer something to humanity. He's going to offer humanity a cure for cancer. I've been to the Masonic research clinic and I swear they can cure cancer, make limbs re-grow and even bring back people from the dead."

A sharp intake of breath went around the room. This last point had not been yet discussed, but Hunter felt they had every right to know.

"That is an unholy thing," said Rebecca.

"Wait. What?" said Marla.

"Brothers Kaufman and Cook call it the Sign of Hiram. It's an implant in your forehead that supposedly directs the brain to cause chemicals to be manufactured in the body that cures disease. But don't ask me, because for the life of me, I can't understand how this thing can bring back people from the dead. I used to think it was scientific, but it's got to be magical," said Hunter.

"Well, if you ask me, to bring people back from the dead, it's got to be more than magical," said Kenneth. "Or maybe I'm wrong, maybe it is magical."

"It's demonic," said Rebecca.

"I don't understand," said Marla. "You saw evidence that the... what did you call it?"

"The Sign of Hiram."

"Right, that's right. You saw evidence that this Sign of Hiram actually worked?"

"Yes."

"You saw it regrow a limb?"

"Yes, well no, I didn't actually see it regrow a limb."

"Uh-huh. And how do you know it cured cancer?"

"Well, I saw the boy before and after."

"Are you sure?"

Hunter hesitated.

"Well, now that you ask me... I didn't actually see him before and after."

"And the person who was supposedly brought back from the dead?"

Hunter's mouth hung open. No, come to think of it. He hadn't actually seen the person before and after, had he? Come to think of it, he had seen none of the people beforehand, or really after-the-fact, had he? Son of a bitch. Was it possible that they had conned him? No wait, there was that one horrible burn victim in the beginning. But he actually hadn't seen her cured, had he?

"I know where you're going with this because it's a fact. I didn't see any of the people before and after. I just saw them after. And I saw one horrible burn victim they said they would cure, but I didn't actually see her cured either."

"Could you have been bilked?"

Hunter felt like a fool. He'd taken Brothers Cook and Kaufman at their word. God, was he stupid or what?

"Yes, I guess I could have."

Ashley broke in.

"Okay, but what if it was real?"

"Yeah," said Kenneth, "but bringing back someone from the dead?"

"How about if we break in and do a little snooping around?" said Marla. "That way we can find out for ourselves."

"Now that's what I call an idea," said Kenneth.

"Their security is too tight. You haven't seen that building," said Hunter.

"There's no need," said Rebecca. "I can feel it in my spirit."

"Are you sure?" said Ashley. "What do you feel, Rebecca?"

"That it's not real."

"Wait, how exactly does that work?" said Marla.

"It's too hard to explain right now. You're just going to have to trust me on this one."

Hunter didn't want to go into his idea that he could implant the Sign of Hiram into Enid's forehead and save his friend. It's not that he doubted Rebecca, he just held on to the vague hope that he could save still Enid.

"We've got to split up our forces," said Hunter. "Because we have two enemies to deal with. We've got Hiram Abiff on the one hand and Eva Morgan on the other, and they won't be in the same place. And I've got to get hold of Rebecca's father to get in touch with Mr. Chirac, quickly, so I can find out where Eva Morgan will be tonight, so that Marla and Rebecca can take her out."

"Wait," said Marla, "shouldn't we be on the team taking out Hiram Abiff?"

"I agree," said Rebecca, " and I want Mr. Chirac's head."

"Look, I'd like your help in taking down Mr. Chirac and Hiram Abiff, but the meeting is an all-male affair. I mean, it's the Masons, and Masons are men only."

"That's bullshit," said Marla.

"Hunter's right," said Kenneth.

"Yes, he is," said Enid, shaking his head. "In fact, I'd be amazed if they let you into the building when Hiram Abiff comes back."

Hunter hated the fact that they were bickering, but it just couldn't be. The women had to take out Eva Morgan, and the men had to take out Hiram Abiff. They could like it, or not like it, but they just wouldn't let women in.

"I want to get my hands on Chirac's neck," said Rebecca.

"We need Chirac to find out where Eva Morgan is," said Hunter. "That's all there is to it. Now, I've got to call Rebecca's father, set up a meeting for tonight and make him our counter proposal. I would like to have Eva Morgan in the bag by then. Can you do it?"

Marla looked at Rebecca, who said, "Yes."

"Are you sure?"

"Yes."

"Wait a minute, Rebecca," said Marla. "You don't know what this woman is capable of, and I do."

Rebecca unbuttoned her shirt and showed off her scar from the goblin that very first night.

"I saw her face, I saw her in Borgo, and I've seen her in my dreams. Oh yes, I definitely know what that woman can do."

"But Rebecca," said Hunter, "can you guarantee me you can capture her? I need to know that if I am to make a bargain with Mr. Chirac."

Rebecca seemed to think about that. She looked at Marla and Marla looked back at her.

"I don't know if we can guarantee that we can capture her. But at the very least, we can kill her or die trying."

"I can second that motion," said Marla.

"All right then, I'll call him right now. But Rebecca, I told them you're with me doing some research on the goblins, and that you are fine. Be prepared to take the phone from me and confirm this."

"I can't talk to him right now. I just can't."

"You've got to do it. I know it will be hard, but you've got to do it. But under no circumstances can you agree to go home. It's not a favorable time for you. Besides, you're safe with me. Can you do that for me?"

Rebecca thought about that for a while, and then slowly shook her head yes.

"Okay, then I will talk to Rebecca's father, so everyone be quiet."

He withdrew his cell phone from his pants pocket and dialed the number for Rebecca's father. One ring. Two rings, he picked up.

"Hey Brother Frank, how are you?"

He had the phone on speaker phone so that everyone could hear the conversation.

"I've been trying to get a hold of you for two days to get an update. Where the hell are you? And where's my daughter?"

Hunter motioned to Rebecca to get over to the phone.

"Hi Dad," she said without being prompted.

"Rebecca? Is that you? Are you okay?"

"Sure. Hunter's been taking great care of me. My arm is healing nicely, and I'm safe."

"Well, when do you think you'll be home?"

"Two days from now. After you've finished all the fuss at the Masonic Temple."

"Brother Frank?" called Hunter. "I need to get hold of Brother Chirac."

It stuck in his throat to call him Brother Chirac.

"Well, call him."

"I don't have his number."

"Ah, I see. Well, wait a minute. Hear it is, let's see, its area code 666..." and he rattled off the rest of the number "... but why do you have to get a hold of him?"

"That's Tyler's business, brother Frank."

"Oh, I see. Well, what have you been—"

"Doing? That, too, is Tyler's business. Goodbye, Brother Frank."

Hunter closed the connection and dialed Mr. Chirac's number. After a long ring, just when he was about to hang up, Spike answered.

"Yes?"

"This is Brother Ian Hunter. I'd like to speak to Brother Chirac."

"He's busy right now."

"Tell him this is an emergency. I must speak with him. It concerns Masonic business."

"Hold the phone just a sec," said Spike.

Hunter walked away from the group to get a piece of paper off the kitchen table and an ink pen to write any information Mr. Chirac gave him.

"Yes, Mr. Hunter?"

"Where will Eva Morgan be tonight?"

"Pray, what has she to do with our union to defeat Hiram Abiff?"

"Because she's part of it."

"Ah, yes, I see. But Mr. Hunter, she will be too much for you to handle. You see, I so foolishly gave her the Blazing Star of Freemasonry to gain power for Hiram Abiff to bring the Nephilim into a new body. Tonight, she will perform the ritual at midnight."

"She has the Blazing Star of Freemasonry?"

"Yes, and I am afraid that tonight she intends to harvest that power for her new master, Hiram Abiff."

"Where will she be?"

"You intend to do what?"

"We intend to capture her for you."

Mr. Chirac went silent for a moment, then he spoke.

"Interesting, Mr. Hunter. An ambitious plan. Need I say that I must have the Blazing Star back?"

"We'll get it for you."

"Very good. You will find Eva Morgan at the following address. Are you ready to take down the information?"

"Yes."

"Très bien, 14367 Mullhaven Drive. It is in Detroit."

"Got it, and the chair's mechanism is ready?"

"Indeed. It is activated by the remote that was included in your toolbox. But Mr. Hunter?"

"Yes?"

"This trick will only work once, I am afraid. Hiram will catch onto it and use his rather extraordinary powers to subvert it. Do you understand?"

"Yes."

"Good. About that man from your side…"

"I am working on it as we speak."

"Don't just work on it, Mr. Hunter, or I shall claim you."

"That's all I can do—" but Mr. Chirac had already hung up.

Hunter turned to find the entire assembled group staring at him. Marla and Rebecca looked worried, Kenneth and Enid looked nonplussed and Ashley just looked curious.

"Well, how did it go?" asked Ashley.

"It went well," said Hunter.

He gave them the piece of paper with the address on it. Rebecca took it and let Marla see it.

"She'll be there performing the ritual to harvest the Blazing Star of Freemasonry's power at midnight."

"You feel up to this girl?" said Marla.

"Yes. I feel like I was born for it," said Rebecca.

"The only question I have is whether she'll have goblins present."

"I think we have to assume that she will."

"Well," said Marla, "let's go shopping for some clean clothes to wear and then gun up for tonight."

Rebecca looked at her curiously.

"What?" she said.

"I've been wearing the same clothes for days now and I'm tired of it. If I'm going out, I'm going out with new clothes on."

For the first time, Hunter saw a grin creep across Rebecca's face. It lit her up, so that she looked almost human. The last few days had been hard on Rebecca, harder than most. Battling with the goblin in her father's house, her spirit captured by Eva Morgan, and then, to top it all off, enduring the agony of Sodom Shackles. And the death of Pastor Mark. Yes, she'd been through a lot.

Hunter glanced at Enid. He knew what a sacrifice that he would have to make. Better to turn into a monster in Mr. Chirac's residence than for Hunter to have to kill him. Hunter felt proud of his friend. But he still wondered if the Sign of Hiram would work. Rebecca's visions or intuitions were not always one hundred percent accurate, were they? What if the Brothers Kaufmann and Cook were not just putting on a show? What if the Sign of Hiram really could cure a person? Would that be enough to save Enid from turning into a monster?

"Hunter?" asked Kenneth.

Hunter realized he had been thinking so much he couldn't hear Kenneth until just now.

"Sorry. What?" he said.

"You really think those two women can take down a monster like this Eva Morgan?"

"I don't know Kenneth. I sure hope so."

"Hey, listen to me," said Enid, "now that the three women folk have gone to pick up clothes and more supplies, least ways we menfolk can talk."

"Enid, I sure do love it when you talk southern," said Hunter.

"Yeah, well, pull up a chair, so I don't have to crane my neck so much, and I'll talk some more."

Hunter did just that, and sat down immediately across from Enid, next to Kenneth.

"Look, I told Kenneth what I planned to do, but he had the worry that I won't make it that long before I turn."

"That thought had occurred to me," said Hunter. "That's why I only told Chirac that I was working on a substitute from our camp."

"Good, but listen to me while I'm still me. Hunter, while the womenfolk is off killing Eva Morgan, and you're off taking care of business with Hiram Abiff, who you plan on having sit with me?"

Hunter thought about what Enid said. In the end, he had to admit he hadn't thought about it.

"Well, I have. You're going to have to let Miss Ashley sit with me."

"What?"

"You heard me. Kenneth isn't too much pleased with it, either. You're going to have to leave her with a gun or two, and instructions to shoot to kill."

"Whoa—" said Hunter.

"There's no whoa about it. She's going to have to be prepared to kill me, Hunter, and that's a fact. It's, as you would say, an irresistible fact. While Eva Morgan is busy with the ritual, and you and Kenneth are out preparing for Hiram Abiff, Ashley will be all alone with me."

Hunter considered that. The only person left was Ashley. He would have things to do apart from the mansion. Ashley would have to be left all alone with Enid. He was right. All alone with Enid was fine, unless he started to turn into an alien creature.

What was he going to do about that?

"Wait. What about Darryl and Eddie?"

"Sweet Jesus, I forgot all about them. I'll call them," said Kenneth.

Problem solved.

But Hunter could not get over the feeling of what if Moser turned into an alien while they were there? Would three of them be enough to kill him?

80

Marla aimed her Mossberg 590 Pump Action 12-Gauge shotgun and dry fired it. The click was smooth, and the trigger pull was good. Rebecca similarly dry fired her Sig Sauer M400 assault weapon and found the rifle a delight to shoot. They were each equipped with two Smith & Wesson M&P Shield pistols and one micro-compact lightweight Kimbers in their ankle holsters. Besides this, they were each armed with DK & AJ blades tactical combat survival hunting and neck knives.

"You sure you have enough firepower?" said Hunter.

"Not yet," said Marla.

She reached for a Sig Sauer MPX Sub Compact machine pistol. Handing it to Rebecca, she got one for herself. She also picked out several magazines, which she handed over half of them, and then pocketed the rest. They wore cross belt ammunition carry-alls.

Hunter thought they looked like they were going to war, and they were. They were going to war for all of humanity against a great evil in the singular person of Eva Morgan. He wondered again if they had enough firepower.

Rebecca passed out the grenades.

They were dressed in black and gray camos, and each had their hair tied up in a bun with a black cap to top off their ensembles.

"Ready?" said Marla.

"Ready," confirmed Rebecca.

Darryl and Eddie were watching them with approval. Kenneth and Ashley stood there, nervous for them, but hopeful. It was seven o'clock and the full October night was upon them. It was an unusually warm night, and they were thankful for that.

"Good luck," said Hunter awkwardly.

Marla gave a thumbs up to that as she shouldered her ammo bag.

"We'll be back. Don't you worry about that," said Rebecca.

But it worried Hunter. It worried him that two of the bravest women he had ever known would walk out that door, maybe never to be seen again. Hunter walked with them to the garage, but Rebecca stopped at the door.

"Look, I just wanted to say I'm sorry," she said as Marla opened the door to the black SUV.

"Sorry? Nothing to be sorry about. I just wished—"

"Let me finish. You've been a stalwart through all my ranting and raving and I've been a bit of a… bitch. So, I'm sorry."

She kissed him briefly on the lips and turned back and loaded her stuff into the vehicle. Marla grinned at him, waved and started the SUV. Rebecca stared straight ahead. Then, they opened the garage door and pulled out.

Hunter touched his lips briefly, wondered what that was all about, smiled and went inside as the door closed.

****

The night sky was inky black as they drove in silence, and the moon was a nacture giant. Clouds were scattered across the firmament, almost invisible in their vaporous enigmatic states. The skyline of Detroit went by in darkness, lit only by the brightness of casinos and office buildings. Marla and Rebecca kept their thoughts to themselves for the longest time. The car's GPS said five miles to travel until they reached their destination.

"What do you suppose that she really is?" said Marla.

"A demon," said Rebecca. "She's a demon from the pit. A monster, that beneath her human form is something awful."

"She's a shapeshifter, too. Like, one time she's a woman, and one time she's a snake and sometimes she's... smoke, or fog or something like that."

"Yes," said Rebecca as she checked her G2 X-Caliber tranquilizer gun one last time. "We've got to catch her in her human form and knock her out. If not, we shoot to kill with our other weapons."

"That makes sense," said Marla. "It won't make Hunter happy, but there will be nothing else we can do. What do you think of his plan?"

Rebecca looked at her for a long time and then looked out into the night.

"50-50," she said. "It all depends on if we're lucky or not. I can't determine if her goblins are there, and I think a lot depends on that."

"Yeah, they're the thing that worries me the most, too. How many of them there are will be critical. Because they all will have to be killed before we can get to Eva."

"Wait a minute, do you think if we kill Eva, that the goblins will turn to dust?"

"Now there's a thought," said Marla.

"I wonder how many of them there will be?" asked Rebecca.

"We're about to find out," said Marla, just as the GPS announced they had arrived at their destination.

"Well, this is grim."

"Isn't it, though?"

They'd pulled up in front of an abandoned warehouse, with rows of broken windows like shattered teeth. Marla navigated the last block without headlights along the length of the building, which was long and dark and empty. There were no lights on anywhere in the building, and no streetlights that lit the outside or the inside. Marla pulled on her night vision goggles and Rebecca did the same. The building came into a stark relief as green hues brought it into focus.

"Are you ready?" said Marla.

"Let's do it."

As they got out of the car, the overhead dome light did not come on, since they had taken the bulb out and put it in the glove box. They had their ammo bags slung over their shoulders and crossed bandoleer style ammunitions pouches for backup. Also, they had their rifles and their pump shotguns and their tranquilizer guns — they were ready for anything. But as they walked toward the warehouse, they felt a sense of uneasiness settle over them. Marla held her pump shotgun at the ready and her tranquilizer rifle on a sling. Rebecca had her tranquilizer gun at the ready and her SIG on a sling around her shoulders.

The door swung open when Marla gave it a gentle push. It didn't make the screeching sound that she would have expected if it hadn't been opened recently. That was a good sign, she thought. It meant that someone had come and gone through this doorway. It didn't have to be Eva Morgan, but Marla was willing to bet her last dollar that it was. She motioned for Rebecca to follow her in.

The two women were left with a conundrum, though. Where was Eva? The place was so big that it could take them half the night to find Eva.

"We should split up while we're searching the place; it's faster that way," whispered Marla.

"I don't think we should split up ever because it's safer that way," Rebecca whispered.

"We're going to have to split up to cover enough ground."

"You remember what happened to me last time I tried to go solo?"

Marla thought about that.

"Lead on," she said finally .

Rebecca looked at which way to go, but the truth was she didn't know. She closed her eyes and thought for a minute, two minutes more and then opened them and started going in an approximately easterly direction toward the river. Marla covered her flank as she did so.

They were in an open warehouse empty of anything but I-beams and a few boxes. Dust was everywhere, but there were no footprints. All of which told Rebecca that Eva had ported into the warehouse when she planned to work there, if she was there at all.

Mr. Chirac was not to be trusted. Of that, Rebecca was sure. But could they could trust him to have told Hunter where Eva Morgan was? Rebecca just didn't know, but she had a feeling, just a feeling that she would find Eva Morgan if they kept going east.

Coming up to a door, Rebecca and Marla stopped. Rebecca leaned her head against it, and she heard nothing for two or three minutes and finally gave the all clear sign. She opened the door, and it opened onto a hallway where there were three doors on one side, two on the other and another door at the end. She didn't like it. Rebecca looked at Marla and she was closing the door behind them. When she caught her eye, Marla nodded, and Rebecca approached the first door.

She slowed her breathing and then opened it. A vast open space awaited her, filled with old furniture. There were chairs and tables stacked at odd angles, mirrors and credenzas that looked like they were ready to fall over. It was packed to overflowing with odds and ends that were just broken. They lay bathed in the green light like someone's discarded possessions. Rebecca decided that there wasn't enough spare room to have a ritual in there, so she closed the door.

Marla tried to open the second door on the left side, but it was locked. She looked up at Rebecca, but Rebecca was staring at the door at the far end of the hallway. There was a faint light that was shining from the bottom of the door that she hadn't noticed. She looked back at Marla and pointed to the door. Marla nodded back at her and advanced alongside of Rebecca.

They walked past the fifth door and finally arrived at the end of the hallway. Always, Marla kept an eye on where they had been, paranoid that something would jump out at them when they turned their backs. She wasn't about to let that happen, though. So, she kept watch.

Rebecca took another deep breath and put in her earplugs. Marla did the same. The light was definitely shining through the bottom of the door, so she flipped her night vision goggles up and Rebecca did, too. She slowly opened the door to a room full of goblins. Marla brought up her pump shotgun. Together, they started firing.

The goblins howled at the eruption of gunfire. There were eighteen of them, and it enraged them. They were not as tall as a short man, covered with sprouts of hair, and their arms reached to the ground. Green from head to toe, they had huge yellow eyes, pointed ears, and teeth that would rip a head off. The stench in the room was overpowering, and it was all Rebecca and Marla could do to keep from gagging.

They were confused by the crack of Rebecca's semi-automatic

firing, and the booming of Marla's pump shotgun rounds at first. Green goblin blood was everywhere. There were five of them down in about as many seconds, but the rest of them attacked as packs. They split up so that six of them attacked Marla and seven of them were after Rebecca.

Rebecca mowed down three of them, but the others split again. Marla could barely keep up with the shotgun, but she kept firing and firing. The hairy beasts were frighteningly fast, and one broke through the line and swung a claw at her, but she ducked, fell on her back and pumped a round in and fired. The others moved in for the kill.

Ducking under a goblin's attempt to separate her head from her shoulders, she poleaxed him and then fired directly into his hideous face. She turned just in time to get struck on the left shoulder by another and narrowly missed getting her heart ripped out.

Rebecca leaped back as two goblins came at her, but with her right hand she fired her SIG Sauer and blew the first one back into the second one. She saw Marla go down and two beasts that were about to pounce on her and fired a spurt of ammunition into them before turning around just in time to have her SIG knocked right out of her hands by a screeching goblin.

Marla dropped her Mossberg and took out her twin Smith and Wesson MP Shields and began firing away at the last goblin. Five shots and it was down. Another hairy beast was rising, but she got to her feet and fired a round into the back of his head. She saw Rebecca about to get eviscerated by a screaming monster and fired six rounds into him to be sure he was dead, and he would have fallen right on top of Rebecca, but she rolled out of the way.

The room smelled of cordite and gun smoke and goblin guts.

Rebecca got to her feet while Marla scanned the room and reloaded. She extended her left fingers and pulled them back again to make sure that they were still working. Just then, a goblin raised its head and shrieked, and Rebecca whirled to defend herself, but Marla pumped a round from her reloaded shotgun to its face. The room fell into an eerie silence as the women surveyed the room.

The smoke was so thick that you could barely see. Through the haze, though, could still be seen the bodies of the goblins. Their hairy arms twisted at odd angles. Bullet holes ripped through their mangled bodies as the putrid aroma of their carcasses drifted through the air.

"Thanks," said Marla.

"Thank you," said Rebecca. "What is this place?"

"You got me," said Marla.

In all the fighting, Rebecca had not looked around the room, which was enormous. Now she did, and she felt sickened by what she saw. There were operating type tables with bodies half-finished for transforming them into hideous apparitions. They were half-human and half-monsters, and Rebecca felt her stomach roil at the sight of them.

"What on earth?" said Marla.

Rebecca walked toward the tables, shaking her head. Her hair had fallen to one side, having lost several bobby pins when she fell. Marla walked backwards, always conscious of something coming up behind them. They stopped when they stood in the middle of a field of human detritus. Here they saw the animals that were sawed up and transplanted to their human hosts, vivisection style.

"What the hell are these things?" said Marla.

"I don't know," said Rebecca. "They're like demons from the pits of Hell."

"Remember the Borgo Pass?" said Marla. "They're like creatures taken from there."

Rebecca turned toward Marla.

"Yes, they are."

Marla turned back the way they had come. She looked at the goblins and then turned thoughtfully to Rebecca.

"What do you suppose they were here for?" she said.

"I don't know," said Rebecca. "Waiting for their mistress, maybe?"

"Well, we certainly made our presence known to everyone in the building," said Marla. "They ought to be showing up here any second now."

"Unless Eva hasn't shown up yet."

"You think?"

Rebecca shrugged.

"I don't know," she said, "but I say we don't stay in one place too long."

"Lead on, then. This place is giving me the creeps."

Rebecca wound her way in between the goblin bodies and Marla followed, always covering her backside as they went.

81

Hunter was restless.

He turned to Kenneth.

"You ready?" he said.

Kenneth turned to Ashley and gave her a hug.

"You're sure you'll be okay?" he asked her.

She looked at Enid, still trussed up in the chair. She glanced at Darryl and Eddie; Darryl was talking to Enid.

"Yes," she said finally.

"You're sure?"

"Yes, I'm sure."

"Well, I'm ready then," said Kenneth.

"Good."

"One thing, though."

"What's that?" said Hunter.

"How come we ain't all gunned up like the ladies?"

Hunter grinned.

"Because I don't think that the Freemasons would appreciate us loaded with all that hardware. Otherwise, I'd be for it."

"So, I've got to leave the shotgun at home, then?"

"Well, I'd bring everything in the car, but I'd only take a pistol or two inside with us."

Kenneth looked through the assortment of firearms.

"If you don't mind the suggestion, Kenneth," said Enid, "I'd take along two of the Springfield Armory 1911 pistols if I was you. And load up with plenty of ammunition."

Kenneth considered the suggestion and agreed.

"Thanks," he said.

"My pleasure," said Enid. "I only wish I was going along with you."

"Me, too, cousin. Me, too."

"I'll bring him home safely, Ashley," said Hunter.

"You better," said Ashley.

And with that, they headed out to the massive garage, and were gone to the Detroit Masonic Temple.

****

It was a massive building in the darkness, all lit up for the grand opening tomorrow night to make sure that all the lighting was just so. Hunter pulled into the entrance to the parking lot, waited to be approached by the security guard, identified himself and Kenneth, and then drove away to park the car. He stared at the building for just a little while.

The Detroit Masonic Temple was a massive building. There was something like one thousand rooms in the temple, it rose fourteen stories above Detroit, the excavation for the foundations required the removal of nearly one point six million cubic feet of earth, three point nine million bricks were used in building it, the exterior contained nearly one hundred thousand cubic feet of stone, and the structural steel used in the building's erection weighed in at just over sixteen million pounds. Hunter was in awe of the sheer scope and size of the building. A feeling of dread began to settle over him at the task ahead of them.

"Do you think that the girls are okay?" said Kenneth.

"I don't think that they'd like it if they heard you refer to them as girls," grinned Hunter.

"Yeah, well, old habits die hard. What do you think?"

"I think, as gunned up as they were, that I'd hate to stand in their way."

"I just don't know how that will stand up against magic," said Kenneth.

"Well, they're about to find out."

They got out of the car and walked the rest of the way to the Masonic Temple. As they walked up the steps, Hunter suddenly remembered seeing the larger-than-life picture of Eva Morgan that occupied the center of the vestibule as they walked in the doors. But when they walked in the doors, it surprised them to see workmen putting the finishing touches on a larger-than-life sign saying, "Welcome Supreme Grandmaster Hiram Abiff." Hunter stopped and gawked at it.

Brother Frank Mihaloff strode over and pumped Hunter's hand.

"My God, am I glad to see you," he exclaimed. "How's my daughter?"

"In good hands, Brother Frank," Hunter said, shaking his extended hand, "she's keeping Ashley and Enid company. Enid's a little under the weather, so he invited Darryl and Eddie Moser—they're cousins of his—over to sit with her. Kenneth is filling in for him."

No, Brother Frank didn't know, couldn't even imagine the trouble with Enid Moser was that he wasn't sick—he was turning into an alien.

"Oh, that's awfully nice of them," said Brother Frank.

The problem was that Brother Frank was spellbound. Hunter was fairly certain that he had told Eva Morgan everything about where Rebecca was and Eva Morgan had ported over to the mansion and, if not for Enid, would have killed her. Eva Morgan was a witch, a real high functioning witch that Hunter did not want to meet face to face without a .45 caliber to fire at her head. He wondered if she was here tonight. Looking around, he couldn't see her, but that didn't mean she wasn't.

"Yes, wasn't it? But now we have Masonic business to attend to. Shall we walk around and see what you've done to the place, and I will comment on the security features?"

"Why yes," said Brother Frank, "follow me. Will Kenneth be

following?"

"At a distance," said Hunter. "He's acting as my bodyguard tonight."

"Any luck with whom the witch was?" asked Brother Frank.

That was what he liked about Kenneth. He followed quietly along, minding his business while checking to see if anyone was eyeballing them that shouldn't be.

"No. And I wish you wouldn't talk about it here where people can hear," said Hunter.

They wound the way through the throngs of Masons that were there for the night's festivities. Apparently, the welcoming of Grandmaster Hiram tomorrow night was a big event. There were caterers in the mezzanine, banners strung decoratively between the rafters of the place and little balls of light were glowing everywhere. There was even a band playing St. Elmo's Fire.

"I'm sorry, but I am concerned about our security."

"Let me be concerned about our security. What about the news? Who's handling that?"

"Our front office handles all that."

"I should have been told about this."

"Well, you weren't there to—"

"That is enough," said Hunter. "I would like to see them right away. You don't seem to realize what a perceived threat he is to the rest of the world."

"But—"

"Now. I would like to see them now."

"But why?"

Brother Frank seemed to take offense at Hunter's insistence. He had already handled this, so what was the push for security with the news office? But Hunter was trying to get rid of Brother Frank, Brother Kaufman and Brother Cook.

"Because I said so."

"Brothers Kaufman and Cook would like to see you."

"They can wait until later. My primary duty is to the security of Grandmaster of the World Hiram Abiff, and everything else is second. Now I repeat, can you please introduce me to the front office, or do I have to find them myself?"

Hunter knew there was a danger with the spellbound, and he did not want to be clubbed on the head by Brothers Kaufman and Cook. That was what the real danger was. If Hiram Abiff had given them specific suggestions that he was a traitor to their cause, well, so much for that. That was where Kenneth came in, but he just didn't know how many spellbound there were, so he just wanted to get in and out. Plus, he didn't know how far his peremptory tone would get him before Brother Frank turned on him.

"Yes, but Brothers Kaufman and Cook wanted to see you—"

"Brother Frank, perhaps I wasn't clear enough. I wish to see the people in the front office first."

He could see it in the big man's eyes, the uncertainty bordering on belligerence. But, finally, he broke.

"Yes, yes, I'll show them to you right now."

And Brother Frank led them down a hall to the magnificent offices. Everything was redone and polished. The hotel truly looked like a magnificent hotel lobby.

"Here they are," said Brother Frank, when they had gone to an offshoot of the main desk. "Now, if you'll excuse me, I have things to attend to. Big night tomorrow. Is there anything else you wish me for?"

"No, thank you," said Hunter with a smile. "You've done more than enough."

Brother Frank left them as a man hailed him from across the lobby.

"Now, what was that all about?" said Kenneth.

The two men in the office waved, and Hunter waved back.

"We just had to get rid of him as quickly as possible. He's spellbound. In fact, the entire Temple Guardians are except for Mr. Chirac."

"Okay, so where are we off to from here?"

"It's a secret place that I think the Templar Guardians have forgotten about or relegated to obscurity.

"Where's that?"

"The Templar Library."

Kenneth shrugged. This entire building was a mystery to him. There were rooms upon rooms, and he thought a man could get lost in here without half trying.

"Lead on, Macduff," he said.

Hunter took an elevator to the floor where the Templar Cross hung and where the suit of armor stood. It was an isolated alcove, away from the bustle of the first floor. He took a deep breath, glanced around him once, and placed a hand on either side of the shield and twisted it first to the right, then twice to the left, then three times to the right and one last time to the left. The wall behind the knight opened inward into darkness. Hunter went in, followed by Kenneth. Once inside, Hunter pushed on a square and compass on the wall. The door swung shut, shrouding them in darkness, but the second the door clicked back into place recessed ceiling lights sprung to life.

"Well, that's nifty," said Kenneth.

"Yeah, isn't it though?"

They were in a square room with no exits. The floor was the tiled black and white, so familiar to Hunter as a Masonic pattern, but the room was void of furniture. The only unusual element to the room was that it was empty. Hunter walked toward the East wall and extended a hand toward it. He remembered his conversation with Brother Mihaloff.

"Yes. My your uncle Bartok's design. He was, as you are now, charged with protecting all items of importance belonging to our order. And there never was a man more suited to the task. He had an amazing and complex mind. I do not understand how this lock works any more than I can explain the Tyler's sword you carry. We, the other members of the Temple Guardians, protected the secret of Hiram Abiff. Your uncle protected the order itself, as you do now."

"Against what?" asked Hunter.

"Behind this wall lie many centuries' worth of secrets, brother, beginning with the writings of a Templar monk named Archambaud and continuing in an unbroken line straight through to your uncle Bartok. Secrets such as these are, to the enemy, worth killing for. But open the door and see for yourself."

Hunter shook himself at the memory. He hesitated, then withdrew the sheathed dagger from his belt and stood up. With a silent prayer for continued sanity, he slid the blade into the slot and heard a soft thrum, like the muted reverb from a sixties band. A soft click when it was finished followed this, and the panel swung inward.

Once again, Hunter was in the inner sanctum of the Templar Guardians. Journals under protective glass, cassette tapes, paintings of men from ages gone by, and the photographs. Each one was priceless because they documented the astonishing life of Hiram Abiff. There were swords and shields, maces and pistols, knives and helmets. Newspaper clippings gone yellow with age and even a microfiche reader. A place for a researcher to get lost for hours on end. Somewhere in this maze of articles and journals lay the answer to what Hunter was looking for.

"Well, shit," said Kenneth, "it's like a museum within a museum."

Hunter looked at him curiously. He hadn't thought of that, because that's exactly what it was—a museum within a museum.

"You know, Kenneth, you're exactly right. And that's what it is. A museum within a museum," said Hunter.

"Well, what are we looking for?"

"It's hard to explain."

"Okay, try."

"All right, I'll try. It's like this, Hiram Abiff is isolated in the town of Borgo, and he can't get to our world. What did the Nephilim have that held him back?"

"Wait, I don't understand what you mean," said Kenneth.

"All these years that Hiram was in this world, newly two thousand years... until, in nineteen forty-six or forty-seven, the Nephilim exiled him to Borgo. You with me so far?"

"Yeah, I guess so."

"What I'm trying to wrap my head around is how the Nephilim exiled Hiram to Borgo. Do you understand what I'm asking?"

"This Nephilim, he was the fallen angel, right?" asked Kenneth.

"Exactly."

"And the Nephilim couldn't control Hiram, so he got rid of him in the town of Borgo?"

"Yes," said Hunter.

"And you're trying to understand, if I understand you right, how we exiled him to Borgo in the first place?"

"That's what I'm trying to understand. Let's say that what Mr. Chirac did to the chair doesn't work. What is our backup plan?"

"Now I get you," said Kenneth.

"I'm thinking that somewhere in these notes, one of the Tyler's for the temple guardians had to come across the Nephilim's secret."

"Understand what you're looking for now, but how we supposed to find it out in the short period of time that we've got?"

"We've got to think of why," said Hunter, thinking out loud as he talked, "that the Nephilim placed Hiram in Borgo in the first place. Maybe there was some weakness that he knew of that could take Hiram down."

"I don't understand," said Kenneth.

"Let me make it clear, then. The Nephilim didn't need to put Hiram in Borgo to prove his powers, he already had those powers to begin with. And when he was screwing around with Hoover, let's just say that he did that because he could. You see what I'm saying? There's no real reason that the Nephilim placed Hiram in Borgo that we can think of. Unless he was concealing a weakness of Hiram. Weakness that was so devastating to Hiram that he couldn't let it out until it was a moot point., I know what I'm trying to say, but I'm not saying it very well."

"Let me try to rephrase it for you then," said Kenneth.

"Please do," said Hunter.

"You're looking for some evidence as to Hiram's weakness. Does that about sum it up?"

"Yes, I think that says it nicely."

"And you're not sure where to begin because there's so much stuff that you could get lost for days just trying to find one piece of paper."

"That's right."

"Well, might I suggest we look for papers in the nineteen forty-five, nineteen forty-six range, because that was the year, if memory serves me correctly, that you said that Borgo was created."

"Maybe we should include nineteen forty-seven."

"Let's get to it then, because I don't feel none too good about leaving Ashley, Darrell, and Eddie with Enid right now."

Hunter thought about it for a little while and had to agree with Kenneth. He didn't know when it would turn, but it was going to be soon.

82

Eleven o'clock and still nothing. Hunter was fascinated, but weary. Kenneth was methodically plodding along, reading paper after paper slowly, turning pages one at a time. It frustrated Hunter; it seemed like they would never come to the end of the line. He yawned.

"I wish we would've remembered to bring coffee," he said.

Kenneth didn't answer; he was busy reading something. The air in the room was still, and Hunter got the creepy feeling that Kenneth, too, was spellbound.

"Kenneth?"

"Just a minute."

Hunter felt a little better with Kenneth answering him. It was creepy with no noise except what they would generate. The long rows of books and papers just seemed endless. He wondered if they had done the right thing concentrating on the era that they were thinking the Nephilim had created Borgo. It was a shot in the dark, anyway.

"I think I have something," announced Kenneth.

"What is it?" said Hunter.

"It's a little hard to explain," said Kenneth. "Why don't you let me read it to you and see what you think."

"Okay, do it."

"I've got to stretch my legs first," said Kenneth as he unwound his long legs from their cramped position. "Man, this hurts my eyes."

Hunter waited impatiently for Kenneth to begin.

"I don't know if this is anything," said Kenneth. "It's hard to read, because I think it's in old English."

"Get on with it," said Hunter.

Kenneth shrugged his shoulders, rotated them to the back once, and read from a sheaf of papers.

"I don't understand," said Hunter when he was through. "This just tells about how the Temple Guardians got their start."

"Yeah," said Kenneth, "but what's on the back is what's significant."

"What?"

"It was written, I think, by the one called Lycenius."

"Go on," prompted an exasperated Hunter.

"It says… let me get this right… it says, 'Call on the Lord in faith to be free."

"Wait, so? That's maybe a generic thing, like a slogan of the Temple Guardians or something. And isn't that a lot earlier than the time frame we agreed on?"

"I followed it backwards because of something else I found on the back of this later manuscript."

"What?" asked Hunter.

"Let me read the second clue out loud for you," said Kenneth.

Resigning himself to Kenneth's slow reading, Hunter slumped back in his chair and signaled for him to begin.

When Kenneth was through reading, Hunter protested, "But I already had a copy of that."

"Ah, but did you have what was written on the back?"

"What was written on the back?" asked Hunter.

"It says, 'Call on the Lord in faith to be free."

"But we already said that might just be a slogan."

"Uh-huh, but it also says, 'To send him back to oblivion."

"It really says that?"

"Yep."

"Oh my God, that's the clue that we've been looking for," exclaimed Hunter.

"Well, that when combined with the third…"

"There's a third?"

"Yep, and all in Mr. Bartok's handwriting," said Kenneth.

Hunter fell silent for a second. Could it really be true? Was the old man saving his bacon yet again? He breathed a sigh of relief.

"What? Really? Are you sure?"

"One thing I know is that old man's handwriting."

"Well, what does it say? And don't read the whole missive to me. Just the ending."

"I really think I should read the whole thing, Hunter. It's got something valuable in it."

"Okay," said Hunter, "just make it quick, will you?"

1945

I write this out of a sense of desperation, a sense of being lost. I cannot die, and what is life if one cannot die? Where an end would give meaning to life, a life that could move onto something glorious, I shall not have that opportunity. The spirits are mostly quiet now, so I can think. In moments like this, sanity is precious to me. Yet, I think I am mad if I think I am sane at all. There can be nothing ahead of me—no death but only stepping stones to complete insanity. I long for total oblivion, where I can think of nothing. Why do these spirits call to me with their maddening chittering? Why am I tormented day and night by their psychotic ravings? Why is my mind filled with these demented speculations of stripping the skin off of grown men and women? Why do I long for the flesh of youth to devour?

I must be delirious—yes, that's it!

These phantasms that haunt my every waking minute. Ghosts and demons and specters claw at me, always they claw at me. Why can I gain no surcease? Why? Why? Why?

Hiram

Hunter read and reread the note written in 1945 that said it must have been written by Hiram. He shook his head.

"He must truly be insane," he said.

Kenneth just shook his head.

"I think you could rightfully say he has a screw or two or three loose."

"How many spirits do you think he's got going on inside of him?"

"Well, considering he's been around nigh onto three thousand years, I'd say a lot."

"My God," said Hunter.

"Yep. Did you read the back?"

Hunter turned the paper over on the back and it said, "If you've found this piece of paper, I assume you're as desperate as I think you are. Whatever it takes, shove him back into the one place he wouldn't expect. May God be with your souls. See my earlier notes. Bartok."

"That's what set me to thinking. We've got to shove him into the Borgo Pass, whatever it takes. And, most important, is we have to invoke God's name when we do it. Does that make sense?"

He couldn't quite wrap his mind around the idea that Bartok had come up with the same plan that he had. Except he had put the caveat that he had to invoke the deity's name while doing it. Why on earth would he have to invoke the name of God while doing it? But he knew the old man well enough not to question him.

"Yes," he said. "Come on, Kenneth. Let's call it quits for the night and hope that the women were successful. We've done enough damage for one night. You know, I never would have found these if it were not for you."

"Well, it would have taken you a mite longer is all," said Kenneth, and he gave a rare grin when he said it.

They made their way out of the underground library to the door that separated them from the lobby. Past the door to the empty room, Hunter looked at his watch. It was eleven forty-one. Walking to the door that would finally let them into the main Masonic hallway, they opened it and stepped outside, only to find Brothers Kaufman and Cook waiting for them. Brother Kaufman was pointing a nine-millimeter pistol at them.

"Going somewhere?" asked Brother Kaufmann.

Hunter felt his stomach tighten. How could he have been so stupid as to open the door without preparing for it first?

"Hello, fellas," said Kenneth from somewhere behind Hunter. "It would help if you had the safeties off on those weapons before aiming at someone."

Brother Kaufmann looked down at his pistol just as Kenneth shoved Hunter to one side and shot him in the stomach with a Glock sub compact 26 Gen 4 9MM with a sound suppressor. Brother Cook reached for a pistol beneath his coat and Kenneth shot him, too, twice. The noise was suppressed, but seemed like cannon fire in the echoing space. Hunter was shocked—he was literally numb.

"Come on," said Kenneth, "let's move these boys back into the room we were just in. Hunter, snap out of it."

"Sweet Jesus, Kenneth, you shot them. Where did that pistol come from?"

"Oh, Enid is always trying to get me to use Springfield 1911s, but I figured they was a mite too big for this job. The sub-Glock is my preference for close-in work, especially with the suppressor. I had it out and drawn while you were thinking of opening the door. Now, come on, let's get these boys into that room and out of the way before someone sees us."

For a second, Hunter hesitated, the fact of two dead men lying there in front of them on the floor too much.

"Hunter, snap out of it and give me a hand. Get that door opened at least. What do you think they intended to do with that pistol they had pointed at us? Greet us and say, 'Welcome to the Detroit Masonic Temple?'"

That was enough to bring Hunter back. The reality of their situation was that Brothers Kaufman and Cook meant them no good, and they were spellbound. Hunter and Kenneth would be as good as dead if all they meant to do was keep them for Hiram Abiff. The fact was that Hiram Abiff was coming tomorrow night, and that spelled disaster for the entire world if Hunter didn't get a move on.

He stepped to the knight, placed a hand on either side of the shield and twisted it first to the right, then twice to the left, then three times to the right and one last time to the left. The wall behind the knight opened inward into darkness.

They dragged the bodies into the empty room, and the door closed behind them and the lights sprang on. Hunter lay down the body of Brother Cook, and withdrew the dagger from his belt, inserted it into the slot and when the panel slid aside, they dragged the two men inside.

"We can't just leave them here," said Hunter.

"Wake up," said Kenneth, "the end of the world is coming tomorrow night and you're worried about two dead bodies left here overnight?"

Hunter looked up at Kenneth and said, "You know, you're right. It was just so sudden how you shot them that I got—"

"Don't think about. Come on, let's you and I get out of here and get gone before Brother Mihaloff catches up with us."

"Yes," said Hunter as he pulled his own Colt .45 pistol out from beneath his coat and started walking.

When they got to the final door, Hunter took a deep breath, tightened his grip on his pistol, and opened the door. But this time, thankfully, there was no one there. They immediately started walking down the hallway.

About halfway to the exit, they unexpectedly met Brother Mihaloff, who looked startled to see them.

"Watch it," said Hunter.

In response, Kenneth grasped his pistol that was in his pocket now. He had kept a watch all the while they were walking for just such a contingency as this. Brother Mihaloff was with three other brothers, and Kenneth wasn't sure if they were spellbound or not. There were so many people around that he didn't think they would try anything, though. But if they did, he was ready.

Brother Mihaloff surprised them by nodding vaguely at them, but walking away. He glanced back once at them, though, curiously.

"I see that Brother Mihaloff is curious about how you're still alive and walking about unmolested."

Hunter almost jumped out of his skin. Mr. Chirac had come on them so quietly that even Kenneth was surprised. But he recovered quickly enough.

"Yes, well, there's two more dead men that were just as surprised," said Kenneth.

Mr. Chirac's eyebrows shot up.

"Why you southern gentlemen never cease to surprise me. Does Brother Mihaloff know about their untimely quietus?"

"If you mean, does he know they're dead, the answer is no."

"Far be it from me," Mr. Chirac said, "to apprise him then. But, en ces moments difficiles, je tenais à te faire part de mes sincères condoléances."

"I'm not sure what that last meant, but what you said."

"We've got to be going now," said Hunter. "Is there something that you wanted?"

"Only to tell you, that my associate Ricci will be in this," here Mr. Chirac waved his hand around at the Masonic Temple, "building to shoot Hiram Abiff in the head when he bows and takes the chair. You should be close enough to him to have the remote go off so that he can be propelled backward into the chair at that precise moment. If you don't, we are all in for rather a bad time, I am afraid."

"Why can't you push him back into the chair when it is activated?" asked Hunter.

Mr. Chirac smiled rather piteously at him. He was as tall as Kenneth, but whereas Kenneth had unruly brown hair, Mr. Chirac had jet black hair that swept back from his forehead. He wore an immaculate suit, whereas Kenneth wore only jeans, a flannel shirt, and a bomber jacket. Kenneth was out dressed and out classed with his work boots and Mr. Chirac's polished shoes. Hunter felt similarly out of his element.

"Mr. Hunter, that is for you to do," said Mr. Chirac. "I am restricted from certain activities. That is one, which is why it pains me to say that I need you. I have wired the mechanism to go off and the chair to spill Hiram backward at the remote signal, and I assure you that the other chair will not open. Is that not quite enough? You must ensure that he goes backward into the abyss."

"I don't understand, but I'll do my part. I'll figure out a way to get close enough to shove him through. Trust me."

"That may be harder than you think, Mr. Hunter. Remember to activate the chair at the exact moment that he is shot and then shove him through and all will be well, that is, if your lady friends are successful in capturing or disrupting Eva Morgan. If not, well..."

"How did you know about—"

With a simple wave of his hand, Mr. Chirac walked away

"Strange fella, isn't he?" said Kenneth.

"Yes, he is, only he's not a fella."

"Yeah, which explains my desire to shove a shotgun under his chin and pull the trigger."

"Come on, let's get home and see if the women were successful and if Enid... stayed human for the night."

83

Rebecca and Marla were lost in the maze that was the warehouse. Their night vision goggles were active again because of the lack of light. They wound their way through, always on the alert for danger. Because the last run-in with Eva's goblins had been enough to keep them aware of their surroundings. They went through door after door, some opened, some closed until at last they came to another closed double door with a sliver of dull light shining out from underneath it. One last time, they checked to see that their safeties were off.

The plan was for Rebecca to open the door slowly, and Marla to enter next, whether with guns blasting or quiet like a mouse. It all depended upon what was in there. Rebecca took a deep breath, looked at Marla, who nodded okay, and slowly turned the knob.

The doors opened up onto a huge warehouse room filled with boxes stacked to the ceiling. Rebecca and Marla looked at each other. Rebecca nodded for them to go forward. They wound their way past oddly shaped crates reminiscent of the ending scene of Raiders of the Lost Ark. There were so many crates and boxes that it was hard to see their way through to where they were going. They trekked to the left and had made it about a quarter of the way through the crates when they heard a noise. Rebecca held up her hand and stopped.

It was a faint noise at first, and then it grew to something more tangible. A buzzing, almost a humming noise. Rebecca craned her neck, but couldn't identify it. She looked quizzically at Marla, but she shook her head.

In the green-yellow light of the night vision goggles, the world was a distorted view, but still representative of what was there and you still couldn't see around the corners, which was frustrating. But the stink that now permeated the whole place was the smell of goblins —a mixture of rancid meat and decay. Rebecca's skin prickled at that awful smell. It became almost overpowering.

"You six guard the circle while the rest of you spread out, while I attend to the Blazing Star. We must have this just right before the master arrives in this new world of his."

Rebecca stiffened. She knew that voice. The witch, Eva Morgan. The woman who controlled the goblins. The witch who had nearly taken her soul that night recently at Hunter's mansion. The woman who was here tonight to harvest the energy of the Blazing Star. The woman they had come to stop.

Marla heard her voice, too, and recognized it. She felt a stiffening of her spine, a tightening of her grip on the tranquilizer gun. That witch, tonight, would get repaid like she never dreamed. She thought she was invincible, but she wasn't. The problem was, she had to get past the goblins to do it, and they were coming her way right now. She could hear their lumbering footsteps coming at them. Marla looked at Rebecca for directions what to do.

By way of answering, she motioned Marla to stay down, put her earplugs in, and stepped out into from behind the row of boxes they were hiding behind, and switched from her tranquilizer gun to her SIG Sauer semi-automatic rifle and shot a surprised goblin full in the face. She kept going forward up the rows of boxes and ran smack dab into another goblin and fired off a three-round burst into its throat. Green goblin goo ran everywhere, and the stench was overpowering. She advanced further and when two goblins came, she laid them low with a double tap to their chest and one to the head for good measure. The noise was deafening. She was a one-woman machine of death.

One came at her from the side and swiped at her. She ducked and fired, missed and fired again, this time hitting it in the side and sent forth a gout of goblin blood. But while she was gunning him down, another reared up, fangs barred and grabbed her from behind. She dropped her SIG Sauer, and grabbed a knife from her belt, spun and stabbed upward, pinning its lower jaw to its upper. Next she took and a handgun from her waist and fired four bullets directly into its chest.

Suddenly, several boxes came tumbling down on her head. As she reflexively thrust up her arms, three goblins came scrambling over at her. She reached for her SIG Sauer semi-automatic machine pistol, but she was too late.

"Stop."

The goblins tumbled over themselves in their efforts to stop, but crashed into each other instead. Rebecca found herself surrounded by fallen goblins and confronted by Eva Morgan. She tried to lift her SIG, but Eva waved her hands and she found she could not lift her arms or move.

"Well, well, at long last you are mine," she said.

Rebecca spit at her, but the distance was too great.

"Oh, come now, is that the best you can do? You've come all this way by yourself. I imagine to gun me down?"

Eva threw back her head and laughed. Her laughter had a musical quality to it. She waved her hands again, and Rebecca's mouth was sealed. She struggled, but could do nothing to open it. Eva walked towards her as goblins surrounded her, growling and spitting.

"My, my—is there something you wished to say to me? What's that? Nothing, because you can't talk or move? I could kill you with a movement of my finger, do you know that? It's easy. And all those guns, all that armament would be useless to you."

Eva walked around behind Rebecca, studying her.

"Such a pretty woman," she said, and then, suddenly, she stiffened. Surprised, she was at a loss for words for a moment, and then, as she stumbled forward, she started to say, "You bitch..." as first the one tranquilizer dart and then a second tranquilizer dart pieced her back.

The spell broke on Rebecca as Marla's darts pumped enough tranquilizer to put down two horses. She raised her SIG Sauer and sprayed the three goblins in front of her. It was a mess, with green goo spattering all around. Rebecca heard Marla's shotgun firing rounds at anything that moved and, freed from the duty of cleaning up goblins for a minute, she wound the cable that she had brought with her around Eva's hands, feet, and arms. Next, she stuffed a rag in her mouth and tied it off behind her head. Finally, after checking around her for goblins, she tied a bandanna around her eyes.

As she was finishing, two more goblins burst on it her, but Marla finished one off with a round from her shotgun and Rebecca finished the other off with her SIG. Rebecca took her earplugs out of her ears and Marla did the same.

"I'm going to check for the Blazing Star while you guard her body," said Rebecca.

"Good. If she moves, I'm going to plug her, though."

Rebecca wound her way through the boxes toward the back of the room. It was a long way, and she was constantly on the lookout for goblins. But she didn't see any and was relieved to finally make it to the cleared semi-circle where Eva Morgan was to activate the Blazing Star. She could see the box that she took it out of, and the five pointed chalk outline with various symbolic deity's names inscribed on the floor. There was earth piled up at one corner of the chalk outline of the start, water at another, a burning candle at another, air at another, and a figure of something representing spirit at the final point of the pentagram. In the center, though, was the shattered crystal of the Blazing Star of Freemasonry. They had broken it into a million pieces by a stray bullet.

"Well, so much for that," said Rebecca, as she scuffed the magical circle with her boot, breaking its power. She did that for a few minutes, then satisfied that the circle was irreparably wounded, she turned around and made her way back to the place where Marla stood guard over Eva Morgan.

"The Blazing Star of Freemasonry?" asked Marla.

"Shattered by a random bullet," said Rebecca. "We might as well bag her and get out of here. You think that horse tranquilizer will keep her down long enough?"

"Oh yeah," grinned Marla.

"Well, let's get her wrapped up and out of here."

Marla took out of one of her pockets a large black plastic bag with air holes in the top while Rebecca did the same. While Marla covered the top half of her body with it, Rebecca did the same with the bottom half. When they were done, Eva looked like a rolled-up piece of carpet wrapped in plastic bags. Marla took the top half and Rebecca took the bottom half and they began carrying her out to the car, all the while ready to drop her and start firing at goblins or anything else. They struggled to get her near the entrance and had to put her down so they could catch a breath.

"Man, she's heavy," said Marla. "That witch must weigh two hundred pounds."

"It's just that she's dead weight. We should have given her that tranquilizer after she walked to the SUV."

"Yeah, come to think of it," grinned Marla.

"You ready for the last segment of the journey?"

"Yeah, I don't enjoy staying around here any longer than necessary."

They checked around for anyone, anything, but seeing nothing, they each took an end and lugged the tranquilized body of Eva Morgan the rest of the way. When they'd finally made it to the SUV, Marla unlocked it with the remote, and, taking a deep breath, they lifted the body in and arranged it.

"Well, that does it," said Marla. "Let's get out of here."

Marla went to the driver's side and got in seat belting herself in place when she heard a vicious growl. She saw Rebecca turn in the passenger's window's side where she had her hand on the door handle. Marla immediately reached for her pistols, having laid the shotgun on the seat beside her, but the seat belt got in the way. She unclipped the seat belt buckle and opened her door, grabbing her shotgun on the way. By the time she ran around the side of the SUV, Rebecca had fired a round into a goblin that was assaulting her. Its rheumy eyes and distended jaws were all that Marla saw. Then there were three of them attacking her at the same time.

Everything slowed down for Marla. She raised her shotgun just as another goblin appeared and knocked the rifle from her hands. Surprised and shocked at the swiftness of the attack, she grabbed for her pistol with her left hand and just as the goblin's hairy body came at her, she jammed the pistol under its chin and fired off three quick shots as it fell against her. In the background, she heard the explosion of Rebecca's SIG as she fell. As she scrambled out from under the fallen goblin, she saw to her horror that Rebecca had gunned down two of the goblins, but the third was on her. She fired five shots in rapid succession.

She hurried over to the goblin and forcefully kicked him off

Rebecca. What she saw horrified her. It covered Rebecca with green goblin blood. And then she saw her move beneath it all, and she gave a sigh of relief.

"I wish these things would die without this stinking goblin blood being spattered all over," Rebecca said.

She sat up and wiped her SIG off.

"Lord God, how I hate these things," she said.

Marla laughed.

"Girl, I thought that you'd bought the farm. Glad to see you're alive."

"Duck," said Rebecca.

In a rapid motion, she brought the SIG up and fired off a burst of three shots as Marla plastered herself up against the SUV, and turned around with her pistol. A hairy goblin had just opened its mouth with its hideous fangs to take a bite out of her. Instead, Rebecca's shots had gotten it right in its massive face.

Marla stared at Rebecca.

"Let's get out of here," she said. "You can clean up later."

84

When Hunter and Kenneth pulled into the garage, it was well past midnight. The girls had already checked in with them by cell phone, and they were successful. They got out of the car just as Ashley Hillis came out of the mudroom door and hugged Kenneth.

"I was worried about you," she said.

"Hey, what about me?" said Hunter.

"What? Oh, you can take care of yourself. It's him I was worried about."

Kenneth walked Ashley into the house with his arm about her, and Hunter followed. He looked around for Rebecca and Marla, but didn't see them.

"They're in the basement checking on that witch-woman," said Ashley.

"Is she—"

"She's all right," said Ashley.

"No, I meant is Eva Morgan all secure, is all."

"Uh-huh," said Ashely. "Sure, but her and Marla have her roped up tight and covered with black trash bags like you said to."

"Well, that's good. How's Enid?"

"Yeah," said Kenneth, "how is the old coot?"

"Still human, if that's what you mean. Although when I stepped out of the room, Darryl said that he saw purple worms go through his eyes once. Eddie was looking away, so he didn't see them. By the time he looked back, they were gone."

Hunter and Kenneth exchanged glances. Not good. Not good at all. But how fast Enid would turn was anybody's guess. He could turn that very night, or in one or two days, or even a week. There was just no way to know for sure. Hunter dreaded with every fiber of his being the change that was to come. He wished that the Sign of Hiram was real, but it wasn't. It was just a show put on for his benefit, or was it? Just trying to figure this out was giving him a headache.

"Come on, let's go see him, Kenneth," said Hunter.

"He's asleep now," said Ashley, "Darryl and Eddie are keeping a close watch on him, after that purple worms through the eyes incident."

"All right, what say we check in on the women?" said Hunter.

"Why don't you go without me?" said Kenneth. "I'm tired and I need to turn in. Ashley, you coming with me?"

"Do you mind?" she asked Hunter.

"Not at all. He deserves it and so do you. I'll find my way to the basement and see our guest."

"Good night, Hunter."

"Good night, Ashley, Kenneth," he said.

Suddenly he thought of Rebecca as the two walked towards the stairs, and he wished that kiss meant something more than it did. He waved hello to Darryl and Eddie and they waved back, and he began walking toward the basement stairs. It was funny how he was growing accustomed to the old mansion. As he walked down the stairs, he considered this. And suddenly, he felt very proprietary towards the old place. He wanted, for the first time, to have it be his; he didn't want Hiram Abiff to come back and lay claim to it and everything else in the world. He thought of Rebecca and truly didn't want her anywhere near Hiram Abiff.

He got to the bottom of the stairs, turned left and walked to the freezer where Pastor Mark's dead body was, and he shivered. They didn't want it to decompose, so it had been the logical place to put it, and it was cold, but not cold enough to cause death. Because of that, they had put Eva Morgan's tranquilized body there, too. Hunter opened the door and went inside.

The women were just on the verge of vacating the premises. There was Pastor Mark's body with a blanket over him, and Eva Morgan wrapped in black plastic beside him. It was odd seeing them that way. There were shelves and chemicals that Hunter didn't know stacked on shelves that would probably go bad in the warmer temperatures of the heated basement, but were safe in the refrigerated environment. And there were other things in boxes that Hunter didn't know what they were. Bartok had been a strange man, and he saved peculiar things.

"Hey, it looks like you really were successful," said Hunter.

Marla grinned.

"We were just giving her another injection of horse tranquilizer. We figured it couldn't hurt, and if it did, oh well," she said.

"Could we talk outside?" asked Rebecca. "It's freezing in here."

"Sure," said Hunter.

They went outside of the room, closed it and locked it, and walked back the way they had come. When they got to the kitchen, Hunter stopped and said, "Kenneth and Ashley went to bed already. Enid's asleep, and I think Darryl and Eddie are taking turns, one sleeping on the couch and the other sitting up with Enid, just in case. I'm going to check in on them and I'll be right back."

Marla said, "You want something to drink, Rebecca?"

Hunter came up on Eddie awake in the chair, and Darryl was stretched out and snoozing, his shotgun next to him. Stretched out like he was, he must have been six foot four. Sand colored hair and jug ears, he was the penultimate southerner to unsuspecting Yankee eyes. He was quick for his size, Hunter remembered, and a crack shot.

"Eddie," Hunter said, "how's the old man?"

"Well, he's sleeping a bit too comfortably, if you know what I mean."

A puzzled Hunter raised his eyebrows.

"No, I guess I don't know what you mean."

"When was the last time he went to the bathroom?"

Hunter stared at Eddie for a moment.

"I don't know, Eddie. I suppose he…" and he trailed off.

Bartok had quit going to the bathroom, too.

"Ahh, shit," he said.

"Exactly," said Eddie. "According to Ms. Ashley, it's been two days since he's been to the bathroom, and that ain't healthy, Hunter. It ain't healthy at all."

This was bad, really bad.

"And, well, he shouldn't be sleeping so easily, all roped and tied up like that. He ought to be... uncomfortable, is what I'm saying. He's been sleeping ever since you left."

Not going to the bathroom, sleeping a lot. Those were the signs all right. The change was coming on. Enid sure as Michigan weather was unpredictable, and it was too far gone to stop it. If, that was, they ever could. He felt a remorse come over him like when Bartok was changing, and he had to watch. There wasn't anything they could do except wait, and hope that he didn't change too early, in which event they would have to shoot him.

"Eddie," said Hunter slowly, "I know he's kin, but—"

"Way ahead of you. If we have to put him down, we will. You got to remember, we're Mosers, and your uncle Bartok taught us good. You understand?"

Hunter nodded.

"But Eddie, one thing I don't know if you know, is just how suddenly it can come—the change, I mean. I was there for Bartok, and I kept thinking he would get better."

"Go on, say it."

"Don't look in his eyes, Eddie. They trap you, his eyes I mean. It's hard to explain, but they do."

Eddie nodded.

"Yeah, is all you wanted to say?"

"No, when he turns, he'll... umm... shed... his skin, and well, this thing will come out of him that will be all tentacles. Do you know what I mean?"

"No, but I'll tell Darryl."

"And Eddie?"

"Yeah?"

"You'll want to pull the trigger before that... umm... happens."

"Okay."

"And keep pulling it until the slide cocks back and the pistol is empty. I mean that Eddie. Pull the trigger until the slide cocks back empty."

"Got it. And Hunter? Thanks."

Hunter looked at Enid, peacefully sleeping in his straight-backed chair, and shook his head.

"Old man, what did Bartok get you into?" he said under his breath.

He walked back into the kitchen where Rebecca and Marla were drinking coffee, looked at them and smiled a weak smile.

"How's Enid?" said Rebecca.

"Fine. He's fine."

"How is he really?"

"He's not so good."

"In what way?"

Hunter pulled out a chair, then changed his mind and walked over to the countertop and poured himself a cup of coffee. He looked at them both for the longest time before speaking.

"He hasn't gone to the bathroom in at least two days, and Eddie finds it disconcerting that he's sleeping so well, all trussed up like he is."

"So?" said Marla.

"That's the same thing that happened to my Uncle Bartok before I had to shoot him because he was turning into an alien."

"What?"

"It's a long story, Marla. It was terrible."

"Anything we can do?" said Rebecca.

"No, I'm afraid not. I wish there was. Thanks for asking though. You know, I love that old man. I really do."

"I'm sorry, Hunter."

"Yeah, thanks. Sorry to wax emotional, it's… the enormity of this whole thing is just now settling on me."

The house descended into silence for a minute than two. It was an odd thing. Hunter was just getting used to the general noisiness of the place, and then this. Enid Moser as an alien. Well, he'd make a good alien.

"Hunter?" said Rebecca.

"Yeah, well… I think we've figured out what we have to do to put down Hiram Abiff once and for all," said Hunter.

"How?" said Marla.

Hunter walked back to the table, pulled out a chair, and sat down. Suddenly, he felt as if a weight had lifted off him. He noticed that all this time, the grim certainty that Hiram Abiff would win had been nagging at him all this time. He felt that there was nothing they could that would stop him, like they had just been going through the motions. Now, with the fact of Enid Moser going to turn seemed to settle it in his mind that they would go down fighting. That maybe Hiram Abiff would come through the Borgo Pass with all the powers of hell at his beck and call, but he would not let that stop him from trying.

"The opening of the Empty Chair is critical," said Hunter. "Mr. Chirac has altered the mechanism so that when we push the remote actuator button, that the only one chair will open so that when Hiram Abiff goes into the Borgo Pass, it will close with him in there."

"Sounds like a plan," said Marla.

"But there are several flies in the ointment. One, we must push him into the Borgo Pass, so we've got to be close enough to him to do it."

"Okay," said Rebecca.

"Two, we've got to keep him in the Borgo Pass for a minute for the chair, or the doorway to close on him."

"Wait," said Marla, "who exactly is going to keep him there?"

"I think Kenneth and I have solved that, thanks to my uncle Bartok. We've got to push him into the Pass in the name of the Lord."

"What kind of bullshit is that?" asked Marla.

Rebecca gave her a look.

"Marla, don't take the Lord's name in vain. Besides, it makes perfect sense."

"It does? How?"

"It just does. There's power in his name."

Marla looked dubious. She had grown to like Rebecca, she truly did, but she didn't understand the religious thing. She found it... mystifying in the extreme. So instead of disagreeing with her, she just nodded.

"Go on," Marla said to Hunter.

"Well, Mr. Chirac's bondservant, or familiar, or whatever he is, is supposed to shoot Hiram in the head."

"That won't do it," said Marla grimly, "from what I've heard about from Traverse and the others, he just reassembles around the wound."

"Yes, he will heal, it's true, but it just might stun him long enough that if I shove him at the right time, it will give the chair time to close and lock him into the Borgo Pass, and remember what your father said," here he nodded at Rebecca, "anything in the Borgo Pass when it closes will be destroyed in the fires of hell."

"Can you get close enough to him to shove him?" asked Rebecca.

Hunter thought about her question. It had been the one aspect of his plan that had bothered him from the moment he conceived of it. What if Hiram didn't allow it? What if Hiram suspected something was wrong?

"Yes," he said, but he sounded a lot more confident than he felt.

Then he asked them how they captured Eva Morgan, and their exploits horrified him. In the next room, Enid dreamed inhuman dreams.

85

The town of Borgo was in chaos, and Hiram liked it that way.

Monsters from the bottom level of Hell were feasting on the living and the dead. Gigantic bat creatures were swooping down from the skies and capturing those unfortunates who tried to escape from the military complex, where other mutations were biting and clawing at them. The viaduct was where they had set up headquarters so long ago, and they just could not understand how this was no longer their haven. The town, with its picturesque shops, tree-lined streets and lampposts that perennially gave off their warm glow at night, was a distant memory. People running for their lives replaced them. The twilight of Borgo was full upon the men and women of Borgo, and it was terrifying.

Morning came.

Still, the mysterious fog did not dissipate. It became thicker, more sinister, wrapping its tendrils around everything that moved, concealing the horrors that could not die. The screaming was less, but omnipresent. The devils that haunted Borgo were still hunting, still grasping at every living man and woman that cowered in the darkest shadows.

Hiram Abiff did not concern himself with this world anymore. Tomorrow night, he would leave Borgo far behind. Tomorrow night was the evening that he would enter the real world, the world of men.

No longer would he be trapped in this dreary, artificial world. No longer would he be suborned to their attacking him day after day with their tiresome weapons, their rifles, their tanks, their artillery, their flame throwers, their poisons, their doomsday machines. All that was past for him now. He had defeated everything they had thrown at him.

And he had defeated every demon that had infested him over the last three thousand years.

Memories flooded his mind, back from the time when he was a brilliant architect, lauded by everyone, when King Solomon himself had so valued his services that he had begged him to construct the temple to his God. And he had supervised the construction of that oh so magnificent temple. The 70,000 porters he had at his command, 80,000 men he had supervised, the 3,600 supervisors that worked directly for him. He had been called the Great Architect. Cedar planks from Tyre, stone from the quarry, brass by the ton, chalcedony, pearl, onyx, diamonds and silver and gold, had been brought to him to decide where in the Temple it would go. The fabrics of purple, blue and crimson yarn, and fine linen that his men worked with- ah, he remembered. And the craftsman who could work with any kind of engraving that could execute any kind of design that he gave them. Of course, there were the plans of King David, embellished and enlarged upon by King Solomon, but the great work of accomplishing everything would not have been possible without him directing everything.

Hiram began to build on the second day of the second month in the fourth year of King Solomon's reign. The building was to be of the proportions of ninety feet in length and thirty feet in width. The portico was to be across the front, extending across the width of the temple, was thirty feet wide and thirty feet tall, with an inlaid inner surface of pure gold. The larger room was paneled with cypress wood, overlaid with fine gold, and decorated with palm trees and chains.

It was a magnificent structure, magnificent.

But Hiram had one fatal flaw —his pride. It was pride that took him down. King Solomon would not promote him to royalty, and he felt he deserved it. Why should he, Hiram, the magnificent Great Architect of the Holy Temple, not be royalty? He petitioned the King, and when the Temple was three quarters of the way finished, he found out that the king would not approve his petition.

Hiram was furious with the king's response. Only the King could be so callous. Only the King could be so utterly dismissive.

That was when the dark magician had first come to him. He had listened sympathetically to Hiram's cause. He had said how unfair the king was being. Hiram was the driving force behind implementing his grand scheme. Hiram, of course, had agreed. Who was the king to turn down his petition? Who was this king to act so peremptorily towards his request to be admitted to the ranks of royalty?

That was when the magician had asked him if he would like to rise to the ranks of royalty. Yes, of course, said Hiram. Then we should do something about it. Would he be willing to do something extraordinary? What did he have in mind? Hiram asked.

And that was the beginning of the end for Hiram. The magician spoke of the slight alteration to the temple, a little room in the temple's heart. A little room where something would be installed and they could worship another god—the Nephilim darkness. Hiram, to his everlasting regret, had accepted the offer.

Before he could complete the room, though, he was killed by three Fellowcraft Masons. They wanted the word for a Master Mason so they could receive higher pay. But Hiram had refused to give it to them because he was so arrogant. They had worked on the separate room, the secret room, and he promised them Master Mason's wages, but he was having second thoughts. They tried to get it out of him, but he hadn't budged. To his everlasting regret, three thousand years worth, he refused to give them the Master Mason's word. All he had to do was give them the Master Mason's word, and they could have received Master Mason's wages, but he hadn't. They had killed him for it in their frustration with a blow to the head.

He had awoken sometime later, a new creation of the Nephilim.

Re-created out of whole cloth to be a man again, but a man without a soul. An empty vessel that every demon could enter whenever they wanted. And so, for three thousand years, he had been home to every demon, every evil spirit that mankind could ever dream of and some that were even worse. They haunted him; they made him do things he would never dream of doing. The Nephilim would laugh when he begged for mercy, to be set free, to die. The Nephilim was all powerful. The Nephilim had dark magic at his beck and call. The one thing he could never do was materialize in the material world.

Meanwhile, Hiram was taunted by the spirits that inhabited his body. When he materialized in front of the president, it was a mistake. He freely admitted that now—it was a mistake. But fiends that the Nephilim could never understand had inhabited him. So what if Hiram killed the president's guards? Hiram was possessed by monsters that tormented him day and night. Sometimes he could barely keep his sanity.

The Nephilim had punished Hiram for that one slip; that one slip relegated him to the town of Borgo, and he had for seventy years been captive here. He could never forgive the Nephilim darkness for that.

His brother had somehow escaped the non-material world where God had commanded that the Nephilim must stay as their punishment for having disobeyed. And he had promised that he would take the Nephilim darkness into the land of the living where he yearned to be. But he, Hiram Abiff, had finally, after three thousand years, before he could escape, had consumed the Nephilim darkness. He had accomplished something that had never been done before in all of recorded history. He had eaten a Nephilim, and the result was that he could finally return to the land of the living as master of all that he surveyed. Nothing could stand in his way.

He would have his revenge at last on those who possessed souls; on the men, women and children of the real world. At last, everything that he desired would be his. He would crush the living and rule the world. With his Masons at his command, nothing could stop him. Five million Masons at his beck and call, and more to follow. They had infiltrated every level of government, every organization, in every country.

The entire world would bow before him.

But first, he would have his revenge on the brother that would have brought the Nephilim back. Yes, Mr. Chirac would be brought up on charges before his Masonic Court, so that all of Masonry could see what happened to those who disobeyed him. He would spellbind every Mason at the Detroit Masonic Temple, and they would take Mr. Chirac and flay him alive.

But first, he had a little surprise for the one called Hunter.

86

Ricci lay on his stomach in his small room, painfully reliving the moments of his punishment. He had no regrets about having done what he had done. His sister, Rebecca, was his secret, and it was worth dying for or worse. That girl must be protected at all costs.

He looked at the clock on his end table and it was five o'clock, time to get up and get ready for his meeting with Mr. Chirac. Slowly, he raised himself off of his bed and sat up. He flexed his massive muscles and cracked his neck. His back was still painful from the flaying he'd received from Spike. The little man had enjoyed it. Ricci would remember that.

His clothes were laid out for him. A black turtleneck sweater, black pants and black cushioned shoes were what clothes he wore on a mission like tonight. A black Navy coat and a pull down cap completed his ensemble. He was to go to the Detroit Masonic Temple carrying his weapon in a large case, speak to no one that he didn't have to, and proceed to the secret room in the Unfinished Auditorium that only he and Chirac knew existed. Spike had already taken care of the workman. He was, in his own way, a devious little bastard that Ricci knew he would have to handle in his own good time.

Ricci put on his pants and shoes first. They were the least painful. His undershirt, and finally his turtleneck sweater, which was immensely painful to put on, followed this. He had a mirror on his dresser and he considered himself. Looking from side to side, he was at last satisfied. He would not give Mr. Chirac the satisfaction of seeming in pain. The rifle was propped up near the corner of his bed. The case was beneath his bed, and he bent down painfully to pick it up. He straightened, placed the case on a chair, and retrieved his rifle. It was a CheyTac Intervention, a deadly American 7-round, detachable single-stack bolt-action sniper rifle made by CheyTac LLC. Even at night, it had a high accuracy rate and could hit a target. It had a flawless design that moved a .408 round down range well over at 3,000 feet per second. They designed the cartridge for accuracy by balancing the linear and rotational drag, helping the bullet to fly farther. CheyTac Intervention held the world's record for the best group at a distance of 2,321 yards.

It was a fine rifle, but it would do no good against a man like Hiram Abiff. He could blow his head off, and it would simply reassemble. It was pointless to shoot him at all. He would die to all the assembled Masons, and then after a reasonable time where all the Masons looked at him in horror, his head would re-form, he would stand up to gasps of incredulity and be healed. Ricci's part was all for show. He would shoot the man. It would do no good, and that would be that. The Masons would think he was a god—the Great Architect of the Universe.

And then what? He would co-opt the Masons, spellbind them into spreading out to control the world. He would introduce the Sign of Hiram, the miraculous healing device that he and Brother Mihaloff had cooked up to save the world. But when everyone in the world had one—except those that didn't go along with his new world order —they would be used to control the people of the earth.

Ricci didn't like the plan.

Under Hiram Abiff's strategy, Rebecca would have no chance. She would be one that didn't go along with having the Sign of Hiram implanted in her forehead, and thus would be relegated to... what? Death? Or worse. Ricci didn't know what he could do to stop Hiram.

He knew what Mr. Chirac had in mind for Hiram. Ricci would shoot Hiram. Hunter would activate the chair to open and would shove Hiram through the opening, but he had the nagging feeling that it wouldn't work. What if Hiram Abiff didn't allow anyone to sit near enough to accomplish shoving him through the opening? Or what if

Hiram Abiff knew in advance of Mr. Chirac and Hunter's plan?   And what if he took steps to prevent it? There were too many variables to contemplate.

With a sense of dread, he packed the rifle away in its case, shouldered it, and headed off to his six o'clock meeting with Mr. Chirac. He had the feeling, the very real feeling, that Mr. Chirac, for the first time in his long life perhaps, was afraid of Hiram Abiff. Ricci had never known Mr. Chirac to be fearful of anyone.   Ricci remembered twisting Hiram's head so that it was oblique to his body, and how he attempted to straighten it at Mr. Chirac's request. But Hiram's head had ballooned in size before he could get to it, causing Mr. Chirac to change his mind. In all of his exposure to magic, Hiram was still the strangest that he had ever seen. His body seemed to be made of... Ricci did not know what.

Spike was waiting for him outside of Mr. Chirac's impressive double doors. The little man had puffed out his chest and was acting like Mr. Chirac's personal butler.

"You're early," said Spike.

Ricci reached out and grabbed him by the neck. He picked him off the ground and swung him to the side. Spike hung there, choking. He brought his hands up to his throat and kicked his feet, but still Ricci would not let go.

"Don't you ever tell me I'm early or late," said Ricci. "Do you understand?"

Spike sputtered and turned red, but he could not respond.

"What's that you say?" said Ricci. "I can't hear you."

Suddenly, he let Spike go, dropping him to the floor.

Coughing, Spike still couldn't talk. He tried to form words, but they would not come. The double doors swung abruptly open of their own accord.

"Ricci," said Mr. Chirac from his desk, "it's good to see you back to your own self. Bienvenue à la maison. Come in, come in, my friend."

He accepted the invitation and stepped into the room. His flayed back still pained him, but it was healing. Spike had applied some of Mr. Chirac's cream to it. He didn't know what it did, but its soothing qualities had tempered his raw back and gradually even scabbed it over. But it still hurt. It wasn't an act of kindness, though. Mr. Chirac had ordered it, which did little to cover up the disdain he felt for the little man. Ricci carried his rifle in with him, like it was an appendage.

"Now Ricci, since I will be not attending the... um, festivities associated with the grand entrance of Monsieur Abiff, you will act as my sole representative."

Ricci hadn't bothered to sit down, and Mr. Chirac had not invited him to. It would be a grave insult to sit when Mr. Chirac didn't ask you, and Ricci had been punished enough. He grunted at Mr. Chirac's instruction that he would be his sole representative. Somehow, he did not expect Mr. Chirac would be there tonight, in case things went really, really bad.

"Spike will be in attendance in case something should go wrong," said Mr. Chirac.

Ricci remained silent. The little man had regained his composure, although he still struggled to speak.

"Permission to come in, sir?" croaked Spike from the doorway.

"What? Oh, my goodness, where are my manners? Yes, oh do come in. How thoughtless of me not to invite you."

The little man came in, rubbing his throat, glaring at Ricci as he did so. Ricci did not so much as glance at the guttersnipe.

"Now, you have something to add, Spike? I await it with bated breath."

Ricci caught the tension in the air even if Spike didn't. He had hated Spike since the day that Mr. Chirac had first brought him on. There was no use for the little man that he could see. He just occupied space. It would have been just fine with Ricci if Mr. Chirac used him to feed Lily, Mr. Chirac's black panther.

"Well, sir, I was just going to ask if we should clear out after Hiram was shot, or if we should stay around for a bit and see if he gets up."

Nearly a full minute passed while Mr. Chirac steepled his fingers and seemed to consider.

"What do you think, Ricci? I assume Spike is saying that he is... concerned... you might... miss. Hmm?"

"At that distance, I don't miss."

"Yeah, but Mr. Chirac, don't you think—"

"Yes?"

Mr. Chirac arched his right eyebrow. Spike caught the sudden menace in the expression.

"Uh… nothing. Really, nothing."

"No, no, please continue your jeremiad, Spike. j'attends avec le souffle bated."

"Huh?"

"Pray, continue."

"No, I think that was all."

"Are you sure?"

"Yes."

"Well, good. Now why don't you run along and await Ricci in the hallway? And Spike?"

"Yes, sir?"

"Never question my judgment again. Is that understood?"

"Uh… yes sir."

"Good. Then run along and wait in the hallway. And Spike?"

"Yes?"

"Close the doors on the way out, will you?"

And, as if he had been given a way out, Spike nodded vigorously and backed out into the hallway, closing the doors behind him.

"You see, Ricci, what I have to put up with when I am without your services?"

Ricci grunted.

"Yes, well, appropriately said. Now I have just one thing to discuss with you before you go on your mission. I deeply regretted the need to discipline you, but I must have total obedience. Do you understand how vital that is to me?"

Ricci nodded, and he said, "Yes."

He knew how important it was, but he would not give up his sister. He just wouldn't. Death was a preferable alternative.

"I simply will not tolerate disobedience. Do you understand?"

"Yes."

"Good, now when you return, we will discuss at further depth why you felt it necessary to meet with that… that hillbilly. Is that understood?"

"Yes."

It was at that moment, as he walked out the doors, that Ricci knew that his fate was sealed. Death was a preferable alternative. It really was.

87

Hunter slept fitfully that night. Hiram, the destroyer, kept swirling around his nightmares. The spectral phantasm of Hiram coming through the Borgo Pass and into the world of the Detroit Masonic Temple kept haunting him. Hunter pressing the button that would open the Empty Chair and it wouldn't work. Hiram smiling at him with that beneficent smile that seemed to say, "Did you really think that would work against someone with my ability to read your minds? That you could stand up against me? I am Hiram Abiff, and for three thousand years I have waited for this day, and I will not have you take it from me. Now die, little worm."

And Hiram Abiff had opened his mouth, distended his jaws wide and—that was when he would wake up, gasping for breath.

The dream was so real. When he'd calmed down, he wondered if Hiram Abiff were intruding into his consciousness, because it was virtually indistinguishable from the waking world.

When he finally got back to sleep, he didn't dream for a while, but then it started all over again. This time, he dreamed that the horse tranquilizers had worn off Eva Morgan. She'd woken up to find herself gagged with a plastic garbage bag over her head, cloth stuffed in her mouth and tape wrapped around it. And a piece of tape over her eyes. She tried to scream in rage but could only manage incomprehensible noises.

To his surprise, even strapped in as she was, Eva Morgan was not finished. She silently wove a spell that burst her bonds and freed her from her constraints. It ripped away the trash bags that were over her head. She sat up in the freezing cold of the storage room, and her eyes flashed with anger. Rippling with rage, she stood up and when she stepped up to the storage room door, she threw her arms wide and sent a burst of red energy that blew it right off of its hinges.

Then Hunter woke up again in the dark, sweating, his heart palpitating. He swung his head from side to side frantically. Nothing. Yet it was so real—it couldn't just be a dream—could it?

He dressed hurriedly, put on his shoes and went down the hallway past where Enid and Ashley slept, past where Rebecca and Marla slept, and made his way down the stairway to the living room where Enid Moser sat bolt upright in the chair. At first, he thought he was awake, but his eyes were still closed. Eddie sat across from him in the chair, while Darryl slept on the couch.

"Everything okay, Hunter?" Eddie asked.

"Did you hear anything strange coming from the basement?" he asked.

Eddie looked at him curiously.

"No. Why, should I?"

"No, I guess not. It's just that I had the strangest dream."

"The way things are going, Hunter, I'd take that seriously."

"I'm going to check things out in the basement."

"No. No going anywhere alone. Take one of the women with you."

"They're asleep, Eddie. I wouldn't want to wake them up for nothing."

"You're not listening. If you had a dream about something happening in the basement, then take it seriously and don't go down there alone. Savvy?"

Hunter was about to object, but he thought better of it.

"Thanks, Eddie. Now that I think about it, you're right. I'll take both of the women with me."

He turned around and went back up the way he had come. He went down the hallway and stopped at Rebecca's door, lifted his hand to knock when it opened. Rebecca stood there pointing a SIG Sauer semi-automatic weapon at him.

"I—" began Hunter.

"Don't bother. I already know. You woke up with a bad dream about Eva Morgan, right?"

She moved out of the way for Marla, and Hunter stepped aside. Both were fully dressed and ready for action.

"I just—yes, I woke up with a bad dream about Eva Morgan. She was waking up and—"

Marla headed for the stairs carrying her horse tranquilizer rifle in her right hand and with her shotgun on a strap on the other.

"Come on," she said, "we're wasting time."

Rebecca hurried after her. Hunter picked up his Colt .45 on the way off of the kitchen table. They stopped in front of the basement door, and Marla nodded, so Rebecca swung the door open after unlocking it. She stepped aside and Marla slid into the opening with the tranquilizer rifle. Some lights were still on, casting the entire laboratory in an eerie glow.

"Clear," said Marla at last, and walked down the basement steps with her rifle held out before her.

Rebecca went next, her SIG Sauer semi-automatic in the ready position. Hunter followed, but Rebecca held up her left hand to stop him. Marla had stopped before them and Rebecca stopped, too. The two women waited a minute, then continued on their way past the tables full of beakers, test tubes, and reagents toward the storage area. Hunter followed them, the Colt .45 gripped tightly in his right hand. They wound their way past the tables and fume hoods, the bookcases and the specimen trays until at last they reached the cold storage room door. It was still closed, just how they had left it.

"What do you think?" said Marla.

"I think we should open it," said Rebecca. "Only this time, you do the opening and I'll stand by ready to blast her. I'm tired of trying to tranquilize her."

"Wait," said Hunter, "shouldn't we—"

"No arguing about it, Hunter. Marla, get ready and open the door. Hunter, stand back."

Hunter ignored her. He had to see what was in that room. He held his Colt .45 at the ready. No one was prepared for what was inside. There, standing inside the doorway, in a swirling mist of cloud colored vapor, was Pastor Mark.

Rebecca lowered her gun.

"Pastor Mark?" she asked. "What—"

The loud report of Hunter's .45 shattered the air. One round, two rounds, and then a third. The first round was in Pastor Mark's face and the second and third went high into his body. Rebecca turned around in shock and Marla didn't know what to do.

"Get out of the way," shouted Hunter as he fired until the firing pin landed on empty. Pastor Mark's body fell to the floor with a thud. Pastor Mark's face was barely recognizable with the massive hole blown in his head by Hunter's Colt.

"What have you done?" shouted Rebecca.

Hunter was already reloading his Colt.

"He was dead, Rebecca. You know he was dead when he hit the ground from the second floor of Bartok's house. You know that—it broke his neck. Think, Rebecca, did he look alive to you?"

Marla's shotgun fired with a loud boom. While Hunter had been talking to Rebecca, Pastor Mark's reanimated body had slowly stood up. Marla blew his head completely off before he could take one step. Blood and gore spattered the storage area. A shocked Hunter and Rebecca pivoted to Marla and then back to Pastor Mark's now decapitated body. It was incredible. What in the world was going on?

Pastor Mark's bullet ridden, decapitated body floundered around for a minute, and then slowly rose again.

"What the hell?" said Hunter.

Rebecca, with a newly determined look on her face, raised her SIG Sauer and stitched Pastor Mark's body from his chest to his legs, blowing him into bloody pieces. She waited to see if the pieces would reform again and rise, but the quivering body parts seemed to have lifted for the last time. Rebecca stood there, her chest heaving, her face a mask of terror and resolve.

"Well," said Marla, "that was interesting."

No one said anything else for the longest time. They just stood there, waiting expectantly for whatever would happen.

"I- I-," began Rebecca.

"I know," said Hunter in a shaky voice. "Come on, we've got to see for ourselves whether Eva Morgan is even still here."

"Watch yourselves," said Marla. "Hunter, you'd better let Rebecca and I go first. No offense, but we've got bigger guns."

"Y'all okay down there?" called Eddie.

"Yes, Eddie. Go back to watching Enid."

"Okay, as long as you're okay, down there."

Marla said, "That guy is smart. Didn't come downstairs, even with all the shooting going on. Didn't leave his post."

Hunter thought about that. Eddie was smart, there was no denying it.

"Come on," said Rebecca, pointing ahead, "I can see her, just where we left her."

Rebecca, Marla, and Hunter moved forward through the cold storage area. It wasn't far from where Rebecca had indicated. There was Eva Morgan's body, tied up with tape over her eyes, a wad of cloth stuck in her mouth and tape around it, and garbage bags wrapped over her body to finish the whole thing off. Rebecca looked back at Pastor Mark's decapitated, destroyed body apprehensively, but he didn't move. Hunter looked back at Pastor Mark, too, and then back at Eva Morgan's body.

"I don't understand," he said at last.

Marla poked at the bag, got no response, and seemed mystified.

"I'm going to shoot her again with tranquilizers," she said, and before anyone else could object, she fired a tranquilizer dart into her thigh. She lowered the gun and said, "That ought to do it."

A stunned Hunter looked at her, and then at Rebecca. He had an uncomfortable thought.

"What if," he said, looking at the unfortunate Pastor Mark's body, which lay in pieces, "what if it wasn't Eva Morgan who reanimated Pastor Mark's corpse?"

"Well, if not her, then who?" demanded Rebecca.

"Hiram Abiff," said a subdued Marla.

"Yes, Hiram Abiff," echoed Hunter. "He is here, or he's got enough power that all the way from Borgo, he's able to reanimate the dead."

"It was awful seeing Pastor Mark standing there. I couldn't breathe for a moment," said Rebecca.

"Yeah, well, it didn't do me any good either," said Marla.

"Let's get out of here," said Hunter. "I don't feel comfortable down here."

They left the storage room and Rebecca locked it behind her. No one looked at or did anything with the body parts of Pastor Mark. It was too depressing. They looked away when they passed them. Pastor Mark was gone, and there wasn't anything to be done about it.

Marla led the way, and Rebecca followed, but Hunter hung back for a minute. Rebecca noticed and stopped mid-way on the stairs.

"What," she said.

"How did Hiram get past the wards?"

Marla stopped at the top of the stairs. She seemed confused, and then she got it, and when she had it, she looked more confused.

"That shouldn't be possible," said Marla.

"Exactly," said Hunter.

"Maybe wards will stop a witch, but they won't stop Hiram," said Rebecca.

"That's what I was thinking," said Hunter. "Maybe we're not as safe here as we thought."

"Well, shit," said Marla.

"Come on," said Hunter, "we better go check in on Enid right—"

"Hunter," screamed Eddie, "come quick."

Marla, Rebecca, and Hunter scrambled up the stairs. They ran through the kitchen, through the dining room and to the living room, where they saw Darryl and Eddie pointing their guns at Enid Moser. Kenneth ran to the top of the stairs in his jeans and nothing else other than his sub-Glock pistol in his hands.

"What is it?" he yelled before Hunter could ask the question.

"His eyes," said Darryl.

Enid looked right at Hunter, Rebecca and Marla. His eyes were bright blue, not the purple snakes that Hunter had half-expected. They shone like blue fire.

"Do we shoot him?" asked Eddie.

Kenneth came down the stairs to join the rest of the group, and Ashley followed him. The group formed a half-circle around Enid.

"I see you have assembled your whole band around you," said Enid, in a familiar voice.

"That ain't Enid talking," said Darryl.

"No, it isn't," said Hunter. "It's Hiram Abiff."

Silence settled over the room as Hunter made his solemn pronouncement. Enid stared at the men and women, one at a time that gathered around him.

"I'll see you burn in Hell," said Marla.

"Oh, I remember you, you're the child that escaped from Borgo," said Enid.

It was terror inspiring to hear Hiram Abiff's voice come through Enid Moser's body.

"I will come for you," said Enid. "I will find you and flay you alive."

"You were in my dreams," said Rebecca hoarsely. "You drifted in and out of them like smoke."

"So that was you I felt," said Enid. "Well, don't worry my dear, I will come for all of you. Tomorrow night will be your last night on earth."

Enid's eyes rolled back, and his head dropped forward.

88

Hunter slept in his clothes until eleven o'clock. He couldn't help it. He stayed up watching Enid with Darryl and Eddie until his eyes wouldn't stay open any longer.

Waking up on the couch in a sitting position wasn't a pleasant way to wake up for Hunter. He found out quickly that he ached all over. He found Eddie and Darryl had gone upstairs to sleep and Kenneth and Ashley had taken their place. Marla sat in a chair next to them and Rebecca was in the kitchen getting coffee. Enid Moser sat in the same place, in the same position. He still slept. Hunter knew some terrible changes must be going on behind those closed eyes. He looked around, blinking, and noticed that Kenneth had his Mossberg across his knees, Ashley had a .9-millimeter Glock laying on her lap and Marla had a shotgun held up high next to her shoulder.

"Well, hello, sleepyhead," said Kenneth. "If you didn't wake up soon, I would have to kick you."

"Yeah, coffee first," said Hunter. He stretched. "You people are sure loaded for bear."

"Here's the coffee," said Rebecca. "You drink it with cream and sugar?"

Hunter yawned. He seemed to do that a lot lately.

"Yeah, thanks."

"I'll get another—don't worry about it. You just wake up."

While Rebecca got another cup, Kenneth continued.

"Look, Hunter, we got to figure out what to do with ourselves. What's the plan for today?"

Hunter drank the rest of the coffee in a hurry. He stood up and stretched again. Man, it would be a long day.

"All right, let me take a quick shower, and I'll be back, and we can figure this thing out."

He went upstairs to shower, got some fresh clothes, and entered the steaming shower. Lord, that felt good. It was morning, and all the memories of Pastor Mark's reanimated corpse would not leave him, though. They had desecrated the man's body unmercifully; he thought. As the water poured down on him, he considered what power Hiram Abiff had to have to reanimate Paster Mark's lifeless body. It must have been astronomical to be effective over the miles and through the Borgo Pass. And to project his voice through Enid Moser's body, he had to have an incredible power to do that. Somehow, it didn't seem enough to shove him through into the Borgo Pass. It would be better to blow up the Empty Chair just like Kenneth had said. But he knew Hiram would just find another way in, and that would be disastrous. No, better to deal with him here and now.

He turned off the water and toweled off. The steam had built up in the bathroom, because he had forgotten to turn the fan on. He was about to turn and towel off the mirror when he saw the message appearing on it. He froze. Appearing as though by magic, the words formed, and he read them, standing there stark naked. It said:

Tick-Tock.

> *Your last day on earth as a free man.*
> *Tomorrow, you will be my slave,*
> *and so will your friends.*
> *Tick-Tock.*

He felt a sense of horror come over his entire body. Suddenly, he realized it was true. If he failed in what he was trying to do, all would be lost, and he would be enslaved to this ghoul Hiram Abiff. He thought of Rebecca. Oh God, she would be, too. He just couldn't allow that to happen.

Getting dressed, he couldn't get Rebecca out of his mind. She was as tough as nails, but he remembered the kiss she had given him on their way out to capture Eva Morgan. When he thought of it, he was more determined than ever that he wouldn't let that happen. He would have to shove Hiram Abiff back into the Borgo Pass and shut the door after him, so that the denizens of the Pass could devour him.

After he finished getting dressed, he exited the bathroom, walked down the hallway, and was about to turn into the stairway when he was stopped by Rebecca's voice.

"Hunter?"

He turned around and saw Rebecca standing there.

"Yes?"

She stepped close to him and looked into his eyes. He felt oddly uncomfortable, like he was standing too close to a fire and might get burned.

"How are you feeling?"

"Okay, I guess. What with the whole thing with Pastor Mark, I—"

"Don't go there. That was awful."

"Yes, it was. It felt surreal. And hearing Hiram talk out of Enid's mouth was bizarre. It seemed somehow sacrilegious."

Rebecca was quiet for a minute. She had something she wanted to get off of her mind, Hunter guessed, but she couldn't figure out how to say it.

"What is it, Rebecca? Is something on you mind? You can tell me, I —"

"Oh, shut up," she said.

And to his surprise, she kissed him again. This time, the kiss was long and hard. It lasted for almost a full minute before she broke it off.

"Now, get going, before I change my mind and deck you."

Baffled, Hunter finally nodded and turned to go, but at the last minute he turned and reached for her again, and kissed her hard in response. In a minute, when he was through, he looked at her.

"I guess I better go downstairs, or risk getting hit by you."

"You'd better."

He grinned, and, not bothering to think of the improbability of what had just happened, he turned and this time walked down the stairs with an odd smile on his face. When he got downstairs to the kitchen followed by Rebecca, who sat down, he looked at Kenneth, who had an odd look on his face.

"What?" he asked.

"Nothing," said Kenneth, "but if you are finished with your shower, I'd say we get down to business."

"Yeah, I guess we'd better," said Hunter, and he sat down, too.

"Well, what's the plan?" said Kenneth.

Hunter took a deep breath, tried not to look at Rebecca when he glanced around the room at the assembled people.

"What gives, Hunter?" asked Marla. "Are you sure Rebecca and I can't help?"

"I'm sure. You wouldn't make it to the tenth floor; in fact, tonight is an all-male night, so I doubt if you'd make it past the front door. Besides, who'd watch Eva Morgan?"

"There's that," agreed Marla, "but I don't have to like it. Why don't we just fill her full of lead and kill her? End of problem."

"I told you—we've got to have someone to give to Mr. Chirac in trade. And Eva Morgan's it. That was his price for making the Empty Chair mechanism to work."

"I still don't like it. All the action will go on in the Detroit Masonic Temple while we're babysitting her."

"I don't like it either," said Rebecca.

Ouch.

"Look, I don't see any way out of this. You can't be guarding Eva Morgan while you're at the Detroit Masonic Temple. You just can't."

"Next topic," said Kenneth. "That one's done with. What are we going to do about Enid?"

Hunter glanced into the living room where both Darryl and Eddie sat. Enid hadn't moved or changed position since Hiram Abiff had possessed him.

"I guess we still watch him."

Ashley spoke up for the first time.

"Hunter, what Kenneth means is he wants you to say it," she said.

"What?"

"That it's okay to kill him if he turns."

"Oh, Jesus. That's putting it rather starkly, don't you think?"

"It has to be said," she said, gently.

He considered it and realized for the first time that he didn't want to say it. He didn't want to say it was okay to kill the old man. But to turn him over to Mr. Chirac was something he wanted to do even less. Weren't there any other choices? Hunter turned to Rebecca.

"Rebecca, isn't there any chance that the Sign of Hiram—"

"No. He didn't want it, and I'm sure. It was a con job. It doesn't work. It just doesn't," she answered.

"Okay," he said, "then if he turns, we kill him, Kenneth. I don't like it, but there it is."

Kenneth nodded and got up to go relay the message to Darryl and Eddie.

Rebecca laid her hand on Hunter's arm and squeezed.

"It was hard," she said, "but it had to be said."

Kenneth came back and sat down. Message delivered. Moser was kin to those two men. They didn't like it, but like Rebecca said, it had to be said. The thought of killing Enid Moser was anathema to Hunter. He was an old friend. But if it came down to it, and he was turning into an alien monster that could harm or even kill them, well, then there was just no choice. It was him or them. And besides, by that point, Enid Moser would no longer be Enid Moser.

"So, you two," here he nodded at Rebecca and Marla, "will have to stay and watch over Eva Morgan. Ashley and Darryl and Eddie will watch over Enid's changing status. I don't envy any one of you for your jobs. Meantime, Kenneth and I will go meet with Brother Mihaloff and hope that we can figure out how to get close enough to Hiram to shove him through the Empty Chair opening, because right now, I don't have a clue how."

"You've got to be close to him, since you're a member of the Temple Guardians, right?" asked Kenneth.

"I guess so, Kenneth, but I don't know. Hiram's supposed to be coming through the Empty Chair portal at eight o'clock is all I can say for sure. For the rest of the arrangements, we'll have to find out from Rebecca's father, Brother Mihaloff. If he hasn't discovered the bodies yet of Brothers Kaufmann and Cook, in which case we'll be arrested upon going in."

Hunter found that oddly amusing, and he smiled. He stopped when he realized the others didn't find it the least bit funny.

"Sorry, it must be the stress," he said apologetically. "Kenneth, I don't feel like we should go unarmed, but they'll have heightened security at the doors, and I don't think they'll let us pass them with firearms."

Kenneth thought about that for a minute.

"Which doors will they be at?" he asked at last.

"I think at the front doors. That would make sense, right?"

"Yeah, well, we'll have to retrieve Brothers Kaufman and Cook's sidearms, I guess. That way, we can get past the guards at the front entrance."

"What? They're..."

"Dead? Yeah, I know. They've got no use for them. They might smell a little, I don't know about that, and they're probably stiffer than all get out, but we can always hold our nose until we get out of that secret room that you call a library."

Hunter was uncomfortable pillaging dead bodies, but it was all there was, really, when you got down to it. He couldn't think of any way to smuggle firearms into the Detroit Masonic Temple except to pillage weapons that were already in there.

"Okay, I give. We will have to scavenge them. But they won't do us any good against Hiram Abiff. We can shoot him all we want, but it won't do us any good."

"I'll vouch for that," said Marla, impatiently drumming her fingers against the table until she realized she was doing it. "But it might do you some good against the spellbound; you don't know how many of them there are. There might be twenty or thirty or even fifty of them."

Rebecca looked both grim and determined.

"Look, we should at least try to get into the Masonic Temple. We could help. There's nobody better with a gun than Marla, and I'm a close second. Besides, there are enough secret passageways through that place that I'll bet we could get in and hide in the unfinished theater or the Hiram Abiff theater or whatever they're calling it now."

"Okay, but what about Eva Morgan?" said Hunter.

"We'll tranquilize her ass into oblivion. As it is, I'm not sure how she's breathing, we've given her so much of the stuff. We'll give her a couple of more before leaving. She'll be fine, believe me. And we can have Darryl and Eddie take turns watching her while Ashley sits with the other and keeps a gun on Enid."

Hunter looked dubious. He looked at the grandfather's clock, which rang twelve o'clock noon. Time to decide. He'd already decided once, but was Marla right? The extra guns would come in handy, no doubt about it.

"Rebecca," he asked. "Are you sure you can get into the tenth floor of the Masonic Temple without being seen? And while you're at it, can you smuggle weapons in?"

For the first time in a long time, Rebecca smiled, and it was a radiant smile at that.

"Trust me," she said. "Come on, Marla, let's go tranquilize the hell out of Eva."

As Rebecca got out of the chair, Hunter realized for the first time just how resolute she was about beating Hiram Abiff, and it gave him hope.

"Well," said Kenneth, "I feel right good that we got beat on that one."

"Kenneth," said Hunter, "those horse tranquilizers give me an idea."

89

"Have you seen Brothers Kaufmann and Cook?" demanded Brother Mihaloff.

Hunter looked at Kenneth and then back at Brother Mihaloff. They were dressed, as everyone was, in tuxedos for the grand occasion of Hiram's coming.

"No, why? Are they missing?"

"They are," sputtered Brother Mihaloff. "I haven't seen them since yesterday. They just up and vanished."

"Maybe they had car trouble?" suggested Kenneth.

"What? I hardly think so. They could have called. They were supposed to be here by now. I could have missed them yesterday, since we were so busy with the arrangements, but they should be here or called. I've tried calling them, but it goes directly to voice mail," thundered Brother Mihaloff.

"Well, if I think of something, I'll let you know," said Hunter. "There certainly are a great many guests."

Just then, three men intruded into their conversation. The tallest of them said, "So this is the Fountain Ballroom, eh? Worshipful Brother Jack Walters here of Pittsburgh, and these are my associates Worshipful Brother Eugene Davis and Worshipful Brother Joseph P. Stone, Jr. How do you do?"

"Oh," said Brother Mihaloff, "so... pleased to meet you. I'm Past

Master Brother Mihaloff and this is... well, they seemed to have moved on..."

And moved on they had. They were walking toward the elevators. Hunter looked over his shoulders at the crowded fullness of the Crystal Ballroom and saw Brother Mihaloff frustrated by being the good host. It was impressive, Hunter had to admit. Seven hundred and fifty luminaries from the Masonic world all gathered together in the Crystal Ballroom for dinner. Then on to the Unfinished Theater, now named the Hiram Abiff Theater, to receive the World Grandmaster Hiram Abiff.

There were more than the seven hundred and fifty men from around the world. There were an additional roughly four thousand Masons, bringing the total to nearly five thousand Masons that would assemble in the room known as the Masonic Theater, ready to receive their Grandmaster. This would, Hunter knew, be a function of what was known in Masonry as the Blue Lodge, the core of all Masonry. The Scottish Rite, the York Rite and the Shriners were adjunct degrees. You had to be a Blue Lodge member to be in them, but there was no higher degree in all Masonry that the exalted position of Master Mason of the Blue Lodge. That was as high as it got.

That being said, no mere Master Masons of the Blue Lodge were invited. Only those members who were Past Masters of the Blue Lodge and were exalted members of the Scottish Rite, the York Rite, and the Shriners were invited. The real brains of Masonry. And these were invited from all around the world.

As Hunter and Kenneth walked to the elevators, they nodded and were greeted by members from India, from places as far away as Malaysia, from the great continent of Africa, from Russia, from a veritable cornucopia of locations from all over the globe. It was dizzying the number of people that they had met already. When they got on the elevator to take them up, there were ten more people to shake hands with and get acquainted. To his amazement, the reticent Southerner seemed to take to the meeting and greeting just fine.

Just as the elevator doors were closing, Brother Mihaloff squeezed in.

"Excuse me," he said.

"That's all right, brother," said a warm imitation of Santa Claus, complete with a potbelly and even a white beard.

"Yes, sure, come on in," said another tall, thin man. "Welcome, brother."

Hunter could not believe how often the Masons used the word "brother." It was like a code word. Every time that they didn't know what to say, they just simply added in the word "brother," and that seemed like it made it okay.

"Thank you, brother," said Hunter. "Come over here, Brother Mihaloff."

Brother Mihaloff squeezed back, exchanging greetings along the way.

"I thought you would follow us," said Hunter.

"I couldn't get away. I envy you," said Brother Mihaloff. "Now about Brothers' Kaufmann and Cook."

The elevator doors closed, and it made its slow ascent toward the Hiram Abiff Theater.

"Yes?" Hunter said.

Brother Mihaloff leaned in close, as though to whisper. Although the Masons were so busy talking to each other, no one else noticed.

"I don't know where they are," he said.

"All right, I'll check as soon as I inspect the Hiram Theater. They can't have gone far, though. I assume you've checked all the emergency rooms?"

"Yes, I've had Dr. Smith check them with no results. I've got people calling the police now, but so far, with no luck."

"Well, where could they have gone?" asked Kenneth.

"I don't know, I just don't know. I've got so much to do, now I've got to handle their stuff as well. Can you please check on them and see what you can find?"

Just then, the elevator arrived at the floor where the Hiram Abiff Theater was located. The men jostled past Brother Mihaloff, Hunter, and Kenneth to get off. They turned sideways so that they could get off last.

"How's Rebecca?" asked Brother Mihaloff.

"She's fine. Ashley Hillis is her new best friend. She's almost healed up from her encounter with the... you know."

"I'll call her when this is all finished. Hiram Abiff is finally coming, Hunter." He leaned in close and whispered, "All will be better when Hiram is here. Are you ready for that?"

Hunter and Kenneth had stepped off the elevator, while others piled in. Brother Mihaloff stayed inside and let them in.

Hiram Abiff was coming.

"All will be better when Hiram is here. Are you ready for that?" repeated Brother Mihaloff.

The doorway closed on an almost maniacally smiling Brother Mihaloff.

"Man, I tell you," said Kenneth, "that is one weird dude. And he'll call for his daughter when it is all over? Shit, man, that's callous. That's just callous."

"That is not the half of it, Kenneth."

Hunter looked around at the newly christened Hiram Abiff theater. It was truly a magnificent sight, and he felt a dread in the pit of stomach looking at all the beautiful architecture prepared for this being from another world.

The sculpted ceilings, the chandeliers, the wood-paneled walls; everything was tailor made for expensive elegance. There was recessed lighting in the ceiling, wonderful designs of nymphs and gardens, and beautiful sconces on the walls, with hidden lights that fountained colors. Rows of royal blue, sumptuously appointed seats, carpeting fantastic in its intricate silver and maroon displays. The cushioned, velvety colored seats were sectioned off with golden, braided ropes. And the elevated seats framed by wooden grandeur, high on the walls where one could have an operatic view of the stage, were breath-taking.

The stage itself was a masterpiece of artistic opulence. It was a reconstruction on the platform of the entire Romanesque room shrunk to fit on the magnificent stage. Hunter could see the four chairs there from where he stood over the heads of the assembled, milling around Masons. He could see the Empty Chair that Hiram Abiff would come through, and he gave an involuntary shiver. These men did not understand the monster that they were letting into their world. The danger that they were admitting into their lives was unthinkable.

Hunter looked at the clock on the wall. The time was five o'clock. In three hours, Hiram Abiff would come through the empty chair, and the world would change forever. Hunter looked at Kenneth, and Kenneth looked back at him, thinking the exact same thought as him.

Were they doing the right thing?

They were letting a demon into their world unlike anything the people of this planet had known. By all rights, they should just blow the chair up; but if they did that, Hiram would just find another way in, and at a time and place when they would least expect it. No, better to deal with him, if it was at all possible to deal with him now, on their terms.

It was now five fifteen p.m. In two hours and forty-five minutes, Hiram would arrive. Hunter wondered if Rebecca and Marla were in place.

90

Rebecca pressed the two stones that were astride the section of the wall, and the section swung away, revealing an entrance. After a quick glance around in the night, she stepped inside, followed by Marla. They put the rifles aside and slid their night vision goggles on and fired them up. The faux door swung closed, and they were in darkness. They were in the Detroit Masonic Temple. It was six o'clock. Outside the Temple, darkness reigned.

Marla brushed off the cobwebs.

"They don't use this much, do they?" she said.

"Not in the last seventy years," agreed Rebecca.

In the green-yellow light of the night vision goggles, all around them were stone walls. Passageways turned to the right and left, and one led to a stairway straight ahead.

"Come on, this way," said Rebecca.

"Where are we?"

"In the walls, where no one would ever think to look for us. They'll take us all the way to the tenth floor, but we've got some climbing to do."

"How'd you ever find out about this?" said Marla as they began their climb.

Rebecca stopped on the stone stairs and seemed to drift away for a minute.

"When I was a little girl, my father used to take me here, but I would always have to wait in the hallways while he had his Masonic meetings. One time, an old, really ancient man asked me what I was doing. I told him I was waiting for my father. He asked me how long my father would be, and I answered that I didn't know. He sat down on the bench next to me. We chatted back and forth for a while. I got the feeling, I can still see him in my head, that he knew these 'vast Masonic secrets.' I think he did, thinking back on it. He told me stories about the Masons and while he was talking, I interrupted him and mentioned these secret passageways that supposedly connected the entire Detroit Masonic Temple.

"I asked him where they were and he said, well, they were everywhere. I said that was cool. He said there was one nearby. He said nobody used them anymore, most likely they were forgotten about. I said no way and demanded that he show me one. He said he couldn't, but I wouldn't let it go. I kept at him and at him, and he finally yielded just to shut me up. He looked around with a mischievous glint in his eye and said we were sitting near one right now. He said, yes, we were, and stood painfully up, and asked me what I was waiting for and we walked over to the wall, and he pressed two masonic ornaments and bingo a door opened. We were about to go in when the door opened and the other Masons were going to come out, so he shut it and held his fingers up to his lips and then he walked away.

"I never told my father about that entrance, but every time that we went to the Temple after that, I would disappear down that rabbit hole. Over the years, I explored pretty much all of it. We can go anywhere we want undetected."

"Wow," said Marla.

Rebecca shrugged and said, "We've got a long hike ahead of us. We better get going."

The two women went up the long, winding, sometimes confusing flights of stairs. They were monotonous stone steps. The stone steps were fresh, hardly used at all. Or they were just plain forgotten. At each floor, hallways branched off to the left and the right. Once, Marla saw a light down one of them and couldn't believe it, but Rebecca seemed not to notice in her continual push for the Unfinished Theater —now known as the Hiram Abiff Theater. They stopped at the fifth floor to catch their breaths.

"Man," said Marla, "how would you ever know where you are at with no lights and all?"

"I used to go by flashlight when I was growing up. In all the times that I did, though, I told no one else about the secret stairways. I don't know why. I guess it was because there weren't any other kids that came or were allowed. These became my secret knowledge."

"Well, it sure is creepy," said Marla. "What with no lights and all. By the way, I saw a light on in one of the third or fourth floors. How come there are none on in the main stairways?"

"Oh, there are lights in these stairways, but they burned out long ago. There used to be three more on, but, well, they just got too old. No one knew about them to change them, so they burned out and weren't replaced, so..."

"Okay, I'm ready to get back to it," said Marla.

"All right, let's get to it."

And Rebecca led the way.

Up they went through the musty corridors. They lost track of time, they just silently counted off the steps.

"Let's stop here," said Rebecca.

"What floor is this?" asked Marla.

"I think the ninth floor."

Marla looked at her watch. The time read six forty-five. They seemed like they had been there forever, trudging their way toward who knew what. Marla thought back to the night when President Usman had first told her about the mission. He had obviously never intended for her to come out of the town of Borgo. He had intended for her to die there. A faceless death. Hiram Abiff awaited her in that place, and that was a certain death sentence.

Only she hadn't died there. Because of this woman, Rebecca, who had gotten her out of there. She would follow this woman into Hell and back. And that's where they were going—to Hell, to the entryway into the Borgo Pass, the Empty Chair, where Hiram Abiff would come out of and step onto the world stage. Returning to the world, he was exiled from when he was sent by the Nephilim Darkness to the town of Borgo, Michigan. Only now, he was to be free.

"The ninth floor," said Marla. "Only one more to go."

"Yes," agreed Rebecca. "Just one more to go."

"You scared?"

"I think I was born to do this. But I'm scared for Hunter and Kenneth. They're the ones on the front line for this."

"What if every one of the Masons becomes spellbound, including Hunter and Kenneth? Did you ever think of that?"

Rebecca took in a deep breath before answering.

"We put every bit of the firepower we've got into Hiram Abiff. Maybe, just maybe, that will break the spell long enough for Hunter to get his wits about him again to push Hiram back through the Empty Chair and finish him for good."

"Sounds like a plan. Let's get going."

With a new sense of purpose, they attacked the stairs. Carrying their rifles in one hand and pulling themselves along by the railing with the other, it was no surprise that they made it. The air smelled somehow fresher when they got to the tenth floor.

"All right," said Marla, "where to from here—to the left, or to the right?" asked Marla.

"To the left," said Rebecca. "There's a place we can set up our shots there. A little room there, that we'll see, but I think that—"

"Wait a minute," urged Marla. "I think I saw a light go on—"

"That will be enough, ladies," said a voice behind them. "Just walk toward the light, nice and slow, with your hands held high."

Rebecca and Marla froze. They both turned around at the same time to see a grinning Spike pointing a gun at them. Somehow the little man's eyes glowed red in the darkness, and Rebecca knew he could see in the darkness. Rebecca hesitated.

A deep bass came out of the darkness ahead of them.

"I'd do what Spike says," said Ricci. "He's small, but he's got an itchy trigger finger."

At that point, Rebecca and Marla knew they were sunk.

"Just carry the rifles in their cases into the room. That way, we've got one of your hands tied up with carrying them. You can lift the other hand in the air, though. And I've got a gun on you, so try nothing."

Rebecca thought desperately. How could she get out of this one? They were trapped in an ugly situation, with no escape.

"You listening?" asked Ricci.

Rebecca turned around and Marla followed. They raised their right hand.

"That's my girls," said Spike.

In the darkness, everybody moved forward. There wasn't any room to maneuver in the narrow confines of the passageway. There was nowhere to run and nowhere to hide, and certain death if they tried anything. So, they walked forward, not submissively, but they walked forward. Ricci's massive shoulders led the way. His bald head gleamed in the green-yellow light of their night vision goggles. As they approached the door, both Rebecca and Marla lowered their right hand and turned their goggles up on their heads. Ricci opened the door all the way for them, stepped back, and they went inside.

The room they entered was small and lit by a single bulb. There were two chairs, one-on-one side, and a bench with a high-powered rifle on the other side.

"Have a seat, but lay your rifles down and keep your other hands held high. Spike, watch them real close so that they don't grab those pistols or those knives they're carrying. Now, lay the rifles down. Go on now."

They complied. Rebecca and Marla both kept an eye for any opening, but they weren't given any. It was frustrating for both women to be so close, but there was nothing they could do. They were caught, and all they could do was follow orders.

"Now, Spike?"

"Yes?"

"Relieve them of their weapons. Carefully, slowly. Any sudden moves and I might be tempted to fire. You got that, ladies?"

The little man grinned and advanced on the women. Just the sight of him alone was enough to give Rebecca the creeps. Spike stopped and leered at them.

"What's the matter?" he said. "You think because of my size, I ain't too smart? You think you can maybe attack me while I'm disarming you? You think that—"

Those were the last words that Spike said. Because Ricci reached out with one massive hand and snapped his neck. He held him upright for a few seconds before the stunned women, and then dropped him.

"I never liked him anyway," he said. "Now you put him in the hallway where he's out of the way, and you two will have to man this place while I go down and deal with Hiram."

He put his gun away inside his coat. The two women just stared at him.

"Come on," he said, "we ain't got all day."

Marla hopped up and dragged Spike out into the hallway and dumped his body. Then she came back into the room, picked up her rifle case and opened it.

"Mine's better, in case you want to use it. Remember, the time to fire at Hiram is when he sits down in the chair, not a second before. Got it?"

Rebecca, who had sat there staring at Ricci the whole time since he had offed Spike, wanted to know, "Why are you doing this?"

"Because somebody's got to make this world safe from a monster like him, and I don't think Hunter can pull it off. And no offense, but that hillbilly that you guys got running interference for him ain't going to cut it neither," said Ricci matter-of-factly.

Standing up, Rebecca walked over to him. The disparity in their heights made him have to look down at her.

"I don't understand," she said.

"You don't have to," said Ricci. "Oh, and shut off the light before you open the shooting window, will you?"

And he left them there, as confused as the moment that he had snapped Spike's neck.

"I kind of like him," said Marla. "Now, where's that window?"

91

The plan was this—Brother Mihaloff was to act as the presiding Worshipful Master, with Hunter as the Tyler. Two others were brought in to replace at the last minute, Brothers Kaufman and Cook. They were introduced as Brother McKay and Brother Coil. They were to perform the Senior Warden and the Senior Deacon's role, respectively. Dr. Smith was the secretary, and Kenneth was assigned the role of Treasurer. That made up for the gap in attendance caused by the mysterious illness that caused Mr. Chirac to be absent and the complete disappearance of Brothers Kaufman and Cook. When Hiram arrived, Brother Mihaloff would step down to the Senior Warden's chair and take Brother McKay's place. It wasn't too bad or too hard to understand, but Brother Mihaloff had gone over the arrangements and places for everyone some fifteen times that day at least.

The whole thing was to take place on the elevated stage at the Hiram Theater, which was laid out in replicate form to the Romanesque Temple. The Worshipful Master's chair was in the East, the Senior Warden's chair was in the West, and the Senior Deacon's chair in the South. The Empty Chair was in the North. The bulk of the stage was empty space, except in the middle of it all, was the Masonic Altar, with a Bible placed in the center of it, with the Square and Compass, so central to Freemasonry, on top of the open Bible. The Treasurer and the Secretary sat on the left-hand side of the

Worshipful Master's station and the right-hand side, respectively.

The problem for Hunter getting to Hiram to shove him through was that the Tyler's position was on the far side of the stage, away from the Empty Chair. But Brother Mihaloff soon solved that. Brother Mihaloff had informed Hunter that he would initiate the brief ceremony by saying that someone sought admittance to the Lodge. Then after Brother Mihaloff's customary instructions to the Tyler to make sure that he wasn't a cowan or an eavesdropper at the door, Hunter would proceed to the Empty Chair. There, to the surprise of the assembled Masons, Hunter would step to the Empty Chair, bend down and pull the secret lever, and the Empty Chair would open and out would step Hiram Abiff.

The thing was, that no one except Brother Mihaloff, Brother Smith, Hunter, and Kenneth knew anything at all about what the whole thing was about. They thought they were going to see a new morality play. There was a buzz going around to the assembled seven hundred and fifty Masons who sat in the audience. No one knew really about what they were going to see, yet they were fairly excited about it. Such a worldwide gathering was really unprecedented in Masonic history. To have Masons gathered from every nation where they had a presence was truly remarkable, and the excitement in the air was palpable.

It was seven-fifty p.m., and the tension Hunter felt was unbearable. He was backstage, and Brother Mihaloff was checking his uniform and his jewels of office over for the hundredth time. He looked over at Kenneth, who stood stone-faced in line as Brother Mihaloff checked him out, too. Hunter peered out over the audience to see if he could see where Ricci was to fire the shot from, but he couldn't see any sign of him. He was worried, because if Ricci didn't shoot Hiram in the head, then all bets were off, and he would have to improvise. Looking back at Kenneth, he saw the grim set of his eyes and nodded. This would be a long night, whatever the outcome.

****

Rebecca and Marla had a perfect view of the stage. They were high at the back of the auditorium, behind a remarkably smoky glass window, which was made to look like a design decoration. The window slid up, so that they had a ledge to place their rifles on. When they were through shooting, they would slide it down and be done with it. That was the theory anyway. The Masons below in the dark auditorium wouldn't see a thing.

Hiram Abiff would step out onto the stage from the Empty Chair, and two silenced shots later, his head would explode. That would stagger him just enough to allow Hunter to shove him back through the Empty Chair and the Borgo Pass would consume him. Rebecca wished she felt confident that's how it would go down. She wondered if Hiram would immediately, as his first action, use his black magic on everyone in the room, rendering them spellbound, thus effectively neutralizing Hunter. Then where would they be? Hiram would then become the most powerful man on earth, having an army of Freemasons to do his bidding.

Rebecca felt guilty, though. The Sign of Hiram would work. She had lied to Hunter, but for a good cause. Enid Moser had asked her to concoct the story about it being a fraud because he didn't want to be saved if it meant using black magic. He would rather die as a decent man, never having been touched by Hiram Abiff's sorcery. He would rather be traded to Mr. Chirac than endure living a life based on Hiram's torturous device. Besides, if Hunter was successful, then the Sign of Hiram would cease to work, and that was victory enough for Enid Moser.

They had the lights out, and their night vision goggles activated so they could see clearly and their two rifles were ready. The rifles were suppressed, so there would be little sounds to identify them by.

"Just ten more minutes to go," said Marla.

Rebecca just nodded.

She wished Hunter luck with his self-appointed task, but more than that. She thought of how she had impulsively kissed him at Bartok's house. Was it just that he looked like her dead fiancé? Or was it more than that? She felt strangely attracted to him, but that had to take second place now to the job at hand. Besides, if they weren't successful, then Hiram Abiff would own this world.

Would he really be the anti-Christ? Rebecca thought about that—was it really possible that he was the devil, or a surrogate of the devil? Really, was that even remotely possible? All the dreams she had concerning Hiram—could they be real? Could Hiram Abiff's coming really portend the end of the world?

No, it couldn't be, but it might be. She remembered what it said in the Book of Revelation. There were just too many discrepancies. Hiram Abiff was born in the Middle East. That much was true. The Bible referenced "the beast" in Revelation, pictured as an individual, the man who was the political leader and head of a beastly empire.

The beast would receive a deadly wound to his head, and it would be miraculously healed. He would supposedly exert mesmeric authority over the entire world and demand the people worship him. He would wage war against God's people. But was that Hiram Abiff?

Rebecca believed that the beast in Revelation was the Antichrist, the one who will "oppose and will exalt himself over everything that is called God..." He would also be called "the man of lawlessness" and "the man doomed to destruction." Or was Hiram an impostor as Hunter had said, imitating the beast just to gain control, and would he then abandon them to pursue goals of his own? Her head spun with the variations.

Just concentrate on your job. Fire at his head. The bullet would do the rest. But, according to the Bible, his head wound would heal. Rebecca felt uneasy about this, though. His head would heal, just like in the Scriptures. Was that a coincidence?

"Marla?" she asked.

"Yes?"

"Suppose we peppered him with shots instead of two rounds to the head? I'd really like to keep firing at this monster. But Hunter wouldn't like that. Stick to the plan, stick to his plan."

"Yeah," said Marla, "so?"

"We'd better stick to the plan."

Rebecca wondered where Ricci was right now.

****

It was ten minutes to eight o'clock, the hour when Hiram Abiff could leave this blessed world of Borgo behind him. He paced impatiently in front of the Empty Chair. When that chair came down, he would exit the town of Borgo, and that was the last time he would ever set foot in this blessed place. He would walk through the Borgo Pass, and he would finally step out through the opening caused by the other Empty Chair, and that would be that.

Stepping onto the stage, he would take his place as the rightful ruler of the world-wide assembled body of Freemasonry. Eva would have harnessed the power of the Blazing Star. The Borgo virus would have infected every conceivable computer in the world to make them ready for their savior—Hiram Abiff in the flesh. Hiram would be the savior of the world, and he would be invincible.

His horrible eyes lit blue behind his glasses with the excitement of it. He rubbed his hands together with glee. He would take their world to whole new levels of necromancy. His magic would be expansive, powerful, limitless in scope. Their whole word would be at his mercy.

He planned to make them pay for all the indignities visited upon him. The merciless villagers of the Gadarenes, the tormenting children of Galilee, the imprisonment in the ruins of King Solomon's temple for which he wished the Roman garrison that had imprisoned him were alive today so he could kill them all over again. All the memories came flooding back to him. He thought of that little man, Robert Louis Stephenson, and all the trouble he had caused him. All because of that book The Confessions of Mr. Hyde.

He thought back to the most troubling man of all—Jesus. Jesus. He remembered looking at him from his rock prison, where he was tortured by the Nephilim darkness. Jesus, who could have set him free from the demons that afflicted him. Jesus who could have given him surcease from a life of pain and agony, but he didn't. He didn't even know that he was there. Or worse, he knew, but he did nothing.

Five minutes until eight o'clock.

He couldn't stand the waiting. It was sheer agony to stand there when he could walk through the Borgo Pass and be free. When he could make the quick trip through that tunnel between worlds, and step out through the other opening and he could breathe the air of a non-created world again. For seventy years, he had breathed the same stale air of the town of Borgo. But at last, at long last, he would breathe it no more.

They, all the people, were the re-animated dead in Borgo. Each of them, born again after death in order to be killed again and reanimated. An endless cycle of life and death. Hiram could have destroyed them all if he so wished, instead of having them continually come back to life. His power, it seemed, was endless. He had not yet thought of the things he could do with it.

He would begin, though, by basking in the admiration of some seven hundred and fifty Masons, then he would immediately go to the assembled five thousand in the main Masonic theater. Hiram was so used to hiding from people in his past that to finally be worshiped as a —dare he say it—as a god would simply be his crowning achievement. He would wallow in their admiration.

Soon, though, he would have to enforce discipline on all those billions of people who disobeyed him. Yes, and the Masons would have the Sign of Hiram emblazoned on their foreheads and they would live forever.

Those who did not, would become the walking dead.

92

The auditorium was deathly quiet. The lights were dimmed, and the seven hundred and fifty gathered Masons were expectant. Slowly, the curtain raised on the lit stage. Brother Mihaloff sat in his elevated chair in the East, the Worshipful Master. Lord of all he surveyed. Hunter as the Tyler, sitting near the stage's edge. Brother McKay sat in the West and Brother Coil sat in the South. Kenneth sat to the right of Worshipful and Dr. Smith, as the secretary, sat to Worshipful's left. The Empty Chair sat alone, with no one sitting in it, as was customary in the North.

Hunter stood and gave the sign of a Master Mason's duegard to the Worshipful Master.

"An alarm has been raised at the Inner Door, Worshipful," he said.

"Who comes here?" asked Brother Mihaloff.

"I don't know, Worshipful, it is most strange. The alarm seems to come from the Empty Chair."

This was not standard Masonic ritual. Something strange was afoot, and those in the seven hundred and fifty man audience suddenly came alert. Where on earth could this be going? They all, to a man, listened more carefully.

"What? The Empty Chair, you say?" said Brother Mihaloff.

"Yes, Worshipful."

Again, the duegard of a Master Mason.

Now, Hunter had the attention of the full retinue. An alarm from the Empty Chair? Unheard of, in all of Freemasonry.

"Brother Senior Warden?"

Brother McKay stood and gave the duegard of a Master Mason.

"Worshipful Master."

"The Tyler says that an alarm has been raised from the Empty Chair. Do you know who goes there?"

The Senior Warden looked dubious.

"No, Worshipful."

Again, the duegard of a Master Mason.

"Brother Senior Deacon?"

Brother Coil stood, looking as mystified as the Senior Warden. He really did not know what was happening. He assumed they would simply reenact a Masonic ritual, declare the whole of the auditorium now open in the Master Mason degree, and welcome all the dignitaries.

"Uh… Worshipful Master."

Here he gave the sign of the Masonic duegard.

"The Tyler says that an alarm has been raised from the Empty Chair. Do you know who goes there?"

"No, Worshipful."

Again, the sign of a Masonic duegard.

"Most strange," said Worshipful Brother Mihaloff.

He conducted himself in an almost regal manner, showing restraint for the growing sense of excitement he felt. In a moment, he was about to introduce to the assembled Masons a three-thousand-year-old man. It was the culmination of his life's work. Brother Smith felt the building excitement, too. Hunter seemed quiet, subdued, as befitted a man who was about to introduce to the world the greatest man that ever lived. Little did Brother Mihaloff know the cause of his unease.

"Brother Tyler," he said in a solemn tone, "proceed to the Empty Chair and see who goes there."

Once again, the sign of a Masonic duegard.

Now, the curiosity of the assembled Masons was seriously piqued. The assembled Masons leaned forward in their chairs to see whatever was happening. Nothing like this had ever before happened in all

Masonry, and to say that their interest was aroused would be to put it mildly.

Hunter walked across the stage, trying to fight back the panic that was rising in his gut. He glanced at Kenneth, only to see the man nodding at him to continue. It was with an odd sense of horror that he completed the distance remaining between him and the Empty Chair. He stood before it, thinking of all the centuries that it had been called the Empty Chair, devoid of its meaning until this very night. Hiram's Chair—it would forever now be known as that. Hunter felt a sense of impending dread descending on his shoulders. In a minute, he would let mankind's worse nightmare into the room. Screaming seemed the only thing to do.

He wondered again if he could somehow—but no; he had to do it. If he didn't open the chair, Brother Mihaloff would. If he tried bolting it closed, then Hiram would just find another way through and any chance of destroying him would be lost forever. There was only one opportunity to eradicate Hiram Abiff, and that was to let him in.

Hunter kneeled down in front of the Empty Chair and pretended to inspect it.

He stood and addressed Brother Mihaloff in a voice as steady as he could. Making the sign of the duegard, he began:

"Worshipful Master, there seems to be a mechanism at the base of the chair. I don't know what it's for. But there is a lever, hidden in the recesses."

"Well, pull the lever, Brother Tyler. Let us see what it's for. Perhaps it is the lever which opens it, and we can see who seeks further enlightenment in Masonry."

"Yes, Worshipful."

The sign of the duegard to the Worshipful Master, and then, taking a deep breath, Hunter bent down, and after a moment's brief hesitation, he pulled the lever, and the Chair opened. The Chair lowered all the way. Hunter imagined the magical signal sent through the Borgo Pass to the other Empty Chair in the town of Borgo, and then the Empty Chair opening in that city. Hiram would begin walking, walking the careful thirty-two steps through the Borgo Pass.

Surrounded by the dead in the Pass, the demons and the monsters screeching outside the membranous reality, howling to get fresh meat when they saw Hiram walking through, but unable to break through.

Hiram would walk, even now, through the Borgo Pass. Hunter stood up and back.

He saw him coming. His short stature, his nearly balding head horseshoed by a ring of hair. Now he could see his glasses shining like twin quarters. His average width shoulders and his slightly bowlegged walk.

All belying the fact that the most dangerous man in the known universe came up out of the shadows and onto the stage. He smiled at Brother Mihaloff, he smiled at Dr. Smith, seemed puzzled by Kenneth, but when he turned to Hunter, he smiled a radiant smile. The Empty Chair slowly lowered back into place.

Hunter panicked for a moment. He almost pushed the button on his automatic remote for the Empty Chair before Hiram sat back down in it. He withdrew his hand from his pocket. That would never do, because Hiram had to be seated in the Empty Chair or it would never work.

"Worshipful Grandmaster of the World, Hiram Abiff, sir, at your service," he said, and the crowd gave an involuntary gasp.

He gave a slight bow to punctuate his statement.

"Worshipful Master, I introduce to you, and the assembled Freemasons from far-away lands, the Worshipful Grandmaster of the World, Hiram Abiff," said Hunter.

Immediately, the Worshipful Master Brother Mihaloff stood.

"Brothers," he said to the officers of the lodge, and to the entire assembly, "please stand to give honor to the Worshipful Grandmaster of the World, Hiram Abiff."

At first no one in the audience gave credence to what he said, but gradually, with Hiram Abiff facing them, and Brother Mihaloff raising his hands in encouragement, they rose to their feet. First one, and then another. When Brother Mihaloff clapped, they did, too, without knowing exactly why. The applause began as first one man clapping, and then another. As it gradually reached a crescendo, everyone was on their feet and clapping wildly. Finally, Brother Mihaloff held up his hands. Into the silence that followed, he spoke.

"Brothers, it is my honor and privilege to introduce to you Grandmaster of the World, Hiram Abiff. Let us now be seated and let him speak."

Confused, but willing to play along, the men sat, as did Brother

Mihaloff and the officers. Hunter stayed by the chair, awaiting the moment Hiram sat down.

Hiram waited until silence ensued before he walked to the center of the stage. He had his hands clasped behind his back. His eyes flared suddenly bright blue, and just as suddenly the audience fell under his spell.

He turned his head and Brothers McKay and Coil were under his spell. In fact, only Hunter and Kenneth were not. Hiram smiled at the two of them. He turned back to the audience.

"Gentlemen, you are the leaders of the Masonic world, and I congratulate you one and all for coming. What I am about to tell you began a long time ago—nearly three thousand years ago, in fact. For that is the time that I come from. From the time of King Solomon's Temple. I was the architect behind the drawings. I was, as you say, the Great Architect."

Here he paced back and forth before the mesmerized audience. He totally ignored those Masons on the stage, and instead was focused on the people before him.

"Several of you find that hard to believe; that I am a three thousand year old man, but I am."

Hunter was amazed by the ease with which he had spellbound them. One minute they were men with critical reasoning faculties; the next they were like brain dead zombies—seven hundred and fifty of them. He looked out over a veritable sea of the spellbound. Hunter wondered if shoving Hiram back through the chair was even possible.

"Yet, I was an unrecognized genius in my time. I was building King Solomon's Temple. When he asked me what reward I would like for my efforts when the Temple was complete, I did not hesitate. I asked to be made royalty. I thought that was a reasonable request for someone such as myself to ask. The merest 'yes' was all it would take, a simple signet ring affixing a seal to a document, and voila, it would be done. But he would not. I was taken aback by that."

Even as he spoke, Hunter realized that this was the first time that he had heard the Hiram Abiff story. Should he believe it or not? What if Hiram was lying? What was the purpose of telling his story, anyway? Was it self-vindication?

"Let me be honest, I was crushed by that."

Was he telling this story as a purgative, for the first time that he had ever told this story? Or did he feel the need to tell this story for some other reason?

"I was lower than you'll ever know. I wandered around that night, an inconsolable man. I went from place to place, despondent about ever achieving my goal of ever becoming royalty. And then, that was when the magician found me. He soothed my every fear. He told me that if only I would do something for him and his master, that he would cause a spell to be cast on King Solomon. This spell would make him see reason, would turn his judgment around, and he would make me royalty.

"I at first demurred. I wondered if it was even possible. He assured me it was. Just build a small room in the Temple and place what came to be known as the Blazing Star of Freemasonry in it. That was all, just that simple little room and I would become royalty. And, to my everlasting regret, I agreed.

"Yes, I left that meeting with renewed vigor in my step. Just one little room hidden away in the Temple and put something in there and I would be royalty. But on my way home that night, I met with three Fellowcraft Masons. Three workmen, that I did not know, who demanded of me the word of the Master Mason, so that they could get paid the wages of a Master Mason. I refused them, of course. In the end, after beating me most severely, 1 was murdered in cold blood. But I still would not give them the word of a Master Mason, not to save my life.

"They hid my body in an effort to conceal the murder, but other Fellowcrafts soon discovered where they had lain the body. When King Solomon came to see my body, he cried out because of my death, and because they would have to finish the Temple without my guidance. He demanded to see who was responsible for the murder, and the three Fellowcrafts were brought forward. Then King Solomon decreed that the three Fellowcraft who murdered me would suffer horrible deaths for it. But I was dead; I was beyond caring.

"But when King Solomon left my body in that grave and returned with his retinue to their home, my nightmare was about to begin."

****

"When is that guy going to shut up and sit down?" whispered Marla.

"I don't know, but I sure hope it will be soon," murmured Rebecca.

They sat leaning forward on the window ledge, rifles pointed at Hiram's head. The room was dark, and the only light came from the stage below. Through their rifle's scopes, they could make out Hiram's head, which was their target. As he paced back and forth across the stage, they tracked him.

"Hunter is seated near the Empty Chair," said Marla.

"I know."

"I don't know if he's close enough."

"He'll stand up when Hiram comes back."

"Rebecca?"

"What if he can't? What if he's spellbound, too?"

"We'll have to wait and see."

But that was the very possibility that worried Rebecca.

93

Hunter listened as Hiram detailed how he had been brought back to life by the magic of the Nephilim Darkness, only as a man without a soul. How the Nephilim darkness had endlessly tortured him for not completing the room in the Temple. How the Temple had been destroyed. How he could not die. Demons had infested him because he was soulless and because of that powerless to prevent them. More and more demons would come and go in his resurrected body, and he simply could not stop them.

How he had been given a second chance when the Jews rebuilt the second Temple, and he had failed at that, too. How the Roman soldiers had locked him in the catacombs beneath the second Temple and how their chains had held him until he had been freed by the Knights Templar.

On and on, layer after layer, detail upon detail, would he never tire and sit down? Hunter grew increasingly nervous. He couldn't think of anything except pushing the automatic button in his pants pocket when Hiram did finally sit down.

He went on and on about the torture he endured, and he grew quite animated about it. The audience was eating out of his hands as he regaled them with the tale. Hiram was reliving the experience in the here and now. He looked over at Kenneth, who seemed just as tense as he was.

Still, Hiram droned on.

Hunter didn't know how much time had passed. He literally lost track of time. It was like he was in a time vortex with no way to get out.

"Hello."

He felt like jumping out of his skin. Hiram Abiff was right in front of him. But that was impossible. Hiram Abiff was still standing up, pacing the stage, telling his story to the assembled Freemasons. Was he hallucinating?

"You can't be here..." he sputtered.

Hiram looked at himself pacing the stage, then looked back at Hunter and smiled.

"I assure you I can be in literally two places at once if it suits me."

Hunter cringed back in his chair. This was impossible, simply impossible.

"You are right now thinking that it's not possible. Such an easy man to read. Why, when I am finished with retelling that story to the audience, I shall reassemble into one man so I can walk to the chair, sit down to their thunderous applause and get shot in the head. Mr. Chirac's man Ricci shall pull the trigger and do the deed, and I shall wait a minute and then reassemble my head, to the amazement, to the utter joy of the assembled masses. And then, with that coup d'état complete, when I have resurrected myself yet again, I shall be accepted for the miracle man that I am. We shall then go introduce myself to the assembly of five thousand Freemasons in the Detroit Masonic Theater and act this whole morality play all over again. When that is through, we shall have done quite enough damage for one night, eh, Hunter?"

Hunter's mind was spinning. Still, the doppelgänger of Hiram lectured on while the other Hiram stood talking to him. What if he shoved the wrong Hiram through the Empty Chair when it opened? Could he really multiply himself endlessly?

"You can't win, Hunter, you truly can't. I have had three thousand years to plan this out, and my powers, which were minuscule in the beginning, have grown to immense proportions. In the end, you and yours shall be my slaves."

Kenneth stood up and pulled out the nine millimeter that he had taken off of Brother Kaufman's dead body and went to fire at Hiram, but Hiram simply raised his hands and froze Kenneth in his tracks.

"Sit," he commanded, and Kenneth sat. "Now put the gun into your mouth—"

"No," shouted Hunter.

"Why?" asked Hiram.

"Because it's unnecessary. I'll behave."

"Oh, you'll behave anyway," said Hiram, "simply because I'll compel you to, or I'll squash you like a bug."

His glasses glowed blue so that his eyes disappeared.

"No wait," said Hunter urgently. "I'll comply because... because you'll squash me like a bug if I don't."

Hiram's glasses became clear again, and he actually smiled

"You may put the gun," he said to Kenneth, "back where you took it from. You see, that wasn't so hard, was it? I rather like being the master of this world. Now, it's a terrible thing what the women have done to Eva Morgan. Horse tranquilizers? Oh, but I shall awaken her when I'm through here, and she shall take her revenge on the two women in the most creative ways. Now, it's time to wrap up my tale of woe, and sit on my chair, I think."

And the audience burst into such thunderous applause that Hunter turned his head to see the double of Hiram take a deep bow. Something about Hiram building a third Temple in Jerusalem. He turned again and saw that the other Hiram was smiling. He looked again, and the Hiram, who had been addressing the audience, walked directly into the other Hiram, and then they merged. It was incredible to see. Then he raised his hands and the other on the stage officers walked toward him, with Brother Mihaloff leading the way.

Again, Hunter got the feeling of surrealness. How could this be happening? And yet it was happening. He was about to play his part in the greatest morality play ever conceived. Hiram Abiff would be shot in the head, and in the brief space of his time to reassemble, Hunter had to activate the chair and shove him through and pray that Mr. Chirac had done his part.

"Brothers, we are gathered here together to celebrate the life of our Grandmaster of All, Hiram Abiff," shouted Brother Mihaloff. "We shall keep silence until our next meeting in the Detroit Masonic Theater of five thousand Freemasons, where we shall unveil a special surprise—

the Sign of Hiram."

The Sign of Hiram.

The implant in the forehead, thought Hunter, that would forever enslave them to Hiram's will while promising them to cure all diseases and to prevent all diseases. The lure of living forever.

"And now and forevermore," intoned Brother Mihaloff, "we shall have a new location for the mastery of the Lodges. We shall designate the Empty Chair, which shall be lifted to be the highest chair in the lodge, the seat of our Grandmaster Hiram Abiff."

Again, the thunderous applause, but this time, Brother Mihaloff raised his hands for silence.

"Brothers, would you all please stand with me in silence, as Grandmaster Abiff takes his rightful chair, the Empty Chair, which shall forever more be called the Chair of Hiram?"

As one, the audience came to their feet, and the Officers lined up on either side of the Empty Chair. Hunter felt a sudden fear seize him. In a few moments, he would have his opportunity to accomplish putting Hiram Abiff back in his chair or not.

Hiram held up his hand, and the room fell silent.

"Fellow Masons," he said, looking directly at Hunter, "it is with great pleasure and humility that I accept your invitation to be your Grandmaster. Soon, very soon, we will unite all Masonry under one banner. I will re-write the Charges of Freemasonry. No longer will we be divided into Scottish Rite and York Rite and Shriners and so forth. We shall be united into one Freemasonry. One fraternity of Man that will represent the consolidation of power of the entire Masonic world and you, the seven hundred and fifty of you, will become leaders in my organization, the one true Masonry.

"Seven hundred and fifty strong. You will transform the world. We will become truly a force to be reckoned with, and we shall lead the world. Those that obey us will be gifted with the Sign of Hiram. Those that will not obey, will feel our iron heel."

Again, the Masons, spellbound to the last man, burst into applause. Hiram raised his hands to quiet them down.

"And now, I shall ascend to the Empty Chair which shall henceforth be known as Hiram's Chair in my honor."

While the rest of the group stood at attention, Hiram beatifically smiled at them all, and then he broke out into an evil grin.

Hunter wondered what it would be like to have the whole place spellbound before him. He wondered at the three-thousand-year-old man, with such evil intentions for his reality. There was only one chance to stop him, and he resolved to take it. He reached into his pants pocket and put his finger on the automatic button that would send the Empty Chair backwards.

"Oh, and Hunter?" asked Hiram just before sitting down.

It was with a sinking feeling that Hunter answered, "Yes."

Hiram waved a hand and suddenly Hunter was paralyzed. He literally could not move a muscle.

"You shall stay as you are. Your plan, while a good one, is not to be. You see, I rather like you immobile. And then when we are through getting me seated, and I am made the official Grandmaster of all the World's Freemasonry, we shall have a first Masonic trial.

"You and your friend Kenneth will be the first people to be executed for treason against me. Do you think you can have a fair Masonic trial with any of these men? Hmm? I think not. They are, as you would say, zombies. Oh yes, did I not tell you that, besides making all the assembled Freemasons helpless before my supreme will, that I can read minds? Really, all you people are too pathetic."

****

At that exact moment, Ricci was walking from the back of the auditorium towards the stage. Hiram would have noticed that and wondered what went wrong with their plan, but he was looking at Hunter. But Ricci was coming for Hiram Abiff. He'd seen enough of life to know pure evil when he saw it. Hiram was no good for this world, Ricci was certain of that.

As he strode down the center aisle towards the stage, he thought of all things that he could have been, if only things had turned out differently. His whole family had thought he must have died in that prison fire, so improbable, so long ago. That was for the better. It was better that they thought he died that night than knowing the agreement he had made, and learn of the life he had lived. He had made a deal with Mr. Chirac—a deal with the devil. And for making that deal, he had been set free the night that the prison had burned so long ago.

He heard Hiram Abiff prattling on and he just knew what he had to do. Making the steps that led up from the auditorium floor to the stage, he climbed them. Always cognizant of his surroundings, Ricci felt a burning in his chest. It was the symbol of his power that Mr. Chirac had implanted in him, and he felt the pain of the original searing moment when it had cauterized itself into the skin of his chest. Only three inches in diameter, it was Mr. Chirac's mark of ownership that was blistered into his bosom. The symbol of his power had such an awful sound to it. He had the magic of the Nephilim burned into him.

Footsteps firm as he walked up the steps, he climbed the rest of the way to the stage. With a grim set to him, he continued walking.

****

"He's walking to the chair now," said Marla, aligning her scope to Hiram.

"About time," said Rebecca.

They were two sharpshooters, tracking their target, when an enormous mass of humanity momentarily filled their screen. In a second, it was gone.

"What was that?" said Marla.

"Ricci."

"What's he doing on stage?"

"You've got me," said Rebecca. "But he's out of our line of vision. That's what counts."

"Now if Hiram would only sit down."

****

Hunter was immobilized, and he had experienced nothing like it in his life. How was Hiram able to magically induce that with a wave of his hand? Hiram was like nothing he had experienced before in his whole life. He couldn't move, not even an inch, but he had to because everything else depended on it. He strained, but he just could not do it. He tried to exert himself, but nothing moved. What was wrong with him? As Hiram neared the Empty Chair, he had his finger on the button to activate it that would make it lean back, but he couldn't move his finger at all.

He concentrated, but it was no use. His fingers, his whole body, was paralyzed. There was no way he could move them. He was going to let everyone down. Rebecca and Marla expected him to activate the chair and shove Hiram through. But he wasn't able to do it.

Suddenly, an image of Rebecca at the mercy of Hiram Abiff came to his mind, and he recoiled at it. He could never let that happen, never. He concentrated all his will power on the finger that was on the button. No use. It wouldn't budge. The picture in his mind of Rebecca at Hiram's beck and call, a slave to his every whim, wouldn't leave him. He tried again and again. Finally, he got his index finger to move a little. Thank God, that was all he needed was that one finger if only he could activate the button.

Hiram turned before the Empty Chair and sat down. Hunter could only move a finger, but he had to try. Maybe the Empty Chair falling back would be enough.

Two silenced shots made through way through the auditorium and suddenly Hiram's head exploded. The assembled Masons stood, too stunned to react. Brother Mihaloff and the other officers, except Hunter and Kenneth, reacted in grim amazement as Hiram's head, now a bloody mess, sprayed over the chair and the wall behind. Pieces of his flesh and bone were everywhere.

Hunter struggled with his finger, trying to push the button, and he was almost there, but not quite. Ricci came up to him then, a hulking menace with a purpose. He almost had it when Ricci reached into his pocket and finished squeezing the button for him.

"Tell Rebecca I love her," said the big man.

As the chair finished lowering, Hiram Abiff's head began to reassemble. Like little sparks of dark light uniting, they slowly came together. First his eyes, and then his nose. The officers of the Lodge now stepped back, their hands to their mouth. The audience was coming alive in confusion as Hiram's spell was temporarily thwarted by his premature death. Shouts from the assembled members who were stunned by the bewildering circumstances. They were just seeing Hiram's head assembling.

Ricci glanced at Hunter.

"You tell her, you understand?"

Hunter blinked his eyes in acknowledgment. He wanted to say that he understood, but that Hiram Abiff must be pushed back into the Borgo Pass that was now opening behind the chair.

"I got this pal," was all Ricci said as he rushed forward toward the now flattened Chair.

Hiram Abiff registered his astonishment as Ricci grabbed him up and literally ran like a footballer headed toward the goal line into the Borgo Pass. A few seconds later, the Empty Chair closed. Hunter could see vague outlines in there, Ricci holding tight to Hiram, Hiram screaming in frustration as the door to the Borgo Pass finished closing.

Brother Mihaloff, coming out of a trance, as did all the rest of the assembled Masons, said, "What just happened?"

Hunter was too shaken to answer immediately, thinking instead of the awful fate Ricci had to endure. Anyone caught in the Borgo Pass when the Empty Chairs closed was doomed forever. The membrane that protected those in the Pass would dissolve, and all the monsters of Hell would come after whoever was inside. They would be forever at the mercy of demons that ripped and clawed outside, looking for someone to devour, someone to eat.

Finally, when he had a few seconds to gather his thoughts, he whispered, "Nothing happened. Nothing at all happened."

Hunter knew at that moment who had fired the shots that took Hiram Abiff down—it was Rebecca and Marla. He thought again of Ricci, who had given up this life, for a life of endless torment at the hands of the demons of Hell.

94

It was only the second time that Hunter had been to Mr. Chirac's home, and this was by far the grimmest, because this time he had to go inside. Kenneth and Marla were at the step before the door with him, and Darryl and Eddie in the truck had their guns trained on Enid Moser and Eva Morgan, both of whom had been tranquilized to hell and back. Rebecca was at home again, taking care of her father, who was recovering from years of being spellbound.

A tall, thin man answered the doorbell after he rang it a second time. He had a hairless pate and giant wire-rimmed glasses that made him look more than a little odd. He was maybe fifty years old. His attire was odd, too, in that he wore all black—black coat and black tie, a black shirt with black opal cuff-links, black pants and shoes. Hunter had the distinct impression that they were dealing with an undertaker, except that his eyes were all black too—not a hint of white showed anywhere at all.

"Yes?" he said.

"I and my guests are here to see Mr. Chirac."

"And whom may I say is calling?"

For a moment, the man's all black eyes held him; he found it hard to think.

"Just say that Hunter and his two friends, Kenneth and Marla, are here to see him. We bring two gifts, which Darryl and Eddie are in the car guarding until we go in."

The man nodded, then closed the door and disappeared from sight.

Marla said, "You think he's going to let us in?"

"Oh, I think so. Otherwise, we would never have found this place," said Hunter.

"Be quiet, someone is coming," said Kenneth.

Sure enough, the door opened again. Standing inside was the tall man.

"Mr. Chirac says you may enter."

"I'll have Darryl and Eddie bring the gifts in, too," said Hunter.

The man looked confused for a minute. His face was that of a predator in black, and Hunter involuntarily took a step back, away from the door.

"I'll see if that is acceptable," said the man, and he closed the door again and left.

"He sure is creepy," said Marla.

"Creepy is definitely the word for it. I get the distinct feeling that we interrupted his reading How to Murder and Eat Your Guests when we arrived," said Hunter.

"You talk too much," said Kenneth.

"Sorry, force of habit," said Hunter. "When I'm nervous, I talk."

When the butler—if that's what he was- came back and opened the door, he said, "You may come in, and your friends. Bring the presents, too."

Hunter motioned to Darryl and Eddie that things were okay, and they opened the car doors. He and Eddie went back to help them carry out the appointed tasks of carrying Enid Moser and Eva Morgan. Kenneth helped him with Enid Moser, whereas Darryl and Eddie carried Eva Morgan. Both were heavily sedated with the horse tranquilizers. Eva stepped aside to let them carry them in first, where they met the man in black and followed him down the elegantly appointed hallway.

The air in Mr. Chirac's house was suffused with the light odor of lavender. The champagne-colored rug made no sound as they walked down it. Marla glanced up occasionally as she followed the men at the chandelier-like fixtures on the ceiling that had the delicate look of suspended ice crystals, arranged in a circular halo of soft pink light. In a living room off to one side, Marla could see a glossy black piano so polished that she watched a curved image of herself move across its side as she went by.

They eventually came to a pair of exquisitely appointed doorways bracketed by rosewood marble, which the tall dark man stopped at and knocked.

"Mr. Chirac, your guests are here," he announced.

After a slight pause, a mellifluous tone said, "Excellent. Do come in."

The double doors opened of their own accord. The tall man didn't touch them. Hunter was sure of that. But Hunter didn't really expect anything else in Mr. Chirac's uncanny residence.

He sat behind his desk, but stood at their entrance, and motioned them in with a graceful arc of his hand.

"Come in, come in and welcome. I assume you've brought me some token of your feasance to me?"

Hunter and Kenneth laid out Enid Moser in the center of the room, and Darryl and Eddie arranged Eva Morgan right beside her. Hunter stood and stretched his back. When did Enid get so heavy?

"No," Hunter said, "I'm fulfilling a bargain, but not a signed document."

"Ah, details. Now Hunter, perhaps you can introduce me to our guests.

"This is Marla. You've already met Kenneth, and this is Darryl and Eddie."

Mr. Chirac seemed to study her as he rose behind his desk. He took in her sleek black hair, her lovely face and her beautiful figure. His dark, attentive eyes took in the fine lines of her neck, the sheen of perspiration in the hollow of her throat, and noted how her breasts pulled tight the fabric of her shirt. He nodded an unconscious nod of approval as he discreetly followed the inward curve of her waist and the outward flare of her hips.

"May I say, Hunter, that you introduce me to the loveliest of women?"

If Marla was affected by his attentions, she didn't show it. Hunter tried to ignore Mr. Chirac's predilection for beautiful women. He had to concentrate on what he came here for, get it over with. He thought again of Ricci's sacrifice, of Enid Moser's impending offering of himself, and he steeled himself.

"I've brought you Eva Morgan," he said.

"Yes, I see," said Mr. Chirac as he finally took his eyes from Marla.

"I'm sorry about Ricci."

Here, Hunter got the shock of his life, as Mr. Chirac's face took on a cheated look, a hateful visage that was so unexpected he took a step back. His face, he would later swear, took on a red cast, his eyes turned bright yellow, and then, just as quickly, it was gone. But the vitriol in his voice remained.

"I shall never forgive him for that act of desperation."

"It was the only way," Hunter recovered and said, "that it would get done. Hiram had me paralyzed, and the entire group of men were under his spell. How could Ricci be unaffected?"

Hunter didn't want to think of Ricci's sacrifice, but he did.

Mr. Chirac seemed to draw inward at that, and he paced behind his desk. At one point, he stopped his pacing and lifted his right hand to his lips. "Ah, the sigil, of course. The symbol of..." here he seemed to realize that he was talking out loud and caught himself.

"So, in your opinion, it was the only way to stop Hiram Abiff?" Mr. Chirac said.

"Mister, I was there," said Kenneth unexpectedly, "and I can guarantee you, there was no other way."

Mr. Chirac reluctantly took his eyes off Hunter and turned to Kenneth.

"You seem to appear in the most unexpected of places," he said. "But whom, pray tell me," and here his eyes bored straight into his, "shot Hiram Abiff if Ricci was on the stage."

"Well—" said Kenneth, but Marla interrupted him.

"I did," she said. "Me and Rebecca. We were both in on it."

"Ah, a remarkable shot, Miss Marla, but then did you also kill my man, Spike?"

There was a certain undercurrent to Mr. Chirac's question. A matter of payment, if Hunter was believed, but Marla's answer relieved him of that consideration.

"No," she said, "that was all Ricci's doing. Not saying for his role in Rebecca and Sodom's shackles that she wouldn't have loved to do it, but, like I said, that was all Ricci's doing. He said that he never liked that man, anyway."

"I see," said Mr. Chirac. "Ah well, mourir et se reposer en paix, no?"

"Anyway, I brought you a replacement for Ricci, as per our agreement," said Hunter.

"Ah yes. But my agreement was for living replacements only."

"Oh, he's alive, all right. In fact, he so didn't want to come, that we had to dose him with horse tranquilizers before we could load him into the car, same as Eva Morgan."

Both Eva Morgan and Enid Moser had the upper parts of their bodies covered with pull downed black trash bags, so they couldn't be seen. Mr. Chirac came out from behind his desk to examine them.

"Fascinating. Mr. Hunter, I didn't think you had in you to turn over a confederate so willingly."

He was doing it because of his promise to Enid, and it was killing him to do it. When he thought of the old man beneath that trash bag, it was agonizing. But he'd decided that he was going to do it, so he gritted his teeth and carried on.

"He was," he said, "a lot more irritating than you know. I hope you put him to good use."

"Oh, don't you worry, I shall," said Mr. Chirac, in a way that foretold the evils that he intended for Enid Moser.

"The Blazing Star of Freemasonry was destroyed in the fight to capture Eva Morgan," said Hunter.

"Yes, how unfortunate. Now Miss Morgan shall have to pour payer le joueur de cornemuse, as they say, or, as you say in English, to pay the piper."

Kenneth said, "Well, if that completes the transaction, we've got to be going, Hunter. We've got business to attend to."

"Yes, well, goodbye Mr. Chirac. I hope I never see you again in this lifetime," said Hunter.

"Of course, you may bring your lovely assistant at anytime," here he nodded at Marla. "But I wouldn't count on it. We shall see rather a lot of each other, I suspect. Francois will show you out now."

Hunter saw with alarm the movement in Enid Moser's trash bag.

The tranquilizer must somehow not be as effective on Enid as it was on Marla. Perhaps it was because of the change. Hunter desperately wanted to leave before he had to answer that question.

Francois was leading the way, and the others marched out the door behind him with Hunter bringing up the rear. Just as the others were leaving out the front door, Mr. Chirac came out and called, "Hunter?"

Reluctantly, Hunter fought the urge to run. Instead, he turned around and said, "Yes."

Mr. Chirac came up to him, towering over him.

"Aren't you forgetting something?"

"What?"

"Tsk, tsk, Hunter, why you are forgetting my ghost box."

Hunter thought about the Ghost Box, now an almost useless device with the Blazing Star of Freemasonry destroyed.

"I'm going to get to that in a few days, Mr. Chirac. I've got things to wrap up."

"Just don't forget, Hunter, you owe me."

"I said I would," said Hunter stiffly.

"Good," said Mr. Chirac, "then until we meet again, I bid you au revoir."

Hunter could not believe his good fortune. When he walked down the others in the car and got in, he was never so happy in his entire life. Marla was behind the wheel and Darryl and Eddie were in the SUV that followed. Kenneth was sitting in the back, and he slid into the seat next to her. He looked at Mr. Chirac's house and wondered about Enid.

"You saw Enid was waking up, didn't you?" said Kenneth, leaning forward in the seat.

"Yes, I could see that."

"Do you want to stay and watch the fun?"

"No, I believe we'd best get out of here while the getting is good. Things are going to get ugly when Enid wakes up and turns into an alien."

"Yep, I'm guessing so. Miss Marla, would you mind terribly beating it real fast?"

Marla looked in the rear-view mirror at Kenneth's smiling face, and then she floored it and headed out of the neighborhood as fast as she could.

95

It was ten o'clock in the evening at the house, and Rebecca was home taking care of her father, who had a nervous breakdown after the incident at the Detroit Masonic Temple. Dr. Smith was under some of care, though they wouldn't say what. Darryl and Eddie were asleep, since they needed it from so many hours watching Enid, and Kenneth and Ashley Hillis had gone to bed early. That left only Hunter and Marla awake in the Bartok mansion.

For a long while, Hunter just stared out the big picture window leading out to the front lawn. He couldn't stop thinking about Enid, he just couldn't. That old man had been his salvation after Bartok's death. He'd straightened him out, that much was for sure. What did it matter if his mannerisms were those cultivated in the Deep South, because they had grown on Hunter. He'd rather fancied that his Southern accent was affected, but not too much. He'd turn into a good alien monster, he decided, and, if he was lucky, kill Mr. Chirac. Afterward, he felt sure that the house on 666 Blood Road would just vanish, and Mr. Chirac would never be heard from again.

"Hey, you just going to stare outside the window all night?" said Marla.

He turned and saw her standing behind him in jeans and a denim shirt, her lovely dark hair pulled back in a ponytail, and her face was beaming.

"No, I was just thinking about Enid," said Hunter, and he walked back to the couch and fell into it.

Marla followed, but sat in one chair opposite him. She considered Hunter for a while. He had a faraway look in his eyes.

"Rebecca said for me to tell you she would take care of her father for a while, and that she won't have to time to see you."

From the startled look on Hunter's face, she knew she had hit a nerve, so she took a chance and told him.

"Look, did anyone ever tell you were the spitting image of her dead fiancé?"

"Well, Pastor Mark said something about it, but—"

"But nothing, Hunter, get over it, get over her. She was just re-living the past. She never got to say goodbye to him. That was her way of saying goodbye. You know what I'm saying?"

"But—"

"I know, I know. She kissed you a few times, is that it?"

"Well… yes, she did, but—"

"Like I said, that was her way of saying goodbye to an old flame. Just drop it, okay?"

Hunter looked down at his hands and didn't know what to say. So, she used him. That was it?

"So, what are you going to do in this big old house, now that everybody's leaving?"

"What?"

"Kenneth and Ashley are going home, Darryl and Eddie are going back down south. So, like I said, what are you going to do with yourself now that Enid's gone?"

Hunter had never thought about it. Now that this quest of his was over, he didn't know what he would do. Bartok's dead, Enid's gone forever, and he had this big house to take care of that he just couldn't let go.

"I don't know," he said eventually, "go back to researching and writing paranormal books, I guess, although it seems so lame now that I know what the paranormal is really all about. What about you?"

"Me," she said, "I've been giving that very topic some thought. I can't go back to government work, that's for sure—not that my agency would want me, now that I've been disavowed by the president, that is. He told me to vanish into the void after this assignment was done. Little did I know he meant it literally, that he didn't expect me to come back. I wouldn't vote for him if he was the last man on earth."

Hunter grinned.

"May I take that as a recommendation?" he asked.

"Yes, you can take that to the bank. Speaking of which, do you mind giving me a ride to the bank tomorrow—there's a chance that they haven't drained all my bank accounts yet."

"Sure. What are you going to do with yourself? I mean, if you don't have a place to stay, you can stay here. I've certainly got the room."

"Thanks, I'll take that under advisement. As to what I'm going to do with myself, I don't have a clue."

"You could always partner up with me and write paranormal books," he said.

"I don't think I'd be any good at it."

"You might be surprised, what with all you've been through."

"You think so?"

"Hey, would I lie to you? Besides, I'm sort of shy a partner right now."

"I'll think about it," she said.

Hunter smiled and then looked away. He thought of Enid again and Uncle Bartok. His mind drifted back to Townsend Mountain. To the monstrous Major Albert Magnus Hillis that was trapped beneath a few tons of cement. Good, the world was better off not knowing about him. He thought back to of the army of automatons that was trapped with him. There was something that pulled at the back of his mind. Something…

Then he realized it with a start. They'd closed the opening to Townsend Mountain, but there was another way in.

Hunter sat bolt upright.

Another way in, another way out.

Suddenly, Hunter didn't feel so safe anymore.